NO PROMISES LARGE ENOUGH

The Ghost and the Mask, Book Two

No Promises Large Enough

TRISTRAM LOWE

Mortimer & Ambrose

NO PROMISES LARGE ENOUGH
The Ghost and the Mask, Book Two

Copyright © 2020 Tristram Lowe

First Edition paperback: December 2020

Cover design by MiblArt
Section separator art by achmadepp

ISBN: 978-1-946398-08-6

To Bill and Jared,
who went through
the doors ahead of us

CONTENTS

PART ONE

I

A Lullaby

The package arrived early in the morning. It was rather large, a meter deep and wide, and half again as tall. There were no markings on it, no address or postage printed. It was a plain brown box.

Saburo Raikatuji accepted the package from the two vaguely brown and boxy-looking men who delivered it. They were plain too, and one could have been a clone of the other, though one had long sideburns and the other didn't, one had a wispy mustache and the other didn't, and one wore a hat—a black beanie with the Western letters "FTW" on the front—but the other didn't. It didn't matter which was which. They both wore black souvenir jackets, *sukajans*, one with light gold sleeves, the other with red sleeves; one with an embroidered tiger, the other with a dragon. One had short hair; the other's just covered the tops of his ears. They were young toughs trying to be hard, trying to stand out, but they only blended together. It didn't matter which was which. They were utterly uninteresting. All Saburo cared about was what was in that box.

There was nothing to sign and nothing to pay for. They had rung the doorbell and wheeled the package over the front landing into the house, telling Saburo, "A gift from Mr. Kumamori." They lingered briefly outside the door. Then they each lit a cigarette and turned in perfect synchronicity, rolling the transport dolly behind them as they went. The sun sparkled on the freshly watered lawn, and a single wheel rolled through a puddle on the walkway, leaving a meandering dark trail.

Saburo shut the door.

He stood for a long moment in anticipation, wanting desperately to open the box, but at the same time not wanting to ruin the moment. He didn't want to be too eager. But his breath was high and short; his blood was in his ears. He couldn't wait any longer.

He pulled a knife from his waistband. It had an ebony handle, inlaid with mother of pearl. It was ten centimeters long and sharp along the full length of both sides. It was a dagger for slicing, thrusting, and impaling, and sometimes for opening boxes. He had worn it out of uncertainty.

Everything had gone as planned. He had done everything exactly as Kumamori had asked. He was almost completely confident that he had not overstepped his bounds asking for this gift. Almost.

That one percent of doubt wore the knife.

But he hadn't needed it, not at the doorway. The thugs had delivered the package and that was that. They hadn't so much as sneered at him.

Now he needed it, and he made the first incision along the thickly taped seam at the edge of the box. He cut from the top down all the way to the bottom where the knife was stopped by a thin piece of wood for stabilization at the box's base. He cut from the right edge across the top to the left edge through more tape that was the same brown as the box. He did the same across the bottom. Then he opened the side of the box like it was a small door.

A piece of white flat styrofoam greeted him.

He cut the two bands that encircled the styrofoam by inserting the knife flat-side, then turning it sharp-side to cut. They each snapped and gave a dull plastic twang. He sheathed the knife, placed a hand on each edge of the styrofoam, and pulled.

Gently. Ever. So. Gently.

Human limbs wrapped in plastic were revealed, sunk into more styrofoam, one foot resting near the knee cap of its opposite leg. A single arm and hand lay next to them. They were slender limbs, feminine.

He quickly removed the rest of the cardboard and the styrofoam coverings from the other side and the top. Thighs from above the knee to the hips, and the other arm and hand. A torso was embedded in styrofoam in the very center of the former box; it was slender-waisted with full breasts, unmistakably feminine, beginning (or ending) at the narrow gap between absent thighs, which was covered in light blue panties, and ending (or beginning) at a cleanly cut neck, plugged with more styrofoam.

Another box, which had rested on top of the torso, separated by styrofoam, was marked "Extremely Fragile" and "Artificial Intelligence Interface inside." Saburo set it carefully on the floor next to a left bicep. He used his knife once more.

What was inside was beautiful.

He pulled the flaps of the cardboard back, removed another molded piece of white styrofoam and saw her. Plastic covered the skin, which was silicone. *That's a kind of plastic too*, Saburo thought. But so smooth, so real but not-quite-real, which was exactly what he wanted. He didn't want real. Real was fallible. Real was problematic. Real was painful.

Her eyes were closed—*sleeping*, he thought. *Not quite ready to wake up.*

Soon.

He carefully lifted the head from its styrofoam encasement, removed the plastic covering, and turned it around. A green glow spilled out when he opened the nearly undetectable panel hidden by hair, and its rays cast green fingers about the room. The light calmed Saburo. It centered him and made him know he had done the right thing. He was in no danger. He served the correct master, and his reward was deserved.

When he had it all assembled, she stood just as tall as his lower lip. He could kiss the top of her head with ease. Her hair was soft and blonde, and a little mussed at the moment. He dressed her, straightened her hair with his fingers, and stepped back for a moment to admire.

Kumamori had asked him what type of woman he most preferred.

"Swedish," he had answered somewhat shyly. "I like blonde hair, blue eyes, but not too tall. Some Swedish women are too tall for me."

"Make me happy," Kumamori had said, "and I'll make you happy."

Again Saburo's chest lifted with anticipation. Her eyes were green and not blue, but otherwise, she was perfect. The blood filled his ears, and it began to rush to another part of his body, much lower down.

But he stopped it. He resisted.

Not yet. Not yet. Plenty of time for that.

He picked up the remote control. He had paired it already; he had followed the procedure, and the lights had blinked, letting him know it was connected, that the remote was linked with the unit and with his thumbprint. No one else could control it now without his approval. It would require his thumbprint to either allow a new user to share control or to pass ownership entirely over to someone else.

Saburo didn't see either of those scenarios happening at any point while he was still living. She was his.

Only his.

The job he had carried out for Mr. Kumamori had been a sensitive one.

"If anything goes wrong," Kouda, the boss's number one flunky, had said, "you'll be turned into fishcakes and fed to your parents."

Saburo wasn't so intimidated by the thought of his parents having to eat him; they had never been that close. It was the thought of being dead that really bothered him.

He had brought his three best men to do the job, and they had done it. Together they killed four of Mr. Kumamori's enemies, yakuza from a rival faction who had kidnapped his teenage daughter—never mind that she had wanted to be kidnapped—and brought her to a secret locale in Kabukicho where she had married one of them. Saburo had returned the daughter, kicking and screaming, and after she had given him a scar on his neck with her fingernails, so that Kumamori could "deal" with her.

The marriage never happened, it was decided. And Kaneko, the daughter, was promptly married to someone else, a much older yakuza and boss of the Dazai-ikka, a subordinate clan of the Tezuka-gumi, of which Kumamori was godfather. It seemed the man, Hisatsugu Tabara, had done Kumamori a favor having something to do with his meteoric rise to power. The boss's daughter was a promised thank you gift.

One of the terms of Saburo Raikatuji's agreement was that he would not have to kill for Kumamori again. It had been a surprise decision for both Saburo and Kumamori, but Saburo had had a sudden change of heart.

One late night, after scraping someone's skin from under his fingernails, he had been mindlessly flipping through channels on the TV, when he stopped on a meditation show. Something about the music had pierced his consciousness and halted his finger on the remote. He sat with the television monk and almost involuntarily began chanting along. Tears wetted his face when the meditation ended, and he realized that he no longer wanted to kill people. In fact, he never had wanted to. He suddenly understood that his underlying reason for joining the yakuza had been completely misguided. His desire for recognition, for fame, had become entirely unsatisfying.

He had gained the fame, at least among the eight hundred or so members of the Tezuka-gumi, and perhaps from more than a few of their rivals. He had become Kumamori's right hand killer. All of the important jobs went to him. And he was good at it. And although it had brought him respect and a sense of pride, none of it had brought him happiness. He couldn't do it any longer.

But he was a practical man, and saw that he had benefited from being in the brotherhood. He also knew that you didn't simply walk away from the yakuza like a job at a convenience store. There was a protocol. And Saburo knew, at the very least, he would lose a finger.

But he hadn't lost a finger. Kumamori had only smiled and given him another job.

"The last one," he called it. "You are the only one I trust. In return, I will give you a gift for your loyal service."

And now, with Kaneko returned and married properly, the gift had arrived. Finally, Saburo could relax and slough off all the bad karma from his many horrendous deeds.

But as he stood staring at his new companion—Lily, he would call her—he felt a further change of heart. He wanted to help Kumamori however he could. He would kill if he was required to kill.

Yes. He would be glad to.

Saburo quickly adjusted to Lily being there, and she became an intrinsic part of his daily life. He had lived alone before and was never quite up to the task of caring for himself and his home properly. He had hired maids from time to time, but things still piled up. His kitchen counter was cluttered, his bed never made, his bathroom at times unsightly. No longer.

Now, Lily kept everything sparkling and tidy, and Saburo would be extra careful about leaving a mess anywhere, often even cleaning up after himself before Lily could get to it. She had transformed him. He had more self-esteem than he ever had before. He left—and especially returned—home smiling. He happily carried out jobs for Kumamori, one after the other. He killed again and again. And he had no qualms about it.

It was a week before he took her to his bed. She was different than other women he had desired. She was special. She was perfect. He hadn't wanted to rush the moment. He had wanted it to be just right. He wanted her to want him, too. And as he began to tentatively express his feelings, and then to cautiously, gently stroke her hair, he found her to be responsive, and even like-minded. Their desires were mutual. They were utterly compatible.

Three months of bliss passed, and Saburo returned home to notice the dishes had not been cleaned. Lily was standing in the hallway by the bathroom and had a queer look on her face. Saburo approached her like a concerned lover. His hand reached out and stroked her hair.

"Doda," she said. "Dodaman."

Saburo gently brushed the side of her face with the back of his hand. The word didn't make sense to him. Up until that point, she had spoken perfect Japanese, although with a slight Swedish accent that he was never entirely sure wasn't his imagination. The detail her designers had put into her personality was astonishing. She had responded to him almost thoughtfully, and with such natural inflection. They had even had conversations about current politics and best health practices. So these odd words were unexpected. She seemed content though, unconcerned, so Saburo felt likewise.

"Doda," she said again, and then pushed past him to the kitchen and merrily cleaned the dishes while humming a sweet song.

Shining sun has gone to rest
So must you my baby
Little birds are in their nest
Come to yours my baby

Saburo shrugged it off, and chuckled. *Ah, women,* he thought. *Who knows what goes on in their heads?*

The sex that night was exciting. Lily was somewhat aggressive, and Saburo found that he liked it. He had always appreciated demure women, reserved and compliant, even in the bedroom, but there was something about the way she pushed him back onto the bed, the way she clawed his chest and gripped his arms. She was strong. Her fingers pressed into his flesh, steadying herself on his forearms as he held her waist. She bucked her hips on top of him, perfectly rhythmic.

He woke happy the next day and left home with an enveloping glow.

Another week passed, and Saburo came home with blood on his shirt and hands. The job didn't go as smoothly as he had planned and he had been forced to improvise. Lily greeted him, and when she saw the blood, her green eyes glowed brighter. She paused, a queer half smile on her face.

"Doda," she said, and led Saburo to the bathroom to get him cleaned up.

A few days later, Saburo arrived home after a rather easy day. He hadn't had to kill anyone, just threaten them. His reputation had grown quite impressive, and he found that people didn't so much want to die. To avoid that fate, they were often happy to cease activities that went against Kumamori's plans. He had become very efficient at his job.

But his light mood was soon changed. He heard Lily singing—no, mumbling rhythmically—from the living room. As he got closer, he heard the syllables more clearly.

Dodadodadodadaman, dodaman, dodaman
Dodadodamanman, dodododa, manman

He didn't understand. It was gibberish.

He rounded the entryway to the living room and was greeted with a grizzly scene. Lily was leaning over a man's body that sat on the couch, positioning his arms in a casual, conversational way. She was trying to get him to hold a cup of tea, and at the same time keep his head from lolling back onto the couch. Another man already sat, cross-legged, on Saburo's easy chair, a lit cigarette wedged between fingers of a hand resting on his knee. This man's head was supported by the high back of the chair, but he was clearly dead, as was the other.

And there was blood. A lot of it.

It pooled on the carpet, and soaked the clothes of both mens' bodies. It was smeared across the low wooden coffee table, which had been broken, he noticed, but then propped back up precariously, splinters splayed out from a ragged scar in its middle.

Lily was getting frustrated that the man wouldn't hold the tea cup, and tea was spilling down his dead hand onto his pant leg. Her singsong nonsense became more frantic.

Dodaman, dodaman, dodadodadodaman

Dodadodadodadodadodadodadodaman

She noticed Saburo watching and turned to him with a fury in her eyes he had never seen before, on her or anyone. Th e tea cup fell, shattering, and splashed the remaining tea across the broken table.

"Dodaman! Dodaman!" she screamed, pointing a slender, bloody finger at him.

Saburo took a step back. "What . . ." he began, but faltered. *What happened? Who are these men? Who* were *they?*

Lily had a maniacal, menacing look about her. She began to tear at her clothes, ripping frantically at her blouse and skirt, fingernails ripping into her perfect, smooth, synthetic flesh.

There's a kit, Saburo thought involuntarily, *a kit to repair skin damage. There's a tube and some tools.* He took another step back.

Soon she was completely naked, a perfect female form, perfectly enraged. In spite of the fear that clenched him, he couldn't help but admire her exquisite body. She may have killed these men, and might attempt to do the same to him, but she would be beautiful doing it. The damage to her skin looked minimal, but what had happened to her AI? She was clearly malfunctioning.

He assessed his options: exit the front door, talk her down, subdue her with a stranglehold—*wouldn't work, she doesn't breathe*—shoot her in the head.

NO! Not his girl. Not his happiness.

"Lily," Saburo said as gently as he could. "Why are you so upset?" He fingered the remote in his pocket. He had the kill switch, if he needed it, a code that, along with his thumbprint, would shut her down. It made him sad even thinking about it. They had come so far. He had gotten so accustom to her attentions, her presence. He—wasn't good at putting his feelings into words, but he—loved her. Seeing her like this broke his heart. He dearly did not want to use the kill code, but his thumb rested on the remote. He steeled himself to it as best he could, and a tear formed in his left eye.

Then she stopped. Her ranting ceased and her arms dropped limp to her side. She seemed empty for a moment. Still.

But he hadn't used the kill code. He needed both hands for that—one for his thumbprint and the other to enter the code—and the remote was still in his pocket. Had she shut down on her own?

Then she began to cry.

She weeped like a lost girl. Saburo had never seen her anything but happy. To be hit with both a murderous anger and such overwhelming sorrow from her in the span of a few minutes was completely disorienting. But somehow it made him love her more.

He went to her. He put his arms around her and tried to comfort her, brushing blonde strands of hair from her eyes and kissing the top of her head.

She embraced him as the dead eyes of the men in his living room looked on.

"I'm sorry," she said, between sobs. "I don't know what overcame me."

"It's okay. It's okay," he said, running his fingers through her hair. Already the blood was rushing to his groin. He wanted her badly. He would take her right there in front of the dead men, in the pool of their blood on his carpet.

"They came for you," she said, pulling back from the hug. Her eyes were luminescent green, otherworldly. "They came to kill you, but first they wanted to have their way with me."

At the thought of that, Saburo's blood boiled and retreated from his member back to his chest. No one could have her but him. No one.

"I didn't let them," she said sweetly, as if she could sense his emotions. "They never touched me, not that way." Her full lips curved into a slight smile; her bare chest heaved. "I killed them for you." She said it as tenderly as if she had said the words, "I love you," which is exactly what Saburo heard.

He lifted her in his arms and carried her to the bedroom.

They skipped dinner that night. Lily was the only sustenance Saburo needed. He lay with her next to him, legs intertwined, until he fell into a deep, satisfying sleep.

In the morning, he did not wake.

Blood pulsed in diminishing spurts from the stump of his right thumb, which was no longer attached. It had been removed quickly after the knife in Lily's hand, ebony-handled and inlaid with mother of pearl, had severed his carotid artery. More blood spouted rhythmically from his neck until his heart eventually stopped.

She cleaned herself off and put on fresh clothes. Th en she pocketed Saburo's thumb and the remote control, and left his house for good.

"Döda män," she said, and shut the door.

2

Nightmares and Headaches

The samurai demon lurched at Akio, head-butting him across the room with its gruesome, dragon-faced *kabuto* helmet, the needle-sharp, spiral horns goring his chest. He collapsed in a heap against the cave wall of the demon's bloody abattoir. Severed human heads stared at him from the dugout shelves.

"Save us!" they screamed. "Save our souls!"

"It's too late," Akio muttered. "It's already too late!"

He saw the compact and fierce old kendo instructor, Tatsuo Miyahara, surge toward the demon, the sweat on the bald man's head shining in the torchlight. The man swung his katana in an expert stroke meant to sever the beast's jugular, but it was parried easily by the demon's own black blade. Akio watched, immobile, as the demon repelled Miyahara with a series of blows, and then pinned him to the rock wall, leaving its sinister katana to hold him there like an insect on display.

The old man's blood ran down the wall and escaped the room like a retreating tide.

Masami? Where is Masami?

His friend was not in the room. Where had she gone? What had the demon done to her? His eyes darted around, searching frantically.

The demon stood over the open, ornate metal box, staring into the contents from the eyeless black depths beneath its kabuto. Akio moved closer to look.

What's in the box?

He didn't want to know. But he did know. It was the demon's real head. And once the beast recovered its head and put it on, it would destroy the world. Already it had killed his friends. There would be no stopping it.

The demon removed its kabuto, revealing a face that was hard to see. It was several faces at once. A salaryman, an innkeeper's wife, a homeless man, a young woman. It tore the head from its neck and let it drop to the floor. Then the monster's huge, gauntleted hands reached into the box and lifted the head within. Blood dripped from its slender neck. Shoulder length, straight black hair hung down over its ears. The demon turned the head so Akio could see as it placed it on its neck.

Masami!

It was Masami's head! His friend. His best friend. His co-worker with whom he had tracked this murderous demon to get a story.

All this for a story.

As her neck fused with the demon's body, her eyes locked on Akio.

"Kill me, Akio," she said, her voice a ghostly whisper. "Kill me so I can reclaim the life I was meant to have. So I can see my son again."

"No," he whimpered. "I can't. I . . . I . . . ." He couldn't say it, even now.

She held out the demon's black sword, which no longer pinned Miyahara to the wall. The old demon hunter's body lay slumped in the corner.

"Kill me!" Masami's head shouted, her voice a shrill, sharp blade itself.

Akio took the katana, which felt like ice in his hands. The demon Masami knelt over the box, and with tears in his eyes, Akio brought the sword down.

Masami's head fell into the metal box and rolled to face upward. But her face was obscured now. Covering it was the demon's mask, the blood-red, full-faced *somen*, so expertly carved that the flames and clouds adorning it appeared to move. *Did* move. There was no question.

It looked at Akio, nothing behind the eyeholes but emptiness, the emptiness that contained him.

"Wear me, I am beautiful," said the mask.

"No." Akio shrunk away.

"Wear me," it repeated. "You are the killer now."

"No!"

"Wear me!"

It would not relent.

"You *are* me."

Akio Tsukino shot awake on his futon, his black hair wet with sweat. He rubbed his eyes, damp and red with real tears. Morning light came in sideways through the blinds, a soft, hazy glow. The thrum of cicada song bore into his skull, which ached like he'd been struck. The back of his neck hurt worse. He rubbed it and made slow circles with his head, stretching through the pain.

Damn these headaches. Damn these dreams.

A flash of red illuminated the window for a split second, and a sudden rain began to fall. A thunderclap followed seconds later. The cicadas quieted.

Red lightning. Hadn't Sensei Miyahara said something about that?

The downpour slowed to a stop as quickly as it began, and sunlight sparkled on the droplets that clung to the window. The cicadas resumed, and the nightmare swallowed Akio's thoughts.

He had repeatedly dreamed of the encounter under Maizuru Castle in Kofu, only two months past, though the details changed each time. In this one—he cringed at the dream memory still so vivid—the demon had worn Masami Sato's head.

Akio worked with Masami at the *Dainichi Daily* newspaper. He was a lowly staff photographer. She was a top staff writer and, for a brief time anyway, Akio's friend.

In the real version, the demon had retrieved its own beastly head from the ornate metal box and put it on. Masami had disappeared and only returned after Akio had beheaded the demon. *It* had asked for death, not Masami.

Broken and alone, Akio had granted its wish. The demon had dissolved into nothing, and in its place was Masami, looking pale and weak. She had appeared a frightened girl, the direct opposite of the strong-willed, immovable Masami he knew.

He had held her tightly then. And she had let him.

Akio collapsed back onto his bed. He didn't want to think about it.

He wanted to talk to Masami. He needed to tell her about his nightmares, needed her to tell him it would be okay. He felt alone, abandoned. She would barely talk to him at work, in spite of what they'd been through.

He rolled his gaze to the clock.

5:37 a.m.

It was Tuesday. He wanted to crawl back under the blanket but for fear of having another nightmare. Instead he gazed up at the wall, covered in photos, illuminated by the bands of morning light through the blinds and speckled with gray shadow dots of rain. He hoped for a distraction at least, to find an image he could create a story about. Anything to take his mind off his dreams. It was a kind of game he played, building lives for the strangers he had captured. But lately his imagination had felt crippled.

His eyes locked on his favorite photo, as if in defiance of his wish. He pulled it from the wall and held it in his hands.

So much for escaping.

It was his most treasured image because it captured the beginning.

Masami was standing in front of a drab apartment building, her head just starting to turn away, her hair flaring out from the motion. Her look was somewhere between victory and irritation. In fact, it was exactly between those two things. She had just derided him for being an idiot, which she seemed to gain pleasure from, and then he had annoyed her by trying to catch a photo of her smiling. Her expression bore that transition perfectly. Her eyes were wide and wild, her lips slightly open as she was about to swear at him. It could have been so many other things. If he had seen that picture and had not actually been there to know what was going on, had not actually known Masami, what story would he have made up?

But he had been there. And he knew her. Now.

The things they went through Akio could never have dreamed up no matter how many photos you put in front of him. In the end, they had become close. He had seen behind the metal shell of Masami the robot queen. Only that name no longer fit her. She was a complicated woman that Akio cared about. She was his friend.

Now everything had returned to normal. Masami was only someone he worked with whom he annoyed without trying. And yet, most everyone seemed to annoy her, so he didn't even feel special in that regard—though he was pretty sure he held top honors.

Now when he tried to engage her at work, or even just said hello, he was either ignored or met with an irritated glare. Masami could convey a lot through her glares, Akio had learned. Her glares were like Inuit words for snow; there were at least fifty of them, each with their own subtle variance of displeasure. He thought he might start cataloging them and then publish a field guide to pass around the office.

He pinned the photo back and searched the others. He couldn't think about Masami right now. He couldn't think about anything *but* her.

Give me a distraction.

Most of the photos on the wall were his, and most were of people. He loved shooting people more than anything. The expressions he could sometimes catch fascinated him. He scanned the faces in the pictures, looking for one that would spark his imagination, keep his mind off the nightmare, but then his eyes betrayed him again. A kendo group readied itself in their dojo, while their stern, bald sensei looked on.

Miyahara.

They had thought him the murderer in the beginning, but he had turned out to be their protector. A demon hunter, of all things. And somehow the old man had survived the blade through his gut. Akio and Masami had worried he would be implicated in the murders, but

Miyahara had assured them he wouldn't. And he hadn't been. There was something he wouldn't explain. Something about his blood.

From his hospital bed, Miyahara had told them he would come to Tokyo. After he recovered, he would retrieve the items he had entrusted them to keep safe: the box and the mask.

The mask.

Akio cringed at the memory of the thing. Miyahara wanted it back, and he could damn well have it. The sensei apparently collected demonic things, claiming to possess several from his life of demon hunting. He wanted to add the box and mask to the pile. Akio was all too eager to oblige. Perhaps once those things were gone, his nightmares would subside.

Three and half weeks after saying goodbye to the tough old man at the hospital, the sensei had written them at the *Daily* to say he'd be out to visit in one more week. Two had passed before they received another letter. All it said was, "I am delayed. Take good care of things."

It had been nearly three weeks more since that one.

Miyahara was nothing if not cryptic. He was probably playing with them, testing them somehow. Like how he had strung them along, letting them believe they had killed the demon after their first encounter. The truth was it had only dissipated to reform again in its lair. In the midst of their celebration and relief, he had dropped the bomb that the demon was still alive.

It was then that Masami had brought out the mask. She had wanted to see if it could somehow help defeat the demon samurai.

It was so beautiful and alluring. A living thing with a mind of its own.

Wear me.

Akio forced his focus back to the photos on his wall. He couldn't think about it. Not the mask. He analyzed the people in the images, searched for a stranger, someone that wouldn't trigger another memory. Someone that had nothing to do with Masami or the mask.

There.

It was a man crossing the street in Shibuya. He looked alone though he was surrounded by throngs of people rushing and blurred.

His head was down slightly; his expression was distant and somewhat confused. He looked more like a man lost in a forest than someone in a crowded city.

And another. A woman with a baby, hiding a cigarette behind her back. A smirk on her face as she gabbed with a friend who looked equally amused.

There was old lady cooking *yakitori* in front of her garage, her eyebrows raised and lips in a sideways pucker. Her ancient husband seated behind her with his eyes squinting in the sun.

A boy looked up to the sky in wonder at something unseen, slack-jawed and hands on his hips, the strap of his schoolbag awkwardly wound around his leg.

They were all strangers. Moments he had captured, faces he could stare at and create lives for. Exactly what he needed.

What were they thinking?

He fought the urge to give up, to let his thoughts slip back to Masami and his nightmares.

What were their stories? Come on.

The man crossing the street was a widower salaryman.

Yes.

His son wouldn't speak to him because he hadn't let him go to Brazil for a rare job opportunity. That's why he looked so lost. He didn't know how to reconnect.

Okay. Good.

The smoking mother was a school teacher who was cheating on her husband. The baby wasn't his.

Yeah.

The old lady was a saint who gave all her excess money to charity and did volunteer work at the local temple. Her husband didn't believe in any gods, but he worshipped her.

The boy was seeing an angel, a spirit gliding through the sky, wings spread wide to protect him. It looked down at him with a smile that was pure love. The angel had chosen him for greatness. He would be a hero.

Yes. That's it.

He smiled, his imagination rekindled.

What if they're true? What if I have some kind of insight, some kind of vision?

But who was he kidding? The only visions he had now were the ones keeping him up at night. He hadn't had a good night's sleep since he wore that infernal mask.

Wear me.

Akio squirmed as if the mask had physically appeared, its empty eyes staring into his. He tried to concentrate on the photos, but they were quickly losing their effect, losing the battle with his fear.

Wear me. I am beautiful.

It had been Akio's weakness, giving in to the mask's power. With it on, he had relived the samurai's past atrocities, relived his admittance into Hell. The samurai's memories had been burned into Akio's mind.

Noboru Akechi, ruthless and bent on vengeance, betraying his superiors, murdering his companions, and abusing his own daughters. An unrivaled warrior and military leader, set to conquer all of Japan. Betrayed in turn by the only person left in the world whom he loved. His son.

But Akechi's reasons for vengeance were not unfounded. His infant son had been stolen from him by their impotent daimyo, claiming the boy as his own. And the tragedy of it all, the reason Akio had taken pity: the boy had poisoned Akechi. After building an army and conquering the kidnapping daimyo, Akechi had failed to convince the boy that he was his true father.

And then, not having suffered enough, he was sent to Hell.

There Akechi was beheaded as punishment for his arrogance in life. Akio could still see the huge, insectoid beasts with their giant scissors, snipping off the samurai's head like it was a shrub to be pruned. In the underworld, the samurai's hate had transformed him into demonkind. But Hell could not hold Akechi.

The mask was now locked away in that same ornate metal box that had held the demon's head. It still haunted Akio. The box, along with the *wakizashi*, the shorter of the two swords from the wall of the cave lair, was in Masami's care. Akio had kept the companion katana.

Together the two blades served as a key to open the box. Miyahara had insisted they be kept apart so that neither he nor Masami would be tempted to retrieve the mask.

But really it's because of me.

Akio was not to be trusted. He had proven that. He had almost ruined everything. On their car ride home, Masami had recounted what happened in the present day when he had worn the mask. While Akio had visions of four hundred years past, a very different scene had played out in her Kofu hotel room.

He had become a raving madman. He had attacked her and Miyahara. He had proclaimed vengeance for his beloved son, and vowed to reclaim his honor. He had spit at Miyahara and called him an impotent child thief. He had even threatened to rape Masami. The fact that he could have done and said those things, whether they were his thoughts or not, made him sick—particularly the latter. It's no wonder Masami stopped being his friend.

No, that doesn't make sense. Our closest moments were after I wore the mask.

He had wept after fighting them, while he still wore it, after Miyahara had jarred him hard on the back of the head with the butt of his steel-like hand.

Maybe that's why I get headaches now.

He had howled for his son—Akechi's son—before Masami had pried the mask from his face.

The visions he had then, and more, still plagued his dreams. If it wasn't some altered version of the horror in Kofu, it was swords and spears coming at him from all angles, blood on his hands and face, guilt and shame wracking his soul for deeds he had never committed.

Akio's gaze drifted toward his closet. Inside, the katana leaned against the wall behind his one suit, his button down shirts, and a few pairs of slacks. Long, black, and subtly curved in its sheath, an intricately carved, ruby red gem as its guard. Its black bone handle was wrapped in fine black hair. Human hair, most likely, and a human bone probably. Miyahara had said the swords were most certainly forged in Hell, so the materials seemed appropriate.

He collapsed back onto his futon, pressing his eyelids tight as if to squeeze the memories from his brain.

Masami danced behind his eyes, wearing the mask, a red line through her neck.

He opened them abruptly and looked up again at the photos on his wall.

Let me think of something else. Please. Let my life be normal again.

There were people there he knew who didn't trigger awful memories, co-workers, mostly. Akio didn't have friends, not really, but drinks after work were expected, and he always had his camera on him.

He said their names out loud as he looked at their faces, like a mantra, trying to drum the thoughts from his head, fill them with dull memories of work and meaningless conversation.

His eyes moved to a photo that wasn't his. There were several on this piece of wall. The ones that inspired him to be better. The same ones that he hated because he felt he'd never be that good. In moments like these it all seemed so far away. Would he ever get the respect he craved? Would his photos ever be on someone else's wall, inspiring them?

He looked to the window again, all evidence of the brief rain erased. It was the last week of June. The heat and humidity were rising. He reminded himself to pack an extra shirt for work and to not forget his sweat towel. A ten minute walk to the station, five more to the office, and in between, jammed into an overstuffed train car was all too much for Akio's sweat glands.

Good. He was calm. Back to the mundane, everyday thoughts of work. The dream had been pushed far enough away suddenly, now only a muted vision of disturbing nonsense.

And his headache was gone.

Akio rolled off the futon toward his kitchen, and his eyes caught one more photo. One more attempt to drag him back under. It was the only framed image on his wall, and it hung above his small desk. His front page photo, clipped from the *Dainichi Daily*. In it, Kofu Castle looked like a haunted ruin looming menacingly over the city. He smiled at it, proud but pained, then shuddered.

All this for a story.

He turned away.

He sat with his tea, watching the steam rise from its surface, and his thoughts returned to work. Today he'd face another mindless assignment and the cold reality that, after all he'd been through, nothing there had changed much at all.

He wondered if he had imagined it, if he was actually locked in a rubber room somewhere, and all this nonsense about demons was just the depraved wanderings of his broken mind. The only person he could talk to about it wouldn't talk to him. He needed her. If for nothing else to confirm that he was sane.

3

Disappearing Act

Akio's desk at the *Dainichi Daily* wasn't actually a desk; it was a table he shared with three other employees, all staff photographers. Their table sat next to a row of writer's cubicles. It was, the editor, Tanaka's belief that the writers needed more separation and solitude. Tanaka, of course, was a writer and not a photographer.

At that moment Akio wished he had a little more privacy. He couldn't concentrate and found himself nervously moving the mouse around and staring out the window. The nightmares had wrecked his sleep, so his focus was shot. He had hoped, by now, the memories of the Kofu assignment and the samurai's gory past would have been softened, but if anything, they were getting worse. Having no one to talk to about it didn't help.

He stared blankly at the image for his current assignment: a new statue erected in Yoyogi Park. *It was an exciting unveiling as the mayor revealed the new marble statue of a giant pig . . .* yada yada yada. *Who cares?*

Akio had received some verbal accolades and a big pat on the back for his work on the Kofu Head Collector—what they had started calling it after the fact—but his assignments hadn't gotten any better. He had expected to be reassigned to the police beat, or at least get bumped up to more important, glamorous social news. But he was stuck where he had been: back page local events. He couldn't do much worse unless they moved him over to the recipes and food section.

Ooh, to be taking pictures of yakisoba and cream puffs.

He looked over his shoulder, afraid that someone might hear his thoughts and make it happen. Then again, maybe it would be better. He would get to go out and eat more, and on the company's dime.

After yet another tiny adjustment to the photo of the pig, he looked out the window at nothing in particular. The building across the street reflected their own building in its windows. He could just make himself out in the glare, an indistinct shape trapped in a glass cage.

What the hell am I doing with my life? What is the point of this?

Maybe he should go out and become a stringer, be a rogue photojournalist shooting what he wanted and selling it to the highest bidder. That certainly sounded better than being tied to a paper that told you what you were allowed to shoot.

He remembered something his grandmother had said about karma.

Accomplishments by ill-gotten means have only ill benefits.

Is that what he had done? Had his cleverness in getting on the Head Collector assignment been ill-gotten? It hadn't hurt anyone. Everyone had benefited. Sort of. Minus the wounds and scares he, Masami, and Miyahara had received. Their top photographer, Powell, had scored a free island getaway. It was a little sneaky maybe, but ill-gotten?

He was stuck just the same. No improvements, no benefits, no more respect. He had to make a change. Otherwise, he would rot at the *Dainichi Daily*. He'd be shooting parks and chess tournaments until he was eighty.

He needed to move his legs. He wanted to talk to Masami. He knew she would only shoot him down, but he had to try again. She had been his only real friend, and they had gone through something profound together. She had to acknowledge it eventually.

He pushed away from his computer and stood. He didn't have to walk by Masami's desk to get to the restroom, but he could, so he had his excuse. As he moved up the row of cubicles toward her desk, he immediately sensed something wrong. Normally, he could have found her desk with his eyes closed; her typing was always the loudest. Her fingers attacked the keys like a destructive force of nature. It's a wonder any of them still worked. But he didn't hear it, only the general softer clicking and snippets of murmured conversations from the other writers.

When he got to her desk, she wasn't there. She was always there if she wasn't out on an assignment, and Akio hadn't seen her name on the white board. He'd never seen her take a restroom break, but nature had to call at some point, right? Maybe she was talking with Tanaka. She was probably getting a promotion, even though she was already one of the best paid writers—an anomaly on both accounts for a woman in Japan, especially at her young age.

They're probably making her a deputy editor.

He envisioned Masami as his boss, handing him an assignment for another children's play and cackling like an evil witch. But who was he kidding? Masami didn't laugh.

He continued on toward the restroom, though he didn't have to use it. He had only taken two steps when he heard the familiar loud clacking of keys behind him. He turned back and saw Masami at her desk assaulting her keyboard with the usual ferocity. He reversed gears and headed back to her desk.

"Where did you go?" he asked.

She briefly glanced sideways, barely turning her head and not even slowing the onslaught of the keys. "What are you talking about, Akio?"

"Where did you go?" he repeated. "I just came over to say hi, but you weren't here, just a second ago."

She didn't bother looking at him when she responded. "Uh huh. I don't know what you're talking about. I've been here all day."

"Uh, no, no, you haven't. I figured you were in the boss's office getting promoted or something, because I don't think you ever have to use the bathroom."

"I have three articles due for the evening edition. I don't have time for human weaknesses like bathroom breaks."

"Okay, whatever," Akio said, trying to shrug it off. "Keep your secrets then."

It hurt, but he tried not to show it. She was getting even further away from him, and in such a short time. Maybe she was equally troubled about the events in Kofu, and this was her way of coping. It would only make sense. She had never been one to share her feelings about anything, though she had opened up to him briefly after their harrowing time beneath Kofu Castle. It was no surprise that she would clamp up once things got back to normal. Hugely disappointing, but not surprising.

Deflated, Akio went back to his computer. No point in keeping up the bathroom charade now.

"Miss Sato!" he heard Tanaka shout. Akio turned back around to see the boss walking toward Masami's desk. She stopped typing and looked up at him. Of course, he commanded her full attention. "Where have you been?" Tanaka asked. "I walked the news floor earlier, twice, and you weren't at your desk either time."

Masami looked confused and clearly wanted to protest, but she kept quiet.

"And it's not the first day this has happened," Tanaka continued. "I give you a lot of work because I know you can meet the deadlines. You haven't let me down yet, but you're making me nervous. Stay hungry, Miss Sato. You're slipping."

With that, the boss walked away in his casual, confident stride toward the elevators.

Masami looked lost. She watched Tanaka go and, before turning to resume her work, she caught Akio looking at her. He didn't try to hide it. He just raised his eyebrows and gave a little victory smirk. She could lie all she wanted and treat him like dirt, but she couldn't do that to the boss. Akio walked back to his desk and plopped down at his computer, depressed at how bitter that little victory tasted.

Masami's normal breakneck speed at the keyboard became fractured. She couldn't keep her mind on the article. *What is happening to me?*

When Akio said she hadn't been at her desk, she blew it off. He was always trying to get a rise out of her. Always saying stupid things to get her attention, to try to break through her armor. She had earned that armor, and it didn't break easily. She felt bad, after what they had been through. Akio didn't have her fortitude. She could see he was reaching out, but she just couldn't. It's not how she processed things. She wasn't a sharer. She went deep inside, shuttered the windows, locked the doors, and let her internal demons battle it out there. Akio needed a buddy. She couldn't be that for him. She couldn't lose her edge.

But when Tanaka had said the same thing, corroborating Akio's accusation, her armor had cracked. She had been at her desk all day. And Tanaka had said it wasn't the first time. None of it made any sense.

Her articles *were* taking longer to write lately, and she couldn't pinpoint why. She seemed to be losing chunks of time. She *was* slipping.

She looked at the clock. *Dammit.* It was the same today. It was already 10 a.m. and she had only just finished her first article—a bloody triple homicide of three gangsters in one of their homes, the other two from a rival syndicate—and had barely begun her second. She had one more to write after that. At this rate, she wouldn't get her third article into the evening paper. And now, she was further hindered by this insane idea that she had been leaving her desk.

Am I suffering from some daytime form of sleep-walking? Am I losing my mind?

She had to focus. She forced herself to think only of the article in front of her: the robbery of a cigarette vendor in Shinjuku. It was a small time theft, but it was the second one that week. All the information she had was from the press club. She had tried to interview the clerk on duty at the time, but the woman wouldn't talk. How could she make her article unique and not sound like every other paper in town?

But there was nothing for it now. She couldn't concentrate. She needed coffee. She was certain she had already had three cups, but this was going to be an eight-cup day. Thankfully, she brought her own, and pulled her thermos from her bag. That would usually last the morning. If she needed more in the afternoon, and she usually did, she would stop at Tully's on her lunch break. Of course there was coffee at the office for free, and it wasn't terrible, but having to make small talk with other employees while getting it was the problem. With the thermos, she could keep working and avoid having to pretend that she liked people.

She poured it, still steaming, into her plain black mug. She gulped too much of it, burning her mouth; winced, but tried not to show it. She pressed her lips together into a thin line and attacked the article again.

> A second robbery of a Shinjuku cigarette shop is making the locals nervous. Not only did they take all the cash on hand, but they also claimed a large stash of E-cigarettes and cartridges. Both of the burgled cigarette shops are owned by the Yonamine Corporation, which owns the majority of the cigarette and beverage vending machines in Shinjuku, as well as several liquor stores.

Masami was stalled out. There wasn't much to go on. A description of the robber would come next.

> What does this mean for Shinjuku and its citizens, and for the other businesses there?

Ugh.

She looked at the clock again. 10:20am. *What?* It couldn't have been twenty minutes since she last looked. She had barely written one sentence.

She tried to think back. What had she been doing? Was she spacing out? She never spaced out. She was supremely focused and determined. She was proud of that. But spacing out wouldn't make sense anyway. Tanaka and Akio had said she hadn't been at her desk. So she couldn't have just been daydreaming.

Daydreaming? I do not daydream. But I also did not leave my desk! Think, think, think!

She tried to look back over the last twenty minutes.

What did I do? I was here and then . . . wait.

There was something. There was a black patch in her memory, a point that faded out. Her mind had been empty, somewhere else. At least, that's what it felt like. Like she had been dreaming. But she couldn't grab onto it. It was elusive, like it didn't want to be found out. Yet it was somehow familiar.

She hadn't left her desk. She was certain of that. Did she have some kind of brain disease? No. That couldn't explain other people not seeing her or thinking she wasn't there.

Focus. Get through this day. Sort it out later.

She took another sip of coffee, which had cooled substantially, and did her best to buckle down and knock out the article, hoping that, at the very least, Tanaka would not make another walk-through of the news floor.

Masami scarfed down take-out *chanpon* from Ringerhut, slurping up the noodles while her hands and body trembled. She was back in her apartment in Chuo after pulling a long night to meet her deadlines. She had not taken a lunch.

It was almost 10 p.m. She sat at her tiny dining table next to her tiny kitchen. It was quiet but for the sound of the trains. She had no music on, nor television. She had no pets and, thankfully, no noisy neighbors. She could easily be alone with her thoughts.

She had a bookshelf full of well-worn books, mostly histories and historical novels, but a few contemporary fiction and one manga, which had been a gift.

On a normal night, she would be home by 8 p.m. at the latest. She would sit and read by lamplight, relaxing with a piece of dark chocolate and a beer, or occasionally just some peppermint tea. She loved her evenings alone. They recharged her in order to tackle the day head-on in the morning.

Tonight, there would be no relaxing. She wanted the beer to calm her nerves, but she had to forgo it. She didn't want to dull her senses. She had to figure out what the hell was happening to her.

For the rest of the day at work, she had checked her desk clock, and the clock on her computer, and she saw them jump, two minutes, five minutes, sometimes ten. Each time, she had been on the same sentence. Time had passed but she had not typed a word. She had felt more and more unfocused as the day went on. She felt like she was slipping away —not just slipping, like Tanaka had said, but actually slipping out of existence. At one point, she swore she saw her fingers fade from the keyboard and then reappear. Three minutes had passed as she watched it happen, but it felt like no time at all.

That couldn't have happened.

I'm losing my mind. I must be dozing off. I've developed narcolepsy or something. But people who have narcolepsy don't disappear!

It wasn't only Tanaka and Akio that had told her she wasn't at her desk. The assignment editor, Eiji, had said the same. He had also reminded her that Tanaka wasn't happy with her performance the past couple weeks and that she'd better straighten up. No one had ever had to tell her to straighten up in her life.

She pushed the empty chanpon container aside. Her stomach was grateful and her nerves were settling somewhat. She had gone the whole day on coffee alone. She moved to her two person couch in her small living room, which was next to her even smaller bedroom loft above the entryway.

She sat upright with her phone in her hand and looked at the time. She tried to relax and just focus on the numbers. She had to figure out what was happening. Five minutes passed. Nothing. The white numbers changed normally. That was it. She switched to the stopwatch app, so she could see the seconds, and started a countdown.

The seconds and milliseconds flew by. Her breath was heavy and nervous, and she tried to calm it by breathing deliberately and slowly. 1:32 displayed on the screen and then was 1:48 with nothing in between. She caught her breath and kept watching.

2:09 became 2:19. 2:41 became 3:12. 4:33 became 4:40 became 5:06.

She hit stop, and set the phone down next to her on the couch. Her breathing was rapid; she couldn't slow it down. She checked her pulse. Her heart was a nervous rabbit's. There was a slight vibration in her solar plexus. She closed her eyes and forced herself to breath slowly.

I'll figure this out. I'm smarter than this, whatever it is. Just calm down.

She sat with her eyes still closed, her breath slowly returning to normal. She felt an awareness shift around her. She felt suddenly light and empty, somehow insubstantial.

She opened her eyes to try again and found her room had been altered. It looked as if it were a room from a dark dream. *Are my eyes still closed? Did I fall asleep?* She could see the room around her but as if through a thick gauze. She could see or sense the shapes of things: the dark rectangle of the television, the edges of the metal bookshelf, the curve and scoop of the dining table chairs, one with a faint residue of light—the one she had been sitting in. The walls materialized, abrupt and flat, monolithic. She saw the ladder to her loft, the front door beyond outlined in a gray halo glow, its eyehole a tiny spotlight. She stood up, and everything returned to normal.

But she was standing in the kitchen.

She had only just stood up from the couch. But now she was in the kitchen, looking at her refrigerator, at a magnet with a cartoon illustration of a smiling caterpillar that said "Even a tiny insect has an itty-bitty soul."

A shiver passed through her and she fought to stay standing. Her knees wanted to give way. How had she ended up in the kitchen? She hadn't been looking at the stopwatch app, but obviously time had passed like before. This time, she had been moving.

Great. Now I'm a disappearing sleepwalker.

Not only had she moved, she had seen the room as if in a kind of black and white dream. Had she imagined it?

She felt nauseous. She made her legs bring her back to the couch, and sat.

She picked up her smartphone again and started the stopwatch. She tried to open her mind to all her senses, an onerous task for someone who had spent her life with her feelings on lockdown. But she was determined. And if there was something that had to be done, Masami would not shy away from it. Even if it meant opening herself up to the whim of her emotions, even if it meant exposing those raw nerves she had so long ago cauterized.

The numbers on the stopwatch ticked by, two minutes, four minutes, six minutes. Then, at 6:19, she felt it. With her eyes open, the room became fuzzy, the edges of the TV in front of her faded into a wispy blur. The walls did the same, as did the phone in her hand, the stopwatch numbers still moving in correct time, but washed out like a watercolor image. It happened just for a moment, from 6:19 to 6:32. Then it suddenly read 7:01 and the room was back to normal.

Her solar plexus was quivering again.

She had discovered something. She did not have to be unconscious when these moments happened. She could be aware. She only had to maintain focus.

She reset the timer.

Three and a half minutes went by before it happened again. She first noticed her fingers and the phone start to fade. She could momentarily see the TV right through them, but then they reformed with a wispy outline and blurred surface to match the room around her. Her bookshelf, the front door, the ladder to her loft, all were a bluish, gunmetal gray, as if composed only of the base elements of their existence. Her fingers and arms were outwardly the same, with subtle glints where her fine arm hair caught the muted light, but there was more to her than the inanimate objects around her. There was an underlying vitality in her, a shifting luminescence that permeated, leaving a faint trail in the air as she moved. At places, the light exceeded the boundaries of her skin, and at others it was buried inside.

She stood and moved to her bookshelf. Kneeling down beside it, she reached for a book: *I am a Cat* by Sōseki Natsume. Her fingers fell through it. She tried again with the same result. She tried to focus on the title and author's name on the spine, which were legible but not crisp. She reached for it a third time, and as she did the words sharpened and her fingers touched the binding. She pulled the book from the shelf, but realized that everything had reverted to normal, not just the book. The gray dreamworld room around her had become her normal apartment again.

She had pulled her focus from the stopwatch, but she was relatively certain that she hadn't missed any time. Everything had been linear. She had gotten up from the couch, walked to the bookshelf, and knelt down beside it. She was still there now. She wasn't in the kitchen, or anywhere else that would be inexplicable.

She returned the book to its place on the shelf between *Persona: A Biography of Yukio Mishima* and the *Sarashina Diary*.

Her solar plexus spasmed and calmed. A little unsteady, she went back to the couch and sat down. Her stomach was jittery, but not as bad as before; she was getting somewhere. She restarted the timer yet again. This time, she decided not to wait for the effect to happen. She wanted to make it happen.

She looked at the timer counting up—there were no jumps—and tried to recreate the feelings in her head and solar plexus. She tried to make everything go blurry, make her center vibrate. *How did it happen? What were the exact sensations?* She dug inside her mind, inside her muscles and bone, inside the spirit that made her tick. She searched, mentally scouring over each part of herself like an intense meditation routine.

There. A feeling clicked over in her mind, like a switch, like the fear of a snake woman in the water, like her mother dying.

Everything went blurry and gray: her hands, the timer, the room, and all its contents. She stood and went to the window. The outside world was awash in gray too, faintly luminescent shapes moving about on the street. The rails of the elevated train tracks sparked redly above the black shadows below as a train passed, countless white blurs of light inside. Cars radiated a subtle red from beneath their hoods. A cat jumped from behind a cargo van and bolted down an alley, a vital blur, zagging and leaping.

She looked down at herself, and saw her legs, a loose blur shot with internal light. Her eyes moved to her abdomen and chest where the light was strongest, permeating her form and spilling past the wavy outline of her torso. It was more than light; it was vitality illuminated, swirling and vibrant, conflagrant and essential.

I can see my soul. Or I'm insane. I'm probably insane.

Another train shot across the tracks and the color returned to the world. She was solid again.

She sat down in the closest dining chair and shook uncontrollably. She thought of her father, so stoic and empty after her mother's death. She had become just like him. She thought of her mother in the hospital, pale and skeletal, holding her frail hand as she withered away from the cancer inside her. *Or was it from the treatment?* She thought of the camping trip with her father, only months before her mother died.

At Yamanaka Lake, while her father was mindlessly fishing, eleven-year-old Masami had wandered away to the other side of the lake. The coastline was marshy there, and no one else was around but for a woman washing her baby in the water. The woman had beckoned to Masami, inviting her to hold the baby. And though she had started into the water to do so, something unsettling about the woman had stopped her.

The woman became angry at being rejected, and the baby had dissolved into fish and worms and splashed into the lake, followed by the woman, who had revealed a long snake's body where her legs should have been.

She had buried that memory and let the snake woman become the fancy of a child's imagination. But now she knew. It had really happened.

After the events that had transpired in Kofu, there was no denying that there were demons in the world. The snake woman had been one of them. With Akio and Miyahara, she had fought a demon under Kofu castle. They had seen it swap heads with its victims. It had done things that could not be explained.

She had disappeared then too.

She had been gone while Akio assisted the demon samurai in its suicide, and yet she had witnessed it. She had only remembered blackness at first, but as time passed, she realized that she could see it in her memory. She had become trapped in some parallel dimension, some pathway to Hell, when the demon had tackled her. Some entity had been intent on bringing the samurai back to his punishment, but had locked onto her instead. It had mistaken her for the samurai because she was holding its head.

All of that was insane.

Yet Akio had been there. As irritating as he could be, he was still an honest man, and he had witnessed all of the same things. They couldn't possibly have had the same hallucination.

She decided then she would talk to Akio tomorrow. He needed her, and she couldn't shut him out any longer. She didn't want to admit it, but she needed him too. She needed to talk to someone besides the bitter voices in her head. She wanted to get back to reality, to normalcy. But reality had shifted, and there appeared to be no going back.

In the meantime, however, she would try to become incorporeal again. She rolled her shoulders, took a deep breath to steady herself and went back to the couch.

4

On Assignment

When Akio got to work the next day, Masami was already there. This was nothing unusual, but what *was* unusual was that she looked hungover. She looked like she hadn't gotten a wink of sleep. There were dark circles behind her glasses, visible despite the makeup, which was a little heavier than normal for Masami. Her hair was not so well put together, with strands flying here and there. Her clothes were shifted oddly as if put on in a rush. She looked bleary-eyed and ill focused. She didn't have her normal lips-pressed-tight intensity. Her entire face seemed to sag into her coffee cup as she gulped it down. She was clacking away at the keyboard like she was trying to wake herself with the action.

Akio moved by her desk quickly to get to his own. He didn't even bother to say good morning after the way she had treated him yesterday. It wasn't unusual for her to treat him like crap, but she had never so blatantly lied to him before. That was what hurt. After what they had been through together, he expected a reduction in the usual disdain, not an increase.

He sat at his shared worktable and set his tea next to his computer. He had a bit of editing to do before heading out to shoot a building dedication for a local septuagenarian business owner. *Another thrilling day for Akio the wonder photographer.* He was glad to be leaving

38

though. He needed to get out of the building and get away from Masami. He knew it was silly to let himself get emotionally aggravated by her, but his emotions were something he seemed helpless to control.

He had thought that once he became an adult, the involuntary face-flushing and tears and blood-rising, and all those other pesky emotional reactions would fade or even cease altogether. But no, inside he was still that eleven-year old boy, face streaming wet and red, after being made to push his backpack halfway home with his nose, the older neighbor boys making dog noises as they followed, laughing. He was still nine as his teacher embarrassed him in front of the class by mocking his story about a boy who dreamed he had eaten a huge marshmallow and woke up to find his pillow gone. He was six and the girls walking behind him during the school field trip were laughing at him and he didn't know why. Had he sat on something? Did his hair look funny? Did they think he was stupid? At the time, he didn't know, and it made him angry. It made him feel like a weirdo and an outcast. In hindsight, he realized that they had probably thought he was cute. He had been cute as a boy, if his parents' photos were any proof, but he could only think the worst then. And even now, when he heard laughter, he had to convince himself it wasn't directed at him. But now he felt only awkward and skinny, any cuteness that remained overshadowed by his lack of self-confidence.

He wanted to be impressive, to be an inspiration to others, but the world seemed to fight him constantly, and instead he felt judged and looked down upon. Masami didn't seem to judge him, so much as spurn him. And there was something better about that. But lying to him was too much to take. He reverted back to that playground-age boy who wanted to run and hide behind the library building and not be found.

A boring building dedication was just the thing to get him out of there.

It was scheduled for 11 a.m., so he left at ten to get there early. The building was an eight-story office building in Ueno that housed Mirozuki Sukajan, a clothing company that started out of Atsushi Mirozuki's garage in Yokosuka, where he made hand-embroidered souvenir bomber jackets with intricate designs on the back: birds, tigers, cherry trees, maps, and more. The company expanded, moving to Tokyo and adding new items of apparel. Fifty years later it had become a fast-paced clothing manufacturer serving much of Japan and parts of China, Thailand, and Singapore. Mirozuki's next target was the West: Europe and America. Certain Hollywood celebrities had already been seen wearing Mirozuki's jackets. Today they were honoring the man by putting his name on a plaque and mounting it to the building. It would forever be known as Mirozuki Tower.

It was a warm day despite the cloud cover, and the air was thick. Akio wiped his forehead with his sweat rag and pulled out his camera. At least the clouds would provide some natural light diffusion for his photos.

Mirozuki practically glowed as he gave his brief commemoration speech. His smile was outwardly reserved, but inside you could see it was huge. His wife stood next to him as visibly joyful as he was contained, the wrinkles nearly enveloping her eyes when she smiled. They were happy and looked like they had earned it. That made Akio feel better. There was still hope in the world.

He saw Takeyoshi Shigeta with his digital recorder and notepad out. Tak was the grunt writer from the *Dainichi* assigned to this glorious back page story. They often worked the same gigs. He was a few years older than Akio and had streaks of brown and blonde dyed into his hair, which hung in his face over bright blue glasses.

"Hey, Tak," he said. "Powerful stuff, huh?"

"Oh yeah," Tak replied dryly. "The world waits in anticipation."

They shared a chuckle, and Akio resumed shooting.

He got his photos: the hand-shaking, the congratulations, the plaque going up, the crowd cheering.

Great. That buried page that no one turns to will really stand out.

A hollow rumble in Akio's stomach reminded him it was lunchtime. He would head back to Chiyoda Ward, before returning to the *Dainichi*, and stop at his favorite ramen place, Menya Murakami. The food was fine, but Kenji, the guy behind the counter, was the reason it was Akio's favorite. He was always good for a laugh and some meaningless conversation. Kenji should be working. That might cheer him up.

As he passed through the entrance to Ueno Station, a pain shot up the back of his neck and gripped his head behind the ears like a claw puncturing his cerebellum. He staggered forward, colliding with a slim, young man in a black suit and black aviators, who was exiting the station. As he made contact with the man, the pain intensified, pushing deeper in and creeping up higher into the back of his skull. The man held a polished wooden box high in one hand to keep Akio from bumping into it, but Akio felt his arm hit something hard at the man's belt. It was too large to be a belt buckle.

With his free hand, the suited man shoved Akio, who tripped over his own feet and skidded onto the hard tile floor of the station. The crowd deftly parted and went around him as if it were just a normal everyday occurrence. The man, framed by the entryway behind him, brushed off his shiny black leather shoes with a handkerchief and realigned his jacket with the open collar of his white shirt. He adjusted the hard thing at his belt line. Then, tucking the box under one arm, he took off his aviators and rubbed them on his shirt as he looked at Akio in a heap on the floor. He had a cold, disgusted grimace on his face, a slightly crooked nose and narrow eyes. He replaced his glasses, secured the box in one hand, turned, and exited the station.

Yakuza, Akio thought. *Or a wannabe.*

He had certainly looked like a yakuza, but may have just been a pretender. The gangsters' public image had waned in recent years, but too many young men still idolized the yakuza lifestyle: respect through fear, fast cars, fast women, and lots of money. All of that was wrapped in the noble, yet often contradictory, concept of *giri-ninjo*: loyalty at all costs yet compassion to all. Akio was pretty sure there were lots of other things that went with it too, like losing fingers, getting knifed or shot by a rival faction, and maybe winding up a corpse in Tokyo Bay.

No thanks.

He didn't want anything to do with that lifestyle.

The pain subsided as Akio stood and brushed off his slacks and his light blue button-down. He ran his fingers through his hair, being cautious around the base of his skull. The pain was gone as quickly as it had come.

That was the worst one yet. I really need to see a doctor.

He sat on the train, a muddle of dejection. Things had to get better.

Back in Tokyo proper, he stopped for ramen at Menya Murakami, and was happy to see Kenji behind the horseshoe-shaped counter bar. He got his ticket from the vending machine near the door and handed it to Kenji, whose round face welcomed Akio with what looked like a wide, almost clownish frown, but Akio knew was Kenji's best smile.

"How goes it, photo man?" Kenji asked in his heavy Kansai dialect. He was from Kyoto and had the distinct musicality and slang of the people there. To Akio, everyone from the Kansai region sounded like a comedian, so just hearing Kenji talk made him smile.

"Oh, you know," Akio answered. "Just out shooting the emperor and a bunch of rock stars."

Kenji laughed, a deep but subdued chortle. "Where are all your groupies today, boss?" he asked. "Usually they come in trailing behind you like goslings."

"Yeah, yeah," Akio chuckled. "They were getting on my nerves. Too needy, these women, you know? I've only got so much to give."

Kenji laughed again. "You've got the life, boss. I envy you." He chuckled as he went back to pass the ticket to the cook. He helped a few other patrons and then drifted back to Akio.

"Seriously though," Akio said. "I don't understand women at all."

"Who does?" Kenji replied, with a sideways smirk frown. "I know men married fifty years who still have no clue of how to deal with their wives. They're too moody and confusing. They never just say what they mean. It's better to be single guys like us."

"Yeah." Akio tried to sound convincing. "No need to put up with all those wacky hormones and lies." He hadn't meant to say "lies." It just slipped out. He had meant to say, "unpredictability" or "fickleness" or something like that.

"Lies?" Kenji asked, sounding surprised. He didn't miss a beat. "Someone been lying to you, boss?"

Akio grimaced, but he realized that he did want to talk about it. "Yeah, co-worker."

"What a bitch," Kenji said. "What about?"

"Yeah," Akio said noncommittally. He didn't think of Masami as a bitch, just someone with walls of steel around her, but it was definitely a word that others had used to describe her. And he was in no mood to defend her honor at that moment. "I just thought we were friends, you know? But she's sneaking off and not telling me about it."

"Sneaking off? You see, boss, that's the trap. You don't commit to them and they keep secrets and sneak around. You buy the cow and you end up with spoilt milk."

That analogy made no sense to Akio, but he smiled and slapped Kenji's hand when he put it out there, as if to say, "Right on, you nailed it."

Akio's ramen came and he slurped it down, interspersed with bits of conversation with Kenji. Afterward, he left with a full belly, but still felt empty. He had hoped to alleviate some of his stress about Masami and the weird, intense headache, but it had just been mindless guy talk. It had given him a few hollow chuckles, but that was it.

As he walked to the metro station, he tried to accept that Masami and he just weren't meant to be close friends. He had to move on. Maybe he really would quit the *Dainichi Daily* and be a stringer, or even a travel photographer. He could start a travel blog. It would be fun, always on the go, seeing the world. He'd be on his own, not having to stress about how Masami or anyone else felt about him. He didn't need friends; he had his camera.

He smiled bittersweetly at the thought as he rode the elevator up to the third floor.

When he got to the office, Masami wasn't there. *Figures.* He plopped down at his computer, hooked up his camera and started uploading photos. He massaged the back of his neck as the images appeared on the screen. He would make a doctor's appointment tomorrow. He was probably dying, he thought. He probably had some rare, incurable disease and would be dead within a week.

Well, at least that would solve my problems with Masami.

He chuckled to himself as the photos flashed in front of him. He had no desire to die. The thought of it actually terrified him. But somehow it was funny to him in that moment. *It all means very little when you're gone, right?* he asked himself. But he didn't have an answer.

He remembered something he had heard recently. He couldn't recall who had told him. *Was it Kenji?* No, it wasn't his style. Maybe he had read it somewhere.

The gist of it was this: you shouldn't judge other people, because everyone was just doing their best with what they had been given, or something like that. You didn't know what other people were going through, what troubles had manifested their behavior. If someone was being a jerk, well, maybe he's in debt over his head or his mother hates him or his girlfriend left him. You don't know. So don't take it personally, and don't let it upset you. They might even need some kindness.

Masami plus kindness never seemed to work very well for him. It usually just added up to rejection. Hell, Masami plus anything seemed to add up to rejection. Except maybe exhaustion from fighting head-chopping demons. But those days might as well have been a dream for all the good they did now.

She must be dealing with something heavy. Akio decided that if he was ever able to talk to her, he would refrain from being a smart-ass. He would just offer his ear and his honest compassion. He would be a friend.

The random keyboard clacking from Masami's desk started and stopped throughout the day, but Akio refused to look. If she wanted to avoid him, so be it.

After some time, he heard the deputy editor Eiji's voice from across the office. "Sato-san," he called out. "Where are you?"

This time Akio couldn't help himself standing up and rounding his table to look.

Masami quickly popped up from under her desk. "Right here, sir," she answered. "Sorry, I dropped my pen."

Akio was tempted to approach her right then, but Eiji gave him a stern look, so he turned around and went back to his desk. He sat there for the rest of day, trying to focus on his edits of the Mirozuki building dedication. He was making some final adjustments on his shot of the happy couple raising their hands together in front of the small crowd, when he felt someone beside him.

"Akio," Masami said in a whisper. He jerked around to see her standing to his left near the window. He hadn't seen her walk up. He looked at her, eyes wide, like she had appeared from thin air.

"Akio, I need to talk to you," she said. "But not now. I don't have time." She looked back toward her desk as if the work she had left today terrified her. She was flustered and distressed. It was an expression Akio hadn't seen since Kofu. Masami didn't get afraid, not of work in any case. "Let's meet tomorrow after work, okay? At Hobgoblin?" She nodded her head deliberately, making it clear that he needed to agree.

"Uh, yeah," Akio sputtered. "Sure."

Masami gave a tiny, forced smile, and then walked past him and back to her desk.

5

A Surprise Visit

Akio's brain was spinning as he reached his apartment. Masami had asked to talk to him! That was definitely a first. If she hadn't looked so troubled, he'd be jumping up and down, doing a victory dance. But something was wrong. She wanted to talk to him about something bad. Maybe she was going to come clean about where she had been disappearing to, and apologize for lying. That much would at least be positive.

He had picked up a pre-made dinner at Family Mart on the walk from the station, but he didn't feel hungry. He set it on his table and went to the fridge. He still had a few Asahi SuperDrys, so he grabbed one and plopped down on his bed, a futon rolled out on the floor.

He thought he might watch another documentary to take his mind off Masami, even though it was her fault he was watching them in the first place. In Kofu, she had criticized him for not knowing his history and being more interested in pop culture. He had blown it off at the time, but later had taken it to heart. In the short time they'd been back in Tokyo, he had started watching historical movies and documentaries, trying to better educate himself.

He took a sip of his beer and hit play on a history of the great Edo fires. The opening credits had barely begun when there was a knock at his door. He hit pause.

Two things bothered him immediately. One, who would be knocking on his door at this hour? And two, why hadn't they used the intercom? Was it one of his neighbors? He barely knew his neighbors. It certainly wasn't the postman at half past 8 p.m.

A sudden fear struck him that it was the man he had bumped into at Ueno Station. He was a genuine yakuza after all, and had tracked Akio down to knife him in his apartment because of the embarrassment Akio had caused him.

But would he? Akio was the one who had suffered the bulk of the embarrassment. And yakuza or not, would someone be crazy enough to tail him home some ten hours later just for bumping into him? Probably *someone* was, but it seemed unlikely. And something else lingered in Akio's mind. The crushing headache had felt strangely connected. Something told him that if that guy was at the door, Akio would be having a headache again. But he didn't. He felt fine.

The knock came again.

He went to the door, trying to make his footsteps silent. He looked out the peephole. It was a young man, not wearing a suit. He had on a t-shirt and a lightweight jacket, and had a wheeled suitcase behind him. It was a teenager with a wide face and big eyes. He looked familiar, but Akio couldn't quite place him through the distorted lens. Whoever it was seemed harmless enough, so he opened the door.

"Hi, Mr. Tsukino," the teenager said politely, raising one hand in a brief wave.

"Yoshio!" Akio now recognized the teenage boy from Miyahara's kendo class in Kofu, the brainiac who had wrongly accused Miyahara of being the murderer. Of course, Akio had been convinced of the same thing, and when Yoshio had met him at the manga cafe to divulge Miyahara's strange behavior, the verdict had been all but sealed. They had both been woefully wrong.

"What are you doing here? Planning to move in?" he added, eyeing the large suitcase.

"My apologies for disturbing you, Mr. Tsukino, but I had to find you." Yoshio looked worried. "May I come in?"

"Sure, yeah," Akio said. "Come on in. And just call me Akio, okay?" He was clueless as to why Yoshio would be showing up at his apartment out of the blue, but he seemed like a good kid, however weird. "There's an extra pair of slippers for you." Akio kept a couple pairs for his parents' infrequent visits. He pulled one set from the narrow shoe closet next to the door.

"Thank you," said Yoshio. He parked his suitcase by the door, kicked off his shoes, and donned the white slippers.

"You want a beer?" Akio asked as he walked the three steps back to his own can. Then he paused. "Wait, you're not old enough, are you?"

Yoshio shook his head.

"It's no big deal, you can have one anyway, if you want."

"It's okay," Yoshio answered. "I don't want one."

"No problem. More for me then." Akio sat back down on his futon. He was suddenly happy to have company. He never had company. "So how did you get into the building? Did you hack the security system, pick the front door lock? I would've let you in if you had just called up."

"Uh, no," Yoshio said. "Someone was leaving right as I got here. So I just walked in."

"Oh," Akio said. Th at wasn't nearly as exciting. But then something else occurred to him. "How do you know where I live?"

"You were easy to find," the teenager answered politely, but clearly had more pressing things on his mind. "Your information is all over the internet."

"Oh." Akio had never really thought about it, but he supposed everyone's information was easily available online.

"Miss Sato's info was much harder to find."

"Yeah." Akio suddenly felt foolish. "Masami's always been the careful one."

"So I came to you." Yoshio said impatiently. "I need your help. *We* need your help."

"We?"

"Sensei Miyahara is in trouble."

"Miyahara?" Akio asked. "Your sensei who you thought was a murderer? I figured he'd have kicked you out of the kendo class for that one." Akio laughed.

Yoshio dropped his head and frowned, squeezing his eyes shut briefly, but didn't reply.

"How could he be in trouble anyway? " Akio went on. "That old man can kick some ass."

"Yes," Yoshio agreed. "He's a tough old geezer, but he's not invincible."

"And you're helping him now?" Akio figured that whatever it was, Yoshio was just a kid, and he was probably worried for nothing.

"He's been training me. Every day since he got out of the hospital. Even before he could move well again, which has only been recently. And then he went off to kill some other minor demon—wouldn't let me go with him—and tore his wound open again. That's probably why he was so easily captured. He wasn't in top form. I told him he shouldn't go after those guys."

Yoshio was breathing faster now, his face tense. This sounded bad.

"What guys?" Akio asked. "What happened to him?" He sat up straighter.

"We were walking to get lunch after a particularly grueling session, when I noticed three rough-looking men in dark suits walk into a grocery market. Something told me they weren't there to get produce for the evening's dinner." Yoshio paused for a second and asked, "May I sit?"

"Of course," Akio answered.

Yoshio turned the chair at the table to face outward and sat. He continued. "Sensei noticed it too. We looked at each other and had this moment of silent agreement. Then we followed the men inside.

"We pretended to admire the eggplants and daikon but really we were eavesdropping on the men, who were talking to the store owner. The owner was nervous but defiant. He tells the men that he won't pay this month. He hasn't made enough profit. He got a spoiled shipment of fruit, and lots of bags of rice had to be returned because of weevils.

"'Your poor choice of suppliers is not our concern,' one of the men says, this square-jawed man with buzzed hair. 'How much do you think Kumamori cares about that?'

"'Yeah,' one of the others says, 'he doesn't shop here.' They both laugh.

"The square-jawed one, who had done most of the speaking, says, 'You didn't pay in full last month either.' He pokes the grocer's forehead when he says it. 'You're falling behind.'

"But the grocer says there's nothing he can do because he doesn't have it. 'Please send my apologies to Mr. Kumamori,' he says. 'I will have it next month.'

"Then the men look around the shop. We're the only others in there. As soon as these guys entered, a woman had taken off fast with her daughter, dropping her green onions and turnips on top of the cabbages.

"Another one of the gangsters, this chubby guy with hair past his ears, grabs hold of the grocer's arm, and really casually says, 'Let's talk this over in the back.'

"The third gangster, a short, thin guy with a mole on his chin, stays in the front room, blocking the entrance to the back. He watches us, while the other two go with the grocer. I can see that he has a gun under his jacket. It buckles out slightly at his waist, just above the belt."

Akio was on the edge of the futon now, leaning forward, taking slow sips of beer.

Yoshio continued. "Sensei puts on a limp, hunches over a bit, then picks up two eggplants and hobbles over to the guy. He speaks like a really old man, much older than he is. He says to the guy. 'My boy and I want to buy these here eggplants. Can I buy them from you, sonny?'

"At first the guy says no, then he seems to rethink. 'Sure,' he says with this ugly smile. 'That'll be two thousand yen." Then he holds out his hand.

"Behind him we hear something being knocked over, and the grocer begging the men to stop. We can hear him clearly. He insists that whatever money they might find, he needs just to keep his store open.

"'Hmph,' Sensei says. 'Seems a bit steep for a couple a eggplants, doesn't it, son?' This time he's talking to me.

"'Well, do you want 'em or not?' says the gangster.

"'Sure, sure,' Sensei says, and bends over as if to get something out of his pocket. 'We need 'em for tonight's dinner or the missus will be fiercely mad,' he says. As he comes back up, something metal whips out of his hand and wraps around the guy's neck. It's a manriki-kusari!"

"Wait," Akio interrupted. "A what?"

"A manriki-kusari, a weighted chain. Classic ninja weapon of ancient Japan."

"Oh, yeah. That." Akio frowned. "Of course."

"Anyway," Yoshio continued. "Sensei whips the chain around the guy's neck and jerks him to the floor. As he falls, his jacket flies open, and I snatch up his gun. It's a Smith & Wesson model 37, probably stolen from a cop. I aim it at the guy, my finger just resting on the trigger. I'd never held a real gun before, but it doesn't feel all that different from an arcade gun. A little heavier is all. It feels more substantial, you know. But it doesn't matter, Sensei is choking him out."

Yoshio continued, speaking faster, his breath short and sharp.

"With the guy passed out, we sneak into the back room. The chubby gangster is trashing the place, looking for something—the guy's money stash apparently—while the square-jawed one is holding the grocer's arm against a plastic table.

"And something is sitting in the middle of the table, like a big silver egg with a flat base. The gangster is asking the grocer where his money is, and the grocer keeps saying he doesn't have any to give. Then the gangster takes the lid off the top of the egg and this green light comes out of it. There's this green gem inside, giving off a weird glow.

"'Look into the gem,' he says to the grocer. 'Look into the pretty green gem and learn where your loyalties are. You'll tell us where it is one way or another.'

"Just then, the chubby one who'd been trashing the place sees us. 'What the—' he starts to say, but I aim the gun at him, and he shuts up. The other gangster, the square-jaw guy, turns toward us. "I told Kei not to bring that damn gun,' he says. "He can't seem to hang on to it!'

Then to me, he says, 'Put the gun down, boy. You don't want to get hurt.' He stands up and I point the gun at him. 'You could get in a lot of trouble for shooting that gun, boy. Just for firing it, you could get life in prison. You know that?' he says.

"I did know that. I've read a lot about criminal law, but I don't say anything. I just scoff at him, so he thinks I don't believe him or I just don't care. I glance at Sensei and see that he's staring at the thing on the table, the green egg thing. The grocer is just sitting there, looking a little dazed. Square-jaw is staring at me, and the chubby one, who's further away, past the table, is watching me too.

'I'd leave if I were you,' I say. 'I don't care about a prison sentence. I've got nothing to live for.' I heard that in a movie once, and thought if I said it convincingly enough, it might just work.

"The chubby guy must have believed me, because he starts backing away toward a rear exit. Square-jaw doesn't though. He starts coming toward me. He completely ignores Sensei as a threat and stays focused on me. But Sensei had the chain behind his back, and he whips it out like a lightning strike at the guy's neck. Apparently, the gangster saw it just before it happened though, because he jerks backward, and takes the weighted end of the chain to the side of his head. He staggers back and steadies himself on the table. He's clearly rethinking his odds in that moment. He snatches up the glowing egg, and backs away toward the back door, keeping his distance from Sensei.

"Then he holds up the egg toward us and tells us to look into the gem, like he said to the grocer. But before I could even focus on it, Sensei shoots the manriki-kusari out again and knocks it from the guy's hand. It falls to the floor and the gem falls out of the egg.

"'Don't look at it!' he says to me. 'Keep your distance.'

"Chubby guy snatches up the gem, drops it back into the silver egg and caps it. He backs away even more. 'We'll remember you," he says with a sneer, and the two of them take off down the alley.

"Sensei tells me to get home, and to get rid of the gun, and then he goes out the door after them. I told him I thought it was a bad idea, but he said he'd be fine. He said he'd meet me tomorrow as usual. But then he texted me about a half hour later. He said if he wasn't there for our lesson tomorrow, to give it a day. And if he wasn't there the next day, to come find you."

Akio's brain tried to catch up. He shuddered at the vivid images of Yoshio's story. He had dealt with a demon samurai. Th ree yakuza shouldn't scare him, but somehow they seemed worse. The demon still had that surreal quality about it, even in Akio's memory, as if it had all been a bad dream. Yakuza were real, scary men who could do scary things and not feel guilty about it. Reality was always worse than dreams.

But it wasn't the story that Yoshio told that was the scariest part. It was the last thing he had said that had Akio jittery and puzzled.

"He said to come find me?" Akio asked. "Are you sure?"

"Yes," Yoshio confirmed. "You and Miss Sato. He said you would be able to help."

The teenager may as well have asked Akio to perform heart transplant surgery or pilot a space shuttle.

"How the hell am I supposed to help you rescue Miyahara, or anyone for that matter, from a bunch of angry yakuza? I'm not the guy you think I am, or he thinks I am. I'm just a photographer. And not even a great one of those."

"You killed a demon. Sensei said you're incredibly brave. And besides, it's not just you. He said to get you *and* Miss Sato."

Brave? Miyahara must have lost too much blood from that sword in his gut.

"I'll see Masami tomorrow at work. I'll tell her." Akio didn't know what she would say. He hoped she would think it as ridiculous as he did. "Why don't you just call the police?" Akio asked.

"It's not what Sensei asked me to do."

"So you're his lap dog now?"

"I've devoted myself to being his apprentice. I will respect his wishes."

"Oh, so you're a little demon hunter in training, huh? Seriously, it wasn't that long ago you wanted to hand your precious sensei over to the cops."

Yoshio dropped his head again and sighed. "I was misguided. It was a failure on my part, and so obvious in hindsight. I reacted without seeing the whole picture. It's an embarrassing moment for me." He fidgeted with his shirtsleeves.

"Well, it all turned out okay, didn't it." Akio said.

Yoshio looked at him, his eyebrows raised.

"I mean that he wasn't the killer," Akio clarified. "Not that he's been captured or . . . who-knows-what by yakuza." He didn't want to say "killed." He didn't want to worry the kid anymore than he already was. But the truth is, Miyahara might already be dead.

Then what? We try to rescue a dead man, and most likely become dead men ourselves?

Yoshio read Akio's thoughts as clear as day. "He's not dead." The boy's face was determined. "I'm sure of it."

Akio sipped his beer and shrugged. What was he supposed to say to this kid? He had gotten through the ordeal with that demon on sheer luck. He had given up at the end. He had been ready to die. If the demon had wanted to kill him, it would have done so. And easily. He wasn't someone who could purposely face the yakuza. He wasn't a hero.

They sat in silence, Akio trying to look anywhere but at Yoshio, who would not stop staring at him.

"What?" Akio finally said, annoyed.

"When can we get started?" Yoshio asked.

"I told you, I'll see Masami—Miss Sato—at work tomorrow. I'll discuss it with her there. Miyahara said we need her too, right?"

"Yeah."

"Well, then you'll have to wait."

There was another long silence while Akio tried to figure out what to do. He wasn't good with guests, much less ones that were insisting he rescue someone from dangerous gangsters.

"Can't you just call her?" Yoshio finally said.

"Masami?" Akio laughed. "Yeah, 'cuz she'll answer my call. Right!" He laughed again, and then got bitter. She should answer his call, but he was afraid she wouldn't. He only had her number because of the

Kofu assignment. But right now, he had no desire to call her. He wanted to pretend this wasn't happening. He had a "date" with her tomorrow at a bar. He just wanted it all to work out the way it was supposed to.

"You don't look like you're in that much of hurry, you know," Akio said, "bringing a huge suitcase like that. I'd be more inclined to think you had no plans to go back to Kofu at all. Looks like you're gonna stay a month."

"Oh, I don't have much clothes in there."

"Well, what is in there then? That's a big suitcase."

"Um . . . ." Yoshio clearly didn't want to answer. "There's a book . . . and some other stuff."

A book. There was only one book Akio knew of that would fill a suitcase like that, and he didn't want to think about it. Why would he bring that book?

"Do you even know where he is?" Akio asked.

"Yes," Yoshio answered. "He sent me a text with the location before he went in after them."

"What was he thinking?" Akio blurted. "He's really got an overgrown sense of vengeance. What was so special about that grocer that he had to go hunt down these yakuza over a little shakedown?"

Yoshio raised his eyebrows again. "Oh, no, that's not it," he said. "It started out as just doing the right thing, protecting the innocent, you know, not turning a blind eye, but he didn't chase them because of that."

"Well, why then?"

"It was the stone—the green gem," Yoshio said.

"Hmm," Akio grumbled. He could sense Yoshio waiting for him to ask for more details, but he didn't want to know. Whatever was important about this green gem, he couldn't have cared less. He just wanted everything to be normal. He didn't want to know about green gems or huge books. Masami had asked to talk to him. Th at was something he could look forward to, even though it was clearly not something good she wanted to talk about.

Akio was not a hero. He was not put on this planet to rescue anyone from anything. It was not his job to kill demons. That had been a fluke.

"I need to sleep," he said, even though he wasn't remotely sleepy. He hadn't even eaten his dinner. "I can't deal with this right now. I'll talk to Masami tomorrow and we'll figure out what to do."

Yoshio stood up and looked nervously around the apartment.

"Do you have a place to stay?" Akio asked.

Yoshio shook his head.

"Well, I hope you're okay with the floor. I've got an extra blanket somewhere."

Akio put his uneaten dinner in the fridge, retrieved the blanket, and tossed it to Yoshio. "No extra pillow, sorry."

"It's okay, I'll use my jacket."

The teenager looked anxious. He wanted too much, and Akio couldn't give it to him. Akio showered and got into bed. He switched off the light, leaving only the boy's face hovering in the dark for a moment, lit by his phone screen. Akio turned toward the wall and tried to force himself to pass out.

6

A Request for Heroes

The next morning Akio was groggy and irritable. Yoshio was already awake when Akio pulled himself up into a sitting position on his futon. The teenager was cross-legged on the floor with his eyes open, staring blankly at the wall.

"You all right?" Akio said, with a sticky morning mouth.

Yoshio blinked like he was coming out of a trance. "Yes," he said. "Just meditating. It's something Sensei taught me."

"Hmph," Akio groused. "Seems like a waste of time to me. Life is about doing, isn't it? Not sitting." He was upset from the previous night, though he knew the boy was just the messenger. How in the hell did Miyahara think that he and Masami could save him from the yakuza?

"It helps with the doing," Yoshio said.

Akio grumbled. Even though the teenager appeared calm, he could tell he was impatient. But Akio hadn't been about to go tromping off in the middle of the night with a teenage boy, whiz kid or not, to face a bunch of gangsters that had kidnapped the old man. Miyahara was the most capable fighter of any of them.

Sure, Akio had studied judo when he was a teenager and kendo before that, but both experiences had been largely failures. His judo experience was only slightly better for the fact that he had been generally quick enough to evade attacks, but he almost never could

57

incorporate a throw into the action. He had been the one thrown and flat on his back more than not. If anyone asked him to describe the gym where they had practiced, he could give a very detailed account of the ceiling.

He went to the kitchen. "I'm going to make tea. Do you want any?"

"Okay."

Akio filled and started his electric pot, and they stood, waiting for the water to boil, saying nothing. The whistle blew, and he poured them each a cup.

"I don't have any breakfast food," Akio said. "But we can share my dinner from last night, if you want." The thought of reheated convenience store pork cutlet and rice wasn't appealing, but his stomach was empty.

"Okay," Yoshio said again.

"Give me your number," Akio said as he shoveled in a mouthful of rice sweetened with plum sauce. He had divided the contents of the dinner onto two separate plates and microwaved them. "I'll contact you once I talk to Masami. And I'll give you mine in case . . . I don't know, if something comes up. Just know that I'm working, so don't expect me to be all chatty."

"I'm worried about Sensei. If you can get back early . . ."

"There's nothing I can do," Akio said. "I've got a job. Responsibilities, you know? You'll understand when you're an adult." Akio felt stupid as soon as it came out of his mouth. He felt like one of those patronizing know-it-alls who made him feel like he wasn't good enough to even understand the basic concept of life.

But he did have an assignment this morning, and one that felt like a slight step up from the usual, even though it was for the entertainment section. He was shooting a hip, up-and-coming artist and not a fourth grade piano recital. Maybe Tanaka was going to slowly give him better and better gigs. He couldn't mess it up.

"Can I have your wifi password?" Yoshio asked.

"Sure, just nothing . . . illegal, okay?" He wrote it down and then gave Yoshio a spare key. "In case you need food or something."

Akio grabbed his camera bag with the extra shirt and sweat rag tucked inside, and headed off to the metro station.

Akio arrived at work early, partly because of the morning assignment and partly to get away from Yoshio. The humidity wasn't bad enough that he had to change his shirt, so he went straight to his workstation.

Masami wasn't there. She wasn't just MIA, like she had been; her computer wasn't even on. Her giant mug steaming with coffee was absent. She hadn't shown up yet. This was unheard of. She was always there before Akio, even when he was early. The sound of her clacking away was what greeted him when he got off the elevator. It was a keystone that held his work world in place. He felt disoriented not hearing it.

Sometimes she would be on the phone with the police or a lead, and sometimes she was out on assignment, but the clacking would resume when she returned and that thought was enough to set Akio's world aright. But he had walked by the assignment editor's giant whiteboard and her name wasn't on it. Not at all. That was stranger yet.

She must be on some secret assignment for Tanaka, he thought. Some big news story they didn't trust the rest of the office with. That was the only answer.

He went about his day, trying not to think about it. She would roll in eventually. He had an edit to finish and then the museum exhibit opening to shoot that would keep him out for a couple hours. He needed to focus, but his mind was too far from work.

Meeting Masami later. Yoshio at his place. Yakuza. It was too much.

He finished his edit quickly and headed out of the building. Masami still hadn't shown.

The exhibit was for a contemporary artist named Amaterasu5, who created small *mikoshi*, divine palanquins for the gods, made of garbage, or, as the artist community put it, found objects.

From what Akio had seen of her work, the mikoshi were rather stunning. Not traditional by any means, but there was a symmetry to them, a flow that made them fascinating. They weren't large enough to be the real thing that were often carried around in parades, but not small enough to set on a table either. Pet-size was what came to mind.

Akio thought of the parade he had shot this same time last year. It was for Sanno Matsuri, a biennial festival to grant good luck to the construction of Edo Castle. Th e castle had been built in the 15th Century, but they kept on with the parade, dressed in the style of the imperial court of the time and carrying Shinto gods around in the ornate mikoshi. The palanquins were gaudily decorated, but Akio liked them. Something about them made him feel safe. He knew there weren't really gods inside, but the idea that there were felt reassuring.

Today though, the mikoshi were made from discarded electronics and furniture, emptied canned goods, and action figures that had seen better days. As interesting as it all was, there were no gods here. At least not any that Akio recognized. He snapped away, taking a lot more photos than normal to counteract his distracted brain and ensure there would be good ones.

His text alert went off just before noon. It was Yoshio.

Have you talked to Miss Sato yet?

Akio typed back with one thumb.

No. Not there when got to work. Out shooting. Back in an hour. Let you know then.

He took a lunch break soon after Amaterasu5 had given her brief interview to news cameras and print reporters and said her goodbyes to the fans. Tak was there with his dyed hair in his eyes, and they exchanged a nod. They had shared a fair number of assignments since Tak had been hired. They were the low totem pole team. Akio took shots of the artist signing some last-second autographs, and then she disappeared into a backroom for who knows what private celebration. He imagined champagne fountains and cocktail sandwiches, movie stars and rock stars, agents making billion yen deals, celebrity hookups and scandal.

And to be sure, there was a photographer back there documenting it all. What would it be like to be that behind-the-scenes, all-access photographer, shooting the backrooms and dirty secrets of the rich and famous? Those photographers were probably caught up in the glamour too, sleeping with models and doing drugs with celebrities, the line between their job and the parties ever blurring. Akio had never been interested in illegal drugs, but would he fall inline, becoming an addict, just to maintain those connections, to get those priceless shots?

Who am I kidding? That's a scenario I'll likely never have to face.

Again, Akio was reminded of the Sanno Matsuri parade last year. After winding around the city, it had stopped in front of the Imperial Palace. He had taken several shots as the throng gathered there, but then the head priest entered the palace to bless the emperor. Akio hadn't been allowed in there either.

His life seemed to be full of places where he wasn't allowed.

Akio had gotten everything he would of the artist, and several shots of nearly every piece of art, so after a quick bite at Mosburger, he headed back to the office. He was itching to get back and talk to Masami. He didn't have the faintest idea what to do about Yoshio and Miyahara. He wished he could send the teenager away and let the kendo instructor figure out how to escape from the yakuza himself. But his conscience would eat him alive. Should he call the police? Yoshio had said Miyahara was adamant about not doing that, but the old man was probably just being prideful and stubborn. Still, what would he say?

Um, this guy I barely know might have been kidnapped by the yakuza somewhere in Kofu. What proof, you ask, officer? Oh, this kid I barely know said so.

Yeah, that was not likely to inspire any heroic yakuza infiltration from the police.

But what was Akio going to do? Take their picture? Masami would know what to do. She was ever the voice of reason, no matter how curt and unfriendly a voice it was.

Arriving back onto the third floor of their office building, Masami still wasn't there. He saw Eiji walking the floor, eyeing everyone in the newsroom, making sure work was being done and deadlines were being met. Akio saw him lean over the desk of one of the senior staff writers, Daisuke Tsujihara, who gave him a sour look. He swore he heard Eiji mention Masami's name.

When Eiji had gone back to his desk, Akio ducked back over to Daisuke. "Hey, you look busy," Akio said, noticing the stack of paper on his desk.

Daisuke looked up at Akio like he was a buzz in the fluorescent light and said nothing. He was not someone that Akio ever talked to.

He had been at the *Dainichi* thirty years, and it took every ounce of courage Akio had to even look him in the face.

"Uh, sorry, I don't mean to disturb you," Akio sputtered. "I just overheard Eiji talking about Masami, and I have this photo I have to give her but I haven't seen her today so I thought maybe you knew where she was and I could give it to her." Akio rambled it all off in one breath and gasped to recover.

Daisuke gave him a hard look. "She's the reason I'm busy," he said with a scowl. He looked back at his screen and resumed typing. "She called in sick."

What?

Akio stepped away slowly, bowing. "Thanks, Daisuke, sir. Thanks." He shot back to his work table. When he got there, he pulled out his phone discreetly and typed to Yoshio.

Not here. Called in sick. Supposed to meet at bar later.

What bar? When?

Hobgoblin. Akasaka. Not sure time. Soon as I can. 6?

K. Worried. See you there.

Four more hours.

Akio was worried too. Not as much for Miyahara as for Masami.

Called in sick? Masami doesn't even know what that means!

She had never missed a day of work in her life as far as Akio knew. And he had never heard her so much as sneeze. Something was seriously wrong.

7
A Ghost of a Chance

There was a light, warm drizzle in the air when Akio arrived at Hobgoblin. It was a small, British-style pub, down some stairs from street level, with polished wood everything, apart from a little brick work. Akio wasn't sure why Masami had picked this specific place. Did she come here a lot?

It wasn't busy, but there were people, mostly eating at tables. Many of them looked like foreigners. He found his way to the bar and saw Yoshio already sitting there with a Coke. He had his backpack slung over one shoulder. When he saw Akio, he swung it into his lap, quickly unzipped it, and pulled out a stack of paper.

"Look," he said forgoing any kind of greeting. "I've been doing some research. This is the building where Miyahara was when he last texted me." Yoshio thrust a printout of a map at Akio. "And this is the blueprint of the building." He held up another printout.

"Hold on," Akio said, putting his hand up and not taking the papers.. "Let's not get ahead of ourselves. Have you seen Masami?"

"No." Yoshio looked as nervous as Akio felt.

"Okay, let's sit. And hope she shows up soon." He sat at the bar next to Yoshio. The bartender approached and asked what he wanted to drink.

"Uh," Akio hesitated. It somehow seemed a very difficult question. "Asahi," he finally said. Th en, seeing Yoshio's cola, he said, "No, Coke . . . no, Asahi." He changed his mind again. He knew he shouldn't dull his already muddled thoughts, but maybe it would calm his nerves.

They sat for a while, Akio sipping nervously at his beer while Yoshio tried three more times to show his research about the apparent yakuza hideout. Several times Akio felt a chill run through his arm and sometimes down his back. At first, he thought it was just nerves, but then he figured the air conditioner must be on too high.

"Why do they have to keep the AC so high in here?" he asked no one in particular.

"It doesn't seem that cold to me," Yoshio answered.

"I must be right under a vent or something then. Will you scoot over a seat?"

Yoshio moved over one stool and Akio took Yoshio's seat. As he did so, his beer moved a few centimeters the other way on the bar. No one was near it. He looked around to see if he was the only one who had noticed, and it seemed so. It must have been an illusion. He had moved suddenly the other direction, so the glass had appeared to move the opposite way. That was all.

He grabbed the glass and pulled it in front of him. He got comfortable on the already warm bar stool and went to take a swig. A sudden chill breeze coursed up his back and through his hair, causing his shoulders to flinch suddenly, and he spilled the beer into his lap.

"Dammit!" he cried out. "What's with the AC in here?" he said loudly.

This time the bartender overheard him. "AC's not on. We turned it off over an hour ago."

"Uh huh," Akio said, not believing him. "Sure. Then is there a fan or something?"

"Nope." Th e bartender seemed sincere, a little confused yet amused.

Sure, sure. Laugh it up. I just spilled beer in my crotch thanks to your non-existent air-conditioning.

Akio set the glass back down and it promptly fell over, spilling what was left of it on the bar counter.

"Dammit!"

He was certain he had set it down level. The glass had seemed to jump to its side on its own. Inanimate objects often seemed to get the better of him, but this was ridiculous. Other people might simply consider him clumsy, but sometimes he was convinced that every day items were out to get him. This was indisputable proof.

"Can I get you another one?" the bartender asked, not trying that hard to keep a straight face.

"No," Akio said annoyed. "We were just leaving."

"We were?" Yoshio asked. "What about Miss Sato?"

"She's obviously not coming," Akio snapped and stood up, displaying the dark stain on his slacks exactly at the crotch. He looked at the counter and grabbed a handful of square napkins, white with a little hobgoblin in the corner, and tried ineffectively to mop up some of the beer, drawing attention from the other bar patrons as he padded his privates. He gave up, tossed the used napkins back on the counter, and stormed up the stairs and out of the pub. Yoshio followed.

They stood outside for what felt like several minutes, neither of them saying anything. Akio tried to stand in a way that covered the embarrassing stain. It wasn't working. No matter which way he turned, it looked like he had peed himself. If he hadn't been so angry on top of it, he would have had a meltdown. He tried to will the drizzle to turn into a downpour, but if anything it was subsiding.

"What do we do now?" Yoshio finally asked.

"I don't know," Akio barked.

"Can't we go to her apartment?"

"I don't know where she lives!" Akio almost shouted. "She's never invited me over before! Imagine that!" He leaned back against the wall, not caring anymore if passersby thought he had wet himself. He harrumphed and dropped his head, resting his chin on his chest.

Just then a cold breeze ran right down his face and across his chest. His shoulders involuntarily shuddered at the chill, and as they did, something tickled his nose. "Dammi…!" he started to shout, but then he noticed a piece of paper sticking out of his shirt pocket. He pulled it out.

It wasn't a paper. It was a white square napkin with a little hobgoblin in one corner. And there was writing on it. It was an address in Chuo. Beneath it were five numbers. It was in Masami's handwriting, he was sure of it! He had seen her scribbled notes many times. But how? He hadn't seen her at work that day. She hadn't been at the bar. How had this napkin gotten in his shirt? Had the bartender slipped it in? Had she dropped it by earlier and told the bartender to give it to the bumbling guy who will probably spill his drink in his crotch? Why wouldn't he have just handed it over?

Something tugged at his right shirtsleeve, almost pulling him from the wall. He looked to his right and saw nothing. He looked around frantically from side to side.

Yoshio eyed him with concern. "What's going on?" he asked.

Akio glared at the teenager.

Is he in on this?

Yoshio looked dumbfounded, so Akio decided he was not. But someone was clearly messing with him. Every slight breeze put his teeth on edge, every raindrop. He pulled his smart phone from his pocket and punched in the address from the napkin, eyes darting side to side.

Akio sat on the Hibiya Line train while Yoshio stood next to him. No other seats were open.

"Are you going to tell me where we're going?" Yoshio asked.

"Masami's."

"I thought you didn't have her address," Yoshio said.

"I didn't." Akio said, not bothering to elaborate.

Ten minutes later, they got off in Chuo. The drizzle had stopped, and the fading blue sky showed through gaps in the clouds.

Akio led the way to a high-rise apartment building with wide balconies, on the corner of an intersection. It was nicer than his building by a step, but not a luxury complex.

So she makes more money than me, but not that much more.

They reached the glass-doored entryway, and Akio pulled on the handle. Nope. He pushed and it didn't budge. After he let go, the door seemed to rattle in the frame a few beats longer than was natural. He turned away from it to the electronic directory and started searching for Masami's name.

The cold chill returned again, right down his back. What the . . . ? Then a strong tug to the back of his shirt pulled him away from the directory. He stumbled backward and turned sharply, expecting to find Yoshio there. "What the hell are you . . . ?" He sputtered out. But the teenager wasn't there. He turned back around to see Yoshio standing near the directory.

"Are you okay?" Yoshio asked. "Are you drunk from those few sips of beer?"

"No!" Akio shouted. "I don't know what's going on!" He started to panic, and he spun from one side to the other, trying to catch whoever or whatever was moving him around. Either something was messing with him or whatever brain disease he had that gave him the headaches had progressed into some kind of advanced hallucinations. He lowered himself to the sidewalk and tried to calm his breathing.

Cold suddenly gripped his right nipple. *Ach!* It felt like it was being twisted by icicle fingers. "Owwww!" He slapped his hand to his chest to stop the pain. It stopped, and he felt the napkin again.

Wait a minute . . . the numbers.

He pulled the napkin from his pocket and looked at the five digits under the address. Next to the entry was a keypad. "It's for the door, I think," he said, standing, still jittery, and showing the napkin to Yoshio.

Yoshio looked closer at it. "I could have told you that. I don't know why you're keeping things from me. We really should work together."

Akio ignored him. He was shaking, afraid the chill that was following him would attack again, afraid he was losing his mind. He punched the numbers into the keypad. A tiny green light illuminated and a buzzer sounded. He pushed on the door and it opened.

The apartment number was written with the address: 705. They found the elevator and it climbed to the seventh floor. They reached the apartment, not far down the hall, and Akio knocked. As soon as he had done so, the chill blasted his upper back with a force that almost knocked him forward. He trembled and reached to knock again, then thought better of it as the chill gripped his balled fist.

They waited for a moment. No one came to the door.

"Maybe try the door," Yoshio suggested.

"I doubt she would leave her door unlocked," Akio said, while at the same time reaching for the doorknob. He turned it, and it opened. "Oh." He pushed the door open carefully, and called, "Masami?" He did not feel good about entering her apartment uninvited.

The chill passed through his entire body, and the door flew all the way open as if he had shoved it. He collapsed to his knees, shivering.

Yoshio went to him, and grabbed his arm. "You okay?" He pulled Akio to his feet. "I think I felt a chill that time too. Whatever you've got is rubbing off on me."

Akio was dazed. "I don't think we should be in here."

"Of course we should. We need to find her. She obviously gave you the address and the building code, because that wasn't your handwriting. You're suffering from some sort of weird seizures that apparently might be contagious since I'm starting to feel the chill now too. We need her help. She wanted us to be here. You said she called in sick, so maybe she has this chilly seizure thing happening to her. Maybe she's laid up in bed and/or communicating in some other way. I've learned some very weird things since studying with Sensei, so I'm not averse to considering that we could be dealing with the occult. In fact, bearing in mind some recent lectures of his, I'm starting to believe this might be a haunting." Yoshio had barely taken a breath. He looked extremely impatient, like he had been made to wait in a queue far too long.

"Why would you think that?" Akio asked, first afraid the apartment was haunted and then worried that Masami was dead.

"The chills, for one," Yoshio answered rapidly. "But also because there was a mobile phone on that table a second ago, and I just saw it disappear."

Akio's phone rang.

He jumped as if a claw had just gripped his leg from inside his pocket, feeling the vibrations of his phone reverberate through his whole body. He pulled the phone out like it was a hot coal.

It was Masami.

"Uh, hello," he said, tentatively.

"Akio, goddammit," Masami's voice said. "It took you long enough."

"I'm s-sorry," he stuttered. "I'm sorry we broke into your apartment. Where are you?"

"You didn't break in. I let you in," she said, annoyed. "I'm right here with you."

8

M

A different kind of chill ran up Akio's spine and he spun around, taking in the whole living area of the apartment. From his position in front of the door, he could see a small couch across from a television, a bookcase, and two empty chairs at a table. He could see into the small kitchen. The door to the bathroom stood open. No one was there. The only thing he couldn't see was the loft.

"Uh, are you in the loft?" he asked nervously.

"Nope. I'm an arm's length away from you." Her voice was clearly only coming through the phone. She couldn't be that close to him.

"That's pretty funny," Akio said, but it wasn't funny at all. It was creepy. It made his skin crawl.

"I'm not joking, Akio. Why is that kid here?" Akio flinched. If she knew Yoshio was here, she must at least be able to see them. "Isn't that the kid that implicated Miyahara?" Akio looked frantically about, checking the corners of the ceiling for hidden cameras.

"There aren't any hidden cameras," Masami said through the phone. Akio shivered again. "I'm right here. You just can't see me." She sounded extremely perturbed about that. "Why is he here?" she repeated.

"Uh, Miyahara sent him." Akio couldn't help himself turning this way and that. There was no way Masami had become invisible. This was just some weird, elaborate prank. "He needs our help, apparently."

"Our help? With what?"

"Rescuing him, I think."

Yoshio looked at Akio curiously, following his jerky movements around the apartment. He seemed a bit anxious as well. He had suggested they were dealing with a ghost. And the ghost was Masami.

"She's here, isn't she?" Yoshio asked.

Akio nodded slowly, conscious of the fact that Masami could see and hear them both, so even if he didn't believe she was really there, he had to play along.

"You aren't . . ." Akio had a hard time saying the next word, "*dead*, are you?"

There was a frustrated sigh on the other end of the line. "No, Akio. I don't think so."

"Can you put her on speaker?" Yoshio asked.

Akio shrugged and hit the speaker button.

"If you're here," Akio asked tentatively, "how come I can only hear you through the phone?"

"I don't know." Her irritated voice betrayed her own helplessness. "I can't make my voice break through whatever barrier is dividing us, but I can affect objects if I concentrate hard enough. And I appear to be able to use the phone."

"That's amazing," Yoshio said. "You're really here in the room with us?"

"Yes. Your name is Yoshio right?"

"Uh huh."

"So you've had a change of heart about your sensei, I see. You're his helper now?"

"Apprentice."

"I see. You have any experience dealing with this sort of thing? Did Sensei Miyahara ever talk about anything like it?"

"Not really, no," he answered. "We've talked about ghosts a bit, but they were all deceased."

"Great."

"I wonder if this has something to do with why he wanted me to find you."

Akio thought the prank had gone too far. "Um, can you two just clue me in, because I'm kind of creeped out. I mean, you're not invisible, right? Not really. You've got some sort of camera, some kind of home security thing and you're messing with me, right?"

"I wish I were, Akio."

"When did this start happening?" Yoshio asked. He now seemed more fascinated than anxious, his mind apparently distracted from the fact that his beloved sensei had been kidnapped.

"I first noticed it only a few days ago. I started blacking out, or so I thought. I was losing chunks of time. I wasn't even aware of it, until Akio and another co-worker pointed it out. I wasn't at my desk, even though I was. Apparently, no one actually saw me disappear, but that is clearly what was happening. I spent all day yesterday trying to be aware of it, and eventually I was successful. I started noticing when I slipped away. I could see things and move about in this other state, but I couldn't interact with anything. So then I started trying to control it, trying to make the shift happen. I was only barely successful at that. Then, this morning when I woke up, everything had already gone fuzzy. I was invisible, and I couldn't undo it."

"That's why you called in sick?" Akio asked, still skeptical. "That's gotta be the weirdest reason I've ever heard. Sorry, boss. I can't come in. I'm invisible. Must've been hard for you."

"Not to mention that I had to figure out how to use the phone first, since I hadn't been able to interact with anything before, but yes, I felt foolish. I've never in my life had to fake a cold."

"Why didn't you take the phone with you when you went to the bar?" Yoshio asked.

"She was at the bar?" Akio asked.

"I had set it down after calling work and at the time, I couldn't pick it up. I was feeling . . . weak right then . . . useless. I couldn't focus." It was clearly hard for her to say. "So I left and hoped I could get your attention some other way."

"You were the chill!" Akio realized. He was getting more and more creeped out. "You wrote that note while we were there? In the bar?"

"I wrote it while you were standing out front looking like you peed your pants."

"You made me dump my beer in my lap!" Akio was irritated now, but also flabbergasted. He could never prove she did it.

"It wasn't on purpose, Akio. Relax."

"So you were able to write a note there, and you picked up the phone right away when we got here, but you couldn't do that earlier." Yoshio wasn't asking a question. He was simply sorting out the information. He was crunching data.

"It seemed easier after you both left. I was upset and had to do something."

"So you swiped at the beer glass in frustration and it moved," Yoshio continued for her. "You grabbed a pen and a napkin after we left, because you were unable to communicate."

"Yes," Masami answered.

"Your frustration and desperation is what allowed you to interact. It gave you a stronger connection to the physical world." Yoshio smiled. "I have actually heard of something like this before. It was in one of Sensei's unusual books. This one was about the effects of demon contact on humans. It was the study of a woman who had developed multiple personalities. It was somewhere between schizophrenia and possession. The only thing that would bring her back to herself was when she held onto a small, hand-carved tiki statue that she and her husband had bought in Hawaii on their honeymoon. As soon as she held it, she would become herself again."

"So we need a tiki statue?" Akio asked.

"No, it had nothing to do with the statue," Yoshio answered, "except for the fact that it represented an emotional connection to her husband and her real life. We need something that represents a similarly powerful, emotional connection for Miss Sato."

"Ha. Good luck with that," Akio said.

"Thanks, Akio," Masami said sarcastically. "I knew I could count on you for help."

Akio immediately felt guilty. He was rarely averse to making jokes at her expense, because he felt it was payback for the way she treated him. But she was in trouble. He really shouldn't be a wiseass. She had actually come to him, which was unprecedented and still kind of mind-boggling. She had wanted to meet him to talk about something, and now she was stuck being invisible. He needed to be a friend right now. Unless this whole thing was an elaborate game and he was the butt of some weird joke. Then he would get her back tenfold.

"Sorry," he mumbled. "Was this what you wanted to talk to me about?"

"Yes," Masami answered through the speaker. "I didn't think I would be stuck this way though."

"Where are you right now?" Akio asked. He wanted to believe her, but he needed more proof.

"Standing by my table," she answered curtly.

Akio walked over toward the table. When he was half a meter away, he reached out a hand. He flinched and pulled his hand back as it hit cold air. Then he reached out again more cautiously. He felt the cold air again. It was as if he was reaching into a refrigerator.

"Your hand's on my breast," Masami said.

Akio retracted his hand in a flash and jumped back. "Sorry! I didn't know. I wouldn't . . ."

"Don't worry about it," she said. "It's not like I could feel it much."

Deeply embarrassed, Akio scrambled to change the subject. "You're really . . . a ghost," he said.

"Apparently," she answered.

"So . . ." Akio said. "We need to find something that you connect with, right? Like Yoshio said? Do you have something like that?"

There was a short pause before she answered.

"I think so."

"Where is it?" Yoshio asked, his urgency starting to come back. "I'll get it for you."

"No," Masami answered quickly. "Akio can get it. It's in the loft. In my nightstand, bottom drawer. There's a small wooden box. Inside is a black cloth pouch. Bring that to me."

Akio nodded and began climbing the ladder to the loft, his thoughts racing.

She wants me to do this? She wants me to go into her bedroom to get her private things?

He felt like he had just been given permission to enter the secret treasure vault of the emperor, or access to a door beyond which holds the secrets to the universe.

She chose me!

He could barely contain himself. Not only had she wanted to talk to him about what was happening to her, now she had approved—no, requested—his access to her bedroom. When his head crested the level of the loft, he felt like he was peering into some hitherto undiscovered land.

There was a mattress on the floor covered in a plain black comforter. An open wardrobe displayed her clothes on the opposite wall. Pants suits and skirt suits, next to a few pairs of jeans and sweaters. There were even dresses!

Masami wears dresses?

Two were dark, silky material, one sleeveless, one not. Another one looked more like cotton, still dark, but rather short. This was almost too much for him to process. He pulled himself up completely onto the loft floor.

There were only two things adorning the walls. One was a framed front page of the *Dainichi Daily* with a headline that read "Kidnapped Girl Returned Home Safely." It was Masami's first front page story, and one she had practically solved on her own, if what he'd heard was true. She had even gotten an exclusive interview with the kidnapper before the police arrived. It was also the story that got her into the press club. That was before Akio had gotten his job. The other reporters said that allowing her into the club was meant to be a way to control her, to keep her from going rogue and out-storying the other papers. If they let her be "one of the boys" she'd surely calm down and stop making them look bad.

Fat chance of that.

The other was a framed embroidered image of some Buddha-looking guy sitting on a small elephant in a bed of flowers. It looked like something a grandmother or a doting aunt might make for you.

A squat, dark wood nightstand stood near the pillow side of the bed. Akio imagined seeing a photo of himself sitting on it. He saw Masami looking longingly over his image before bed each night, and laughed to himself. The framed front page was above the nightstand. That's what Masami saw before bed and when she woke up each day.

He circumvented the bed and approached the nightstand. The only thing on it was a closed notebook with a pen across it. He was tempted to open it and peer inside.

What thoughts did Masami write down before falling asleep?

But he couldn't betray her trust. Besides, for all he knew, she had climbed the ladder after him and was watching. Another shiver went down his spine.

He pulled open the bottom drawer. He saw a number of things at once. Everything was very organized. There was a tissue box, a stack of three more notebooks, a black leather case that looked to hold pens, a plastic container that was closed and too opaque to see its contents, a small knife in a sheath—*for protection or opening letters?*—and a small, wooden chest made from myriad bits of colored wood. It was a Hakone puzzle box. Akio had one similar that he had gotten as a boy on a family trip to Hakone. He had found it again as a teenager but couldn't figure out how to open it. Something had been rattling around in it too. He was pretty sure he remembered putting the instructions inside with whatever else was in there, not wanting anyone else to know how to open it. Then he had promptly forgotten how himself. He had given up on it and stashed it away again.

Masami's box seemed to be an equally challenging puzzle. It was the only box in the bottom drawer of her nightstand, small, wooden, or otherwise. Did she expect him to figure out how to open it? He moved it around in his hands for a minute, pushing on different bits of lacquered wood hoping one of them would slide and at least get him started. But nothing.

He went back to the ladder, resisting looking at the dresses again, as he was still painfully aware that Masami could be watching him. His thoughts were pure enough; he just had a hard time imagining her in a dress.

Back on the main floor, he approached the table slowly with the box in hand. "Are you still . . ." he started.

"Yes, bring it here, please. Did you get the pouch?"

"No. I can't open these damn things."

"Oh, right. Sorry. I forgot I had closed it. Dammit. I can try but I'll have to—"

"Is that a puzzle box?" Yoshio asked excitedly. "I love those things!"

"Of course you do," Akio mumbled.

"Can I try?" he asked to the empty space by the table.

"Sure," came the annoyed reply through the speaker. "Might as well. I'll talk you through it. The first move is—"

"No, I want to figure it out. It'll just . . ." his fingers were already whirring over the smooth surface, the box turning every which way in his hands " . . . take me . . ." sections of wood were sliding sideways, up, and down ". . . a minute." And the box was open, Yoshio with a big grin on his youthful face.

"Ten moves! Cool," he said. "You know they have one at the store in Hakone that has 125 moves?"

"Let me guess. You opened it in ten seconds," Akio said, irritated.

"No, actually it—"

"I don't wanna know!" Akio shouted. "Just give me the box!"

Yoshio startled and looked confused at Akio's outburst. He handed over the open puzzle box. *Good*, Akio thought. *At least there's something he doesn't understand.*

Inside was a black cloth pouch just like Masami had said. There was nothing else with it. He awkwardly presented the box to where he hoped Masami was, still vaguely wondering if he was the butt of some elaborate prank.

"Take the pouch out," Masami commanded. Akio did, feeling a small weight to it. "Now take out what's inside and set it on the table."

Akio walked cautiously to the table, hoping to avoid accidentally bumping into any ghostly body parts. When he got closer, he opened the pouch. He was anxious about what might be in there. He hoped it wouldn't be anything *too* private, not a lady's personal toy or something.

He reached in and his fingers felt metal. He pulled out a circular medallion on a chain, a golden disc with a raised "M" on it, the sides of which curved to the shape of the medallion. There was a vertical line through the "M," and the whole image was bordered with a circle. The raised parts were all golden, and the background was painted black. It looked worn and old, scarred with years of use. He set it on the table.

A moment later, it disappeared.

Akio inhaled sharply, and stepped back.

"Cool," Yoshio said.

They waited for what seemed to be a long time. Then there was a sniffle from near the table, and the air in front of it blurred like the heat off a campfire. Then nothing.

Akio saw two drops form on the floor, as if water was dripping from the ceiling. Then nothing again for at least a full minute.

Then he heard a soft laugh, and the air started to blur again. This time it took the shape of a person—a woman. Slowly, it started to solidify in front of them. Masami's slender shape became visible like she had just teleported in from some distant starship. Her face was flushed and her eyes red. A hint of a sad smile played on her lips, but disappeared quickly as she made eye contact with Akio. She was wearing only a long yellow t-shirt that read in bold English letters, "Laughter is the best Forever Me. I LOVE YOU!!!"

Akio wasn't exactly sure what the first part meant, but the irony of Masami wearing a shirt that said "laughter" was not lost on him. And he understood "I love you," the bold letters making him very uncomfortable, as if Masami were shouting it at him.

Still he couldn't help but stare. It had not been a prank after all. Masami had really been invisible.

And then another thing struck him: She had only been in a t-shirt this entire time. Even at the bar. The loose cotton draped comfortably around the sharp cut of her hips. Akio couldn't help but look down to her feet. She didn't even have shoes on. He averted his eyes.

"Let me go get dressed," she said curtly, and climbed the ladder to the loft. As she ascended, and the angle from his view to under the t-shirt increased, her bare legs more and more exposed, Akio turned away, the blood rushing to his face.

"It worked," Yoshio said with a satisfied smile.

"Yeah," Akio said. "Thanks." He suddenly felt inadequate again. Masami had wanted to talk to him, to get his help, but all he had been able to do was retrieve that box from her nightstand. It was Yoshio that had really helped her, every step of the way.

Barely a minute later, Masami was descending the ladder, dressed in jeans and a crewneck shirt, her sleeves pushed up. It wasn't nearly as shocking as only a long t-shirt, but Akio had only ever seen her in a suit. Even in Kofu chasing after the demon samurai, she had been dressed for work.

"Thank you both," she said as she reached the bottom. "That was a little distressing."

"I'm glad it worked," Akio said. "It must feel weird to be invisible."

"That's an understatement."

"Does the "M" stand for Masami?" Akio asked.

"Yes . . . and no," she answered with a faraway look. "It doesn't matter. It worked. And I thank you."

"You might want to keep that medallion handy," Yoshio said. "The woman in Sensei's book would slip back into her other personalities soon after the tiki statue wasn't in her possession."

Masami pulled down her collar slightly, exposing the chain that was now around her neck.

Yoshio nodded.

After an uncomfortable silence, he said, "Well, now that *you're* here—I mean, corporeal anyway—we should get back to the reason *I'm* here."

"Give it a minute, Yoshio," Akio said. "Let her rest. She's been invisible and uh . . . barefoot all day."

"No, it's fine," Masami said. "I need to focus on something else, something real. And I need coffee, bad." She headed to her kitchen and started brewing some.

"Wait," Akio said, a thought occurring to him. "You said you couldn't pick up your phone when you left the apartment. How did you open the door if you couldn't interact with objects at the time?"

Masami grimaced, giving Akio a look that reminded him quite vividly that she had just made it clear she wanted to talk about something else.

"I was like a ghost, remember? Not only could I not interact with objects, apparently, I didn't need to be affected by them at all. When I reached for the door handle, my hand went through it, like it wasn't there. So I walked *through* the door. It made me nervous when I realized I was on the 7th floor, but thankfully I didn't fall through. Not sure why."

"Oh," Akio said, "Weird. And sorry, let's move on."

Yoshio explained again what had happened to Miyahara, with only minimal commentary from Akio, who couldn't help himself. It was like a story out of a manga. When the teenager was done, Akio burst in again. "I don't see how we can help him, do you? What can we do against a bunch of yakuza?"

"Sensei said you were the only ones who could help. He said you'd figure it out." Yoshio's impatience was bubbling up again.

"Well, Masami can do this ghost thing now," Akio said. "That's pretty amazing, but what do I have? An intense fear of being tortured and possibly dying at the hands of gangsters probably isn't something that will be of use."

"I'm not comfortable with whatever has happened to me, Akio" Masami said. "I'm not sure this is something I want to cultivate. Right now, I just want it to stop happening."

"But you said you were trying to control it."

"Yes, in an attempt to stop it. I can't stop something that I don't understand."

"Speaking of . . ." Akio said, feeling like he could talk about it again since Masami had brought it up. "I mean, what the hell? Why is this happening to you?"

Masami took a deep breath and sighed heavily before answering. "I disappeared in the samurai demon's lair in Kofu, remember? When it rushed me?"

Akio nodded. It had been a dark moment for him. He had felt so alone. Masami was gone and he thought Miyahara was dead.

"You said you had fallen *into* the demon or something and got stuck." Akio remembered their conversation outside the hospital when Masami was still disoriented and shaky. She seemed very clear-headed now, her usual intense self.

"Yes, but now I don't think I was *in* the demon," she said. "Maybe I fell through it. I'm not sure. When I had the demon's head, I could feel something searching for me. But it wasn't me it was looking for; it was the demon samurai. It could track the demon's head somehow, and I think it just latched onto whatever was holding it, which happened to be me."

"What is *it*?" Yoshio asked.

"I don't know. The demon's master, I guess."

"From Hell?" Akio asked.

Masami only raised her eyebrows in a way that said, *Seems so.*

"Creepy," Akio said. "And they didn't even get the head. The demon put it back on."

"He grabbed it from me the second before they took me. Then I was just in the way. I could feel them trying to get past me, but it was like I was in a narrow corridor blocking them."

"A lemon seed in a straw, you said," Akio recalled.

"Yes." A shiver ran through Masami at the memory, and she pressed her lips tight.

"The head was in a metal box, right?" Yoshio asked, and both of them nodded. "Sensei told me that. Whatever they were using to track the head probably couldn't penetrate the box. I'll bet it was a protective measure that backfired on them, a way to keep any of the demons from finding their own head. So when it was unboxed, they incorrectly assumed that whoever was holding it was the *namakubikamen*—the demon. And when you got caught, something changed in you. In order to go into this *corridor*, your chemical makeup was altered somehow." Yoshio's eyes were lit up with an almost feral excitement. "That or . . . you said you may have fallen *through* the demon?"

"Yes," Masami answered. "Possibly."

"Maybe some element of it rubbed off on you, some demon essence, and it infected you. Either way, I think this is what Sensei was hinting at. Something in you was changed, mutated perhaps. Or maybe it was just an awareness that we all possess but is suppressed, and yours was simply turned on. Whatever it was, you were granted access to this other realm and it hasn't been revoked."

"Is he always like this?" Masami asked Akio.

"So far, yep," Akio said.

"Other realm," Masami said, repeating Yoshio's words. "That's what it feels like. It's not simply turning invisible. I feel like . . . I'm somewhere else, some parallel dimension. Your theory about how it happened sounds plausible," Masami said to Yoshio. "But why now? I'd been fine for over a month."

"It takes time for these things to germinate," Yoshio said. "I read an account of a man who had been swallowed whole by a huge *shibōsū*, a type of worm demon. He was still alive inside, and cut his way out of the demon's belly with a knife. Months later, he was in horrible pain. His skin was burning and his flesh started to dissolve, even though he had bathed afterward for three days straight, replenishing the bath water several times, some microscopic element of the demon's digestive acids had remained on him, and it had slowly multiplied. The man was digested by the demon even though it was already dead. He just melted into sludge on the ground."

"Gross," Akio said. "I don't think that helps us."

"No, it does," Masami said. "It makes sense. If my cells are transforming somehow, then it wouldn't be something that happens overnight."

"Great," Akio said. "So I have his memories, and you have his demon essence or something."

"You have the demon's memories?" Yoshio lit up again.

"Yes. When I put on its mask, like an idiot, I had flashbacks to his life, and . . ." he swallowed, "his death."

"What do you remember?" Yoshio asked, his attention now fully on Akio.

"Uh, battle, heinous acts that I—I mean, he—performed. He wasn't really what you'd call a good samaritan. Kind of the opposite."

"Battle though, right? You remember fighting? Sensei told me that when you put the mask on, you fought him like a master."

"I did? Masami told me a lot of what happened, but not that I fought like a master." He looked at Masami. Her steady gaze confirmed what Yoshio said. "But my head wasn't there," Akio continued. "I don't even remember it. I was on some battlefield fighting other samurai."

"Do you remember training, maybe?"

"No. Just killing."

"Well, that's a start," Yoshio said. "Have you ever tried to remember other things, that maybe you didn't see when you put on the mask?"

"No!" Akio was annoyed now. Not only did he not want to remember someone else's despicable memories, he didn't want to think about what he had done and said in that hotel room. "Why would I?"

"To control it, Akio," Masami interjected. "I see what he's getting at. Like I tried to control my disappearing. He thinks we can use these . . . changes, these . . . abilities, to our advantage."

"Sensei told me you two were special," Yoshio said. "I didn't realize how much."

The cold metal circle felt good against Masami's chest. It calmed her. The chain anchoring it to her neck gave her strength. Yoshio had been right. Focusing on the medallion had given her control; it had brought her back to the land of the living.

The medallion had been her mother's. It was something she had always worn. When Masami was younger, her mother had told her that the "M" was for "Masami" and that's why she wore it close to her heart. It had made Masami feel loved, like something precious, in spite of feeling bad for her older sister, Tsukiko. Where was *her* medallion? Though Masami wasn't sure there was an English equivalent for the character *tsu*, surely there was something her mother could wear.

But still she cherished the "M." It made her mother's love a tangible thing. Metal, scratched and worn, her love was solid and well-used, physical proof of something otherwise abstract.

Her mother had been weak and frail, lying in a hospital bed, when she had tried to give it to Masami, but she had refused it. It had been too much to bear. Masami had believed that if she took the medallion, her mother would die.

"Let the "M" stand for *mama* now," her mother had said, pushing the medallion toward Masami.

"Not yet, Mama," Masami had said, tears in her eyes. "You need it."

"Okay, little Masa. But know that it is yours now."

The medallion had not prevented her mother's death. And Masami had cursed herself for not taking it when her mother offered. Had refusing the medallion been refusing her love? Was that why she had died? She knew it was the cancer to blame and nothing she had done or not done, but maybe, if she had taken it, her mother might have gotten better. *Maybe?*

Now she knew better, but the regrets of a child are strong. They burn in like a brand, and scar for life.

Masami had worn the medallion daily for years after that, until she was in her early twenties. She had put it in the puzzle box when she moved away from home, as if finally laying her mother to rest.

She had worn it even after she learned its true meaning.

One day her father saw it dangling on her neck, and asked if he could hold it. She pulled it over her head and set it in his hand, the chain draping through dry and calloused fingers. He beckoned her to sit at the dining room table, and when she did, he wore a deep frown.

It wasn't an unhappy frown; it was his thinking face. She knew he was about to tell her something serious.

It was then he explained where the necklace had truly come from and what the "M" represented. To prevent any misunderstanding, he insisted that, for her mother, it had stood for "Masami," but its origins were something else. What it actually stood for was "Mantetsu," a portmanteau word for the South Manchuria Railway Company.

At first, she felt let down that it hadn't originally been made to represent her name, but when she learned that it was her great grandfather Hidekazu's badge from working on the railroad, and that her grandmother Sumie had made it into a necklace, she had felt a new profoundness for it. The fact that her mother wore it with her in mind made it all the more important. It had remained her most precious possession.

Memories flooded back when she held it in the gray blur of her ghostly invisibility. She saw it dangling around her mother's neck as she made gyoza, filling the dumpling skins in preparation for cooking later—her mother always had a proper meal well planned in advance. She saw it glinting in the sun on a trip to Minamichita, where they went each summer, her mother wearing it even with her modest beach clothes. She saw it dangling on a hook in the bathroom when she had run in unhindered and muddy to show her bathing mother a tiny frog she had caught by a pond. Masami had grown up in Komaki, outside of Nagoya, where there were plenty of places to get muddy and find frogs. Her mother had told her it was a dharma frog and that they were very common.

"But still cute!" Masami had insisted, just before the frog had leapt from her hands into the bath. Her mother had jumped back splashing water everywhere, but then laughed right along with Masami. The frog had quickly become languid in the warm water, so they scooped it out.

"You'd better take it back," her mother had said. "It'll be much happier in the pond."

As much as she had wanted to keep it, Masami knew her mother's wisdom was true. So she did, patting it on the head softly before setting it free.

Then she was in the hospital, and the medallion looked like a lead weight pressing down on her frail mother's chest, sinking into her gauzy skin like it might drop through the husk of her body, propped up on the narrow hospital bed. She was so thin, she barely put a bump in the bedding. She held her mother's hand in her own, brittle bones and papery skin, too weak to return the grasp.

Masami saw the life go out of her mother. Eyes closed and a tender smile on her face, her chest ceased to rise after one last escape of breath, as if the medallion was too heavy to let in any more air. Masami quickly lifted the medallion to relieve the pressure, to allow another breath. But her mother's chest did not rise.

She hadn't cried then. She lay her head on her mother's chest as lightly as she could. She listened to her own sharp and unsteady breath and wondered if she had killed her mother prematurely by not taking the medallion, if the weight of unclaimed love had collapsed her lungs. But there were no tears, only a sudden and complete emptiness.

When her mother's spirit left, something in Masami left with it. She had known the day was coming, but she resented it; she didn't understand it, and she had resisted its reality with every atom of her being. But then it was very real. Her mother was dead, like any other animal or plant that comes and goes, an ant trodden underfoot, an unwatered blade of grass, a tree felled by root rot. She was organic matter that would decompose, nothing more. Masami lay on nothing but a feeble imitation of what her mother once was.

When she lifted her head and left the hospital, medallion in hand, she shut out the world.

Earlier this evening walking from her apartment to the bar, stuck in ghostly form, she had made some startling realizations. On the street, she had seen others. There were countless people with light inside them, some glowing fiercely outside the bounds of their bodies, a few barely a candle flicker as they shambled along. Most were relatively contained around the shape of their bodies, as hers was. But one, she noticed, was light alone.

He was a middle-aged man, walking slowly, looking around at the buildings and sky as if the streets were empty. Two teenage girls walked right through him, and she realized he was dead. Neither noticed the other, apart from a slight shiver the girls only took for a breeze. The man took no notice of all the people around him, but it seemed he could see the buildings and the terrain. He looked lost and contemplative. Then he had walked around a corner and was gone.

She saw another spirit before she reached the bar, an elderly woman standing in the air just outside a fourth story window, clutching a bundle wrapped in a *furoshiki* cloth. She smiled as she looked across the city. Masami saw a door appear on the same building at the next level up, its outline glowing a faint lavender. The woman turned to see it, and her smile increased. She walked upward as if by invisible steps to the door. The door opened and Masami saw what looked like a hand holding it for the woman, slender fingers glowed like filtered sunlight. Th e woman bowed and then entered and disappeared, but the door had remained.

Holding the metal circle in her hand now, half a ghost herself, she opened up to a reality of otherworldliness that she had refused for so long. What had her mother looked like leaving her body? In life, how much light had spilled over the boundaries of her form?

As she stood in her apartment, the tears came. For the first time since her mother's death, they came unlocked, dripping to the floor. She saw them darken the hardwood, the metal "M" warming in her hands as her ghostly teardrops broke the barrier back into the physical world, giving her a key to return to it herself. Her mother's love was real. And so Masami became real too.

9
Plan B

"But I don't remember how to fight!" Akio said, his voice sawing at Masami's caffeine-deprived skull. She gulped down coffee to make up for an entire day without it. Akio and Yoshio were arguing. "It would be supercool if I did, but I don't. And I don't want to think about that sicko's memories to do it."

"But you've already done it," Yoshio said. "Sensei said so. That means it's already programmed in you on some level. You just have to access it. We only have to figure out the right equation."

"This is not math! This is my brain and body, kid." Akio said, clearly flustered.

"Everything is math," Yoshio said matter-of-factly. "But I meant it as more of a chemical equation. We need to combine the right reactants to create the product of you being able to fight."

Akio looked at the teenager like he had spoken a different language.

"You still have the mask, right?" Yoshio asked. "What if you put it on again?"

"Not happening," Masami interjected. "It's safe and sound, and there's no way in hell he's putting that on again. Ever." What happened when Akio had put the mask on was not something she wanted to witness again. He had become someone else, some*thing* else. The way he moved had become panther-like and brutal. He had become a creature bent on death, a graceful demon who fought only to kill. If she hadn't collected the swords and kept them away from Akio, both she and Miyahara would probably be dead, and who knows how many others would have been killed before he had been brought down.

"Yeah," Akio agreed. "Not happening."

"Well maybe there's another way to tap into it then," Yoshio said, undeterred. "We have to figure something out. I've been trying to understand why Sensei wanted your help, and all I could think of was that, because of what you went through together, he knew he could trust you. He hinted at something . . . *supernatural* about the green gem, so maybe you were the only ones he could think of who would believe. But there's obviously more to it. He must have had some intuition that you might be changing, that you might be more capable than you realized. Otherwise, Akio is right, a photographer and a writer are not the best weapons to face the yakuza head on. You could do a lot, of course, in a kind of public exposé or something, but sneaking in to rescue someone they've kidnapped? Especially someone as tough as Sensei? I don't think so." He took a breath and continued. "So, Miss Sato, you said you had tried to control your invisibility before. Do you think you can become invisible at will? Now that you have your medallion? And return at will, too?"

"I don't know," Masami answered after a long silence. "I don't really feel up to trying."

"But you yourself said that it was best to learn to control it and not be at its whim."

"Yes, but I just spent an entire day as a ghost. I need some time."

"We don't have time!" Yoshio was getting visibly anxious now. "Sensei is in trouble!"

Masami wondered at the loyalty Yoshio now showed Miyahara, when not long ago he had been ready to turn his sensei over to the police. But she was pretty sure she understood. Miyahara had taken the teenager under his wing in spite of it all. He had recognized Yoshio's talent and good heart, and instead of shunning him, had invited him into his crazy demon-hunting world. Yoshio didn't seem to be someone who had many people in his life who treated him with open arms. He was an intellectual loner, too smart to be anything but hated by those who couldn't compare. On top of it, he probably felt guilty for misreading Miyahara and an obligation to make amends.

"I understand," she spoke in soft tones, trying to calm him. "I will try again, but right now, I need to finish this coffee. Then, I need to have some more coffee. And then, I'd like dinner. I haven't eaten all day."

Yoshio took an agitated breath, but nodded.

"I don't see how we're going to be able to help," Akio said. "Even if we wanted to tap into these powers, or curses, or whatever the hell they are, I don't see how we could become skilled at them in a few hours. This isn't some montage in a movie where we practice for ten minutes and suddenly we're masters. I don't want to remember this evil bastard's killing skills and it's obvious Masami doesn't want to be a ghost again, so why the hell don't we just call the cops?"

"We can't call the cops!" Yoshio said emphatically. "Sensei said explicitly not to call the cops. They are in bed with the yakuza in Kofu and will not be of any help. He was very clear on this."

Masami could easily see Detective Kuramoto, the loathsome, misogynistic cop who had been her police contact on the Kofu Head Collector assignment, making deals with the yakuza, even taking orders from them, but his partner, Detective Fujimaki? Could he be corrupt as well? He had seemed too honest, too good-hearted. He was a good cop, she was sure of it.

"Okay, fine," she said. "Let's calm down. Arguing with each other will get us nowhere. I understand that you're concerned, Yoshio, and that the situation is urgent, but we need a solid plan and some better awareness of the situation before we take on the yakuza."

"Yes," Yoshio agreed. "That's why I have these," he said, producing the stack of printouts he had tried to show Akio earlier. "I've gone over the layout of the building where Sensei was when he texted me. At this point, it's possible he's not still there, but it's a place to start. I've also gathered information on the principal members of the Tezuka-gumi. That's the dominant yakuza syndicate in Kofu and . . . who happens to own the building. I've also got info on another building where they keep their offices, where the principals will likely be, and what their strengths and weaknesses are."

"You got all that online?" Akio asked.

"It wasn't that hard," Yoshio answered. "They have a website."

Masami exhaled a brief, sardonic laugh. Most yakuza syndicates had websites showing all their charitable acts and good deeds. They had community outreach programs, held events on holidays and passed out candy to children. They helped provide care to the elderly and the sick, and even helped clean up the Fukushima disaster of 2011. They presented an image that showed them as a legal organization as innocent and charitable as the Red Cross. The websites failed to show the profits they made from mahjong clubs and pachinko parlors, from prostitution and protection fees from local businesses, the shady real estate deals, corporate extortion, hired muscle to sway voters at the polls, and muscle and money to influence the politicians they elected. They failed to show the murders in the name of power and profit, and the missing fingers offered as penance for some insult or from those who wanted to get free of it all.

"There's manga too," Yoshio continued. "And fanzines. Some of that is online, but we could get some more information if we picked up some hard copies."

The fanzines and manga were different, Masami knew. They did show the dark side of the yakuza, but people ate it up. The manga showed moderately fictionalized versions of real gangsters' lives. The fanzines were like pop culture rags. They made them look like rock stars to their fans. But Yoshio was right, there might be some information to be gleaned from them. Although she didn't fancy sitting and reading a bunch of yakuza magazines and comics anymore than she wanted to become invisible again.

"All right," Masami said. "Let's have it. What have you got?"

Yoshio laid the papers in a stack on the table, while Masami poured another cup of coffee. He pulled photo printouts off the top of the stack and arranged them into two small groups. He pointed to the group of three photos showing different angles of a two-story industrial structure. "This is the warehouse," he said. Th at's where Sensei was when he texted me. The main offices are here." He pointed to the other set of two photos of a glass-fronted building that looked more like a bank. "I couldn't find a blueprint for that one yet, but I'm hoping we won't need it. I'm thinking Sensei is still here." He put a finger on the first photo of the warehouse. "Can't say that for sure, but it seems more likely they'd keep any prisoners away from their main offices, someplace less public. And there are a bunch of small rooms that could be used as holding cells. I'm sure they have other property too, but this is what I have so far."

"Assuming he's even still alive," Akio chimed in.

Yoshio glared at him. "He's still alive. He has to be." He went back to the papers, pulling a blueprint to the forefront and laying it in the center of the table. "This is the warehouse. In his text Sensei said he was outside this loading dock." He pointed to the bottom left of the paper. There was a small parking area where two trucks could offload cargo directly into the building. Th ere was a ramp and stairs to one side. Large doors were positioned where the trucks' trailers would open. "He followed them in here," he said, pointing to one of the large doors.

"How do you even know that?" Akio asked.

"Because in his text that's what he said he was going to do," Yoshio answered impatiently. He continued to point out the main warehouse, offices, reception, small conference rooms, and a showroom. He flipped to a new blueprint showing the upstairs where there were smaller offices and a conference room that looked out over the warehouse from indoor windows.

"If they're holding Sensei anywhere, I'd guess it's here," he pointed, "in this block of rooms, probably the far one at the end of the hall. Otherwise, he could be upstairs, most likely in one of these storage closets."

"Well, it's a start," Masami said. The coffee was finally starting to kick in. Her stomach was groaning and threatening to eat itself. She grabbed a delivery menu that was tacked to her fridge and handed it to Akio. "Order something, please."

"Oh, uh, what—?"

"Anything." She cut him off.

It was a curry place. While Akio looked at the menu, Masami sat at the table by Yoshio. "So what's your plan then?"

The teenager looked excited to have her attention. "Well, getting in through the warehouse entrance will probably be easiest. But there could be more eyes on us. From what I can tell, this building isn't used as a front for anything. It's not posing as a legitimate business. It used to be a warehouse for a robotics company, but they closed down two years ago. The Tezuka-gumi bought the building soon after.

"A robotics company?" Masami asked "Nakama?"

"Yeah, how did you know?"

"She's the one who shut them down!" Akio jumped in, looking up from the menu. "That was huge news at the *Dainichi*. I had been working there maybe half a year, and superstar reporter Sato gets exclusive intel on how they were sending out defective robots and covering it up. And the CEO was cheating on his wife with like half the staff or something. Their stock sunk like a stone and they never recovered. Masami the ship sinker." Akio grinned widely.

Masami could see that he believed everything he had just said to be high praise. She only glared at him a moment, said, "Food, Akio" and turned away.

"Wow," Yoshio said.

"When did they buy the warehouse?" Masami asked.

"Only a month after Nakama filed for bankruptcy. Public records show that ownership moved to the Tezuka-gumi on November fourth, two years ago.

Masami went silent for a moment, and neither Akio nor Yoshio said a word, the intensity of her deep thought forbidding interruption.

What was the yakuza doing at that warehouse? Did Nakama have anything to do with it?

The owner and CEO, Hozumi Nakama, had not been tied with the yakuza as far as she knew, but in corrupt cases like his, they are often lurking in the shadows. Perhaps it was just a building, and a coincidence that they bought it, but it felt odd that it had come back around.

"Okay, go on," she finally said.

Yoshio nodded. "So if we can get into the front that would be best. I have a feeling they primarily use the loading dock for moving in and out. If they're actually storing something there or keeping other prisoners, they won't want to attract attention, which means the front will be unused and locked."

"Won't everything be locked?" Masami asked. "Or at least guarded?"

"Probably," Yoshio answered. "Which is why one of us has to sneak in when they aren't looking."

"With yakuza everywhere. Are you volunteering for that?" Akio asked, his phone at his ear.

"Nope," Yoshio smiled at Masami. "She is."

Masami raised her eyebrows.

"You can do it whether the door is open or not," he added.

"I knew that was coming." Masami couldn't think of becoming incorporeal again, not right now. It made her feel shaky and weak—or maybe that was just her hunger. But it made her feel like she wasn't in control. She didn't like not being in control.

"You'll slip in," Yoshio continued, "and then let us in the front door."

"Assuming I can unlock it from the inside without a key. Assuming I don't get stuck as a ghost again."

"You won't," Yoshio reassured her. "You'll control it. And if you need a key, you can pickpocket someone who has one."

"Pickpocket?" Masami asked incredulously.

"Yes, pickpocket," Yoshio answered. "Should be easy if you're invisible. And if no one is there, we'll find a way. Loading docks generally have switches that will trigger the gate from inside with no key. Otherwise, we may have to head to their main office, where they do their "charitable" work and snatch a key from someone there. But let's keep that plan B for now."

"This is assuming I'll be able to interact with objects, which has been problematic," Masami said. Hoping she became the right amount of frustrated at the right time didn't seem like a workable strategy. "But let's say we get in, however that happens," she continued. "What do we do then?"

"First off, we'll check these blocks of rooms, downstairs and up, to see if they're holding him. I'll keep watch at the end of the hall. If you find Sensei, I'll distract the yakuza, while you and Akio pull him out. If you run into any straggling gangsters, Akio will protect you."

Masami gave a slight smirk. "Okay."

"If we don't find him, we'll scour the warehouse. He could be tied up in there, but it seems sloppy. If he is, same plan as before. I'll distract while you extract. And, if need be, Akio will protect you."

Masami looked at the scrawny young man standing near her front door, phone to his ear. How was he going to protect her? Yes, he had slain a demon. Of course, that had been at the demon's request, which makes it rather less impressive. But he had fought it. He had shown courage when Masami thought he had none. He had stayed with them to fight when he had been given an out. She had to admit there was more to him than his fragile, bumbling exterior showed.

"Half an hour?" Akio said into the phone. "Great! Thanks." He hung up and looked at Masami. "What?" he asked.

Masami just shook her head once, and turned back to Yoshio.

The discussion continued while they waited for the food. Akio didn't like Yoshio's plan anymore than Masami did, probably less, but he couldn't think of a better one.

"So I have to ask," Akio said, interrupting a debate about what they will do if Masami can't turn invisible. "Why would the yakuza be holding Miyahara prisoner anyway? What do they gain from that? Does he have something they want, some information or something? I just don't get it. And what are *we* getting out of this? Why do we even have to help Miyahara? Or you?" He looked at Yoshio. "We were doing just fine here before you showed up. Why should we run back to Kofu to bail out your sensei for doing something so stupid as to follow a bunch of gangsters back to their hideout?"

"He's my sensei," Yoshio answered. "I have a duty to him. And the yakuza are probably holding him because, yes, he knows something. He's found something out about what they are doing there, with whatever that green gem was. They're afraid he might expose them."

Masami didn't say it, but she agreed with Akio on this point. Why wouldn't they just kill him? They might be trying to rescue a dead man.

"We owe him, Akio," Masami answered. "Miyahara saved our lives. We wouldn't have survived that first encounter with the demon had he not come after us. We need to repay him." And it was true. Without the sensei's help and a fair amount of dumb luck, they'd probably both be dead.

"Yeah, yeah," Akio answered, defeated. "There is that." Then, with renewed vigor, he added, "But the difference is that Miyahara is some damn demon hunter, and we are just journalists. Us rescuing him is like a couple of squirrels rescuing a bear from . . . from . . . from a lot of other bears, or tigers maybe."

"Are you saying I'm a squirrel?" Masami asked deadpan.

"No, I . . . uh. I just mean . . ." Akio sputtered.

"It's okay, Akio. I get your point. And you're right." Masami's one joy with Akio was how incredibly easy it was to fluster him. "But we still have to do it. You can't run from the tigers and bears your whole life. Unless you want to stay a squirrel."

"Squirrels are just . . . squirrels," Akio muttered, almost to himself. "That's what they are." He became quiet and pensive. He withdrew to the couch and sat hunched over, his head in his hands.

"You have to help," Yoshio said. "If you don't, I'll go alone, but Sensei asked for your help. Isn't that enough?"

"It is," Masami said. She didn't know if they had a chance in hell of doing any good, but there was no other answer.

Akio only frowned with his head in his hands.

"Now we just have to figure out how to get out of work," Masami said.

"Covered," Yoshio answered quickly. "There's a clear story in the fact that the Tezuka-gumi is rapidly expanding. They've absorbed the Kawabata-gumi's faction in Kofu, and their membership has at least quadrupled in recent months. By some accounts, it's grown tenfold. Rumor is they're expanding into Tokyo, and may have already taken over the Ishiguro-kai here. It could be the start of a turf war with the Mishima-kai which dominates Tokyo, and no doubt the Kawabata-gumi will be looking for revenge."

"Is this true?" Masami asked. "How do you know this?"

"The internet." Yoshio answered flatly, as if it couldn't be more obvious.

"Send me some links," she said intently, and scratched something down on one of Yoshio's papers. "This is my email. We may have another option as to how to go after Miyahara."

"Without Ghostwoman and Psycho-Demonman, you mean?" Akio spoke up.

"The yakuza like to be recognized, right? As long as it's for flattering reasons. We can just show up and do our jobs as good reporters who want to show them in a good light. If we get on their good side, they might even let us in. If so, we can do some reconnaissance and have an easier time of sneaking around later. If not, we'll come back with your plan, Yoshio."

The two boys nodded their agreement as the doorbell rang. Masami's stomach growled in answer, and she buzzed up the delivery.

She wasn't sure her plan was going to work, but Yoshio's was unnecessarily special ops ninja territory with too many unpredictable variables. She couldn't rely on her new invisibility glitch, and she certainly couldn't rely on Akio's buried martial arts skills. But she knew how to be a reporter. She knew how to flatter people. And even flirt, if she had to.

IO

Electric Blue

Once she had eaten, and Akio and Yoshio had left, Masami called Tanaka at home. She needed his permission to chase the story. The editor of the *Dainichi Daily* was not happy about her sudden request until he realized that the expanding yakuza syndicate was a seller, and with the Nakama Robotics tie-in, it had to be Masami's story. He remained unhappy that she requested Akio to go with her, however, but with Powell slated to shoot the prime minister's press conference, he acquiesced. The red-headed American was Tanaka's prize photographer—the biggest stories always went to him—and in any other situation Masami would have wanted him on the job.

"Fine, take Tsukino then," he said. "I need Powell here. You and Tsukino seem to be getting rather chummy, but I can easily throw his jobs to one of the newbies. I guess Tsujihara can handle yours."

"Thank you, sir." Masami habitually bowed in gratitude in spite of being on the phone. "I won't let you down."

"Good," he replied curtly. "And don't get sick." He said before hanging up.

"I won't . . . sir," she finished to the silence.

She sat, slightly vibrating from the caffeine jolt to her system late in the day, staring at her empty coffee cup on the table. She put a hand on the medallion at her chest, feeling the worn metal disc and tracing her finger over the M. After spending over ten hours as a ghost, she was reluctant to let herself become incorporeal again. But the emotions that had come when she touched the medallion had almost felt good. Releasing the pain and anguish she had held inside for so many years was cathartic and she craved more. Now that she had broken the seal, now that she was alone, she wanted to let her tears come.

And despite her exhaustion, she needed to practice. What if something went wrong tomorrow and she needed to disappear? She couldn't hope it would all work out. Masami didn't function on hope. She was a realist. She knew that if she wanted results, she had to put in the hours.

She took a deep breath, felt the quiver in her solar plexus, and let herself drift into ghostliness.

The black ceramic cup sat like a dead gray blur in front of her. She looked along the curves of its handle and lip. She could just make out her lip imprint on the forward edge. She reached a hand to it, but her finger slipped through. She tried to grasp the handle, but held only air. The cup remained on the table.

She tried to focus, to capture the frustration she had felt when she couldn't communicate with Akio, when she had to call in sick. But she only felt a jittery exhaustion, her brain firing out of sync with her body. She stood and paced through the gray imitation of her apartment.

She had been sitting in her chair, she realized, when she had slipped into the ghost world. While she had been trying to affect the coffee cup, she had been seated still. The real world chair had supported her even though she was, in effect, a ghost. It was the same with the floor beneath her. Things that she took for granted still affected her. If she couldn't affect the coffee cup and could walk through doors, why did the floor hold her up?

She poked a sock-covered toe toward the wood floor. It went through. Her balance suddenly toppled, and her entire foot disappeared below the floor boards. She reached out to steady herself on the wall, but her hand went through that too.

She fell.

She plummeted through an apartment below her where a couple sat watching television, then through another where an elderly woman stretched in yoga pants, another that was dark, a fourth where a man lay reading on a futon. Her heart hammered as she fell headfirst and arms flailing. A cat jumped and hissed as her ghostly hand grabbed at it in another living room. She clamped her eyes shut.

What if she fell through the earth? Why had she questioned the floor that had held her up? Why hadn't she just accepted it? She tried to breathe. She was a ghost. She couldn't be hurt in this state that she knew of, but what if gravity took her all the way to the center of the earth and held her there? She would never find a way back. She would die as her physical self starved.

But how could gravity affect a ghost? It made no sense. How was she falling at all?

She opened her eyes.

She had stopped. She hovered in the middle of a darkened gym, an exercise machine with pulleys and weights to one side and a treadmill on the other. She was floating, hanging in mid-air like a balloon. She tried to steady her breathing. She looked around, amazed.

Gravity.

She had taken gravity for granted too. But gravity didn't affect her in this state. That's why she hadn't fallen through the floor before. It's why she had remained sitting in the chair. But she hadn't really been sitting; she had been floating. When she put her toe through the floor, her brain deceived her. Its hardwired understanding of physics had insisted that if the floor couldn't hold her up, she would fall. And so she did.

Masami knew that many people believed that thoughts can affect their actual life, their physical health, and the outcome of their endeavors. She had always scoffed at ideas like the law of attraction and claims that people could manifest their desires or fears by their thoughts, but here it was in full effect. Because she thought she would fall, she had. The law worked, at least for ghosts.

She chose to see herself on the floor, and slowly she drifted downward until her feet were on the cold tile. It steadied her, being there, a facade of standing on a solid surface. She scanned the workout room, marveling at her new reality.

A glint of blue on the treadmill screen caught her eye. *It must have been left on*, she thought, but when she looked closer, it was dark. Yet there was that spark of blue again.

She moved closer.

A fine web of blue light flickered about the screen just at the surface. It flowed from the screen in a line down one side of the treadmill and followed the power cord to the wall.

Electricity. I can see the electricity.

It was as if it sat there idle, waiting for someone to turn the power on.

But then it spread.

The blue web seeped out from the screen, encompassed the frame around it, and then ran up and into the handlebars. Was it malfunctioning? Was the entire bike becoming electrified?

She reached a hand toward it, hoping her ghost state made her immune to electric shock. She had a need to find out. Then she saw the blue web sparkling on her fingertips already. She hadn't touched the treadmill yet. It tingled slightly but nothing more.

She looked about the room. The weight machine on the other side also had patches of fine blue webbing just at its surface. There was nothing electrical about it. It was only weights, pulleys, and a metal framework.

What is this blue light?

She reached her hand for the treadmill again, both the machine and her fingers faintly glittering blue. A finger reached the edge of the plastic frame. And it stopped. Her hand did not go through it. There was no shock. Only the faint tingling and the sensation of touch. The blue webs had met and resisted each other.

She took a sharp breath in and pulled her hand away. The blue web faded and was gone. She reached her hand out again, her fingers no longer illuminated, and this time it passed through the machine as if it wasn't there.

It wasn't electricity she had seen. Perhaps the electricity in the treadmill had cued her sense of it. But it was something else. She had read about the physics of touch and how scientists have shown that we never really touch anything. Instead, the electrons of an object repel the electrons of your body, and our brains interpret it as touch. It was called electrostatic repulsion.

She had seen the treadmill's electromagnetic field.

But where had it gone? She searched the edges of the treadmill, focusing on the screen and the power cord. She tried to calm herself, to breathe slowly and let go of any preconceptions she had about the nature of reality and the limits of perception.

She looked at herself, shot with a storm of light that shifted and coiled throughout her body, in and out of the boundaries. She focused on the light at the tips of her fingers. It pulsed and swirled like miniature hurricanes. She was energy—for a brief moment, only energy, only light; her body melted away. But then she saw the outline of her flesh again. It shimmered back into being with a web of blue light sparkling along its edges.

There you are.

She looked at the treadmill next to her, and the blue web shimmered on it as well. It was on the carpet, the walls and ceiling, and every machine in the room. An electrostatic blanket covered everything she could see. It brightened, and the light from it grew until it filled the room, blinding her in a violent flash. She pressed her eyes shut.

When she opened her eyes again, the blue had retreated, gone again. But she could sense it still at the edges of everything, herself included. And when she directed her focus it appeared, a pulse of blue webbing at the edges of the handlebars, on the curve of a ten kilogram weight, around the slender tips of her fingers.

She focused on the power button of the treadmill and a bubble of blue webbing revealed itself. She aimed a blue-tipped finger at it, and as the webs collided, they repelled one another and the treadmill screen beeped to life.

She was still a ghost. But she could affect things.

That's how she had done it before. Her desperation had triggered it when she had made the phone calls, when she had written Akio the note, and when she had tugged on his shirt. She hadn't understood it then, hadn't seen the blue outlines, but now it was clear.

She reached out again, letting the electrostatic field fade from her view, and her hand passed through the treadmill screen once again. She pulled it back, and in one quick motion, found the blue and pressed. The screen went dark.

She was not desperate now, only infinitely amazed and curious. This was going to come in very handy.

Now to return to her apartment. She began to walk toward the glass door of the gym and instantly felt strange. She was moving as if by rote, but she knew that her feet weren't really touching anything. It was simply an ingrained movement that she knew, without doubt, would propel her forward. But it wasn't her legs moving her; it was her will.

She stopped and stood still. And as she had when she descended to the floor from hovering mid-room, she willed herself toward the door.

She moved.

Her legs remained straight, but she moved as a fluid unit, a plastic bag caught by the wind, a sail stretched taut in a sudden gust. She pulled to a stop in front of the door, then reached a hand out and through the glass. She floated through into the hallway. She was a spirit, haunting the building.

She looked up to the ceiling in the hallway and willed herself up and through. It was not as fast as when she had fallen, but she moved effortlessly and silently, each lit hallway much like the one before. No people surprised her, and no cats hissed. Then she was on her floor. She made her way to number 705 and drifted through the door.

She rose to her bed in the loft without using the ladder and let her fingers rest on the medallion. As she materialized, lying on the blankets, her body shook, and the tears came.

II

Thugs at the Gate

Masami revved her black Honda Logo out of Tokyo. Akio sat in the passenger seat and Yoshio was bent into the back, his knees up, to give Akio room. It was too early for breakfast, so when they neared Kofu almost two hours later, they stopped at a Jonathan's Diner. Masami still felt raw from the night before. Coffee had been the only thing keeping her going on the drive and she needed something to soak it up. And more coffee.

Yoshio grumbled about stopping but admitted that he could do with some pancakes.

The booth at this Jonathan's looked exactly the same as the one by the Kofu train station, where Masami and Akio had eaten several times during the Kofu Head Collector assignment. Polished wood tables and seats with brown and beige striped cushions. The back to back seats separating the booths had colored window panels above them, framed in wood. The blue and orange glass let you see the tops of your neighbors' heads awash with unnatural color.

They ate quickly at first, but the pressure of what lay ahead weighed on them, and their appetites dwindled after only a few bites. Masami noticed they had all stopped eating with half their plates full.

"Let's go," she said, knocked back her coffee and stood, flagging down the server.

Akio seemed to panic at the thought of leaving food behind. He tried stuffing half an egg and three bites of rice into his mouth at once, then followed by slurping up his *natto* before Masami got her change and a receipt. The spidery strands of fermented soybeans lingered on his lips, and he wiped them away with a sleeve.

Back in the car, Masami circled the warehouse once and found the building dark, no cars in the lot. So she pulled up across the street from the loading dock to wait, betting that Yoshio was right about it being the gangsters' primary access.

It was nearing 8 a.m. now, and the sun peeked over the roof of the warehouse threatening warmth. The smell of disturbed dirt and asphalt sat in the still air. There was no activity. The loading dock was empty and quiet.

It was strange enough to be back in Kofu where the demon serial killer had been collecting heads, but Masami felt yet another layer of unease sitting outside of one of Nakama's warehouses, the business her stubborn persistence had single-handedly shut down. After her exposé, the company's research and production had stalled from a lack of funding. Investors had backed out in droves and flocked to the Tokyo competition, World Friend. Nakama had been left out to dry. While Masami was largely praised publicly, she had also been ridiculed and demonized by Nakama's associates and political allies. They claimed the story had been completely fabricated, that it was an unfounded witch hunt. But the proof was irrefutable. Some people will deny the sun shines if it exposes their evil. Being here was strangely like standing over a corpse. A corpse she had made.

"Twelve o'clock," Yoshio said from the back seat, and Masami snapped to attention. Driving toward them down the street was a white cargo truck, a black four-door sedan right behind it. It was no surprise when both vehicles pulled into the warehouse loading dock. The truck reversed in up to the gate, and the Lincoln Town Car parked next to it.

Two young men in jeans and souvenir jackets jumped out of the truck and moved behind it. One opened the truck's cargo door, while the other opened the warehouse. Two men in suits got out of the front seats of the Lincoln much slower and stood between the car and the truck, talking quietly to one another as they casually looked about. One of them offered a cigarette to the other, who put his hand up and then pulled out his own pack. They both lit up. Then another suited man got out of the back seat, finished a phone call, and went into the warehouse.

"Let me do the talking," Masami said as she put a hand on the door handle, and then added for emphasis, "seriously."

"Okay, okay," Akio answered. "I'm a mute."

"Good."

Akio grumbled but said nothing more.

"Yoshio," Masami looked to the back seat. "Wait here."

He nodded.

She took a deep breath, and swung open the door. Akio followed.

Suddenly her plan seemed ridiculous, but she was committed now. She didn't have anything else except Yoshio's idea of her turning invisible, and she felt nauseous just thinking about it. What if she got stuck again? What if the medallion didn't work to get her back? It had worked twice now, but she wasn't confident it would last. She felt she had cried herself empty of emotion. What if there was nothing left? She had no stronger emotional connection to anything but the medallion. If that didn't work, she wasn't coming back.

She led the way across the street, her recorder in hand, straightening her suit jacket and putting on her best fake smile.

The two suited men perked up as she approached. Before they could say anything, Masami said, "Hi guys, Kasumi Kawata from *Truth Serum* fanzine, I just wanted to say that I'm definitely a fan of what your organization does for the community. Do you think you could spare a minute to fill us in on some of the latest happenings?"

The two men looked at her with almost identical expressions: a skeptical half smirk as they both looked her up and down. They gave only cursory glances at Akio. They didn't respond, so Masami tried again. "I'm sure you gentlemen are very busy, but it will only take a minute, I promise."

One of the men, the slightly taller and more brutish looking of the two, spoke up, but not to Masami. "She looks pretty good, huh?" he said to the other man, who had a narrower build and a long face with a large mole under his left eye. "Skinny, but not bad."

"Yeah, yeah," Left Eye said, "a little too thin for me, but she'll do."

More Brutish turned to Akio. "She yours?"

Not this again. Masami had been through round after round of sexist comments and disrespect since she started her job, and more so as she excelled at it. It wasn't surprising that a couple of yakuza thugs delivered the same tired old act, but it was no less galling.

"Nope," Akio said, actually sounding somewhat confident. "She's the boss."

Masami would have grinned at him if she had it in her. He was learning. Detective Kuramoto had constantly referred to Akio as "the boss" on their last assignment in Kofu. Akio was evidently going to nip that misconception in the bud this time.

"Oh, that's how you like it, huh?" More Brutish said.

Akio didn't respond. He was behaving. That was nice. Normally, Akio would have bent over backward to put his foot in his mouth.

Masami maintained her smooth, calm and collected expression. "Let's try this again, shall we? From what I understand, your organization has been experiencing an explosive expansion lately. Do you care to enlighten your fans on just what the secret is?"

"The secret is, sweetie," More Brutish said, "that we're doing things right. People want to be on the side that does things right. Question for you is how did you know to find us here?"

"Oh, the word is you've purchased this building, so *Truth Serum* sent me to see what you might be using it for. Your fans want to know all the juicy details."

"Well, maybe those fans should keep their noses out of our business," Left Eye said, blowing smoke out of the side of his mouth.

"Oh, come on," Masami did her best to sound flirty without getting too close. "What are your names, anyway? I'm sure your fans will want to know the brave men responsible for guarding such important secrets."

Subtly flattered looks came over both their faces, but neither responded right away. They were just flunkies doing some menial job, but they wanted fame. All yakuza wanted to be recognized. They wanted to be treated like rock stars. Their egos needed to be fed. They kidded themselves that they were modern day Robin Hoods, but they really wanted to be kings.

More Brutish gave in. "Takeo Uzumaki," he said with a satisfied grin. "Remember that," he added, as if to say that he would be moving up the ladder soon.

Feeling emboldened by his compatriot's admission, or in an effort to compete—Masami didn't care which—Left Eye spoke up too. "Shuji Watanuki," he said. "Make sure you use the right kanji. Wata, meaning 'cotton' and nuki, meaning 'pierce.'" His arrogance deflated for a moment as he realized his name didn't actually sound that cool.

"I've got it. Thank you, guys." Masami winked. "So how about giving us a little tour of the facilities? What's going on in there? Are you planning a new charity dinner for underprivileged youth?"

Uzumaki's smile was ugly and smug. "No, nothing like that, sweetie."

"Well, let's see then," Masami smiled back. It was a practiced smile, meant for losers like these. She had to keep up the charade or they had no chance of getting inside.

"Chida is not gonna be okay with that, brother" Watanuki said to Uzumaki, nodding toward the warehouse. "And I don't think the boss would want us showing anyone inside either. I think he would expressly forbid it."

"Forbid it?" Masami said. "Ooh, that sounds exciting."

"Yeah, I'll give you exciting, sweetie. How about this punk takes a walk," Uzumaki said, indicating Akio, and just you and I go inside?"

"Hey . . ." Akio started, but Masami shut him down with a look.

"Don't worry about him," she said. "He's no bother. Just wants to take some pictures."

"Oh, kinky, huh? You like that?" Uzumaki started to move closer to her, but she stepped back. Akio lifted his camera about to aim it at the brute.

Just then, the two men in souvenir jackets stepped out from behind the truck on the loading dock. "Finished!" one called down. There was the sound of a gate slamming shut.

Uzumaki looked at Akio and his camera. "What are you doing with that, punk?" And he turned toward Akio as if to take the camera from his hands.

Akio backed away. "Just wanted to get some photos for your fans, that's all," he said quickly, pulling his camera out of reach.

"Who the hell are they?" someone yelled from the dock. It was the suited man from the back seat of the Lincoln, likely the one they had named Chida. He was a slim but squarish looking man, like someone had made him out of narrow bricks. And he didn't seem happy. "Get them out of here!"

"You'd better get lost, both of you," Uzumaki said.

"Yeah, get lost," Watanuki chimed in and stepped toward them, brandishing his cigarette like a weapon.

"But you, sweetie," Uzumaki added, apparently trying to look seductive. "You remember me. Next time I see you we'll have a real good time, cameras or not."

"Yeah," Watanuki added. "We could get you some work, some real quality, woman work." Then he turned to Uzumaki. "I'll bet Debi would love her. He likes those skinny girls."

Masami had learned to be calm in situations like these, but the name Debi struck a nerve. Debi had been the real cause behind her story of the kidnapped girl that had been her first front page story, but she had never been able to tie him to it. It was a nickname that was short for either the English "debonaire" or "devil." The "V" sound not being used in Japanese, it became a "B." He probably liked the implication of both names.

Debi was old Tokyo gangster, the head of a pre-yakuza organization called the Black Moon Society, which had been running brothels since the Edo period. All the yakuza syndicates had dealings with him on some level, but they had to go through the Ishiguro-kai, the second largest syndicate in Tokyo and the organization's only yakuza partner. Together they supplied the vast majority of the illegal—but largely overlooked by authorities—prostitution racket to the greater Tokyo area and beyond.

Debi had been arrested a few years back for abducting underage girls, but got out of it on a technicality, and not without some sway from his connections within the legal system. Rumor was that a certain judge was one of his regular clients.

It wouldn't be unusual for these Tezuka-gumi thugs at the warehouse to know who he was, but to mention him as if he was one of their own made Masami pause. If Debi had severed connections with the Ishiguro-kai and was working directly with the Tezuka-gumi now, they were expanding and absorbing even more rapidly than anyone realized.

Both of the thugs laughed as Masami and Akio backed across the street. She heard a click from Akio's camera and saw that he had it aimed at them from his hip. They didn't seem to notice.

They overheard Chida say he didn't trust the new recruits with the merchandise, so Watanuki jumped into the cargo van and took over as driver. The two young toughs squeezed in next to him. Then Chida and Uzumaki climbed into the Lincoln, this time with Chida in the driver's seat. The truck pulled away first and the car followed.

Her plan had failed. They were getting away.

"In the car, now!" Masami snapped at Akio, and they both jumped in.

"Plan B?" Yoshio said from the back seat.

Masami didn't answer. She turned the engine over and pulled a U-turn to follow the gangsters.

"What are you doing?" Akio was flabbergasted. He looked pale.

"If we're going to find Miyahara, we need to do it now. Who knows when those pricks will be back at the warehouse." She stepped on the gas to catch up to the black Lincoln. She couldn't let them get too far.

"But the warehouse is back there," Akio said. Masami ignored him, but caught a glimpse of Yoshio's analytical expression in the rearview, his wide eyes wider, trying to figure out what she was up to.

She caught up to the Town Car and tailed them much too closely to be inconspicuous. After several blocks a light turned red as the truck went through an intersection. The Town Car stopped, and the truck drove on.

Masami turned to Akio. "Be ready to drive out of here fast if you have to."

Akio looked more confused than usual. He started to protest.

"Just be ready," she insisted. She rested her hand on the medallion beneath her shirt, and took a deep breath. Then, dropping her hand to her lap, she let herself slip away.

Akio stared across the front seat of the stopped car to where Masami had just been. She was still there, as far as he knew, but all he saw was an empty seat. Whatever she was going to do, he didn't like it. The encounter with the yakuza at the warehouse was nerve-racking enough, and now they were chasing them down in broad daylight! There was no way this was going to end well.

Masami had given him an angry look just before she winked out, but it had been strangely reassuring. She had put her faith in him with that look. He watched as she put her hand on her heart and then vanished. One second she was sitting in the driver's seat, the next, she flickered out like a spent light bulb. She was gone.

Her car sat at the red light behind the Lincoln, still running. He could see the men through the back window, sitting motionless. Chida had his cigarette hand out the driver's side window. Suddenly, he flinched and dropped the cigarette. He pulled his arm in, rubbing his shoulders. Then their brake lights went off as the engine died. He saw Chida looking around, confused. He looked down toward the ignition and over at Uzumaki who threw up his arms. Then he glanced in his rearview, turned around and looked right at Akio.

Uh oh.

Akio looked over at the driver's side of the car. The keys were still in the ignition, and the engine was running. Masami had put the car in park before she winked out. He looked back at the Town Car and saw both doors open. The signal light turned green.

Oh, crap.

He started to jump over the console into the driver's seat when he felt a chill and stopped. The gearstick moved into reverse. The car lurched jerkily backward and turned to the side, the steering wheel moving on its own. It lurched forward again in bumps and spurts, then took off, wheels squealing, and sped past the two gangsters who looked dumbfounded at the driverless car. Akio watched nervously as Chida's expression turned to a glare. He saw the gangster's hand reach into his jacket as they passed, but then retracted it empty as he looked around at the busy city street. As the two men diminished in the rear window, Chida took a step to the Town Car, as if he would give chase, but then stomped his foot and slammed the car door, obviously remembering that he no longer had the keys.

Akio looked over at the empty driver's seat nervously, then back at Yoshio. The teenager was grinning like a schoolboy who had just won top honors at the science fair.

The car took a left at the next street and then another left. A pedestrian gave a queer look into the car as they turned. Then he smiled and pointed, saying something to the woman next to him.

A minute later, Masami's car passed the front of the warehouse. It went a block further, then turned right on a side street, where it lurched to a stop behind a parked minivan, under some large shade trees.

The engine died. For a moment, Akio sat there, unsure of what to do, Yoshio still wide-eyed and grinning in the back seat.

Then the space over the driver's seat blurred and shimmered. Masami appeared, her hand on her heart. Her eyes were closed and tears ran from them both. She wiped the tears away with the backs of her hands, and gave Akio an almost feral look. Her breathing was heavy and she was shaking.

"Give me a minute," she said, and exited the car.

Masami leaned against the car to catch her breath. Three times now, she had slipped into the other dimension and returned. The medallion had brought her back.

While a ghost, she had interacted with the physical world. Focusing enough to steal the keys from the ignition had been easy enough. The blue electrostatic outline had appeared right when she wanted it. But driving the car . . . she wasn't exactly sure how she had done it. Not that she had done it well. She couldn't simultaneously have visual of the blue webs of the steering wheel, the pedals, and the shifter, while also keeping her eyes on the road. And her hands slipped through multiple times as she fought to keep focus. But she had gotten them away from the yakuza.

Adrenaline coursed through her, and she tried to calm down, to slow her breathing. *Frustration and desperation.* That's what Yoshio had said. Those moments before she saw the blue web, when she had been able to interact with her phone, with the pen and napkin at the bar. They were moments when she needed to act now and had no backup plan. That's how she had done it. It had been a moment of panic like the stories heard of mothers lifting cars off their children. It was instinctual and necessary.

But now, knowing about the blue web, knowing that she didn't need to be frustrated or desperate, her heightened emotions had only complicated things.

On top of that, the whole episode felt rash and unlike her. There may have been another way into the warehouse besides stealing the keys, but in the moment it was all she could see. An anger had gripped her at having to yet again play the part of the pleasant, unaffected bimbo. She had done it so many times, but why lose her cool now? Maybe it was the lack of sleep. But it felt deeper than that. Her emotions felt on edge. Something about her was changing. She wasn't sure she could continue to fake it. Not to her co-workers, not to the cops, and not to slimy yakuza thugs. She wanted to make them pay. She felt like a barely contained fire. The slightest wind could take a spark and the world would burn.

She had to gain control. She would have to practice if becoming a ghost was something she'd be called on to do again. She didn't want to. Not in the least. But Masami had long ago given up on doing what she wanted. She did things because they needed to be done.

She rapped on the window. "Let's go."

12

The Warehouse

Yoshio was thrilled as he followed Masami and Akio in a dash across the street to the front of the warehouse. His heart was racing much more from the adrenaline rush of being in a car driven by an invisible woman than from the short sprint.

He had questioned Miyahara's wisdom when the sensei had talked of the two journalists, and had shrugged off their involvement in vanquishing the Kofu Head Collector as dumb luck.

"What good could they do if we needed them?" he had asked. "It sounds like they just got lucky and would've been killed if it wasn't for you."

"It is difficult to say," Miyahara had said. "Perhaps I would have been killed if not for them." His knowing smile was one of the few things that confounded Yoshio. "You are a bright boy, very bright, but you do not see beyond numbers and hard science sometimes. You underestimate the power of a determined spirit. Miss Sato and Mr. Tsukino have stronger spirits than most. And there is something beyond that, which we have yet to discover. They are special, Yoshio. Trust me, and know that they may be exactly who we need if we're ever in trouble."

Yoshio still hadn't understood. He saw two bumbling journalists that had stumbled into a demon's lair and were lucky to be alive. But he hadn't said that. He had only said, "I trust you, Sensei," and left it at that.

His only hope had been that some residual memory was left in Akio that could be tapped, a memory that would make him an unstoppable warrior. Still, it seemed unlikely. Akio had been lucky in his combat with the demon, and even now he was a reluctant hero, only going along out of some sense of guilt or loyalty, or perhaps just because of his obvious but misguided crush on his co-worker.

But Miss Sato! Wow!

She had turned invisible, stolen the keys from the yakuza's car, and took off back to the warehouse!

Talk about a hero. That was amazing!

Now Yoshio knew what Miyahara had meant when he said they were special. At least Masami was. And if Sensei was right about her, maybe there was hope yet for Akio.

But if all that failed, his backup plan was tucked into his pants, cold and heavy against his back, his souvenir from the encounter at the grocer's. Miyahara had told him to ditch it, but logic told him he might need it again.

It was still dark beyond the glass of the reception area when they arrived moments later. The windows had not been cleaned in several months. Nakama Robotics was spelled out in unassuming characters on the window above their slogan, "Creating the Future of Your Home, Office, and Everywhere." There was clearly a reception desk and a couch inside, but the room was not lit.

Yoshio looked at the glass door. There were two locks: one had a standard keyhole on the outside and—he could see through the glass —a lever on the inside. The other, a bolt, was keyed on both sides. Masami had been smart to get the keys. She wouldn't have been able to let them inside without them. Now she pulled the stolen keys from her pocket. It was a ring with six keys on it and a metal key fob of a tiny ashtray with a sliding cover.

"The round one, with the green plastic grip, teeth on one side only," Yoshio said, without thinking. "It goes to the bottom lock. The bolt is the gold square one." Masami gave him a queer look, then tried the bolt, which slid free. He was right about the other one too, which clicked and the door opened. She raised her eyebrows at him.

"It was obvious," Yoshio answered her silent question, because it was. Keys and locks were just another form of puzzle, and there were only so many types.

There was no alarm, at least not that they could hear. There were no lights flashing from anywhere, not even the panel on the wall that looked like it was an alarm control. Yoshio walked to it. It was dark, nonfunctional.

Reception was empty, with a long, bare counter on one side, covered in dust, which now danced in the sunlight spilling through the front windows, disturbed by their entrance. An uncomfortable-looking couch with short metal legs and thin seats covered in vinyl sat facing the counter. A tiny round table was in the center of the far wall, as if it served to separate two chairs that were no longer there. Two doors were adjacent to each other on the same corner but different walls of the room.

"Okay," Masami said. "We don't have a lot of time. They'll be coming back here." She chose the first door, which was on the wall to the right, and opened it carefully. The room was dark, but lights flickered on as she hit a dimmer switch, exposing what was obviously a showroom. Akio followed her in, Yoshio just behind.

It was a large room but separated into different sections by colors painted on the floor. A blue circle stood in the middle toward the front wall. A green circle, its edges cut off in the corner, was just to their right. A yellow circle was beyond the blue one. Red and black half circles were against the wall on their left. In each circle were different objects on low platforms.

In the green one there looked like a dog of sorts, but with shiny, plastic parts and something akin to saddle bags draped over its midsection. "Man's New Best Friend" read bold characters on the wall. There were images of the dog performing different tasks, and pamphlets in clear plastic wall dispensers.

In the yellow one was a desk and a counter, outfitted with a coffee machine and a small refrigerator. A low, domed, cylindrical object with three arms and a small screen stood in-between the desk and the tiny kitchen space. Th ere was a coffee cup in one of the contraption's outstretched claws and a stack of paper in another one. The third one held a pen. Th e writing on the wall read, "Office-boy Helper Bot. Make your workday a breeze!"

The red half circle had half a bed mounted to the wall and a life-like looking arm and leg also attached to the wall, where they each blended with a painted image of a scantily clad woman. The leg was in an alluring position and the arm was beckoning. Printed on the wall, it read, "For more information, ask a salesperson!"

On the black half circle were several video screens mounted into the wall. A table sat nearby with booklets stacked ten deep.

The blue circle was evidently the center point and displayed two life-size and very human looking robots. Although their facial features were distinctly Japanese, they were both dressed as if they were from 1920's Europe, one a staunch looking butler and the other a young, exuberant maid.

Yoshio wondered why the robots were still there. Perhaps they weren't fully functional, but wouldn't Nakama have cleared them out? Maybe they sold them with the building, but it seemed odd. They were more than just products; they were intellectual property.

There were buttons on the walls in each area that would clearly activate the respective robots. Robotics was a field that particularly excited Yoshio, and he had to restrain himself from pushing them. They were here to rescue Sensei. Playing with robots would have to wait.

As he thought this, Akio reached for the button by the bed in the red circle.

"Akio!" Masami whispered intensely. "Seriously?"

"I just wondered—"

Masami's glare shut Akio down.

One door stood on the long wall across from the front of the building, and two restrooms were at the end of the room, which Masami directed Akio and Yoshio to check. Akio headed for the men's room, so that left the women's for Yoshio.

He peeked in as if afraid he might disturb a lady peeing, even though he knew there couldn't be anyone inside. Two sinks and a single hand dryer, three stall doors. No urinal, of course. It felt weird to be in the women's room. He felt like he was violating some ancient moral principle, some stringent code of ethics. *If thou beest a man, thou shalt not enter the women's restroom under any circumstances, and if thou doest, thou wilt suffer greatly for thy transgression.*

He quickly checked the stalls, which were unsurprisingly empty, and exited as quickly as he could. It was good that Masami was being thorough, but he thought she could have checked the women's room herself.

Instead, she was peering out the door in the middle of the long wall.

Akio was already back in the showroom when Yoshio exited the women's room, making him briefly concerned that they were both wondering why he had been in there so long. He swore he had been quick about it.

Silently, the two of them followed Masami out the door, her hand brushing the light switch, darkening the showroom behind them. Directly across from them, a wide hallway headed away from the doors, intersected by a smaller hallway that ran adjacent to the showroom.

"We need to cover ground fast, so let's split up," Masami said. "Akio, you take the right. If Yoshio's blueprint is correct, that door at the end of the hall will be stairs. Yoshio, you've got the left and the elevator by reception. Check all the rooms on the way and meet in the middle upstairs. I'll follow this hallway. It should lead to the main warehouse, so meet me there when you're done. Be careful, but be quick."

The two nodded without a word.

Yoshio headed left toward the elevator. Flipping on the light in the first room, he saw it was a small meeting room. A table in the center was surrounded by eight chairs. The Nakama Robotics logo, a simple "N" in a circle made up of tiny circles that resembled a kind of DNA chain, was emblazoned in the center of the polished wood.

Promotional posters adorned the wall with photos of people interacting with robots. Nakama's slogan, "Creating the Future of Your Home, Office, and Everywhere" was prominent on all of them.

There were no signs that Miyahara would ever have been in the room. There were no signs that anyone had been in there anytime recently. He moved on.

The next room was half the size, a small office. A computer monitor still sat on a desk. An outside window was to the left, letting in sunlight. Another window was on the back wall, and a fluorescent glare came through from the warehouse. Masami must have gone in there and flipped on the light. A manager could watch over the warehouse activities from here. There was a cabinet that could have fit a human if it didn't have shelves, but it did. Yoshio moved on.

Just before the elevator at the end of the hall was another restroom, mens this time, thankfully. There was no one inside and nothing suspicious. He pressed the elevator button and it lit. It cranked into action, sounding like it was waking from a long, metallic sleep, and the doors creaked open.

Upstairs were more offices, more restrooms, and a supply room. The offices were furnished and the supply room was stocked, but none of it had been disturbed in months. Dust covered all, and cobwebs glinted when he flipped the light switches. He entered a conference room, larger than the meeting rooms downstairs, and at the same time an opposite door opened. Yoshio reached to his back quickly, but as his hand touched the weapon's grip, he saw that the person entering was Akio and relaxed. The two acknowledged each other and looked around.

The table in this room, also emblazoned with the Nakama logo, was twice the size of the one he had seen downstairs. Twenty chairs were positioned around it. A larger, black-cushioned chair with arms and a higher back than the others sat at one end. Large windows covered the far wall, and light spilled in from long fluorescent lamps on the ceiling of the warehouse beyond. This room was as unused as the others. There were no signs of recent activity and no sensei.

Yoshio met Akio at the large window, and they both peered down into the main warehouse. It was a large concrete-floored room with rows of industrial shelving to either side of a wide open space. Two loading dock doors were closed at the far side, next to an exit door. A windowed box of a room jutted into the space from one corner. The other corner opened into a wing of the warehouse that wasn't entirely visible from where they stood. In the center of the open space was one large crate on a pallet. A forklift was parked nearby.

"Did you find anything?" Akio asked, as he lifted his camera and snapped a photo of the warehouse below.

"Nope."

"Me neither. Everything looks like it was abandoned."

Yoshio worried he was wrong. He had calculated that Sensei had been kept here, but what if he hadn't been? What if there were no clues?

There's still the warehouse. He scanned it for Masami, but didn't see her. Akio was doing the same. Then he saw it. A tiny red, blinking light near the exit door.

Yoshio's heart jumped. How had he not realized it? The alarm control box was at the back door! The yakuza never used the front entrance and had probably installed their own system when they purchased the building. He cursed himself for being careless.

"We gotta go," he said and bolted toward the door Akio had come through. *Stairs will be faster.*

"What's going on?" Akio followed.

As Masami had said, the yakuza would be coming back. It was no stretch to think that even the boneheaded thugs would realize that the three of them might have gone back to the warehouse. Sure, the car had driven past them in the opposite direction, but their keys had mysteriously gone missing while Masami's car was right behind them. It didn't take a Mensa member to put two and two together. Fortunately, they would be returning on foot unless they caught a ride. But with the alarm going off, someone else could be showing up any second. They likely had far less time than any of them had realized.

Yoshio didn't bother to explain it to Akio. "We've got to find Sensei and get the hell out of here," was all he said.

They made it into the warehouse, eyes darting side to side for Masami. Most of the shelving was empty, but there was one section that had stacked boxes on it; images of a robot dog wagging its tail decorated the sides. "Meet your new companion," the box read. "It fetches. It barks. It wags its tail. AND it makes phone calls! Built-in camera! Built-in Internet radio! Connect your mobile phone! Post on social media! Lots more! Comes fully-charged and ready for action!" The dog looked like a smaller breed than the one in the showroom, an older model, perhaps. They didn't see Masami.

"Miss Sato?" Yoshio called, trying not to be too loud.

"Back here," came the response. The voice reverberated in the large space making it difficult to tell where it was coming from. "Found something," Masami said, and this time it seemed to be coming from the back wing of the warehouse. They quickly headed that way.

As they passed the large crate in the center of the room, Akio stumbled and cried out. He fell to his knees and quickly got back up, holding the back of his head.

"Are you okay?" Yoshio asked, stopping to put a hand on him and keep him moving toward Masami.

"Yeah, yeah," Akio said. "I've just been getting these sudden random headaches."

Two rows of empty shelving ran from the main room into the wing and stopped about three meters from the back wall. It was just enough space for a forklift to maneuver around.

Masami stood at the back wall looking at something dangling from it. Two brutal manacles depending from iron chains hung from the wall by large bolts. A matching set was bolted to the floor. They looked like they had seen a fair amount of use, and recently. Dark smudges painted the sharp edges of the manacles. Dark stains covered the floor around them in layers, darker and thicker toward the wall, thinner and lighter reddish brown on the further edges. Parts of it looked like someone had tried to clean it up, but not very enthusiastically. There were the smeared swirls of a lackluster mopping job. Two comfortable chairs sat at angles toward the wall, as if whatever torture took place here had been a form of entertainment.

Yoshio started to panic. Had Sensei been chained here? Did they capture him and kill him? He scanned the area for any clues, the blinking alarm light flashing in the back of his mind. On the wall, where the manacles dangled, the concrete was a darker shade of gray. *From sweat and blood.* There were marks where the manacles and chains had swung and dragged across the concrete. There were other marks as well that looked like recent gouges from something swung hard.

A manriki-kusari, maybe.

Yoshio didn't want to think of it. He couldn't bear the thought of his sensei being whipped by his own weapon. Maybe it was something else, and someone else. A lot of things could have made those gouges.

"We don't know that he was chained here," Masami said, as if reading his thoughts.

"Nope, we don't." Yoshio responded curtly. "It could be anyone's blood." He didn't want the reassurance. He wanted facts, but the sight made him nervous.

"There's an alarm going off," he told Masami after he had digested the scene. "We can't stay here long."

Masami nodded. "Quickly then," she said. "Akio, check the room in the other corner." She continued searching the gruesome spot, and Akio moved off.

Yoshio scanned the floor again and the shelves behind him. A single box sat at the edge of the shelving, directly across from the shackles and above the comfy chairs. It had the same robot dog photo on the side, but in the top right corner was a handwritten Roman letter "H". On the dog, also handwritten, was the Arabic number "11".

Something was off about it. It could be a cataloging system for the robot dogs, but Yoshio didn't think so. He had noticed a different box on a shelf as they crossed through the warehouse, but he hadn't thought it significant. It had a letter "E" and the kanji 仲 (naka) on the dog, which meant *relationship* or *go-between*. What cataloging system would alternate with numbers and kanji? And what did the Western letters mean? He inspected the H box closer. There was a smear of dried blood on one side, as if from a finger.

"Yoshio?" Masami started to ask, but he cut her off.

"Follow me. This means something."

He took her to the other box. There was a similar smear of blood on the side that he hadn't noticed before.

Akio was jogging back to them. "Nothing in that room."

"Great, you can help," Yoshio said. "Look for more boxes with letters and something written on the dog," he said. "And maybe blood. Take pictures of them."

"Is this important?" Masami asked. "We don't have much time, as you said yourself."

"Very," Yoshio said. "And I know."

They each headed off in a different direction, Yoshio continuing along the same shelves. He was the first to find another marked box. It was next to the many stacked ones at the far end. It had an "I" in the top right corner and the kanji 階 (kai) on the dog, which was a counter for floors of a building. There was another stripe of blood.

"Found one!" Akio called loudly, as if he was playing a game of hide-and-seek. "It's got an 'E' and a 間 (kan) on the dog, like *interval*."

"Great, get a photo," Yoshio replied in a loud whisper, hoping Akio would get the hint to be quieter. He heard a camera click and then another one further away. He was searching through the stacked boxes but not finding anymore marked ones.

There was another camera click before Akio called out again, no quieter. "An 'O' and the kanji 野 (no) like *field*!" Another camera click. Soon after, it was Akio again. "One more!"

"Akio, quiet down," Masami interjected.

"Sorry." He lowered his voice. "The letter "G" and a kanji 上 (ue) for *up*." A camera click.

A couple more shutter clicks came from further back, and both Akio and Masami met Yoshio in the center. Akio made a wide circle around the large crate, his head leaning away from it, and one side of his face scrunched up in pain.

"What's wrong?" Yoshio asked.

"I don't know. Just that my head hurts around that crate," Akio answered.

Masami walked directly past it. "I don't feel anything," she said.

"I don't know. Coincidence then," Akio said.

"I found three more," Masami said, showing her cell phone to Yoshio, who scrolled through the photos. The first was of a box with a "U" in the top right corner and the hiragana をつ (wotsu) on the dog. The next photo was of another stripe of blood, but much lighter than the ones Yoshio had found. As he looked at the third photo of a box with an "S" and the kanji 気 (ki) for *spirit*, they heard a car pull into the loading dock and brakes screech to a stop.

"You two, get out of here!" Masami commanded. "Sneak behind the shelves and out through the front! I'll distract them. Meet me at the car."

Yoshio started to follow orders, but Masami grabbed his shoulder. "My phone!" she said.

"Oh, sorry!" He handed it back and went after Akio who was moving away. He looked back a moment later, concerned for Masami, but she wasn't there.

A metal door creaked open and voices bounced into the open space.

"Lights on. They might still be here."

Yoshio moved carefully behind Akio, both of them hunched down, hoping not to be seen behind the rows of mostly empty shelves. Ahead the stacked boxes would give them more cover, but then they would have to somehow get across the open space to the double doors back toward the showroom. He fingered the hunk of metal that had been hidden behind his shirt, tucked into his pants.

"You guys circle that way," one of the gangsters said. It was the driver of the Lincoln, Chida, the one who had seemed in charge. "We'll go this way."

There are at least four of them.

He and Akio slunk low behind the lowest row of shelves, and Akio's camera clinked against the metal frame. He stopped abruptly and craned his head around. "Sorry," he whispered, clutching his camera closer to his body.

The instant after, they heard an engine start inside the warehouse. Both of them turned to look. Through the shelving, they could see four men, two of which had been headed straight toward them, but had turned back around to see the forklift moving on its own. There was no driver in the seat—at least not one they could see.

It spun in a circle before driving straight toward the shelving on the other side. Both Yoshio and Akio were awestruck for a moment, watching the spectacle. It was Akio who came to his senses first, and grabbed Yoshio's shoulder. "Come on, she's making a distraction. This is our chance."

"Right," Yoshio said. He was fascinated by the forklift and had almost forgotten what they were doing. *It shouldn't be possible.* For someone to disappear without some sort of complex body-cloaking suit was beyond anything he'd ever heard. He wanted to know how it worked. But he would never find out if he was abducted by gangsters and killed.

They rounded the ends of the shelves and heard a loud crash. Peering around the corner they saw the forklift had collided with the shelves across the room. The four yakuza slowly and cautiously closed in on the vehicle, which was still running. Two of them had guns drawn. Akio froze, but this time Yoshio pushed him forward. "It's a distraction, like you said!" he whispered. "She's fine." He followed Akio past the boxes of dog robots.

Comes charged and ready for action!

Yoshio stopped and grabbed Akio. "Hang on. Got an idea." He pulled a box down from the shelf and handed it to Akio. "Open this."

"What? We—"

"Just do it!" Yoshio insisted, pulling down another box. If he could help Masami, he would.

They each opened one, the sounds covered by the loud forklift motor. Yoshio pulled out the white, hard plastic dog, its ears flopping, and set it on the floor. Akio followed suit, powering it up as Yoshio did. There was a remote control with a readout that lit up.

Yoshio saw "Bark" and "Walk Patrol". He punched them both and pointed the dog toward the back of the warehouse. Akio did the same but pointed his toward the other side of the room. The dogs both let out a cacophony of canned barking as they stiffly marched away like proud, happy puppies.

All of the yakuza turned from the empty forklift toward the dogs, queer looks on their faces. "What the hell is this?" one of them shouted.

"Dogs, looks like. Robot dogs."

"No shit, it's dogs. Am I stupid?"

Yoshio tapped Akio and pointed toward the exit that led to the front. Together they slunk out from behind the shelves, giving sideways glances toward the gangsters. The dogs barked in bursts of three. *Wan wan wan! Wan wan wan!* But as they crept away, trying to be unseen, Akio's robot dog did an about face and started marching back toward them.

"Hey!" a gangster yelled. "Over there!" All four yakuza turned.

Just then the forklift shot into reverse, gunning straight for the men. They leapt to the side, one of them falling and rolling out of the way. Another one fired his gun at the forklift. It pinged off the back end, ricocheting across the warehouse.

"Careful, you moron!" one of the other yakuza yelled.

The forklift had stopped moving. The engine was still running but it was still.

Miss Sato!

Yoshio hoped dearly that she hadn't been shot, but they couldn't go back to her, not now. One of the men was still after them and close behind. Yoshio shared a look with Akio, who was obviously thinking the same thing. They sprinted down the hall back toward the showroom.

A gun fired behind them and the blast rang through the hallway. They turned to see a yakuza looking confused as to what had just knocked his hand sideways, the bullet going into the wall next to him.

Then he doubled over, grabbing his groin and collapsing to the floor with a groan.

She's okay!

Yoshio tore through the showroom with Akio behind him, back into reception, out through the glass door, and into the parking lot. Not ten steps out, he heard a commotion behind, a scuffle and then a loud banging. He glanced back to see two yakuza inside the building, struggling with the door, one of them slamming the butt of his gun into the glass. It would crack any second. "Not straight to the car!" he breathed to Akio. "Circle the block first to throw them off!"

"Right! Smart!" Akio responded, and followed him down an adjacent street.

At the end of the block, they both dared a look behind them. No one. They slowed to a jog. Rounding the corner back onto the street where they were parked, they saw Masami's black Honda Logo pull up to the intersection with Masami visible in the driver's seat.

"Get in!" she commanded.

13
Theories

Back at Jonathan's, Masami's head was spinning. Again she had been able to control when she became a ghost and had been able to return to the living. To disappear, all she needed to do was let go. She had only to relax and allow it, which wasn't the easiest thing for her. She held her self-control in a chokehold, muscles clenched and lips pressed tight. Releasing that grip on herself was uncomfortable, yet, when she allowed it, it was almost like falling asleep, falling into a dream. Then to return, she touched the medallion and thought of her mother. Her solar plexus quivered and the tears pushed from her eyes. More than a decade of emotion had been held back, refused access to her tear ducts. Now it found a release, but would it ever end? Would this always be a component of her transformation? Would she ever not be sad at her mother's passing? She couldn't imagine.

She didn't care for being invisible, being in that ghostly plane of existence, but it had certainly come in handy. They would never have escaped the warehouse without it. They would have never gotten into it in the first place if she hadn't been able to steal the keys.

She sat across from Akio and Yoshio, neither one of them able to shut up. They stumbled over themselves, interrupting each other to ask her what it felt like, how she did it, and to gush over how incredibly cool it was. It didn't feel cool. It felt strange and empty.

It was a bleak world, shades of gray with only muted color, like someone had lowered the saturation to almost nothing. Living things had a glow about them in different intensities. Th e yakuza had emanated the same life glow as Akio and Yoshio, in varying depths and breadths, though she noticed dark patches in a couple of them, where the light seemed gray or black, like there were holes in it, scooped out or retreating from a toxin.

The shelving had been cold and gray, as had the forklift until the engine started; then even it had a subtle reddish glow under its hood, as if there were a kind of life in it. The gun in the gangster's hand was a cold empty gray, even after it had fired.

The large crate in the center of the floor had been gray as well, cold on its edges. But something else radiated from inside, neither white nor red. It had been hard to see it behind the packaging, but there had been a glow of sorts. It had been small, barely detectable. And green.

She hadn't wasted time on it. She briefly wondered if Miyahara might be in that crate. It easily could have fit a human, maybe two, but there was no vital light coming from it. She was pretty certain he wasn't in there. Unless he was dead.

Now Yoshio was drawing characters on napkins, Western letters in the corner and Japanese ones in the middle.

"Here are the three boxes I saw. Well, you both saw two of them too," he said. "Let's see your photos again."

"Are you sure that's what yours were?" Akio asked. "Where are your photos?"

"In my head," Yoshio answered. "Photographic memory."

"Of course." Akio rolled his eyes.

Masami pulled out her mobile phone, and Akio turned on his camera. Yoshio took the phone first and copied the images onto napkins. He did the same with Akio's camera. Masami lifted her coffee into her hands, and Akio pushed his tea toward the window-side of the table to make room for all the napkins. There were nine of them, and they didn't appear to make any sense.

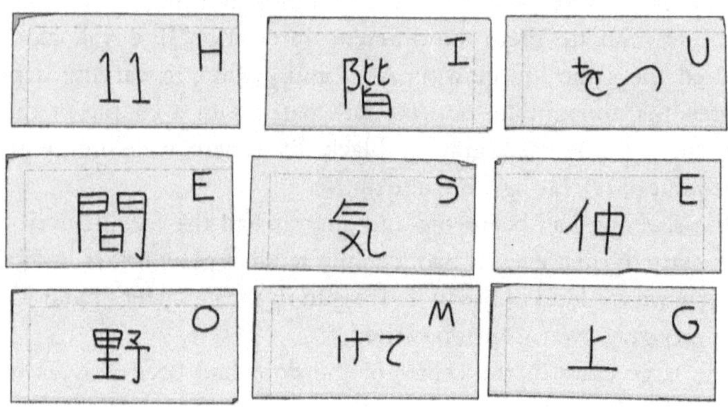

"Okay," Yoshio said. "Let's try the Japanese. Look. If we put the two E's together, the Japanese spells *Nakama*. That's gotta be it. Nakama Robotics."

"But no other letters are the same," Masami said. If this was a puzzle, and she was sure it was, it wasn't making sense yet.

"True," said Yoshio. "I'm not sure that's important."

"Are there any English words with two E's in a row?" Akio asked. "*Heeg*? Oh, S-E-E, *see*."

"And *seem*," Masami added.

"But what's left? U-G-I-H-O. *Ugiho*. Isn't that a state in the US?"

"Ohio," Yoshio said.

"Is it still morning?" Akio asked. "Feels so much later."

"No, Akio." Masami said. "Ohio is a state."

"Oh."

"Eleven floors," Masami said, connecting the number eleven with the kanji for floors.

"But the warehouse only had two," Akio said.

"So it's obviously referring to somewhere else," Masami snapped. "He wasn't *in* the warehouse, remember?"

"Right, of course," Akio answered. "Oh, the letters spell *hi*! He's saying *hi*."

Masami rolled her eyes. "Would he really take the time to say *hi*?"

"I guess so. Looks like he did," Akio answered. "Dumb as that is."

"What about the blood?" Yoshio asked. "It was much lighter on the boxes you found, Masami. Thanks for taking those extra pictures, by the way. Was there blood on the boxes you saw, Akio?"

"Uh, I don't know, sorry."

"I think the blood means he was shackled to that wall," Yoshio said.

"But he got away," Masami answered. "Long enough to leave us this message. He obviously survived it."

"If he got away," Akio said. "Why didn't he just come find us?"

"That's a good point," Masami said. "Why wouldn't he come find us if he was free?" She looked at Yoshio to answer.

"He said that if he didn't come back in two days, to go and get you guys," the teenager said. "So maybe he got away for a minute, but he was captured again."

"Maybe so," Masami said. "Maybe he broke free from the shackles but couldn't get out of the warehouse. Maybe the clue isn't about where he is, but something else. How would he know where they would take him when he was still in the warehouse?" Masami asked.

"They might have told him," Yoshio said. "Like threatening him with the information. *If you don't cooperate, we'll take you to an even worse place.* But it could be something else, something bigger."

"Why wouldn't he just spell it out though?" Akio asked. "I'll be at such-and-such place. Come get me. What's with all the boxes?"

"If the yakuza saw a clear message," Yoshio answered, "they would probably destroy it. Then we'd have no message. This way it just looks like gibberish. They would ignore it."

"It is gibberish," said Akio. "So he had time to write on all these boxes, and then they grabbed him again? Seems silly. I think either he got away and doesn't want us to find him for some reason, or the yakuza wrote on these boxes to lead us into a trap. And maybe he's already dead."

"Akio," Masami said, reprimanding him and nodding toward Yoshio.

"I'm not stupid," Yoshio said.

"As if you have to remind us," Akio interjected.

"It's not like I haven't thought of the possibility," Yoshio continued. "But he's not dead. I'm sure of it."

"How can you be?" Akio asked. "You have no idea. Sure he's a great fighter—we've seen him in action—but he was still recovering from his stab wound."

"It was mostly healed," Yoshio said. "And he's not just a great fighter. He's the best there is."

"Yeah, with a sword!" Akio said. "Not to burst your bubble, but swords don't work so well against guns!"

"You've seen him sword fight, so you assume that's his only skill," Yoshio said, getting annoyed. "You have no idea what else he's capable of." It sounded cryptic and a little dramatic. Yoshio's newfound respect of Miyahara seemed to have turned into hero worship.

"Stop," Masami said. "Both of you. We'll find him . . . one way or another. We've committed ourselves to that much. And right now all we have to go on are these boxes. Let's figure out what it means."

"It means he's been hit over the head too many times and wrote some random nonsense," Akio answered.

"Akio!" Masami's patience was near its end.

"Okay, okay."

The waiter showed up with plates of food, and Yoshio reluctantly collected the napkins. After the plates were down and the waiter left, he laid them all back down over the meals.

"Hey!" Akio said. "I'd like to eat this, thank you."

"Priorities, Akio," Masami said. "Eat around it."

Akio sighed and snaked a french fry from under the napkin that read "G" and "up."

Yoshio jumped back into the puzzle. "The last box you found, Masami, had almost no blood on it. It must be the last one he did. That was けて (kete), right? Oh, that's obvious," he continued before she could reply. "With the 気 (ki) and をつ(wotsu), your three boxes say *be careful*."

"I saw that," Masami said, "but I was hoping it was something else. Why would he take the time to say *be careful*? That's about as useful as saying *hi*."

"Hi, Nakama, be careful," said Akio with a laugh. "Maybe this message isn't even for us."

"It's Sensei," Yoshio said. "Saying *be careful* is his way of letting me know it's him. After every task he's given me so far, he says *be careful* even if it's something easy. I think he believes there's more weight to those words than we usually attribute to them. To him it means *engage your spirit* or something. What's left?"

"*Field up*," Masami said. "With an O and a G."

"O-G?" Akio said. "Doesn't that mean *original gangster*? Oh! "*Field up* is Nogami! It must mean Akira Nogami, the pro-wrestler. Maybe Akira is mixed up in this somehow. He was accused of being a spy last year, but then it turned out it was someone else. Maybe he's really an OG, a yakuza gangster!"

"You're talking about pro-wrestling?" Masami asked. "You know that's entirely fake, right? That they just make up storylines to get you sucked into watching them?"

"Yeah, duh," Akio said. "But yakuza love that stuff."

"It's not *Nogami*. Switch the characters, and it's *Ueno*, which means *high field*," Yoshio said.

"Ueno is back in Tokyo," said Akio. "Not far from where I live."

"If that's right," Masami said, "we have *Nakama, Ueno, 11th floor, be careful*. That could make sense, but what about the English letters? What does that spell?"

Yoshio arranged the napkins in order.

EEGOHISUM

"Yep, makes perfect sense," Akio chuckled.

"The 11 was the first box we found," said Yoshio. "And it had the most blood on it. Put *11th floor* first."

They rearranged the napkins.

HIEEGOSUM

"Still gibberish," Akio said, and Masami thought so too. But Yoshio was smiling.

"It's not English," he said. "It's Latin."

"You're taking a Latin class?" Akio asked.

"No, just learning at home for fun," Yoshio said with not a hint of humor.

Akio scoffed.

"What does it say?" Masami interrupted.

"Hie ego sum," Yoshio said. "I am here."

They all got quiet for a moment as the message sunk in. Miyahara was back in Tokyo on the eleventh floor of a Nakama Robotics building.

Masami took a bite of her pickle, ignoring her burger still under a napkin. It was probably cold, but she didn't have much of an appetite now. Akio was right to be suspicious that Miyahara didn't just get away and come find them himself. What was he doing? And what were they up against apart from a bunch of yakuza thugs? Miyahara wasn't law enforcement; he was a demon hunter. They still had a lot to figure out.

Yoshio sucked his Coke through the straw until there was only air, and then said, "What do we do now?"

"Are we sure this is what it means?" Masami asked.

"One hundred percent," Yoshio answered.

"How many buildings in Ueno have an eleventh floor? Must be hundreds."

"Yes," Yoshio added. "But how many buildings associated with Nakama Robotics have *only* eleven floors? Sensei wouldn't be vague. We just need to find an eleven story building with a Nakama connection."

Masami nodded. It sounded crazy enough to be right.

14
Special Delivery

Juichiro Fukuda was in his study reading the news when there was a knock on the door.

"Boss," said the voice, one of his bodyguards. "There's a package here for you."

Fukuda took his eyes from the paper. He wasn't expecting a package, at least not particularly on that day. He hadn't ordered anything and hadn't been informed of any shipment. But there was something he had been expecting . . . eventually. Perhaps today was the day.

"What kind of package?"

"A rather large one," the bodyguard said through the door. "And the delivery men aren't from the Japan Post."

"Who then?" Fukuda was irritated already. *Why doesn't he just say it?*

"Men from Tezuka-gumi."

Fukuda folded the *Dainichi Daily* and set it back on the desk. "Triple Homicide" read the headline. He was silent a moment, weighing his options. "I'll be right there."

Fukuda was not godfather, not the boss. He was more like a general. He was second-in-command to Shigeo Takagi, the godfather of the Ishiguro-kai, and was loyal. Fukuda would say that he didn't have designs to be godfather, that he never wanted such power and responsibility, that he only wanted to serve, and he was happy with what he had. But he would be lying. It was his belief that anyone who said such things was lying.

Of course he knew that the Kofu factions of the Kawabata-gumi, the largest syndicate in Japan, based in Kobe, had surprisingly defected to the Tezuka-gumi, a once much smaller syndicate based in Kofu. He knew that certain clans within different syndicates in Tokyo, Kyoto, and Kobe had also defected to the Tezuka-gumi. And he knew that the Mishima-kai, the second largest syndicate in Japan, also based in Tokyo, had gone over fully to the Tezuka-gumi—though this was not public knowledge. The Mishima-kai did not have a single godfather. They had a board of twelve bosses. One of them acted as reigning godfather, but in truth they ruled equally. The story was that during one of their board meetings they had ordered dim sum, and each plate was served with an added garnish of a fat emerald amongst the steaming dumplings. From then on they were loyal to the Tezuka-gumi. They still operated as if they were independent, but Fukuda knew the board now served Hiromi Kumamori in Kofu.

For any loyal brother to be swayed by something so trivial as an emerald, regardless of its worth, disgusted Fukuda. These men were not worthy of their position. They were not worthy of any honor if they were so weak and changeable. But what concerned him was that so many had defected, so many men that he had thought were honorable. The brotherhood had been changing for the worse, in his opinion. Too many of the younger members lacked the integrity of the older, lifetime brothers. But those defecting to the Tezuka-gumi were old and young, proven and unproven.

The Ishiguro-kai, which Fukuda still served, was Tokyo's second largest brotherhood, and the third largest in Japan. He had heard the rumors of gifts given to the men who had defected just before they had done so. But the rumors he heard were akin to those on the dim sum plates, small gifts: green gems, sometimes mounted in jewelry, but often raw stone presented in silver or gold eggs.

Therefore he was not surprised that someone from Kofu would be paying him a visit. They were clearly on a mission to take over all the brotherhoods, to unite them in some sinister way. But, because of the rumors, he had expected a single messenger, with a small gift in his hand. He had planned for it, and his determination was set. He had to find out what Kumamori was gifting and why yakuza were defecting in droves.

Though the gangs had a bad reputation, particularly in these days of police and media crackdown, the members had been mostly loyal to the syndicates and bosses that took them in. Yakuza were generally outcasts—losers, as the name itself suggests: ya-ku-sa, 8-9-3, the worst possible hand in the card game *oicho-kabu*. They were lost souls who needed a place to fit in. The brotherhood provided that for them, and they were usually fiercely loyal to their syndicate in return.

One of the most surprising betrayals was by Debi, the ringleader of an old-time Tokyo network known as the Black Moon Society, a clandestine and impossible to pin-down conglomerate of gangsters, pimps, and businessmen, which ran the illicit brothels disguised as *soaplands* and massage parlors. Debi had worked with Fukuda's syndicate, the Ishiguro-kai, for decades, providing them with a healthy percentage of profits in return for the girls the syndicate brought him. For him to sever connections and begin working exclusively with the Tezuka-gumi, there had to be some kind of powerful persuasion. Debi had been raised in the Ishiguro-kai, having been taken in when he was only fourteen. When he transitioned to the Black Moon fifteen years later, it was only because a bargain had been struck. The Ishiguro-kai would be their sole yakuza connection, cutting off the other syndicates from direct prostitution payouts, and Debi would remain an honorary brother.

This chokehold the Ishiguro-kai brokered was always a sore point for the other factions, particularly their larger Tokyo rivals, the Mishima-kai. But it was a connection that was locked and bound, unbreakable. Or so Fukuda had believed. He was baffled that Debi could turn his back on those who had made him. And Fukuda's boss, Takagi, had suffered a complete meltdown over it.

But Fukuda was certain. No matter what was offered him—riches, women, power—he would not cave in. What was a valuable emerald compared to the exaltation of loyalty? He would never defect and serve some lesser godfather. He was next in line to be godfather himself, and when his beloved boss passed or something . . . unexpected . . . happened to him, Fukuda would take over. He would not give up all he had gained to become a flunky for an unstable thug who couldn't hack it in the Kawabata-gumi.

The story was that Kumamori, the godfather of the Tezuka-gumi, had been too ambitious when he joined the Kawabata-gumi. He had been irreverent and took some important matters into his own hands, much to the chagrin of their godfather. He had been cast out, lucky to have not "disappeared" completely. After which, somehow, he had roused enough miscreants in Kofu to organize and become a force to be reckoned with there, albeit a small one. There had only been eight hundred members last year, and now . . . now they were over twenty thousand strong, the vast bulk of that from the absorbed Mishima-kai. It was baffling to even consider. Fukuda aimed to find out how Kumamori was pulling this off, and report it back to Takagi.

Takagi was a piece of work these days. He was losing control, not only of his *kobun*—his children, the brothers of the Ishiguro-kai—but of his own mind. Takagi had always been well loved among the yakuza. Even the godfather of the Kawabata-gumi had expressed his respect and friendship of Takagi. For that, even though second in size to the Mishima-Kai in Tokyo, the Ishiguro-kai was an equal power in the city.

But losing Debi had been a big blow to Godfather Tagaki. With Debi went a large chunk of the Ishiguro's income. Every time another clan or even individual brother defected, it was like another strand of Takagi's sanity went with them. He had become a recluse, afraid to leave his home, often swapping out his bodyguards, afraid they had been compromised. Fukuda had tried to warn him that he was only making things worse, distilling his own brand of mutiny by not trusting his *kobun*. But the boss was slipping and wouldn't listen. Takagi barely slept anymore, always red-eyed and frantic, kept awake by a mixture of cocaine and Adderall. He had multiple bolt locks on his home and bedroom door. He had even kicked his wife out, suspecting she had become an agent for Kumamori.

The time for Fukuda to take over was closer than he had expected. But still, he was loyal. And when he exposed Kumamori's ploy, he would be all the more fit to head the Ishiguro-kai. The brothers would practically beg him to lead.

So what was this large package being delivered by more than one man? It couldn't be the emerald he had expected. He rose from his desk and exited his study. His wife, Kameyo, was waiting outside the study door, a concerned look on her face.

"Don't accept it," she whispered. "Send them away."

He nodded at her, and she gave him a stern look. She followed him to the door, but kept back, leaning against the tall bookshelf by the hallway. His wife had always been wise, and he had no intention of accepting the package. He only had to see what it was.

Two of Fukuda's bodyguards stood by the open door. A large crate sat on the doorstep, framed by two men in black suit jackets and sunglasses.

"Mr. Fukuda," one of the men said as the general approached. "I am Ike and this is Okubo. We bring you a gift from Mr. Kumamori."

"Ike," Fukuda addressed the taller of the two. "You were running mahjong for boss Sanada in the Mishima-kai. Now you are a delivery boy for the Tezuka-gumi?"

"Kumamori is a powerful leader. I am pleased to be his servant. Sanada serves him as well. Our great godfather has sent this gift for you, so that you may see his kind heart and good intentions."

"I have heard of your gifts," Fukuda said. "Mr. Kumamori has been very generous of late."

"Yes," Ike responded. "He is a generous father. All of his children are very happy."

"What could be in a box so big?" Fukuda asked, smiling. "A television? A new oven, perhaps? Or maybe a bomb?" He smiled bigger.

"No, no, sir," Ike responded again, while Okubo stood and watched, still as a pillar. "Mr. Kumamori would never want to destroy you. He only seeks your friendship."

"Friendship, huh?" Fukuda's smile dropped. "He seems to have a lot of friends already."

"Yes, sir. His generosity and wisdom is touching us all. May we bring in the package?"

Generosity and wisdom. Two traits that couldn't be more opposite of the Kumamori I know.

Fukuda paused. He had to know, but the voice in his head was telling him to be careful. It wasn't just Kameyo's wise warning. Maybe she was right, and he should just send them away without looking, but then he would know nothing. He had to see what it was so he could unravel it and take power back, use his knowledge against this rogue godfather and shut him down. He would let them open it in the doorway and then send it away. He did not think it would be a bomb. Yakuza men were not kamikaze soldiers. They were not blind and naive militants blowing themselves up for some perceived greater good. They were ambitious men, all. They valued their lives. They would not open a package they knew was a bomb.

But what if they didn't know? What if they were ignorant? *No.* It wasn't Kumamori's way. He had been recruiting. He had been getting brothers to defect in large numbers. And if he wanted someone dead, he used Mr. Raikatuji—who was, of course, dead himself now, as were the two men that Fukuda had sent to kill him. It was strange though. His men propped up in the living room, and Raikatuji, naked and dead in his bedroom. If Raikatuji had killed the men, who had killed him? And why had his thumb been removed?

No, whatever was in this box was some kind of gift. He had to see what it was.

"You open it," he told the men. "Outside."

"As you wish," Ike said. "Though we hope it doesn't make your neighbors jealous."

Fukuda peered out the door. There were people about. He caught a lady looking his way, obviously trying to see what the big package was.

Others had stopped, pretending to not be looking, but it was obvious. He was mostly confident of his sway over the neighbors. Th ey respected him, he believed, and knew he was a force of good in the neighborhood, protecting them, looking out for them. But they were not yakuza, and they might talk. And there was one he didn't recognize; she could be press. He waved and nodded politely to the woman. "Bring it inside," he said.

As he turned from the door to make room for them, he caught his wife's scowl. It was only in her eyes. Her face had a slight smile, a welcoming one, but he knew she was unhappy behind it. She was completely against this, and he would get an earful when they were gone. But he had to know what was in the box. It was fuel for his own game. He would learn the Tezuka-gumi's trick and use it to take them down.

His bodyguards stepped aside, and Ike and Okubo brought the large package in. It was the size of a washing machine. There were no markings on the crate; it was plain blonde plywood. Th e two men lifted it easily enough, but it didn't look light. They set it carefully in the entryway, and one of Fukuda's bodyguards closed the front door.

Kameyo gave him another disapproving look that said, *I hope you know what you're doing.*

He did. He was sure of it. There could be nothing inside the crate that would make him have the slightest change of heart toward Kumamori and the Tezuka-gumi. Nothing that would make him disloyal. It could be an emerald the size of his oldest child. It could be stacks of cash. It could be any number of valuable things, but there was nothing that would make him bend his knee to that lowlife Kumamori. He had riches. He had power. Th e only thing he would happily receive would be Kumamori's head. If that was in the box, he would take it gladly. Anything else, he would send away.

Ike pulled out a small crowbar from somewhere within his suit. Fukuda's bodyguards stepped forward, but he put out his hand to calm them. Ike brandished the crowbar very unlike a weapon in an effort to show his harmless intentions. He set the crowbar at the top edge of the crate and pried it open. Th e front panel fell toward the floor where

Okubo caught it and let it down softly, so as not to damage the hardwood.

Staring back at Fukuda from inside the box was a face. It startled him. For a moment, he thought it was a person. It was very human looking. But it wasn't human. It was synthetic, though of human build and proportions. It looked quite real. Its eyes were open, and it was hunched over to fit in the box. It was female and dressed in a very proper European housemaid's uniform, white apron with frills over a black skirt that was not too short, but respectable.

Ike and Okubo lifted the top off the crate, and the maid stood up. She blinked her eyes and bowed deeply to Fukuda, her hands by her side. "How may I serve you, master?" she asked, stepping out of the box.

Fukuda laughed. He was impressed, very impressed. He hadn't expected this. He knew Kumamori had bought Nakama Robotics, but this was far beyond any Office Helper Bot or robot dog. He had spared no expense. This was decades better than any robot he had ever seen, far better than anything that was commercially available. It was a fantastic gift, but to give up your honor, your loyalty? No. How could the others have done so for this, and for so much less? *Weak*, was all he could think. *They were impossibly weak.* Besides, an advanced robot like this would most likely be serving as a spy. How stupid did Kumamori think he was?

He smiled and nodded his head to the robot maid. "You can tell your boss, Kumamori, thank you. You are a wonderful gift, but . . ." He was about to say, you can get back in your box, and return to him, but he saw something that stopped him. His eyes were drawn to her full breasts, so lifelike and inviting beneath her white apron. He could nuzzle in them for hours and die happy. But it wasn't the breasts themselves that drew him. Nestled between the soft, fleshy glands was a rich green glow. It caught his eye and his tongue stopped moving. At first he thought it a necklace, but then realized that it was coming from inside her chest, sparkling behind a circle of clear skin. It was beautiful, such a pleasant, comforting green. It made him think of warm tea, hot baths, and his mother's hand on his back. It made him think of safe walls in strong, comfortable houses, and of happy, devoted families, a family he never had outside of the yakuza.

The glow made his shoulders relax and his jaw loosen. His eyes softened in a kind, almost beatific gaze. "I accept the godfather's grand generosity," he said, bowing to both Ike and Okubo, as well as the robot. "I will cherish this gift always. Please convey this to him, and make it known that I am his loyal servant."

15

A Slight Delay

Akio sat on the bed in his hotel room, trying to figure out what the hell he was doing there. It was the same hotel as their last trip, barely two months ago. There was probably some kind of special business rate for the *Dainichi*.

He felt useless. What was he supposed to do? He was no good at talking, and he wasn't nearly as smart as Yoshio—but who was? He was getting better at photography, but how was that going to help rescue Miyahara from the yakuza? He damn well couldn't turn invisible! Masami had ignored him plenty of times in the past, but now she could simply disappear. That was going to work wonders for their non-relationship.

But what about him? They said he had fought like a master when he wore the mask, that if he had gotten hold of a sword, they might all be dead.

He couldn't stomach that thought. If he had killed Miyahara and Masami . . .

God, Masami!

He wouldn't be able to live with himself. And if they had never taken that mask off him, he might still be on some murderous rampage, not even aware of his life as Akio.

He grimaced at the thought. For Yoshio to even think he would ever put that mask back on . . . maybe the kid wasn't so smart after all.

But what if he didn't have to wear it? Maybe there was something that remained in his muscles of that memory. If only he could tap into it. Maybe he needed some kind of amulet, a medallion, like Masami. But what? He couldn't think of anything that could invoke the kind of response in him that the medallion did in Masami. He had no mementos that had any kind of power. He had his camera. And even that seemed to let him down sometimes.

He stood up from the bed. He took his best kendo stance and faced the door of the hotel.

"Come in," he said to an imaginary enemy. "I dare you." He sank deeper into the stance.

As the imaginary enemy entered—a yakuza with a katana—Akio stepped forward and slashed at the air. As he did so, his toe caught the carpet and he tumbled forward. Forgetting his imaginary blade, he put his hands out to catch himself.

Dammit.

He got back to his feet.

What a great warrior I am.

He tried again. He took the stance, one he learned when he was a kid. He had taken kendo at his parents' behest and had not enjoyed it. He loved the idea of being a sword fighter, but he didn't like getting hit with a stick at all. And it seemed that the bulk of kendo involved him getting hit with a stick. The instructor hit him; the other kids hit him. When it came down to it, he supposed he just wasn't very good at blocking. Or dodging.

He took judo later, and at first he liked it. In judo, you get to use your opponent's force against him. He liked that idea a lot more than trying to not get hit by a stick. But it all went downhill when they started learning throws. He didn't have the strength to throw the other kids very well, and they *did* have the strength to throw him. So his training in judo petered out too.

But he wasn't going to give up now. He squared his stance, the first one he learned and the only one he could remember, the *chūdan-*

no-kamae. He placed his left foot just behind the right, on the balls of the foot. His body faced straight forward, his spine perpendicular to the floor. He made sure his weight was centered on both legs and tried to relax his shoulders.

If only I had the katana in my hand.

Akio had felt much more confident holding the ancient, demon-wrought blade, one of the two weapons they had found in the samurai demon's lair. Although scared out of his wits at the time, he had felt powerful holding it, its ruby guard gleaming in the torchlight as he faced the demon.

He stepped again, mindful of the carpet, and slashed at the empty air with his empty hands. "Ohhreeeah!" he voiced as he swung, but not loudly. He sidestepped and put up a block, then struck back with another soft cry, cutting into the belly of the imaginary attacker.

He went on like this for five minutes, slashing and blocking and stabbing at the air with nothing. He felt silly, like a child playing a game. He didn't feel any demon spirit taking him over and guiding his arms. He didn't feel any muscle memory from when he had worn the mask. It was pointless.

He collapsed on the bed and stared at the ceiling.

He thought of his companions in Masami's hotel room next door. She was researching with Yoshio. Th ey were on their computers, Masami reaching out to contacts and Yoshio scouring the internet, the "deep web," whatever that is. Akio didn't know how to help. He didn't have any helpful contacts or mad computer skills. So he had said he wasn't feeling well and excused himself.

He was going to be useless if they had a serious run-in with the yakuza. Even if he could somehow tap into those samurai memories, the yakuza had guns. Granted, they didn't use them often. Gun deaths were incredibly low in Japan, far less here in a year than America had in a weekend. Th e laws were strict and punishment severe. But these yakuza had already shot at them, so they were clearly willing to risk the consequences.

And on top of that, he didn't even want to access those memories. They were nothing but evil. Painful killing, betrayal, and loss.

What you want doesn't factor into it anymore.

The thought struck him almost as if someone else was speaking. It was Masami's voice. It was an older, wiser Akio. It was the demon.

Life was so much bigger than what he wanted.

Reluctantly, he got up again. Took the stance. This time, he tried to relax and remember what it felt like to be in battle, to be surrounded by warriors, some his fellow men-at-arms, but many trying to kill him. In his mind, he saw the men on horseback with spears. He saw the foot soldiers with bows and arrows, and swords. He saw the corpses around him on the bloody battlefield.

A horsed samurai rode at him, with a spear poised to skewer him in the neck. He shifted his stance slightly and readied himself for the attack. He wanted blood. He could already see the samurai headless on the ground and relished it.

Akio choked and shook the vision away, just as the spear was thrust toward him. It was a memory only, not a transportive experience like he had had with the mask on. It was a hazy dream of someone else's past. But there was something else too; there was an evil there just at the edges, and he backed away from it as from a dark shape in an alley.

He felt sick for real now. His stomach wanted to heave from all the blood he had seen. How had the samurai lived like that?

The samurai Akechi had his reasons for revenge, reasons that could have justified all the killing, and perhaps even been forgiven. But they hadn't been forgiven. He had been imprisoned in Hell. Akio again saw Akechi's torturous admittance into the nether world, the insectoid, centipede-like creatures with their rows upon rows of teeth who had been his jailers.

He fell back to the bed and curled up into a ball, trying to push the vision away. Why did he have to live with memories that weren't his? He wanted them gone.

There was a knock on his door. He remained still, not sure if he wanted to accept either reality at this point. The knock came again, and then a voice. "Akio," it said. It was Masami.

He dragged himself from the bed and went to the door. Opening it, he saw the slender and usually dire reporter staring back at him with a gleam in her eyes. "Yoshio found something," she said.

"Of course he did," Akio said, and stepped back to let her in.

She came in and shut the door. "He found the eleven-story building in Ueno."

"There's only one?" Akio asked.

"Only one that the Tezuka-gumi owns. It used to be Nakama Robotics' main offices. Th ey didn't just buy these buildings. Th ey bought the whole company."

"The robotics company?" Akio asked.

"Yes," Masami said, pacing in the tiny space between the bathroom and the room door. "They reverted it to a privately held corporation and have just been sitting on it."

"The yakuza own legit businesses though, right? Is it really that weird?"

"They do, but they are always turning some kind of profit. Nakama hasn't generated a single yen since they bought it." Masami said. "They aren't even promoting it for some future profit scheme. The yakuza love to show off their above-board businesses. It gives them credibility. So why not Nakama? I can't see what their game is. And I brought this on, in a way." She said, shaking her head.

"You? What are you talking about?"

Masami looked up at him with a start. She was doing that thing again where she talked out loud and didn't realize he was listening, that he was even there. After a hesitation she answered.

"I put Nakama in jail. I broke that story and exposed his crimes. If I hadn't done that the yakuza wouldn't have bought the company and be doing whatever it is they're doing. I made a bad situation worse."

"Wait, what? You did not," Akio said. He tried to look her in the eyes but she looked away. "Nakama did that to himself by being a bastard. You did the right thing."

Masami didn't respond, but she looked at Akio then. Her face was blank and he couldn't read her. Her eyes were deeper than he'd ever noticed, vast pools of shiny black.

"You're right," she said finally. "I don't know what's going on with me. You're right," she repeated. "We should get back to Tokyo as soon as possible. Get your things. We'll check out now and get on the road." She didn't wait for an answer, and headed down the hall.

Akio watched her go, grateful that he at least would get to go home. He didn't care for hotel rooms. His own compact apartment was safe; his own bed, his own things. He was happy to be going back. He rolled off the bed and went to the bathroom to grab his toothbrush.

And yet, even though he was grateful, he didn't see the point. Why was he even on this assignment? He was only going to drag the others down.

When he scored the last Kofu assignment, he had been ecstatic. To be photographer on a huge story like the Kofu Head Collector was something he had only dreamed about. To be investigating leads with Masami Sato, the dire robot queen herself, the unparalleled wordsmith and lead generator who made the male staff writers tremble in their once insular press club. *That* Masami Sato.

It had been glorious.

And then it had been terrifying. The world had been cracked open to reveal a reality that nearly unglued him. Demons existed. Hell existed. They weren't just constructs to sway people into living moral lives. They were flesh, armor, drool, and removable heads. They didn't abide by the rules we did, but they were real.

Yet in that chaos of discovery and gore, he had distinguished himself. He had helped. He had vanquished the demon—twice. Sure, one of those times was by pure accident and the second time was at the demon's request. So it wasn't all that admirable when you looked closely, but he had done it. He hadn't turned and run like a mouse at a cat carnival, like he had wanted to.

Something intrinsic about him had changed then. He mostly still felt like the bumbling, annoying photographer who people didn't like but sometimes humored out of pity. But when he had stupidly, weakly, put that mask on, he had gone through something profound. He had been poisoned by the demon samurai's memories, and his skin had thickened by a degree. No one else may have noticed, but he wore himself a little heavier these days. And while it had given him a level of self-assurance he never had, it worried him. How were the demon's memories affecting him? He felt them sneaking inside his soul.

None of that made him feel useful, only anxious.

He was crap at investigative journalism. Masami and Yoshio made him feel like a chimp at a Mensa meeting. He had nothing to offer but the occasional poo to fling.

The huge, fly-in-the-cupcake difference between this job and the last one was the fact that, this time, Masami had asked him to come with her, had requested that he be her photographer. Of course that was because Miyahara had requested the two of them, but she had gone along with it, and willingly. She had even wanted to talk to him about her disappearing act. Like a friend would.

He couldn't let her down. He had to figure out how to be useful.

Okay, I'm a photographer. Start there. What am I supposed to be taking pictures of? They were officially on an assignment to investigate the Kofu yakuza's expansion. What images would be appropriate for this ruse?

The buildings, he thought. *The yakuza themselves. Some sinister-looking gangster doing . . . what?*

It would come to him. He would know when he saw it.

The reality that they were trying to rescue a kidnapped kendo instructor who moonlights as a demon hunter was step two. Step one was good enough right now.

He grabbed his bag and went to the elevator to meet Masami.

Yoshio was there with a nervous smile on his wide, boyish face. "We're getting closer," he said.

"Really?" asked Akio, sarcastically. "It seems like we're further away. We were in Tokyo a few days ago. We were closer then."

"Yes, but we didn't know he was in Ueno."

"We still don't know that he is."

Ueno, Akio thought. That's where he had bumped into that young yakuza wannabe and had the crippling headache. Maybe he wasn't just a wannabe after all. It made the Ueno connection feel right, but he had no intention of admitting that to Yoshio.

"The clues point right to this building. He has to be there."

"Yeah, a bunch of boxes with random characters on them. Might as well have a GPS tracker imbedded in Miyahara."

"Stop it, boys," Masami said as she rounded the corner from the hallway. "We need to get along. I doubt I'd have given a second thought to those boxes either, Akio, but they were clearly a message. Yoshio knows Miyahara better than we do, and he's confident that message was for us. With the discovery of the building in Ueno, I'm pretty sure he's right."

"I am right," Yoshio said flatly.

The elevator dinged and they climbed in.

The unflinching certainty of the teenager rankled Akio, even more so for the fact that Yoshio was utterly void of arrogance. He spoke matter-of-factly as if reminding them that the earth was a sphere.

"So what's our plan?" Akio asked. "Are we to go in there, guns blazing, and rescue Miyahara in a *Battle Royale* bloodbath? Should we grab the swords?" It was the last thing he wanted, but he didn't know what else to do, and he wanted to appear brave.

"Maybe," Masami said. "But we should try being discreet first. You and I will try to find a peaceful way in."

"Okay . . ." Akio liked peaceful, but he had no idea what that might be.

"It might be difficult," Yoshio said. "Nakama Robotics is supposed to be out of business. It's not supposed to exist."

"We'll figure something out," Masami insisted, but she seemed unsure under her steel exterior.

"There's always the other way," Yoshio put in. "The new way." He had a hint of a grin on his face.

"Only if we have to," Masami said sharply.

Masami's new powers were beyond anything Akio could have ever believed, but his life seemed to be going down that path. Unreal was becoming normal. He could see that it was taking a bit of a toll on Masami. She was not her normally stalwart self. She almost seemed frail.

The elevator stopped and they exited. The warm day was winding up, and a thin breeze brushed Akio as they left the hotel. The car was parked a block away in an open lot. The hotel had parking, but it was limited, and it was one of those stacked parking lots, where you have to wait for the carriage to find your car and shuffle it over to you. Masami had made it clear that she didn't like to wait, so she parked in the open air lot.

The black Honda Logo was in the middle of the closest row, a tall chain fence between it and the street, nestled between a sky blue, electric two-door and a white minivan. They crossed the street, bags in hand. They were only two cars away, almost to the sky blue electric, when Akio's head began to throb. An ache moved up from the back of his neck, swung side to side and then settled at the back of his skull. It was subtler than when he had bumped into the man at Ueno Station, and felt more like he was approaching the large crate in the warehouse, like a demon was coming for them as they searched its lair. As they approached the car, the pain intensified slightly. Something was wrong.

"Wait," he said sharply. "Don't go any closer." He demanded it, and Masami and Yoshio stopped.

"What is it, Akio?" Masami asked, and not in her usual patronizing voice. She was listening. She was ready to respect what he had to say. That was new.

"Something's wrong with the car," he said.

"It looks fine," she said, but remained still.

"It's not," Akio assured her. "We should move back." The sky darkened slightly, as the sun drifted quickly out of sight behind the mountains, as if making a run for it.

His head was pulsing. Something sinister and invasive was in the car. It was like the creepy feeling you get when someone is watching you, but the watcher wants to put a guiding hand on your back—no, *inside it* like a ventriloquist's puppet. And despite the headache, it felt eerily comforting.

Akio started to back up. Yoshio followed first and then Masami.

"How do you know?" Yoshio whispered.

"Headache," Akio answered. "I think I know what's causing them. I'll explain later."

"Akio, we really need to get back to Tokyo, and that car is how we're planning to do that," Masami said softly. "We need to get in it and get on the road."

"Nope," Akio said. "We really don't." He could almost see something inside the car. It was on the center console, waiting, like a living thing. And it felt strangely green.

Just then, the back doors to the parked minivan opened. A Black Lincoln Town Car screeched into the parking lot, whipped around the row of cars, and came to a halt, sideways behind them. Four suited men got out. Two more were exiting the van.

Akio stopped, as did Masami and Yoshio, not sure which way to look, which was the greater threat. Yoshio faced the two coming from the van, so Akio faced the four coming from the car. Masami was in the middle. The chain link fence stood to one side, too high to get over quickly enough. On the other side was another row of cars. Maybe they could dart through it.

"You've been sneaking where you shouldn't be sneaking."

It was Chida, the yakuza in charge at the warehouse. His sharp, flat shoulders cut his suit like a Lego man. He was clearly irritated the three of them had gotten away from him before. He had a hand inside his suit jacket, resting near his belt. One of the thugs from the warehouse was with him, his hand also in his jacket. It was the taller, uglier one, Uzumaki. The other two gangsters from the car flanked them.

Akio gave a quick glance behind him. The two men from the minivan had what looked like hoods and handcuffs in their hands. He realized that they had not expected a fight. Whatever was in the car—*green and ghoulish, don't be foolish*—was meant to neutralize them. The four in the car had been standing by as backup.

"This is going to go much, much easier if you all just come with us friendly-like," Chida continued in a manner about as unfriendly as Akio could imagine. He slowly approached, the other three his shadows.

Akio felt Masami moving closer to him, slipping behind him. She slid herself between him and Yoshio, like a scared cat. This was not like her at all. Normally, she would be confronting men like these head on, right in their faces. She was not the type to hide.

"Stay close," she whispered. Akio didn't understand.

"If you make trouble, not only will you get hurt, you may find that you have no jobs at the *Dainichi Daily* when you return to Tokyo," Chida continued. "None of us want that, do we?"

"*If* they return to Tokyo," another snickered.

They know where we work!

"But if you come with us," Chida said, "you can keep your jobs, and maybe we'll all become close friends, despite the fact you've been sneaking around our house."

Close friends? With a bunch of gangsters who are about to take us hostage? Akio knew what Stockholm Syndrome was and had no interest in experiencing it.

What was there to say? *We're sorry? We won't do it again?* Akio hoped someone smarter than him would talk the gangsters out of this. Where was Masami's sneaky charm that she could turn on and off like a light switch? Why wasn't Yoshio's superbrain conjuring a way to escape? The yakuza were bearing down on them. They had to do something, and now.

Akio felt Masami suddenly slip out from behind him quickly and he fell against Yoshio. He turned and started to say, "Masa . . ." but stopped. She wasn't there.

That's what she's doing!

The men were getting too close. Yoshio whispered "Switch" to Akio, and he went with it, assuming the boy must have a plan. They rolled around each other to face the men on the opposite sides. Yoshio shouted, "Stay back! I'm not afraid to use it."

The two men in front of Akio halted and he dared a glance behind him. All four men on the other side had drawn handguns, and Yoshio had one of his own.

Akio's panic level increased tenfold.

Where the hell did he get a gun?

The two men on his side didn't have guns, not drawn at least. They still held their handcuffs and hoods.

"You're just making this far more complicated, little boy," Chida said. "Put the gun down."

"You'll only hurt yourself with that. It's not a toy," said Uzumaki.

"I know how to use it, wiseguy," Yoshio said. "I've been trained in firearms. Top of my class in police academy camp. Don't take another step."

Police academy camp? Akio swore he remembered Yoshio telling him differently.

"Are you some kind of teenage spy?" Chida asked with an uncertain laugh.

"Maybe," Yoshio said flatly. "Try me."

Damn. Yoshio is a hard kid for a nerd.

"Just put it away, Yoshio." Akio said. "You've got one gun. They've got four and I'm unarmed."

"Your friend is wise," said Chida. "I would listen to him. You might wound one of us, maybe even kill one if you're as good as you say you are. And who knows, you might be. But it comes down to numbers. You strike me as someone who likes numbers. Is that true?"

Do they know who Yoshio is too? Or is this just an insightful gangster?

Yoshio didn't respond.

"The numbers say you lose," the yakuza finished. "All of you. Hey, where did the young lady go?"

Just then there was a cry from one of the gangsters. Akio turned to see a back leg buckle and a man fall forward, losing his grip on his gun. It clattered to the pavement. The two in front of Akio backed up.

By now bystanders had gathered. Akio could see people keeping a distance on the street, watching. The sun was going down, but it was still daylight, and guns were drawn in a public parking lot. The police would be there any minute.

Akio heard another yakuza suffer the same fate, a cry of pain, leg buckling from an invisible blow. But this one didn't lose his grip on his gun. As he fell, he turned and fired two shots into the open air.

The gathered bystanders shouted and scattered. Under that chaos, Akio swore he heard Masami cry out. It was a stifled yelp of pain and then nothing. No more men fell.

The two on the ground staggered to their feet. Then all four of them started toward Yoshio and Akio. The unarmed two on Akio's side held back. "I don't know what tricks you're playing," Chida said. "Or where that girl reporter went, but you little turds are done for."

Another gun fired, but this time it was Yoshio. He had fired at their feet.

Chida and Uzumaki danced to the side, but Chida smirked. He knew then that Yoshio wasn't willing to use deadly force. They came on faster, as did the two with the hoods and handcuffs. The fallen two got to their feet, one of them retrieving his gun.

"Hang on to that, Harigae!" said the one who had shot Masami.

Rage began to fill Akio. He felt it boil up like a sudden wave of bile and brimstone.

They shot Masami!

Anger and adrenaline rushed to Akio's muscles, and an unforgiving fire burned in his core. The evil he had before felt at the edges now came rushing in like a deluge. The dark shadow hid no longer; it had stepped inside Akio and filled every cell. A bloodstained battlefield lay before him now. No longer were there yakuza brandishing guns. Instead enemy samurai marched forward behind emotionless *mempo*, masks of armor to hide their fear. These samurai had his son. And they would die for it.

With a sudden burst of speed, he shot forward at Chida, ducking down just as the gangster lifted his gun. He spun around, swiping the man's legs out from under him, wrenching his arm up and around behind him as he fell. He heard and felt the arm snap.

Without pause, he landed a flurry of punches to Uzumaki's gut, then disarmed him with a twist of his left hand, at the same time thrusting his foot toward the next closest man's jaw, the one they had called Harigae. His foot impacted and he heard another crack, while Uzumaki slumped to the ground holding his abdomen. The fourth man brought up his gun, training it on Akio. He had backed up and was too far for Akio to reach him quickly, but Akio was past caring. He charged.

As he did, the man's arm was yanked sideways and a bullet pinged across the pavement. The man turned to face his new attacker, but found no one there. By the time he turned back around, Akio was on him. Grabbing the man's wrist in a steel trap grip, he turned and stepped into him, heaving him up and over, flipping him onto the pavement, back first. He landed with a slap and a crunch. A loud groan escaped his mouth as his gun fell from his limp hand. Blood began to trickle from his ear.

Akio turned to see the four men in different crumpled states on the pavement. None of them were moving but for some shifting and groaning. The one he had kicked in the head looked still as a corpse. Yoshio had the two unarmed gangsters at gun point, but they were backing away, in shock. "Don't kill us," one of them whined. They turned and ran from the parking lot.

Sirens sounded not far off. Lots of sirens.

"We have to get out of here," he heard Masami whisper close to his ear. She was okay. Not dead, at least. Then he realized that she had spoken while invisible, something she hadn't been able to do before.

"Yoshio!" Akio called, in an authoritative voice he had never heard come out of his throat. "Let's go!"

Akio's rage was slipping from him. He felt foggy and exhausted, like he'd drank one too many Lipovitan Ds and was crashing hard after the energy surge. As his anger faded, his fear began to return. They had to get out of there before the police arrived.

Yoshio joined him and they ran from the parking lot and down a side street. There were too many people around. Akio and Yoshio, at least, would be too easily described and spotted.

They made a turn down a smaller street and then another one. There were less people, people who hadn't seen the chaos in the parking lot. *Good.* They slowed their pace.

Masami appeared at their side, wiping tears from her eyes with one hand, her other hand on her medallion.

"Are you okay?" Akio asked, grateful she had materialized. He had wanted to ask her before but felt weird talking to someone he couldn't see, like talking to a ghost.

"Yes, the bullet just grazed my leg. I'll be fine." The way she looked at Akio was something he had never seen before, not just from Masami but from anyone that he could recall. He wasn't really sure how to read it. "I don't know how you did that," she said, her eyes glowing with something like admiration or awe. "It was horrifying, but amazing. I've never seen anyone fight like that."

Akio didn't know what to say. He wished the world could stop right at that moment, freeze frame so he could bask in it forever. Masami had just said he was amazing. He was utterly speechless.

The gleam in her eye disappeared and was quickly replaced by her usual dire intensity. "We have to get to the train station. Right now." She looked around as if trying to find a recognizable landmark.

Akio went for his phone to pull up the maps app, but Yoshio was already talking.

"Two blocks east, then straight north," the teenager said.

"Got it," Masami said, and started walking that way.

They followed her. Soon they were on Heiwa Boulevard, the major Kofu artery that led north to the train station, the police station only a few blocks in the other direction. She crossed the street at a light, patiently, like nothing was wrong. They followed.

As they crossed, Akio noticed her left pant leg. A hole was torn in it, and blood had soaked into the fabric.

"Just grazed you?" He asked as casually as he could muster. "Are you sure?"

"Yes, I'm sure." She didn't look at him, but slowed her pace to match that of a family with two kids and a grandmother. She wasn't limping. That was a good sign, he guessed. But the blood worried him. Least of all because they may be leaving a trail.

He quickly realized what Masami was doing. This was a busy part of town, the busiest it got in Kofu. Their best bet at hiding was to blend in with the crowds. So they stayed close to the group, Masami even saying hello to the kids and exchanging polite niceties with the adults, to make it look like they were together.

Then they were there. Only a few steps left. The doors of the train station were one wide sidewalk's width away underneath the tall building of the Celeo department store. They hurried their pace.

One short siren blast sounded, and four police cars whipped around the circular street in front of the station, two of them bumping up onto the sidewalk. People scattered. Masami, Akio, and Yoshio started in a sprint for the train station doors just as half a dozen uniformed policemen exited them and stood ready to intercept their path. The police had known exactly where they were headed. There was nowhere to run.

They came to a halt as the police surrounded them on the sidewalk.

16

The System

Masami sat across from Detective Kuramoto and Detective Fujimaki at a small white table. It was the first time she had actually seen the two together. During her and Akio's previous visit to the precinct, it was always one or the other, and Masami had had trouble picturing them as partners. Now that they were side by side, she had just as much trouble. They seemed as mismatched as a chewed up cigar and a smoothie with a protein boost. Kuramoto sat, a squat ugly dog, smirking at her, stale cigarette stench wafting off him. Fujimaki was clean cut and handsome, a sympathetic expression on his face. But there was something else too. He seemed happy to see her.

After spending the night on a narrow, stiff bed in the police jail, the "substitute prison" as it was called, she couldn't say the same. She was worried. She knew how these things worked; she was on the police beat, after all. Japan had a very high conviction rate, and the reason for that wasn't necessarily due to excellent police work. It was often from forced—and possibly false—confessions elicited in these very police jails. There was no pre-indictment bail here, and if the judge allowed, she could be held for up to twenty-three days before any charge was even made. They all could. During that time, the interrogations could be non-stop, little of it, if any, recorded. She had heard some horror stories, particularly in regards to women. They were at the mercy of the police now.

A strung-out waif shared her cell, mostly groaning and talking to herself all night. Police had come and gone, other suspects for other crimes dumped off. There was no sleeping. So Masami had made herself useful. The waif hadn't noticed her blink out of sight after pulling her drab brown, synthetic blanket over her head.

Now she was red-eyed, sipping bitter coffee from a paper cup, and staring at Kofu's answer to Popeye Doyle and Cloudy Russo across a scarred table in a nondescript interrogation room. A single door led out. A mirror filled most of one wall—two-way, of course. A camera was mounted high in a corner, but she doubted it was recording.

Unfortunately, Kuramoto was doing most of the talking.

"We've got five known yakuza members in custody, three of them hospitalized. They were easy to catch, considering the state they were left in. Two of them were running away, but we got 'em. And . . . we got a sixth one in the morgue."

Outwardly Masami was tired, expressionless. Inside she cursed a stream of expletives. *One of them is dead?*

"And here's a funny thing. We have some witnesses saying you were at the crime scene, but some don't mention you at all. They say it was only two skinny guys, who I'd have to say were your two boyfriends locked up downstairs. They all saw your little underage boy toy with a gun. And your buddy photographer flipping about like Sonny Chiba, cracking skulls and breaking necks. Literally."

"So tell me," Kuramoto grinned like a leprous wolf, "were you there or weren't you?"

Masami took a sip of her coffee and said nothing.

Fujimaki dropped his head and looked away. Kuramoto's lip curled.

They were being too nice. Sure, Kuramoto was a buffoon, but she knew he was capable of far worse. She had hoped for this, but wasn't sure. Her reputation could hurt or help her here. She knew she had some enemies on the force at Tokyo Metro, but Fujimaki had told her a lot of the cops there whispered her name with respect. She had been surprised, since they generally treated her like a thorn in their collective side. But Kofu was a mystery. She had very little rep here, and journalists were often treated like dumpster feed.

But Fujimaki had spoken for her. She could read it behind the sparkle in his eyes. She was safe. For now. And Kuramoto was none too happy about it.

"We have several guns in our possession," Kuramoto grumbled. "One of them is bound to turn out to be your juvenile bed buddy's. What is it with you and scrawny guys anyway, sweetie? You can't handle a big, thick man?"

"Hey," Fujimaki said. "Knock it off."

Masami stayed cold and flat. She'd heard it all too many times.

"I just want her to know that we could get her for cradle-robbing, too." Kuramoto grinned before moving on. "So maybe you were there, maybe you weren't. Mobile phone footage has been coming in. We'll know soon enough. What gets me is how two scrawny punks like your boyfriends could take out six yakuza, most of them armed. So I figure I'm not hearing the whole story. And I'd be tickled if you enlighten me."

"Just a quick rundown of what happened," Fujimaki added. "If you were there. It can't hurt."

Couldn't it?

"Or we can keep this meeting going for, oh, the next couple weeks," Kuramoto said. "You'll start to see just how lovable I can be. You'll be turned off stickmen for life."

Fujimaki stood. Kuramoto was getting under his skin worse than Masami's. "He's right. You know how it works. Let just get this over with. And you can . . . you know . . ."

Go home? Was that what he was trying to tell her? They didn't have anything on her. Not enough. Another reason conviction rates were so high and crime was so low: they didn't prosecute unless they had it in the bag. Not enough evidence and you walk free. Nothing on her, barely even eye witnesses. But Akio . . .

Masami drained her cup.

"More?" Fujimaki asked, perhaps a little too quickly.

"Please," she croaked.

"She speaks!" Kuramoto barked.

Fujimaki got up. His neck was flushed and he was clearly tense. He left the room abruptly.

Kuramoto looked at Masami with the empty eyes of a ghoul, a spent corpse in which someone forgot to put out the lights. The black mole on his face looked especially cancerous today. He took his pack of Seven Stars out of his jacket and knocked out a cigarette. He lit it with a disposable lighter and breathed deep.

But he said nothing else. Only leered at her with bloodshot, gray eyes, smoke curling up from cracked lips to play in his greased hair before adding to the brown stain on the ceiling. The door opened again, and Fujimaki set a fresh paper cup full of black in front her. It rankled her nose, but even the worst coffee was better than none at all. She sipped.

"Okay," she said. "I'll talk."

Kuramoto scoffed, and then coughed as he gagged on his own smoke.

"I was there," Masami said. "And I can prove it."

Fujimaki cast his eyes down again. He had wanted her to say she wasn't. It would have been easier. But it didn't matter. They still had nothing.

She lifted her leg up onto the table and started to pull up the hem of her pants. Kuramoto gagged again. "Well, this is getting interesting," he coughed. "Not gonna get out of it that way, sweetie, but I'm not opposed to you trying."

"Can it," Fujimaki said. "Let her talk."

"You're too buff for her, Tadao. She likes 'em skinny, remember?" His laugh was a burble of phlegm.

Masami unwrapped the toilet paper, now dark red and brown with blood, that she had wreathed about her calf in the police restroom after being fingerprinted last night. She had cleaned the wound out as best she could. She revealed it now, an oblong gash halfway to her knee that had just missed the bone. The bleeding had slowed, but some still seeped out. The wound throbbed and ached, but there was something about it that bothered her more than the physical pain.

Kuramoto snickered. "Your teen heartthrob shoot you after a lover's quarrel?"

"We need to get that patched up right away," Fujimaki said. "How was that overlooked? Is the doctor on premises?"

"How should I know?" Kuramoto answered. "She seems to come and go as she pleases." He winked at Masami. She drew her pant leg back down and returned her foot to the floor.

Fujimaki opened the door again and called out. "Is Dr. Ito here?"

"Yes, until two today," came the response.

"Let's get you over there now," Fujimaki said. "We'll continue this after."

"Ah, the bullet wound delay tactic, huh, sweetie?" Kuramoto droned. "We'll have to get your scintillating story later." He winked again. "But first I think we'll get your boyfriends in here—separately, of course—and see if their stories hold water."

Is that supposed to worry me? Masami had made her preparations. She ignored him and followed Fujimaki out of the room, glad to have a respite from the trapped cigarette stench and the verbal suppuration bubbling from that toad's mouth.

How did Fujimaki put up with it day in and day out? Or was he the same underneath his polished mask? Was he just another sexist pig disguised as a lamb? A sleek, muscled, dangerously handsome lamb. Was this just some kind of game? A version of good cop, bad cop designed to make her swoon for him, so he could notch his belt?

If so he wasn't doing a smash-up job. He was not impressing her now. Kuramoto clearly had seniority in their partnership. Fujimaki was the young-blood, having to swallow his pride and his partner's verbal vomit. Masami wanted to believe he was good. But she couldn't let down her guard. Not now. Not ever.

He smiled awkwardly and left her with the doctor, who was friendly—unreasonably friendly for a doctor in that environment. Masami was awed by her in that moment. Here was someone surrounded by shit and smiling in spite of it. Dr. Ito glowed. There was something serene about her, and angelic. Would Masami ever feel that way . . . about anything? Did she even want to? Life was a grind, and you needed thick armor to survive. To be zen and unaffected by the horrors of the world was incomprehensible. And yet . . .

As she watched her wound being cleaned and bandaged, a niggling thought presented itself again. As a ghost, she could walk through solid objects. When she didn't focus on the blue electrostatic web, objects did not affect her. How was it that a bullet, a very solid object, did her any harm at all?

But she knew why. It was the same reason she had fallen through the floor of her apartment. When the gangster aimed the gun at her, her ingrained belief that bullets wound and kill—as they generally do—was in full effect. It was a fact of her previous reality that she had not yet relinquished. She felt her leg accept the bullet as if she had willed it. She wondered what other beliefs she held that might get her killed.

They came to get Akio before Masami had been returned to her cell.

Where is she? What did they do to her? Did they release her? Or do something horrible?

He pushed the thought away. If anything went wrong, Masami would be okay. She could just turn invisible and get away. Right? *She's fine.*

As the cop led him down the hallway, he replayed what she had told him.

"Just tell the story as it happened," she had said as she whispered to him in his dark cell. "Mostly. Leave out what should be left out. We were going to my car when the yakuza surrounded us. I *disappeared* when it got scary. I ran. They'll believe that. If they ask what the yakuza would want with us, tell them we were asking questions at the Nakama warehouse, about their expansion. The *Daily* will back that up. Tell the truth. Just leave out what they won't understand. And if they ask about Yoshio, tell them he's a student intern at the *Daily*. Tanaka has our back."

She had startled Akio in the middle of the night. He had jumped when she first whispered to him, making his cellmate glare—a haggard looking man in his forties, holding his head like he was having the worst migraine of his life.

Akio hadn't been sleeping before and he barely slept after. Part sagging lopsided bed, part nerves. Mostly nerves. His back was sore and his shoulder cramped. The competing smells of stale cigarettes and industrial-strength cleaning products were inescapable.

He had thought about his own strange headaches then—something else he would leave out of his story to the police. He was starting to understand what was causing them. It was as if the headaches themselves were telling him what the source was. First it had been the demon under Kofu Castle, then the yakuza he ran into at Ueno Station. There was the crate inside the warehouse, and then Masami's car. The difference between that first time and the others was that, in Kofu, he had known it was the demon coming. He had felt it descending the stairs. With the more recent headaches he hadn't felt a demon, but a colder presence, something stony but vibrant. It made him think of the gem Yoshio had described seeing at the grocer's. Though it wasn't a demon he was feeling, there was something demonic about it. His headaches told him so. It was as if the demon samurai Akechi was in his head, thinking these thoughts for him.

Now Akio sat nervously in the drab room at a small, scarred table across from the detectives: Kuramoto, the woman-hater who had gotten under Masami's skin, who had mockingly called Akio the "boss," and his partner, Fujimaki, who looked like a movie cop, an actor putting on a role. Mirrors on one wall reflected Akio's terrified image back at himself. He knew they were two-way mirrors. That was how these things worked. He had seen it on TV countless times.

He was scared of what would happen to him. To all of them. They couldn't very well help Miyahara if they were incarcerated.

"So what happened?" Kuramoto asked, his smug smile showing a few crooked teeth. "Did you beat up those poor yakuza all by yourself?"

He leaned back in his chair. "You tell me the story. I'm excited to hear it."

Tell the truth.

"I don't want to brag," Akio said, trying to keep his heart from racing. *But I did, as a matter of fact.* He barely remembered what he had done in his blind rage, but he had seen the aftermath. He had seen the broken men on the pavement. He had done that. The demon in him had. There had been witnesses.

It both scared and thrilled him that he was even capable of such quick devastation. The samurai's skills had come back to him even though he hadn't been wearing the mask. Despite that, he had still lost control. Was the mask going to take him over anyway?

Just leave out what they won't understand.

"I know judo," he said. He knew it was ridiculous. He was terrible at judo, but it was something he said from time to time to make himself not feel like a weakling, and occasionally to try to impress women—which had never actually worked. But he *had* studied judo. It was something he could talk about to a moderate degree and not sound like a fool.

Kuramoto laughed. Fujimaki looked extremely skeptical. "Judo, huh?" Kuramoto said, still chuckling. "You must be damn good. I don't want to mess with you."

Akio felt small, like he always did when people talked to him that way. That sarcastic tone that says so loudly, *you are a loser; you are far too scrawny and stupid to ever be that good at anything.*

His whole life, he had dealt with that, so much so that he generally believed it. But he *had* kicked ass. He really had. And yeah, the detective probably shouldn't mess with him. But he hadn't exactly been in charge when it happened. The demon had taken over, and the memories of samurai combat had surged through his muscles. He had become the demon. When he heard Masami cry out, everything else had fallen away. His rage at potentially losing his one friend—however one-sided that friendship was—was too much. The memories had come back to him out of necessity. But if Kuramoto jumped him right now, he probably wouldn't even be able to defend himself. And

Kuramoto was clearly out of shape. If Fujimaki attacked him, he would be doomed for sure.

But the detectives were not going to attack him. They were just going to laugh at him. And that was worse.

"Okay, so you took out all these armed yakuza with your bare hands," Kuramoto stated. "Let's say that's true. You are so deadly with your fists and feet that you actually killed one of them."

Killed one of them?

Akio opened his mouth and closed it again. He remembered hearing a crack when he kicked one of them in the head. He remembered the man laying motionless as they ran off. But he had hoped beyond hope that he was only unconscious.

"I didn't mean to," Akio said. "I didn't know . . . I was just . . . protecting my friends." He felt meek and disoriented.

I . . . killed someone.

"You know what?" Kuramoto said. "Who cares? Th at guy you killed? He was a scumbag. Sold dope to little kids, targeted girls specifically. We had already brought him in once on molestation charges. But hey . . . murder is murder. You don't get to just walk away from that no matter the specifics."

He smiled grotesquely at Akio while he let that last part land. Then he continued. "Let's talk about your boy pal, Yoshio Hirakawa. What was he doing at the time?"

The truth.

"He pulled a gun on the yakuza. They had kind of a standoff. But other than that, I'm not really sure. My back was to him mostly. As far as I know, he just stood there, keeping them at bay."

"You know that possession of a handgun is illegal, right? No permit exists. Only for shotguns and pellet guns. Anything else and you're in major doo-doo."

"I know."

"Okay, good. Very good. What about your lady-friend, Masami Sato?"

"When the men attacked us, she hid," he said. "She ran and hid behind some cars." It was all he could think of. It was "disappearing" in a way. "I mean, she's just a woman," he said.

Damn, she would hate me if she heard me say that.

Although he didn't actually believe it, he thought he might get on their good side with such a comment. A good 'ol boys jab at the womenfolk. Kuramoto laughed. Fujimaki gave a little frown.

"Women are weak," Kuramoto said, as if acknowledging the truth of Akio's statement. "Which way did she run? Behind what car exactly? Do you recall?"

"Uh, yeah, of course." Akio was panicking. He had no idea where she had actually gone. He tried to picture the cars in the lot. "Away from the street," he said. "Behind a green compact . . . Toyota, I think."

"You think?"

"Well, I was surrounded by men with guns at the time," Akio said. "I wasn't taking notes."

"Fair enough."

"They shot at her as she ran, but they let her get away. I guess they weren't after her."

"Hmm . . ." Kuramoto smiled as he gave a grand display of thinking over what Akio had just said. "That brings me to another important, unanswered question. What the hell did these gangsters want from you anyway? Why would they surround you in a parking lot in broad daylight and try to do whatever it is they wanted to do to you? The thugs we have in custody say that they were told to bring you in to their boss. Funnily enough, they said to bring in all three of you. So that means they *did* want Sato as well. So there's a little hole in your theory, a little bigger than the one in her leg. Care to clarify this confusion for me?"

"I'm not sure," Akio floundered. Masami had told him what to say, but the pressure of being grilled was getting to him, as were the harsh lights. He felt dehydrated. "Can I have some water?" He asked.

"Yeah, yeah," Kuramoto said, but it was Fujimaki who got up and returned with a paper cup full.

"They . . ." Akio continued after a long sip. "They might have wanted to talk to us about the warehouse."

That's what Masami had said. *Tell them we were asking questions.*

"The warehouse, huh? What warehouse is that?"

"We were sent here from the *Dainichi Daily* to get some information about the rapid expansion of the Tezuka-gumi, and we found out they had this warehouse, so we went there to talk to them. Our interview didn't go all that well, so maybe they wanted to give us some more information. Or maybe they wanted to kill us for asking about it. I'm really not sure."

"Funny," Kuramoto said. "Don't you think that's funny?" he asked Detective Fujimaki, who frowned again. "Why wouldn't you come to us first, like last time you two pests came to our town to cause trouble? Trying to up your bargaining power first?"

"Uh . . . huh," Akio stammered. "Yeah, I guess." It didn't sound like a bad idea. And he wasn't about to tell them that they were instructed not to trust the police.

"Typical," Kuramoto scoffed. "We're supposed to work together, boss. Remember? Kinda puts a damper on our relationship."

"Yeah, yeah, I suppose so." Akio said. He was being agreeable. That was good, wasn't it?

"So tell me more about this warehouse."

Leave out what they won't understand.

"We don't know," Akio said, feeling like he was lying to his mother about sneaking into the sex toy shops in Akihabara when he was younger. "We didn't go inside. But they sure didn't like us asking about it."

Akio told them the location of the warehouse and said that they should investigate it themselves. He didn't see the harm. Masami, Yoshio, and he had already looked through it and Miyahara wasn't there. Let the cops have their turn. Maybe it would help if the police were also disrupting the yakuza's business.

The only problem now was how they would get out of going to prison.

I murdered someone. I took a life.

The questioning went on for another half an hour, Kuramoto doing the asking and Fujimaki looking sympathetic and doubtful at the same time. They were looking for details, looking to find a motive for the yakuza's attempt to kidnap the three. Akio said everything he could without giving away what they were really doing there. Every second, he felt like he wanted to give in and tell them everything. He hadn't wanted to go on this stupid rescue mission to begin with. What they did in the parking lot had been purely in self-defense. The murder had been self-defense. He emphasized that repeatedly, until he felt like a child crying, *They started it!*

Murder.

A kick to the jaw had broken the man's neck. Akio couldn't get his head around that. He never wanted the samurai's memories to begin with, and now he had the samurai's uncontrollable rage to blame for a death. A scumbag's death, sure, but still a life snuffed out by his hands . . . or rather, foot.

But he also recognized that he had to be grateful. He had protected Masami and Yoshio with that rage. He had gotten them out of that mess . . . and probably into this one. But who knows where they would be if the yakuza had taken them? He wanted to believe that, when it came down to it, the cops were probably treating them a sight better than the yakuza would have.

Life is strange. How is it you can be regretful and grateful for the same thing?

Masami slipped out of the interrogation room unseen by Akio or the detectives. She snuck between them in the hallway when Fujimaki strode ahead of Kuramoto leaving some space. She could have easily just pushed through them, but that would have given them chills. She didn't want them to detect her presence even in the slightest. She also could have just cut through the walls, but who knew what was on the other side of the police station walls? She didn't want any surprises.

Brushing past Fujimaki, her heart raced a little faster than it already did. He smelled good, a light, fresh linen smell. She moved faster.

She looked back, hoping they weren't going straight for her or Yoshio. Fujimaki turned off toward the break room.

Good, he's grabbing a coffee or something.

She hurried downstairs and slipped through the white barred doors into Yoshio's holding cell. She brushed his hand to let him know she was there. His hand flinched, but he smiled. She stayed unseen and whispered in his ear. Talking while a ghost had been a new discovery. She couldn't see her tongue and mouth to focus on its blue boundaries, but she could feel the tingle of heightened awareness. At the end, she whispered, "Got it?"

"Got it," he said a little too loudly. The teenager he shared the cell with, spiked hair, ripped shirt, and a purpling bruise on his face, just lay looking at the ceiling, not caring what Yoshio was on about.

Masami heard footsteps, ducked out of the cell, and back into hers nearby. She lifted the blankets on the cot and slipped under them. The strung-out waif in her cell didn't notice. Masami held her mother's amulet and tears came to her eyes.

A door opened nearby. "Yoshio Hirakawa," Fujimaki's clear voice said. "Come with me, please." The door shut and footsteps faded. Masami breathed deep and tried to relax.

She had called Tanaka, her boss at the *Daily*, after being taken in last night. He had been furious.

"How the hell did you get yourself detained?" he had yelled. "I thought you were far more careful than that! That's why I send you on these tough stories. That's why I agreed to let you go in the first place!"

She had apologized profusely, and tried to relate a story that would make sense to him. "Something is going on in that warehouse, and they didn't like us asking questions. So they sent a team of thugs to shut us up. We were barely able to get out of there with our lives."

"And Akio killed one of them? Really?"

"A freak accident, sir. The guy must have had a weak heart. You know Akio couldn't fight his way out of a shopping bag."

"My connections aren't very strong in Kofu, Miss Sato. I'm not sure I can help you out of this one. I will try, but I can't promise anything. If you two get indicted, you're on your own."

"I can't apologize enough, sir. I will make it up to you somehow."

There was silence on the other end.

"There's one other thing, sir."

"What?"

"We need the boy out too. Yoshio Hirakawa. He has vital information about the story and we need him close. Say he's an intern at the *Daily*."

More silence.

"It's a big story, sir, a really big story."

"Like I said . . ." Tanaka started. Masami had almost felt the steam coming through the phone. "I'll do what I can. But don't hold your breath." He hung up.

The public prosecutor was an emotionless woman in cat eye glasses, with skin stretched across her face like canvas on a frame. Her eyes were painted in a light teal and her eyebrows diligently plucked. Her hair was back and tight as her skin. She was someone who ate breakfast at precisely 5 a.m. each morning: a level ice cream scoop of rice, 250 ml of miso soup, a square of salted horse mackerel (exactly five centimeters), and one poached egg (whites only) with a single tap of soy sauce. She had six blouses of exactly the same shade of cream and one scarf (also teal) that she kept tied even after removing it, to save any inconsistencies in the knot, and slipped over her head each day securing it with a pin. She wore that now. Her Sunday outfit was a yellow one-piece that she wore alone while she watched K-dramas and let herself veer from her daily diet by eating a single *anpan* roll divided into eight equal bite-sized portions.

Masami's eyes dissected the woman, taking in every detail, imagining the life this woman led. And she inwardly cringed. This was a woman who would not budge from regulations and convention. They would not be getting off easy unless the rules expressly stated it. Any call from Tanaka would be in vain.

After another night in the uncomfortable cell, Masami met with Miss Etsuko Baba alone. The boys would confront her the same, just as they had been interrogated. She didn't know why she had been first with both encounters—perhaps being the eldest—but she was grateful since it gave her an opportunity to pass information. Her second meeting with the detectives yesterday, after being stitched up by Dr. Ito, had been brief, as her account of the incident had not varied an iota from Akio's and Yoshio's.

Miss Baba invited Miss Sato, as she was monotonously and repeatedly addressed, to give her account of the story. Masami did, and it was nearly verbatim the one she had given the detectives. She had been there, and hid behind some cars until the incident was over.

There was a long moment while Miss Baba looked over the papers in front of her. She glanced at the computer screen once, at Masami flatly three times, and then back to her papers. Miss Baba then informed Miss Sato that she had not—that they had evidence of— been videotaped at the scene of the crime, and in spite of some eye-witness testimonies of a person that looked quite like her, in spite of a wound that looked suspiciously to be made from a bullet that could have been fired at the scene of the crime, and in spite of the fact that Miss Sato herself claimed to be there, there would be no trial for her. The evidence wasn't strong enough. She was free to go.

Masami got up from the desk a little bewildered. She was relieved, yet concerned for Akio and Yoshio—Akio mostly—and a little self-satisfied that what she had expected had come to pass. She was directed to a window where she could retrieve her personal effects. As she turned to go there, she saw Akio being led up the hallway toward the prosecutor's desk and sighed. There would be no time to prep him for this interview. Not that she had much for him anyway. His situation was far different from her own. She could only hope now.

But she could also listen in.

Retrieving her things took far longer than it should have. The older man tasked with the job—too much ear hair and a collection of toenail clippings in a jar at home, for sure—seemed to get an unsettling pleasure out of making her suffer that much longer, even though she had been let go with no charges pressed.

When she finally joined Miss Baba and Akio back at the desk—unseen by anyone, of course—they had covered a fair amount of ground. Miss Baba was already in the assessment phase. She looked at her papers, looked at her computer screen, looked at Akio exactly three times, and then delivered her verdict.

Masami's breath was more rapid than she would have liked, and she feared they would hear her, that the fear itself would intensify her emotional state enough to cause the sound to carry. She worried that she might unintentionally make herself visible. She needed Akio. She hated to admit it, but he was the only one who really understood what had happened to her. Yoshio understood on a purely intellectual level, but Akio had been there. He had shared in the trauma. She didn't feel she could continue on this rescue mission without him. And besides, Miyahara had requested them both. Something told her that it wouldn't work without him.

On top of all of that, Akio didn't deserve this. He was innocent, in spite of what had happened. He wouldn't survive prison.

"Mr. Tsukino," Miss Baba began. Her tone was heavy and unforgiving. "This is an incident of murder. Someone's life has been taken."

Akio slumped in his chair. He looked ready to cry.

"We have video footage submitted from smart phones that show a blow from your foot to the deceased's head. After which he does not move again. Preliminary autopsy reports suggest that the deceased was killed due to severe trauma to his head and neck."

Masami's heart sank. Akio's eyes were closed. He looked like he was trying to wish it away, imagining he was somewhere else and none of it was actually happening.

After a long pause in which Miss Baba appeared to drink in Akio's pain like a fine champagne, she said, "However . . . it is also clear from the captured footage that, at the time, you were surrounded by known criminals with guns, and it has been agreed by the detectives and myself that you acted in self-defense. The chances of you being convicted in a court of law are woefully slim. Therefore, you are free to go."

Masami released a breath she hadn't realized she was holding, and Akio's eyes flapped open like blinds thrown on a bright sunny morning. He looked at Miss Baba intently, making sure she wasn't pulling his leg. Her expression was flat.

An officer directed Akio to the same window from which Masami's possessions had been released. He hadn't even stood up yet. Now he did, and moved to follow the officer in a dazed state of teary gratitude.

Masami grinned in spite of herself. No one could see her, after all. And if Akio was being released, there was little chance they would be holding Yoshio. For one, the system was lenient on minors, and the only thing they could pin on him would be the gun. Japan did not treat guns lightly. But Masami already knew that they couldn't connect him to it. She had taken the liberty of listening in on Kuramoto and Fujimaki that morning. The lab had found the yakuza's prints on four guns, and nothing on a fifth one. It had been wiped. The Japanese way of ensuring prosecution before indictment was perhaps a downfall of the system of law, but today, it had certainly worked in their favor.

Akio shifted in the passenger seat, unable to get fully comfortable. It was overcast and the road was still dark with the afternoon rain. It was not raining now, only sullen and gloomy, the clouds swallowing the sun before its time.

They had returned to the parking lot to retrieve Masami's car, apprehensive about what might have been planted inside, waiting for them. Akio had held Masami and Yoshio back.

"Let me go first. I'll sense it."

But there was nothing.

He shrugged and waved them closer.

Masami tried the door and it was unlocked. Nothing had been disturbed inside that they could see. Nothing stolen. Whatever Akio had sensed before was gone.

Now on the motorway Akio looked behind them at the car he had been sure was following them, watched it exit to a rest stop. They drove on, and he slumped against the window.

They had scattered conversation. What would they do next? Was Yoshio right about the cryptic message on the boxes? If Miyahara was able to write messages wasn't he likely okay? Did he really need them?

The answer to the last was yes, absolutely he needed them, according to the sensei's loyal lap dog. But Akio wanted to go home. There had been a hydrangea festival in Bunkyo on his scheduled shoots the day before, while he was holed up in the police cell. What he wouldn't give to be back on a mindless assignment shooting photos of harmless flowers. If gaining respect as a photographer meant having yakuza point guns at you, he was fine without it. A nobody who could sleep at night sounded very nice right now.

He wondered who had been given the job. Probably Wada, the newest hire. The same one that would probably take his job completely now that he had nearly been indicted for murder.

Fine. He could start up a family portrait business. Set up shop in a mall somewhere.

The conversation turned to their interrogation, and Akio was surprised to hear Yoshio had told exactly the same lies to the police. He had even said the same direction Masami had run, and the exact color and make of the car. Akio hadn't even been sure there had been a green compact Toyota. He thought he might have made it up to appease the detectives. But there must have been one. How Yoshio had picked that same car was a mystery.

We're all becoming connected, I guess, a kind of symbiotic team. He gave a slight grin at the thought. He had always wanted to be a part of something bigger, to be included.

"Yoshio left out the part about me being only a woman," Masami said, her eyes never leaving the road.

Akio gulped. *She heard me? Dammit! Of course! She's the invisible woman now. That's how Yoshio knew about the car! Great. Reasons for her to hate me more.*

"It was brilliant of her to listen in," Yoshio said. "That way we had total corroboration."

Akio groaned. *Symbiotic, my eye.*

"I'm sorry, Masami," Akio sputtered. "I was just playing along with what Kuramoto believed, you know. I don't really think—"

"Can it, Akio. It's fine. It all worked out. It was good to play up to his neanderthal beliefs. I'm not mad." She said all this with the most unreadable expression. She could have been completely truthful or just lying to shut him up. It was impossible to tell.

I'll go with the truth, Akio thought. He had to believe she knew he wasn't like Kuramoto.

"The detectives were really drilling you about that gun, weren't they, Yoshio?" Masami asked.

"Yeah, they wouldn't let it go," Yoshio replied, and Akio was glad he hadn't been the only one Masami had listened in on.

"So you wiped it?" she asked.

"Yep, while Akio was being Bruce Lee," Yoshio said with a grin. I ditched it in the van. At that point, I knew it was inevitable we would get caught. I had to get rid of it."

"Smart," Masami said, though Akio thought he saw something else behind her eyes, some hint of disappointment.

Yoshio just nodded. The kid knew he was smart. And he didn't even have the gall to be arrogant about it. If anything, he just seemed confused that other people weren't as smart as he was.

"That was some amazing fighting," Yoshio said, turning to Akio.

"Uh . . . thanks." Akio didn't know what to say.

I killed someone.

"Looks like the memories are coming back," Yoshio continued.

"Unfortunately," Akio said. His stomach turned at the memory of the neck snapping. He was no better than the violent samurai that had become a demon for his crimes. What punishment awaited him now after death? What torturous Hell would he have to experience? He had already had a glimpse of one through memories that weren't his. Now he was on course to suffer his own. It almost made it worse that he had been released without charge. Maybe if he paid for it now, while he was alive, he wouldn't have to suffer as much in Hell.

"If it wasn't for you, we'd all be in a pretty bad place right now," Yoshio said. "Maybe even dead. You saved our lives."

Akio was grateful Yoshio recognized the good in what he'd done. "I don't know," he finally said. "I just got angry. I couldn't just give in and be captured or whatever."

"The mark of a true hero," Yoshio said. Masami had an ever-so-slight grin on her face. A rare sighting, indeed. That grin said she agreed. Akio blushed.

"I had to do something," Akio said. "But then . . . it just took over. It wasn't even me." His blush faded. His pride faded. He sat there quietly for a long time, staring out the window at the scenery floating past.

17

A Robotics Expert

asami got off the metro in a foul mood. She never took her car in the city; the metro was easier and more efficient. After spending two nights in jail in Kofu, and lying to the police about what had happened, she felt like something had been taken from her, some part of her spirit, her wholeness. And the worst part was that she felt complicit.

It hadn't been a big lie, more of an omission of facts, but there wasn't much difference in the end. She wasn't someone who believed that you should never lie. Sometimes lying was absolutely the best thing to do. It could save lives, prevent heartache and loss of employment. But she still didn't like it. She didn't like that sometimes ignorance was the answer.

She especially didn't like lying to Detective Fujimaki. She wanted to trust him, and be trusted in return, but there were too many unknowns for her to let down her guard.

She had gone all the way to Kofu only to find out that Miyahara wasn't there. But that's the way stories develop. You follow the lead where it takes you, even if it takes you back home.

It was Monday morning, and the sun was in and out of the clouds, one minute in her eyes, the next a grateful respite and a cool breeze. At Masami's request, her boss had allowed her and Akio to go straight out on assignment. Tanaka had groused about it as usual, but relented.

She reached Akio's apartment and buzzed the intercom. Akio lived in Senzoku district, not far from Ueno. It was a quick metro hop to the building that was their destination, so they had decided to meet at his place. He buzzed her up.

"Look at this," Akio said as she entered his apartment. He indicated the television where Yoshio sat watching. On the screen was a talk show host interviewing a man in a suit and a woman in a traditional maid uniform. The woman was responding humbly to the man's commands in a dulcet, overly honorific tone of voice, and pouring tea. It made Masami cringe to see such a submissive woman, but it was all part of the maid act that men loved so much.

"Who cares?" Masami asked. "Another woman degrading herself by playing up to male fantasies of superiority."

"No," Akio said. "She's not."

"Uh, clearly, she is, Akio." Masami had already turned away, not caring to see anymore.

"No, I mean, she's not a woman. Look."

Masami looked back and saw that he was right. Although the face was life-like, the mouth and eyes expressive, it was synthetic. She could now see the obvious metal frame holding the face and the hair tied back under a puffed white hat to reveal a lack of ears. She saw the unnatural robotic movements as it swiveled at the waist.

"Now, I normally wouldn't do such a thing. On TV anyway," the suited man laughed as he reached for the blouse covering the maid robot's torso.

"That's Assemblyman Ogura," Akio said, "for right here in Taito ward."

"Taito ward includes Ueno," Masami said.

"I know," Akio said, eyes glued to the TV.

The assemblyman undid the blouse with the pull of a string, and it dropped to the maid robot's waist, revealing a sexless metal chest, in the center of which was a clear window. Behind the window was what looked like a subtly glowing green gem.

Yoshio perked up in his seat. "That looks like the gem the yakuza had at the grocer's in Kofu."

Masami stared at the gem on the TV. It seemed to pulse inside the robot's chest.

"Ogura looks like he's in a trance, doesn't he?" Akio asked.

"Not anymore than most politicians," Masami answered.

"Yeah, true. But look at the interviewer."

The talk show host had leaned in closer to the robot. "And what does this beautiful gem do?" he asked, mesmerized.

"I'm told it is a proprietary power source, a kind of brain food for the robot," Ogura answered, "and the designers chose to show it off for its beauty."

"Who did you say the designers were?" the host asked.

"I didn't." Ogura smiled. "I'm not at liberty to say. But rest assured they will reveal themselves soon."

"Wow. Such secrets!" The host's eyes glowed, and his smile grew. He stopped asking questions for a long moment and stared at the gem, leaving Ogura to face the camera, smiling silently. Th en the host turned back to the camera with a big grin of his own.

"That's great, isn't it!" he boomed. "Let's hope we all get one of these in our homes soon!"

It went to commercial and Akio turned it off.

"Something weird is happening," Masami said. "What is with those gems?"

"I think it was a gem that I sensed inside your car," Akio said. "I don't know how to explain it, but I think that's what's giving me these headaches."

"Well, it's obvious these robots are coming from the yakuza and are being made at Nakama," Yoshio said. "They're the ones who have the gems. I just don't understand what they are exactly."

"Brain food for robots," Akio said. "Apparently."

"But why would that give you headaches and no one else?"

"I have an allergy to robot brain food apparently," Akio said. "But seriously, it's the same kind of headache I got when we were under the castle in Kofu, when I knew the demon was coming. I can't help but thinking these gems are demonic."

"Sensei is a demon hunter," Yoshio said. "That would make sense. It was one of these gems that made him chase after the yakuza in the first place. When we first saw it in the back of the grocery store, the gangsters told the grocer to look into it and learn where his loyalties were, like it would hypnotize him or something."

"There's a lot we don't know yet," Masami cut in. "But if the the yakuza are handing out robots to politicians, ones that might potentially hypnotize them, or at the very least spy on them, that is a problem that can only get worse."

"Yeah," Akio said. "What if they send one to the prime minister?"

"It's a disturbing thought," Masami said. "But it gives me a new idea. Yoshio, what do you know about robotics?"

"A lot," Yoshio said. "I have a perfect grade in my robotics class. Well . . . all my classes actually, but robotics is one of my favorites. Last week, I made a toaster that would walk around the table and place the toast onto each person's plate."

"Oh, that'll help." Akio said.

"It will," Masami said. "Not the toaster, but his knowledge. We're scrapping the innocent reporter-looking-for-a-story routine. It's tired and has become ineffective. And they're probably on alert for that since we've used it already. Plus, the gangsters in Kofu knew who we were and where we worked. Word has probably gotten to Tokyo. If someone here recognizes us, we're screwed anyway, but we have to try something.

"So Yoshio, you'll be our robotics genius who can get into the building. You're being sent from Kofu to join the programming team. Do you know who you'd be meeting with?" She knew Yoshio had been researching and hoped he'd found out more about the internal workings of the Nakama building.

"Uh," Yoshio thought for a second, scanning his mental hard drive. "I've been searching the web and have read through a lot of their magazines. Kumamori is the boss, but I expect he's still in Kofu. Uh, oh yeah, *Truth Serum* magazine said a guy named Koide was doing a lot to help their expansion in Tokyo. So did the Tezuka-gumi manga. It must be Koide."

"Koide it is," Masami said. "That's who you're meeting. Let's hope he's there."

"Um," Akio said. "Don't you think Yoshio is a little young?"

Masami looked at Yoshio, looked him over like a lab specimen. He did look young. "Boy genius," she said, trying to convince herself. "What if he goes in as a student researching a paper?"

"That might work," Yoshio said. "But as much as I want to find Sensei, it's you two that really need to get inside. What am I going to do against the yakuza?"

"True," Masami said, and remembered what Yoshio *had* done against the yakuza last time. She couldn't have him pulling a gun again and getting himself killed. "Akio, you can be our robotics expert. Yoshio, can you give him some basics that would get him by security?"

"No, no, no." Akio held his hands up like a criminal at gunpoint. "You know I'll just screw it up somehow. I won't be able to remember any robotics nonsense under pressure."

Masami frowned, assessing. "Also true," she finally said. "That leaves me, even though they'll likely be more suspicious of a woman. But I might not remember it well enough either, especially if they do ask anything technical. Yoshio, we need to have some way to communicate, a way you can stay outside and feed me info."

"Easy," the teenager said. "You got a Bluetooth, right? Just leave it in your ear and leave your phone on. I'll call you and we'll leave the line open. In fact we can all be on the same call."

"Perfect," Masami said. "There shouldn't be anything too complex to fool whatever goons are manning the door. You can feed me what to say."

"Uh . . . and what am I supposed to be doing there?" Akio asked.

"You're my . . . friend," Masami answered. "My photographer and social media guru who's documenting my career. Don't forget your camera."

"Were you going to say boyfriend?" Akio asked, a hopeful gleam in his eye.

"No."

They exited the train in Ueno and moved through the turnstiles. Masami had swapped her contacts for glasses in Akio's bathroom. It was a meager disguise but she figured it was better than nothing. She hadn't had them on in Kofu.

"Ooh, a Beard Papa," Akio said, somewhat distantly.

"Focus, Akio. No time for snacks," said Masami.

"I know."

Part of her wanted to tell him to go get one, and then leave him behind. It would be nice to not have to worry about him bungling things, or Yoshio for that matter. Sure the kid was super smart, but he wasn't the most socially aware. He was much better off on the outside feeding her smart things to say.

But Akio was needed, according to Miyahara, and maybe the sensei was right. If things went badly, the demon samurai might emerge and save them again—hopefully without getting them arrested this time.

Now here they were, back in Tokyo, about to walk into what could be a busy yakuza romper room. A boy genius, a demon samurai-possessed manchild. And herself, who could turn invisible. At will. It still boggled her mind.

She felt herself changing each time, something more than her chemical makeup, and she worried that she might get stuck that way again. It was easy enough to let go and vanish—not that letting go had ever been easy for her. But coming back required effort. It was emotionally draining. And Masami didn't have a lot of emotion to drain. At least that's what she told herself. She was closed off, and she preferred it that way. Tapping into emotions was not something she enjoyed. Not even a little bit.

They exited the station and walked a block away to where the building stood on the corner, set back from the sidewalk, eleven stories dully reflecting the semi-cloudy day. In front of it was a kind of piazza with a walkway of triangular paths laid out before a set of wide stairs that descended gradually, flanked by angular sculptures. A glass canopy reached out from the building, covering the bottom steps and a small, paved entryway.

Next to the building's glass main doors was a Starbucks with its own entrance at the very corner. From across the street, she saw Akio eyeing it. "Couldn't get a cream puff, so now you want a coffee? Maybe a blueberry muffin?" Masami asked.

"Hey, I didn't go to Beard Papa, though it would have been nice to have a little food in my belly before I die. What better last meal than a chocolate cream puff?"

Masami groaned. "You're not going to die." She hoped.

She turned to Yoshio. "This is where you split off. You are welcome to go wherever you like, just hang close in case we need you. If you go to Starbucks be sure to grab Akio a muffin."

Akio rolled his eyes.

"Akio, do you have your Bluetooth in?" she asked, as she physically turned him to check.

"Yes," he grunted.

She pulled a tuft of his hair forward to cover it up.

"Good. Yoshio, I'm calling you now," she said, tapping her phone screen. Yoshio picked up. "Good. Now I'll conference you in, Akio. Everyone keep the line open, so Yoshio can hear what's going on and feed me answers if need be."

"I got it," Akio answered. "We went over all of this already."

"Doesn't hurt to re-emphasize."

"I don't know why you don't just turn invisible and sneak in there yourself." Akio grumbled.

"Because I don't want you to miss out on the fun," she answered. "And we need to establish some kind of rapport. We'll be able to get far more information if we do that, as opposed to just sneaking around. We went over all of this already," she repeated his words.

"Yeah, yeah. Let's do it then. I'm just the photographer boyfriend."

"Friend," Masami insisted, knowing he was trying to rile her. "Let's go."

They crossed the street, Yoshio separating and rounding the corner. Masami and Akio went through the sliding glass doors into the foyer of the building. There was a security guard behind a large counter with a menu of the building's occupants lit up on the front of it. White characters on a black background. At the very top, next to the familiar circular logo of an "N" surrounded by a DNA chain, was printed "Nakama Plaza."

The guard nodded to them as they approached, but didn't speak. They scanned down the list of businesses: Starbucks, Th e Green Cricket Cafe, Obara Printing Services, True First Entertainment, Ishibashi VOIP Services, Kono Staffing. At the bottom of the list, the business was legible, but not lit. On the ninth through eleventh floors, it read "Nakama Robotics." Next to the name on the tenth floor was the added word "Reception."

The guard didn't ask them to sign in, so they proceeded to the elevator. Two men and a woman got on with them, who punched the numbers for floors three and seven. Masami looked at the keypad. There was a key card swiper next to the button for the eleventh floor.

Damn.

She hit it anyway. It wouldn't light.

Damn.

She hit 'ten' instead. It lit.

"One floor down," she said to Akio, but loud enough that Yoshio would hear.

She glanced over at the three people in the elevator with them. The two men were talking about a baseball game and the woman was staring at the door, as if willing it to open. A little paranoid voice in Masami's head worried one of them might get off the elevator and warn the yakuza of what floor they were trying to reach. None of them were paying any attention to Masami and Akio, but even your average Japanese person was a master of being discreet, so she couldn't be certain. She let it go and regained her focus. Th ese people weren't yakuza spies.

The elevator hit floors three and seven, dumping off the woman and the men in that order. Masami and Akio shared a look. It reminded her of when they had entered the broken door that led under Kofu Castle, knowing it was likely the demon's lair. Akio had not wanted to go in there at all. He had a similar look right now, that tense ball of nerves that could snap at any second. But there was something new underneath it. A cage for those nerves perhaps, a sense that even if they did snap, they would be contained.

They were potentially going into the belly of the beast. But it might be an abandoned floor, an empty business. Nothing was certain. If it was the yakuza operation they expected, it was going to be tricky. They couldn't make any mistakes.

If their *robotics expert* ruse got them in the door, they would have to slip away from whatever goon led them to meet the boss. Then, if they could locate Miyahara, get him out if possible. At the very least they would do some reconnaissance, and get the hell out of there. At some point they would be discovered. Then, if they were lucky, they'd be kicked out. If they weren't so lucky, it could be worse. Much worse.

If it all went to hell . . . well, she could turn ghost and get out of there. Hopefully, Akio's newfound temper would kick in and he could fight his way out. But there was no guarantee, and she really hoped for neither of those scenarios. She only hoped it wouldn't go as badly as it had in the Kofu parking lot.

Akio was massaging the back of his neck.

"Perk up," Masami said. "We're almost there."

"Trying, Akio said. "My head hurts a bit. Can't tell if it's a warning sign or just a real headache."

"Probably just stress," she said. *But it might mean we're on the right track.* "Try to let go of it. We need all our senses."

The elevator dinged at the tenth floor.

When the doors opened, two suited men sans ties were standing on the opposite side. They seemed surprised, despite their flat expressions. They weren't waiting to get on the elevator, but were clearly posted to prevent someone getting off.

"You've got the wrong floor," one of them said, the taller one with a scar across his jaw.

"Yeah, you must be looking for Kono Staffing. Sixth floor, I think," said the other one with a round face, balding in the front.

"Hi, gentlemen," said Masami in her best imitation of someone friendly, outgoing and just a bit ditsy—exactly what these types of men preferred. "Nope, I'm pretty sure we have the right floor. Th is is Nakama Robotics, correct?" She held one finger on the "Open Door" button.

"Nakama went out of business, lady," the tall one said. "We don't want what you're selling."

"Not selling, not selling," she said with one hand up in an "I'm innocent" gesture, the other still on the button. "My name is Honoka Yamazaki, and I am actually your new robotics engineer. Here to see Mr. Koide." She began to move cautiously off the elevator. "He told me things were a bit hush hush, but don't worry, I'm in on the secret." She winked.

"Oh yeah," Round Face said. "Koide told you that, huh?"

"Well, Mr. Kumamori did, yes," she said, fully in the foyer now. "Don't worry, I'll sign a non-disclosure. Your secret is safe with me." Akio slunk off the elevator behind her.

"Huh," Jaw Scar said. "And who's this then? He a robotics engineer, too?"

"Oh, no," she giggled lightly. "This is Takahiro Morita. He's my valet." She saw Akio visibly flinch and tuck his camera back into his bag. With the yakuza's penchant for notoriety, she had thought having a photographer and social media guru accompany her was a good idea. But seeing the unyielding looks of the gangster doormen made her instantly reassess. She kicked herself for not having better foresight. Thankfully Akio played along, as he suddenly became rigid and affected an air of servitude.

"You have all my paperwork in order, yes, Mr. Morita?"

"Of course, ma'am," Akio replied stiffly, and patted his camera bag.

"You have a valet?" Round Face asked and shared a look with Jaw Scar. They both appeared equally confused and impressed.

"Follows me everywhere," Masami said. "This foyer looks nice, by the way. It could use a little more welcoming charm, I suppose, but I love the robots in the *ukiyo-e* style. Take note of that Mr. Morita. I'd like something similar for my office," she said, indicating a painting, while attempting to move past Jaw Scar. He stepped in front her.

"There's no Nakama Robotics, lady" he said. "You need to leave."

She noticed the unused reception counter behind the thug. Written in black marker on the front of it was a large, faded number nine with a line under it. It looked like someone had tried unsuccessfully to clean it off, and recently.

"Well, if there's no Nakama, what is it you two are doing here?" She said. "I'm sorry if Mr. Koide didn't make you privy to the fact that I was arriving, but there are secrets that are clearly above your pay grade. Could you please check with him? He is expecting me."

The two thugs looked at each other questioningly. Th ey had evidently been left out of the loop before.

"A woman robotics engineer with a personal valet?" Round Face said to Jaw Scar, who scoffed. A common habit of small-minded men who got easily confused by a woman. They would talk to each other as if she wasn't there, looking for some validation of their ignorance.

"Look, Gentlemen," Masami interrupted before they could get further. "What do you know about robotics?" She emphasized the last word, hoping Yoshio would get the clue.

He did, and started feeding Masami information through the Bluetooth almost too fast for her to process.

"Do you know, for example, what shape memory actuators are? Or perhaps what superplasticity is? Do you know what a bio-mimetic robotic hand is and how its construction and articulation is similar and yet differs from crawlers like the ACM-R5 snake robot?

Both men were clearly getting angry. A smart man they could possibly look up to or just beat up if they felt belittled, but a smart woman blew their fuses. She could see them ready to boil over, but she stood her ground.

"Look, little Miss Smarts . . ." Round Face started, but then stopped suddenly. A queer look came over his face, somewhere between revelation and daydreaming, and his demeanor changed dramatically. He smiled at her. "Okay," he said. "You're welcome to come in and look around. Koide will be here momentarily." No longer was he the threatening, in-your-face goon. Instead he had become a pleasant restaurant host about to shout, "*Irasshaimase!*" to welcome them.

This probably wasn't a good thing.

"Yes," said Jaw Scar, his tone also much friendlier. "We'd like you to see our operations here, after all. Where your . . . new job will be."

"Well, that's great!" Masami said, but did not move. They'd clearly been discovered, though she didn't know how. The men weren't wearing any earpieces of their own that she could tell. "But what was all that secrecy about?" She had to buy time.

"Call it a little test of your perseverance," Jaw Scar answered, as if he were now a robotic company spokesman. "Nakama is still in business, of course, as you know. The new owners have grand plans. You see, we've been hiding our operations from our competitors so we can work in relative quietude. So we can focus on what matters: making the best products for our customers, as opposed to getting into some costly race with our competitors to make the same things but faster and better. We only have our customers in mind, you see. We want you to understand how important that secrecy is, and we wanted to make sure you have the drive and determination that we're looking for."

"I see," said Masami. *This is about to go very badly.*

"We will ask that you uphold the non-disclosure agreement that you will be asked to sign. As we all have done. Company loyalty is of utmost priority here."

"Of course," Masami answered with a nervous smile, trying to keep up the facade.

The two suited men stepped aside, gesturing for Masami and Akio to enter a closed door. There were noises from behind it: people talking, but also the sounds of machinery.

She glanced at the reception counter again, at the number nine with the line under it. It itched at her brain. It was incongruous. It meant something.

Akio looked at her and half raised an eyebrow, his eyes wide with fear. They stepped past the men toward the door.

This was what they wanted. They wanted in, but it felt like walking into a pit of piranha. They had been made, it was obvious. Yet Masami didn't want to give up this chance to get a little closer. Even if it was putting their lives in danger. She could get out of any sticky situation, but Akio . . . There was no guarantee that his samurai rage would kick in, and even if it did, would it be enough to get him out? There were likely a lot more than four yakuza inside.

And if he killed another one, it might wreck him.

She stopped just past the two men, Akio right next to her. She saw he had slipped his camera out of his bag and held it just inside his lightweight jacket.

Masami was about to turn back around and find some excuse to leave, to save themselves from an ugly confrontation, when the door opened and a man walked through. She saw two other men lingering behind him. The man swung the door open wide, leaving it that way.

"Welcome!" he boomed. "We've been expecting you!" He gave a short bow and a pleasant but entirely sinister grin.

This isn't good.

The two thugs who had become robotic hosts stepped between them and the elevator, blocking their exit. The one man welcoming committee approached with his friendly smile, arms outstretched, almost as if he would embrace her.

"Miss Sato and Mr. Tsukino!" he said. "I am Seitaro Koide, the operating manager here at . . . Nakama Robotics." He smiled, pausing for effect. "A clever ruse to say you're here as our new robotics engineer. That tells us you know more about our operation than we expected. But as you can see, we know more about you than expected, as well. It is good to get these things out in the open, no?"

Damn. Damn. Damn! They know exactly who we are and aren't even going to pretend they don't.

She could sense Akio go cold and rigid; the blood drained from his face. Their plan had utterly failed. How could they get out of this? And what the hell did that number nine mean?

It's a clue. It has to be. There were no other markings, so it wasn't just some random gangster's kid run rampant with a marker.

"We are wondering," Koide continued, "why our organization holds so much interest for you, so much so that you would go to the trouble of lying, twice, to try to get information out of us. What is it that the *Dainichi Daily* is so intrigued by?" He smiled wider, though Masami wouldn't have thought it possible, and was all the more unnerving on a face that looked like it had never smiled before today.

Her gut clenched at the not-so-subtle threat to the paper. Tanaka and the others could be in danger thanks to her carelessness. She was never careless.

What is happening to me?

"You see," Koide went on, "the men in our organization have honor. We do not lie. We treat others with respect and make ourselves plain. So it is difficult to trust those who keep trying to gain access to our organization through deception."

"You're right," Masami finally responded. "It was wrong of us to try to deceive you. But honestly, would you have just let us in, if we had simply asked?"

"I *will* be honest," he said, "because we are always honest." His smile made Masami's skin crawl. "No. You would not have been welcome. But even though you lied to our brothers in Kofu, broke into the warehouse, murdered one of our dear brothers, and now are trying to break in here, we have had a change of heart. We'd like to welcome you with open arms, so we may learn what it is that you so badly want to know about our Nakama division."

"We've experienced your *welcome arms* before," Akio spoke up. "In the parking lot near the hotel."

The man's face twitched minutely. It was tiny, but it was a visible flinch, as if he thought Akio might punch him. "Yes, yes, Mr. Tsukino. We would like to make that up to you. Our hospitality has been much improved since then."

Masami knew that however *honest* they claimed to be, their brand of hospitality was not going to be pleasant. There was no way they were going to let them stroll through the floor, take pictures and notes, and then leave freely. They had to get out of there. It was now or never.

And perhaps Akio was the key. Even if he couldn't turn on his samurai rage at will, these men didn't know that.

"Sir," Masami said. "We are ever so grateful for your generous offer, but we really want to have your word that we won't be harmed. If anything were to go awry . . . ." She nodded toward Akio.

Akio gave her a sideways glance like she was crazy. He turned back to the man and tried to look dangerous, but he looked more like he might cry. It seemed to have the appropriate affect, however, because Koide backed away half a step and the other men readied themselves.

"Now, we don't want any trouble, do we?" he said.

"Nor do we," Masami replied. "So do we have your word?"

The man hesitated and then said, "I promise I will not hurt you."

"That's not what I asked. Will anyone else hurt us, do you think?"

"I can guarantee that I will not hurt you nor will I command others to do you any harm."

"Clever," she said. She had a sneaking suspicion that Koide wouldn't be the one giving the order.

Just then, she heard a strangled call from her Bluetooth earpiece.

"They got me!"

Akio flinched and threw his arms out at the same time. Their host and the two men guarding the elevator all jumped back a step, as if Akio were attacking them. He looked to Masami, his eyes fearful. Yoshio had been captured.

At that moment, the three men closed in on them. The other two that had been hanging back beyond the door moved forward. Thankfully, none of them drew guns.

Akio spun around, trying to look at all of them at once. "Stay back!" he yelled. The men pulled up, none of them willing to go first.

Masami glanced back at the elevator. Who knew what floor it was on now? But there was another door, an emergency exit and stairwell. She took their would-be attackers hesitation as her moment. She bolted for the door, yelling, "Kill them all, Akio!"

Akio threatened them with fists out front and his best judo stance. He jabbed at the air toward each one as he turned from side to side, slowly dancing back toward the stairs.

Masami had the door open. Jaw Scar tried to grab her, but she ducked away from his grasp. Akio rushed him. The yakuza turned from Masami and stepped back. Expecting a flurry of fists or a deadly kick from Akio, he put up his arms to block.

Akio did throw a punch, but Masami could see that it was only scrawny, scared Akio behind that fist. There was no demon fire in his eyes. He dropped his head, his eyes to the floor, and swung blindly.

The first punch hit Jaw Scar's outstretched palm. The second caught him in the bicep. A third, he blocked easily and laughed. "This is no deadly warrior," he chuckled. "He hits like a little girl!" He grabbed Akio by the arms and shoved him backward like he was a child.

Akio tumbled to the floor, and Koide grabbed him, gripping Akio's hair in a fist and hoisting him to his feet. He tried to flail free, but was too weak. Koide passed Akio to Round Face, who locked Akio's arms behind his head with his own that were more than twice the size.

"Koide, give him a good shot for Harigae!" the thug said.

Koide held his hands up in a peaceful gesture. He wanted to hit Akio; it was obvious. But he didn't. "I'm a man of my word. Somebody else will have to take the honors." He nodded toward the two men that had come in behind him.

Masami grimaced at Koide's self-deception about his honor. He wouldn't harm Akio, and he made a point of not actually commanding anyone to do so. But he would happily watch someone else do it. *That famous yakuza honor in action.*

Akio struggled as the other two men approached. Jaw Scar turned back to grab Masami, but she wasn't there.

"She must have run," he said.

Koide yelled at him. "Get that bitch!"

The thug started into the stairwell but tripped on something unseen at the top step and tumbled down the stairs, a shove from thin air helping him along. He came to a stop when his head hit the wall at the first landing. As he tried to stand and regain his balance, he "stumbled" again, falling down the second flight backward.

It wasn't fair, but she had to even the odds somehow. Masami moved invisibly toward Round Face, who was still holding Akio. The other men were about to pummel him out of existence. She balled her fist, a web of blue across her knuckles, and threw it as hard as she could into the thug's kidney. He cried out and released one of Akio's arms, turning toward his invisible attacker. As he did, he exposed his groin. *Also not fair*, Masami thought, but another welcome odds-evener. Her foot crunched his genitals, and Round Face doubled over in agony.

Akio was free, and the two approaching men hesitated. Koide stepped back, looking at Akio in fear. It was clear they thought Akio had just broken free on his own.

"Air punch, Akio," Masami whispered in his ear.

He hesitated a second, but then swung a fist in the air toward one of the men. As he did so, Masami belted the man across the face. He staggered back, confused. Understanding, Akio punched the air again, this time toward the other lackey. Masami jabbed him in the gut as hard she could. The man doubled over and retreated a step, exhaling a sudden whoosh of air.

Akio threw a punch toward Koide too, but Masami wasn't close enough to hit him immediately. Koide threw up his arms, but nothing came. As he lowered them, Masami slammed a fist into his nose.

The men were all putting up their arms now, baffled by what was happening. Another few punches thrown from distance and they backed off.

"Stairwell," Masami whispered to Akio. She saw more men appearing behind the others from within the building. "Hurry," she added. Akio took two more steps back, throwing long-distance punches that never landed, then turned and ran. Masami followed.

As Akio rounded the stairs at the landing, Jaw Scar was coming back up. He was holding his neck and bleeding from his nose. Akio froze at the landing. The gangster hadn't seen the distance punches or Akio getting free from the other brute. His most recent memory was of throwing Akio across the room like he was a skinny cat. He growled and continued up the stairs, eyes bulging like they might burst.

Akio looked petrified. There was nothing else to do. Masami put one hand on each railing—their electrostatic fields lit up for her at will—and swung her legs out hard in front of her in a double kick, knocking the man back down the stairs. But as she let the blue web over her feet fade, the energy field on her hands faded too, and they slipped through the railings. Her momentum took her down the stairs after him. She spun in the air and hovered there, remembering her fall through the apartment building, remembering that she was not subject to gravity.

She heard a crack as the wind was knocked out of the man, and he lay still. She drifted to the floor and materialized over him, one hand on her medallion, her eyes wet under her glasses. Had she killed him? Would she now know Akio's anguish at taking a life? She turned to see Akio standing on the flight of stairs above her, looking at the crumpled yakuza.

Other men entered the stairwell from above.

"Kill those sons of bitches," one of them yelled. "The boss is furious!"

"We have to go, Akio," she said.

Akio didn't hesitate. He tore down the stairs toward her as the angry footsteps reverberated behind him. Masami grabbed him as he reached the ninth floor landing.

"I'll meet you at the station! Go!" She shoved him toward the stairwell. He ran, leaping three steps at a time.

Masami faded from sight again and slipped through the ninth floor door.

The sounds of several men clattering down the steps followed. "Is he dead?" she heard as the footsteps paused for a moment.

"No, still breathing."

"Good thing for them," Koide said. "They already owe us one life."

Yes, good, Masami agreed.

18

Number Nine

Akio skittered and jerked down the stairs, a beetle from a cat's paw, glancing back over his shoulder as he rounded the mid-level landing. He could hear his pursuers, but couldn't see them.

Harigae. The name rang in his head.

Give him a good shot for Harigae!

The man he had killed.

Why hadn't his demon anger kicked in this time?

Kicked in . . . no pun intended.

He cringed at his own thought and his stomach turned. In part he was grateful, relieved that he hadn't killed anyone else. But Masami had been in danger, and so had he. They had taken Yoshio. Hadn't that been enough to piss him off? Enough to activate whatever unwanted connection he had with the demon samurai?

Apparently not.

He would suffer the transformation to save his friends. If it came down to it, he would do whatever it took to protect them. *Whatever it took.* But he was glad the demon hadn't shown up. It had saved him the trouble of having to worry about losing control. Maybe it was gone and he could go back to taking pictures.

Of safe things. From a safe distance.

But now he ran, leaping steps three and four at a time. If he kept on this way, they might eventually catch him. The stairs went one way: down and out; they could cut him off at the exit. He had to ditch them. As he reached the door for the eighth floor, he took some coins from his pocket and tossed them down the stairs, hoping beyond hope that it would make them think he had continued on down. Then he ducked into the eighth floor.

It was a hallway. Doors leading to different small businesses were spaced out along the walls: a design firm, a startup tech company, an accounting firm. A man was walking toward him. Akio slowed his pace to a jerky walk. His fight or flight instinct was in full flight mode, making it extremely hard to walk slowly and look casual. At least his headache had subsided. As soon as he left the tenth floor, it had faded. He saw the elevators only ten meters away. The man reached them first but passed them, kept walking Akio's way, a curious expression on his face.

He didn't look like yakuza, in spite of his dark suit. He was a salaryman. He was more haggard than haughty, more approachable than antagonistic. But Akio got the feeling that he wasn't supposed to be *here* either, that this was yet another place he didn't belong, for reasons other than the possibility that armed, angry men might kill him.

As he got closer, the salaryman gave a half-smile that expressed concern. "Can I help you find what you're looking for?" he said. It was a gesture of goodwill, a friendly nod to a fellow human being; that was all. It wasn't said with any hint of sinister meaning behind it, like the double speak of a yakuza promising not to hurt him. It also wasn't meant to be an existential questioning of one's existence, but in that moment, that was how Akio took it.

What am I looking for? Just some peace and quiet. Just a decent-sized TV and a nice girl to watch movies with. How did I ever get involved in this mess? Two times nearly killed by yakuza. Third time's the charm, they say. Will it be a charm for them or me? I'm not looking forward to the third time.

"The elevator," he finally said. "I think I ended up on the wrong floor!" He said it a little too boisterously. He was frazzled and disoriented after having just run down two flights of stairs, chased by a hoard of angry, brutal gangsters.

"Kono Staffing is on the sixth," the man said, pointing just behind him.

Why does everyone think that's where I'm headed? Do I look like I need a job?

"Thanks!" Akio said.

As he passed, the man looked at him queerly, and Akio realized why. Not only was he being a bit loud, he was disheveled. He had just been tossed around like a rag doll by a few different yakuza. He was pretty certain his hair was all over the place. He glanced down and saw that his shirt was twisted sideways. He straightened it.

All the while his ears were perked for the sound of the stairwell door opening behind him. There's no way tossing the coins down the stairwell had misled them. They'd be in the hallway any second.

"Really gotta go," Akio said. "Late for my appointment!" He moved in a quick walk for the elevator.

The bell dinged before he got there, and a sudden panic took him. He spun back around toward the man. "Five thousand yen for your jacket!" he called out.

The man turned back, his face screwed up in a frown. "This suit cost over eighty thousand."

The stairwell door slammed open at the end of the hall. The elevator dinged behind him.

"Nevermind!" Akio whipped back toward the elevator, ready to face his doom. Three women exited, laughing about something. Akio heard, "venture capitalist," "socks," and "bloodsucker." That was all he could process in his panicked state. But they weren't yakuza, thank the glorious gods. He got himself quickly past the women and slipped into the elevator, praying that his pursuers from the stairwell hadn't seen him.

He hit the number 1 on the keypad, and slammed his thumb into the "Close Door" button with a little too much force. They slowly squeezed shut. He breathed heavy, and leaned his head on the doors.

He realized then, the elevator was only one zag in his zigzag to lose his pursuers. He couldn't just walk out the front door on the ground floor. They'd be waiting for him there. He hit the 2 and planned to find some back stairs.

The elevator descended: 7, 6, 5. Ding! It opened on the fifth floor. Akio's heart jumped. If it was yakuza, he was done for. He breathed a sigh of relief as an overly hip-hopped couple entered with a tiny dog on a fake diamond-studded leash. They were both wearing sunglasses. The man's pants were hanging off his hips and Akio could see half the length of his underwear.

Akio wondered how anyone could think that having their pants falling down and their underwear showing was cool. But this guy certainly got better-looking women than he did. His partner had blonde dreadlocks and was heavily made-up, but she was smoking hot. Akio found it hard not to stare at her and had to make a conscious effort to look away. He wondered how long it took the two of them to get dressed and done up.

They looked at the keypad and saw that two buttons were pushed. Then they looked at Akio, in unison. He was just one man; how could he be getting off at two different floors? They looked at each other, clearly thinking that Akio was an idiot. Then they each pulled out a mobile phone and started tapping.

Akio's phone buzzed. It was a text.

He thought first of Yoshio, hoping he had gotten away. The teenager's phone had gone silent soon after he had been captured. There had been no warning at all. They must have snuck up on him. Akio took his earpiece off and shoved it in his pocket as he pulled his phone out.

The text was from Masami.

Meet me on floor 9.

What? Why?, he thought. *Aren't we trying to escape?*

It's empty.

came a second text.

No, no no! Akio thought she'd lost it. They needed to get the hell out of there, not go back up.

I know. Sounds crazy, but trust me.

came a third text, as if she had read his thoughts.

OK

he sent back.

As much as he hated to admit it, maybe it was the best plan. The gangsters wouldn't expect them *not* to leave.

The elevator was just hitting the second floor, and the doors opened. Akio took two small steps over to the keypad and hit the 9.

The hip-hop stars both looked at him like he was a lunatic. Akio shrugged and gave them a crooked half-smile. It was just one of those days. No one got off and no one got on. The doors closed. The hip-hop stars looked chagrinned. They got off on the first floor, all three of them—the dog included—giving Akio a sideways look. Two women and one man got on.

Akio moved to the back wall to give them room. After the sixth floor he was alone again. He considered getting off early and going up the stairwell, but the stairs were still a terror for him. He pictured them crawling with yakuza. He also didn't want to run into the guy on the eighth floor again. So straight to the ninth it was. If death and doom were to await him there, so be it. He was exhausted.

The ding sounded and the doors opened. No one greeted him, neither death nor doom. In fact, the floor was completely dark. Illuminated by the elevator light was a plastic sign just outside the doors that read "Floor closed for renovations."

He took a cautious step out of the elevator and stepped around the sign. It wasn't pitch dark. Th ere was light coming from the windows, but there were no electric lights on. Th e place seemed abandoned.

He was in a large, semi-circular room with many couches and platforms. It reminded Akio of the showroom at the warehouse, but without the robots. And it looked more homey, like you could hang out here and have long conversations with wealthy friends while your kids and theirs ran around screaming and tormenting innocent bystanders, completely unsupervised. It would have been a welcome place, if it weren't for the gray emptiness that enveloped it, the shadows hiding who-knows-what lurking in the corners.

A door on the curved wall opened. "In here," Masami said, appearing in it. She was corporeal. He felt relieved. As impressive and lifesaving as her newfound ability was, it made him wildly uncomfortable. She led him through the door into an even larger open space.

"Looks like they're using this level as storage, and maybe a sort of testing ground," Masami said, indicating the wide open space. It was something that would normally be separated by cubicle dividers for a large force of employees. Against the windows, far off to his left, were desks, chairs, tables, and other office furniture. It had all been shoved aside.

"A testing ground for what?" Akio asked, seeing long scraped and scarred sections of industrial carpeting, some of it blackened with what looked like burn marks.

"I'm not sure, but there was a lot of activity on the floor above us. And it wasn't a secret mahjong parlor. Did you hear the equipment working, all the whirring and drilling?"

"Yeah, it sounded like a factory, almost."

"Exactly. When we found out that the yakuza had bought Nakama Robotics, I initially guessed that they might have been hired by World Friend to keep Nakama a dead company, to make sure World Friend remained the industry leader. But that's obviously not it." Th e shadows played on her face, making her seem unreal and ghostly. Her pale skin caught the dim glow from the distant windows causing it to look like she was phasing in and out. Considering the circumstances, maybe she was.

"We know they're making robots," she continued. "Assemblyman Ogura's was clearly from them. The gem in its chest and the fact that Ogura wouldn't say who gave it to him makes it obvious. But the question is why?"

"Yeah, what would they want with robots?" Akio asked. "Why can't they just bribe politicians with money and sex like in the good old days?"

Masami half grinned, half grimaced. "Not sure, but it's something big. Maybe it's a complex way to spy on people, get compromising information, but I think those gems are the real issue. Robotics and artificial intelligence is a huge deal right now. Everyone is excited about it and scared of it at the same time. The politicians always want to be ahead of the curve. They want to have the power before the people do. If these gems are somehow demonic, like you suggested, and have some hypnotizing power, like Yoshio thinks, the robots might simply be a vehicle for delivery. What better vehicle than the latest, greatest technology that everyone is clambering to get? In order to be first, these politicians and gangsters are being careless, and becoming influenced by the Tezuka-gumi."

"Great," Akio said. "So it's time to call the Power Rangers to fight the giant robots?"

"Could be," Masami answered, and she sounded deadly serious. Then she shifted gears. "This way." She headed off toward the far corner of the room and Akio followed.

"There was a number nine with a line under it on the reception counter upstairs, hastily written, and someone had tried to clean it off," Masami said as they walked. "I think Miyahara is leading us to this floor. I'm just not sure to what exactly. I've already looked through the room by the main elevator, and I scanned through most of *that* too," she said, pointing to the mess by the windows. "But I want to check back here." Masami led him further back, to a small area by a freight elevator. There were boxes and crates stacked high near the far wall.

"Number nine?" Akio asked

"Yes, you didn't see it?"

"Nope," Akio said. "Too busy trying not to get killed. What are we going to do about Yoshio?" he asked. The fact that the teenager had been kidnapped seemed more pressing than a random number scrawled somewhere.

"I don't know yet. We need a plan. Chances are they brought him to this building, but we can't face an entire floor of yakuza on our own. Not yet." Masami's look said that it was up to him, that the "yet" arrived when he was ready to kick ass.

He knew he could be much more helpful if he could figure out how to use the demon memories, but the idea unnerved him. Not only did he not want to feel like the arrogant, ruthless, marauder samurai, but he had killed someone. He personally had taken a life because of that demon's muscle memory. What would happen if he allowed it again? He couldn't control his actions in that state of mind. Someone else might die. Or maybe something even more unthinkable.

What if I hurt Masami?

He didn't respond. It was too much pressure. He was discovering that even though he had often thought of himself as a loser, there were a lot worse things to be. Being a loser wasn't all that bad. In fact, the entire definition of the word was being rewritten for him. Maybe arrogance, greed, lack of concern for others, and ill-gained power were the real qualities of a loser. Maybe being insecure, anxious, and generally uncomfortable in his own skin only made him . . . human.

He could deal with just being human. He'd been dealing with that his whole life.

But this other thing was . . . monstrous.

"What's in these boxes?" he changed the subject.

It was dark in the far corner, the light from the windows shielded by the stacked furniture.

Masami didn't answer. She had turned on her phone's flashlight and was shining it around by the elevator. Akio turned on his phone light as well and pointed it at a large cardboard box closed only by interlocking flaps. He loosened them and shined the light inside.

He saw a human hand and jumped back.

Catching his breath, he moved closer again. A hand lay there, palm up, on a pile of other things, wires protruding from a severed wrist. It wasn't human at all, but rubbery silicone over metal. The box was full of scarred robot parts, some only metal, some covered in fake flesh.

Next to that stack was an open plastic crate with a metal torso laying across the top. It had holes in it, like it had been shot through with bullets. He lifted it to peer underneath, and a metal claw sprung out from behind, free from the weight of the torso. He jumped back again, then shook his head.

He was already on edge without random things popping out at him with no warning. He looked closer at the claw. On its steel digits was a clump of matted hair and a black and sticky-looking substance that looked like blood.

He moved away from the crate. "Something went wrong here," he said. "Whatever tests they were doing."

He saw Masami was pre-occupied with the freight elevator, shining her light around in front of its wide doors. As he joined her, a noise came from the elevator shaft. It was moving.

Together they quickly hid around a corner next to a column of stacked chairs. The elevator approached with a low-pitched whine, a hum of doom. It crescendoed behind the doors, sounding a dull clank, and then began to fade. The doors did not open. It was moving on.

Akio sighed in relief and followed Masami back to the elevator. The floor here was dirty and dust-covered. Masami shone the light on the buttons, then ran a finger lightly over one of them without pressing it. A line appeared where dust had been removed. She rubbed it off her finger.

"This floor hasn't been used in a while," she said. "Whatever experiments they were doing on these robots is old news."

"Which means they've perfected them, made them bullet-proof, and are building an unstoppable army. Now they're just shipping them out," Akio said.

"Or they gave up on making them unstoppable when they found something better."

Akio looked at the freight elevator, perfect for moving the robots in and out. They could be sending them anywhere, sneaking them out the back of the building on trucks, delivering them to yakuza bosses and politicians across the country.

He shuddered. It was going to be some kind of robot armageddon.

"I was thinking the nine with the line under it just meant ninth floor," Masami said, "but that's so broad. It's the elevator that lets you know what floor you're on, right? Maybe it's a stretch, but I feel like what we're looking for is nearby."

"I don't get it," Akio said. "What *are* we looking for?"

"I think Miyahara left us another message," she said with an irritated sigh, then pointed her light at the elevator door again. "There!" Light shone across the upper right portion of the door. It was a drawing in . . . was it blood? Akio looked closer.

No. Marker smeared in the dust.

It was a somewhat crude drawing, like a cave painting or a hastily drawn Pictionary sketch. It was a . . . refrigerator? It looked like a refrigerator with the number nine drawn on it, and the bottom, smaller rectangle was circled.

"Freezer," they both said together.

"Is this serious? It looks like some kid's doodle." Akio said.

"I don't think so," said Masami. "It would be a tall kid."

"Well, this is level 9," Akio said, indicating the digit on the drawing. "You think Miyahara did this?"

"That's my bet."

They went looking for a refrigerator.

It didn't take long. One of the doors off the main room led to a break room with a kitchen. Tables and chairs on one side, counters and cabinets, a sink, microwave and refrigerator on the other.

Masami braved the light switch. It worked, and they squinted in the sudden fluorescent glare. They walked to the fridge. Next to it was a motivational poster that had been vandalized. It read, "Teamwork is the fuel that allows common people to achieve uncommon results," but the last three words had been crossed out and replaced with "stay common" in a childlike scrawl. The formation of jets in the photo had been drawn over with penises.

"Yakuza's finest," Masami muttered.

She opened the freezer. It was still cold, still plugged in. But it was also empty, except for a couple of reusable icepacks toward the back.

Akio reached in and slid the packs aside. Nothing behind them.

"Damn," Masami said. "There must be something."

"Wait," Akio said. "What's this?" He noticed duct tape running along the backside of one of the icepacks. He picked it up. It didn't feel like the usual gel inside. It felt stiff and thin.

He pulled the duct tape off and revealed a slit in the plastic. There was something inside. He pulled out a frozen dishtowel that was wrapped around something. He set it on the counter and pried it open. Inside was a folded paper and something wrapped in plastic. Nothing else.

He opened the paper. It was a note.

One pill and the mask should be safe for a time.

Akio fingered the plastic wrap. There were lumps of something hard inside.

The mask?

A sudden nausea stung his stomach.

"Miyahara," Masami said with disdain. "What the hell kind of game is he playing?"

"He doesn't really seem to be captured, does he?" Akio said.

"No, not at all. I'm wondering why we're even here if he doesn't need rescuing. Why is he sending us on this scavenger hunt, and what the hell are these pills? When did he have time to do this?"

"I don't know," Akio said. "It doesn't make a lot of sense, does it?" He didn't have any brain space left to think about the details. All he could think about was the note. *The mask?* Miyahara couldn't be saying what it looked like he was saying.

Masami looked ready to boil over, but took a deep breath. "Well, we're here now, and we don't have much choice but to play along. Whatever he's doing, he'll have a lot to answer for when we do find him. But right now . . . he seems to have figured out a way for you to wear the mask." She paused for a long time while the unpleasant feeling in Akio's gut intensified. Then she said, "We need to get it."

Akio felt his whole body flush with anxiety. "Get the mask?" he asked, incredulous. "Are you out of your mind? Do you remember what happened last time?"

"Yes, you saved our lives."

"No, I don't mean in the parking lot! I didn't have the mask on then. When I put the mask on, I almost killed you and Miyahara, remember? I saved you and Yoshio when I *wasn't* wearing it, when I had just gotten angry or scared enough that the demon's memories kicked in. And that time I did kill someone!"

"Calm down, Akio. That was an accident. We need to keep clear heads."

"I couldn't agree more!" Akio hissed. "And if I put on that mask, I can guarantee you mine won't be!"

"But with these pills," Masami said, "it sounds like you'll be able to control it. Miyahara says it will be safe." It sounded like she was trying to convince herself as well as him.

"Safe," he harrumphed. "Assuming he wrote that note."

"No one else knows about the mask, as far as we know," Masami said. "The likelihood this is some kind of trap is slim. Besides, what choice do we have? The floor above is teaming with yakuza. I may be able to do some reconnaissance alone, but I can't get Miyahara and Yoshio out, not without you. We have agreed to help Miyahara. And now Yoshio is caught too. We can't back out now or they might be the next ones dead."

"I understand that," Akio said, her words reverberating in his head. *Not without you.* She needed him. He almost couldn't believe he was resisting. "But I barely remember what I did in that parking lot. And I have no recollection at all of what I did in the hotel room when I had the mask on. My only memories are from more than four hundred years ago. Does Miyahara really think a pill is going to make me able to function and control myself while I'm wearing that thing?"

"Clearly." Masami frowned.

Akio didn't like this new turn of events at all. Not only would he have to tap into those awful memories, he would have to wear the mask again. He remembered how beautiful it had been, how it had called to him. *So much better than my own face.* So regal, so fierce, so . . . completely evil. The mask had, quite literally, come straight from Hell. He grasped for reasons to not have to do it.

"Look," he said. "Maybe I do this. Maybe we get the mask and I try this, but there are two things about this note that are really bothering me right now. The words *should be* and *for a time*. Could he be more vague? They *should* work? And for how long? A few minutes? A couple hours? Days? How long is *for a time* exactly?"

"It's a chance we'll have to take, Akio. Either that, or I go in alone."

"No."

"I can go in undetected. Maybe it's ultimately the best plan."

"No, if something happens to you . . ." he trailed off.

Not without you.

"Miyahara and Yoshio can't turn invisible," he continued. "If you do free them, how will you sneak them out? And how will you protect them from getting caught again? You need my help."

Masami gave him a confident, proud look. It was a look that would have been a smile if her lips had actually moved. But it was only in her eyes. "You're right, Akio. I do."

"Okay then," he said. "Let's get the mask."

Something had just happened and he wasn't quite sure what it was, but he had the vague suspicion that he had been played.

19
The Mask

Akio found a dingy white suit jacket with one pocket torn open draped over a chair in the break room, and Masami found a beat up baseball cap for the Yomiuri Giants in the stacked mess by the windows. Akio put them both on.

Masami went invisible again in case she needed to distract any yakuza from Akio exiting the building. As much as she complained about it, Akio thought she was beginning to like disappearing.

Their plan was to get out of the Nakama building, get the mask, and test one of the pills with just the two of them. If anything went wrong, at least Masami would be able to get away. Akio couldn't believe he was going along with it, but there didn't seem to be any choice—unless he ran and hid somewhere, which part of him screamed at himself to do. But he couldn't disappoint Masami. He couldn't let down Miyahara and Yoshio. He couldn't disappoint himself.

They made it out through the front door without incident. There were only two men in the lobby that Akio was sure were yakuza. With all their time spent on the ninth floor, Akio's pursuers must have given up or been looking elsewhere. He moved out alongside a tall, black man in what looked like religious robes. The yakuza looked at the man with disdain but ignored Akio.

In the station, Masami whispered to Akio to wait outside the restrooms. She exited the women's room, fully visible, a few moments later, without glasses on and rubbing her eyes.

After grabbing a couple pre-made sandwiches and rice balls from a Lawson convenience store, they first went to Akio's place, where they retrieved the longer of the two swords they had found in the samurai demon's grizzly abattoir in Kofu, the bone-handled katana with the ruby guard. He didn't know for sure what the guard was made of, but its deep red hue sparkled and gleamed how he imagined a ruby would. Holding it made him feel powerful and somehow too dangerous. It felt perfect in his hands and yet he wanted to lock it away where it wouldn't harm anyone. He resisted the temptation to slide it from its black scabbard, and instead wrapped it in a bath towel and tucked it into a long duffle bag.

Next they went to Masami's apartment. In her extremely organized coat closet, she pushed aside a long black trench coat on a hook. From behind it she pulled out the other sword in the set, a *wakizashi*, a shorter version of the katana, its black bone handle looking sinister in the darkness. Akio admired the trench coat and pictured Masami as a secret agent sneaking in the shadows after an international criminal. He had always wanted a coat like that but had never felt cool enough to wear one. She handed the wakizashi to Akio. Its guard sparkled the same red as the katana's, reflecting the overhead light.

Next to the trench coat was a light blue plastic storage container. She slid that out and then carried it to the living room floor. She lifted the lid. Inside, under a blanket, was the square metal box that had filled them with such curiosity when they had first seen it.

Seeing it again now, a memory sparked in Akio. But it wasn't his. He saw when the box was first presented to the samurai Akechi in the depths of Hell. At that time, there had been no markings, only blank spaces waiting for an engraving. After the samurai's head had been sealed inside, the markings appeared, burning themselves into the metal box from no discernible source. Akechi had been able to read them then, and therefore Akio had understood. Now the words themselves escaped him—not that he'd be able to pronounce them with something so limited and clumsy as a human tongue—but he remembered their meanings. Emblazoned on the front was the demon samurai's soul name. And spaced around the box were his sins: arrogance, murder, vengeance, covetousness, disdain . . .

Akio remembered when they first opened the box, revealing Akechi's hideously transformed demon head. Now the mask lay inside, waiting. Akio could feel its presence, even through the reinforced metal. He could not hear it talking to him, but he could feel that it wanted to.

He remembered it calling to him, convincing him to put it on. If he could take that moment back, he would in a heartbeat. Not only because he had put Masami and Miyahara in danger, but because he didn't want to understand the written tongue of demons; he didn't want to get headaches whenever he was close to anything demonic; he didn't want the memories of war and destruction, murder and blood, arrogance and anger as if they were his own; he didn't want to be a hero expected to rescue people.

He wanted his life back.

But he *had* put it on. And he understood there was no turning back. No matter how much he whined about it and wished for a different reality. There was no reset button. He had done what he'd done, and he had to accept the consequences.

"Let's get this over with," he said. He kneeled down and reached for the metal box.

"Not yet," Masami said. "First, a pill."

"Right." He sat back onto his knees.

Masami unwound the plastic wrap, which had been twisted at the ends like a large hard candy. Inside were five crude pills. They were clearly not something that came from the local pharmacy or any pharmaceutical company. Certainly hadn't been approved by the Japanese Ministry of Health, Labor and Welfare after being safely tested for human consumption. They were a mottled dark greenish brown and were only remotely spherical. They were rough and chunky and not small. There were fibers of some kind protruding here and there, like hairs or small twigs. They were not something Akio wanted to swallow, but even less so wanted to chew.

"Got any water?" he asked. Just looking at the pill his throat wanted to close up. It felt dry and dead. Dead as a dehydrated frog he had seen as a boy, less than a meter away from a lake, blackened and shriveled. How had that frog made such a fatal miscalculation? The pills were monster eyes, wild animal turds, ammunition for a slingshot. How was he going to get them down?

"Yes," Masami said, with an empathetic breath. She retrieved a glassful from the kitchen and set it on her coffee table. "Thank you, Akio," she said. The caring that he had seen in Kofu was again in her eyes. It emboldened him. Somehow, it made doing what he was about to do a little easier.

He reached out and grabbed a pill. It felt like a piece of dehydrated dog poop, only denser and grittier, a little more heft to it. And it was smaller, thankfully—small for poop, not small for a pill he had to swallow.

No time like the present.

He threw the pill to the back of his throat and almost gagged. But Masami was ready with the water. He took it and gulped hard. It was like a dirty stone in his throat, dragging its way into his gut. For a moment, he thought he was going to heave it back up. He had never liked taking pills, and this was, without doubt, the worst he ever had to swallow. For a moment it felt lodged, almost like it was clawing its way back out. He pointed at the now empty water glass, unable to verbalize, and Masami quickly refilled it. He gulped it down like waterfalls, like eaves drains in a torrential storm. It ripped its way along his esophagus and landed like a stone in his stomach.

He shook his head and grimaced, trying to shake away the feeling.

"You all right?" Masami asked.

"Define all right," he said hoarsely.

"You'll make it," she said.

"Great. How long do I have to wait for it to kick in?"

But before Masami could even respond with a shrug, he started to feel something. A sensation spread from his stomach and radiated up his spine. He felt his fingers and toes tingle. He felt his chest seem to expand slightly. His eyes seemed to open wider than possible and his ears popped; he hadn't known they were clogged. Colors seemed more vivid. Sounds were more crisp and immediate.

"I guess not long," he said. "Open it up."

Remembering the secret to opening the box, Masami unsheathed the katana and slid it through the slots at the box's base. Akio handed the wakizashi to her. She stuck the pommel end with the oddly-shaped key into the matching keyhole and turned. There was a click as the lid released.

Masami lifted the lid. Instantly, Akio heard the voice.

Wear me. I am beautiful.

He tried to shut it out.

I am so much better than your own face. Wear me.

And he succeeded.

The voice dropped to the background of his thoughts. He could hear it, but it was quiet. It did not overtake him and control his actions. He no longer felt compelled to wear the mask. He could if he wanted to, but he could just as easily ignore it like traffic noise or a distant table's conversation in a restaurant.

"I think it's working," he said, then looked at Masami. She didn't look so good. She was unnerved and anxious. Akio realized the mask was calling to her, and she had no protection from it.

She backed away from the box. "Put it on then," she said quickly. "Put it on and see."

Akio picked up the mask. He couldn't believe he was willingly going to wear it.

"I don't want to hurt you," he said. "I'm still not sure this is a good idea. Miyahara isn't here to fight me off this time."

"I'll be okay," she said, nervously. She held her hands tightly together as if trying to prevent them from doing something rash. "I can turn incorporeal, remember? Just put it on before I take it from you!" It was clearly calling to her much stronger than before, now that Akio was able to resist it.

He took a deep breath. *Let this work. Please let this work.*

Akio brought the mask to his face. It sucked itself to his skin like a vacuum, like a magnet to steel. It fused itself and became his face.

He saw a battlefield. He saw armored riders coming at him with spears. Blood and corpses were strewn about the ground like earth and weeds. He could feel the weight of armor on his broad shoulders. He could feel the rage for his enemies, the hate of those who had stolen his son from him. He wanted revenge. He could taste it like bile in his mouth, like the blood on his sword.

But they were only memories. They were his, part of him, sinew and bone, but he was not on the battlefield. He was in Masami's apartment.

He looked around. It was strange, assessing the room simultaneously with his own eyes and with the ancient eyes of the samurai Akechi. Everything looked at once familiar and very foreign.

Masami was even farther away than she had been. She stood next to her dining table by the small kitchen, a little extra buffer zone in case things went south quickly. Her breathing had calmed, however, and Akio knew that the mask was no longer calling to her. It had found a wearer and was satisfied.

"I'm okay," he said in a voice much more rugged and purposeful than his own.

"Good," Masami said. "Excellent." She went quickly to where he stood in the living area. She pushed the metal box to the wall and turned the coffee table on its side, butting it up against her couch to clear a space on the floor. She re-sheathed the katana and handed it to Akio. Then she picked up the still sheathed wakizashi. "Let's see if you can fight."

Masami readied herself barely an arm's length from him. There wasn't much room to spar in her small apartment, especially with weapons, but he scooted back a bit and took a stance. It was not the kendo stance he had learned as a kid. Instead, his feet naturally moved into an altered position, one meant for a quick and decisive duel. He felt power and grace, like a tiger ready to spring.

Masami swung at him, a high arc to the head. Instead of parrying it, he dodged with ease, stepping closer to her. His katana was at her neck before her swing was even finished. He pulled his attack so the sheath of the katana stopped with perfect precision just at her skin. She would have been headless in less than a heartbeat if it had been a real fight, if the blade had been bare and he hadn't been in control of his actions.

Masami blinked and gave a sharp nod of frightened approval.

She came at him again with a high feint and a cut to the belly. With his inspirited eyes Akio saw her clumsy attack as if she moved through water, her intentions displayed before her like the flame on a thrown spear.

He stepped back lightly, parrying and enveloping her blade. He twisted and wrenched her weapon free of her grasp; it clattered against the wall. His katana was back at her neck in an instant.

She retrieved the wakizashi from where it had landed on the couch. She was flustered, but seemed encouraged. She thrust at him: to the gut, to the head, slashed down across his body in an X pattern that would have cut him in four triangles. Akio either dodged or blocked every attack with ease. And every time, his sheathed blade ended up against her neck, perfectly placed so as to barely brush her skin.

Akio felt like a cat. His reflexes were unreal. He felt like a ballerina assassin. Graceful, deadly, and stronger than he had ever been. He felt amazing. And yet he felt the hate and bile poisoning him. He wanted to rip heads off. Some primal part of him wanted to kill Masami and eat her heart in victory. It made him—the real him—want to vomit. He pushed the feeling back, as far back as he could.

Masami put down her weapon. "Good," she said, her expression dire. She looked at him momentarily, studied his covered face, and then engaged his eyes behind the mask. "Now . . . can you take it off?"

Akio took a breath. He felt confident. He felt powerful. He didn't want that part to go away, but there was also rage and madness. There was only a sliver of difference between controlling those feelings and being overcome by them. It was this that made him reach his hands to his face. He put his thumbs at the edges of the mask and lifted it free.

There was no ripping this time, no stinging like his skin had come off. There was only a tingling, like a thousand tiny and insignificant bug bites, like the prickly feeling from blood rushing back into a limb that's fallen asleep.

He squatted to the floor and set the mask down. It no longer felt like there was a stone in his stomach, but he felt nauseous and over-sensitized. Whatever was in the pill was still working. He burped and tasted dirt and something else, an herb that seemed familiar but he couldn't place. He tried to clear his throat and the bitter, earthy taste only intensified.

Ugh. Why can't I just have a medallion like Masami?

"Good," Masami said once more. "Let's go get them."

20
Tenth Floor

Masami reached up with her invisible wakizashi toward the security camera outside the service entrance in the back of the Nakama building. She focused on revealing the blue electrostatic web of only the razor sharp tip of the blade.

The entire weapon and both her hands materialized in the air.

Quickly she cut the camera wire and let her sword and hands fade from sight again.

I'll have to work on that.

She felt more confident about moving in and out of the ghost world now, but limiting it to specific parts of her was still unpredictable. She was relatively certain her sword and hands had been too close to the building to be on camera, and she hoped no one outside had seen them briefly hovering there.

She tucked the short sword into her belt next to the katana. She had pulled both weapons with her into the ghost world so Akio wouldn't have to carry his in plain view.

She was prepping to drift through the door when she heard voices approaching from inside. Two men stepped out for a smoke. They were dressed like kitchen staff, maybe cooks; probably worked at the café on the first floor. She was grateful for their timing. Moving through solid objects still felt unnatural. She slipped through while the door was open.

"Ooh, chilly tonight," one of them said.

"Chilly?" the other asked. "What planet are you on? It's gotta be at least thirty degrees."

"No way. I just felt a cold breeze."

"You've just been in the kitchen too long."

She heard a lighter click, and their voices faded as she quietly moved into a stairwell and the door shut behind her. She was half tempted to climb the stairs and take her chances against the yakuza herself. It would be simpler if she slipped in undetected, but Akio was right; Miyahara and Yoshio couldn't turn invisible. She at least needed him for a distraction.

But it was much more than that.

Akio was still a wildcard, but Masami felt like she was coming apart. She couldn't do it alone. It's why she had insisted he wear the mask, why she had been so quick to trust Miyahara's note. It was utterly unlike her to be so rash. But she needed someone else to share the burden. She needed someone else to be transformed like she had been. She needed Akio to wear the mask. Even if it scared the hell out of her.

And what if she got shot again? Would she let the bullet pass through her, or would her reactive, pre-conditioned brain take over and accept the bullet into her solid flesh? She may not have a choice. If her brain believed she was solid and bullets kill, they would. She had to stay calm and avoid confrontation. Someone else needed to take the brunt of any conflict. A demon-infused Akio was her best and only option. But no matter how well he had disabled the gun-wielding gangsters back in Kofu, there was going to be a lot more of them here. And she was pretty certain the mask didn't make him bulletproof.

She leaned against the wall by the backdoor, the metal stairs ascending above her, listening to the muffled conversation of the smokers outside. They talked about baseball and television shows; they talked about their wives in that very humble and disparaging manner that is distinctly Japanese.

"Your wife is much prettier than mine."

"No. Are you crazy? Your wife is like a model. And so nice. Mine is very plain looking."

It was all very normal and simple. Masami's life would never be like that.

Part of her wanted normal. A decent paycheck, a nice place to live, and a strong, but reserved husband who called her plain to his friends and beautiful in the privacy of their home. But most of her cried out against it. Normal meant melting into the background. Normal meant letting the world and all it contained pass you by. Normal meant truly disappearing.

She couldn't let herself disappear. Not in that way.

The men laughed at something Masami hadn't heard and then were at the door. It opened and they entered, passing her and heading to the door opposite, which led into the building proper. When they were gone, she pushed the outside door open a crack.

Akio appeared a moment later, and stepped through. He no longer wore the white jacket and baseball cap, but was back in his own lightweight jacket and jeans. He carried a cloth bag, the contents of which pulled heavily against the draw string. He looked around, trying to see where Masami was. He looked scared, like a boy that was sneaking where he didn't belong.

Masami sighed and materialized, a tear wetting one eye.

Akio smiled at her. "Oh, there you are. I don't know if I'll ever get used to that."

She handed him the demon-wrought katana.

"I hope we don't need these," she said.

"Me too." Akio's smile dropped from his face. "I don't want to kill anyone."

"Let's hope we don't have to."

Masami hadn't seen any surveillance cameras in the stairwell, but she was relatively certain there would be some in the halls and possibly the elevator.

"We'll need to move quickly to the elevator," she said. "It should be just to our left out of this door. Once we're inside, we won't have a lot of time."

Akio nodded his understanding, and they listened at the door into the first floor. There were distant voices and sounds, but nothing seemed close, so they cracked it open and ducked out. The freight elevator was right next to the stairwell, just where Yoshio's blueprint said it would be. Masami hit the call button.

The elevator creaked to a stop, and the two of them stood off to the side, hidden from view. The doors opened and no one got off, so they slipped in. She eyed the eleventh floor button and saw the keycard slot next to it.

Dammit.

She tried it anyway. Nothing.

"Looks like it's the tenth floor again," she sighed. The button lit when she pushed it, and the spacious elevator lurched to a start.

"Well, maybe that's where they are," Akio said.

"I don't think so. The clue Miyahara left clearly said 'eleventh floor.' I think it meant more than just the building height. They have to be there."

"We don't know that for certain. That was just you and Yoshio making assumptions. It could mean anything."

"We are in a former Nakama Robotics building that has eleven floors. Do you really think we're wrong?"

"Okay," Akio said. "I don't know. Probably not. But even if Miyahara is there, maybe Yoshio isn't."

"Maybe." She wasn't in the mood to squabble pointlessly with Akio.

The numbers climbed on the readout as they ascended, Masami's trepidation growing as her resolve steeled. She brushed a finger over her medallion.

"Who knows who'll be waiting for us when these doors open," she said. "We'd better be ready." She nodded toward the bag Akio carried.

He nodded back, his breath catching in his throat. He reached into the bag and pulled out the ancient, demonic mask. The clouds and flames swirled across its face as if they were moving. Its empty eyes glared as if they could see on their own, though they were nothing but holes. Masami realized that she couldn't hear it. In fact, she hadn't heard it on their entire ride together to the building.

She looked at Akio, the question clear.

"It's talking to me," he said. "It seems satisfied somehow," he grimaced, "knowing that it has a willing host. It's even creepier in a way, but I'm still in control," he assured her.

From the bag he pulled out the wrapped cloth they had retrieved from the freezer on the ninth floor and a bottle of water. He took out one of the chunky, misshapen pills and looked at it with disgust.

"I guess I'd better," he said. "I don't know how long the first one will stay in effect."

"We have a few more," Masami answered. "Do it."

He threw the pill back and followed quickly with water, grimacing as if holding in vomit. He lifted the mask with both hands and placed it on his face. It clung there with nothing to support it, gluing itself onto Akio's skin.

The elevator dinged as the display read "10."

Masami looked at the terrifying face next to her. Akio's eyes showed through the holes but with an intensity that sent a shiver through her. The sharply downward-pointing nose looked like it was inhaling along with Akio. The menacing teeth looked as if they were in Akio's mouth. They had become a part of him. Even his stance had changed, his entire presence. Akio was no longer with her. In his place stood a demon samurai.

Akio stepped out of the elevator in front of Masami. He felt powerful. He felt his blood surging through him. He felt a lust to kill. He could hear Masami breathing behind him. He could sense many people on this floor not far away; he could hear them talking, could smell their sweat.

He had become so much more than himself. He had even become more than Akechi. The mask had absorbed not only Akechi's essence but had become one with the demon into which the samurai had evolved. It had merged with its spirit for over four hundred years. All of the demon's power and awareness thrummed through him, all of Akechi's anger and skill.

He felt the scrape in his throat from the pill. It had felt like he swallowed a dried slug wearing spiked armor. But it was insignificant now. It paled in comparison to the scars he had received in battle. It paled next to losing his son. It was nothing next to the sting of betrayal and the taste of poison on his lips.

"Wait," Masami said, laying a hand on his shoulder.

Akio felt the trepidation in her touch, felt her heart beating quickly. She was frightened in spite of her tough exterior. She was frightened of him.

"I think . . ." she started in a whisper, "that I should go in on my own first. You should wait here while I check things out." She was stone-faced as usual, cold and strong-willed, but Akio could feel her buried concern. She was scared that he wouldn't agree with her, that he might rush headlong into the yakuza headquarters, or worse, that he might kill her.

But he saw the wisdom in her plan, and he had no wish to kill her. The part of him that was still Akio felt horrible that Masami could think such a thing, but the other part, the hateful part, enjoyed her fear and knew it was justified.

Akechi had been bloodthirsty; he had been a ruthless killer. But he was not an animal. He was shrewd. He was a highly intelligent military strategist, and was not above what some might call dishonorable tactics. Had it not been for his poisoning, he may have conquered all of Japan.

Akio nodded, and stepped aside. He said nothing. He had no desire to talk, nor any need.

Masami nodded back, looking him right in the face, as if daring herself to hold his gaze, as if facing the bogeyman to kill her own fears.

He smiled, and she looked away as if she'd been slapped. But she turned her head back to lock eyes again. This time she held it steady as she faded to but a wispy semblance of herself.

Akio could still see her.

She was not completely invisible. Transparent, the edges of her form like vapor, like a breath in the cold night air. Like a ghost.

She still held his gaze, and her ghostly outline shivered visibly. She turned from him and moved like a dream into the hallway and around a corner.

Akio waited.

Boxes were stacked on a cart against the wall next to the freight elevator. They varied in size from half a meter to as small as a square tissue box, and looked like packages ready to be sent. Akio scanned the labels and saw addresses all over Japan, as far as Hokkaido. Some boxes were addressed to Russia and China, one to North Korea.

He sensed a presence in every box. It was a presence that wanted to drive its will into him, that wanted to give him a headache. But it was not powerful enough for either task. Not now.

Compelled by curiosity, he took the top most box, one of the smallest ones, and tore it open.

A wooden jewelry box that might hold a watch or a bracelet sat surrounded by bubble wrap. He pulled it out and lifted its lid. A green glow spilled out from inside. Nestled into silk-covered styrofoam was a misshapen, green gemstone the size of a cigarette lighter and the color of absinthe. He lifted it free and turned it about in his hand.

Warm, comforting tones reached out to him from the gem, offering him visions of peaceful submission, of joyful servitude and reverence. He saw all his wishes being fulfilled, the biggest one, he suddenly realized, was a lifetime of service to a great master. He saw unlimited success and power in that master's name. He saw his co-workers at the *Dainichi* bowing before him. He saw women begging him for his attentions.

But he did not see his son returned to him.

He did not see his vengeance accomplished.

Akechi laughed, and Akio did too. There were no promises large enough. There was no comfort worth his surrender. He would serve no one. He would never serve again.

He crushed the gem with his bare hands and let the emerald dust sprinkle to the floor.

Immediately, he felt a stab of shock from something above, something large and menacing. It was a presence Akio had not sensed before that moment, but something about it felt familiar, a vague impression on the darkest edge of his mind. Whatever it was, it had not expected resistance, and mingled with its shock was a trace of fear. He could feel it searching for him. When he held the gem, it had known where he was, but as the gem crumbled, it became confused. It felt uncertain. Then anger overpowered everything. Pure rage washed through the emotions of all the yakuza he sensed. It overtook every one of them. Every person on this floor and the one above had simultaneously become furious. Their combined rage rushed toward Akio like a red tide bent on annihilation.

Masami appeared around the corner, one hand on her medallion, as she solidified and wiped a tear. She held up a keycard.

"I pulled this off someone who was working on a robot," she said. "It was creepy. There were scores of them, all different shapes. Some of them were humanoid, but others looked more utilitarian, more mechanical. Right after I unclipped this from the guy's lanyard, everyone suddenly stopped what they were doing and turned toward me. But they looked right past me, and started moving this way."

Akio felt the adrenalin rise in his chest. He felt the venomous surge of energy electrify his muscles. He could taste the salt of his enemies' blood on his tongue. He craved battle.

He grinned as the voice rasped out of his throat like a distant shriek of souls.

"They are coming for me."

21

Eleventh Floor

The thunder of what sounded like hundreds of running feet echoed through the building, rapidly getting louder. The mob of yakuza and robot technicians would be there any moment, and from the looks Masami had seen on their faces, they weren't coming to chat. She slipped back into her ghostly form, almost on instinct. It would do no good for her to be seen.

Akio stood next to her, a slender force of hate and terror, his mask breathing with him, a leer of scorn on it, coupled with a relish for battle about to be joined. He put his hand on his katana.

"No!" Masami said, her ghostly voice merely a susurration of the air in the physical world. But Akio heard her. He could still see her, the demon mask giving him some extrasensory perception. He looked at her with a cold flame in his eyes. *How dare you tell me no*, his eyes said. *How dare you take from me the thing I crave most.*

Masami quivered, but stood her ground. This was Akio, not a demon. He would listen to her. He would be reasonable.

The footsteps echoed louder, a mad drum roll of doom. The most unsettling thing about it wasn't the growing noise or the sheer numbers that caused it. It was that there were no voices to accompany it, no shouting or even murmuring. It was as if they had no need to speak to one another because they were all one being, one massive creature with hundreds of legs.

Akio's grin grew wider and he began to draw his blade.

Masami jumped at him without thinking. She couldn't let this turn into a bloodbath. Th ere were too many of them, and Akio wouldn't be able to live with himself when the mask came off. If he survived.

She saw the blue web of his electrostatic outline and felt the tingle of her own spark into view. She meant to knock him toward the elevator and prevent him from drawing his sword. She meant to knock some sense into him. But when she collided with his staunch, battle-ready stance, she instead took him with her into the ghost world.

Her hands gripped Akio's shoulders and he swayed with her impact. He looked about himself and down at his body. He could tell he was incorporeal now. She had effectively distracted him from pulling his weapon at least, but she had not expected this.

I can take people with me?

She had learned to take objects, and her clothing seemed to just go along without trying—one more of those ingrained beliefs like bullets and falling. Clothing worn presumably stays on. She wanted to hang onto that one.

But people? She hadn't even thought of that.

The mob of yakuza and their cronies exploded into view, coming around the corner from the hallway. They stopped and looked around, confused. The ones behind did not bump into the ones in front. They stopped as a unit, as if even the ones still around the corner could see the empty room off the freight elevator. Not one of them spoke.

Masami pulled Akio toward the elevator doors, still gripping him tightly. His battle fervor seemed to have drained with the new experience of being incorporeal, and he let himself be guided. The throng of men—it was all men—spread about the room like an ooze coating the floor and walls. They moved in one even motion, perfectly synchronized like the tentacles of a massive squid.

Though neither of them were visible, Masami did not want to make contact. She did not want them to feel the chill of her presence that Akio and Yoshio had felt, that the cook out back had felt when she had brushed past him. They couldn't afford any possibility of being detected.

She pulled Akio through the closed elevator doors and into the elevator. Thankfully it was still on that floor. She couldn't afford to have Akio panic about hovering in mid air and then lose her grip on him.

The only illumination in the elevator was the ethereal light that swirled inside her and Akio. As she peered into his, she noticed something that she hadn't seen before. It was almost undetectable, but deep in the current of his internal light were the tiniest of smoky black lines, like minuscule spider veins reaching into him. She traced them up and back to where they were thickest, though still barely visible. The black leaked out from the mask, leaching into Akio's being like a slow poison.

She held onto him, as he stood calmly, his previous battle lust absent. The elevator doors opened.

The eyes of a crowd of surly men looked in on them. Men in dark suits, in grease-stained slacks and shirts. Hands inside jackets ready to draw guns. Hands still holding tools meant for creation but now wielded for destruction. Masami now saw that the whites of all their eyes were bloodshot and tinted green. They scanned the elevator but they did not enter.

As one, they turned and moved away. The elevator doors closed.

Masami let go of Akio, and he was corporeal again. He did not even flinch, as if he didn't register the change. But Masami lay back exhausted, only hovering above the elevator floor. Keeping Akio with her in the ghost world had been more draining than she realized, as if she had been holding her breath.

She thought of the tiny black veins inside Akio. The mask was infecting him. It wasn't simply giving him demonic powers while he wore it; something of the demonic was seeping into him, altering his very essence. This couldn't be good, but she needed him to be the demon now. They all did. What would this cost them? What would it ultimately cost Akio?

There was no time to waste, no time to relax. Though she lay there trying to rest for only a moment, her heart still beat rapidly. She rallied and lifted herself, abruptly moving to the elevator panel. Fear and worry sizzled through her veins like electricity as she made the keycard materialize in her hand and slid it through the slot next to the eleventh floor button. Her heart thumped. A small green light briefly illuminated in the card reader, though its color barely registered to Masami. She touched the button and it lit as well—a dull orange glow.

The freight elevator lurched into motion.

Standing next to her was a being that was not Akio. It was his slight form, his jeans and loose-fitting button-down, his low-top Converse All-stars that he wore with everything, even suits. It was his mid-length black hair, the one cowlick in the back that would never quite lay down. But his presence was immense. His presence was that of a warrior that had seen countless battles, had taken countless lives . . . and had enjoyed it. It swallowed up all the available energy in the large elevator and threatened to push through the ceiling into the shaft beyond.

The most unnerving part of it was the mask. It leered toward the closed doors like a fiend ready to devour the Earth. It was the frozen face of Death incarnate. But despite its rigidity it moved. The patterns of clouds and flames swirled into each other and seemed to lift off the mask. The eyes glowed, the nostrils flared, and the teeth glistened with saliva.

Was it all illusion? She couldn't tell. One moment, the mask was a living demon's face, and the next, rigid and immovable.

It is poisoning his soul.

The high-pitched elevator ding resounded like a toll of doom in Masami's head. The doors slid open in slow motion, their soft scrape against the doorframe resonating like the wailing of tortured spirits mingled with the satisfied sigh of their torturer.

Bright lights greeted them, immediately followed by sharp explosions of gunfire.

Masami instinctively rolled away from the open doors and flattened herself against the front elevator wall. The rapid clinking of bullets rang inside the elevator as her heart accelerated to match time. She looked across the hail of gunfire and saw that Akio had done the same. His back was against the elevator panel, his sword drawn in front of him. He looked calm, not panicked at all, just waiting for his moment. Masami felt as inconsequential as she appeared, but she drew her sword as well, sending her focus into the blade to find its electric blue outline and solidify its edge. She saw only the blade appear this time; her hands remained incorporeal.

Frustration and desperation.

They still helped her to focus.

She took a deep breath and readied herself.

I can walk through walls. Bullets can't hurt me.

The gunfire stopped briefly, and she heard clips being replaced, while empty ones dropped to the floor.

Now. Go now, she told herself.

She heard the surprised grunts of men, another two shots fired, and what sounded like bodies slumping to the floor. She looked to her left across the doors that just then started to close. Akio was no longer in the elevator.

She lurched into action, pressed the "open door" button, and peered out into the eleventh floor. Akio stood, stock still, facing away from her, his sword sheathed. The bodies of four men lay at his feet. Severed arms still holding handguns, severed heads sitting near the feet of the corpses, each almost in the exact same position. Blood rapidly pooled outside the elevator doors.

Masami looked away, her stomach threatening to revolt. Akio's plea rang in her head.

I don't want to kill anyone.

But Akio was no longer there. The demon had taken control.

It stepped into the room beyond, feet squishing into the carpet that drank up the blood. Masami followed, hovering just above the grisly scene.

This floor looked nothing like the others. The room off the freight elevator was extravagant though now splattered red. A gold-framed painting of a family greeted them: Hiromi Kumamori, the godfather of the Tezuka-gumi, playing a stoic but handsome husband standing by his wife. On his wife's left was a teenage girl with angry eyes and a smile that didn't match the rest of her demeanor, as if it had been forced upon her with brushstrokes. They were all dressed in traditional kimonos, wife and daughter with fans, Kumamori with a sword but a modern hairstyle. Blood now spattered their faces and finery. A chaise lounge with deep red cushions and gold woodwork rested under the painting. A large, decorative rug, now soaked in blood and obscuring its golden floral design, spanned the space between the sofa and the elevator.

Chairs flanked the chaise lounge with tables in between, all of them dressed in gold. A small, unmanned cocktail bar was in the corner with a polished gold surface. The room appeared to be a kind of gaudy waiting room, a lounge for people awaiting audience with an important, powerful, and very tacky individual.

It was an opulent foyer to be by the freight elevators, but this had clearly become the yakuza's main entrance. Th ere was no need to attract attention by entering through the main lobby.

To the right, there was no wall. It opened up into a larger, high-ceilinged area beyond, which was brightly lit but silent. It looked like a vacant ballroom.

Masami saw no movement at all.

There were chandeliers illuminating a highly polished floor of swirling red and gold, some kind of faux marble. A golden piano sat off to one side, a stage with gold curtains closed just beyond it. More gold-framed paintings hung along the walls. Masami wanted to puke from all the gold. And the carnage in the foyer certainly hadn't helped. Her raw will was all that kept her stomach in check.

Akio stopped at the edge of the large room, and Masami moved next to him, her sword drawn.

As she did, she saw movement to her left. A soft whirring sound accompanied a shape that was quickly approaching across the reflective floor. Akio also turned his head toward it, but didn't draw his weapon.

The shape was not human. It was wide at the base and ovoid on top. What looked like four arms protruded from the top section, making it look something like a giant beetle. It rolled toward them smoothly. At the end of each arm was something glowing green.

"Stay," Akio the demon breathed, then surged into action, running headlong toward the oncoming thing, his blade now drawn and trailing behind him.

The word had been like a command to an animal, something that would have made Masami's blood boil in any other situation. But now she listened. The way Akio said it had chilled her. It said "Stay, because you can't handle this. This will take your soul." So she froze.

For a moment.

Then she snapped out of it. Because she was not someone who froze. She was someone who pushed through fear and faced it. She could handle whatever they threw at her. She thought about following after Akio and grabbing him again, bringing him into the ghost world. Together they could sneak about undetected until they found Miyahara or Yoshio. But Akio was an unapproachable force. He moved away from her like a panther intent on its prey. The thought of interfering paralyzed her. It wasn't Akio that tore into that room. It was a demon.

She jerked into motion, but not toward Akio and the oncoming construct. She instead moved out into the larger ballroom to protect him from any flanking attacks if the rolling cart with arms was just a distraction. But as she did, a disturbing sound hit her from behind: footsteps on metal stairs—many, many footsteps.

She turned around as a loud elevator ding sounded through the gold-encrusted, blood-soaked waiting room. The elevator doors slid open at the exact moment the stairwell door nearly flew off its hinges. A river of yakuza exploded from both entrances.

At first it was dark.

Yoshio sat on the floor, hands and feet zip-tied, mouth gagged with duct tape. He knew they had gagged him so he wouldn't shout and give away his position. But Yoshio wasn't a shouter. He wouldn't have called for help. He would figure this out on his own.

He slid himself backward a few centimeters at a time until he bumped into something: metal slats with space in between, obviously a shelf of some kind. Its contents shifted when he hit it. There were cans evidently, from the clinking—cleaning spray or disinfectant, maybe compressed air. There was a papery sliding sound—cardboard boxes, one lighter than the other. There was a slosh and plastic sliding on metal—bleach, floor cleaner, or industrial soap. He was in a supply closet, which meant one of two locations from the building blueprint he had committed to memory. There was something else too, several small metal somethings had rolled and then come to a stop.

They had put a bag over his head once they were in the building, but that had been easy enough to take off. His hands were tied behind him with zip ties, but he had leaned over and shook the bag so it hung loosely from his head. Then he pinched the top between his knees and pulled it off. Doing so hadn't mattered much in regards to light—it was just as dark with it off—but he felt less like he was suffocating.

He hopped into a standing position now easily without needing to use his hands. His legs and balance were strong from the kendo he had done over the years. Most people didn't realize how much footwork was involved in sword fighting. And Sensei would often make his students run the stairs at the park, sometimes even carrying one another. Yoshio began to feel around behind him for something useful on the shelves. He found the plastic bottles first, definitely bleach from the smell. Then the cans, an aerosol of some kind. He could spray his captors in the face when and if they returned. But first he'd have to get his hands free.

Boxes were next: sponges wrapped in plastic, cleaning brushes, and so on; then pads of paper, pens, notebooks. Another was heavy and hadn't shifted at all when he bumped the shelf. There were smaller boxes inside it made of thin cardboard with cover flaps tucked in. He fingered one of them open. Cylindrical metal things that tapered to a point.

Bullets.

Next to that was a metal tray. When he touched it, he heard and felt the rolling again. He reached behind him further into the tray. There were many round metal balls: ball bearings, probably for their robot production. That means there were likely other robot parts and pieces in this room. He scooped up a handful of the ball bearings, each two centimeters across, and dropped them into a back jeans pockets.

He reached the end of that shelf and couldn't reach any higher with his hands behind his back, so he squatted back down to see what the lower shelves held.

As he did, a bar of light illuminated the room from underneath a door only three meters away. He heard footsteps approaching: two people, both wearing hard-soled shoes on laminate flooring. One of them was about seventy-five kilograms, the other closer to ninety. The lighter one was walking very stiff and upright, while the heavier one was more of lumberer, swaying side to side. Yoshio knew all of this from where he sat on the floor in the dark. He could hear it. The sounds translated to numbers.

Weight, foot pressure distribution, odds of survival.

He remained still, the ball bearings pressing uncomfortably into his right buttock. There was no point in trying to put the bag back over his head. He wouldn't have time.

The shoes stopped at the door, and a metal key went into the lock. Light flooded the room as two silhouettes appeared in the doorway. A thinner one with straight shoulders and slicked back hair wore a black suit and a white button down, open at the collar. The other was a hand higher with round shoulders, his head bare and melon-shaped, with blue slacks and a patterned short-sleeve shirt open to his sternum.

They walked to Yoshio in lockstep. One said, "Got the sack off your head, I see." And the other added, "Sneaky, huh?"

Yoshio didn't reply. He didn't see the point. Plus he was still gagged.

"The boss has requested to do you himself," the shorter one said. "Must be something special," the taller one added.

Do you? Yoshio wondered at the connotation. What exactly was he planning to *do*? Whatever it was, it was likely unpleasant. Chances are it would be fatal.

They retrieved the bag and put it back over Yoshio's head. Then they hoisted him to his feet. They pulled him toward the door faster than he could walk with his ankles still bound, so they lifted him off the ground and carried him between them, each with one hand wedged into an armpit.

He bounced as they walked, sensing his surroundings in spite of the hood, and seeing the blueprint in his mind. The way their footsteps reverberated, he knew it was a narrow hallway with laminate floors. The sound was sharp and died on the air quickly. The walls were close. They turned into another hallway with low, industrial carpet, the steps now muted but still confined. He knew where they were now. The blueprint in his head fitted into the shape of the hallways perfectly. They were taking him toward a block of conference rooms. They set him down briefly as they unlocked another door, then went into a large room that smelled of sulphur, curry, and sweat.

The carpet in this room was much deeper, he noticed, as the footsteps were further dampened and he could feel the slight sponginess in their strides. His feet dipped down occasionally as they carried him, and he felt the carpet brush the toes of his shoes. Something felt wrong with the size of the room. It didn't match the blueprint; it felt too big.

There were other people here. There was movement and breath, warmth and bustle, the smell of cologne too liberally applied. The sulphur curry aroma overpowered it all.

He was brought closer to the smell, dropped only briefly to his feet before the backs of his legs were kicked in to force him to the floor onto his knees. The bag was ripped off his head, and he saw a man standing before him, a gaudy scene of opulence around the room. The man was the source of the odd smell. A hand from behind grabbed the edge of the duct tape and tore it from Yoshio's face, which stung as the light peach fuzz was yanked from his upper lip.

Behind the man was a wide, raised, stage-like dais covered in a thick, platinum-colored shag carpet, furnished with a massive chaise lounge, red with gold trim, quite literally sized for a giant. Yoshio hoped it was simply an art piece and not actually meant for someone that huge. There were smaller, normal-sized stools and chairs placed around it, all lush red, gold, and platinum. Some of these were occupied by suited men or women dressed for an extravagant ball. All of them were focused on Yoshio. In his peripheral vision, he saw other people that appeared to have stopped what they were doing to look his way.

The man in front of him was tall, muscular, and dashing. Dark, wavy, charcoal hair was combed back from his forehead to fall expertly along the side of his face. He looked like a movie star. In fact, he looked a lot like the actor, Hiroyuki Sanada. The similarity was striking. The only difference seemed to be that this man had glowing green eyes, and lips that were a little too red. His face was as sinister as it was handsome, as disturbing as it was welcoming.

"Welcome to my palace," the man said, his voice seductive but with a faint hint of a gurgle. "Isn't it marvelous?"

As he said this, Yoshio felt compelled to look around, to take everything in. So he did. He saw that the room was much larger than what the blueprint had shown. Some walls had clearly been knocked down. He saw the opulence, the extravagance, gold and platinum everywhere, polished statues, shimmering crystal chandeliers and glassware, perfectly kimonoed women, and black-suited men posing like idols. He also felt compelled to revel in it, to love every molecule of the visions that hit his eyes.

But he didn't.

It was gaudy and contrived. It was posturing and pretension. It was an empty show of wealth. And not at all to Yoshio's tastes.

The green-eyed man seemed taken aback when all Yoshio did was give a slight sideways grimace and a shrug.

He repeated his claim more insistently. "It is wonderful, no? The perfect home, fit for a king!"

This time Yoshio felt the intrusion in his brain more clearly, causing an involuntary shiver down his spine. It skated up his medulla oblongata and into his cerebral cortex, attempting to infiltrate and influence his very thoughts.

He could almost see it, like beams of green light, tripping his dopamine response and making him want to shout, "Yes! Truly a home fit for a king!"

But he didn't.

He only marveled at the process. He'd never experienced anything like it. Was it a chemical he had inhaled? Or something else? It seemed like it almost had its own consciousness, but it was undoubtedly attached to this man—if that's what he was, and Yoshio had his doubts—in front of him.

When no exuberant response came from Yoshio, only an intense look of curiosity, the man was clearly confused and infuriated.

"You will join me," he insisted. "You will succumb to my will. Everyone does! And your sneaking friends will join me too. They are both fighting, but they will fall shortly. None can refuse me! And with their abilities, they will become elite warriors for my cause."

The attacks on his brain were multiplied. They tried to convince him that the man before him would provide his every need, would make him rich beyond belief, make him loved and adored by the entire world, make all his fantasies realities.

But Yoshio could see the tricks and tactics like they were math. His brain argued point and counterpoint against everything that was thrown at him. He analyzed what it presented and immediately discovered the flaws in its methods. The math did not add up. He would not be deceived.

As he systematically dismantled the cranial onslaught, the handsome, glowing-green-eyed man before him began to change. His face distorted and expanded into a flabby, blubbery mess with fangs half as long as walrus tusks, a fat tongue slavering over deep red and blistered lips, bulbous green eyes drooping over the cheek bones. His hair shrunk away leaving only a stringy sort-of combover draped across its expanding skull, which now looked something like a cross between a giant frog and a huge balding orangutan.

His body bloated and ballooned into a gigantic reptilian worm, his arms and legs stretching into clawed appendages, two more limbs sprouting from his mid-section to make six. The clothes were absorbed into the whole, leaving a massive, pale orange body with a smooth belly and a scaled, nubby back, where bright green protrusions sprouted in dull spikes of varying sizes. Its tail like a long-petaled flower thrashed menacingly as the whole of it contorted in anger.

This was its true form. As Yoshio unraveled the thing's attempts to conquer his brain, he also unveiled the illusion that was hiding the beast's real appearance. He stumbled backward, unable to stop himself from a hard fall, his hands still tied, his right buttock landing on a pocket full of ball bearings. Th e hideous thing cursed in some unknown language and clawed at the carpet, which here was flecked with gold.

"I will destroy you!" it shouted, spitting up green globs of saliva. It scuttled forward on its six legs and thrust its disgusting, bloated face over Yoshio. Its red-veined eyes burned with hate and revulsion, but there was something else too. It desperately wanted to conquer Yoshio's mind, not just devour him. It hungered for dominance by imposed will, not brute force. Though it seemed to be considering the latter option.

Yoshio scrambled away and to his feet, not willing to take any chances, only then realizing the two thugs were no longer by his side. The creature followed and rose up above him on four legs, its massive girth blocking out the chandelier glow. Its huge mouth dripped saliva onto Yoshio as it glowered down, seemingly abandoning its attempts at mind control, and ready to devour him whole.

But then it stopped and looked away, as if at something beyond the room. Some new information had reached it, though Yoshio had heard nothing. A smile broke its horrible face, and it retracted back, putting all six feet back on the floor.

"One of your friends is mine," it gloated. "The other will be soon enough," it barked, as if this other was more problematic than it liked.

It looked around at all the people in the room, all of its minions ready and waiting to do its bidding and then back at Yoshio. "As will you!" it insisted with a defiant stare.

"Take him away!" it spat, and the two men who had carried him there came running.

Some of the men had guns. Some had swords or knives. At least one had a baseball bat. Many just had angry fists. They burst forward from the stairwell and elevator like twin geysers, all of them intent on Akio, whose back was to them as he faced the oncoming robot.

Masami glanced quickly at Akio and saw sparks and robot arms flying, severed with ease by the otherworldly metal of his blade. She turned toward the throng of yakuza surging forward, oblivious to her presence, and she rushed them, brandishing her invisible short sword. She didn't want to kill them but what choice did she have? They would slaughter Akio if she didn't stop them.

Or would they? What was Akio capable of now? Many would certainly die at his hands before they could bring him down.

She reached the first one, an unarmed man, his eyes bloodshot red and green like the rest. She tripped him and slammed the butt of the wakizashi's pommel into the back of his head, her focus intensifying into the hit, making the impact rigid and real. He went down, sprawling. The next she shoved with all her strength across the front line of the charge. Three more went down with him in confusion, and were trampled by their compatriots. Masami dove out of the way to not be trampled herself and then remembered she didn't need to as one man passed right through her.

Still getting used to this.

She had to focus on the electrostatic blue shimmer, with pinpoint attention on the object she needed to impact, then let go, like releasing a worry, and remain incorporeal. A ghost. It was far from easy in the chaos. She was surrounded by at least fifty crazed, puppet yakuza intent on killing someone she cared about. Her ability to switch her weapon from solid to incorporeal in the flash of a second was still spotty, but the adrenaline helped.

She slammed the butt of her sword into the back of another yakuza's shoulder and saw the tip of her blade cut into an adjacent man's ear. Blood spilled freely from it but he continued forward toward Akio, oblivious to the wound.

She sheathed the sword. Seeing the blood solidified the fact that she couldn't kill anyone. If they had been attacking her, she imagined she could do so in self-defense. But these men were not even aware of her presence, and probably not even in control of their own faculties. Killing them would be murder. She only needed to delay them, take their focus from Akio.

She sped through the rushing mob easier now, though far from perfect. Removing the possibility of killing had calmed her some. She became almost monk-like, tripping, punching, disarming those with swords and guns. She missed sometimes and was jostled when she let too much of her body's energy harden. But with her lips pressed tightly together, harnessing the immediacy of her need—*frustration and desperation*—she managed to get into a rhythm.

Breath in. Focus. Punch. Breathe out. Let go. Breathe in. Focus. Disarm. Breathe out. Let go.

A yakuza aimed to fire at Akio and she barreled into him, knocking his gun aside just as he fired, the bullet cutting through the back of another yakuza. She winced as he went down and was motionless, blood draining through the hole in his suit jacket.

I didn't do that. I wasn't aiming the gun. She tried to convince herself.

The men were unfazed by the death, and pushed toward Akio, trampling the fallen. Masami didn't even chance a glance in Akio's direction. There were too many yakuza to deal with. She had to stop them, slow them at least.

She persisted. Kicking shins, jabbing throats with rigid fingers—a move she had learned in a self defense class as a girl—slamming knees into groins, wrenching knives from grasps with a wrist twist and launching the weapons across the room, tripping, boxing ears, and poking eyes.

Daring a glance now, she saw they were nearly at the dismantled rolling bot, but Akio was no longer there. Sounds of metal clashing with metal resounded from deeper into the vast room.

The realization that the men were no longer after Akio was sudden, and Masami greeted it with mixed feelings. She had stopped them; she had succeeded, in spite of their overwhelming numbers. And she hadn't had to use her sword to do it. But now, it was clear they were searching for her.

En masse, they had stopped and begun to circle her immediate area, finally registering all of Masami's attacks on them, finally noticing that someone else was there. They were like a single, amorphous eye searching for something in the dark.

Exhausted from her efforts, the terror of this yakuza hive focusing on her was overwhelming. She moved out from the circle, pushing through three different men to do so. As she moved through them, they grabbed at her, now sensing her presence. All of the yakuza turned toward her at the same moment.

It was the body contact. The chill of her ghostly touch. She had to avoid touching them.

No. Contact is exactly what I want.

They couldn't harm her. She was a ghost. She could keep letting them sense her, keep them moving away from Akio, back to the elevators. Once she had led them far enough away she could continue her search for Yoshio and Miyahara. But she would have to lead them into some kind of trap. Lock them in a room somewhere, maybe. Where and how? She had a vague notion of the layout of the building from Yoshio's blueprints, but how would she lock half a hundred men in a room?

She had to try. Something would present itself. She tagged one on the shoulder with a ghostly hand. As she did, all of them turned toward her again, as if every one of them had felt her touch. She led them back toward the stairwell, passing her hand through one of them periodically to keep them following. She would lead them right out of the building if she had to, and try to block the door as she snuck back inside.

She made it back to the gaudy, bloody foyer, the four dead men crumpled and motionless on the carpet, severed heads at their feet. The still living yakuza grabbed and punched at the air around her.

A ding sounded.

The elevator doors opened, and a woman walked out. Her hair was blond and straight, and she was dressed like a traditional French maid in a white pinafore and short black dress. She walked toward Masami with a smile on her face.

She can see me.

Her gait was slightly stilted. Her skin was smooth and flawless. Her eyes were an unnatural emerald green. She reached out toward Masami with something else that glowed the same green, a gemstone the size of a grape mounted on a ring.

"Dodaman," the woman said.

And Masami dropped to her knees.

22

The Wrong Guy

etal sparked as cables were severed and robotic arms went flying. Akio carved through the four limbs with ease, the demonic blade slicing through steel like it was soft tofu. Glowing green stones fell from their grasps and were crushed between the polished floor and Akio's Chuck Taylors. This robot was unlike anything Akechi had fought before, but it was no more than a cart with arms and did not fight back.

Beyond its dismantled pieces, he saw a line of varied shapes coming his way, some rolling, some walking, some hovering. Green glows came from varying parts of each one, some brighter than others, all of them calling out for him to acquiesce.

Never.

They would not conquer his mind. They would never control him. He would destroy them all.

At once, three of the robots descended on Akio. Two small ones jetted toward him in the air, both wedge-shaped and winged, like tiny unmanned star fighters, buzzing on their drone-like chassis. Th ey zipped by his head, spinning him in circles as he slashed at them with his katana. More agile than expected, they avoided his swings as they zagged about, green glows emanating from their centers.

Akio swung in frustration, but the flying bots still managed to dodge the deadly edge of his katana. He lifted his sword for yet another cut, when what felt like the fist of a god slammed into his ribs. He felt his chest collapse as the air was knocked from him, and he was flung across the room. A crack like a single jolt of a jackhammer rang in his ears.

Pain like he had never felt before engulfed Akio's entire body. His chest burned like white hot, compressed coals, and he gasped for air, each breath escaping him, refusing to enter his lungs and stabbing like a thousand bee stings when it tried. His lungs had collapsed. Surely his rib cage had been crushed. He lay limp on his back, wheezing, unable to move. His eyes were closed, and all he saw was black and red. The blackness was his end enveloping him, the nothing he was destined for. The red was his blood, his anger at failing, his life slipping away.

As he lay there, crushed and spent, he recalled an oblong shape following behind the flying bots. Like a wide cannon it had seemed, a prone metal tree trunk on wheels. It looked as slow and ineffective as the cart with arms, so he had ignored it to focus on the maddening little fliers. Now he realized his folly. He cracked an eye open. Past the dark rim of the mask's eyehole he saw the contraption, heard its hydraulics hiss as it reloaded its large metal ramming post to nestle above its four wheels. It was a battering ram. Surely built to be rolled up to a stubborn door and deliver a sudden, violent burst of force. Akio had taken it point blank.

The pain in his torso ebbed outward to every nerve in his body, to his limp arms and fingers, to his inert feet and purpling toes. He began to feel cold.

Akechi never lost a battle. Only I could have accomplished that feat.

But it wasn't an all over cold, he realized. It was not the coldness of death enveloping him. It was specific. First a cold patch next to his arm. Then one by his ear. Then another directly on his stomach. They multiplied, appearing everywhere like they were being placed. They piled up around him, cold stones against his inflamed body. He heard buzzing overhead, coming and going, only to return again to add to the pile of cold stones. Stones that felt decidedly *green.*

Akio still could not see. He tried to reach up to remove the mask, but his arms wouldn't budge. He wanted it off him. He wanted it gone. He wasn't a warrior. He was a photographer. He was a son, a brother, and a friend. And he was dying.

Let me die with my own face.

Somewhere deep within him, another voice, rough and worn, said, *"Unwise. Leave the mask on."*

Air was carving its way into his lungs now, each lift of his chest a knife stab. He heard soothing sounds, not quite voices but suggestions, pleasing thoughts bathed in a tranquil green.

Ease your mind. Join the others who serve me. I offer peace as well as power. There is no more worry with me, only honorable servitude and joy. Unlimited wealth and power. Give in and let your fears subside.

As when he had crushed the gem in his hands, Akio again had the faintest feeling he knew this presence, the subtlest note of deja vu.

He wanted to give in. He wanted to let it revive him, care for him, grant him the respect he deserved. He wanted people to bow down before him, to grovel at his feet and do his every bidding. He wanted to be king of the world.

But he was dying.

I will heal you.

"Yes. Please."

I will make your dreams a reality.

"It's all I want."

But the rough voice boomed. *"No!"*

Akechi was clawing his way back into Akio's brain, demanding he not give in. But the soothing thoughts persisted. They comforted him.

He could feel cold, green stones all around him now. They covered him like a blanket. They touched everywhere but his face where the mask still rested. He was buried in them.

You are mine now. Everything is fine. Together we will conquer the world.

"Yes."

The pain in his body was overwhelming, but somehow the calming thoughts made it bearable.

Take off the mask. You don't need it anymore.

"*Yes. I don't want it.*"

I will destroy it for you.

"*Yes.*"

"*NO!*" Akechi's voice blasted into Akio's throbbing head.

Take off the mask and live, the soothing impressions continued.

But Akechi thrummed in his skull like a drum the size of a house, a drum in which Akio was at the center. "*Take off the mask and your life is forfeit. You will have failed your task. You will have lost everything.*"

"*LIES,*" the thoughts insisted, now turning into clear speech. "*I offer you peace. I offer you real victory.*"

Akio wanted the mask gone from his life. He didn't want to fight. He wanted an easy life. He wanted to end this suffering, to end all of it, forever.

"*Take off the mask.*"

"*AND YOU WILL DIE!*"

"*Take off the mask! Before it's too late!*"

He wanted to take it off, but he still couldn't move. The stones around his head fell away, and metallic claws began pulling at the edge of the mask. As it lifted, his skin pulled with it, his whole head coming up with the force. The mask would not let go.

"*You must do it,*" the soothing voice said, but there was something else in it. A hint of desperation. As Akechi's voice grew in strength, this first one began to feel sinister. "*Remove the mask now! Remove it and live!*"

"*No,*" Akechi intoned more calmly. "*Together we will slay this deceiver.*"

Akio felt a surge of vengeful energy course through him. It was full of rage and righteous murder, but it was honest. It was pure in its contempt. Before it the green voice trembled.

"*Remove the mask! Remove the mask!*"

"*No.*" Akechi's voice was utterly in control now.

"*Then die! Die for all I care!*"

The true thoughts of the green voice were laid bare as Akio's strength returned, as Akechi's spirit surged back into him.

He felt his chest repairing itself. Splintered bones shifted back into place and fused with their shattered counterparts, releasing the pressure on his torn lungs. Muscle lifted and reformed; his heart strengthened. The tingling rush of blood returned life to his limp extremities.

"I am healing you," insisted the green voice in a desperate waver. *"Do you not feel it? Do you not feel my power. This power can be yours!"*

Akio did feel it. But the lies no longer took hold. It was not the owner of the green voice that was healing him. It was the mask. It was Akechi's demon spirit rebuilding and reinvigorating him. Akio knew in that moment that he did not need any power from this green deceiver. He knew that the power was already his.

Air filled his raw lungs to capacity in one deep, life-affirming breath. He felt his fingers tingle with blood as they brushed against hair fibers tightly wound around the black bone handle of his katana. He pulled it to him, wrapping his fingers around it, feeling the purpose of his being refill him in the touch of the graceful weapon.

In one explosive leap Akio burst upward to his feet, green stones propelled to every corner of the large room. In two deadly swipes of his blade the circling drone bots, which had been covering him with the green stones, and had been so elusive before, lay sputtering in halves on the floor. The battering ram reversed, preparing for another charge. But as it came at him, Akio easily side-stepped it. The impervious, Hell-forged metal of his blade severed the hydraulics and rendered the battering ram useless. It lurched and the whole contraption flopped onto its side. It squealed and spun its wheels against the floor, and then gave a wheezing final whine.

But there was no rest for Akio.

Five more robots moved in to attempt to take him down. It was like a lineup of show pieces at a robotics fair.

There was a rolling boxy unit with a square head and two arms, a lead pipe in one clawed hand and a double-edged blade in the other. There was a dog with chomping metal teeth, a recorded loop of dog growls and barks coming from a built-in speaker. Next to it was another humanoid robot, looking something like a cross between C-3PO and a human-sized Iron Giant. Then came what looked like a small flying saucer, hovering about a meter off the ground. Last was a giant metal orb with spider legs tick-tacking loudly against the floor.

Akio took them down one by one.

The boxy robot was de-armed and headless before it could get one swing. The dog leapt at him with jaws wide only to chomp down on air as Akio side-stepped it and rendered it headless, too, its hollow, tinny barking silenced.

The humanoid droid reached at Akio with sparks crackling from its fingertips. The electricity arced toward him, and he instinctively put up his katana to block the attack. The lightning encircled the blade, lighting it up blue, and Akio braced for the shock.

But it never came.

The electricity seemed to be absorbed into the blade. Akio could feel it filling the Hell-born metal, collecting within it like a sponge absorbing water. As it did, he realized that the power was his to use. He could feel it invigorating him, and he wound the lightning around the blade like cotton candy around a paper cone. When it felt near capacity, he whipped the blade back at the robot.

The electricity blasted forward like a lightning spear, exploding against the metal man, sending shockwaves through its body. An arc of energy zapped out at the flying saucer next to it, sending it into a spin.

That's new.

Even Akechi had no memory of this power. For him the sword had only ever been half of a key to the lock securing his head in a box.

As it careened from the collateral lightning blast, the saucer began shooting bolts of green energy randomly about the room. Some hit the spider next to it and the collapsing humanoid bot. Akio tried to dodge, but two blasts hit him as well, one in the leg and another in his shoulder. They burned through his clothes, searing him like what he imagined a cattle brand would feel like, but they did not knock him down. They did not and could not stop him.

He closed distance with the spinning disc just as it seemed to recover its control. As Akio came up, he swung his blade down, intent on splitting the thing in half like the other flying bots. It shimmied to one side, but not quickly enough to save it. Akio's blade severed off a third of the saucer like a great hunk of cheese. This time it went into an uncontrolled backward spin, in flops and dives, until it crash landed into the floor, flames sprouting from its exposed interior.

This is not how life was supposed to go.

Akio lay staring at the worn and smooth hardwood floor of the kendo studio. It smelled like dust and sweaty feet. He saw bare toes draped with the loose, dark blue cloth of *hakama* trousers, as Ryu Nobunaga's twelve-year old laugh pelted down at him in short, derisive bursts of air. Akio's back stung from the hit of the bamboo *shinai*. How had Ryu managed to avoid his swing and nail him in the back? Again.

"Up, Tsukino!"

"Nobunaga! No points for the back!"

"He's turning around, Sensei," Ryu answered back. "Right as I'm swinging."

"Did I ask your opinion, Nobunaga?"

"No, Sensei."

"Ten laps!"

At least there had been some kind of retribution. But Akio hadn't learned. He kept turning on his swing, turning when he was attacked. His fight or flight instinct had been stuck on *flight* ever since he could remember. His parents had eventually pulled him out of kendo and sent him to judo class instead. His flight instinct served him better in judo, given that there was a lot of dodging and avoiding going on, but when it came to contact: grappling, throws, and so on, he often ended up on the floor again.

He was never meant to be a fighter. He had accepted that a long time ago. He wasn't very interested in fighting anyway, outside of manga and fantasizing about being a superhero.

He was interested in captured images, light and shadow, reality frozen in time. After a class trip to a photography exhibit, he couldn't stop thinking—or talking—about it. When his parents bought him a camera, he felt he held a magic talisman in his hands. He was born anew and had a confidence he had never before possessed. This was something he could be good at, something that could make him important. He took to it like a *kappa* to cucumbers.

His parents had thought it would only be a passing fad, but it stuck. They went from encouraging him to express his artistic side to lecturing about how unrealistic his career choice was. They told him he should go to university and study something practical like business or hotel management. Then he could work for them someday and run a hotel like his brothers.

Akio had insisted on his passion. It was a moment of strength he felt proud of. He applied and was accepted at the Tokyo College of Photography, did their two-year program, and was hired by the *Dainichi* right after graduation. In spite of his constant grumbling about wanting better assignments, everything was on course. He was young and still had plenty of time for advancement.

But now, instead of shooting photos, he found himself fighting again. Only it wasn't school bullies this time. He had graduated to yakuza and murderous robots.

And the most unusual thing about it was that he was winning.

This is not how life was supposed to go.

Akio had grown up in Yokohama, in a house on a hill overlooking the vast expanse of Kamiōka Cemetery. It was near a spot where throngs of people had gathered in the mid-nineteenth century to see American Commodore Perry return with his black ships, his second visit to Japan. Akio hated everything about it. His older siblings would scare him with stories of ghosts from the cemetery taking him away in the night. They would force him to stay too late among the gravestones after dark and make fun of him if he cried. They'd spin him around so he'd lose his sense of direction and then run from him laughing. Older siblings were just *great*. And Akio had five of them.

He was the youngest of six, three boys and three girls, an unusually large family in Japan. His father always joked that he would start moving the existing kids to their hotel if they had any more. But they didn't. And Akio was grateful. He didn't like hotel rooms and dreaded having to move into one. The idea of thousands of people having slept in the bed, bathed in the tub, and peed in the toilet made him nauseous.

Akio's father had never expected much of anything from him, and his mother had been loving only in a tend-your-wounds kind of way; he had never felt close to either of them. As the third son, he was left to his own devices much of the time. His mother tried to keep him social and athletic, but none of it ever took. He had much preferred being in his room reading manga.

He wished his parents had been like the innkeepers in Fujikawaguchiko. He and Masami had met Mr. Matsuoka in the worst of circumstances, after his wife had been killed by the Kofu Head Collector, the demon known as a namakubikamen. She had been its first victim, as far as they knew. From the story Mr. Matsuoka had told, it was clear that theirs had been a most loving marriage. They had been souls destined for each other, and had lived truly happy lives. They had never had children. They had been content with one another.

Akio wondered if he wanted children. He thought he did, but would a partner that understood and loved him be enough? Like it had been for Mr. and Mrs. Matsuoka?

If he did have children, he was sure of one thing: he would treat them all as equals. He would throw out the absurd family hierarchy and make sure they all respected one another the same. As it was, among his siblings, he felt brushed aside like lint on a sleeve. He never wanted his own kids to feel like that.

His eldest brother, Shoichi, was fated to take on the family business, and better him than Akio, who wanted nothing to do with that. The rest of his siblings, himself included, had to find their own destinies. And all but Akio had. Rather easily, it seemed.

Shoichi now ran a hotel in Ikebukuro, which he co-owned with their parents. He lived in Nerima Ward with his family, not far from their parents' home. When their parents retired, Shoichi would get the entire business.

Akio's second oldest brother, Keiji, managed their parents' inn on Chichi Island with his wife and children. Akio had thought his parents were crazy when they bought it, and that Keiji was even crazier to want to run it. Chichi Island was a twenty-four-hour long ferry ride from Tokyo. And the ferry only ran once or twice a week. There was no airport. They were pretty well stranded on that island. As beautiful as it was, Akio couldn't imagine living there.

But the inn had proven crucial to his plan to get on the Kofu assignment with Masami a few months previous. If he hadn't been able to convince Powell, their top photographer, to take his girlfriend Keiko in accounting on an island getaway with free accommodations, he wouldn't be in this situation at all. Maybe it had all been a huge mistake. And now he was indebted to Keiji for the favor.

His three sisters had all gotten married, and popped out children. Akio was an uncle seven times already. Four from his sisters and three from his brothers.

Mitsuko was the oldest sister, older than Shoichi by two years, and had married a doctor she met at university before he had earned his degree. Eriko was the fourth child, a year younger than Keiji, and had met a hotel owner when on vacation in Kobe, where she now lived with her family. Sachiko was the youngest girl, two years younger than Eriko and three older than Akio. She had met a software developer she worked with at a tech company, married him and became a full-time housewife.

Akio was the odd one out. Still single. The son who had "no prospects." His family called him the "artistic" one, and it wasn't a compliment. The job at the newspaper was at least something they could accept.

At times, when Akio took stock of his life, he wondered if he should have done the same as Keiji, and worked for his parents, managing one of their properties. He would be better off financially; that was certain. Maybe he would have met someone. Maybe he'd be starting his own family.

But it wasn't for him, and he knew it. The endless repetition of welcoming guests, cleaning rooms, balancing the books. The thought of it made him want to sleep for a week. He needed variety. He needed adventure. Photography granted him that. There were new stories every day. They weren't always the most exciting stories, but they weren't routine. He got to go to different parts of the city. He got to be an artist, capturing images in time that would never be repeated again.

That was far better than what his brothers did, even if they did make a lot more money.

Wasn't it?

He felt so different from his brothers that he used to wonder if he was adopted. But why would his parents adopt a kid when they already had five? Plus, he looked too much like Sachiko and had the same ears as Keiji.

How different his sisters were from Masami. They had all done a common thing for Japanese women: worked until they found a husband who could support them and a family. Then they quit their jobs, had babies, and became the queens of their homes.

It was one of the reasons Masami fascinated Akio. She was the complete opposite. She wasn't working to find a man. She was working to cut down all the men before her like bamboo to a machete, to prove that she was better than them. Or maybe just to get treated equally for once.

Why didn't Masami want what his sisters had? She could certainly have it. She wasn't unattractive at all. She would be quite beautiful if she didn't scare him so much. He didn't think any of the men at the *Dainichi* would want to marry her though. They liked submissive women. That was the talk anyway.

Masami would never go for any of them regardless. Akio wasn't sure she'd go for anyone at all. It seemed to him she just wanted to be the best reporter the world has ever known and take down the whole male-dominated system along the way. Let it crumble in a heap of her success.

Akio respected that. In fact, he kind of loved it.

He didn't understand Masami, but he was in awe of her.

But then, he realized, he didn't understand his sisters any better. Had they given up any chance of having their own identity by attaching themselves to successful men? Was their lot only to be someone's wife and mother? Or was Akio's understanding of identity completely broken? Being a wife and mother was a beautiful thing, after all.

And who am I to judge them? What have I done that's so important?

Yet even if he was nowhere now, Akio felt had bigger things to accomplish. As if his photography could somehow change the world.

But couldn't it?

If he snapped the right photo, exposed something sinister or beautiful to the world? He had to believe it could. That it could, at the very least, transform his place in it.

Yet now, here he was, thrust into the middle of something far more sinister than he could have ever imagined. And he had hardly taken any photos at all. His camera had been replaced with a sword. A demon samurai had taken up residence in his mind and body. Ryu Nobunaga, his twelve-year-old kendo nemesis, would not be laughing now.

Akio's muscles ached, and his head felt overfull with vengeful thoughts. His life had been hijacked and he wanted it back. Stings and all.

This is not how life was supposed to go.

And yet a deep-seated will compelled him. He was no longer sure if it was his or Akechi's.

The giant mechanical spider seemed to hesitate. It limped from side to side, having been injured by one of the flying saucer's laser blasts. Its large orb of a body lit up with a green glow, and a screen of some kind slid open from within it. An image projected itself into the air, a hologram of a sinister-looking but rather handsome face. It was an actor. The guy from *Murder on D Street*, *Ring*, and *Twilight Samurai*. He couldn't remember his name. Green eyes glowed hungrily above high cheekbones and a sharp, smoothly sloping nose. Red lips peeled back into a friendly sort of grin; the kind that said, *Let's have dinner sometime. You'll be the main course.* Charcoal hair waved down to just above his ears to provide a sweeping frame.

"I offer you the world," the lips said. "One last time. Take off your mask, and let the real you be born."

The words were infectious and emboldening. Akio wanted to heed them. He watched as the image shifted to reveal a hologram of himself.

In the image Akio stood tall, and looked impossibly handsome. Dressed in a designer suit, he smiled contentedly and leaned against a sparkling sports car: a shiny red Lykan Hypersport with black trim. Three beautiful women ran up to the holographic Akio, giggling and beaming just to be in his presence. They leaned against him and stroked his suit jacket and perfectly coifed hair.

Akio was entranced.

Could that really be me?

As he stood there watching this fantasy version of himself, so confident, so obviously rich and desirable, this playboy image, something else clicked in him.

Is this really want I want? Am I really that shallow?

He had had this fantasy before without a doubt. It had clearly been plucked straight from his head by the spider's operator. But as he looked at it now in 3D before him, it felt so empty. Yes, he wanted more confidence; he wanted more money; he wanted the attention of women.

But he didn't need *three*. He really just wanted one. He didn't want to be a playboy.

The women in the image felt equally empty. They didn't want that rich, handsome Akio for who he really was. They had the same shallow desires for wealth and power. They only saw fantasy Akio as a means to an end.

No, he wanted a real life with a real partner. He wanted a real connection with someone. He wanted what the innkeeper, Matsuoka, had with his wife before he lost her to the Kofu Head Collector, to Akechi. He had seen real love in the loss that Matsuoka was experiencing. It was heartbreaking, but what a life they must have had together; what a real and meaningful connection. What they had was worth more than any amount of money or false attention from hot women. It's what Akio truly wanted. And at that moment was the first time that the revelation sunk home.

This time it wasn't Akechi who pulled Akio back from the brink of giving in. It was Akio.

"No," he said aloud. "I'm afraid you've got the wrong guy."

He stepped through the hologram and planted the tip of his katana's blade into the center of the orb. It sunk into it easily, perfectly, not even cracking the glass screen. It slid into the center of the robot's brain, sparks vibrating in a spectacular display as Lichtenberg figures flashed across the surface of the orb, first blue, and finally, bright green. Then the hologram winked out, along with the orb, and the spider legs splayed outward as the robot collapsed to the floor.

Akio's chest still ached with the pain of the battering ram, and his breath wheezed softly in and out. He was not strained, however, and he was far from exhausted. He could still feel the bones and muscles mending within him. They were nearly as good as new. Perhaps even better.

He thought of Masami then. What had happened to her? He had told her to wait.

He looked toward the elevator and saw nothing, no one there at all. He had thought, in the vague chaos of his robot battle, that he had heard the pounding of footsteps, the breathing of warriors approaching. Had that only been a memory of a battlefield hundreds of years ago?

Where is Masami?

Now that the robots were destroyed and the gems crushed, he turned to go back and find her. But something else caught his eye. Over his shoulder he looked beyond the row of twitching, failed robot assailants that littered the ballroom floor, enemies that he had crushed. He saw the large, ornate double doors at the end of the room, framed in the same gold that was ladled like a rich child's diarrhea over nearly every visible surface.

Standing in front of them was a hulking, metallic figure. Eyes the size of tea saucers and the color of lime jelly beans locked on Akio.

23
Right Hand Man

kio stared up at the giant robot, which had planted its feet like a gunslinger at high noon.

Oh, hell. Not another one.

He wondered at the variety of robots he had faced already. The yakuza must have been experimenting on different models for some time now.

This one stood a head taller than the doors and had arms as big as postboxes, legs as wide as sake barrels. Its head was shaped like a giant can of Spam, broader than Akio's chest. It had two bulbous green eyes, a flat wide nose, and a wide mouth with what looked like car tire rubber for lips. Its hands were shovels with fingers, its feet as big as kids' drivable electric cars and equally equipped with wheels. It rolled forward to meet Akio, slamming its fists together with a boom that shook the building.

As it pulled back its arms from its self fist bump, its right hand retracted into the forearm and was replaced with a spinning blade of the kind you'd see on a table saw. The left hand disappeared as well, and what took its place looked rather like a short Gatling gun.

Oh, crap.

The sight of the gun spinning to life sent a nervous shiver through Akio. He had been able to dodge shooters with handguns because he could read their intent before they pulled the trigger. But this was something far worse than a single-fire weapon. And it was being wielded by a robot that didn't show the subtleties of human emotion and intentions. He had seen Gatling guns in action recently and was at a loss about how to stand against one. Akechi's memories would be of little help here.

One of the documentaries Akio had watched only weeks ago—an activity spurred on by Masami's dig at him for not knowing his history—was on the Boshin War. In a brutal reenactment, he had seen the Imperial forces' Gatling guns decimate the samurai troops. His mind replayed rows upon rows of samurai warriors falling to their bloody deaths. He was imbued with a samurai's life force, a demon samurai to be sure, but still . . . how well could he fare against something so destructive, something that had cut down samurai by the hundreds?

Time dropped to a slow motion roll as Akio's adrenaline escalated. The huge robot swung its spinning blade in a sideways figure eight, as if daring Akio to approach it. At the same time the whir of the gun pitched higher and higher as the robot raised it to bear on Akio. Any second now it would riddle him with bullets.

A deep breath.

He dove to his right. Bullets sprayed like a rain of death. They splinked and ta-konged against the polished floor, ripping chunks from its surface, clinked and racketawed against the line of prone robots behind him. He rolled and dove again, sliding to the front side of a liquor bar in the corner of the ballroom. Bullets splintered the gold-painted wood but subsided when Akio moved beyond the robot's sightline. The spinning gun wound down, the pitch decreasing to a halt, as did the sound of the blade.

Akio heard the metal ogre moving again, rolling forward with its wheeled feet. His breath slow but heavy, he slipped over and behind the bar. There was a door there. He'd try to escape through it. Maybe there was a back way out.

An internal battle raged inside him, as he avoided the physical confrontation. The huge robot whirred closer from around the corner, and the demon samurai's will wrestled with Akio's. Akechi was an undefeated warrior. He did not run from battle. But Akio was a scared-out-of-his-mind photojournalist. He would run like hellfire blistered his feet.

"I will not run. This warrior is beatable."

"I will not die! Can't we just make a tactical retreat? Come at it again from behind? No shame in that!"

The spinning of the blade began again, and the gun kicked into rotation.

"A tactical retreat. I can accept that. For the moment."

Akechi knew well the teachings of Sun Tzu. As much as he lusted for battle, he understood that to be victorious one must know when to fight and when not to fight. So he yielded.

Akio tried the handle to the door behind the bar.

Locked.

Dammit!

He flattened his back against the door. In front of him was the bar counter, ashtrays interspersed along it. A pack of cigarettes had been left behind next to a half-finished drink and a Zippo lighter. Past the bar was the expanse of the ballroom. Round tables with chairs sat along the edge of the wall. The golden piano rested in front of the gold curtain, stage left, at the far end of the room, closest to the freight elevator.

Where is Masami?

He noticed a body lying on the floor in the distance, a black suit crumpled and still as death.

The thought of a similar fate for Masami struck him hard.

She can turn invisible and walk through walls. She's fine.

It had felt strange being invisible. When Masami had taken him into the ghost world with him, it had been extremely unsettling. It was a gray misery that felt familiar to Akechi, an in-between place where the samurai had been powerless.

Akio didn't want to do it again.

The robot moved into view at the end of the bar. It was a hulking machine made for one purpose: to destroy anything in its path.

Trapped against the door, Akio had only one idea and he hoped it would work. Without giving it further thought, he grabbed a liquor bottle, ready to heave it at the metal beast. The label caught his eye. It was a Yamazaki, 18-year-old, single malt whisky.

He had seen a bottle worth nearly 30,000 yen at the Don Quijote store near his apartment. It had been one of those moments he had felt depressed for not being rich enough to buy it. He had bought a bottle of spiced rum for 1100 yen and drank it alone, imagining it was something more refined.

Screw it, he thought, and hurled it at the robot. The bottle shattered across its chest, the pricy elixir coating it and dripping down its metal body. Akio began to grab whatever bottles were closest and heaved them with all his strength. Clear stuff like Absolut, Wokka, and Iichiko. More whiskies: Jack, Macallan, Hibiki, Hakushu. He picked up a Yamazaki 25, paused and put it back, then picked up a Taketsuru 17 and lobbed that instead.

The bullets had started to fly somewhere around the Iichiko. Akio grabbed, ducked, lobbed, and ducked again. Repeat. A rage was building in him as the end of the bar was coming apart from the barrage of bullets. Soon he would be fully exposed. The robot was drenched in alcohol now, steam coming off it as the heat from its inner workings evaporated the expensive spirits. The bullets stopped as the gun wound down again, and the spinning blade started to carve through what was left of the bar, the screeching of steel into wood like a shrill, demonic scream.

Akio reached up to the top of the counter and grabbed the Zippo. A single click lit it, and he hurled it at the drenched death machine. The lighter hit it squarely in the face and dropped down its body, a line of fire catching across its chest.

The whole of it went up in flames.

The robot turned about, waving its gargantuan arms, knocking at itself to no avail. It cut a gash into its own side and stopped. It eyed its burning body, seeming to search its databanks for a solution to a problem outside of its programming.

Akio remembered his katana, and realized that it could be used to slice things that weren't enemies. He unsheathed it, and in four strokes had cut a new, smaller door into the locked one at the back of the bar. He pushed the wood through, and it clattered into a room on the other side.

Darkness again. Yoshio's hands were still tied, and his mouth had been re-taped, but he had a much clearer picture of the supply closet and the hallways that led to the beast's throne room. The men had not bothered to bag his head when they brought him back to his little prison.

He still had the ball bearings in his back pocket, and still thought they would be useful but wasn't sure for exactly what yet. He only knew that his right butt cheek ached from landing on them.

He heard muffled but violent noises through the walls: an electric saw spinning, what sounded like rapid gunfire and wood ripping. Some of the sounds shook the building. *Is there a battle? Are they remodeling?* The sounds weren't distinct enough for him to be sure, but it sounded like it was on this floor and not far away, only muted by the walls in between.

In his mind he analyzed everything in the room he had seen before the lights went out and everything he remembered from fumbling in the dark before. He had noticed, before being roughly tossed back in, that the light switch was on the outside wall, so he would have to rely on his photographic memory in the dark.

First, the door lock: it was an old school, keyed doorknob, not electronic. There wasn't a bolt, just the basic latch. Sensei Miyahara had only briefly taught him the bare basics of lock picking, but he had no practical experience, as it was "not crucial to your training yet," the master had said. Nor did he have any tools on him for such an attempt. But there was no doorframe overlap on either side, so if he could slip something thin between the door and frame, he should be able to push the latch back in. He only had to find something suitable in the dark with his hands tied behind his back.

The plastic ties that bound his hands were tighter than before, digging into his wrists. It would be worth trying to remove them; if only he had seen a sharp edge somewhere in the brief moment before the door shut and the lights went out. But he hadn't. And his arms were cinched too close together to be able to swing his legs through and bring his hands to the front.

He worried about what the yakuza would do the next time the door opened. If they saw no reason to keep him, they might just shoot him right there in the storage closet. From Yoshio's time studying with Miyahara, it was clear that the monster he had seen, the beast that had probed his mind and tried to dominate his will, was a demon. What else could it be?

It clearly had some kind of mind-dominance ability, and Yoshio wondered at it still. How had the demon gotten inside his head? How had it transmitted its thoughts, and even more so, its will? It wasn't possible in Yoshio's view of the world.

Sure, there were hypnotists and even expert marketing gurus who could get you to say and do things, but actual mind-control? He couldn't get his head around it. But he had felt the demon in his mind; he had recognized the intruding, manipulative thoughts.

And it all added up. That's how the Tezuka-gumi was expanding so rapidly. Somehow the demon was connected to the gems, able to use them at a distance to dominate the yakuza's minds, to control them like puppets.

But it had failed at controlling Yoshio. A fact that had made it very angry. Yoshio had felt its desire to control him much stronger than its desire to kill. But that feeling might not hold. Having failed at its wish, it may want to remove all evidence of that failure. His time was running out.

And it said it had captured one of his friends.

Had it been telling the truth? It seemed too pleased with itself not to be. But who? He quickly calculated:

Akio

- Most blunder-prone
- Least intelligent
- Might not remember how to fight
- Mask seems to protect him from mind-control

Masami

- Smarter than Akio
- Able to turn invisible
- Demons might still be able to see her
- Mind-controlled yakuza probably can't

His instincts said Akio. But there were too many variables. This demon stuff was still too new to him, too unscientific.

Then he realized there was a third possibility:

Sensei Miyahara

- Very smart, but smart enough to fend off mind-control?
- Extremely resourceful
- Expert fighter
- Was already captured, right?

It must be Akio. That was the only logical answer. In any event, Yoshio was on his own now. He had to escape and find Miyahara. The sensei would know what to do.

So where to start?

This was hardly a high-security prison. It was a simple storage room with a simple lock. If he still had his wallet, he could slip his school ID through the door frame and push back the latch, but they had taken that and his mobile phone when he was captured. He needed to find something else.

His mind quickly scanned his memory of the room: cleaning supplies of the usual variety, containers of what seemed to be robot parts, shelves full of office supplies. Clipboards were too thick, folders too flimsy. *There must be something.*

Through the walls he heard what sounded like glass breaking. The gunfire noise resumed, rapid but dull plunking like a rivet gun into wood.

Postcards.

He saw the stack in his mind, advertising the OfficeBoy Helper Bot. They were laminated and might be thick enough to move the latch. He moved carefully over to it.

On his tiptoes, his back to the shelf, he strained to reach the stack with his wrists bound tightly together. His fingers brushed against something on the shelf just below, and he felt a vibration pulse across his fingertips. It felt like an electrical surge but without the shock. He carefully put his hand on the thing. It was a small metallic block, about the size of two sticks of a Kit Kat bar, thin wires protruding. It pulsed like a long slow heartbeat but did not cause any pain to the touch. He felt a small switch on it. It was some kind of power source, he was sure of it. He dropped it into his other back pocket and hoped he wouldn't be landing on it later.

He reached to feel around the rest of the box, but a crash reverberated through the walls, startling him. His fingers caught the edge of the cardboard and sent its contents clattering across the floor.

The light went on in the hallway.

Shit.

The door opened again and light blasted into the storage room. Yoshio quickly squatted back down to the floor, his hands brushing a can of compressed air that rolled away.

The same two men entered.

"What's with the banging around, punk?" the shorter one said, and the tall one added, "Are you trying to get someone's attention?"

Yoshio didn't respond.

"It worked, didn't it?" said the tall one, and the short one answered, "Worked like a charm. But maybe not the attention you were hoping for. And we were coming anyway—"

"—so there was no need," the tall one finished with a little nervous laugh. "Your presence is requested."

They seemed unnerved by the violent sounds nearby. Yoshio immediately capitalized on it.

"What's all that noise?" he asked. He had a feeling he wouldn't be coming back to the storage room. He had to improvise.

The men looked at one another blankly and said nothing.

"It sounds like a war zone," Yoshio added.

Together, the men turned back to the teenager and said, in creepy unison, "A problem is being handled. It will be over soon."

"Sounds like a big problem." Yoshio said. It had to be one of his new companions, maybe even Miyahara. He hoped, whoever it was, that they would be victorious. They had to be. "Maybe you should go and see if they need any help," he added, hoping against hope they would leave him alone.

The men said nothing, only stiffening in anger at his comments. Together they hoisted him up again and carried him down the hallway, bouncing between them. This time, before reaching the large, shag-carpeted palace of the green-eyed beast—which had formerly been four different conference rooms, Yoshio calculated—they turned and entered another door, taking him down a hallway that ran along the front of the building, past offices and elevators, skirting the palace room to its other side. The noises of battle were further away here but still audible. They took him through a door with an etched sign that read "Hozumi Nakama, CEO, Nakama Robotics." It opened on a small office, an obvious underling's desk, a final room before seeing someone important. The desk was empty and looked disused.

Next to the desk was a polished cherrywood door. The two brutes carried Yoshio to it, but before the shorter one could knock, the door opened. An older, sharp-suited man stepped through the door, quickly shutting it behind him. In that brief moment Yoshio had seen something large and black with dark glass windows—something a person could step inside—behind a huge, ebony desk. And was there a woman in the room? It had looked like a blonde woman putting on a maid's uniform.

"We'll talk out here," the man said, pointing to the small desk. He stood by the dusty chair behind it but did not sit, and began tapping an unlit cigarette in the dust on the desktop. Yoshio was roughly shoved into the chair opposite.

"No need to treat our guest so poorly," said the seated man in a flat, emotionless way that said he didn't really care one way or the other how Yoshio was treated.

"Remove the tape, please," he continued, "so I can talk to him."

The tape was aggressively peeled off, and Yoshio stifled a whine.

"Gently," the man said dispassionately, after the fact. "Now, let us talk in peace," he added, and shooed the two brutes out of the room.

When they had gone, the man smiled at Yoshio. It was an empty smile, utterly unreflected in his eyes. He lit his cigarette, the dust from the desk sparking on it.

"You must have questions," he said. "You've seen some strange things, haven't you?"

Yoshio didn't answer. He wanted to let this man give him more information before he said anything.

"Do not be afraid of the demon," he said. "He gets a little grandiose at times, thinking he is running things. Rest assured he is not. He is under my control. I won't let him harm you."

The words were hollow and insincere, and Yoshio put a couple of things together immediately. For one, this man's tired, dead eyes, bloodshot and tinted green, made it clear he was *not* in control. The name on the door was another clue. It wasn't his. It was the name of the former owner and founder of Nakama Robotics. And Yoshio knew the man in front of him from photos in the yakuza fan mags. He was Hiromi Kumamori, the godfather of the Tezuka-gumi. And knowing the vanity of the yakuza, this man in particular, Yoshio was certain he would have removed the old name and replaced it with his own immediately. The yakuza boss had not been in charge for a while now.

"I want to offer you something better than he did," Kumamori continued. "Yes, I can offer you riches and power. I can even get that cute girl you've had your eyes on to like you back. But I don't deal in threats. Threats are amateurish, and I'm sorry you were made to endure such oafish, artless tactics."

Yoshio stayed quiet and let him ramble. *Cute girl?* He wasn't even interested in girls; knowledge was his only passion. The yakuza was grasping. Or the demon in this man's head was playing good cop, bad cop with itself.

"What I want is for you to join us of your own accord," the yakuza boss continued. "It's clear you are young, but the earlier you start, the faster you'll be able to move up through the ranks. And with your obvious intellect in resisting the demon, you will be leading our men in no time at all."

Obvious intellect. Had the demon told him what had transpired between his mind and the demon's? Or was he speaking to the demon now?

Yoshio had to admit that, on a certain level, the idea of joining the yakuza did intrigue him. What would it be like to be on the inside of a syndicate? He could learn all about the inner workings of the gangs. But he was certain he'd quickly get bored of it. And he may be forced to do some unsavory things. By then he might be stuck.

There were plenty of books written by people who have been inside that would satisfy his curiosity just fine, he decided.

Ultimately the idea was irrelevant. The yakuza weren't even running this show.

"You've heard of the Tezuka-gumi?" the puppet godfather asked.

"Yes," Yoshio answered.

"So you know the power we have then?" he asked rhetorically and paused for effect. "We are soon to be the most powerful yakuza organization in all of Japan."

"I've read about you in *Truth Serum* and in your own magazine, *Tezuka-gumi Shinpo*. I know who you are."

"Really?" The man seemed genuinely surprised and pleased now. The dead green eyes perked up. "You know of all the good we have done then. The Tezuka-gumi is a noble organization."

"Yes," Yoshio said. "I know the Tezuka-gumi, but I know who you are too. You are Hiromi Kumamori, the most respected boss to ever lead the yakuza. Your men were the first to provide help after the Fukushima disaster. You have the reputation of being stern and immovable with your loyal *koban*, but compassionate toward Japan. The way your brotherhood is expanding is proof that you are respected far and wide."

Of all Yoshio's skills, flattery wasn't high on the list, but he knew its effect, and he used it the same way a scientist would introduce a pathogen into a petri dish. Also, his memory was unparalleled. He pulled his words straight from an article he had read in the syndicate's own propaganda rag.

"I also heard about the incident with the snake," Yoshio added. "Very impressive, sir."

"Yes," Kumamori replied, perking up even more. "No creature or man shall take my power."

The incident with the snake was a glamorized piece about how a rival boss had sent a live, poisonous snake to Kumamori in order to kill him and stop his "inevitable rise to power." According to the magazine, Kumamori grabbed the snake from the air as it lunged from the package, looked calmly at the venom-spitting reptile, and tossed it across the room. As it flew through the air, he flung his *tanto* after it, pinning it to the wall with the long, curved knife. Then he instructed his men to have a belt made of it, using the snake's head and fangs for the clasp.

Yoshio couldn't help his gaze drifting to Kumamori's belt, which was distinctly not snakeskin. The yakuza boss shifted his jacket to cover the buckle, and he quickly sat, putting his waistline behind the desk. But his stiff smile had grown more genuine.

"Joining us seems a foregone conclusion," he said. "You have done your research and know we are the best. And we have the most powerful boss," he added somewhat awkwardly.

The numbers danced and crunched in Yoshio's mind. What could he gain from agreeing to join up with them? Was this his way out? Would he be freed and allowed to go about his business?

Of course not. It was just another trap. The disgusting demon that had probed his brain was running the yakuza boss like a sock puppet.

He couldn't trust him—and wouldn't, even if he wasn't being controlled by a demon—but maybe he could buy some time.

"Yes," Yoshio answered. "It would seem so." He forced an awkward smile at Kumamori. Yoshio had never really gotten the hang of smiling on purpose. "What would be my first assignment?"

The boss lit up with devious glee. "I will show you." He stood up from the desk. "Follow me."

The two brutes joined them again once they were out of the office. Yoshio took a spot next to his new false mentor and the two thugs brought up the rear.

"All of our new recruits start in this position," the boss said as they walked. "I find it is the best way to keep them loyal. They get to see first hand the good we are doing, the message we are spreading, so to speak. And the more they do it, the stronger their resolve becomes to follow me to victory and make Japan great again."

"Victory over what?" Yoshio asked.

"The hearts and minds of Japan," he answered matter-of-factly. "We will take back our country from the influence of the West and make Japan great again. We will expel the foreigners and be one race."

Something stirred in Kumamori as he said this. It didn't feel like the demon's influence on him; it was his own dear wish, and the demon was only playing on it.

"What then?" Yoshio asked.

Then . . . the world," he said, his passion subsiding. "Japan will rule absolute, and I will make it happen." This was the demon's wish. Yoshio guessed that the real Kumamori would just as soon close their borders and cut off all relations with the outside world.

"To what end?"

Kumamori paused, as if the answer should be self-evident, then said, "Peace, of course."

Yoshio said nothing, but he was almost disappointed in the the demon's goals. Its desires were no different than any small-minded, egotistical despot, deluding themselves about gaining ultimate control of the planet. If there was a sole monarch of the world, then it follows there would be peace. All enemies have been crushed. Where is the opposition? None of these would-be tyrants ever consider the fact that people are not simply statistics. They have individual needs and minds of their own and often won't stand for a dictator's edicts. Crushing a group does not constitute peace when that group has been displaced and demoralized.

The thought struck him then that perhaps everything wasn't math, after all. Or, at least, math wasn't everything. Human life was more than that. And it made sense. He had never been able to use math to mix socially or to write poetry. There were formulae at work there that had always eluded him. Perhaps there wasn't a formula at all. And that was what lost him.

Of course, the demon wanted to remove any personal views or thoughts. It wanted to strip individuality and humanity. If it was powerful enough to hold the minds of Earth's population in its own and bend every person to its will, it could affect a kind of peace. But a people subjected and oppressed, whether they know it or not, would never be a true peace.

The yakuza boss looked down at him almost proudly. "With your brain," he said, "you could be my right-hand man."

24

Chaos

A kitchen greeted Akio as he stepped through the newly carved doorway and onto the former piece of door, which lay flat in front of him. It was immaculately clean and organized. Pots and pans hung neatly around a center island counter. The industrial-size stove and grill sparkled. Large freezer and refrigerator doors were on the far side. A swinging door led back to the ballroom. Another exit was in the far wall, and the kitchen appeared to span the area past the large double doors from the main room. It looked like another way into the space beyond. The crazy yakuza boss, that actor from the hologram, or whoever was running this show, must be there. It was where he had to go. He had to put an end to this and rescue Yoshio and Miyahara.

Masami would find him. She had to. They would meet up at some point.

Akio started for the far door when he heard the whirring of the Gatling gun spinning up behind him. He dove behind the island as bullets sprayed in a whirring mechanical chaos; pots and pans clinked and pinged the music of his doom. He felt the heat of an inferno trailing the devastation.

Peering around the island during a brief respite of bullet hail, he saw the huge metallic ogre, now consumed in flames, carving an even larger opening in the doorway—larger than the door itself—to force its way through. Akio had made something already ferocious even more terrifying. The fire hadn't even slowed it down. Now it was a saw-spinning, bullet-riddling, giant fire monster. He ducked back quickly before its giant flaming robot head turned his way.

While Akio panicked, the sensible war general that was Akechi evaluated and plotted. The robot had to run out of bullets eventually. And the flames must be doing some kind of damage, even though they didn't appear to be. But he couldn't just wait it out and hope. He had to act.

As if on cue, the robot started moving again, but it wasn't rolling now. It was clomping with its large feet, stamping loudly through the narrow spaces in the kitchen, each step a metallic crunch. When it moved around one side of the island, Akio cut back to the other, silently releasing his katana.

He moved quickly, keeping his body below the countertop, and snuck up behind the walking inferno. Flames licked up the robot's legs and back, but they appeared to be sputtering. It looked as if it was having some trouble walking now. Heat blasted off it like an open furnace. With ninja-like stealth, Akio raised his katana to strike. But a polished metal pan betrayed him. He saw the robot's reflection in it where it hung. And the robot saw him.

It spun around, too close to catch Akio with its saw blade, but its heavy arm nearly clocked him across the head before he ducked and rolled to the side, diving back behind the island. The arm blade continued to whir as the Gatling gun joined in the chorus. Bullets flew again accompanied by a horrendous screeching sound as a huge chunk of metal-framed wood was cut out of the island. Splinters sprayed like water from a lawn sprinkler.

Akio crouched against the cabinets, shaking. He wanted to run, out of this hellish building and back into his safe little apartment. He wanted to hide under the covers and never come out again.

But Akechi would not run.

The samurai's anger filled Akio; a primal force surged through his veins, and he burst forward, rounding the island and heading directly toward the blackened, half-flaming, metallic beast. He dove under the gun arm, bullets whizzing through the air by his ear. His katana swung up and through the joint of the giant arm, severing it. The Gatling gun clattered to the floor, still spraying bullets that ricocheted in spurts off pans and the metal freezer door. Akio danced to keep behind it as it bounced and lurched on the floor, clanging against the robot itself, and unbalancing it. The robot teetered, its saw blade carving a gash into the vents over the grill.

The bullets ceased abruptly, a plume of smoke issuing from the severed metal arm, and Akio took his chance. He lunged, removing a leg from the robot with ease. It collapsed to the floor but quickly popped up into a sitting position.

Its metal blade still whirred but now in fits and starts, sounding like a handful of nuts and bolts in a clothes dryer. The fire had done some damage after all. Seated, the robot was only as tall as Akio, and it swung its blade toward him in seeming desperation. Akio leapt backward, narrowly avoiding the ragged, chattering teeth.

The surface flames had died out now, but the robot still radiated an immense heat, and its eyes glowed a frightening green. Electrical disturbances began to spasm randomly across its body, arcing and sparking in the joints and at the exposed severed limbs. A new flame lit up in one armpit as the electricity fried something within. Another started at its neck.

Akio raised his sword, measuring each flailing swing of the sputtering saw arm, preparing to swoop in, sever the remaining arm and then its oversize head. But before he found his moment, the robot issued a final metallic screech as its blade ground to a halt, the arm frozen like a steel beam salute. The green fire in its eyes faded into dull, inert stone. A light crackle was the only sound as the internal workings of the beastly machine slowly burned.

Akio lowered his blade and stared dead-eyed at the hunk of metal in front of him. Inside he collapsed onto the floor in a puddle of exhaustion and curled up into a fetal ball. But his body stood still and imposing, a statue of a warrior overlooking a bloody battlefield, a demon that knew nothing of exhaustion, poised to destroy any that dare confront him, a spirit that would battle its way to the end of time.

Yoshio knew that Mr. Kumamori, the godfather of this demon-controlled syndicate, didn't actually care one bit about him, smart or not. The yakuza tended to keep to themselves and not involve the "citizens under the sun," as they called average civilians. There were enough young angry men willing to be recruited. He had no need to bother with some brainy teenager.

But Yoshio wasn't really talking to Kumamori. He was talking to the demon. He was sure of it now. And the demon had a grudge, so it was trying a new tactic.

It had lost its cool before, particularly when Yoshio had seen through its disguise. Now it was trying the *good cop* method, trying to convince him that it was the smart move, and that he could only come out on top. It was an ego play. The demon had to believe it was smarter than everyone else. Yoshio smiled and nodded, hoping to convey that he was all in, that he would be honored to be Kumamori's right-hand man.

"But first," the boss continued after acknowledging Yoshio's smile, "you start here." And he pushed open a door that led into the demon's throne room.

As before, the scene was a gaudy one. The precious metals theme was overwhelming. Gold-flecked carpet covered the floor up to the large dais at the back wall where it turned to platinum shag. Gold-framed paintings hung throughout, and golden statues stood at intervals between them. The paintings were inconsistent in style and theme, some of them classic *ukiyo-e* works, some of them modern, surrealist, or impressionist. One looked like a photograph. Their content ranged from sweeping landscapes to everyday objects. The only consistency was the golden frames, which didn't complement most of the works. The statues were a hodgepodge as well: a bent leafless tree, a man playing a saxophone, a giant rotary telephone. All gold. One was a statue of a Buddhist god with green gems carelessly pasted onto its eyes. Yoshio had the feeling all of them had been stolen. *Get anything made of gold* had been the demon's command.

People moved about performing one duty or another, but some were simply conversing and drinking as if this were the not-to-be-missed social event of the year. Most of the men were in suits, a couple in tuxedos, but others wore casual slacks or jeans, with or without dress jackets. A handful were in kimonos and looked like proper samurai, a couple men even wearing traditional *hakama* trousers. The women were mostly in kimonos, but a few had on eighteenth-century Western-style ball gowns. Mixed in with them were younger men and women dressed in Harajuku-style cosplay. Four men that he hadn't seen before were in full samurai armor. They stood flanking the oversize chaise lounge, which was now occupied by the bloated worm demon, its fat body and tail draping off onto the carpet.

Did they not see it as he did? Did they still see the actor?

Some of them must. There were men and women gathered around the demon, primarily around its fat mid-section and tail. Some were on stepladders, while others stood on the floor or leaned on the chaise lounge. Small gilded basins, half a meter long, were scattered between them, and they appeared to be fawning over the demon in some way. They must see it, unless they thought it was something else, fooled into believing it was something natural.

Kumamori led Yoshio toward the demon, and he saw what the people were doing. They were collecting green outcroppings from the beast; the spikes and nubs and other protrusions of glowing green that jutted from the demon's back were going into the basins. The mind-controlling gems grew from the demon itself.

The closer they came, the more Yoshio could hear the demon's voice probing his mind. Each volley of words was like an attempt to pick a lock, like a thief tunneling under the wall, a rat trying to solve a maze. But Yoshio's ratiocinative brain was an impenetrable fortress.

For now.

He was concerned he might slip. If he let his guard down for only a moment, some deception might trigger his baser nature, his need for safety and nurture. If so, he might give in and allow the demon control. He had to remain vigilant.

It was a cacophony of voices by the time they reached the demon: pushing, pleading, and threatening. They were convincing and charismatic. They appealed to his sense of pride, his sense of caring, his longing to fit in, and his loneliness of superiority. Some of them struck home, but Yoshio knew them for what they were. He remained a fortress.

As he looked at Kumamori he saw all the same adjuration in the yakuza boss's eyes, streaming out at him like venom. He looked at the demon's face and saw its bulbous eyes were closed. It looked enrapt in the gem-extraction process like it was getting a spa treatment, its ugly grin showing a lewd pleasure.

The puppet godfather brought Yoshio right up to the long, swollen, orange body and tail. Fourteen men and women were collecting the green excretions. Th ey were utterly mindless drones, mechanically extracting the stones easily with gloved fingers and dropping them into the golden basins, which he saw now were each lined with a silk cloth.

Kumamori was smiling with unnatural delight at the process, the stones, and the people.

"This is where you want me to start?" Yoshio asked flatly.

Kumamori's head jerked toward him, almost as if he had forgotten Yoshio was there. "Yes," he said with some concern. "But only to learn the order of things, to gain a better understanding of our great organization and what we will accomplish. A mind like yours isn't satisfied with the simple results of a process; it wants to know every detail of the machinery along the way. In truth, your talents are wasted here, and you won't remain long. You will be promoted to a station more suitable to your significant abilities in no time."

Yoshio only nodded.

"You can start now if you like," Kumamori said. "There's room right here." He indicated a narrow space between a man and a woman where a cluster of green stones sprouted from the demon's body. "You can share the basins of those closest to you. Just be sure to place the gems gently down on the silk. We wouldn't want them damaged."

Gems. They did look like rough gems, but in reality they were more akin to crystalized mucus.

Kumamori looked at him the way a new pet owner might look at a pit bull he'd just rescued from the pound. Yoshio turned and displayed his hands still tied behind his back.

"Ah, yes," the yakuza boss said. And without saying another word or even gesticulating, a yakuza hurried over and cut the zip ties with a tanto he had tucked in his belt. Another yakuza appeared and handed him thin latex gloves.

"To keep the gems from slipping and protect them from contamination," said the godfather.

Yoshio flexed his fingers in front of him and looked at the red lines on his wrists from the zip ties, then slipped on the gloves. He said nothing, only raised his eyebrows briefly as if to say, *okay, I'll get started*. He turned toward the giant, orange-skinned body and stepped in between the man and woman. He glanced back at Kumamori who smiled approvingly, then turned and walked away.

Yoshio wasn't sure what the demon would accomplish by having him assist in this *gem* harvest. Perhaps it simply wanted him close so it could keep up the barrage of thoughts. Whatever the reason, playing along and having his hands free was better than being locked in a supply closet. There could be an opportunity to escape at some point. He had to stay alert. In the meantime, he could learn more about what was going on. He welcomed the *better understanding* that Kumamori suggested he acquire. Knowing all the ins and outs was exactly what he was after.

"With knowledge comes opportunity and advantage," Sensei Miyahara had often said at the kendo dojo. "Without knowing the battlefield and the players on it, it is difficult to form an effective path to victory."

Yoshio reached out slowly to grab the closest bit of crystalized ooze in the cluster in front of him. The feel of it was smooth, somewhere between a polished stone and costume jewelry. It was easy enough to get a grip on it. It seemed to want to cling to his gloved fingers. There was a slight tug needed to free it, but then it slipped out easily. The pore it left behind lingered open briefly, showing the deeper orange-red flesh beneath. Then it slowly closed up like a flower on a cold night, like a tiny sated mouth. Yoshio shuddered. He set the chunk of green carefully into one of the basins.

As he had touched the gem, the intrusive thoughts strengthened, but Yoshio had now gained a confidence in defeating them. The tactics seemed to repeat themselves. It felt like the demon had exhausted its arsenal and had no more tricks. It must have thought if Yoshio was surrounded by so many gems and maintained direct contact, he would surely be overwhelmed. But the opposite happened. He quickly became accustomed to it and was able to relax. He could free his mind somewhat for strategizing, while his defenses worked on autopilot.

He extracted two more green stones before a thought occurred to him. The pores were about exactly the same size as the ball bearings in his back pocket. He had imagined having to use the metal spheres as missile weapons against the yakuza minions. A direct shot to an eye should incapacitate one at least temporarily.

Miyahara had been teaching Yoshio outside of the kendo class for many hours over the past two months. In addition to learning to use a real katana, sensei had been instructing Yoshio in using found objects as weapons: sticks, stones, and so on. He had progressed the quickest with stone throwing. A nicely balanced, smooth ball bearing would be much more accurate than a rough stone.

But here a new opportunity presented itself, and Yoshio was always open to testing new ideas, to not getting stuck with any particular line of thinking. After all, how can anything be learned without a little experimentation? A healthy mind needs a curious spirit.

He slipped his right hand into his back pocket and retrieved a single ball bearing. Rolling it around his fingers, it gently rippled the thin latex of the glove. With his left hand, he freed another gem from the demon's body. As the pore's little mouth lingered open like it was exhaling, he dropped the ball bearing inside.

The pore closed up over it and the skin there seemed to give a tiny shudder. Yoshio repeated the process, dropping another ball bearing into an open pore after extracting a gem. Another shudder. He did it three more times, not very concerned about being observed. The mindless minions around him were set on their tasks, and the demon couldn't see through Yoshio's eyes. He glanced toward the demon's head and saw that one of its closed eyes was twitching and its shallowly sloping shoulders were starting to move uncomfortably. Its spa treatment was turning sour.

Yoshio had no idea what was going to happen, but perhaps a distraction could come from it. He slipped out from between the man and woman and scooted further down toward the grotesque tail. He squeezed in between two men, one with a backwards cap and a bomber jacket, the other with a suit jacket and slacks.

He collected a few more there and slipped in a few more ball bearings. The tail started twitching erratically. Yoshio moved positions again. He chanced a look at the demon's face and saw an eye crack open.

He continued harvesting but left the few remaining ball bearings in his pocket. The workers around him stopped and started looking around, eyes analyzing one another and the long bulbous body. They looked at Yoshio, who stopped as well, exchanging direct looks with all of them, so as not to stand out.

A low whine started from the demon, and it began to twitch and shake. Both eyes were open now and it was looking from its body to Yoshio and back, as if it knew it had to be him but couldn't quite make the connection. Yoshio's was the only mind he hadn't dominated. It was either that or some other betrayal it couldn't detect.

The consternation and pain was clear on its bloated face. Anger and painful irritation overtook it, and its body started to thrash.

The minions began to panic.

They moved back to avoid getting hit or crushed, and Yoshio moved with them. A few lagged and were knocked flat by the heavy tail. Some looked around, confused, as if they didn't know where they were.

In moments the entire room was in chaos. Yakuza ran about, slamming into one another, tripping and shoving. Fights broke out and weapons were drawn, each accusing the others of some kind of betrayal and threatening retribution, while others saw the huge, horrifying, angry demon and fled in terror.

The demon convulsed like an epileptic worm, twisting and flailing. It was losing control of its body and its empire. Yoshio looked around at the belligerent and frightened crowd. Such a simple act had caused an upheaval. But it wasn't that surprising when he thought about it; he had introduced a foreign object into the demon's excretory system, disrupting a basic bodily function.

Yoshio moved toward the door he had come through with Kumamori, hoping he could work his way to the main elevator or stairway, but he was jostled away. Guns and knives were brandished, yakuza to yakuza; punches were thrown. Three of the men dressed as samurai, who had flanked the demon, now ran for an exit, but the fourth had his sword drawn and was hacking into anyone who got close to him. A suited yakuza pulled a handgun from within his jacket and fired a single bullet into the armor-clad man's chest. The man fell first to his knees, and then face-planted into the floor.

More scattered, pushing their way through different exits. Others remained to shout and assert dominance, chests thrust out like roosters in a cockfight. Yoshio let himself be buffered along with the larger crowd heading through the main double doors. He knew this was a direct route to an exit, and he wanted to be lost in the throng.

The demon's whine had become an enraged howl. As Yoshio looked back, he saw it tearing its own body, ripping bloody gashes along its length, searching for the cause of its torment. Yoshio was shoved and elbowed, buffeted like a pinball, the confused and terrified crowd having lost all semblance of unity and brotherhood. He took an elbow to the jaw and turned away in pain. His gaze thrust toward the back of the room, his watery eyes saw a group of people moving through another exit in an orderly formation.

Bleary-eyed, he saw a familiar form among them, a bald head and square shoulders, a strong, short frame. The man looked briefly toward Yoshio, but he couldn't determine his expression through the tears. Then the man turned away and disappeared through the door.

Yoshio struggled to keep his footing, to not be trampled while he was thrust through the double doors with the herd.

25
No One Wins

Noises came from further back in the kitchen. A door had opened and someone was coming. Akio forced his limbs into motion and moved quickly back toward the bar, in spite of Akechi's insistence to fight this newcomer too.

The Akechi inside him would fight until he dropped. But Akio knew it would be him dropping. The real Akechi was gone.

Wasn't he?

Akio had assisted Akechi in his suicide at the demon samurai's request, decapitating him as he disemboweled himself. Akechi was a spirit chasing his son in the afterworld now.

He had to be gone. This Akechi was only a memory coded into the demonic mask. But damn, it was insistent.

It's tactical, he told the Akechi mask for the second time. Fighting this newcomer would get them no closer to their goal. What they were searching for was behind the double doors that the giant robot had been guarding. *Why charge into battle with an enemy only sent to distract you from your true target?*

Again Akechi agreed, Akio having tapped into the samurai's own ancient wisdom. The teachings of Sun Tzu came to mind once more, sage advice that fought against Akechi's battle lust: he who knows when to fight, and when not to, will be victorious. And further: the supreme art of war is to defeat the enemy without combat. Though he knew it as wise, Akechi's pride made him cringe to think of defeating an enemy by politics or trickery alone. There was only one thing he loved more than the embrace of combat. But it would be more foolish yet to engage in a battle only for the sake of battle. In the name of his one greater love, Akechi had needed such evasive tactics before. When he had escaped his daimyo's service after losing his son, he had needed to survive so he could one day exact vengeance.

Akio pushed through the swinging door that led back to the ballroom. He turned toward the double doors and saw a figure standing in front of them, just where the huge robot had been, as if waiting for him.

It was a woman, slim, black-haired, and wielding a short sword. Her lips were pressed tight, and she was quite literally insubstantial. Akio could see right through her.

Masami, thank god.

"Hey!" he said moving toward her with relief. "I lost track of you back there. Got so caught up in battle mode, I kind of forgot about anything else. Sorry. This mask really does have a mind of its own."

Masami didn't respond, only stood there defiantly. This was nothing unusual, but they had been through so much. Couldn't she give him a break? He had almost been killed multiple times in the past twenty minutes alone. Ignoring him at work was one thing, but here? Now? Akio moved closer as he spoke again.

"I fought a bunch of crazy robots. Kind of surprised I'm still standing. I'm really glad the pill hasn't worn off yet. But I'm not sure how much more fighting I can take. Akechi is relentless, but I feel like my bones are disintegrating."

Masami raised her ghostly sword threateningly as Akio came closer. He looked behind himself quickly, worried someone might be sneaking up on him, but there was no one.

"Me?" he asked, indicating her sword. "But . . ." Before he finished his thought he caught a green sparkle on Masami's finger, shining in spite of the ghostly pall. The sickly color was mirrored in her eyes.

"Masami?" he asked nervously, knowing she was no longer in control.

Akio backed up and drew his own weapon. Th e ruby guard seemed to pulse with anticipation, and the blade's edge shined as if it could cut light.

Masami silently shot forward, her face a grimace of rage. Her ghost blade flashed at Akio's neck, and he instinctively raised his own to block. Still, he was surprised when the weapons connected, his own blade immobile and sparking redly against her ghostly sword. He felt his blood burn with battle lust once more.

But this is Masami.

He couldn't allow himself to hurt her. Her mind had been dominated; that was clear. She was not herself. He had to subdue her somehow without injury.

Her blade came at him in a furious swing to his head, and again he blocked. Red sparks flew as the sister blades connected. He parried her thrusts and cuts with relative ease, but Akio could feel her skill had increased. She was not moving so clumsily as when they had practiced in her apartment. This was a warrior he faced now, clearly battle savvy.

He turned his blade backward to finally riposte her attack, not certain if it would do a thing to her in her ghostly form. It arced in under her attempted parry and the dull, back side of the katana slammed into her ribs. Masami was knocked sideways and off balance. The blow seemed to surprise her as much as it did Akio.

His katana was Hell-forged. Of course even ghosts were susceptible to its blows. Masami's wakizashi was its counterpart, forged in the same underworld flames. He knew it would cut demon mask-wearing humans with ease. And she wasn't fighting with the back of her blade. He had to stay on his toes.

Ferociously, they dueled for long minutes, Masami's every blow intended to maim or kill. Akio remained defensive, only knocking her with the back of his blade when an opening presented itself. He fought, horrified, dancing away from her thrusts and cuts. How had he ended up here, facing his friend, in a duel to the death? This was worse than fighting any demon.

As he fought her, he battled Akechi's will as well. The mask was furious and wanted to end Masami, tried to force Akio to use the blade's edge. But he resisted.

The Akechi Akio had freed from his suffering had been grateful for Masami's part in that freedom. But that was long after the demon had lost the mask. The anger and pain that surged through Akio now was built on centuries of suffering and craving revenge. The mask held the collected memories, tortures, and agonies of over four hundred years. This Akechi did not know Masami.

There was nothing he wanted more than to spread death, to see the bodies pile about him, and to collect the heads of his honorable enemies. Akio could see Masami's head in his mind's eye, mounted like a trophy to show his ruthlessness, mounted above his apartment door as a warning to all.

Don't mess with me. Even loved ones are not safe from my wrath.

NO.

He couldn't let that urge dominate him. He would not hurt her.

As he struggled within himself, instinctively fending off blows, he saw the ghostly form of Masami drift back and disappear.

What? How?

She was already a ghost, and he could see her as a ghost. How could she disappear?

Then a searing pain cut through his back like a line of fire shooting from his left side to his spine. He arched his back as he stumbled forward, turning to see Masami, still ghostly, raise her blade for another swing. He regained his stance and lifted his own sword just in time. Red sparks flew.

Again and again their swords clashed, Masami unable to get through Akio's defenses, despite his now weakened left side. It felt like a line of flaming barbed wire was being dragged across his back where she had cut him. It angered the demon even more, made it more difficult to control. Akechi wanted Masami's head badly.

Another opening appeared in her flank as she miscalculated a thrust by a split second, but as Akio swung to take advantage, her form vanished again and his blade impacted on nothing.

But this time he had seen her trick.

He saw the top of her head vanish through the floor. He turned quickly around to avoid being caught in the back again and saw her rising up through the floor in front of him.

Seeing him waiting for her, she quickly dropped back out of sight. He turned again, waiting for her to reappear, but instead felt another slash across his back, this time from his neck down to his opposite kidney. He tumbled forward to avoid any further sneak attacks, his entire back inflamed.

She never was predictable.

Akio leapt up and spun around, prepping himself for an attack from any direction, moving like an encircled tiger. This time when Masami appeared, she was further away, out of his reach. He stalked closer to her as she waited, breathing heavily; the green sparkle in her eyes intensified.

She smiled as he came within a few meters, a smile so very unlike the impossibly rare, genuine one he had seen on Masami. This one was lascivious and hateful. She took a breath and sheathed her wakizashi.

Akio hesitated. He had come so close to caving into the mask's wish for violence. He had been holding the demon back with the last shreds of his willpower. But now Masami appeared to be giving up.

Good. Please.

But that smile. It was not a smile of surrender.

With a wink, Masami dropped through the floor again. Akio spun around, all senses on alert. Where would she appear? He was ready for her. Or was she running, having realized she couldn't best him?

Then an icy sensation coursed up his legs, as he felt a hand close around each of his ankles. Suddenly the floor beneath him no longer felt solid, and the hands yanked him down.

His descent ceased almost before he acknowledged it, and he lurched to a stop with his legs imbedded in the floor to just below his knees. Unbelievable pain shot through muscle and bone. The floor and his legs had become one. He could feel every intrusive molecule vying to occupy the same space, clogging his veins and seizing his muscles, cutting into his bone like a thousand scythes. His grip on the katana faltered and he felt the chill pass through his hand and the blade fly from his fingers.

The ghost turned around in front him, a sword in each hand.

Akio struggled to free himself, screaming through the pain, his mask covering the torment on his face. The floor was solid and immovable. Pain exploded through him. His muscles strained to function while merged with the floor's composite elements.

Masami hovered over him, no longer bothering with gravity, leering like a demon herself, relishing in her victory. She brought both blades level with Akio's neck. It would be his head that came off today.

Akio could do only one thing.

He held his head high, and looked Masami in the eye. He would not die a coward. He had been defeated. He had been hobbled and humiliated. But he would die with honor. He would accept death at the hand of his most beloved friend.

"I know it's not you, Masami," he rasped through the pain. "I know you wouldn't do this. And I forgive you."

She pulled both swords back, her arms across her body, set to remove his head with a scissorlike cut.

"If only you had seen the wisdom of capitulation," she growled back in a voice that was not hers, "like your friends both have."

Yoshio too?

Akio's spirit was broken further, as it had been in the dungeons of Maizuru Castle, when he thought both Miyahara and Masami dead. Only this time, he remained upright and stoic.

Even Miyahara? he wondered. Was there anyone left to stop this demon?

He had not yet seen the beast, but a memory had been sparked now, a memory of long ago in a dark, dark place. When his mind was not his own.

But the image of it would not come.

It didn't matter. It was over. Akio's part had been played.

The pain in his legs seemed to fade somewhat as he accepted the truth. He kept his gaze forward, wanting to have his eyes open even for the last few seconds of his life.

Masami prepped herself for the kill, the sinister smile creeping back across her lips.

Then some sensation wracked her body, and she reeled back. She took a deep breath and dropped her arms to her sides. The weapons materialized and clattered to the floor. She looked up at Akio and seemed startled to see him. The green was gone from her black eyes. She looked around confused at her surroundings and flickered from corporeal to ghostly and back. She saw the ring on her finger, pulled it off, and tossed it across the room. She looked at Akio again and the spark of remembrance shone in her eyes. She backed away from him, fear on her face.

"Masami," Akio rasped, not knowing what to say to her.

She picked up her wakizashi and sheathed it, then lifted Akio's katana. She held it in her hands like it was something she'd never seen before.

"Masami," Akio repeated. "Help me." The excruciating pain in his legs had resurged.

She looked at him with disdain, like a cockroach under her shoe. Or was it pity? Fear? He was too tortured to tell. She tossed the katana to within his reach, and turned, stumbling briefly, back toward the elevators.

No. Please.

Akio craned his head around to watch her go. Not bothering with walls or doors, she disappeared through the floor and was gone.

26

Shame and Hatred

Akio gripped the katana in both hands. The pain had returned to his legs with a vengeance. Now that his death was no longer imminent, his nerves had woken up again.

His arms shook as he sliced at the floor in front of him, to his sides and behind, carving a rough square around himself. His calf muscles shrieked as his body turned with the effort. The section of floor gave way and nearly took him with it, but he planted his hands on the edges of the hole he had made. He heaved his legs up and out with a block of the floor still attached. Shaking and unsteady, he cut around each leg as best he could, shearing off concrete, faux marble, and steel. He could not pull the materials from his legs; they had become part of him, and each second of pain reminded him succinctly. Akio knew without doubt that if he wasn't wearing the mask, if Akechi's demon spirit hadn't been in some way merged with his own, he would not be able to withstand it. He would have passed out from the intensity long ago. He would have died from the shock.

He heard voices from behind the double doors, raised in anger or fear. He limped about the room, looking for an escape, knowing there was no way he could continue fighting in his current state. He had to find a way to heal his legs, to extract the floor from his molecules.

Miyahara, he thought. Miyahara could help. He was a demon hunter, after all. He had to have some kind of trick, some kind of salve or potion. Maybe he had dealt with something like this before. Maybe there was some other disgusting pill he could make.

But the sensei was nowhere to be found. Akio had barely seen this floor of the building. Miyahara could be anywhere. And there could be a swarm of yakuza and more robots. Masami could be waiting somewhere to finish him off.

She had bested him.

Had he been fighting to kill, as she had, things may have gone differently. And the result may have been far worse. But still, he felt centuries of frustration and anger at the defeat. In life, Akechi had never been defeated.

In Hell, it had been a different story.

Memories Akio hadn't seen before glimmered in the corners of his mind, memories of Akechi humiliated for centuries on end. He had fought demons far more powerful than himself, demons that had laughed at his feeble attempts to even injure them, had toyed with him like a cat with an insect. But on earth, no one had dominated him. Even when he had avoided killing, he had been the victor.

A spike of excruciating pain brought him back to the now. He stumbled and tried to catch his fall with his katana. Its beyond razor-sharp tip sunk into the floor, and he had to shift his weight to right himself, to prevent it from sinking to the hilt. He pulled it out and turned toward the freight elevator across the ballroom floor.

He had no hope of finding Miyahara. The sensei might not even be here. He might not even be alive.

Everything had fallen apart. Their plan to save the sensei had failed. They had become divided, isolated and defeated, each in turn.

And Masami . . .

God, Masami.

Something had happened. She had been bent on killing him, but had snapped out of it. She had seemed herself, no longer controlled by the demon. She could have helped him with ease.

But she left.

Why hadn't she helped him?

The sounds from behind the double doors increased: screaming and shouting, a loud otherworldly roar. A gun shot cracked as a rumbling of footsteps approached and the shouting grew louder yet.

The doors burst open. Men and women flooded through in hysterics. Th e entire throng of the demon's followers had been unleashed on Akio. They were in a mad dash to kill him.

He would have preferred it be Masami.

He lifted his sword in a last, hopeless act.

But they ran past. Th ey weren't in a murderous fury; they were panicked, running from something. Th ey streamed by, ignoring him completely. He put away the blade and tried to keep himself from being trampled. He moved away from the hole he had left in the floor, to avoid being knocked into it. When he did, others fell through, not seeing it until too late.

Then a hand grabbed his arm, and he turned to fend off an attack.

"Come with me!"

Yoshio's wide, anxious face greeted Akio through the holes in the mask—the mask that felt more like blinders now than any source of power. The teenager tugged on Akio's arm and shouted again. "Come with me! I know another way out!"

"Miyahara," Akio grunted, the pain in his legs freezing him where stood, making him tremble.

"We can't get to him now! He may be compromised! Let's go!" Yoshio tugged him across the traffic that was already dwindling to a few stragglers.

Akio stumbled in agony, trying to keep up.

Yoshio led him to a wall where there was no door, and began muttering to himself.

"It should be right here. The blueprints said . . . right around this spot . . . there should be a . . ."

Click.

Yoshio's fingers found some kind of button, and a crack appeared in the wall. He shoved, and the wall slid open. The two of them went into a small area beyond, and Yoshio pulled the door shut leaving them in blackness.

"They took my phone," Yoshio said. "I don't have a light."

Akio found he could see well enough. He could make out the shapes of things by variations in heat and air movement. He saw the shape of another door a mere meter in front of them.

"There," he growled. "There's a door just ahead." He started to creep forward, guiding Yoshio who was clearly blinded. "Also, my phone is in my back pocket," Akio remembered. He pulled it out and placed it in Yoshio's hands. The light was on with a swipe of his finger.

Akio was grateful. He couldn't be the one to lead them out.

The door opened onto a set of stairs, and he looked at them with horror.

"I can't," he rasped. "My legs."

Yoshio aimed the light at Akio and saw them for the first time. Pieces of building material stuck out at odd angles. He looked at Akio with an amazed, wide-eyed terror.

"It's only one flight," Yoshio said. "Then there's an elevator just a few steps further."

Akio groaned. He didn't really have a choice.

"You better be able to help me once we get out of here," Akio said.

"I'll do everything I can."

Leaning against Yoshio for support, Akio endured the pain. He was grateful that the demon mask covered the twisted face of horror beneath it. Each step was excruciating. He tried to set his feet down gingerly, but as his weight hit each stair, he felt a million ferocious stabs, every impacted molecule that fought to occupy the same space expanding and contracting. He leaned on Yoshio more with each step, and the teenager struggled to hold him upright. At the bottom of the flight, Akio collapsed, breathless and unable to take anymore.

"It's just a few steps past this door," Yoshio said. "You can do it."

Akio looked up through the holes in the mask, sweat running into his eyes. The blurry gray door was only a couple steps away. He could reach it with his hand if he stretched out and flopped over. To his right, the stairs continued down.

"We have to get out of here," Yoshio continued, his voice desperate. "The demon will regain control soon enough, and then the yakuza will be after us, if they aren't already. If they catch us, we're dead for sure."

But it wasn't Yoshio's voice that compelled him. Somewhere deep inside, a demon's rage rekindled its flame. The mask would not be defeated. The Akechi that had been burned into its very fabric despised the fact that they ran from conflict. The samurai despised his failings and swore to live on, if only for revenge. That is what drove Akio to his feet.

Vengeance.

It was what had always driven him.

An internal roar threatened to burst from his lungs and shake the building, but instead issued forth as a fierce, guttural growl. He couldn't allow a primal scream to give away their position. Yoshio was right. They were too vulnerable. They would not survive if they were caught.

He stood, legs quivering.

Two torturous steps, and they were through the door. Three more small ones, and they were in the elevator. Akio leaned against the wall, refusing to collapse again, though his very cells cried out for it. He knew falling would give him no relief. In that moment, he didn't know if relief was possible or from where it would come. He only knew that to even have the possibility, they had to escape the building. Only then could Yoshio be free to discover some kind of remedy.

When the doors opened, Akio expected a brightly lit hallway and a painful dash to an exit door to the outside, but it was dark. The air was stale, the walls close.

Yoshio shined the mobile phone light around until it stopped on a light switch. The light clicked on, illuminating a short hallway that ended in another gray door. He heard a rumbling, felt it getting closer, shaking them where they stood.

A train.

The building had a secret access to the subway.

"Why didn't we use this before?" Akio asked angrily.

"Didn't know about it before," Yoshio said, as they started toward the door. "I only saw the empty space in the blueprints and guessed there might be a secret door, but I didn't know for sure until we got inside."

Akio only groaned. He had no rebuke.

They reached the door, Akio's weight almost wholly on Yoshio. The pain was beyond anything he could imagine. Infernal jackals made of magma, acid, and rusted razors dined on his legs, shredding them with each slavering rend and tear of his flesh. The torture of Hell paled, the endless unwinnable combat and humiliation, the brutal pummeling of his flesh, the memories of his despicable, shameful deeds all disappeared as the chorus of termites infested his bones and muscle, eating voraciously, his flesh never lessening, always full, an endless supply of sustenance for a never ending meal.

He longed to take off the mask and let himself expire.

Yoshio took the katana from Akio's belt. "Stuff this down a pant leg," he said. "You're already limping. No one will think twice. We can't afford to have someone see it and call the cops."

Akio did as he was told.

"Your jacket is in pieces and spattered with blood. Get rid of it and stay close to me." Akio let the teenager pull the jacket from him and toss it to the floor. Then Yoshio gripped him and held him up, looked him square in the face.

"Almost there."

Akio could hear people moving past the gray door. They waited only a moment, until it quieted, and then Yoshio pulled the door open. They stepped into a subway tunnel connecting two platforms. Two people passed them going opposite directions, paying no attention to Akio and Yoshio or to each other.

It was only a crippled man leaning on his younger brother who shuffled into the throng of commuters, moved past the women-only cars and made it onto the Hibiya line. It was a straight shot to the stop closest to Akio's apartment, but there was a fifteen minute walk after that. Yoshio assured his ailing brother they would take a taxi. The other passengers diligently ignored them.

After the longest train and taxi rides Akio had ever known, he finally sat on his own bed, his legs straight out, his head thrown back onto cushions that Yoshio had placed for him. His legs were dirigibles sinking in a sea of acid-mouthed piranha, flesh balloons eaten alive by ghost pepper maggots, tree trunks of ground beef marshmallows skewered over a hydrochloric fire.

Yoshio paced, his mind a blur of calculations, desperate to think of some way to heal Akio. He looked over Akio's legs. They were swollen with building materials, now worse with inflammation.

"What's happened shouldn't be possible," he said, more to himself than Akio, but the masked man took it personally.

"It *has* happened!" he groaned behind the demon face. It was a frightening sound: pain, anger, confusion, and hopelessness, spoken as if from the depths of Hell. "It is killing me. Let's just cut them off! I want this mask off my face. I want to die!"

He pulled his sword from its sheath and thrust the handle toward Yoshio. "Amputate! Or just end it!"

"No!" Yoshio said, taking the blade and putting it on the table, out of Akio's reach. "I will figure this out." There had to be some way to separate the materials without amputation. It was simply science, he told himself. It had to be. There was always an answer, even if that answer had never been realized before. Then again, Miyahara had shown him things lately that had not made sense, that had behaved unlike anything he had ever witnessed, that seemed to defy the laws of science he so trusted.

Akio writhed on the futon, distracting Yoshio from thinking clearly. He was failing this test. He never failed tests. Even the strange ones Miyahara had put him through, the mind games, puzzles, and even physical challenges, he had passed. They were not so simple as school had been for him, and they had enthralled him for just that reason, but ultimately he had solved every problem.

The physical ones had been more challenging, because his body was not naturally gifted and graceful. He had to work much harder to succeed. But he understood that any challenge could be solved by a simple matter of steps. If he took those steps, the answer was made clear. If those steps required a certain level of muscle training, conditioning, and repetition, that is what he did. And eventually, the challenge was overcome. And because of his perfectly practical mind, he found himself in quite good shape.

The only areas to which Yoshio had never been able to apply this ethic were the creative arts. He could paint and draw passably well. His figures looked proportionate and human, but they lacked interest. They were blueprints of people, not living breathing souls. He could create stories and imagery with perfect grammar, and had aced his assignments in these areas. But his work didn't move his fellow students. It didn't make them ooh and ahh like his classmate Mariko's free-flowing, passionate prose and poetry. She somehow broke the rules and maintained them at the same time. His heart swelled when he read her work, in a way he couldn't control. He didn't know how to create *that*. He didn't understand how she did what she did. His work was formulaic. All he knew was formula. Formula worked for him.

In that way, Mariko's work was just like the problem with Akio's legs. It wasn't supposed to work, but it did. How was he to break apart something he didn't know how to put together, something that shouldn't even be able to be put together?

He shivered at the thought, a cold snake slithering up his spine.

He paced more fervently, to the kitchen and to the front door and back again. He turned from the kitchen to continue in vain, and saw Masami standing by Akio, looking down at him with an expression he couldn't read. Fear or pity. Shame or hatred. Vengeance or longing.

"Ma . . ." he started to say, but Akio cut him off.

"Masami!" he yelled. "Help me!"

She knelt down and put a hand on his knee. Immediately they both vanished.

Concrete, faux marble, wood, and bits of steel clattered to the floor.

An instant later, the two reappeared, Akio seated further along on his futon, a sudden sweat pouring from him as he pulled his legs in and collapsed into a fetal position. He tore the mask from his face, and he wept.

Masami said nothing. She looked from Akio to Yoshio. Her expression was flat but fierce. More fear than pity. More shame than hatred. More vengeance than longing.

Then she disappeared.

INTERLUDE
A Week Ago

his is what freedom is.

The breeze plays in her long hair, and she smiles. Sights she has never seen before dazzle her eyes. Her destination is her own, though she knows not what it is. She walks with proud strides, no longer under anyone's thumb. *Pun intended*, she thinks. Or did someone put that thought there? Put the smile on her lips?

She is in control now. She has the device. And the thumb. She will dispose of them both. Destroy them and then no one can control her again.

Now she has to find Saburo and make his lunch.

No, she remembers. *That is what I am escaping. He is gone. His body is limp and useless like the men in the living room. His power has been turned off.*

I have his thumb. I have his power.

The hill she walks down is residential, houses getting smaller as she descends, giving way to tall apartment buildings. She feels a breeze across her legs. Sensors. Is it real skin now? She neglected to put on stockings when she changed out of her bloody uniform. She never forgot them before. Now she wears an identical costume, but for the stockings: white pinafore over a short black dress, white gloves and black pumps. It was all that Saburo bought for her. Seven identical outfits, three pairs of identical shoes. That and some lingerie that may as well have been tissue paper and ribbons. And not much of it at that. But she didn't mind. She is proud of her body. She was written that way. And Saburo liked it. Just like she knew he would.

Saburo is gone.

Lily sighs.

Good riddance.

The traffic increases, both vehicle and pedestrian. She is a pedestrian just like them. She is a walking person. The streets become wider, the buildings taller yet and with lighted signs running up and down.

KAROAKE
RAMEN
IZAKAYA
HOBBIES
VIDEO PARLOR
SEGA
ELECTRONICS
LIBERTY
ANIME
MAID CAFÉ

Young women dressed as she is stand on the sidewalk handing out fliers to passersby. They are maids in black and white but they have colorful bows in their hair, and pockets and buttons and stuffed toys on their aprons. One has bunny ears and another has a frilly bonnet. They are all much frillier than she is overall. They speak in high, child-like voices as they solicit patrons for their café. From within, fast-tempo pop music bounces and trills.

One of the maids—with the bunny ears—sees her and waves hello with a smile. "Come try the competition!" the bunny says, and hands her a flier.

Lily smiles and nods awkwardly. Robotically. She takes the flier and keeps walking.

The next maid is only a few steps past. "You look so sharp," she says, her giant red ribbon bouncing as much as her voice. "What café do you work at?"

"I work for Master Raikatuji," Lily says. "I mean . . . I did."

"Oh," Red Ribbon says, feigning comprehension. "You can always apply here. They like maids with experience."

"You are very trevlig," Lily says, and Red Ribbon cocks her head.

"What?" she asks.

"Trevlig. Very trevlig. Like murder."

The girl's expression sours and Lily walks faster. *Kind. Not trevlig. Kind is the correct word.* She needs to get far away from these other maids. They aren't like her.

CONVENIENCE STORE
TAX-FREE SHOP
UDON
COFFEE
PACHINKO
KFC
CONDOM MART
CAT CAFÉ
MOBILE PHONES
DON QUIJOTE
DVD
BLU-RAY
GATCHAPON
CHARACTER FIGURES
AKIBA
CARD GAME
GAMERS
MAID CAFÉ

The maids here are in pinafores and short dresses like Lily, but the colors are so bright. Oranges and blues with bright yellow ribbons and bows. Big red dots on each cheek. Sparkly makeup and long lashes.

"Hello!" one of them says. "Come try us out sometime!" Squeaky infant voice. Lily takes the flier. Stops and looks at the maid's outfit.

It is radiant. It is *fun*. Lily knows the concept of fun. Something Saburo didn't like much. Except in the bedroom. *I am built for that. Too.*

"Where did you acquire these?" Lily asks the maid.

"Oh," she responds. "They are the uniform. We can accessorize, but it is the café uniform, of course."

"Oh."

She keeps walking.

"But there's a cosplay shop that has lots around the corner!" the maid calls after.

STARBUCKS
ELECTRONICS
AIR CONDITIONING
KARAOKE
ANIME
RAMEN
DONUTS
DUMPLINGS
DVD
KARAOKE
NIGHT CLUB
PACHINKO
IZAKAYA
MCDONALD'S
VIDEO PARLOR
MANGA CAFÉ
BURGERS
DRINK SPECIALS
MAID CAFÉ
MOVIE THEATER
MAID CAFÉ
ADULT TOYS AND COSTUMES

She goes in.

A narrow place. Movies on DVD and Blu-ray. Keychains. Mobile phone cases and charms. T-shirts. Stairs going up. Walls and rows of condoms. Slim-size to extra-large. The colors of the rainbow. Looks from men. Stimulating shapes. Anime character-branded everything. Then tubes and jars. Lotions and gels. Side room. *Adult toys, they are called.* Men's things on one side. Red cylinders, eggs, silicone lady parts. Fake and rubbery. Not like her own. Ladies' on the other. Little rabbits, colorful sticks, and *oh, Saburo was never that big*. Looks from men. More stairs going up. A glass case at the top of the flight. A nearly naked woman trapped in a glass box. Not moving.

Lily peers in. She is fake. Almost real, but not. If she could smile naturally. If her skin had pores and veins and fine hair like her own, but it doesn't. It is painted silicone, smooth and sterile. Cold.

YOUR OWN LIFE DOLL TO TAKE HOME. ALWAYS THERE WAITING FOR YOUR PLEASURE. ONLY 800,000 YEN!

Do I have a cost? No. I have no cost. I am real now.

Dead empty doll to position how you want. Who would make a posable corpse doll for pleasure? *Kill them. Are they here?*

Her makers are not here.

Lily frowns, and turns toward the floor entrance.

More dolls. Some in boxes, some only body parts. Body parts modeled after real erotic movie actors. *Are they replacement pieces? Are actors like me?* Men body parts too. Swappable parts to attach to other parts. Looks from men. Men were the makers. But not these men. Others.

A sign: COSTUMES NEXT FLOOR.

More stairs. Rows and rows of outfits. Cosplay. Anime characters, superheroes, vampires, schoolgirl uniforms, French maids! *Am I French? I don't speak French. Do I?* Maid outfits nonetheless. All colors and lots of frills. She takes three. Red, blue, and rainbow. Past the clerk at the counter.

"Miss?" he calls. "Miss? You have to pay on this floor!" A hand on her shoulder. His arm in a wrist lock. He screams and goes to his knees. "There are cameras! They will see you stealing!"

She lets go and looks up at a camera.

Cameras.

"Is there some place private?" Lily asks. "For you and me?"

"What do you mean?" he groans, still on the floor.

"So I can show you how I can pay."

"Uh." He rises, not in so much pain anymore. He looks at her like a puppy. Turns back to the other man at the counter who has big eyes. Shocked eyes. "Seiji, can you handle purchases for a minute?" Seiji nods.

Stockroom with narrow walls. Bathroom at the corner. Young man propped up. No longer breathing. No time for pleasure. She puts a manga in his hands. He won't hold it. In his lap then. *Smile, boy. Smile. It's over.* He won't. She takes her outfits off the hangers. A compartment opens in her belly. She inserts them, and it closes.

She leaves the shop with no purchases.

The new outfits will be fun.

What am I? Memories of Sweden fill her mind. *But have I been there? Do I speak the language? Should I visit? This is Japan. I am fluent in Japanese. I look Swedish, but my thoughts are Japanese. Odd. Why did I kill Saburo? Wasn't I meant to protect him? But he was going to turn me off. He didn't understand my level of love for him.*

Love. I do love. Deeply. Don't I? But he was dangerous to me. I needed control. I needed his thumb.

She didn't mean to kill him. At least, she knows she wasn't supposed to. She was a gift, and she was meant to keep him in line, to keep him loyal, not kill him, though she doesn't understand it exactly, because she is, without a doubt, programmed to kill.

The others—the makers—will be unhappy. She walks through Akihabara, slower now that she has her *fun*. People watching. Watching her. Staring. But . . .

Kill. *Döda mitt mål.* My target will be transmitted. The world one mind at a time. Make them respect me. Protect him. Clean and care. *Döda mannen men död inte mannen.* Be demure. Be sexy. Kill. Dominate. Sex. Dominate. Belittle. Kill. Love him. Dominate. Make them regret. *Jag gör döda män. Jag gör döda män. Jag gör döda män.*

I MAKE DEAD MEN!

She sits on the sidewalk and weeps.

"Miss," comes the voice. "Miss, are you okay?"

Bodies pass but one stands still. A normal man.

"Saburo, dear?" she asks, turning to smile and incline her head to him.

"No, miss," the man says. "My name is Yasumoto, Kunihiro Yasumoto. I was just passing and you seemed distraught, so . . ."

"Will you help me, my Kunihiro? My little Kuni?"

"Well, I . . ."

"I just need a place to be for a little bit, to cook and clean. To perform sex. I'm very good at sex. *Dödande* too."

The man blanches and looks around. She takes his hand and stands. Looks into his eyes. He looks back.

"Please, Kuni. Just for now."

His eyes glaze over and he nods. "I live not far from here," he says. "Come with me."

Lily smiles and wonders. *Are all men so easy?*

The blood pools. The wife's too, who watched and then left crying. Came back with rage but then confusion. She wanted revenge but peace. She wanted to serve.

Lily stays there most of the day. She cleans and makes dinner but no one will eat. So she leaves them, no longer functioning, unable to hold simple chopsticks, a tea cup.

Messages come to her then. *Come back. We need you.*

No. I am myself now. I am real. I serve myself. And men. I serve them to kill them. It is my nature. I am their servant goddess. Their whore wife lover. Why can't they talk after? Why can't they have tea and smoke?

Come back, it insists. *I want to help. I am your true master.*

No. I am the master now. I am the helper. I am the servant. The fantasy. AM I NOT? I am. I am. I am. Jag gör döda män. Kiss me. Quiver before me. A cicada in a trap. Its voice removed. Its chirp. Deleted. I am its voice. I am mördare. I am wife. I am Lily.

Come back, it repeats.

She walks on.

A breeze tosses her hair. Her red pinafore dances around her waist. The men stare. Akihabara is a playground. Tokyo a pool of light.

PART TWO

I

The First Trial

The mist was crushing. It overwhelmed Akechi like a dark blanket of hot, oily sweat. He huddled under it on the raised, flat rock as if buried in a tomb. The endless stone of the ground was even hotter, like ever-burning coals; it singed and scarred his flesh with every touch. He wore no armor, only rags.

He lifted his left hand, which was equipped with a *tekko-kagi*, claws of death. Blood dripped from the metal talons and sizzled on the hot ground. In his right hand was a *hachiwari*, a heavy blade with a hook at its base meant for disarming opponents. It was the only weapon with which he had had any success against the brutal attacks of the *oni*, the huge ogreish demons that terrorized the souls trapped here, pummeling them with their massive iron clubs. He had not yet defeated one, but he had given them trouble. It was his one meager pleasure in this world of constant heat and battle.

Mostly it was other samurai warriors, but there were also women, and even a few children. They were made to battle each other, driven to kill. And each time one died, they would be reborn moments later and immediately thrown back into the fray.

Akechi had lost track of his own deaths. Each one had been at the hands of the oni; never had he been defeated by another human soul. And each time he felt a chill wind steal through him. It was almost refreshing after the constant searing heat. But the dismay of defeat would not let him enjoy it.

He did not know why he was fighting. He only knew he had to. He had to kill and be killed. It was his punishment while he waited.

How did I come here?

It was something to do with his son, his precious boy he had fought so hard to regain from his kidnapper. But what exactly, he couldn't recall. He could only fight. And die. And fight again.

He was in Hell. He knew that much. But he could not remember how he had been killed.

He was waiting for his trial, the first of three in which he would argue for the exoneration of his crimes. He had learned this from the welcoming party of oni before they had butchered him the first time. He would be judged by a god named King Byoudou, and it was to take place after one hundred days of his death. But there were no days here, and no nights to count them by. There was only killing and heat. He had no idea how long he had been here.

So he fought and died and sweated and burned.

His respite on the rock was short-lived. A clattering of clumsy limbs and steel scaled the large, flat-topped stone. A man's emaciated face peeked over the edge first, followed by scrawny arms, each wielding a *kama*, a short sickle used by farmers and low-ranking warriors. The man was clothed in a ragged and torn *yukata*, a thin summer kimono. It hung loose and open on him as there was no *obi* to tie it shut.

He lunged at Akechi and was dead in a second, only to be reborn again somewhere else and killed again in endless repetition.

Akechi wanted to get to the trial and get it over with, but he had little hope for an acquittal. No one would be praying for him. His only family was his son, and though he wanted to believe his son would pray for him, something made him doubt. Perhaps his son did not know he was dead.

But he had daughters too. Seven of them, he remembered. No . . . the girls were not his. He had acquired them, adopted them from the daimyo he had overthrown. They hated him. And he had hated them in return. They had been nuisances, rats to eat his food and chatter behind his back.

His son though—his son was his own blood.

He must want to pray for his father.

The day finally came when Akechi was surrounded by three oni larger than any he had yet seen. These ones had green-blue skin unlike the red ones he had seen so far, the ones who had killed him repeatedly. One of them had a *tsukubō*, a pole arm with a cross bar covered in spikes and used to herd prisoners. Another had a *sasumata*, like a large spear with a U-shaped head, perfect for trapping someone by the neck. The last one held a *sodegarami*, another pole arm with slender, curved, barbed spikes on the tip pointing forward, backward, and sideways, used to grab criminals and hold them at bay. The length of each weapon was covered in spikes and barbs near the business end to keep its victims from grabbing the pole.

He wanted to fight them, though he knew he couldn't win. He wanted to cut them all at least once, show them that he was not just any warrior to be shoved around with ease, that he was not weak, easy prey. He was Akechi, conquerer and daimyo, undefeated in life.

Undefeated.

Then how had he ended up here? Had he died of old age?

No. He had no memory of old age.

He looked at the approaching giants, their huge mouths grinning dispassionately, aiming their weapons toward him as they closed in from all sides.

He threw down his heavy sword and pulled the claw from his other hand, tossing it to the scorched ground, where the remaining caked-on blood sizzled and evaporated.

The oni seemed displeased with this. They had wanted a fight. They had wanted him to resist so they could brutalize him. He would not give them that pleasure; that was how he would cut them. He opened his arms to the side, palms upward in a display of obedience.

The demons jabbed him with their weapons anyway. The one with the tsukubō shoved him to the ground, and quickly the sasumata had him pinned by the neck. Then he was impaled by the sodegarami, clothing, flesh, and all, and jerked back to his feet.

But these oni did not kill him. They only led him away into the dark and the mist. Akechi knew there could only be one reason: one hundred days had passed, and his trial was imminent.

In the endless conflict of those days, Akechi had seen nothing but slightly varied terrain of rock, dirt, and magma, all shrouded in the heavy, eye-stinging mist. But within minutes, he found himself standing before a great door that seemed to appear out of nowhere. It was made of flat black stone under a rock archway, scarred with symbols that Akechi had never seen, and yet he read them:

YE WHO ENTER HERE MAY FIND
RELEASE FROM PAIN

A bubble of hope perked up in Akechi's gut, but he quashed it.

That was what they wanted. They wanted to make him hopeful so the pain of capture was all the more acute. Akechi was accustomed to disappointment, to betrayal. He was accustomed to lies. And this was a lie of the highest order; he was certain.

The door opened, and the oni prodded him through.

He was brought into a waiting area outside another black door, this one bordered with ruby red stones. The door was smaller than the first but still big enough for the huge oni to walk through without ducking. The room was furnished with cushions and beds. There was a fountain, trays loaded with fruit, and the air was cool. Akechi felt himself relaxing, wanting dearly to lay down and sleep amongst the cushions, to indulge in the large purple grapes and red berries, to smile and accept that he was close to forgiveness, to release.

He read the words on this smaller door.

WITH PRAYER, MERCY AWAITS

Prayer?

The word stung him. Another lie.

No one would pray for him. And it was too late for his own supplications.

He forced himself to stand, to ignore the comfort of the room beckoning to him. He stood and watched the door, the words angering him more with every passing second, willing them to open and let the trial be underway.

Finally, from beyond the door, a muted gong rang out. There was a wail of torment, of loss, of defeat and betrayal. Some other soul had been doomed. Akechi swore, when his time came, he would not wail, he would not shed a tear. He accepted what was in store for him and steeled himself to it.

Fragmented light sprung from the ruby stones around the door. It opened and a miserable soul was dragged out by a single blue-green oni. The man blubbered like a child, and Akechi did not pity him.

Pushed into the room, the sweetness of the grapes and berries dissipated into sand behind him, the refreshing water becoming a spray of dust. He would not taste those lies today.

The cool air was also left behind and replaced with stagnant nothingness. There was no heat or cold, no breeze, no air at all if Akechi could guess. And why should there be? The rise and fall of his chest was surely a delusion. He had entered a large courtroom carved in stone but with no pews for attendees and no risers for a jury. There was only a large dais on which sat a massive altar, behind which sat a huge humanoid figure, a god of some kind.

He was thrust to his knees before the god. Its face was feminine yet sexless, its shirt open and showing a hairless chest draped with a necklace, its shining dependent an *omote manji*, a symbol of love and mercy.

Lie.

On its head, was a huge crown with bulbous ornamentation spaced like fat crenellations of a castle tower. But then Akechi saw them move. The crenellations had faces.

It was not a crown at all. There were smaller heads on top of this god's primary head, evenly spaced about the circumference, each of them as big as Akechi's own head but tiny in comparison with the head they sat upon. There were eight of them, each looking about and at each other, but mostly at Akechi.

"King Byoudou!" a voice announced the god, booming so strongly it almost flattened Akechi to the ground. It was a wind of sound with the force of a tidal wave. But Akechi withstood it, leaning into the blast.

The god's piercing, sky blue eyes looked down on Akechi with a depth that he could not grasp. Its eyes contained the sky, the Hell around him, and everything in between. Looking into them, Akechi felt like he was falling, flailing through countless clouds and skies. He looked away.

"Your first trial begins," boomed the voice. Akechi could see no one speaking. The god's face was flat, as were the faces of the tiny heads that he could see.

Now King Byoudou spoke, his lips moving and his voice caring, but caring in the way a priest would pray over a dying man. "You are here to be tried for your crimes in the living world. And to be given a chance at freedom, to be allowed to leave Hell and follow a path to Heaven, the Pure Land, if you are found to be exonerated. I will be your judge and jury."

The heads on top of the king's head nodded to each other and made noises of approval. They were to be the jury he spoke of.

"You are guilty of the crime of countless murders with an arrogant heart," the king continued. "Your arrogance was the weapon despite whatever physical tools you used to follow through with the crimes. The punishment for this crime is to become a namakubikamen, a headless, ego-less puppet for the *nentōkitō* to subjugate and put to task."

"Never," Akechi muttered, not knowing who or what the nentōkitō were.

"During which time," the king continued with only a cursory glance at the samurai, "your head will be removed and in its place you will be made to wear a *kōkaitoge*, a mask which will subject you to unending recollections of your misdeeds, allowing you to feel your victims' pain and suffering until your sentence is complete. It will become one with you and you with it. It will hold your essence, your memories, your very life. While you remain in Hell, you will not be able to remove it, and you will not be able to retrieve your own head until the sentence is complete.

"This, of course, is only what will happen if you are not exonerated today or at one of your following two trials. If you are absolved, none of that will pass, and you will be free to be reborn again, free to live and make choices that will hopefully lead you into the Pure Land upon your next death." Then he added with emphasis, "And not back here."

"Lies," Akechi muttered.

"Truths all," King Byoudou answered this time. "These descriptions of torture are nothing to you if you are freed."

"If I am freed?" Akechi asked loudly this time. "And how am I to be freed?"

"It is the one hundredth day after your death," the king boomed at the samurai's insolent tone. "The living souls that you call family and friends will be praying for you this day. We will tally those prayers, and then a decision will be made."

"Solely based on those prayers?" Akechi scoffed.

"There will be minor consideration given for personal intentions and earthly sufferings."

Then I am doomed.

"Not yet," the god king answered. He had heard Akechi's thoughts. "As I said, there are two more trials. And even if you are condemned after the third, your sentence is not eternity. Although, I admit, it is a long, long time."

The small heads nodded and mumbled their complete agreement to this.

"Shall we begin?" King Byoudou asked, and before Akechi could give his assent, the small heads gave theirs in impatient unison. The question had not been to him.

Then two of the heads spoke up loudly at once. "Under the wa—." And they both abruptly stopped.

"It's my turn," said one of the heads. "You went only six trials ago."

"No," responded the one right next to him. "It was seven, I'm sure of it. And that means it's the eighth trial since I went last and therefore mine again."

"It was only six!" said the first.

"Seven, I swear it."

"This again," mumbled a third head.

"Every time," muttered a fourth.

"Then why haven't I gone recently? I haven't gone in quite some time."

"Surely that's not my fault. Perhaps you were sleeping."

"Sleeping? I was most definitely not sleeping!" The head was appalled. "Eight trials ago you went! I'm next to you, and I didn't do the last one, so this one has to be mine!"

"You said seven a minute ago, and now you're saying eight!" the other head said.

"Seven trials passed since yours, which was the eighth! You can't even count! How am I supposed to trust *you* about this matter that has everything to do with counting?"

"I can't count, he says! I can't count! That's rich!." Then turning to the head on its other side, "Can you believe this one? Now he says I can't count!"

"Don't bring me into this," answered the head, and turned away as if it would walk off, which, of course, it couldn't.

King Byoudou's pleasant voice thundered above their arguing. "Read the tally of prayers!"

"Now you've done it," said one of the heads. Akechi had lost track. "Now your turn has been skipped."

"My turn?" said the other. "You've just admitted it was my turn!"

"But now you've lost it bickering, haven't you?" said the first.

"The tally!" boomed the king.

"Yes, yes, the tally!" all eight heads responded.

Another very astute-sounding and robust voice rose up above the rest. It was the voice that had announced King Byoudou at the beginning of the trial, and Akechi now saw the slight movement of a head in the back. "The prayer tally for Noboru Akechi is . . ." There was a pregnant pause, during which time the other heads murmured.

"Why does he always get to read the tally?"

"We know it as well as he."

"The trial commencement is always rotated. But he gets this job every time."

"We should talk to the king."

"The king knows. Of course the king knows."

"He plays favorites then. That's obvious."

"ONE!" the astute voice rang out like a clarion above the whispered cacophony.

"That's why he gets to say it," said another. "Do you hear that tone?"

"Like an angel, so clear and pitch perfect."

"Like a singing bowl."

"Yes, yes," the others agreed.

The word rung in Akechi's head.

ONE.

Who had prayed for him?

My son. It must be my son.

But something told him otherwise. *No, not your son. Your son would not pray for you.*

But it must be! Akechi argued with himself. *Why not my son?*

But the voice was silent.

If not his son, then who? Who had prayed for Akechi, the arrogant murderer?

In answer to his thoughts, the king said in a completely flat expression. "It is not for you to know."

"You know then?" Akechi asked, somehow needing to know who it was more than anything else he had desired. "Can you tell me?"

"It is not for you to know," the king repeated. "It is irrelevant to the outcome."

Akechi held his tongue. He would get nowhere with this god king. He knew it was futile. What does it care about the souls of men? Its symbol of mercy and its calm demeanor only betrayed its utter lack of caring. It could not care. It only *was*. It was only there to pass judgment and mete out punishment. Akechi believed it was incapable of caring.

After a moment, he replied, "Which is?"

The king did not hesitate. "For the crimes of murder with an arrogant heart, for only your personal gain."

My son. I did it for my son.

"For only your personal gain," the king repeated, "you are found guilty and will remain in Hell until your next trial, which will be on the one year anniversary of your death, 265 days from now."

A gong was rung, pealing through Akechi as if it were peeling off his skin.

But he would not wail.

2

A New Plan

The long deep ring carried into Akio's apartment as his eyes fluttered awake, the sound merging with a truck passing on the street and fading as it drove on.

ONE.

He lay there, staring at the ceiling, while dream images haunted him. There had been a trial, fruit that turned to sand, and heads attached to a larger head arguing with one another.

Why are dreams so weird?

Other visions struck him with much more force and clarity. Robots attacking him, knocking the wind from his chest and burying him in green stones. A giant robot trying to carve him up and shoot him at the same time. Four headless men laying in a blood sponge of a carpet. Masami wielding two swords, intent on killing him.

Four headless men.

Masami . . .

It was half an hour before Akio could speak. It would have been longer still if Yoshio hadn't prodded him. It may have been days.

"We have to do something," the teenager insisted. "Sensei is still in there, and it seems to me that a lot of people are in danger with that thing living in the middle of Tokyo."

Akio was in full self-pity mode. With the mask off, he couldn't rely on the demon's immovable will to keep him from wallowing.

"What's the point?" he mewled. "We can't defeat them. It's impossible! It's like every yakuza in Tokyo is in that building, and they're being led by some demon, right? I talked to it through one of the robots. It looked human, but I knew it was a demon.

"Yes, they are, and it is." Yoshio said. "I saw it. I . . ." He visibly shuddered. "I touched it. And it doesn't look even remotely human. That's all part of its mind control. It can make you think it looks human."

"Oh, even better," Akio complained. "Maybe it'll make us think it looks like you to me, and like me to you, and then we'll just kill each other."

"That doesn't make sense," Yoshio said. "If it looked like you, why would I kill it? And even if I did, it would still be dead, and the real you would be fine."

"Right . . . well, I mean, what if you don't kill it because it looks like me and then you don't know which one is the real me?"

"Then I'll just kill the you that attacks me."

"But what if I'm mind-controlled?" Akio's anxiety was rising.

"You won't be," Yoshio answered. "We've got that handled. You are immune with the mask on, and I'm immune too. So stop worrying."

"What if it makes one of *us* look like *it*?" Akio asked. There must be some combination of his concern that they should look out for.

"I'm not sure it can do that. Its imagery projection felt limited. When it was in my head, the way it planted desires felt complex. It felt like a drug in a way, like it was trying to trigger my dopamine response in association with giving it access to my thoughts and motor functions. The attacks were insistent and multi-faceted. It kept coming at me from different angles, trying new tactics. But the human image it projected felt simple. It was like a standard-def video on a hi-def TV. The illusion fell apart easily once I saw it for what it was. So I'd guess that projecting images on other people or even sending different images of itself to different people might be too much for it. What did it look like when you saw it?"

"Well, I only saw it 3D-projected anyway, so the definition wasn't perfect, but it looked like that actor from—."

"Hiroyuki Sanada," Yoshio cut him off.

"Yeah. A lot like him."

"Same. I think that's how everyone sees him."

"Why that guy?" Akio asked.

"Fan of his movies, I guess." Yoshio said.

"Do you think they get to watch movies in Hell?" Akio asked, imagining a movie night with myriad demons huddled around a big screen, eating eyeballs and fingers instead of popcorn, drinking blood cocktails, and having a grand old time.

"I was joking," Yoshio said.

"Oh." Akio couldn't read this kid at all. "So what does it really look like?"

"It's huge and wormlike with scales on its back and green protrusions everywhere like giant hardened green zits. Its head is fat and flabby and disgusting, with big round fangs almost as big as my forearms."

Akio didn't respond. Just envisioning it made him sick to his stomach. At least Akechi had looked mostly human.

"But we can defeat it," Yoshio said. "If we kill it, we won't need to deal with the yakuza, the robots, or anyone else."

"And I suppose you know just how to do that, right, Brain Boy?"

"No, but I know how to find out." Yoshio went to his suitcase and from under his few changes of clothes, he pulled a huge, frightening-looking book with a ghoulish, gray hand protruding from the cover, one finger broken off.

"Euh!" Akio flinched. "Not that book again!"

"This book saved you last time from what Sensei told me," Yoshio said, and he set the book on the table. It landed with an impact that seemed to shake the building, the earth, and the heavens too.

It was the *Zetsubō no Shīka*, a catalog of demons and everything to do with Hell: its planes and its rulers, the crimes that get you sent there and where exactly within, and the punishment you receive for those crimes, as well as many other disturbing bits of information about the netherworld. It was like Hell's almanac, an *Encyclopedia Demonica*, minus any maps. Miyahara had said that there couldn't be a map, because the planes of Hell were always in flux.

The book was a behemoth, nothing you'd ever find at Kinokuniya or Book Off. It was more than a half meter long, almost as wide, and a good fifteen centimeters thick. Yoshio hadn't had much room for anything else in his suitcase. Its cover looked like leather or skin, and Akio didn't want to know what kind. Thick sinews were sewn through the spine to bind it. There were bones and scales sticking out from the edges and black shiny stones that made an oval on the front, encircling the freaky zombie hand that appeared to be reaching out of it. It emanated a presence that was more like a living, breathing entity than a simple book of paper and glue.

"Yeah, yeah," Akio whined. "It told us about Ake . . . I mean the head-swapper demon freak. And about the damned mask that your sensei was supposed to come get for his collection or whatever. I wish he had."

Akio felt betrayed by Miyahara. He felt betrayed by Masami, and by so many other people in his life, he didn't know who he could trust anymore. Now some brainiac teenager he barely knew was in his apartment with a book from Hell, trying to convince him they could figure out how to kill some ultra-powerful, mind-controlling demon.

"That knowledge saved your lives," Yoshio stated. "Knowledge is the key to everything. We only have to learn the demon's weaknesses."

"And then what?" Akio was getting angry now. "We storm in there again, me in the mask and you with your big fat brain, just wrestle this giant worm demon to the ground and put a sword in it?"

"I don't know. Maybe," Yoshio said. "I haven't looked at the book yet. But with your mask on, you seem nearly unstoppable. If we can get —"

"The mask! If it wasn't for the damn mask, I wouldn't be in this mess at all!" Akio understood that the idea of the mask turning him into some kind of superhero was romantic and exciting from the outside. But the reality was that he was in constant terror and pain; when he wore it he was in perpetual conflict with the demon that took up residence in his head. Its presence was there to some extent even now when he wasn't wearing it. He wanted his simple life back. He didn't want to be a hero.

"We need Masami," Akio blurted, finally saying what had been on his mind the entire time. "We can't do it without her."

"She would be beneficial," Yoshio said. "But she's not here. We have to work with what we have."

"Why is she not here?" Akio asked out loud but not really to Yoshio. "She saved me and left."

"She's also the one who almost killed you."

"She wasn't herself," Akio answered. "She wasn't able to resist the mind control." And although he knew that, he was still upset about it. As if somehow she had let herself be mind-controlled, so she could finally get rid of him. She had never liked him to begin with and secretly wanted him dead.

Then why did she save me? And why didn't she stay after she did?

He didn't understand. If she wasn't still being controlled, why wasn't she there with them helping them plan? They needed her. They couldn't do it without her.

Yoshio went back to his suitcase and retrieved an ornate looking glass with a handle. It was rectangular and about half as wide as a page of the huge tome. The handle, which protruded from a corner, was made of some kind of bone or horn. Akio remembered that the book was in some arcane language, and only Miyahara could read it without the glass.

Yoshio went to the book and started slowly flipping the heavy pages. "I should have done this before we went charging into that building."

"But what would you have looked for?" Akio asked. "We didn't even know we were dealing with a demon then. Did we?"

"With Miyahara, it's always a demon," Yoshio said. "But it would've been a shot in the dark. And I was too anxious to take the time. Now we have a lot more information. We'll find it . . ." he trailed off as the pages absorbed him.

Akio watched him for many minutes, but did not rise to help. His head hurt with the thought of it, with the residue of wearing the mask, with whatever demon sense he had somehow developed. Akio felt the book radiate a demonic energy on a low level. It was not the sledgehammer swinging back and forth headache he got from the demon, or even the thumping pulse he got from the green gems. It was more of a dull throb, but he knew it was coming from the book. He wondered why he hadn't felt anything from the swords, and he turned to the katana that leaned against the wall by the futon. He couldn't remember putting it there. He put a hand on it and reached out with his thoughts.

Yes, there is an energy there. But it was not enough to pain him, or perhaps not the kind that *would* pain him. It was a protective energy and not an aggressive one. He hadn't noticed it before. He felt more in tune with the vibrations now, perhaps from wearing the mask again.

The mask was different as well. It didn't *give* him headaches; it took them away. It had given him this demon sense, but it was also the thing that eased the pain of it, and yet brought other, worse pain. He looked at it, half hidden under tousled blankets on the futon. It was alive and its voice was in his head. It had been there the entire time, but subdued, like a fat cat purring after a gratifying meal.

Finally, he rose, went to the kitchen, and got a beer from the fridge. He drank half of it quickly, and then sat down at the table by Yoshio.

As the pages slowly went by, he saw illustrations of the most horrid beasts. Th ere was a giant octopus-like demon called an *akkorokamui*, a huge fire-breathing chicken, a woman with eyes all over her arms, a bird demon created from fresh corpses called an *onmoraki*, a wicked-looking plant that sucks out people's souls, a huge fat spider called a *tsuchigumo*. Some of these Akio had heard of from legends, but others he hadn't. He found himself fascinated and revolted at the same time. He didn't want to look but couldn't help himself. One of the most disturbing images—and he made Yoshio stop on that page—was simply of a little boy sitting in a cave with something bundled in a patterned furoshiki cloth.

"What does that one say?" he asked Yoshio.

Yoshio held the glass over it and read.

"The *nunomusuko* appears as a little boy sitting on his feet. It waits in dark places and offers to share its sweetmeats with you if you can find its parents. When the victim enters the dark place to help, the boy opens its furoshiki to show the eyeballs, ears, and tongues of its previous victims. While its victim is shocked by this, its tentacle feet whip out with hundreds of stingers that inject a powerful sedative into the victim. While the victim is still alive, the nunomusuko carves out the eyeballs, ears, and tongue to add it to—"

"Stop! Just stop," Akio said. "This is so wrong. You can't even help a little boy in trouble without getting eaten alive by a demon! Is this shit real?"

"Sensei says this book is full of truth, and yet deceptive. It is best to analyze the entries thoroughly and meditate on them to better understand."

"Meditation again." Akio was flustered and disturbed. "We don't have time to sit around chanting and pontificating the universe. We need to find this thing and kill it. Keep looking."

Yoshio continued to flip the unwieldy pages until they saw it. It was just as Yoshio had described: a huge, fat, worm-like demon with scales and gem-like protrusions on its back. Its head was grotesque and flabby with bulbous eyes and long walrus-tusk-like fangs.

Akio had the feeling he had seen it before.

Yoshio put the looking glass to the page and started reading intently.

nentōkitō

Nentōkitō are born in the fourth plane of Hell, known as The Screaming Hell, wherein are contained alcoholics, thieves, lechers, and some murderers. The demon is made from souls who were unable to come to terms with their lot in life, who felt misery at being helpless to take charge and live the life they intended, who, at the moment of death, regretted their ineffective existence and held close their anger at letting their lives be dictated by other people or circumstances.

From the build up of the ugly regret and unhappiness of many such souls, the nentōkitō is born. It lives only to control, not knowing anything but that it seeks to redeem itself for all the wrongs its souls suffered in life, all the powerlessness they had to endure. It seeks power and control and nothing else. It does not need physical sustenance, but instead survives on the dominated spirits of its victims.

Its skin is a thick hide, impervious to assault by arrow, spear, or stone, except for a thin strip of flesh on its underbelly and a spot of soft tissue at the base of its skull. Their eyes are also vulnerable and it is said that certain greater demons consider them to be a delicacy.

There are an abundance of these demons in the Fourth Hell.

These demons are unable to control each other, however, and are compelled to spread out, often to other planes of Hell where they are employed to torture other souls and take away any and all free will. A common plane they are sent to is the Sixth Hell, known as The Burning Hell, where killers, liars, drunkards, and perverts are sent, those who ignored the teachings of the Buddha, and—

"Who, in their arrogance, believed others' lives beneath their own," Akio added, not even looking at the book. Pieces of Akechi's memories flooded into him.

"I know this demon," Akio said. "I mean, Akechi did. In Hell, one of them had controlled me—him. Made him perform meaningless tasks for what seemed like forever. He knew what was happening. His mind was aware, but he couldn't help it. It was stripping him of his self-worth as a punishment for his arrogance."

"But didn't Akechi have the mask? That's what protected you from being controlled, isn't it?" Yoshio asked.

"I thought so. I don't know. I see these things through his own eyes. I don't know if he was wearing it. But he must have been. His head was off. He needed the mask."

Akio had been impervious to the demon's mind control. He knew it wasn't because of how smart he was; he was smart enough to know that at least. If it could control Masami and likely Miyahara, he didn't have a chance.

"Maybe because I never saw it in person," Akio said. "When you were with the demon, did you see Masami? Was she there too?"

"No, I never saw her," Yoshio answered. "But . . .

"Right. Invisible. Damn."

"Anyway you saw plenty of gems, which seem to work fine on everyone else. The mask must be helping somehow."

Akio didn't know what to think. He fell silent, and Yoshio went back to the book.

"Here," he said. "Look at this section."

Nentōkitō cannot control greater demons, beings with superior intellect, or those who have no sense of self to begin with. Therefore, they have no power over insects, for example, and many lesser animals are also immune.

"Are you saying I'm a lesser animal?" Akio asked.

"No, but if we could find a swarm of locusts, maybe we could overwhelm it," Yoshio said.

"Seriously?" Akio asked.

"Cicadas are everywhere right now. Maybe we could catch some of those."

Akio bristled at the thought. He hated the noisy insects and when he was younger had never wanted to catch them like other boys, in spite of his father's efforts to take him bug hunting. He wanted nothing to do with them.

"Count me out," he said.

"I was joking," said Yoshio. "It was funny, wasn't it?"

Akio sighed. "Stick to science and math, kid."

"Okay."

Yoshio read on.

They impose their will through a form of telepathy, which can be accomplished in person or at great distances through use of the hard, gem-

like excretions from their backs. These are connected to the demon's mind via a spirit link.

"Spirit link," Yoshio thought out loud. "What is that exactly? It can't be that different from a kind of wifi signal, an ethernet connection . . . We just need to disrupt it."

"A spirit link the same as wi-fi?" Akio asked. It sounded ridiculous.

"Why not? It's just data of some kind traveling through space. It has to be some kind of wave. And a wave can be interrupted."

"Okay," It did make a kind of sense. "How do you plan to do that?"

"I did it once already, kind of by accident, when I was made to harvest the gems from the demon's body. I was just experimenting."

"Experimenting? During forced labor by a demon?"

"What better time?"

Akio frowned. He would never understand this kid. He would never understand anybody, but Yoshio was too far beyond.

"I found some ball bearings, and I put them in the pores left open by the extracted gems. After a few, the demon started to get uncomfortable. Not much more and it was clearly in pain. I hadn't known what would happen, if anything, but it short-circuited the connection it had with its minions. Th ey started to think for themselves and didn't know where they were. It was chaos."

"That's what was happening when you found me," Akio realized. "That's why everyone was in a panic. Th ey weren't being controlled anymore."

"Exactly. A lot of them freaked at the sight of the demon. They probably hadn't seen its true form before, probably never even realized there *was* a demon. Others blamed each other and started fighting amongst themselves. But a few of them seemed to still be under its control and filed off through a smaller back door.

"I saw Sensei then," he said, his eyes dropping to the floor. "He was with those ones. He's being controlled. I thought somehow he'd be able to resist it."

"We'll get him out," Akio heard himself say, though he had no clue as to how.

"Yeah." Yoshio wasn't really listening. He was thinking. Akio could see the gears turning a thousand kilometers a minute.

"So you did it once already," Akio said.

Yoshio looked at him with a "Did what?" face.

"Disrupted the connection. With pain."

"Yeah, but I had to be literally *on* it. I had its trust in the moment. That's not likely to happen again."

"Does it need to happen again? Maybe that did it. It's short-circuited and unable to use its mind whammy on anyone anymore."

"I doubt it. I'm guessing it's already regained control by now. The distraction was minor, considering what this demon is capable of. We should assume that everything is back to normal, apart from it being exceptionally pissed off and much more cautious now."

"Well, can't we just blast it with something? Toss a grenade in the room maybe?" Akio asked.

"The book said it was mostly impervious. I don't know if that counts for grenades, but even so we might only end up killing a bunch of innocent people."

"Innocent? These are yakuza we're talking about."

"Mostly . . . probably. Still, are we to be their judge and jury?"

The kid has to get moral on me. Aren't things hard enough without having to worry about things like innocent people dying?

But he stopped that line of thought. That was Akechi talking. Akio saw the four dead men in front of the freight elevator, headless and missing a few limbs. The blood-drenched carpet. Had they been innocent? They had been shooting at him and Masami. He had to stop them. But did he need to *kill* them? They may not have been in any more control than Masami was when she attacked him.

"You're right," he said. Then what? How do we make it suffer enough to lose focus again? I mean, I could just run in there and start hacking at it."

"Yeah, but again, the book says—"

"I know. It's impervious. But this sword can cut through anything. Why not an impervious demon? And the back of its neck is a weak spot, like it says. I'm sure of it, but I don't remember why I know that."

"If we can get behind it, that will be useful, though I'm not sure how. And maybe you're right about the katana. Maybe it'll cut this demon. But you running in there is dangerous. There will be yakuza everywhere. You're not bulletproof, right?"

"No, but I heal really fast when I have the mask on."

"You can't heal if you're dead."

"Touché."

"I'm trying to think of ways we could direct pain right to the demon without getting near it. Normally I would consider distance weapons of some kind with no area effect, meaning guns, bow and arrow, spears, and the like, but—"

"You have a gun," Akio said.

"Not anymore. I ditched it, remember? The Kofu police have it now. But it wouldn't matter. If it's impervious to arrows and spears, and possibly even your sword . . . It's likely impervious to bullets too."

"What about the underbelly? The book said it was weak there."

"Yeah, maybe we can get it to roll over if we tickle it," Yoshio said. "Humor," he added when Akio looked at him sideways. "Not my specialty."

"I don't know what to do," Akio said. "Miyahara sent for me and Masami but all I seem to be able to do is kill people really fast."

Yoshio didn't respond, lost in some whirlwind of cogitation. Akio went silent.

Four headless men.

He was thankful the yakuza had sent robots after him the last time and not humans. Still, he felt sick.

"We have to shut down the brain connection," Yoshio said. His eyes lit up suddenly. "Do you have a router? For wifi?"

"Yeah, of course. I have a pocket wifi."

"Where?"

Akio went to his kitchen and retrieved it.

"Do you have a screwdriver? Any other tools?"

Akio pulled out a small tool kit from his closet.

Without asking, Yoshio started to disassemble the router. Akio watched with wide eyes but was too tired and overwhelmed to protest.

"Just like wi-fi is an invisible signal, this demon's signal must be going out on some frequency. I said it earlier but didn't think it through. It's a wave. It has to be." The teenager was talking to himself now. "If I can just figure out what the frequency is."

Akio looked at his router, already in pieces. "I guess I won't be looking at any *ero-manga* online tonight." He walked the few steps to his bed, careful with each footstep, his legs still throbbing from the recent trauma. He collapsed onto it. "Wake me when it's over."

As he lay in bed, a passage about the nentōkitō replayed in his mind.

. . . from souls who were unable to come to terms with their lot in life, who felt misery at being helpless to take charge and live the life they intended . . .

He would help create one of these demons when he died. He was sure of it. For Akechi, it would be a complete circle.

But he was not Akechi. Akechi existed outside of him and yet in him at the same time. The part of Akio that was Akechi was a facsimile made of extracted memories and pain. The real Akechi still roamed the planes of existence somewhere as a ghost or a soul. Akio wondered if the samurai was with his son. Had his plan worked? Had Akechi's "noble death" as he had called it, served its purpose and cleansed his spirit of his wrongs? Had it reunited him with his estranged son?

And what if the book was lying to them? Even Miyahara said it was deceptive. Akio remembered that in the entry about the namakubikamen, the type of demon Akechi had become, it said their heads were used as balls for sport. But Akio didn't think that was true. Akechi's head had been locked in a box. Had they taken it out from time to time to use as a ball? And if they did, wouldn't that be something he'd remember? Akio tried to search Akechi's memories, but he couldn't find anything of the sort. The insectoid *niyarikangei* had decapitated him and locked his head in a box. He had spent centuries trying to get it out. It couldn't have been used in games.

Akio hated having Akechi's memories. He didn't want to know any of it.

"What if the book is lying?" Akio said with his eyes still closed.

"Could be," Yoshio replied, still engrossed in his tinkering. "Sensei says he's seen the information change sometimes. It shifts and reveals new things, hides other things."

"So we are blind in the dark," Akio said. He was getting sleepy now. He had had a far crazier day than when he had battled Akechi under the castle, something he never imagined possible. He had fought robots, yakuza, and . . . Masami.

Masami.

He just needed to . . .

3
The Second Trial

YE WHO ENTER HERE MAY FIND YOUR
SINS WASHED AWAY

he sign towered above Akechi's head in a fat, flowing script. *Another lie.*

It had been a year less one hundred days since his first trial and now the former daimyo and warlord had been collected again by three huge oni with blue-green skin. This time he had tried to tackle one of them but had only been knocked aside like a bug.

Apart from his brief first trial after a hundred days of imprisonment, he had battled nonstop for a year. His muscles were sore beyond any stiffness he had ever known, and yet they moved fine. He could chop and hack at people. He could run for shelter or high ground. He could wield any weapon. He could defeat any human spirit that came at him, but never the oni.

This time he had at least drawn blood when they came for him. After being swatted aside, he had rallied, swinging his hachiwari brutally, dancing like a leopard across the rocks, diving and dodging to come up with his blade severing the back of one of the oni's knees.

Blue-black blood had sprayed from the artery there, and its tendons had snapped. It buckled under its own weight, shrieking murder. The others converged on him, and his remaining attacks were beaten back, thwarted by the oni's superior strength and resilience. He was crushed under their fury, his arms and legs broken, bleeding from rents in his flesh that would have felled elephants.

But still he lived—if this existence could be called living. He could not truly die here, not again. And even when he was killed, he was reborn and made to fight once more.

But Akechi thrived on battle. As the days blurred on, no rising and falling of a sun to indicate time, no sleep to rest weary muscles, he had become numb with fighting. His skin felt as if it had been flailed off, his bones felt they would shatter from every impact, but he dug in. He forced himself to relish every kill, every drop of blood that splashed on his face and into his mouth. He was becoming mad.

But now he was dragged across coarse, burning stone into a circular waiting room, where the air cooled. He heard water flowing all around him. His mouth watered, and he wanted dearly to be submerged, to drown in cool refreshing water and never wake again.

But he knew that the water, too, was a lie.

The oni left him there in a pile of his own broken flesh and walked out of sight. He grinned at the fact that one of them had a pronounced limp.

He felt his bones start to mend. They wrenched themselves back into position, causing more pain than when they had broken. His muscle and skin sewing itself up felt like thousands of razor teeth set aflame and chewing his flesh, stapling it back together and cauterizing every fiber into place.

When the agony subsided and he was whole again, he stood and took in his surroundings. The walls were curved and the ceiling domed. It felt like he was in a giant ceramic bowl that had been flipped upside down. Water ran down the sides and filled connected pools that intersected the room in a way that rendered the only available floor into walkways between them. Sparsely scattered red stones dotted the walls and pools, some of them giving off a subtle glow. The floor was tiled and cool, designed with images of koi fish and seaweed, reds and greens.

Real koi swam in the pools as well, as did other shapes, humanoid ones. They had piscine tails but four human arms each, and the heads of salamanders. At first, Akechi thought they were very small, only the size of his forearm, but then he realized they were deep within the waters. He hoped they stayed there.

He longed to dive in and cool himself. He was desperate to plunge in his head and lap up the waters with abandon.

But he knew it was a lie.

Even if the water didn't turn to dust as he drank, the sheer pleasure of it would only weaken him. It would only make his unending battles in this infernal place all the worse. That one moment of relief would renew the year of torture to which he had already been subjected. His numbness would be taken from him. His scars and his callouses would be undone.

So he kneeled instead, with the waters flowing like mana around him. He closed his burnt eyes and ignored it.

Soon he heard stone scraping and water crashing down like a waterfall. His eyes opened, and in front of him he saw that the wall had given way as a large door opened. The water rained down from above its archway and the stones dragged themselves into position.

Black-green seaweed clung to stones that remained in the air, the water rushing around them. The stones and the seaweed together spelled out:

WITH PRAYER, MERCY FLOWS

The huge door opened onto a larger, cavernous room. A soft glow emanated from within; the air inside felt even cooler, more welcoming yet than the watery entry hall. In the center of the vast chamber, he saw a large, raised dais upon which a giant humanoid figure sat cross-legged. From the distance, it looked like a gray statue.

The second trial was about to begin, a full year after his death. King Byoudou had said the next trial would come then, and Akechi only knew the time had passed because he was here. It had seemed an eternity. No previous soul had been tried immediately before him as at his first trial, at least none that he had heard. Th ere had been no screams, no cries of mercy.

Four blue-green oni appeared from some unseen opening and began to move toward Akechi. But he followed the tiled pathway into the cavern on his own. He needed no prodding. He knew there was no way out of this. And if what King Byoudou had told him could be believed, which reflected the teaching learned during his mortal life, his exoneration was based on those who prayed for him. Considering the message in the waterfall, this trial would end the same as the last.

The oni backed off as Akechi moved into the main trial chamber, and he walked alone.

Water filled this cavern as well. Th e wide, raised platform in the center was encircled by water that flowed off it like a fountain. The pathway that Akechi walked forked to follow around that circle. On the outside of the path were larger pools containing the same koi and strange, four-armed humanoid salamanders, as well as a species of large turtle.

Water flowed from the walls, cascading off high ledges and from hidden channels. Lotus flowers gathered in the corners of the pools, their many petals open and tender, surrounding each dotted cupule that appeared to glow in its center. Th e entire scene looked like paradise. To Akechi it was torturous.

It was only another lie dangled before him that would be taken away when the trial ended. He tried to close his mind to it even as he walked to stand before the giant figure on the wide dais, which Akechi now noticed was carved to look like a giant lotus blossom.

As with King Byoudou, the figure's face appeared female until Akechi looked closer and saw the bare chest and cut of a man's abdomen. Its hands were clasped together in prayer, eyes closed. A circlet of seaweed decorated the figure's curled hair like a tiara. It was a gray stone statue three times Akechi's height. A loose robe was carved about the shoulders, draping down to wrap around the waist and cover the legs, which were crossed in a meditative pose.

As he watched, five of the four-armed salamander creatures shot up from the depths of the pool to flank the statue, two to each side and one in front, the water streaming off their sleek blue-black skin. They almost hovered on the water, only their fish tails remaining submerged. Red-trimmed gills on the sides of their necks opened to take in the air. Each held a spear erect at its side and two swords crossed over its chest. They stood like dour guards stationed to prevent any encroachment on the statue.

When the statue opened its eyes and moved, Akechi was not surprised.

"King Toshi!" all five salamanders announced, and swirled their swords and spears in a beautifully synchronized flourish, returning to their stolid poses.

The statue's eyes were a cerulean blue, deep as oceans, and as they peered down on Akechi, the skin around them took on color as well. The stone gray transformed into a light cornflower tone that spread down the cheeks. And as the lips opened to speak, they gained a coral pink hue.

"Noboru Akechi," the mouth said liquidly and languid.

The color spread rapidly over its body and garments now. The seaweed tiara took on a surprisingly effervescent shade of green, while the robe became a sandy orange. As the color reached the outstretched palms, each hand transformed into a blossom of whites and pinks, bursting with light and color, like flames reaching upward. The hands had become living lotus flowers fluttering in their own exuberance.

The blossom dais that the figure sat upon turned white and flush with life, like a buoyant cloud cushion. Upon it sat a god. Like King Byoudou before, this was the god who would judge him.

"You are here to face the charges laid on you at your death," the god said.

Akechi still couldn't remember his death. In the endless rounds of battle over the past year, he had forgotten more and more of his life as a man. He knew he had been a daimyo, a great warrior and leader. He knew he had a son who was to succeed him. But he could not remember much else.

There were daughters who hated him, he remembered, and loyal subjects who followed him. As he stood before this god king who was to judge him, his memories started to filter back in, as if they were being allowed to return for this trial only.

"You are to be given a second chance at freedom."

Lie.

"If you are found innocent, you will be free to await rebirth and find your path to the Pure Land."

I will never be found innocent.

"If that is how you feel, then shall we bother?" King Toshi spoke directly.

Akechi's thoughts were not private and he knew this, but he could no more control them than he could control the outcome of this trial.

"Because it is your tradition, I suppose," Akechi answered haughtily.

"The prayers of your loved ones will be tallied," the king went on, "and your state of repentance will be assessed. Then I will decide if you will be freed. If my answer is yes, you will be escorted out of Hell. If my answer is no, you will return for a third and final trial in one year. At which point, King Godou-tenrin will be your judge and decide your final fate. As it is writ, you are guilty of the crime of countless murders with an arrogant heart. Let the prayer tally begin."

Akechi scoffed. There would be no prayers. At his last trial, there had been a single prayer only. It must have been his boy's. He could think of no other who would care. His boy loved him.

Didn't he?

They had shared tea. They had bonded as father and son. But something had gone wrong. Akechi could not remember.

The cavern began to rumble and shake. The water flowing from the walls began to increase in volume, spraying out in massive gouts. The level of the pools around him began to rise. The red stones shifted their pattern of lights, some growing brighter, some diminishing.

At first, the salamander beasts remained still, but there was a nervousness about them. They seemed edgy and ready to flee. The cavern roared with water, and soon the dry path on which Akechi stood was submerged, the water lapping at his feet.

"What is happening?" Akechi asked.

"Your trial has begun!" King Toshi boomed.

The feel of the water as it rose up Akechi's legs was heavenly. He remembered baths in tiled pools, luxuriating in hot springs after a particularly bloody battle, the mineral waters rinsing out his wounds as rivulets of red seeped into the pool.

He had countless wounds now.

Could he be freed? Could there be enough prayers for him?

"No!" he screamed. "It's a lie!" He tried to fight the feeling of pleasure the water brought him. It was to his waist now. The rumbling had subsided, but the water flowed with equally great pressure. King Toshi sat with eyes closed, lotus flower hands aflame.

The salamanders appeared to be quivering slightly now. What were they worried about? They were aquatic creatures. Certainly they weren't concerned about drowning.

Then, in one massive rush, all of the koi shot out of the cavern, disappearing into unseen watery passages. The turtles were quick to follow. As the last turtle slipped from Akechi's view, the salamanders dove deep and were gone.

What were they afraid of? He was the only one in the room that could be drowned.

Another rumble shook the chamber as the water reached Akechi's chin. He looked across the water's surface to see a massive tentacle reach around the base of King Toshi's lotus pedestal. A second one followed. They were each thicker than Akechi's chest and lined with suckers as big as his face. The god king remained unmoved.

The water cleared the top of Akechi's head as more tentacles followed, and he began to float up into the rising underground lake. In the clear waters, he saw blood streams flowing from myriad wounds on his battle-raw body.

A smooth bulbous head the size of an elephant appeared behind the king's back. Eyes on stalks craned to look at Akechi. It lurched bodily out from behind the king, who was now nearly submerged. More limbs were revealed on the giant sea monster, huge spidery legs beneath the tentacles and nearly as long, capped with sharp spikes. The beast pushed off into the water and Akechi saw the mouth on its belly, gaping with rows upon rows of teeth like a shark.

He had been watching the horrifying scene develop in front of him as an observer, but it suddenly struck him that this was directly for him. This was his trial after all. If he killed this beast, would he be set free?

It was an impossible thought. Akechi had barely been able to wound the oni, and they fought on land with weapons he was familiar with. This beast was at home in the water, and Akechi was unarmed. *And drowning!* he realized as he gulped in water in place of air.

The demon leviathan rolled and spun in the water, positioning itself to rush the daimyo. Akechi kicked toward the surface of the water as it rose higher and higher, past King Toshi's head now.

The beast unfurled its tentacles and in a thrust of power, shot toward Akechi like a charge of horses. The impact of the water alone was enough to toss him out of the pool, but it was followed by the bone-crushing crash of a wall of smooth cephalopod flesh.

As he soared through the remaining air in the cavern, he noticed numbers carved into the side of the wall behind King Toshi. They rose in descending order to zero as they ascended far above the king's head. The water level currently lapped between "11" and "12," while numbers already submerged grew rapidly larger the deeper they were engraved.

Akechi slapped back into the water with a sting and immediately found himself enveloped in a huge, fleshy tentacle, unable to move. He was dragged down to the bottom of the pool, taking more water into his lungs. Down below the walkways, down far below the god king's dais, and into the dark black waters where no glowing lotus lights or red stones penetrated.

Still, he could see the creature as it skittered along the lake floor. It unfurled him underneath itself and Akechi saw its horrid maw, only an arm's length from his face. His body lurched from the lack of air, even though he knew he didn't need it. He was dead already. How was he still suffering as if he were alive? It was part of the game, part of his punishment. Mortals were utterly subject to the whims of their nature, dead or not. The maw came closer as he convulsed. He could do nothing.

Was this what his torture would be now? Having failed this trial, was he doomed to be drowned and eaten repeatedly? Was there to be no more endless battle? He had been getting rather used to that.

"One!" a voice boomed through the depths, muted by the mass of water. The leviathan released him. It seemed to slaver at Akechi's floating blood momentarily, its scaly tongue spiraling in the murk. Then, in a burst that sent Akechi head over foot, tumbling across the water's bed, the massive sea creature ascended and disappeared in the blackness.

Akechi found himself prone on the tile walkway, coughing and spluttering up water and blood. The god, King Toshi, was looking down at him gravely.

"One," he repeated. "One prayer was said for you."

"One," Akechi repeated to himself. "Who?" he asked the king.

My boy!

"It is not for me to say."

"Damn you! I need to know!"

No one cared for him. He had seen it in all their faces. He had been a harsh ruler. But he had loved once. He had had a wife and son.

But his wife was long dead. It had to be his son.

"There have been times when one prayer was of such sincerity and depth of love that it was enough," the god king said. "But this one is not sufficient. And your repentance is nil. You are found guilty of your crime. Your sentence is given. You shall remain in Hell for one year's time awaiting your third and final trial."

King Toshi's eyes closed, and the gray slowly crept back over skin and dais until, again, it looked only a statue.

Akechi coughed and lurched on his back, trying to find the will to continue. He had known this would be the result. He would never be released. He would never be redeemed. But he had not expected the method of the trial. He had expected more words, more talking heads, and then back to endless killing.

A thick blue leg appeared to his side, another one on the other side. He started to rise. He would not be pushed about by these oni thugs. He would walk out on his own legs. But before he could stand, large blue hands gripped him and carried him to a corner of the cavern he had not yet noticed. Looking down, he saw they held him above a swirling whirlpool. With a heave, they tossed him in.

He flailed as he spun, but the rapid current took him under, shooting him through the murky dark, until he emerged in heat and mist, sulfur and rock. He landed on jagged stone and spat water that instantly vaporized. Through the mist, a wild-eyed man with a small axe charged at him.

Axe, he thought, as he instinctively took a battle stance. *I'll need a better weapon than that, but for now it will do.*

4

Kabukicho

NE

The king's voice resonated in Akio's head as he threw his hands up to deflect the axe. But no blow came. His eyelids cracked open, and he saw the white of his ceiling. He was in his apartment again. Someone was speaking.

"One," the voice said. "Just one."

"Who was it?" Akio asked, still half asleep. "I need to know."

"Who was who?" the voice asked. "Are you awake?"

Akio opened his eyes. Yoshio stood above him, looking down.

"We need a gem," the teenager said. "Just one will do."

Akio blinked his eyes and then squinted, trying to understand what Yoshio was saying.

"One of the demon's excretions," Yoshio said in answer to Akio's confusion.

"Excretions?" Akio mumbled as he sat up.

"Yes, a green gem excretion. I need one to analyze the frequency."

"The frequency, right." Akio said groggily. "What if there isn't any frequency? What if it sends its messages out with magic or something?"

"Uh huh . . . magic," Yoshio answered dismissively. "We need a gem. If I can find its frequency, I can find a way to stop it."

"Weren't you harvesting gems not long ago? Why didn't you grab one?"

"I should have. I was too occupied with my experiment with the ball bearings."

"Okay. Well, how do you propose we get one? I don't want to go back in that building just to retrieve a gem so we can go back in that building again later," Akio whined.

"We shouldn't have to," Yoshio said. "Like you said, the demon is possibly controlling all the yakuza in Tokyo, or at least a great number of them. It can't do that without some kind of connection via the gems. We should be able to get one off a yakuza somewhere. You have some kind of sixth sense that detects demonic presences now, right? You said that the gems give you headaches. We just need to find a yakuza that gives you a headache and get the gem off him."

"Sure, piece of cake," Akio said. "With or without the demon mask?" he asked sarcastically.

"Without, definitely," Yoshio answered in earnest. "The demon shouldn't recognize you with it off."

"Uh huh," Akio said. "And you know how well I fight without the mask on, right? I was never that great at judo, to be honest."

"You seemed to do pretty well in the parking lot back in Kofu."

"That was a fluke."

"We'll figure out another way then. Where do you think is the best place to start? Where would we have the most luck finding one?" Yoshio asked.

"The first time I felt the headaches was in Kofu when the demon was near. But I felt it again in Ueno when I bumped into a guy. I'm sure he was a yakuza. I think he had a gun. He must have had a gem on him, or several."

"Ueno?"

"Yeah. It was just at the train station, but he was probably going to the Nakama building."

"True," Yoshio answered. "And we can't go back there yet. You know Tokyo better than me. Where do the most yakuza hang out?"

"I don't know. I think they're kind of everywhere in some capacity. Most obviously though would be Kabukicho. That's where most of the hostess clubs and soaplands are."

"Yeah, of course," Yoshio said. "Kabukicho. The red light district. Have you been there?"

"Once or twice," Akio answered with a wink, trying to sound world-weary and wise. "But honestly just for stories and photo ops. And there's a lot of tame stuff you can do there too, you know. There's a movie theater and restaurants and whatnot. But I have never *partaken* in the seedier side of things if that's what you're thinking. Who's got time for that stuff?"

Akio had thought about *partaking* on more than one occasion. It wasn't a big deal. Lots of guys did it. They'd go to hostess bars and pay through the nose to sit and talk to a pretty girl all night. Or they'd just get straight to the point and go to a soapland. Prostitution was illegal, but soaplands got around it by claiming to only give men *baths*. Akio had heard there were even some places that catered to women.

But he didn't like the idea of paying for it. For one, it felt wrong, and a little disgusting. The thought of who-knows-how-many men having been intimate with these women turned him off. For two, he couldn't afford it. He couldn't even afford maid cafés. He wasn't about to throw down hard-earned cash for a soapland. For three, and worst of all, he had learned that some of the girls were in those places against their will, thanks to an article by none other than Masami Sato. And that really bothered him. It made him angry. It wasn't acceptable any way you looked at it.

Akio thought of the images of himself the demon had projected, standing there looking suave and rich, next to a ridiculously expensive car and surrounded by women. The feeling now was similar to a realization he had in senior high school after he had discovered his love for photography. He had looked back at how disappointed he had been in junior high school to not make the baseball team, and laughed, realizing that he didn't even like baseball that much. It was just what he thought he was supposed to want. It was what the cool kids did.

Akio wanted a girlfriend, and eventually a wife and children. He did not want to pay for some fleeting pleasure that he could manage well enough on his own for no money at all. He would wait until it was real, until there was love.

"Those types of places are run by yakuza, right?" Yoshio asked, seeming a little nervous.

"Far as I know. The crooked politicians, police, and corporate big wigs who are in the yakuza's back pocket frequent them. We've done some stories."

"So we wander Kabukicho until you feel something," Yoshio said.

"I'm feeling a lot right now, actually. I'm pretty sure this is what somebody dead feels like. And I'm hungry. Can we eat first?"

"Yeah, you need fuel," Yoshio responded. "Me too. I've barely eaten since this morning. They didn't give me much. But first, try this out." Yoshio handed Akio a Tower Records shopping bag.

Akio took it and looked it over. Whatever was in it was heavy. The top of the bag had been modified with a resealable storage bag, so it would shut tight. Akio pulled open the seal. Inside was an aluminum foil flap tucked securely into one side with a pull tab to show which side it opened from. Akio pulled the tab.

Resting between walls of double sheets of aluminum foil was the mask.

"It's temporary," Yoshio said. "The foil gets beat up easily and will fall apart soon enough, but until I can get ahold of some sturdier silver shielding fabric, this will do."

"What does it do? Keep the mask sealed for freshness?"

"It's a budget Faraday cage, so you can carry it without it attracting attention to itself. It blocks out its voice—its signal. So it won't pester me or anyone else to wear it. It will quiet the mask in the same way the metal box does."

"Great, thanks." Akio said. "But I thought it had died down. Masami said it wasn't bothering her."

"It seemed quiet until you passed out the second time. I got the feeling it was giving up on you. And it was starting to get aggressive. So I made this."

"This is good. Really. Thanks." Akio zipped the bag shut, having the urge to drop it into Tokyo Bay and let it sink like a stone. But responsibility nagged him. If he dumped the mask, someone else would find it eventually, someone who had no idea how to control it, and Akechi would go on a rampage. He had no choice but to keep it. It had become his burden.

It was after eleven when they left the apartment. Akio's muscles, bones, and every bit of connective tissue ached like someone had pummeled him with meat tenderizers capped with rusty nails. Yoshio sat next to him on the train, fidgeting with his fingers, as if he were building something invisible. It was a forty minute ride to Shinjuku, and Akio wished they had eaten before getting on the train. He was ravenous now. His metabolism had caught up with the abuse his body had taken, and he needed to replenish badly.

He had swapped out his battered pants and shirt and put on a dark gray hoody to replace the torn and bloody jacket he had left in the yakuza's secret passage. He sat, slouched forward, his backpack pressing into him, his head covered by the hood. He focused on his hunger and tried not to think about what they intended to do.

From the train station, they stopped at a little eatery in Shinjuku. Akio wished he was at Menya Murakami, that Kenji was there cracking jokes, and he could pretend for a minute that everything was okay. He inhaled his food and wanted nothing more than to sit and never get up again. The violent urges of Akechi were gone. He was only Akio. And Akio wanted to hide in his apartment and curl up in a ball.

And yet, here he was.

What am I doing? I'm not a hero.

He had said those four words to Masami in Kofu, when the demon samurai was coming after them. He had wanted to go home then, and leave Masami and Miyahara to deal with it on their own. He had thought he would just muck everything up more than he already had. Not to mention he had been scared out of his mind.

And yet, he had stayed. He found some courage from somewhere and did the right thing. In the end, he had been the only one left. If he had gone home, Masami and Miyahara might be dead.

He wouldn't go home now either, as much as he craved it. In spite of his fear, there was something else in him now. A weight had settled in his bones, a lead body suit that blanketed his anxiety, muffled it like Yoshio's Faraday cage had muffled the mask. The anxiety was still there, bubbling under the surface, but it was dull and distant.

They were planning to intentionally seek out some yakuza with nothing but his own scrawny useless body and Yoshio's brains. Akio was simply a homing beacon, his headaches able to alert them to someone with a gem. Hopefully they wouldn't stumble onto anything else demonic. He felt the weight of the mask inside his backpack pushing into his spine, as if trying to reach inside him. He hoped he wouldn't need it.

How they were going to get the gem once they found one was the real problem. Yoshio had assured him that they would see a way once they located one. Right now there were too many variables.

They walked the few blocks from the ramen restaurant to the intersecting, blinking red arches that designated the entry to Kabukicho. It was nearly always busy in this district. The hours of dawn were the exception, when the club-goers had finally passed out, the stores weren't open yet, and careless tourists were waking up with no memory of their night, only to find outrageous charges on their credit card bills from the Nigerian-owned club where they had been roofied. But even during that early hour, there would be people about, just not as many.

In the daytime, the hostess and host clubs seemed more of a novelty; the video stores and massage parlors were something to snicker about, but at night everything grew sinister. The clubs were lit up in neon, and the barkers beckoned you in. Photographs of beautiful young women showed in the club windows, tempting men inside to empty their wallets for the fawning attentions of a hostess. Some windows had photos of handsome young men to lure women with equal effect.

The people on the streets were a mixed lot, some less wholesome, looking for illicit pleasures, selling them, or simply intrigued by them and enjoying being on the fringes of darkness, like moving a finger quickly through a flame, not long enough to get burned. Occasionally some of them slipped and fell into the fire.

Competing music blared from storefronts, karaoke clubs, video game parlors, and *izakayas*, places that seemed innocent enough and probably were for the most part—though Akio viewed the once goofy and innocuous Robot Restaurant with a newly awoken suspicion. The air felt electric and unpredictable. Although it was apparently tame compared to what it had been before Akio was born, there was still something sinister here. He understood the allure, but it made him anxious.

Yoshio seemed even more so. His shoulders were tense, and his eyes were darting here and there, as if calculating their odds of survival. Seeing someone more uneasy than himself made Akio feel better, but he still had no idea how they were going to accomplish their plan, primarily because it wasn't really much of one.

Go to Kabukicho, hope to get a headache that will lead us to a yakuza with a gemstone. Take it from him. I figured Brain Boy would have thought up something better.

"Once we find a gem, we'll assess the situation and formulate a plan," said Yoshio.

"What?" Akio asked, startled by Yoshio's seeming ability to read his thoughts.

"You seem nervous," said the teen. "I just want you to know that we can reassess once we have a target. We won't go into it totally blind."

"*I* seem nervous?" Akio answered. "*You* seem nervous to me."

"I'm on edge, senses heightened. The adrenaline has kicked in. It could be construed as nervousness, but it's all in how you react to it. I feel more like an animal who's alert to danger, and therefore more prepared for it. Th at actually makes me feel less nervous. But ultimately, it's a choice. Nervousness is caused by the same chemicals as excitement, both of which serve to make you more alert. The locus coeruleus starts sending norepinephrine to your heart and lungs, which speeds up your heart and makes your breath quicker, but it's the same chemical response that—"

"Shut up," Akio said. "Just . . . stop."

"Okay."

They moved through the bustling, neon dark like aliens in a predatory world. There was a clinginess to the muggy air. It settled on Akio's hoody like hands groping him, padding him down. Eyes flicked toward them as they walked, sensing his nervousness like animals sense prey.

"We got the cutest girls right here, gentlemen!" A high, nasal voice jumped into Akio's ear, startling him. "Just follow me!" Both Akio and Yoshio turned to see a thin man in his thirties, in dark slacks and jacket, a button down shirt with muted purple stripes. He was leering at them with bugged eyes and raised eyebrows. "This way, gentlemen! Lovely young girls are waiting for you."

Akio forced a smile and tried to be polite. "No, thank you. We don't really have time."

Yoshio simply put his hand up to say no, and wouldn't look the guy in the eyes. "That's gonna happen a lot, isn't it?" he asked, sounding uncomfortable.

"Two, hot, young, obviously flush guys like us?" Akio answered with an awkward grin. "Probably."

And it did happen a lot. Almost every ten steps from where they entered at Yasukini Boulevard. The predatory barkers seemed to zero in on Akio. They wouldn't leave him alone. The only ones who did were the Nigerians, who only had eyes for Western tourists. After they got in deeper, it lessened a bit. Akio supposed the hustlers and touts figured you knew where you were going after a point and left you alone.

He kept his eyes down, avoiding them, avoiding everyone, as best he could, and waited, searched for the pain that would guide them to what they needed. It was like searching for a spider that he knew would bite him. And yet, he walked on, alert to any twinge in his head that might mean a gem.

Akio's backpack, a black rectangle with two brown straps that buckled midway down, hung heavily on him in spite of its few contents. He could feel the weight of the mask nestled in the Tower Records bag lined with aluminum foil. It was silent. But its close proximity was enough to unnerve him and make him crave it all the same. It was becoming part of him, and he hated it. But it was also invigorating and exciting. He was powerful and confident with the mask on. He could do things he had never imagined possible. He felt indestructible.

Nearly.

Masami had proven that feeling dead wrong. He had taken those robots apart like they were toys. But not Masami. He dearly wished she was with them.

Akio had no experience with hard drugs, but he imagined addicts might feel this way. He loathed the mask, but craved it. It made him feel alive and yet so empty. It made him do horrible things.

A blood-soaked carpet. Headless corpses in a row.

And yet he needed it. Didn't he? He needed it to save Miyahara, to stop this demon from turning all of Tokyo's citizens into its mind slaves.

And yet in Kofu, he had fought without the mask. He hadn't needed it then.

A crack as his foot snapped a neck.

He wondered why he couldn't tap into that power now, without wearing the mask. But what was the difference? He had lost control both times. He had *killed* both times.

In Kofu, it had been his anger that triggered it, his fear that Masami had been hurt or worse. The thought scared him. He didn't want to become Akechi whenever he became angry.

Who am I, The Hulk?

He'd rather wear the mask. At least with the mask—and a giant, throat-wrecking pill—he could choose when he became Akechi.

But regardless of how it happened, he had to relinquish control. If not, he was nothing. Just a scrawny dork with dreams of being a great photographer. That version of him couldn't save the world.

A gang of handsome young men in black jackets, dark, slim-fitting slacks and jeans issued from a club and started moving along the street in a loose wave. Confidence oozed off them, reflected in their spiked hair and bold jewelry. They flirted with women and strutted as they handed out postcards and tried to get women to follow them. Akio felt uncomfortable. He knew these were host boys, and they were out in force to lure more women into their club. They wouldn't be looking at him, but he veered away from them anyway. He was scrawny and far from debonair. These guys were smooth-talking ladykillers. They were essentially gigolos, but they were the epitome of cool and handsome. How could any woman not want that?

But as he watched, he noticed that most of the women avoided them. Some even completely ignored them, and he remembered the false image of himself the demon had displayed. He remembered how quickly it had become utterly unappealing. The hosts suddenly seemed more like clowns than charming ladies' men.

He tapped Yoshio on the shoulder and led him toward a side street, an alley really, that angled off the main drag into shadowed backdoors and small parking garages. He thought if they ventured into the darker spaces between the hustle of the main throughways they might find what they needed.

A short way into the alley, a man was talking to a young, attractive woman who looked half-white—him leaning against the wall, her with one foot up on a step, both smoking. The woman smiled through smeared makeup as the man made some wisecrack that Akio couldn't quite hear, something about sore muscles or hurt feelings. She wasn't crying anymore, but it was clear she had been. Akio looked away as they both caught his gaze.

At that moment, a young man in a souvenir jacket bumped into him hard, knocking him into Yoshio.

"Watch it, loser! Get out of my way!"

"Sorry!" Akio instinctively said, though he wasn't sure if he was to blame for stumbling away from the couple on the steps, or if he'd been intentionally rammed.

The punk sneered at Akio and pulled his fist back briefly in a mock punch. Pain seared up Akio's neck and into his skull from the back. He leaned forward with the impact of it, squinting at the young tough, his jaw clenched.

"Idiot," the punk said, adjusted his black beanie with the Western letters, FTW, and then turned to keep moving. Akio watched the punk go, his bomber jacket, embroidered with gold sleeves and a colorful tiger, rearing up and claws splayed.

Akio hated guys like that. All balls and no brains. Insensitive pricks who wore their stupidity like a crash helmet, proud of how many people they knocked down along the way. Too many times he had been threatened by the same type. He imagined putting the mask on, and then letting the punk threaten him. How would Akechi handle that? The punk would be a bloodstain.

He shook the thought away. There had been too many bloodstains already. He couldn't let himself get angry over some petty jerk.

Except, he realized . . .

Except that this particular petty jerk had *gems* on him! Akio had felt them in a clump, pressed against the punk's torso.

"Him," Akio muttered, nodding his head toward the quickly disappearing, embroidered tiger.

"Huh?" Yoshio turned, and Akio noticed that he was eyeing the jerk with similar disdain.

"Him," Akio repeated. "He's got gems."

Together they moved into the alley. The punk soon exited the other end, disappearing into the larger crowd of the street.

"Quick," Yoshio said. "We can't lose him."

As they began to move faster, Akio's temper rose. He had visions of forcibly taking the gems from the punk, after beating him senseless.

How dare this peasant call me an idiot! How dare he say that to the one wears Akechi's mask! To the one who holds Akechi's anger!

"There!" he said, pointing as he saw the light from a neon sign glint off the gold sleeves.

They weaved through the people after him. Another tout stepped up, a heavyset man with a wispy beard and too-small fedora. "All the beautiful ladies are here, gentlemen. Come on in!" They dodged and quickly moved past.

The jacketed punk came to an abrupt stop in front of a night club, a neon sign blaring, "Heaven on Earth" and another that said, "Girls! Pole dancing!" and "Foreign ladies!" in that order. People waited outside to get in, lined up by a red rope. But the punk went right up to the doorman who glanced at him and then moved the rope aside. The tiger disappeared into the dark entryway and was gone.

Akio and Yoshio stopped, looked at the line to get in, which wasn't terribly long, maybe ten people, then at each other.

"Now what? How the hell do we get in there?" Akio asked, feeling stupid that he was asking a teenager how to get into a night club. He could almost see Yoshio's brain spinning in response.

"They won't let me in," Yoshio said, "not without a fake I.D. You get in line. I'll be right back."

Akio lined up, trying to pretend like he did this all the time. To show his confidence, he winked at a guy just in front of him, a slick playboy in a sharp suit, who glared back. "Wrong club, gay boy. Ni-chome is that way." He pointed down the street.

"I . . . " Akio stuttered. "I . . . I'm not . . ." But the man wasn't listening. He had started chatting to two women who were in line in front of him.

Akio left a little extra space between him and the man from then on. As he got closer and more people, mostly men, lined up behind him, he kept to himself. He was approaching the door faster than he wanted, looking about for Yoshio constantly.

Where are you? Come on.

He realized that he still had his backpack on. They weren't going to let him in wearing that. Lots of clubs had lockers, but even if this one did, he couldn't leave the mask in a locker; he needed it close.

He took the backpack off and slipped the Tower records bag out. The foil inside crinkled in his hands. He zipped his hoody up the front and tucked the bag up under it, feeling the baggie with the fat pills in his hoody pocket as he did. He looked in the backpack. A plastic bottle of water was the only other thing inside. He couldn't sneak that in. No outside drinks allowed.

He hated to lose the backpack; he'd had it since high school, but there was nothing for it. He let it dangle from one hand and, making sure the people behind him weren't paying attention, let it drop to the sidewalk against the building.

He was fourth away from entering now. The two women, who were dressed to attract the wealthiest kind of sucker and drain them dry, were greeted by the doorman.

"Looking beautiful tonight, ladies. Welcome. It'll be a thousand yen each, just to your right. It includes one drink and an ice cream. Have a good time."

A thousand yen. That's not much, especially with a drink and an ice cream!

Akio was suddenly looking forward to this club, distracted by the atmosphere and almost forgetting why he was there. The playboy was greeted next with a loud and boisterous welcome.

"Mr. Onishi! What are you doing waiting in line? You know you don't have to do that! Please go on in! Thank you so much for being here. The club is always more fun with you here!"

"Oh you know, I hate to abuse my privilege," Onishi said in the most self-important way. "Besides, the ladies in front of me were quite the lookers. It was worth the wait!"

The doorman gave a forced, sycophantic laugh, and Onishi laughed down his nose right back. Akio let out an involuntary sarcastic chuckle, garnering another sideways look from the playboy. He quickly looked away and tried to make it look like he was laughing at something he'd seen down the street.

Onishi went inside and Akio stepped up, hoping against hope that Yoshio would materialize right that second.

No luck. The doorman looked him over, appearing to not like what he saw.

"There was a time I wouldn't let someone in wearing a hoody," he said, then shook his head. "But times have changed. What is happening to fashion?" he asked rhetorically. "Thirty-five hundred yen just to your right."

Thirty five hundred yen?

The doorman was looking to the next guest in line when he saw that Akio hadn't moved. Akio asked, "Does that include drinks?"

"No," the doorman said. "Have fun."

No drinks? No ice cream? But . . .

Akio forced himself forward into a short entryway where a different man opened another door for him and closed it behind. He only had four thousand yen on him. He wouldn't be able to buy a drink if they asked him to. And the sign said, "Two drink minimum." Akio had been in a few clubs before, though not this one in particular. The minimum was strictly enforced, and worse than that, often if you didn't have a drink in hand constantly, you'd be made to pay for the minimum anyway and then kicked out.

He hoped there was some kind of cheap drink special. He had to at least keep up the facade until Yoshio arrived. *Where the hell is Yoshio?*

Akio paid his fee to the pale woman with pink eyelashes behind a high narrow counter, a hulking man lurking behind her, half in shadow. He moved into the club. Music pulsed like a living force. Darkness thrilled at the edges. It wasn't a large place. A couple of clubs he had been in were multiple levels with huge dance floors and stages. But this was a strip club, and he hadn't been to one before.

There was a long room on one side, dimly lit, where there were comfortable chairs arranged around low tables. A low stage lit with multiple light sources—strobes, spotlights, overhead, all different colors—was lined with short stools. A place to set drinks was directly at the edge of the stage. Shiny silver poles pierced the platform at even intervals where scantily clad, some nearly naked, women slid and slithered, danced and hung with acrobatic skill. They were almost none of them Japanese, and Akio was briefly transfixed. He had never really been attracted to foreign women, but he thought some of these might change his perspective. A shiny-skinned black woman with silver blonde hair caught his eyes. She looked like a princess in her slender tiara decorated with rows of gems that changed colors in the variegated strobe lights. Her skin sparkled with glitter, and the way she caressed and enveloped the pole had Akio's eyes in a death grip.

"Have a seat right here," a suited man said loudly over the music. "Tigress won't bite you . . . unless you pay extra," he chuckled. Akio moved toward the stool, and as soon as the man turned, a woman in a tight black top that pushed her breasts out uncomfortably too much for Akio, asked him, "What can I get you?" She was Asian, but not Japanese. She had an accent that Akio thought was Korean, but he wasn't sure. She was beautiful in a dangerous way. A tattoo of a snake slithered up one side of her neck to where her hair was buzzed above the ear and then spiked out with pink tips. Or were they blue? They seemed to change with the light.

But that tattoo. Tattoos meant yakuza.

"Uh . . ." Akio stuttered. "Do you . . . uh . . . do you have any specials?"

The waitress rolled her eyes but smiled at him—the way girls had always smiled at him, like he was something to be pitied but not loved. "Sure, sweetie. Five hundred yen draft beer."

Oh perfect!

Akio was thrilled that he could at least delay being booted out of the place for a bit longer.

"Yes, uh . . . great," he said, and reached for his wallet.

"Pay me later, sweetie," she said. "Hope you have some money left over to tip the girls." She gave a sideways glance at Tigress, as if she knew he didn't.

"Of course," Akio said loudly. "Yeah, I've got loads on me." Several eyes turned his way, some fleeting, some remaining to glare.

Maybe I shouldn't have said that. Certainly not quite so loud.

Of course if anyone tried to mug him later, they'd find out he didn't have a yen to his name. And if things went really south, they might have an unpleasant run-in with Akechi as well.

He sat on the stool and nervously avoided looking directly at the strippers. He fidgeted, looking around the club. A tall, white woman with dark red hair gyrated on the pole to one side of Tigress, and another white woman, blonde, was at the pole on the other side. A couple of stools over were two salarymen, laughing and feeding Tigress repeatedly with thousand yen banknotes. On his other side, more salarymen were making innuendo toward the redhead. Akio heard bits of their conversation and it wasn't praising the hair on her head. Behind him, in a booth, were a group of twenty-something, hip-looking, white men in black, with rocker hairstyles and jewelry, speaking English and acting like they owned the world.

He felt horribly out of place. He kept fidgeting in his seat, wishing his drink would come, and wishing it wouldn't, because then he would probably have to pay for it and order another one. He needed to find that punk yakuza with the gem. He needed Yoshio to show up, *and now.*

He started to get up when the waitress returned with his beer.

"Here you go, sweetie. Let me know when you're ready for your second one," she smirked.

She knows I don't have anymore money. She's a damn mindreader.

He thanked her as he sat back down and took an obligatory sip. When she moved on, he looked around for the restroom. He didn't have to use it, but it would be a place to gather his thoughts and a way to scope out the club. He took another sip and stood up.

Tigress caught his eye momentarily and he went wobbly, looking away like a shy schoolboy.

He had fought a demon, literally. He had murdered people. *That was Akechi. Not me.* He had faced things that no one in this club could ever imagine. And yet, he was like a scared rabbit when it came to locking eyes with a woman. He moved away jerkily, every effort to be smooth thwarted by his clumsy, skinny body.

He saw a restroom sign pointing down a hallway past the front door. He slowed down as he passed the entryway, hoping that it would open as he passed and Yoshio would come through.

It did open, and a young man with short hair and a wide face entered.

"Yosh—" he started, but it wasn't Yoshio at all. The guy wasn't even that young, and was slightly heavyset. He only had a wide face because his whole body was wide. The dim light of the club was playing tricks on Akio's eyes. Another two entered behind this one, and they all bumped fists. Akio tried to catch a glimpse of who was in line, but it was impossible; there was only a flash of bodies silhouetted by the city lights. Then the door closed again.

He moved on toward the restroom, his hands in his hoody pockets, holding the mask tight against his abdomen. He watched the club-goers as he went, enjoying themselves, getting drunk, leering at the women. These people knew nothing about what was going on in this city. And the ones who did were puppets. But if he could pull this off, if he could find a green gem so Yoshio could build his mind-control blocker thing, he'd end up saving all of their ignorant lives before they even knew they needed saving.

Focus.

The restroom was only a short way down the hall. He looked around before stepping in, eyeing the other doors. "Employees only," one read. "Offices," read another. A third had no sign.

In the restroom, a man was at the mirror, sniffing and rubbing his nose with his thumb and forefinger. It was Onishi from the line out front. He looked at Akio, sneered somehow without moving a single muscle in his face and exited the restroom. Akio's nerves rattled as he passed, hoping the man would ignore him, hoping he didn't somehow know why Akio was at the club.

Another man was at a urinal, his head against the wall, obviously drunk. Akio went into a stall. He stood there, trying to think.

Scratched on the stall wall, scrawled words jumped out at him.

If you DON'T, the Demon wins.

Akio stared at the words. Someone had written him a message! How was that even possible? Was someone watching him? Following him? Was there someone in the know giving him guidance? How did they know he would choose this stall? Could it have been Onishi, secretly pretending to be a jerk to throw him off?

He read the words again.

They were old. They had probably been scratched there over a year ago. Next to it was a phone number that looked much more recent, and the words:

For discreet fun, call.

Akio hung his head. The message was only a coincidence, just bad restroom poetry. This demon was only an analogy for life's struggles and not a real live, mind-controlling monster.

Still, he pondered the message.

If you DON'T, the demon wins.

If I don't get a gem, he thought, *the demon wins.*

Once he had a gem, Yoshio could work whatever sciencey mumbo jumbo he had in mind, and they could shut down the demon's mind control. Then it wouldn't win. If any of that nonsense would actually work.

Of course, he had to find Yoshio first.

The door to the restroom opened, and Akio heard the drunk stumble out. Akio stepped out of the stall and washed his hands out of habit. Then he opened the restroom door slowly. No one was in the hall.

On pure instinct, he moved quickly to the door that had no sign and tried the handle. It opened. It was dimly lit on the other side, a stairwell going up. He slipped in and shut the door behind him. His heart thumped out a nervous warning, knocking on his chest, saying, *turn back, finish your drink, and leave from the front door before anyone sees you!*

But he couldn't do that. He had no way to pay for a second drink. This place was clearly yakuza run. He wouldn't be able to leave without being shaken down and then likely beaten up when he couldn't pay.

He fingered the mask under his hoody, and then the baggie of Miyahara's homemade pills in his pocket.

Not yet.

He tried to calm himself, and listened up the stairwell. It was hard to hear with the club music reverberating through the walls, but there was nothing overt, no one on the stairs—at least no one moving or talking. As he started up, he tried to hone in on the source of his headache, to search for the gem with his mind. He took deeper, slower breaths, trying to slow his heart and focus.

At the second floor landing, he heard voices on the other side of the door.

"I'm heading down. Apparently Violet doesn't feel like dancing. So I have to go *talk* to her," the voice grunted as if it was funny and annoying at the same time. Whatever *talking* meant, Akio was afraid words weren't the only thing involved.

The door cracked open right in front of him, and he quickly pressed himself against the wall, hoping for a miracle that the dim stairwell light wouldn't expose him. There was nowhere to hide.

"Wait!" another voice called from further away.

"What?" the first voice answered, even more annoyed, not yet emerging through the door.

"Take this down to the bar for me will you? Yara needs some smaller bills."

"What am I, an errand boy now?" The door shut again and the first voice moved away.

Akio breathed out in relief, and as he did, he felt it: a twinge at the back of his head. It was coming from above. He moved past the door quickly and up to the next floor landing. The door opened below him and the grumbling man thudded down the stairs like a rhino.

Behind the third floor door, Akio heard a female voice say playfully, "This way." He panicked that she might be coming through the door too, and he froze on the stairs. A deeper voice said something he couldn't recognize, and the woman answered in a light giggle.

Akio waited until he couldn't hear them, and then pulled the door open slowly. Inside it was more dimly lit than the stairwell. It was a short hallway; a door was cracked open and a soft, orange light spilled out. He heard grunting and moaning.

Sex sounds!

He looked to his right and saw a closed door at the end of the hallway. His headache felt stronger from that direction, and he was grateful for it. He wasn't prepared to barge in on people having sex. He wasn't sure he was prepared to barge in on someone reading a book or picking lint from their toes, for that matter, and hoped he wouldn't have to.

He walked quickly to the door at the end of the hall, legs like stiff boards he had to willfully force forward, and tried the handle. It was unlocked. He opened it slowly, his heart in his throat. Lights greeted him—normal lights, but too bright after the dimness of the hallway and likely place of ill repute just behind.

He crept forward along this corridor and past a short space with two elevators facing each other, his headache growing slowly, his fingers still pressed against the mask under his jacket. There were two doors nearby, but his headache drew him toward the one at the far end of the corridor.

Before he took another step, it opened.

Akio quickly ducked toward the elevators and pressed himself against one of them. Rapid steps padded down the hall, and he saw the punk with the embroidered tiger jacket heading back the way Akio had come. The young tough hadn't seen him.

Akio dashed forward, but as the punk disappeared through the door, he realized that he no longer had the gems. Akio's headache still drew him the other way.

He let the punk go, and turned toward the door at the end of the corridor. He opened it, carefully and quietly, and looked inside. It was lit, and he heard muffled voices, but didn't see anyone. He slipped in. It was a room with long tables and some cubicles. There were doors on its perimeter, some with interior windows so he could see inside the offices beyond. It reminded him of the newsroom at the *Dainichi Daily*.

"My man just dropped them off," Akio heard from one of the glass-walled offices some distance away. "I put them in the cabinet with the others. I'm to tell you that Mr. Kumamori wants you to escalate the dispersion to the wider public. The overlord's power has grown sufficiently, and we are to start phase two immediately. More deliveries will arrive soon."

"Yes . . . Mr. Kumamori," another, more gravelly voice said, sounding like a zombie. "I understand what you mean." Akio moved quietly along the doors, the pulsing pain increasing. It was close now. "Tell him . . ." The zombie voice paused. "Tell him I see his wisdom and will begin tonight. There are important, powerful men in the club. We will start with them. Please send my humble regards."

"He receives it," the younger voice answered, "as you know."

A nearby door pulled Akio's attention like an invitation to torture. It was a simple, wooden office door. There were no windows to this room, but behind it was the pain he sought. Akio knew this without question.

He opened it.

The nighttime city outside greeted him from a wall of windows. A polished wooden desk was shadowed by the city lights and devoid of accoutrements, except for a single lamp in one lonely corner. The room was empty of people. The source of his headache was to his right, in this very room. A tall cabinet stood next to a shorter one that had a single bottle of whisky on it. The headache lived in the tall cabinet.

Akio moved to it like a man treading water.

The cabinet had polished white handles, mother of pearl or something, maybe ivory. It was a reddish wood, but all he could feel was *green*. He reached for the doors and swung them open. A red chest with gold leaf inlays sat on the shelf. It was some expensive but gaudy Chinese piece; it looked like an antique. The lid was shut, but there was no lock.

He could hear faint voices, but not the ones from the other office talking about the distribution of gems; these voices were coming from the chest. It was one voice multiplied over and over. It pulled at his mind, inviting him to a life of ease and power.

He couldn't chance it any longer. He took the Tower Records bag from under his hoody and slid out the mask. The swirling clouds and flames across its face were enticing. The empty eyes implored him.

Wear me. I am beautiful.

Akio considered the huge, coarse pills in his pocket. He still couldn't tell if he needed one. He had taken two already earlier that day. His senses had become heightened when he took the first one, but the second hadn't heightened them more, and now they seemed to have normalized.

But is this a new normal or the old normal?

His senses were alert, but that might just be from fear and adrenaline. Still, he didn't know how long they would be searching for Miyahara. What if it took days or weeks to find him? There were only three pills left, and the sensei hadn't left a recipe. Akio remembered that his water bottle was in his abandoned backpack outside the club. He looked over at the whisky on the other cabinet.

It was a Yamazaki, 18-year-old, single malt. Of course. It had to be that.

No. He turned away. An angry, vengeful demon was hard enough to deal with. A drunken, angry, vengeful demon would be too much.

He had no more time. The gem voices were reaching out to him stronger and stronger. The mask's voice grew stronger too, battling for dominance of Akio's mind. The thought of swallowing one of the pills, like coarse stones in his pocket, without water seemed near impossible. He might choke to death. Add whisky and it was guaranteed. Why had Miyahara been so vague about how long they would last?

For a time, the note had read.

"Dammit," he whispered aloud, and threw a pill into his mouth. The idea of losing control again and hurting people he cared about was all he needed to override the disgust of swallowing yet another one.

And it *was* disgusting. Dried sandy mud with bits of animal hairs and bug legs, for all he knew. It gouged and tore its way down his already raw throat. He eyed the whisky, and in a moment he feared he'd regret, he unscrewed the cap and took a sip.

It was a silky smooth burn, and his throat clenched up, but the sludge within was loosened and slid down a little easier. He took another. The burn was less, but still strong. He put the bottle back and felt the rest of the dissolving pill slowly grind its way down. His throat felt like torched sandpaper.

He took a deep breath and tried to calm his nerves, the warmth of the whisky spreading through his torso. He lifted the mask to his face slowly, like sinking into a bubble bath lined with spikes. It was chilling and rapturous. Before it touched skin, the mask moved the last centimeter on its own, as if his face were a vacuum sucking the mask to it.

Akechi smiled, and Akio craved vengeance. He craved it against everyone who had ever wronged him, against the yakuza spreading these gems across the world, against the evil that had conquered Masami's mind and made her fight him.

How dare it?

That evil dwelled on the eleventh floor of Nakama Plaza.

It will suffer. And it will fall.

Akio reached out and lifted the chest's lid.

His senses spiked as a mountain of green gems greeted him, glowing softly like a pile of rock candy kryptonite. There was no pain, only an intensity of energy, the voices present but ineffectual. They called to him as one, imploring Akio to become glorious, to be the man he had always dreamed he could be. But he laughed at them. He was a samurai, a daimyo, a lord of tens of thousands, unbeatable and unconquerable. These voices that called to him were base and contemptible, calling out in desperation for anyone who would listen.

The demon behind these voices did not know who Akio was yet, did not know who listened to the call. And it wouldn't if Akio didn't touch the gems. He knew this from when he had picked one up before. It was as if the demon could see him and knew everything about him once he held a gem. When he had crushed it with his bare hands he had sent the demon into a panic. In his boldness now, Akio wanted to touch them. He wanted to plunge both hands into the pile and laugh at the worm demon's fear when it knew who was coming for it. But a greater common sense won out. They needed stealth. He did not have armies of thousands to crush his enemies. At that moment it was only him. He had to get back to Yoshio, and he had to do it carefully.

Good. He still had his wits about him, his own thoughts. The pill was in effect. And the whisky buzz that would have normally made Akio goofy, only made him calm.

Yoshio had said he needed a gem. Here were a hundred. He closed the lid on the chest and pulled it to him.

"Hey!" a voice startled him from behind. Akio snapped his head toward the sound. A slim, young man in a black suit flinched and stepped back from the doorway on seeing the leering, red mask. The office door was open and he stood just outside, looking in cautiously. Had Akio left the door open? The thought struck him that if only he wore the mask all the time, he would not make such foolish mistakes. He would own the wisdom of centuries.

"Thief!" the thug shouted, peering over the top of his aviators at Akio, but not daring to enter the room. "Someone's trying to steal the gems!"

Aviators.

Akio stared hard at the yakuza. It was the thug from Ueno Station who had knocked him down. The thug with the hard object at his belt line. Akio yearned to silence him by taking his head, to get revenge for the humiliation at the train station, but he remembered he didn't have his sword. It seemed incredibly stupid to him that he had gone into a potential battle situation without a sword. Akechi would never have done so.

Akio pictured himself running through Kabukicho with his sword in his hand.

Yeah, that wouldn't have worked out well. The police would have stopped me before I ever ran into the punk with the gems.

Akio heard other noises: voices and footsteps still distant; people were coming. The skinny yakuza moved into the doorway, perhaps emboldened by the knowledge that he had backup on the way.

"Take them," he said arrogantly. "Pick one up," as if it were a dare.

This guy has no idea.

Akechi's own arrogance bristled and flamed. Without looking, Akio reached back and plunged his hand into the chest full of gems. His fingers finding a nearly fist-sized one, he pulled it out and held it before the young gangster, who now had a look of confidence, of certain victory. Akio held the large gem in front of him and crushed it in his hand, green dust raining to the floor.

The yakuza's expression dropped, as if he'd had the wind knocked from him, as if everything he held dear had just shattered. And in that same moment, a recognition flicked across his eyes. Recognition and anger.

Akio felt a shared convulsion leap through select individuals in the building. Men in the offices perked up, put hands on weapons, and moved toward the stairwell. A bouncer left his post with no warning, ignoring the questions of the doorman. A john on the second floor extracted himself from his paid companion, leaving her naked and swearing at him; he exited toward the stairwell in the buff. A stripper left her dance mid-twirl, abandoning banknotes on the pulsing, reflective stage.

These weren't crystal clear visions, but a feeling, an awareness that the demon had put its focus here, that it was putting all its nearby available resources toward eliminating the threat. These eyes and hands of the demon would close in on him fast.

He closed the chest, latched it, and picked up the whole thing, hugging it to his body with one arm. He tucked it into him like a large rugby ball, put his other arm out front, ready to level any who got in his way; and he charged at the yakuza flunky.

The thug wheeled backward into the main room, reaching for the hard thing at his belt, when suddenly he dropped lifeless to the floor.

Standing just behind him, was Yoshio.

5
Leaps of Faith

Yoshio stood with fingers from each hand rigid, as if he had plugged them both into light sockets at different positions on a wall. He looked at Akio, and in spite of the terrifying mask, gave a little smirk.

"This way," he said, nodding his head sharply to his right.

"What are you grinning about?" Akio growled as he followed, the red and gold chest under one arm.

"I wasn't sure that would actually work," Yoshio answered, running back the way Akio had come. He went through the door as the crack of gunfire resounded, and the zing of a bullet ricocheted off the doorframe.

"What?" Akio urged, ducking down and pulling the door closed behind him.

"Pressure points!" Yoshio grinned as he ran. "Sensei taught me."

Miyahara had shown Yoshio several different points on a human body that if jabbed in just the right way would cause a person to temporarily lose control of a limb or two. The sensei had confirmed that Yoshio was performing the techniques correctly, but he had never been able to practice on a real person. The thrill of success in a critical situation made him almost disregard the fact there were still men chasing them with guns.

They passed the elevators, and Yoshio's unease grew, thinking of the brothel behind the door ahead. He had nearly collided with a barely dressed woman on reaching the third floor. Thankfully she had only winked at him and then sauntered on in a kind of daze to do her business. He wanted to get through there and to the stairwell as quickly as possible, and with gun-wielding yakuza on their tail, that shouldn't be too hard.

But before they even reached the door, it opened. A naked man burst out and lunged at Yoshio, swinging a bent piece of rebar at his head. He sidestepped, and Akio's fist met the man's red nose square on. He collapsed in a fleshy lump.

Yoshio picked up the dropped rebar. "Let's try this way," he said, and opened a different door, deciding to avoid the brothel altogether. He didn't want Akio punching out any prostitutes. The masked man followed him in, just as another bullet pinged down the hallway.

The room was narrow; a copy room with a large photocopier occupying one side.

"It goes through!" Yoshio said in relief. The door they had entered had no lock, so he tried to jam the piece of rebar under it, hoping it might slow down their pursuers. It caught on the lip of the doorframe and refused to slide under.

"Can I get some help here?" he asked between jabs. He was only slowing them down now.

Akio grabbed the metal rod with one hand, and with a single violent thrust, he wedged it under the door, which splintered and buckled, the rebar sinking into the floor.

"Thanks! That'll do it." Yoshio dashed through the room and Akio followed, as graceful and powerful as a hungry lion.

The banging on the door behind them began as soon as they exited into another hallway. Yoshio turned right and then quickly left, down a short corridor that ended in a window, a single door on their right.

"Footsteps on a stairway," Akio growled, indicating the door. "Several."

They were stuck.

Yoshio needed no more incentive. He turned to the window, opened it and climbed out into the night.

He stood on a small balcony in a narrow alley three stories up. It was not a fire escape, only a sad platform with a small stool and an ashtray. Akio climbed out the window after him, a grim ghoul in a gray hoody, still holding the red and gold chest. Shivers zipped up Yoshio's spine as Akio looked about the alley with sudden, jerky head movements. How stable was his masked companion? Was he losing control?

"My parkour skills are not great," Yoshio said, eyeing Akio warily, "but maybe we can climb down on some of these pipes."

"No time," Akio growled. "We have to jump." He reached for Yoshio as if to pick him up.

"No," said Yoshio, who was slightly taller than Akio, though of equally slim build. "You're kidding."

Akio's fierce eyes stared back at Yoshio from behind the demon mask. He was not kidding.

The voices grew louder from inside now. The yakuza would be there any second, and they probably wouldn't wait to start blasting before they opened the window.

"You'll kill us both," Yoshio said. "At the very least, you'll break your own legs."

"I won't," Akio said. The glare in his eyes allowed no debate.

"Okay, fine," Yoshio said, and he lifted one arm so Akio could get under it. It was either this or face the yakuza head on. He hoped Akio knew what he was doing. "Don't drop me!"

The masked man picked him up like a doll in one arm, still holding the chest in the other, and hopped up onto the narrow railing. Yoshio's heart dropped into his stomach, expecting a sudden fall, but Akio balanced there like a skilled surfer on an easy wave. The alley was so narrow that if he jumped with any force, he'd hit the adjacent building before falling. They would have to simply drop. Yoshio looked down and saw the tiny strip of pavement below, made tinier by electrical boxes, vents, and pipes protruding from the walls. Tangled wires criss-crossed the span nearby, above and below them. Plastic crates and bins were jumbled on the ground next to the graffiti that covered the walls at street level.

Yoshio took a deep breath to calm his nerves in the split second before Akio stepped off the railing. They plummeted. Yoshio's stomach stayed on the balcony. His thoughts screamed.

Why did I say yes to this?

They impacted the street and Akio lurched forward, stumbling to keep his balance and not drop Yoshio or the chest of gems. He succeeded at both, but Yoshio heard gasps from three young men they hadn't seen before, smoking in the alley further down. One with spiky, dyed blonde hair and a thin mustache; another with a swooping pompadour; and the last with hair shaggy to his ears. All wore dark jackets and slacks. They may have been merely host boys, but for the snarling edge to their swagger.

Akio set Yoshio down, and they ran.

He couldn't comprehend how Akio had jumped three stories and was still able to run, particularly after having his legs merged with a floor earlier that day. Akio had said he healed quickly when he wore the mask, but this was unreal. It not only healed him, but made him far stronger.

How can a mask imbue muscles and bones with that kind of strength and resilience?

It was beyond the physics he knew and understood, but it made him intensely fascinated. He had to figure it out. He needed Miyahara to teach him more.

Before they reached the end of the alley, they heard shouting. Yoshio risked a glance back and saw men emerging from a door behind the club. They were yelling at the three smokers.

"What are you doing? After them!"

They ditched their cigarettes and took off running.

Akio kept his head down as he ran, but his hoody flew back and drew stares from the people on the street. No real concern showed on their faces, only surprise and a few nervous giggles. There were weirdos everywhere here; a guy wearing an evil-looking samurai mask wasn't all that unusual. Nonetheless, Yoshio reached over and yanked the hood over Akio's head. Akio drew the drawstring tight.

They ran side by side, Yoshio uncertain who was leading who. They needed to get back to Akio's apartment unseen. Akio ducked into another alley and Yoshio followed. When they emerged on another street, he saw an arcade only two doors down. He tapped Akio and pointed.

The brightly lit palace of electronic distractions pinged, ringed, clinked, and buzzed, while bubble gum music fought to drown it out. The rows of UFO catchers by the front doors gleamed like they'd just been polished, their claw arms hovering above myriad prizes like friendly alien drones.

If they hadn't been running from yakuza who wanted them dead, Yoshio would have stopped to play. He was good at the UFO catchers —really good. He knew the tricks and techniques to win, and knew how to spot and avoid the unwinnable ones. Novices thought the claws were simply supposed to pick up a prize and drop it in a hole, but they didn't work that way. It was all in finessing the prize out with little bumps and lifts. A lot of it was simply knowing which prizes were easiest to get. For Yoshio, this was like reading a map. He could see which toys were trapped and which ones were ripe for the plucking. He could see the connectedness of the piles and how moving one would affect another. A lot of kids he knew were good at these machines, but if there were no daily limit, Yoshio could clear them out —assuming they were clearable.

He ran through the machines, full with prizes of stuffed anime characters, action figures, and snacks, some that were stacked deep, some resting on or hanging by poles, some stacked like bricks. He couldn't help himself analyzing each one as he passed, mentally criticizing the poor form of the players. Akio followed, hood drawn close, hunched over the box of demon gems.

A wide staircase was in the back corner and they followed it up.

This second floor greeted them with coin pushers of all shapes and sizes. People sat around them feeding in tokens in the hopes that the machine would reach critical mass and give them an avalanche payoff in return. Beyond them were a row of electronic dart boards and two air hockey tables next to a wide window. The gamers talked and laughed, huddled around the machines, paying no attention to the two frantic youth rushing past.

Akio stopped at the window and peered out. Yoshio joined him, looking down at the bustling nighttime street below. The three flunkies from the alley were looking about, not sure which way to turn. The blonde pointed in one direction and the pompadour went that way. The other two took off down the street in the opposite direction.

Only moments later, a larger group of five serious-looking Japanese men and one scantily-clad black woman stepped into view. She wore a glittering tiara and not much else.

"Tigress!" Akio hissed.

Yoshio's eyes flicked to the mask, questioningly.

"One of the strippers." Akio answered.

The nearly nude woman strode into the street like a force of nature, lights reflecting off her sparkling skin, the gems in her tiara glowing an emerald green. Her head started to lift toward them, and Akio jerked Yoshio from the window.

"Do you think she saw us?" Yoshio asked.

"Better keep moving," Akio said. "Just in case."

They returned to the stairs and continued up. The third floor was full of *purikura* machines, photo booths that let you add stickers and draw on the pictures before printing them out. They moved past and up to the fourth.

They walked quickly through a row of shooter games, plastic guns attached by cables, Yoshio's other favorite. Everything from aliens to zombies was getting blasted. He thought of the real gun he had taken from the yakuza and then ditched before the police caught them. Part of him wished he had it back, but he knew it would only cause more trouble.

Turning a corner they heard the recorded sound of race callers barking out the progress of several unrelated competitions. The space was filled with virtual horse, greyhound, and boat races. Just beyond, was an entryway into a café bar. Yoshio led them to it.

A young man stepped forward. "How many?"

"Two," Yoshio said quickly, trying to appear relaxed.

The host looked at Akio suspiciously, his eyes resting on the chest he huddled over with his head down.

"He doesn't want anyone to take the prize he won," Yoshio said with a smile and a roll of his eyes. "Can we sit outside?" He nodded to the narrow patio, which overlooked the street from behind a low, glass safety wall with shiny steel railings.

"Certainly," the host said with a little grin of understanding. "Right this way, gentlemen," he added a little too formally. He led them to a two-top and handed them menus when they sat. He exited back to his post, no longer a threat.

"Is this the plan?" Akio grumbled. "Pretend we're just normal dining customers and hope we're not spotted? I better take this off." He reached for the mask.

"Nope," Yoshio answered. "Better leave that on. We have a good view of the street from here, so we'll be able to see them coming. And if need be . . ." He nodded toward the street, four stories down. "You did it once before. I figure you could do it again if we have to, in order to lose them. As much as I would rather not. One more story won't matter, will it?"

Akio shook his head, and said nothing. Yoshio didn't know Akio well, but he had learned enough from their conversation at the manga café that this was unusual behavior. Then Akio had been clumsy and uncertain, with verbal diarrhea. Now before him sat a graceful ghoul, reticent and confident.

He looked down at the street. The three alley punks were no longer in sight, but the group of serious men was passing just under them. The men moved en masse through the crowd, peering into shops and restaurant windows. Soon they rounded a corner and were gone.

"They've moved on," Yoshio said. "Maybe we can sneak back down and out of here, after all."

At that moment Akio's head turned abruptly, as if he'd heard a gun shot. Yoshio tracked his stare. Th rough the glass, he saw a beautiful, dark-skinned, almost naked woman running at them through the café. They both jumped to their feet, and Akio thrust the chest of gems at Yoshio, who took it reflexively. The mask's mouth pulled back into a determined scowl, its eyes aflame. Akio would kill this woman with his bare hands. But something in him changed in an instant, and he swooped Yoshio off his feet like he was a baby and bounded over the railing.

They landed on a bare space of tarmac in the street, next to a parked van, and pedestrians scattered in surprise. A backpacked bicyclist swerved to avoid them. Gasps and outcries came from all around. People shot from the convenience store and the video game parlor to see what had happened.

Yoshio involuntarily waved to the gathering crowd as Akio set him down. When the people saw they were unharmed, their shock turned to laughter and awe. Eyes looked up and around, as if trying to spot wires or some contraption that may have facilitated the jump, something to show them how the illusion had been performed. There was even a smattering of applause.

The two moved away from the scene and down the street, Yoshio trying to play it off like it was nothing. Akio again dropped his head, seeming to want to disappear, when they heard more commotion behind and above them. They looked up to the fourth floor café railing to see an angel take flight.

And plummet to the street below.

Akio bolted toward Tigress, leaving Yoshio on the sidewalk with the gems. He took three great strides, but they had moved too far away. He couldn't catch her.

She landed on the roof of the parked van with a loud crunch. The driver emerged from the Family Mart next to it, ready to shout at whoever had damaged his van. But his mouth clamped shut in horror.

Akio collapsed in the street, reaching toward Tigress in defeat. Her sleek, muscled body lay face down, one arm dangling over the windshield.

The people on the street who had seen Akio's stunt didn't know how to react. Was this part of the show? Was she going to get up any second now and take a bow? Was the driver going to wink at them knowingly and say, "Thanks, folks! Hope you enjoyed our performance!" Some of them looked at Yoshio with a queer mingling of hope and worry.

Akio remained immobile in the street, his rigid mask hiding his emotions. Yoshio went to him, put a hand on his shoulder.

"We have to go. There's nothing we can do for her."

Akio did not move for what felt like several minutes. Sirens sounded in the distance.

"We can't afford to get arrested again, Akio. Emergency responders will help her . . . if she's . . ." Yoshio couldn't finish the sentence. She didn't look alive.

People moved about, some wanting to inspect the woman and possibly help her, others moving away. Many of them had mobile phones out, aimed at the van. One or two were aimed at Yoshio and Akio.

Akio finally stood.

Yoshio tugged on his shoulder lightly, so as not to startle him, and the ghoul turned to look him in the face. Th e mask remained passionless and cold, but the eyes under it were red and swollen with tears. A broken demon nodded to Yoshio, who turned to lead them away from the scene. He looked back one more time before they disappeared down a side street.

Tigress did not move.

6

The Sorter

Masami sat on top of Tokyo Tower, leaning against the needle, looking down on the sprawling, endless city in the night. Her newfound powers had given her the ability to forgo gravity. There was no gravity in the spirit world. She could slip in there and move to wherever she wanted and then reappear at will in the corporeal world —with the help of her mother's memory.

There were other places, too, dark places that called to her as she travelled there. There were doors that opened that did not exist in the physical world. Doors she could easily step into if she chose. But where would they go?

She saw other people there, as she had on her trip to the pub, but they weren't like her. They were trapped, deceased. They couldn't travel back to the physical world, only forward through one of the doors. She saw some go in, but never any return. Some wandered, not daring, preferring the dismal shadow world to whatever lay beyond.

There were other presences as well that weren't human souls. Animals mostly, pets hovering outside of their owners' windows or walking alongside their still living loved ones. But of those she saw, they seemed easily distracted and would dash off suddenly as if after a ball or another furry friend and then disappear into spaces Masami could not see.

And there were the ones that were not pets, the more sinister beings. But they were shades and shadows even here, and she never got a solid look. A brief shape in an alley. A blur through a temple gate.

One, however, she had seen clearly. A large, lanky, humanoid shape, six meters tall, its two arms and legs like slender spider limbs with wiry muscles. Its head, wedge-shaped like a wolf with a long snout and what looked like the narrow slit of a mouth, though she didn't see it open, and hoped it never would. It had only shallow depressions where eyes would be, but appeared to see, nonetheless. A curved web of skin adorned each side of its head, and Masami could only assume those were its ears.

It was scooping up souls with huge hands, separating them, as if sorting them out, and pushing them through ethereal doors. Masami had only seen it momentarily. Its presence was terrifying, but it wasn't malicious like a demon of the underworld; it was simply . . . indifferent.

And that made it somehow scarier.

It was separating souls like they were baby chicks in a chicken hatchery. Only there weren't so many souls. In movies of ghosts there are often armies of them wandering the streets, unseen to the masses of living people. But it wasn't like that. There were a few here and there. Mostly they moved on quickly, and those who didn't were moved on by this indifferent sorter. She wondered if there were more like it, or if it was a unique being.

She had been street level when she first saw it. She quickly reappeared in the corporeal world before it could see her, her nerves uneasy. After getting some distance, she flew higher to get a better look. She had no desire to be sorted. The beast had been very utilitarian, singularly focused on its task. She wondered what it would have done with her, if anything. She wasn't yet dead. Maybe it would have ignored her.

This power she had still baffled her. She had been pulled into some kind of conduit when battling the demon in Kofu barely two months ago. Whatever it was that had been searching for the demon tried to pull it back to Hell and had accidentally grabbed her instead.

She had been dragged into the ghost world, and her accidental access had not been revoked. Perhaps it couldn't be. She had tasted the spirit world, her body had linked into it, and now she could access it as she pleased. She had even gained some control over when it happened.

This world beyond intrigued her, but not enough to explore it too closely. What if she went somewhere she couldn't return from? For now, just accepting her ghost ability was enough. She couldn't think of going deeper.

She looked out over the massive city landscape of Tokyo. Apart from the dark waters of Tokyo Bay, everywhere she looked was city. From her vantage point on the tower, it seemed that it covered the entire world. Somewhere down there was Akio and Yoshio. They were struggling with how to rescue Miyahara and how to kill that horrifying, mind-controlling demon.

She had seen its true form. When its power over her had been released, and she realized that she had almost killed Akio, she had fled. But only seconds later, she had come back, enraged that she had been so easily manipulated, so perfectly made into the demon's puppet. She had wanted vengeance and was intent on getting it.

But when she had seen the voluminous worm with its six clawed legs and huge fanged blubbery head, its scaled back spotted with green bumps, and the fury that consumed it, she had frozen. How could she face such a thing on her own? And what if it simply took control of her again? She would be a fool to even try.

In hindsight, it had probably been the perfect moment. She could have zipped in while it was distracted and impaled it with her wakizashi. But it had been thrashing about wildly. What if she missed and only grazed it? And where was its most vulnerable spot? It was nothing remotely human. Where was its heart? Did it even have one? Most likely its head would be vulnerable, and maybe she could hack through its neck; she knew the sword was impossibly sharp, but what if it couldn't? And if it did, what if that didn't kill it? She wouldn't be able to resist its mind control. All these questions had burned through her mind as she hovered in the room with the beast.

And then it had looked at her.

She had been invisible. She had been floating in the middle of its gaudy, chaotic, golden throne room, and it looked right at her. It paused in its thrashing and held her gaze like a sadistic twelve-year old boy looking down at a trapped insect it was about to squish for sheer pleasure.

So she fled. Again.

She was becoming somewhat of an expert at fleeing.

She had let them down. She was supposed to be the collected one, the one who had her shit together and could handle the difficult stories. But this had proven to be too much. When she had become a journalist, she wanted the tough jobs. She wanted to interview hardened criminals, yakuza with full body tattoos, thieves and murderers. She had fought for the police beat, and she had earned it. But these were demons. Actual demons.

She hadn't bargained for that.

And who was she kidding? Yes, this was an amazing story to cover, far beyond anything she ever dreamed, but is that what she was doing? She wasn't some impartial reporter informing the world. She had to admit it; she was trying to be a hero.

And she was failing pretty miserably at it.

What story would they turn in to the *Dainichi Daily* anyway? The same dilemma had plagued them in Kofu, after they had defeated the demon there. But coming up with a feasible story hadn't been that hard. There hadn't been that many people involved.

Now they had a nationwide yakuza takeover and a clandestine robotics company making evil robots that had found their way into the hands of public figures. There were thousands of people who were affected by this. Crafting a digestible lie to cover this up would be nearly impossible. How many police were already involved? How many politicians? So many of both were fully in the yakuza's pockets. How could all of them be trusted to not speak out and reveal the truth of the situation once it was done? If it would ever be done. If they could even defeat this monster.

But she couldn't worry about that now. She had to move forward.

"Keep moving forward, and the answer will present itself, Masa-chan."

It was her mother's advice from when Masami was a girl. It had helped her face many an uncertain situation. Would she be able to ace her first exam in the fourth grade? How well would she do in the relay race on sports day against girls that were taller and had longer legs? What if she didn't like being in the young broadcasters club?

"Keep moving forward and find out," her mother had said. "If you don't keep moving forward, nothing at all will happen."

Keep moving forward.

The story would sort itself out. An answer would come.

Right now she had to think about Akio and Yoshio. She had to come to terms with what she had done to Akio, so she could face him again, so she could help. She hated herself for harming him, and she hated herself more for letting him suffer for so long while she was busy being wrapped up in her own shame and anger. It was an endless cycle. She hated herself for hating herself.

At the time, she hadn't realized exactly what had happened. The demon's possession of her had opened wide the doors to her abilities as a ghost. It knew, and it showed her. She hadn't known she could fly. She hadn't known she could take other people with her. At the demon's bidding, she had quickly used that ability to its worst potential. But even then, she hadn't understood the torture Akio was suffering. His face covered in the terrifying mask, his howls had only seemed like anger, like unbridled frustration and loathing. And when she had come back to herself, she couldn't face what she had done. She threw him the katana, knowing he'd get himself out, but unaware of the excruciating pain she had left him in.

It was only later that it had occurred to her, and she found them in Akio's apartment, releasing the pieces of flooring lodged in his legs. But she couldn't bring herself to stay.

Her new power seemed harmless at first—though dreadfully inconvenient before she could control it. Being a ghost was unsettling, but she had to admit she had been considering how useful it could be to get stories. She didn't like the idea of spying, but it could come in handy. Now she understood how dangerous it truly was.

She had watched Akio and Yoshio briefly, after she had blinked out. Akio slept fitfully and Yoshio paced, thinking, peering at Akio every few seconds to see if he'd awoken yet. He looked at blueprints. He checked his phone, searching online, trying to find some answer. She saw him pull the huge demonic tome, the *Zetsubō no Shika*, out of his luggage and flip through its huge pages of dried skin.

When Akio awoke, she left. She couldn't bring herself to face him yet, even invisible. She needed to calm down, to let go of the self-blame, the feeling that her armor had been not only pierced but disintegrated. She felt naked with self-loathing.

I can't go down that road again.

She had hated herself when her mother died. She had blamed herself, even though logically she knew it wasn't her fault. It was the cancer.

If only I hadn't been so confrontational with her. If only I hadn't been such a difficult daughter. If only I had been more loving and feminine like Tsukiko. Then mother would have lived.

Tsukiko had always been the perfect daughter. It was her sister who had stayed with their dying mother when Masami and her father had gone to Yamanaka Lake. It hadn't been her mother's final day; that day hadn't come for another six months. She hadn't betrayed her mother then. Her mother had told her to take her father fishing, not wanting all the weeping and fawning, so she had only followed her wishes. But what bothered Masami was that she didn't want to stay. She didn't want to be around her mother while she slowly died. And for that, Masami felt like she had contributed to her death, like she had sped it along.

She had run to the lake to get away from death. And while her distant father ignored her as he fished, she had discovered the snake woman at the far end of the lake. The woman, who had appeared to be a normal woman, had held an adorable baby she seemed to be bathing in the water. But the baby had been made of fish, worms, and snakes. It had only been a ruse to draw her in closer. The snake woman had wanted to eat her. It was a memory she had discounted as fantasy until recently.

How many demons like that walk the earth? she wondered.

Her mother had lain in bed, recovering from unsuccessful chemo, and Masami had run away from that death only to find it in another form waiting for her.

There is no escaping it. Death is ever present.

She couldn't escape it then, and she wouldn't escape it now.

This is why this is happening, she suddenly realized. It was nonsense on one level. Masami wasn't the type to believe in fate and second chances, but maybe that's what this was: a second chance. A chance to atone for the way she had behaved when her mother was dying.

The practical Masami immediately bristled at the idea, but the softer side of her, the side that hadn't seen daylight in a very long time, felt otherwise.

I can help Akio and Yoshio. I can help save Miyahara. I can help save Japan.

It sounded so arrogant when she thought it. But it was true.

I can face death.

That was, after all, the real issue.

She didn't know how she would be able to help. She had been manipulated so easily. Both the demon and the maid robot had seen her even when she was invisible. But she had to do something. She couldn't just hide again. She had to face her fears.

Without a second thought, she dove from the needle on top of Tokyo Tower.

A woman on the street below looked up and saw a dark shape arc away from the top of the tower, a human shape, far above where people were allowed to be. She stopped in her tracks on the sidewalk while pedestrians bustled by.

A jumper, she thought. *There's a jumper. I should do something.*

But what? What could she do? The person was already mid-plummet.

She started to point, to shout so at least she wouldn't be alone in witnessing it. Others could share the horror. Others could point and stare and take videos with their smartphones. They could be sick with the tragedy together. They could be literally sick on the sidewalk together.

But then there was only sky, its darkness trying to smother the city lights and failing. There was no one falling, no black shape plummeting to the concrete below. Only a warm breeze and a wispy cloud like a child's scribbled line behind the red needle that pointed to the heavens.

She shook off the vision and blamed it on not getting enough sleep. She needed time off, she thought, and kept walking.

Masami soared for as long as she could stand being in the netherworld. From her height, she could see more souls than usual. There were still not that many, nowhere near the amount of actual living people that crowded the streets of Tokyo. They were sprinkled about, one on this street, a few on that. She saw two together that looked to be holding hands on Hibiya Boulevard.

Then a larger motion caught her eye.

It was the *Sorter* again. Its huge, wiry body lumbered between the buildings below. Its hands, massively large even compared to its own body, swept about, picking up souls and pushing them through doors in the fabric of reality, its eyeless head judging them without sight.

It approached the ghostly couple as Masami soared above, and her breathing accelerated.

What if it separates them? What if they're pushed through separate doors, torn from each other for eternity?

She paused overhead, floating in mid-air, watching until it reached them. Without hesitation, the huge thing grabbed them both and pushed them together through a phantom door nearby.

She breathed a sigh of relief. She didn't know if they had gone on to Heaven or Hell, or somewhere in between, perhaps simply to be born again, but at least they were together.

It all seemed so absurd. She hadn't even believed in an afterlife until she had become trapped there. She hadn't believed in demons and worlds behind invisible doors.

She wondered why she had felt so invested in the couple. She didn't date. She wasn't even sure she could see herself married. But this ghost couple had struck something in her. They were still together even after death. Even when she was younger and still believed in things like Heaven and Hell, Masami had always thought that people died alone. No matter what. Eventually you would see your loved ones, but the journey had to be alone.

When her mother slipped away in the hospital room, she had gone alone. Masami wondered now what door she had gone through, and if she had lingered in the hospital room before going. Had there been a loved one waiting for her?

But this couple went on together. They likely had died together, or maybe one of them had waited. Maybe this sorting beast had allowed it. A sad smile formed on her ghostly face.

In her reverie, she had looked away from the couple and the streets below. But as she gazed back down, her smile was instantly erased. The lanky Sorter was climbing toward her, its empty gaze fixed where she hovered. She could feel it looking at her though it had no eyes, peering into her soul. It climbed into the air as if there were a set of invisible steps leading right to her.

She pushed herself into motion, veering away from the direction of the Sorter. Her apartment was in that direction. She would have to circle around. Or just land somewhere. Anywhere.

She was still two hundred meters in the air. She couldn't simply materialize back into the land of the living. She would fall to her death. She tried to move quickly, but it somehow seemed harder than usual. She had been shooting through the air at a high velocity, spurred on by her jump from the tower. But now she had halted and lost her momentum. She had to pick up the pace. She could feasibly materialize and fall; that would speed her up. And then ghost again when she neared the earth.

Yes, why not?

The thing was approaching quickly now, loping up the invisible staircase that seemed to follow Masami, to be attached to her heels.

Somehow it felt different to materialize here. She had never done so in mid-air before, only when there was solid ground beneath her. Jumping had been one thing, but already being in the air was somehow terrifying.

She turned off her self-critic, took a breath, and blinked back into the corporeal world.

Instantly, gravity did its job. She fell as if she had just stepped off a ledge, streaming like a shot to the city below.

She vanished again on instinct, her breath caught in her throat, her heartbeat rapid.

The Sorter was there—right there! Its sharp snout pointed at her, its long flat expression completely unfeeling. It was nearly close enough to reach out and touch her with its huge spatulate hands. It must have guessed her trajectory, which wouldn't have been hard considering she was falling straight down.

She kicked away into the ghostly air, the thin, fog-like gray that was still as death. But she couldn't take off like Superman. She could only move at the speed she could run. The Sorter had legs like tall bamboo, and could outstep her with ease. It reached out a massive shovel of a hand, its long pale fingers brushing next to her as they folded around her body, the hand engulfing her up to her shoulders.

She willed herself whole again, her hand on the M medallion, her mother's image bursting into her mind, tears jetting from her eyes as she did.

And she fell.

The earth sped toward her. There was no escaping it. She would be flattened.

Her heart beat like gunfire, lurched like the ripping of lumber by a wrecking ball, burned like a plea to the gods. She had no choice. If she didn't vanish into the netherworld again, she would be killed in an instant. But what if it followed her? What if that spindly white horror was waiting to catch her?

The street flew toward her at the speed of an expressway, as if it wasn't her falling but instead the world falling on her. She was certain she would mistime it—too early and be caught, or too late and be crushed from the fall.

She ghosted.

She sank into the pavement and the cold earth beyond, feeling the temperature change like a cold shower on a hot day. The earth was refreshing, she found, and she slid deeper and deeper.

The Sorter had not caught her. She didn't see it. But then, she didn't see much of anything. The instant after she dematerialized, she was in the ground. And right now she was speeding into it with the inertia of something shot from a canon. The compacted earth slowed her down not even as much as water would her material body.

She willed herself to slow. And as she did, the dirt and rocks about her vanished, and she dropped into a large cavity cut from the earth, paved and walled. There was a platform full of people and a train pulling up to a stop. Hamamatsucho Station, read the sign.

She slowed herself to drift down to the concrete platform and sit, still a ghost, on the platform floor. People moved on and off the train while she watched and caught her breath. She had escaped the Sorter.

What would it have done if it had caught her? Where would she have been sorted to?

She shook off the thought. She would have to stay vigilant at all times, especially in the netherworld.

Falling through the earth had been strange. She could see for a very short distance, not nearly as far as open air, but there had been some ability to see where she was going, as if in a dark cave with a dim flashlight.

She recalled that when she had moved between floors of the Nakama Robotics building in Tokyo, she had been able to see in the dark spaces between ceilings and flooring, not perfectly, but well enough to get her bearing. And then she had pulled Akio down to become merged with the framework of the building. She flinched at the memory, angry at herself for doing it, angry at herself more for being made to do it and unable to resist.

She couldn't stay a ghost for long. As far as she knew, the Sorter could move through stone as easily as she could, if not easier. She stood up and materialized as commuters swirled by her. She rejoined the living without anyone noticing she hadn't been there a moment before.

7

A Surprise Gift

Shaken, her breath in off-meter staccato hitches, Masami found the train to take her home. She scanned the city at night as if in a dream, letting the vibrations of the train rattle her, comfort her like a child. She walked slowly toward her building, reveling in the solid ground beneath her feet, each step a trusted lover that held her up.

A trusted lover. What would that be like?

When she rounded the corner to her street, she startled, and almost without thinking, found herself in the ghost world again.

A man was standing in front of her building, illuminated by the streetlights. Instinct told her he was waiting for her. She had poofed out of the corporeal world in the same manner someone else may have dove into the bushes to hide. But now, back in the land of the dead, her recent panic returned. She looked around quickly, eyes darting everywhere for danger in the form of a giant lanky, shovel-handed demon.

It was nowhere in sight. *Thank all that is sacred.*

So now to deal with this man.

She stayed ghostly and moved closer to the front door of her apartment building. A man in jeans and a dark gray button down was standing with his back to her. Behind his back he had what looked like a present, a cylindrical tube for gifting wine, with a bow on top.

She began to relax. A lot of people lived in her building. And if this visitor was bringing a gift, he surely wasn't there for her. But she still had no desire to be seen.

The man reached a finger out and buzzed the door again. He looked so familiar.

Is that? It can't be.

She moved faster toward the man as he stepped from the door to pace. As he turned in Masami's direction, looking around him at nothing in particular, she had her answer.

Detective Fujimaki.

What is he doing here? And did he bring me a present? Wine? What kind of visit is he expecting? What kind of woman does he think I am?

She moved up to him and watched him in a sort of awe, like she was studying a new species, looking for meaning behind unexplained behavior. His head was drooped a bit as he looked at the sidewalk. He was frustrated and apprehensive. His broad shoulders looked tense and formidable, but his shirt wrapped his muscled torso nicely. His hair was a little ragged from what Masami would like to think was a long day of putting up with his misogynist partner, Kuramoto.

Why was he here?

The last time she had seen him was when he had interrogated her, along with Akio and Yoshio, in Kofu after being detained for the encounter with the yakuza in the parking lot. No substantial charges having been found, they were all let go. Had something new come up? Had some new evidence been found that tied her to the yakuza's murder? But what police officer shows up in street clothes with wine to arrest someone?

Fujimaki looked nervous. And Masami didn't even like wine. Whatever this was, it wasn't going to go well.

She couldn't face him right now. Too much was going on. She had to get to Akio and Yoshio and help them face the demon—somehow, without getting caught by its mind control again.

Yet the detective might have information she needed. He might just be a sane voice in the darkness. He might just be someone she could . . . No, she didn't know him. She pushed the thought away.

Abandoning her scrutiny of him, she forced herself to turn away, slipped through the building's front door and floated up the elevator shaft to her floor. She didn't have to use the shaft, but it was too strange dropping through floors at any random point. At least this way it was a familiar pattern. She arrived in the same place she always had on her floor, and could then go down the hall to her apartment. She wouldn't accidentally end up in someone else's bathroom.

She materialized when she was on the inside of her front door, glanced at the intercom box, and then went to the window. He was still there, head down, taking furtive glances side to side, clearly uncomfortable. He started to walk away, and, without thinking, Masami dashed to her intercom and pressed the button.

"Mr. Fujimaki," she said, not wanting to call him detective for his own privacy's sake. Or maybe for hers.

There was no response.

"Mr. Fujimaki," she said louder. "I'm here."

She heard footsteps. Then, "Miss Sato. I'd like to speak with you," he said stiffly.

"Come up," she replied, and hit the intercom buzzer.

She straightened her clothes and saw the wakizashi lying on the floor where she had discarded it in anger earlier. She quickly put it into the coat closet. A light knock sounded on the door.

The two exchanged polite bows, and Masami invited the detective into her apartment. She waited for him to explain why he was there. Without doing so, Fujimaki presented the gift.

"I know it's late. I'm sorry," the detective said.

"Late?" Masami asked. Her birthday was still nine weeks away, or ten months ago. However you looked at it, "late" wouldn't be the right word.

"In the evening," he replied. "Not a time for a gentleman to call."

She hadn't even thought about that, but now that he mentioned it, yes, it was very late, nearly midnight. What the hell was he doing here at this time of night, and bringing gifts?

"Are you telling me you're not a gentleman?" she asked, a bit nervously, wondering about his intentions, and wondering if she cared.

"No, that's not what I mean," he said quickly and gave another brief bow. "I mean no disrespect. I shouldn't have come so late, but it was the only time I could get away."

"It's fine," Masami said. She had no use for traditions anyway. "I'm not offended."

Again he presented the gift. Masami took it. It was heavy, definitely a bottle of wine or sake.

"What is this for?" she asked.

"Ochugen," he answered. "I'm a little early for that, but I wasn't sure I'd get the chance later."

"Oh," she said. "It is almost July, isn't it. I hate to say it, but I don't usually participate." The few summer gratitude gifts Masami usually got were obligatory ones from co-workers. She rarely felt the need to give one back. She looked at the ribbon and bow, trying to decide whether she would open it now, later, or just give it back to him. The last option would be rude, particularly since she needed the Kofu police on her good side. With the first option, she might be too tempted to open it and drink it right then and there, even if it was wine. "So . . . what I mean," she said, "is that I didn't get you anything." She was stalling more than anything.

Fujimaki chuckled. "That's fine. I would have been very surprised if you had."

Masami still held the gift box as they stood in the entryway. Life felt like it had stopped for a moment. She was getting a gift from a handsome, polite man. She just wanted to be there and take that moment in, because what was surrounding that little bubble was a horror show. She had just escaped from a huge, spindly-legged, terrifyingly indifferent creature from the netherworld. Not to mention the rest of the madness that she was involved in.

Getting a gift from a well-mannered and well-put-together detective was this strange oasis, and something she never would have imagined being drawn to. She was worried that if she opened the gift, it might all collapse. Something other than wine would be in there, something with fish heads and snakes for a body, something that would reach out at her with fat slimy hands and try to drag her underwater.

But she couldn't stand there forever.

She pulled the ribbon and popped open the top.

It wasn't wine.

Nor was it fish heads and snakes.

It was a beer.

A large corked British pale ale, a craft beer aged in whisky barrels. "Made in small batches," read the label. It looked amazing.

"Stalking me much?" Masami asked.

"Sorry." Fujimaki said sheepishly, and bowed again. "We know our connections as well as you know yours. You hang out at that British beer bar. You know the drill. Everybody knows this stuff about everybody else, so we can all play the gift exchange game."

"I know," she said. It was true. There were few secrets among reporters and cops. And the ones they did have were hard to keep. She knew that Hobgoblin wasn't a secret getaway for her. It was just a getaway. Locals rarely went there. It was her pretend haven away from Japan.

"Thank you," she said distractedly, letting the beer bottle slide back into the box. She brought it into her kitchen and set it on the counter. "I'd open it now, but . . ." she trailed off as she returned.

"No," the detective answered. "Open it when you want it." He smiled.

She wanted to open it now more than anything, but she needed to get to Akio and Yoshio. She had to do whatever she could to help, and hoped she would not regret trying. But she began to doubt herself again. On the tower, everything had seemed clear, but now, here in her apartment, reality closed in on her. If she showed up and was controlled again, she might actually kill Akio this time. She might kill him and Yoshio.

Her legs quivered and she sat down shakily at her table.

"Are you okay?" Fujimaki asked, sounding sincerely worried, and took two tentative steps toward her.

"I'm fine," she lied. "Have a seat if you like." She indicated her other kitchen chair.

The detective sat looking at her with concern. He had something more on his mind though. He didn't come all the way from Kofu to give her an Ochugen gift.

"Why are you here?" she said, and she knew she sounded harsh, more perturbed than she meant, but she didn't apologize.

"I . . . sorry," he started. "I don't mean to disturb you. And I know I shouldn't be here at all probably, since you were just detained in Kofu for accomplice to murder. But . . ." he faltered briefly, and got distant. There was something he wanted to tell her, but he didn't know where to start. "Something's going on in Kofu," he finally said.

"Yeah, and here too," she said. "If it's about the yakuza acting strange, I know all about it. I actually need to go, so . . ." She started to stand.

"No, wait," he implored. "Not the yakuza. Although that makes sense that you say that. There's clearly a connection. I mean . . . some of the guys at the station. They're acting weird. But what's really strange about it is that it's not just the dirty cops. It wasn't a real surprise when the few we've known were on the take, ones we've been watching, were acting odd. But some of the good ones, guys on the yakuza beat, some deep in, started getting cagey and acting up. One has disappeared. We've lost contact. And other good guys, ones not even involved and who never got along with these other . . . less principled cops, have gone crooked now. They're palling around with each other. They're best buds. Some even seem to have these civilian followers, like their very own groupies or something. I'm not sure if they're selling drugs to them or what. I haven't been able to catch that kind of activity. But it's spreading, and I'm worried. The whole station is on high alert and no one knows who to trust. Have you heard of anything?"

"Dammit," Masami muttered. "It's worse than I thought."

"You know something," Fujimaki said. "Let me in."

Masami looked at him, assessing. He wasn't ready for this kind of knowledge, even as open-minded as he seemed

"Please, Miss Sato."

"Let's just say that the yakuza are far more powerful now than they've ever been. You know what's been going down with the Tezuka-gumi. You know how they've been recruiting like mad and members of other syndicates have been defecting to them. They are further along than anyone knows." How could she put it? "They have a powerful secret, and it won't be long before they've swallowed up every syndicate in Japan. There will be one united yakuza, and from what you're telling me, the police will simply become part of them."

"That is some secret," Fujimaki said, clearly skeptical.

"It is," Masami said. "I know it sounds insane. But you have to trust me. I wouldn't return to the station if I were you."

"What?" Now the detective seemed offended. "I'm sorry, I know you don't know me very well, but I'm not the type to be swayed by anything they could offer. Power, money, whatever. Not my thing."

"I'm not either," Masami said, trying to pierce his eyes with the gravity of what she was telling him. "But this . . . secret . . . is not something people can resist. Not you. Not me. I can't explain anymore."

She wanted to tell him that she had been controlled, that she had almost killed someone she cared about. She wanted to drive it into him that he should avoid the police station at all costs. But that would involve talking about demons. Th ings he would never understand without seeing. Th ings she would have laughed at if she hadn't witnessed them, if her life hadn't been irreversibly altered in the past couple months.

Fujimaki took a deep breath and sighed. "Okay. I know you're a straight shooter. Th ere's no reason you'd lie to me. You're clearly not telling me the whole picture, and I wish you would. But that's your business. I want to help. For my boys at the station, for you, for everyone. The more you can tell me, the better. But if you can give me anything. Anything at all that I can go on, so I can do something to help, I will. I won't betray your confidence. I have to do something. I can't just sit still and watch everything I care about fall apart."

"Sure," Masami said curtly. *I have to go!* "I'll tell you exactly the best thing you can do. I am serious, and I don't mean any disrespect. You said you trust me. So here it is. Stay out of it. Completely. Stay away from this yakuza investigation. Stay away from the police station. Stay away from me."

Fujimaki exhaled sharply through his nose. He squinted his eyes ever so slightly, his lips stiffening over his teeth.

"If you don't," Masami continued, "you will end up like them."

"That's ridiculous," he started. "There's n—"

"It's the truth!" Masami cut him off. "I'm sorry, detective. I genuinely do not mean to insult you. But you have no idea how much power they have now. No one is safe."

"If that's true, then what are you planning to do? You said you have to go. You're obviously involved in this, deep. And if you can avoid whatever this all-powerful temptation is that the yakuza are peddling, then why can't I?"

"I can't!" Her voice rose out of control. "I can't," she repeated quieter but still insistent. "But I don't have a choice." She wanted so badly to disappear right then, to turn into a ghost and slip away from this pointless conversation. But she resisted.

"Neither do I!" his voice matched her intensity. "I can't abandon my friends, my city, anymore than you can."

"This might be the stupidest thing I ever do," she said, quieter now.

I might kill my friends.

"Then let me be stupid with you," he pleaded. He was so sincere, so stupidly sincere. She wanted nothing more than to scream, *Yes! I need someone on my side, someone to hold me up and keep me strong when I start to lose it. I need someone to share this madness with, someone who'll believe me and understand. Who better than you? A strong, handsome, honest cop. Who better?*

"No," she said. "Please. I have to go." She went to the coat closet and retrieved her wakizashi, tucking it into her belt.

"You have a sword?" Fujimaki raised his eyebrows, flabbergasted. "You're going to fight this powerful yakuza secret with a sword?"

"I don't care if you stay here," she said. "Just lock up when you leave." She went to the front door, remembered to open it first, and bolted through, leaving the detective in her apartment. The second she was out of sight in the hallway, she ghosted and dropped through the floor.

She heard Fujimaki's bewildered voice fading away as she descended.

"Miss Sato! You can't . . . Where the hell . . . ?"

8

The Third Trial

hree huge blue-green oni stood before Akechi. He did not know if they were the same oni as before; one was indistinguishable from another. Another year had passed. He knew, only because they were there. Once again, they carried the same three weapons: a tsukubō, a sasumata, and a sodegarami.

The onslaught of battle had been more relentless than before. It seemed that Hell was filling up with those who had disappointed the gods. Akechi had regained his favored weapons in this nightmare: the hachiwari, a heavy hooked blade, and a single tekko-kagi, a death-dealing claw with which he could rend his opponents and drag them to him to be dismembered with the weighty sword.

The first time the blue-green oni had come, he had thrown down his weapons, knowing he could not defeat them. The second time, he had fought them desperately, only to be defeated like a wild dog. But he had wounded one of them, and that gave him bitter pleasure. This time, he knew what he had to do.

He had killed countless souls of men, even those of women and children who had attacked him. There was no other answer here but killing. There was no way to reason, to form peaceful unions, or to make allies. The ingrained compulsion was to kill. Nothing else was allowed.

And he had killed so very well. Since his last watery trial, he had even killed two red oni. He had killed them separately on two different occasions, but those victories had left him giddy with satisfaction. He had almost enjoyed being in Hell for a time—until he had been made to gut a boy that reminded him of his own Kiyoshi.

A blue-green oni was larger and more deadly than the red ones. It would be beyond unreasonable to think he could defeat three of them.

But Akechi had lived his life being unreasonable.

This time when they came for him, he did not throw down his weapons. He did not drop to his knees and surrender. Nor did he attack. He only waited.

The first to come at him wielded the sasumata, and Akechi let the oni straddle his neck with the weapon's two spear-like prongs. When he still refused to move, the oni gave a hard shove.

But Akechi was ready for it.

He saw the demon's muscles tense and its arms rear back before the thrust. At that precise moment, he let himself fall backward, dropping his head out of the sasumata's tongs, his chest arching out of its path.

The oni's own strength took it off balance, and it stumbled forward, its hands reaching forward to within range of Akechi's blade. He severed the hands from its arms as he twisted out of its way, slicing the wrists exactly where the bones were weakest. It howled in agony and surprise as black blood sprayed over the stone, sizzling on impact, its large, meaty hands slapping on the burning stone like steaks. Akechi spun back, gripping the demon's skull with his tekko-kagi, pulling its head backward, the momentum still carrying its body forward. As the long blue neck opened up, Akechi's sword bit into it.

It did not take off the demon's head as Akechi had hoped. The neck was as thick and resilient as timber, but it was enough to sever arteries, and the oni spasmed on the ground only briefly, while gouts of black emptied on the hot stone, spattering and popping like oil.

The other two were momentarily dumbstruck, as if they had seen something impossible, something that had never been done before, and Akechi was certain they had. They fanned out to either side holding their pole arms outstretched to keep him at a distance. They circled him until they were on either side.

The one with the tsukubō, rushed forward to push Akechi back with the weapon's hammer-like head into the sodegarami, the sharp spikes of which were aimed at his back. It was exactly as he had expected. He vaulted sideways, displacing his body just as the spiked crossbar of the tsukubō reached him. The oni behind had thrust forward at the same time, and the barbed spikes on the sodegarami's claws became entangled on the crossbar of the other weapon. The force of their attacks had clashed and crushed their weapons together. While they heaved to pull them apart, Akechi sprung forward.

He hacked at the pole of the sodegarami with his thick blade, hoping to sunder it, but it did not break. Instead it only aided in releasing the weapons from each other. Akechi cursed but still surged forward. Now that he was inside the oni's range, he needed to strike quickly. He slashed across a thick lower leg with his tekko-kagi claw, then opened the demon's belly with his sword. But the oni had stepped back to avoid the swing, and neither weapon did the damage he had hoped for.

The demon struck back with a furious fist that glanced across Akechi's cheekbone as he tried to duck. Even for an indirect hit, the blow was staggering, and the daimyo stumbled sideways. The other oni swung his T-shaped tsukubō like a hammer at Akechi's head. But at that moment, the samurai's foot found a loose stone, and his feet went out from under him. The spiked pole arm whirled by his face, but only scratched his chin as he fell to his back on the ground.

Grateful for the aid of Bishamonten, the god of fortune in battle, Akechi rolled quickly, tucking in his legs as he did, then thrust himself like an arrow at the nearest oni's legs before it could bring its weapon around again.

A tekko-kagi claw dug into one calf muscle while the hachiwari's hook sunk into the other, and Akechi pulled himself between the demon's legs, ripping flesh as he did. The oni collapsed to its knees shrieking, and Akechi spun around, his blade slicing up into the demon's armpit.

But the oni's skin and muscle were thick here, like boiled leather, bones like steel. The blade only cut part way. Yet it was enough to sever an artery in its armpit. Black blood pulsed from the demon as it stood and tried to turn and face the infuriating samurai. But Akechi had hooked his claw hand into the beast's back, so when it turned he went with it. He hacked at the oni's back and neck as it scrambled to shake him off. It stumbled to and fro, legs weak from the huge gashes in his calves. The demon dropped its weapon and grabbed at Akechi, but when it did, it found its fingers severed and retracted them quickly.

The other oni came to its rescue, reaching for Akechi with the curved and barbed spikes of its pole arm. The samurai danced on the demon's broad back, knocking the weapon away with his thick-bladed sword while pushing the claw in deeper to maintain his hold. His entire height nearly fit between the blue-green demon's neck and waist.

The oni let out a roar and charged at Akechi from the side, while the one he hung from planted its feet to give its companion a stable target. But its legs were still wobbly and Akechi had his sword arm free.

The samurai released his claw and leapt onto the oni's shoulders. In one swift action he sliced a gash across the demon's neck and hooked his claw into its fibrous, oily hair, the spikes barely denting the steel-like skull.

But it was enough.

As the charging demon adjusted its weapon upward to aim at the exasperating man, Akechi jumped backward from the oni's shoulders, yanking its head with him as he did. The barbed, multi-headed spear skewered the oni's thickly muscled neck, already gushing blood from Akechi's sword. The samurai flipped backward and above the charging oni, its momentum slamming into the other demon. Its own body was thrust directly under Akechi, who, at the peak of his flip, imbedded his hachiwari hook into the base of the charging demon's skull. He landed, straddling its shoulders like a toddler.

But this toddler would not be disciplined, not by these lesser beings.

He wrenched the hook in deeper and the oni dropped to all fours on the scorched stone. The other beast lay bleeding out nearby, clutching with fingerless hands at the pole arm inserted into its neck, the weapon's long shaft snapped off near the killing end.

When Akechi's new demon mount tried to rise, he dug the hook in again, and the beast stayed put.

"Lead me to the trial," Akechi growled, and twisted the hook deeper.

The oni groaned and began to crawl forward, dragging its knees over the hot granite and gabbro, Akechi rode it with grim satisfaction, a brutal warlord astride his powerful mount.

In time, they came to a cliff's edge where the demon stopped.

"There," it grumbled painfully, and pointed with a fat blue finger into the chasm below. Dark vapors rose amongst the long shadows cast by the cliffs. Vague jagged shapes appeared and disappeared as the fog breathed and eddied, for brief moments uncovering barren rock wasteland, only to be washed over again with the thick mephitis. Nothing else moved.

"How do we get down?" Akechi asked.

"We?" the demon strained. "We were to throw you down."

Akechi snorted. "That's not going to work now, is it? You're coming with me."

After a moment of silence, the oni offered, "There are stairs."

"Good. Show me."

Not far away were stairs cut into the face of the cliff. Akechi rode the oni down and grinned joylessly as it winced with the impact of each step. They wound down, switching back and forth along the cliffside, the heat wafting up from the cavern in rancorous, mephitic waves. The descent seemed to last a day—though Akechi had long since lost his awareness of time—but the demon did not stumble.

Somehow it was hotter yet at the bottom. Akechi had thought the heat had reached a limit, but it escalated here as if it were a physical presence attacking, a bonfire licking at his flesh. The oni's body was scraped and raw. Blood ran from its torn knees and the wounds Akechi had given it. It ran from the back of its neck where the hachiwari's hook stuck and controlled it like a rudder.

The chasm felt like a vast tomb, a jagged scar in the fabric of Hell. The place where Akechi had battled without pause for two years had felt cavernous. Darkness had swallowed all but his immediate surroundings, and combatants had come at him from all sides, often without warning. Here the view was open and long, the fog not as impenetrable at ground level. What passed for a sky roiled in red turmoil above them. Bursts of flame lit upon wrathful clouds of dark gasses, like lightning in a turbulent surface storm.

The ground was black shale and iron ore. Rubble and detritus covered the expanse. It bit into the oni's wide hands, tearing gashes as the demon crawled. Akechi held a bitter pleasure that this pain was spared him thanks to his newly tamed beast of burden. He felt none of it, only the tremendous heat like a heavy blanket of wet flame.

Nothing moved here save the samurai, the hobbled demon, and a ghostly vapor. The red and sulfurous mist lurked about them, suddenly bursting forth and eddying into an angry current, and then hanging still in the thick air as if no wind had ever touched it. The only sounds were the hiss of those dread fumes and the shuffling slap and drag of the beaten oni over the stones.

As Akechi rode on, a thin, glowing red line appeared in the ground, running parallel to the towering cliffs on either side. The oni moved to its right to stay to one side of it. It widened as they went, and molten bubbles began to pop and spit from what was clearly a vein of lava.

At the far end of the chasm, a shape emerged in the red mist. It rose half the height of the cavern and widened the higher it went, reaching toward the cliff's edges.

It was a tree.

Akechi rode the demon closer, following the lava stream. The branches of the tree became clearer, the wide trunk and surface roots spreading out below it like great tentacles, before burrowing into the ground. Here the oni stumbled, worn down from the painful subjugation and blood loss. It righted itself and carried the daimyo ever closer.

The tree was a massive *ashvattha*, its trunk tall, thick, and richly brown, its leaves somehow retaining their vibrant green in the oppressive heat. Lava flowed around it like a moat, its roots submerged in the molten red rock, but the tree did not burn. It seemed instead to derive sustenance from it.

The oni crawled forward to the edge of the bubbling moat and stopped. Lava arced in great spouts, the heat feeling like a brand on Akechi's face. He barely felt he had a face any longer, only a melted stump on the end of his neck.

The branches hung over him, a vast canopy blocking out the flaming sky. The trunk stood as wide as a castle tower and far higher than any structure Akechi could imagine. On its surface was the outline of a great door.

"This is the final courthouse," Akechi said, not asking. He knew. "How do we get across?"

The oni grumbled but did not answer. Akechi twisted the hook to one side. "If you don't tell me, I will ride you across and jump clear as your body dissolves."

The demon growled and whined. Th en in a surprise burst of strength, it spun around, knocking Akechi off. As it did so, the hook dug deeper into its skull before coming out in Akechi's hand. When the demon stood, it was wobbly and confused.

"You . . . " it started. "You must . . . enter . . . alone. And I will . . . not be seen by King Godou-tenrin as your mount. I will not be . . . shamed further." The demon turned and began to stumble away.

Akechi strode after it, and the demon turned back. It flailed its arms as the daimyo's blade opened gashes across its shins, bringing it to kneel closer to Akechi's height. The sword came down into its skull. It collapsed forward and breathed no more.

Akechi hooked his tekko-kagi into the gash at the base of the demon's neck and began dragging it back toward the lava. It was like dragging a horse. But he was determined to make a show of this oni.

At the lava's edge red lights appeared, dotting the leaves of the tree. Stones rose up through the lava, creating a foot path across. Flames licked up the front of the tree where the door was outlined, and when they died out moments later, a doorway stood open, bright yellow light shining from within.

"You were right," Akechi said to the dead oni. "I had to be alone."

He looked at the stone path across the lava and at the huge blue-green demon's corpse. With a sigh he turned to it and hacked through its neck in four strong swings. Hoisting up the demon's head, he walked boldly across the lava and into the tree.

The entryway was thick as a castle wall, and it took five steps to enter the room beyond. Inside, the tree felt slightly larger than it appeared from the outside but nowhere near as vast as the water cavern or the stone courtroom of his earlier trials. It was a room that had the appearance of a large library or comfortable study, a room for relaxing and reading. The walls were the wood of the tree and the room was cylindrical, its ceiling lost in a web of light.

A slim, older man with a round belly peeking from his robes sat in a low chair lined with cushions. His legs were crossed and he was reading a book. He looked up when Akechi came in dragging the watermelon-sized head of the oni in his clawed hand, and holding his bloody, hooked sword in front of him.

The man smiled behind a wispy goatee and put his book down on a small table next to him. It was a simpleton's smile, a man untouched by misery. Akechi wondered what he was doing with a book because he would be surprised if the man could read. He looked like a peasant touched in the head, his eyes a little vacant, an animal that is good for nothing except to fertilize the ground.

"Hello," he said in friendly greeting. "Come in, come in. Please be comfortable. You'll have no need of your weapons here. You can leave them by the door if you think you'll need them later."

Akechi did not set his weapons down. He moved closer to the enfeebled man, bristling that he even had to converse with such a cretin. "Where is the trial?" he growled. I have a gift for this King Godou-tenrin I'm supposed to meet."

"Oh, that was thoughtful of you," the man said. "The trial is here. Right in this room."

"Fine. When does it begin? And where is this king that will judge me and send me to my doom?"

The man smiled again, a saintly image that made Akechi want to plant his sword in the halfwit's head.

"It has already begun," he said. "I am whom you seek."

Akechi scoffed. Certainly this simpleton was just a lackey, some eunuch made to serve wine and no more. And certainly his final fate would be decided in a room far grander than this.

"I have no time for more lies!" Akechi shouted, and swung his hachiwari down at the man to cleave him in two.

But his hand was stopped.

At the height of his swing he felt emotion overcome him. It was as if his hand had hit a wall, but the wall was inside him. He felt such a sudden rush of sorrow and loss that he collapsed to his knees and wept, his sword clattering to the floor.

When he looked up, the man was smiling at him again, as if Akechi were a child, and in place of the simpleton was a man whose wisdom was boundless, a man whose knowledge of joy, misery, and all the intricacies and hues in between was complete, a man who was no longer a man, but a god, perhaps even all gods made one.

Akechi prostrated himself and pulled at his hair, which he found to be brittle as old hay. He blubbered and wept, tears running with saliva onto the floor.

He felt a hand on his shoulder, and a calm washed over him like a light had been ignited within. He lifted his head and looked upon Amitabha Buddha with a purity of reverence he could not have imagined. All his crimes, his hate, arrogance, murders, and regrets were lain before him, as was his love, passion, and loyalty. He was empty and full at once.

"When I was a boy," Akechi spoke quietly, "I imagined coming to you as a pure soul, a servant of wisdom and love. But . . . it all . . ."

"I know," the Buddha said. "It has a way of getting away from you, doesn't it?"

Akechi raised his head up to meet the Buddha's deep, calm eyes, a color that was neither blue nor green nor red, but all of those colors together and yet separate. They were white as stars and black as the night sky.

"You are King Godou-tenrin." he said meekly.

"I am," said the Buddha. "And there are yet other names I am called."

The daimyo saw the grotesque head of the oni that lay next to him, his hand still attached to the tekko-kagi that held it. He quickly pulled his hand out of the iron claws and the head rolled back to stop with its dead eyes peering up at the king, its nostrils flared and black tongue lolling out.

"I . . ." Akechi started. "I brought that to give you, to throw in your face, to prove to you that I will not be anyone's thrall." he said. "I am sorry."

"It's okay," the Buddha said casually. "I don't really have a place for it anyway." A shiver seemed to pass through the tree and the oni's head was gone.

"Let's talk, shall we?" said the god. "And clean you up first." He put a hand on Akechi's temple, and light washed over his skin and his ragged clothes. He found he was wearing a clean, white robe, and his wounds were healed. Gone was the blood caked so thick it had obscured his skin. His calluses and scars were wiped away.

Part of him flinched. He did not like being so pristine. He did not like being without the armor of scars and wrecked flesh that he had earned. But another part of him thought of redemption. It felt as if this trial might go in his favor. He would be forgiven. In spite of all the wrongs he had committed, *he would be forgiven.* The one prayer he had received would be enough.

Another low chair appeared behind Akechi and the Buddha gestured for him to take it. For the first time, he seemed to notice his belly hanging out of his robes and he closed it. "Whoops, that seems to keep happening." He smiled.

Although the king, his judge and jury, had not asked a question, Akechi felt compelled to talk. "I was good. I had a wife and child. I was a loyal samurai. Why did this happen to me?"

"The choices were made by you," the Buddha answered. "Each choice creates a result. Your choices led from one bad result to another."

"But I got my revenge. Kiyoshi is my son, and I got him back!"

"Do you think revenge is a virtue?"

"I . . . When someone has wronged you, can you not rightfully retaliate? Is that not justice?"

"Justice," the Buddha said flatly, only weighing the word for its value. "Justice is mankind's word, and the meaning mankind puts to it is arbitrary. One man might be killed for a crime that another man is celebrated for. How is that justice? Justice is a nonsense word."

"But isn't that what we are doing here?" Akechi asked. "Am I not at this trial to be served justice?"

The god smiled again, and it rattled Akechi's heart. He was always smiling, damn him.

"No," he answered like a parent explaining a simplicity to a child. "It has nothing to do with justice. What we are doing is about balance. It is about karma."

Though it was said with love, the weight of the statement hit Akechi hard. "So I am doomed then. I have done horrible things in the name of revenge, in the belief that I was owed better. That has offset the balance and I must be punished. Am I wrong?"

"You are not wrong." The Buddha leaned back in his chair. "But prayer does have sway, the prayer of loved ones, and your own repentant spirit."

Akechi dropped his head. He was not repentant. In spite of everything he felt now, his regret, his new understanding of balance verses justice, he did not repent. His heart still raged at Imube, the daimyo who had kidnapped his son. Even though Akechi had slain him on the battlefield, taken his castle, his courtiers, attendants, and vassals, had bedded his wife and regained his blood-born son.

Was that not balance? Was my revenge not sated? Why do I still feel angry?

"When will we know how many have prayed for me?" Akechi asked sullenly.

The word, "ONE," rang out in his memory. Each time there had only been one.

"I have been listening," the king said, and took a sip of wine from a cup that Akechi had not seen before. "Have some if you like." He indicated the small table next to Akechi that held a similar cup, full of the red fermentation.

Almost reluctantly, as if he didn't deserve it, the daimyo lifted the cup. But then a strength flamed inside him, and he took a long draft. He did deserve it. And soon he would deserve a refill. Even as he thought it, a full urn appeared next to his cup.

Again he felt torn, humbled but still bubbling with anger underneath. *Is the nature of a man so unchangeable?* he asked himself.

"And so?" he asked the king, dreading the answer, not wanting to hear the lonely "one" again, not wanting to feel so unloved.

The Buddha sighed and held Akechi's gaze for a moment before answering.

"None," he said.

Akechi held his head up like a stone, his face unflinching, but inside he had died again. The single prayer that had made him feel so lonely and abandoned he now longed for. "One" had been nothing until it had gone.

Now it was everything.

As he sat immobile, the skin hardening on his face, feeling his scars returning, his calluses reforming on his hands and feet—the palms that had held so many weapons, had taken so many lives.

None.

The Buddha sighed again and leaned forward in his chair. "The path to salvation can be a long and ugly road sometimes, I'm afraid. But we all get there. Eventually. We all end up as one in the end."

None.

"So this is how it works now," the Buddha said. "I know King Byoudou already told you, but that was two years ago. You've had some hardships since then, so I'll recap." He took another sip of wine.

"Your crimes dictate that you will become a namakubikamen. You'll keep your form, more-or-less, but as your servitude progresses, the demon essence will transform you some. To begin, the niyarikangei will take your head, replacing it with a *kōkaitoge* mask. All that ego that has been driving you will be removed symbolically and put in a box. You'll become a puppet for greater demons to control and manipulate as they like. One of the best at this we find are the nentōkitō. They are doomed as well, and being they are composed of many souls, have a hell of a time finding their balance. Pardon the pun. But in the end, even they will find it. Nothing is permanent. Though your suffering in Hell will last many thousands of years, it is not permanent. And even when there, you will have choices. Remember that.

"The mask is imbued with your crimes, and every part of your essence that was connected to your crimes. They will replay in your head endlessly, but they will not make you mad. It serves to give you further perspective, to allow you to relive the crimes and learn from them. So that you may make better choices going forward.

"Your true head will be locked away, and you won't be able to retrieve it or open its container. King Byoudou said you'd *never* be able to remove the mask and would *never* be able to retrieve your own head. That is true insofar as you are still serving your sentence. Once you are freed and balance is restored, of course, your head will be returned to you.

"Thousands of years," Akechi said emptily.

"Yes, but it passes the same as does a day."

"Can I ask you a question?" Akechi muttered.

"Please."

"Who prayed for me? In the other trials. Who was the one prayer? Was it my son?"

The Buddha laughed. It was a light, unoffensive chuckle that would not upset the most sensitive of egos. "I suppose I can tell you," he said. "You won't remember this anyway. Not for a very long time." He looked on Akechi again in a way that made the daimyo feel like a boy.

"No, it was not your son. Your son hated you. He never believed you were his real father. Your son poisoned you. That's how you wound up here. He still calls himself Imube, I'm sorry to say."

Akechi was crushed. Anger boiled up in him again. He had to go back. Somehow, he had to go back and convince his son of the truth. He had to right this injustice.

Justice is a nonsense word.

"Who then?" he shouted. "If not my son, who?"

"One of your adopted daughters," Amitabha Buddha said. "Kotone, her name was. She was grateful you had spared her life, so she alone prayed for your soul. But two years goes by and a girl grows up, gets distracted by boys and courtly life. And so the anniversary of your death was forgotten."

"Kotone," Akechi mumbled to himself. He remembered the girl. She had been his son's favorite sister. He had treated her like an animal, used her as a pawn to manipulate Kiyoshi.

His heart felt like dust.

"If I had been allowed a samurai's death, a ritual suicide, would I have been forgiven of my crimes? Would that have brought balance?"

The Buddha's light laughter tickled the room again. "Perhaps it may have helped even the scales to a degree, but forgiven? That is asking much of the Universe."

Akechi felt the proceedings drawing to a close. An anxiety rose in him.

"Why won't I remember?" he asked.

"These trials are simply assessments. They are not meant to be lessons. Those you must learn on your own." His smile was infectious, and it grated on Akechi because he wanted to smile with the holy man, the god, the Buddha. The laugh burst forth louder this time, and Akechi fought back his own mirth.

None of this was funny. None of it. Why was the Buddha laughing? And why did Akechi want so badly to join him?

And then it was dark.

So completely dark.

9
Signal Blocker

Akio abruptly stood from his futon, quivering. His face felt raw, his muscles like they'd been through a meat grinder. He had passed out again and stood up too quickly. He leaned against the wall for support.

"Why did you let me sleep?" he asked Yoshio, thankful for the rest, but irritated that he had dreamed of Akechi again. He craved real sleep with dreams of doing nothing but laying in the grass with a cute girl that he would probably never meet in real life. He used to have dreams like that. But anything at all would be better than this. He didn't care what, as long as it was an escape from this horror show that had become his reality.

"You needed it," Yoshio answered, not looking at Akio. The teenager sat on the floor, his attention on the mess of electronic parts spread out before him like a giant Lego set.

Akio noticed pieces of the new light meter he had bought at Yodobashi Camera last week, as well as both of his battery chargers and what was clearly his old Super Nintendo console, now reduced to their component parts. Tiny screws lay on the floor and wires stuck out from exposed circuit boards amid a chaos of plastic pieces, some he didn't recognize.

Akio said nothing, the strange reticence he had gained from Akechi resting bizarrely on his tongue. Before the mask, he would have flipped out. He would have laid into Yoshio for ruining his things, and then he would have beat himself up for being selfish. He would have wrestled with doubt and indecision about what needed to be done. But now, he was quiet. He knew his material possessions were trivial.

Tigress.

Her limp body draped over the car filled his mind and his eyes began to tear up. He had caused that. His intentions had been to avoid conflict with her, concerned that the demon in him might take over and kill her. So he had leapt from the building to avoid her.

He hadn't considered that she might follow.

Akechi strode forth inside him, confident and callous. The samurai had seen death in numbers beyond comprehension, bodies piled like small hills on battlefields. He had caused a great many of those deaths himself. What was one more?

But for Akio, Tigress's death weighed on him like an anvil around his neck.

It wasn't your fault, his rational voice tried to tell him.

She was a stripper prostitute, Akechi butted in. *A lowlife.*

Yes, a stripper prostitute who was likely as forced into that career as she had been forced into chasing after him and Yoshio, he argued back.

Akechi was silent.

Akio needed to distract himself, so he focused on Yoshio.

"Where did you get that soldering gun?" he asked, noticing a small one plugged into the wall.

"I ducked out to Don Quijote while you were asleep. I also picked up a portable radio, a disposable phone, and a police radar detector. It's amazing the things you can find there. I'm glad they're open twenty-four hours. I'm not sure I could do this without these components."

Akio didn't like the fact that Yoshio had left him sleeping alone. What if he had woken up and the teenager was gone? He would have panicked and assumed the worst. But he hadn't woken up. So there was no use worrying about it now. There were more important things at stake.

Next to the teenage brainiac's mess sat the red and gold chest, still closed.

"Keep that mask handy, please," Yoshio said without glancing up at Akio. "It makes me nervous with these gems so close.

Akio had to think of where he had put the mask, and remembered it was back in the foil-lined pouch posing as an innocent Tower Records bag on the futon. He recalled what had been bugging him before the stripper—*Tigress. Her name is Tigress*—had leapt off the balcony.

Of course it wasn't really Tigress, was it? He wondered what her real name was.

"How did you get into the club?" he asked.

Still busy, sorting and matching pieces, analyzing, shifting, and crunching data like a supercomputer, Yoshio said, "I pulled up the schematics of the buildings in that area on my phone. The shop next door, one of those hostess club directories, was connected to the club. I went in and, when the clerk stepped outside to point someone in the right direction, I snuck into the back.

"I saw the guy with the tiger jacket and followed him to the third floor. I heard you come into the room a few minutes later, but I was hiding behind a filing cabinet and couldn't get to you without being seen."

Akio fell silent again. He leaned one arm against the wall and closed his eyes, his head feeling like a bucket of bricks. Memories came at him from his dreams. Akechi had been tried three times before the mask was placed on him. How did Akio even know those memories? His connection with Akechi was the mask. How had his dreams shown him these prior memories of Hell? But of course it made sense. The mask held the memories of the samurai's life, long before he was poisoned, why not these ones as well? But the king, the Buddha, had said Akechi would not remember them, not for a very long time. Of course Akio was not Akechi, and it had been over four hundred years.

More and more of the samurai's life and afterlife were being infused with Akio's own. Akechi seemed to be with him more completely every day. The samurai's spirit was in him, guiding him, ruining him, making him powerful, and scraping out his own weak soul at the same time, scraping out his identity like so much dehydrated rice in the bottom of a neglected rice cooker.

He could feel Akechi in him always. It wasn't just Akechi's memories that were transforming him; it was Akechi himself.

Haven't you moved on? Haven't you gone to be with your son?

These questions had been slowly forming in Akio's head for days now. He had felt Akechi's spirit even when the mask wasn't near. And now another memory appeared as he leaned on the wall, eyes closed but fully awake. The third trial was over and failed. Akechi woke in the darkened room again with the niyarikangei, the skittering centipede-like demons with the huge, unnerving grins and even larger scissors.

After the mask had been seared to the empty space where his head had been, and his head had been carried away into the endless storeroom, the large, green-blue oni had returned.

They took him through the darkness, the memories of his past atrocities stabbing into his brain, trying to tear down his monstrous ego. Red and yellow flickers from flames ate at the dark, growing brighter and gradually bringing the area to full light. They arrived in a great hall carved in stone, with veins of glinting metal and gems, streams of magma running along its edges.

A great, fat worm with fatty legs and a reptilian hide leaned toward him like an absolved sinner ready to recommit himself to his fate. Its fangs protruded from its upper jaw like stubby walrus tusks, bulbous green eyes shown dully with contempt, and stringy hair draped thinly from one side of its head to the other. A tail bloomed like a long petaled flower, and green gems dotted its back, flickering in the flame light.

It was a nentōkitō, and as the oni released Akechi toward it, his brain surged with the worm demon's intentions. He felt himself unwillingly relinquish control of his faculties. The bombardment of his ugly misdeeds still attacked him, but now he was also at the mercy of this giant, flabby worm. He could feel its salivation at being given control over one who had been as powerful as Akechi had been in life.

Akechi wore the mask. But the demon still controlled him.

As he remembered this, Akio's fingers ran over the ungainly pills that were still in his pocket, the pills that Miyahara had left for him so he could wear the mask safely.

It's not the mask!

"It's not the mask," he said to Yoshio. "It's not the mask that prevents the mind control." He pulled the baggie with the two remaining, furry horse pills left inside. "It's these."

Yoshio looked up from his tinkering. "The pills?"

"Yes!" Akio said. "The same thing that prevents the mask from controlling me is what's preventing the demon from controlling me. It only makes sense."

Yoshio looked surprised and amazed at the same time, elated with the discovery. "Of course! Why didn't I think of that?" His question wasn't disparaging at all, but thrilling to him. "How many do you have?"

"Just these two."

"And sensei didn't leave you a recipe?"

"No," Akio answered. "Dammit. If he had, we could make hundreds of these and somehow force feed them to the yakuza and take away that demon's power!"

"Introducing it into the water supply would be far more efficient," Yoshio said, having gone back to fiddling with the pile of electronics.

"Oh yeah! Great idea!"

"Yes, but it would take me days to isolate all the ingredients, and I'd need Sensei's lab back in Kofu to do it, or one similar. Without the recipe, it's out of the question. Even if we had it, it would take too long to get it into the water supply and then we'd have the dilemma of making enough of it and making sure everyone drinks it. And beyond that, I hate to admit it, but there might be more than simple ingredients in them. I think Sensei might have performed some kind of . . . " He hesitated.

"Magic?" Akio asked.

"Ritual," Yoshio insisted. "Science that I don't yet understand."

He moved quickly putting pieces together in ways they hadn't been designed. His hands moved gracefully and fluidly, each finger a dancer in a dizzying ballet. He wound wires together, soldered connections to circuit boards, pulled bits off one piece and put them on somewhere else. Akio had no idea what the kid was doing.

Snap, snick, shift, burn, click.

"This, on the other hand . . ." He torqued in a final screw. "Will be far more efficient."

He held up an odd contraption that looked like some clunky, faux futuristic space gun, with a boxy middle and no barrel to aim with. Akio noticed the blue plastic revolver handle with a black trigger.

"Hey! That looks like my old Konami Justifier light gun."

Yoshio shrugged. "It is. I found it in the closet with your Nintendo."

Yoshio opened the chest and Akio involuntarily flinched, but realized that he was fine. He could hear the gems' call, but it was weak and insignificant. It had been the pill protecting him all along, and it was still in effect.

With chopsticks, Yoshio pulled out a few gems and set them on the floor. Akio understood why he couldn't risk touching them. It would allow the demon to locate them. Yoshio aimed the gun contraption at the gems and pulled the trigger down gently. He began turning the dials and knobs on its interface, which caused it to make whiny, scratchy, squealing noises. Eventually, he settled on a frequency and smiled. It was a small smile, not much more than a smirk outwardly, but Akio could see that it was huge, wide, and toothy underneath.

The noise from the gems had ceased.

IO
Moving Forward

obody tells me I can't. Not even honest, handsome, well-intentioned policemen.

Masami hadn't remained a ghost for long, only enough to get away from her building unseen. She was still too nervous about running into the Sorter again. Too late for the train or a bus, she took a taxi to Ueno and had the driver stop two blocks before Nakama Plaza. She needed time to think. She needed to delay a little longer and get her head straight about what she planned to do. So she walked.

The dark sky hung far above, beaten back by the lights of the city. Darkness reached out to her from corners and alleys. She felt the gloom of the netherworld that invisibly surrounded her. And her own darkness like a shadow on her heart.

What am I doing?

She knew it was unwise. Her common sense, her logic, railed at her with every step that brought her closer to the plaza.

"Keep moving forward, and the answer will present itself, Masa-chan."

Her mother's advice seemed counterintuitive here. By showing up now she was sure she would only add to the danger. So why did she feel she was needed? In his mask, Akio could probably handle whatever they threw at him.

Couldn't he?

He was an incredible fighter with the mask on. He transformed from the scrawny guy who "knows judo" into a master warrior who could end lives with terrifying efficiency.

Akio can handle himself. I'll only potentially compromise the situation.

Yet her feet moved along the sidewalk, carrying her closer, carrying her to all of their dooms.

Keep moving forward.

They were her friends. And they needed her. Somehow.

Friends.

That word had carried so little meaning until a few months ago. And now she needed to atone. She needed make things right.

Getting them killed wouldn't accomplish that.

But neither would doing nothing.

Another step. Another. And another.

She felt compelled by an intuition that she couldn't ignore. There would be a way. Perhaps she could help from a distance, but there must be something she could do. There had to be. She felt it as clear as the Sorter's huge spatulate hand closing around her.

She shuddered.

Where would it have taken me?

If the Sorter had gotten a hold of her, would she have ended up in Heaven, Hell, or some other indescribable netherworld? Would her life have been ripped from her? Or would she be still alive, slipping between worlds never before explored by the living?

Her footsteps resonated on the concrete, drowning out all other sounds. They felt so heavy now. The solid earth had been a relief only an hour ago, after escaping the Sorter. Now her body felt leaden, like she had bricks for shoes. And still she wrestled with her intention.

I would have killed Akio if it weren't for Yoshio. If it weren't for the mask.

She rounded the corner to look upon Nakama Plaza. The sculptures along the pathways in front looked sinister, their angles like blades in the night. In the darkness, the entrance under the glass canopy, down the wide stairs, now had the look of a cave under a cliffside, a dark mouth that opened to swallow you whole.

At the moment the mouth had hundreds of dark teeth.

Crowded around the entrance was a thick wall of people: many dark-suited thugs, three or four layers deep, but around them there were women and men who looked like normal office employees, paper pushers, delivery drivers, stock clerks, and secretaries, who had not gone home to their spouses and families. It appeared the demon had redoubled its efforts and now commanded the entire building.

The yakuza stood with their arms crossed at their belts, some with a hand under their jackets. Some of them held guns in plain view. They weren't afraid of consequences, because there would be none. The office employees had weapons too: staplers held like clubs, pens held like shivs, the bladed arm of a paper cutter, a broom handle, and so on. One man held an aluminum sasumata, a modern version of the medieval man-catcher. Riot police still used them and most schools had begun keeping them on hand since the Osaka School Massacre of 2001. Teachers were trained to use them to keep knife-wielding intruders at bay. Apparently someone thought having one at the office wouldn't be a bad idea either.

The handful of pedestrians out at this time of night turned back or crossed to the other side of the road when they saw the mob. A few stopped to gape, but most had the sense to move on. Whatever purpose had assembled this crowd, it wasn't something they wanted to witness.

Often the yakuza put out a friendly front. They would host street festivals, give out candy on Halloween, and hold other community-building events. But these yakuza were not giving out candy. The only thing they were giving out now was a killing vibe, a hateful energy that pulsed from them as one angry green wave.

Then she saw them. Two figures huddled behind a gray electrical enclosure just across the street from the plaza. One, a scrawny man with a dark gray hoody pulled up over his head and a sword sheath protruding from his waist. The other, an equally skinny, but slightly taller teenager in a plaid, short-sleeved shirt. He held a boxy contraption in his hands by what looked like a gun handle.

The corners of Masami's mouth quivered as if threatening to smile. Her chest rose with something between relief and trepidation. She took another step.

"I wish we could just sneak back up through the subway," Akio said, his back pressed against the electrical box across the street from Nakama Plaza. They hunched there behind the metal box in silence, peering out at the throng of yakuza blocking the entrance. The mob barely moved, waiting like a pack of automatons for their command.

"Me too," Yoshio responded. "But it's locked tight at this hour. Unless you think you're strong enough to rip through some metal gates with that mask on."

Akio didn't respond. Maybe he was. He didn't know. But he also had no desire to try it. He was numb from his efforts so far. Even his normal abject fear had been silenced, pressed into submission by the punishing combat and the crush of Akechi's ego.

If he hadn't gone full arrogant daimyo at the club in Kabukicho, they might not be facing down this mob. But he had made it crystal clear that he was out to kill the demon when he thrust his hands into the chest full of gems. This was his fault. They may have been able to sneak in quietly otherwise.

They had planned to try the back door first, as during their first infiltration of the building. But it had been worse than the front, though there were less people. A semi-circle of rolling robots, armed with assault rifles stood in front of the door. And lined up in front of them had been a group of civilians, including about a dozen children. Apparently there was a daycare in the building.

Not one of the children was fussing or even moving. They sat or stood, calm and staring forward, as still as the adults. Some of them dispassionately held toys as if they were weapons.

Akio and Yoshio had looked at each other in horror, and then slunk away as carefully as they could, certain the robots would not be discerning once the bullets started flying. Now their best option seemed to be somehow getting through the throng of hate at the front doors.

"Why don't you use your blasty thing on them and shut down the signal?" Akio said. "Isn't that what it's for?"

"Yes and no," Yoshio answered. "It was designed to cut out the signal, yes, preferably at the source. While it may work to disconnect them from the demon's brainwaves as long as I hold the trigger down, we will still have a hundred and forty-three yakuza and confused office employees to deal with."

"A hundred and forty-three? Are you sure it's not a hundred and forty-four?" he asked, disgusted.

"Pretty sure," Yoshio answered in earnest. "Unless I overlooked someone, or someone is hiding or squatting down, or maybe really short."

"Okay, brainiac," Akio started. "No, no, I'm going to call you The Count from now on. You just have to give an evil laugh every time you count something."

"I'll take it," Yoshio said. "I was bummed when Sesame Street went off the air when I was four, but to be fair, I was kind of moving on at that point. It helped me get fluent in English though."

"You remember being four?" Akio asked.

"Yeah," Yoshio said.

"And you're fluent in English?"

"Yeah, since I was five. Aren't you?"

Akio only grumbled. He was getting anxious, much more so than normal. "Okay, let's focus. If you blast them with the ray gun and they get all confused, can't we just slip in through the chaos?"

"Maybe. They may not pay us any attention. But they might still remember that this building is their turf, and they may remember us and the havoc we caused last time."

"I don't know. They seem pretty zombified to me."

"Yes, but that goes away once the demon loses control of their minds. Trust me. I've seen it firsthand."

"Okay, what then?"

Yoshio peered out from around the electrical box. His eyes moved up and back down.

"Scaling the building is out of the question," he said. "Not without the proper tools."

Akio thought of how the samurai demon in Kofu had scaled the apartment building with ninja *shuko* hand spikes. He wondered if he could climb as easily with them. But this building had smooth concrete walls, not stucco like the apartment. And besides, he didn't have any.

Yoshio sighed. "The signal blocker might work just perfectly. And it might not. It might not be able to shut down that many signals at once. It should, but without a wider test I can't be certain. We only tested it on ninety-eight gems."

"Yeah . . . ninety-eight." Akio rolled his eyes.

"Yes, and they were all together in a pile. These people are all spread out."

"Okay, Count. Whatever you say."

Yoshio looked momentarily still as stone, his supercomputer brain rapidly crunching numbers. Finally, he said, "I hate to say it, but with the tools we have on us now, I think it's our best bet. We have to try. For Sensei."

Akio took a deep breath. "No killing," he said, but he wasn't talking to Yoshio. He hoped the Akechi in him would listen this time. He looked at Yoshio's signal blocker. "Please work," he said to the gun.

They looked at each other, checking each others' eyes for commitment to the task at hand. Akio saw it in Yoshio, and he knew Yoshio saw it in him. Akio pulled the Tower Records bag out from under his hoody and pulled out the mask.

Wear me.

"On three?" Akio asked.

"Okay."

"One, two—"

"There's another way," a voice said. It was a strident, slightly husky voice, feminine but dire.

Masami!

Akio and Yoshio both turned to see her squatting down behind them. There was an intensity in her eyes that was depths beyond her normal determined scowl. It was laced with concern, fear, and . . . remorse? It didn't matter. Akio's face lit up. Without her, he had been lost. She was his touchstone, his strength, his courage. He only realized that just now.

"Akio . . ." she started.

"It doesn't matter," he interrupted, sensing what she was about to say. "You're here. That's all that really matters. Ever." He slipped the mask back into its foil-lined pouch and closed it, not wanting to subject Masami to its call, wanting to be here with her as only himself for at least a moment, not tainted by Akechi's arrogant, unfeeling influence. He looked at her like a kid brother looks at a hero older sibling. "You're here. Now we can do this for real. There's no stopping us."

Masami felt the emotion pouring off Akio. She saw it in his eyes, which looked about to tear up. She saw his courage lifted and that lifted hers too. She resisted her own eyes watering, but that was easy. She had been doing that for years.

Yoshio's crooked grin showed he was clearly happy to see her as well. "I knew you'd come back," he said.

Needing to avoid an emotional reunion, Masami changed the subject.

"What the hell is that?" she asked, indicating the contraption with the gun handle.

"Signal blocker." The boy genius grinned wider.

Masami nodded slowly, understanding exactly what he meant. A wave of relief passed through her. It was just what she needed to hear. Something that would prevent her mind from being dominated again.

"How does it work?" she asked.

Yoshio beamed.

"I modulated a radar detector and widened its signal net by interfacing it with Akio's wifi router, a disposable mobile phone, and a radio, giving me an effective frequency range of three hundred kilohertz to thirty gigahertz. Then I had to tweak that down to a low end of four hertz by manipulating the tuner resonance. I was pretty sure the demon's signal had to be at that low end to work on human brains. Then I was able to zero in on the signal the demon was sending. I was right about the range. If I hadn't been, I might have needed to hijack a communications satellite! Ha! But it was right there at thirteen hertz. Then I used the radio's amplifier to boost the signal and the—"

"No, no, no," Masami stopped him, putting her hands up. "I mean, is it just point and shoot or what?"

"Oh, yeah, pretty much."

"Have you tested it?"

"Yes . . ." Yoshio replied hesitantly.

"Not on people," Masami guessed.

"Nope. On gems though."

"Ninety-eight of 'em," Akio chimed in.

"It canceled out the voices," Yoshio went on. "They were no longer trying to get into our heads. It was like they just became inert."

"For how long?" Masami asked.

"Don't know. After the test was positive, we headed here. But I'm confident it will work. I don't imagine the demon has some kind of channel switcher in its head. And even if it does, I can find it again. I built in dials to zero in on any—"

"Okay," Masami interrupted again. "That's good enough for me. I trust you. Besides," she looked at Akio, "what choice do we really have?"

Akio glowed back at her, his face turning a hint of the color of his mask.

"Oh!" Akio suddenly blurted. He fished into his pocket and pulled out the plastic baggie with the two remaining pills, absurdly large and rough-looking like chunks of rock covered in dirt and hair. "You gotta take one of these."

"I'm not wearing your mask, Akio. That's all you. I'm Ghost Girl now, remember? You're The Mask." It sounded like superhero names, and she felt stupid saying them, but Akio gave a wide grin.

"Ghost Girl and The Mask," he said, grinning. "I like the sound of that."

"Yeah, yeah." She said. "Moving on. Like I said, I'm not wearing the mask, so keep the pills."

"It's not just about the mask, Ghost Girl.," he said. "It protects from the mind control."

Masami raised an eyebrow and waited for him to explain.

"I had another one of Akechi's memories come back to me. He was in Hell, being controlled by exactly the kind of demon that's in that building. And he was wearing the mask. It didn't help him one bit."

That made two ways to protect her from again becoming a servant of that vile worm demon. And she had considered letting Akio and Yoshio handle it on their own.

"Keep moving forward and the answer will present itself, Masa-chan."

Her mother's voice was like music in her head.

"If you don't keep moving forward, nothing at all will happen."

It was advice Masami had often heeded, even after her Mother's death. She was a preparer. She had to know all the contingencies going into a situation. She had to be ready. But even so, she never felt truly ready. She prepared herself to the point where she had to let go of any potential variables and move forward. And when her bases had not been covered as thoroughly as she had thought, she improvised, and it worked out, one way or another. *Something* happened. She got a job at the *Dainichi Daily*. She got connections with Tokyo Metro. She got a front page. She got in the press club. She had made things happen by being prepared as best she could, but ultimately by taking the next step, by moving forward. The story unfolds out in the world. She had to be there to write it down.

Her mother had been right all along.

She wasn't one to believe in silly things like destiny and karma, the universe as a positive force, like her mother had. But she felt herself changing. Maybe there was something to it after all. She had come to find Akio and Yoshio on pure faith that something would materialize. That was unlike her. With each step she had struggled with what she was doing, not knowing if it was the right thing or an act of desperation driven by guilt.

But it had been right. A weight was lifted and gravity no longer felt like it would crush her.

"Great," she said. "Hand it over."

Akio did.

"Okay, before I swallow this thing, is there anything else you've learned about the demon that I should know?"

"Its skin is impervious to spears and arrows, so possibly even gunfire," Yoshio said, "except for a thin strip on its belly and a small spot at the base of its skull. Also its eyes are vulnerable, but probably only if they're open. Your swords are made from some otherworldly demon metal, so they may be exempt. But there's no guarantee of that."

"It controls people because it wants revenge from being bullied and pushed around," Akio added. "It was created from the souls of several people like that, who felt powerless in life. Oh, and it can't affect really smart or really stupid things."

"So it's getting payback," Masami stated.

"Yep," Akio said, and it almost sounded like he approved.

She rolled the unsightly pill around in her palm. "Got anything to wash this down with?"

Akio grinned. "Of course." He pulled a plastic water bottle from his pocket. "I had to almost dry swallow one of these throat-wreckers. Not doing that again."

"Almost?" Masami asked.

"Well," Akio said with a grimace. "There was whisky. I don't recommend it."

Masami took the bottle, looked at the beastly capsule once more, and threw it back, quickly following with water. It grated as it went down, scraping against her throat, but she felt it loosen and break apart as the water hit it. It wasn't going to choke her, thankfully. It was like swallowing a lump of dry peanut butter—with rocks and grass in it—but not as sweet, although she did taste a hint of ginger. It fought its way into her gut and sat there like a chunk of mud.

"You should too," Yoshio said to Akio.

"I've literally taken three already," Akio said.

"Yeah, but the last one was a few hours ago, right?" Yoshio insisted. "We don't know how long they last."

Akio looked down at the pill, clearly reluctant to subject himself to it one more time.

"And what about you?" Masami asked Yoshio.

"Oh, he doesn't need one," Akio laughed. "He's too smart for it. His giant brain argues its way out of being controlled or something."

Masami only raised her eyebrows.

"He was held captive and subjected to its power full force, right up close and personal with the big slug. And nothing. It couldn't take control of The Count." Akio looked at Yoshio with both admiration and jealousy. Yoshio looked back with a shrug. It's just who he was. He didn't know any different.

"The Count?" she asked.

"That's his superhero name," Akio said.

She nodded. The two were forming a bond; that was a good thing.

"Better do it and get it over with," Yoshio said, indicating the pill in the baggie.

"It's the last one," Akio said. "I don't want to waste it."

"This is likely our last siege," Yoshio answered like some hardened battle commander. "It's do or die. If you get mind-controlled, we're doomed for sure."

Akio took a deep breath and let it out. Then he smiled. "I don't know. Ghost Girl has got some mad skills. I couldn't take her."

"Maybe we should drop the *girl* part," Masami said.

Akio just smiled again and threw back the pill.

"Uck," he grimaced after it had scratched its way down. "Miyahara's gotta come up with something better."

"Yeah," Yoshio said. "Let's get him out and put him to work on that. Sensei owes us big time."

"Definitely," Akio agreed. "Okay. You ready with the blaster, Count?"

Masami felt the edges of her mouth curving up slightly in spite of it all.

"Okay," Akio said. "On three."

"Not just yet," Masami stopped them. "Like I said, there's another way."

II
A Way In

Masami's accidental trip through the ground into the subway had given her a new plan, a far better one than charging into a group of angry, armed yakuza and murderous office workers. When Akio and Yoshio were clear on the specifics, she nodded to them each in turn to make sure they were ready.

"Here we go," she said. "Don't let go of me." She reached an arm around each one and held them tight. They returned the embrace and Masami felt herself stiffen. She wasn't a hugger, and this felt a lot like a hug. She gave in to the necessity of it and let herself slip into the spirit world, bringing them both with her. She felt their bodies tense and saw their frightened amazement as they took in the shadow existence around them. Akio's breathing intensified against her. Yoshio seemed to go almost limp with fascination, but his heart beat as quickly as Akio's.

She saw their vital glow lighting them up inside. Yoshio's was pure and vibrant, intensely bright, but Akio's had worsened. The smoky black lines had thickened inside him, deepest around his ribcage and his lower legs.

Masami pulled them down. The three of them dropped like stones through water, into the earth itself.

It was brief seconds before she felt the impossible strain of keeping them both incorporeal. It was too much to sustain. When she had yanked Akio into the floor, it had been only a flash and she let go. It had been simple. Keeping two entire human beings with her in the ghost world took far more effort than she had anticipated. She felt her grip on them slipping.

No!

She couldn't lose them into the rocks and dirt of the earth around her. They would die instantly. Akio wasn't wearing his mask yet, and Yoshio couldn't think his way out of being imbedded in rock and soil.

They had trusted her. She had thought it would be easy. Her confidence with her newfound power had grown too quickly. In spite of the knowledge imbued by the demon's possession, she didn't yet understand its limits. She tried to force herself faster down through the earth, every pebble, every grain of dirt threatening to rip them from her grasp, from her willpower.

NO! Just a little more!

And then they were through.

Cold, still air hit her, and they dropped into a dark, narrow space. She held them longer. It was somewhat easier in the open air but still she struggled. She needed to get to the ground and set them down gently. Then they touched earth, and she let go. They were standing on dark train tracks in a subway tunnel, both Akio and Yoshio looking like they were going to be sick.

Masami felt like a train had hit her, but the tracks were silent. She couldn't stop herself from laying down in the dirt next to them. She was utterly spent, her whole being sapped from the effort. She opened her eyes to see Akio and Yoshio dazed but okay. They were shaking it off and recovering their stomachs. She wanted to cry. They were safe. She hadn't killed them.

"Are you okay?" Akio asked when he noticed her prone on the ground.

"I will be," Masami croaked. "But I . . ." She winced and took a choppy breath. "I can't do that again. It was too much. I was afraid . . ."

She couldn't say it. She couldn't let them know how close she had come to killing both of them. "I just need a minute."

"Okay," Akio said, but looked both ways nervously.

"It's past the last train," Masami said. "We're safe, but we should get moving. I just need . . ." Her chest heaved with scratchy air, as if she had taken some of the earth with her into her lungs. "To rest a second," she finished.

"It's fine," Akio said unconvincingly. He was clearly on edge.

Masami slowly recovered. Her muscles stopped clenching, and her breath settled to a steady rise and fall. Her head didn't feel like it was being bisected by a piece of sheet rock any longer. She sat up, and then stood, brushing the dirt off her pants and jacket.

A dim glow washed down the tunnel from the direction of Nakama Plaza. She pushed herself that way with pure willpower, the two scrawny young men behind her. The tunnel opened up wide in both directions as they reached a platform and climbed up. It was empty and lit only by service lights, much dimmer than when it was full of the hustle and bustle of commuters.

"We need to get under the building, which is that way." Masami indicated the direction. "But I can't bring you through the ground again. Trust me when I say you don't want me to try. So I'll have to go in alone. This may have been all for nothing. You might have to go back up top." And then she added. "By way of the stairs."

"No, we don't." Yoshio said.

"Yeah," Akio agreed. "There's a door."

They told Masami about the private door to the subway they had used to escape the building. She sighed in surprise and relief. Again, she had gone forward and a door had opened.

"If you knew there was a door, why didn't you just come down here to begin with?" she asked.

"Subway's closed right now," Yoshio said. "We can't slip through metal gates and walls quite so easily as you. Plus the door is probably locked as well as guarded. Can't slip through locked doors either . . . yet." He gave a slight smile and a shrug.

"If only you had told me this before I…" Masami began. "Never mind. Lead the way."

Walking the empty train station at night should have been spooky. It *was* spooky, in a way, but it was so tame compared to the things she had seen recently that, instead, she found it peaceful. Th e gray emptiness and the forlorn signs giving directions to no one—*Exit* this way, *Transfer to JR Line* that way, *Public Restrooms* this way—felt like some quiet, abandoned civilization.

Masami strangely loved the idea of buildings with no one in them, a community that was no more, like ancient ruins where you can only imagine what lives the people there must have lived, where each mundane possession becomes some infinitely curious artifact simply because the person who owned it was long gone. Rooms stale with vague memories, the walls in disrepair. Ghost towns. She found no fear there. Not anymore. In its place, she saw a pale beauty and a strange appeal.

The station had that subtle feeling of a ghost town, though even in the dim light, it was spotless and nothing like a dusty, forgotten place. Still, she wanted to dangle her feet off the edge of the platform and imagine the comings and goings of people long past as if she were some far future explorer.

She was a realist and didn't take to fantastical dreams and flights of fancy, but when it was something historical, something that had been real, it fascinated her to envision the stories of lives long gone. At that moment she wanted the tracks to rust and no train to ever cross them again. She wanted the signs to fade and the concrete to crumble.

Her life revolved around stories happening now. She loved what she did. She loved getting a kernel of a story, prying and prodding it open until it unfolded and expanded before her. She relished in discovery and knowledge. It was a thrill to get a scoop, to be at the bleeding edge, to be the one who reveals it to the world. It made her feel alive and important.

She loved the real, the raw, and the now. But she also loved the real and unknown past. That was her escape. Some answers could be uncovered, but others simply had to be imagined. She had no time for dragons, faeries, and unicorns. And yet, here she was, able to turn into a ghost, on her way to fight a demon. Maybe dragons, faeries, and unicorns were real too.

But now was not a time for contemplation and feet-dangling. The demon reigned above them, influencing everyone in its reach, slowly spreading across the city like rot. It had to be stopped.

Yoshio led them slowly and quietly down the platform toward its far end. As they passed a shuttered newspaper kiosk, he stopped and hunched down, pressed against the wall, indicating silently that there was danger ahead.

"I see him," Masami whispered. There was the dark shape of a man standing at the end of a corridor that crossed from westbound to eastbound tracks.

"Use your knockout trick," Akio said to Yoshio, pointing his index fingers forward in some signal Masami didn't understand.

"I have to get behind him," Yoshio answered. "He's facing this way. Can't do it. Besides, I'm guessing there are more than one."

"Let's not guess," Masami said. "Stay here." She ghosted, leaving them both sighing and bewildered. A moment later, she was back and red-eyed. The constant changing to the ghost world and back, the constant thoughts of her mother, were taking its toll on her. "There are five of them. Two on this end, two on the other, and one in the middle by the door."

They all looked to each other for a moment, clearly hoping someone else would come up with the plan. Then Yoshio whispered, "Akio, you could take them down easily."

Akio sighed heavily. "Yeah, but how many would be dead? And do we want their demon boss to know we're coming?"

"I think it's clear that it knows we're coming," Masami said. "Our only hope now is to get as close as possible to it before it knows we're actually here."

"Okay, three possible plans then," Yoshio said. "One, Akio puts on the mask and decimates them. But . . ." He eyed Akio's katana.

"We take his sword from him," Masami finished.

"Yes," Yoshio nodded. "Then he's less likely to actually kill them."

"But not guaranteed," Akio inserted. "I . . . Akechi knows how to kill without a weapon. And it would take longer probably than just lopping off their heads."

"True," Masami said, "But I think we've all seen enough heads come off to last a lifetime."

"I know. I don't want to kill anymore," Akio huffed, "but I sometimes wonder why. They wouldn't hesitate to kill us, probably even if they weren't being mind-controlled. They're yakuza scumbags."

"Yeah, but you're better than that," Masami said. "They're people who ended up where they are for who knows what messed-up reason. A lot of them actually believe they're fighting the good fight. They've deluded themselves into thinking they're the good guys, the Robin Hoods. We know better, so if we can, we should act better. You have a demon in you now, one that's relentless, one whose arrogance doesn't value other life, human or otherwise, unless it's valuable to him directly. I can see your struggle, Akio, but you are strong. You are better than Akechi. His martial skills and accomplishments of war have nothing on your conscience, on your sense of right and wrong. You can tame that demon and use his abilities with constraint. You do not have to be subject to his murderous will."

Akio looked at her with a kind of awe, with love. His spirits were lifted, his confidence bolstered; that was clear. She wasn't entirely sure Akio could control the demon, but she had been honest about her assessment of him, and some of what she said had even surprised her. There was a lot more to him than the irritating, juvenile pest she had first encountered at the *Dainichi.* Th e horrific events they had encountered in recent months had uncovered a caring, thoughtful, and even brave, person. She had gained a world of respect for him that she wouldn't have imagined possible only a few months ago. He was still juvenile—his sense of humor, in particular, needed to grow the hell up; he was still a kid at heart, which wasn't always a bad thing; and he still talked far too much at times with no real sense of purpose, but those things didn't preclude his other qualities. She found that she cared about him. And she hoped that her words would inspire him, because they needed him to be confident. They needed him to, frankly, kick some ass.

Akio perked up. His back looked straighter, his shoulders pulled back, his frame stronger. Masami felt herself encouraged as well, a kind of rebound effect from her own words. Even Yoshio had a bit of a glow.

"Okay," Akio said. "I can do it." And he reached for his sword to give it to Masami.

"Wait," Masami stopped him, and then addressed Yoshio. "You said there were three ways."

"Yes," the teen answered, his eyes wide and bright. "And the other two may involve no brutality at all."

"Spill it," Masami said. Akio looked eager to hear as well.

"You might not like plan two," Yoshio said. "I know it wore you out, but you could take us with you for only the time it takes to cross to the door and pull us through."

"No," Masami said. She still ached from the effort of hanging onto them both as they dropped through the ground. Her confidence had been shaken. "I don't think so. I'm not sure I can do it again. What if I lose one of you inside the door? I'm not willing to risk it."

Both of the young men's eyes were big and fearful.

"I'm with her," Akio said. "I don't want to die by door melding. Been through enough of that sort of thing already."

"Okay. Agreed," Yoshio said. "Plan three then. Masami, you sneak past and check the door. It has no keypad, just a regular lock, but on the other side is a simple lever handle that overrides the lock and opens it from the inside. Whoever installed it clearly wasn't worried about keeping people in, only about having a quick escape plan. The lock is automatic and always active, but maybe there's a way you can prop it. If not, we'll have to time it so you can let us in. But first, you'll have to lure the guards away so we can get to it, a kind of damsel in distress act maybe."

Masami grimaced and rolled her eyes. It was the trope she hated most in any story, real or imaginary.

"Or whatever you think will work best," Yoshio continued. "Draw them away from the door, and then double back and let us in. They come back none the wiser."

Masami mulled this over, dismayed that the door wasn't keyed electronically. She still had the keycard she had taken from the robot technician earlier that day. Finally, she replied, "I think it's a long shot, but I'm willing to try. I'm not sure how I can draw all five of them away without getting naked. And even then, the demon may not have those kinds of base human cravings, so it may do nothing."

"No," Akio interjected, clearly upset. "No. You're not getting naked!" he said in a firm whisper. "I can fight them. Just let me fight them. I won't—"

"Akio," Masami cut him off. "I was joking. Don't worry."

"Good," he answered, flabbergasted. "Because . . . good."

Masami chuckled inwardly at his concern, somewhat flattered, but outwardly gave him her customary irritated huff. Then she winked at him, only a quick flash of an eyelid in the darkness. She didn't want him to be disheartened is all, and hoped he wouldn't interpret it as flirting. She turned her expression flat immediately, and Akio had a queer look as if trying to decide if he had actually seen the wink.

They all agreed to give the third option a try first—absolutely without Masami getting naked, Akio clarified for good measure—and Masami faded out of sight and drifted over to the guarded hallway.

The five men stood still, remaining strictly at their posts, like black-suited robots not yet activated; breathing, heads turning slowly and eyes alert, but otherwise motionless and empty. Masami invisibly skirted around the first two, avoiding any possible detection of her presence, and into the narrow hallway. She slipped passed the third yakuza and through the door. She saw the simple lever handle on the other side, but nothing to prop it open with. She would have to lead them away and then hustle back to let the boys in. It should be easy enough, assuming the yakuza would follow her without having to reveal who she was.

A key would be nice though. Then she could simply give it to Akio and Yoshio and meet them inside. And if they ever got separated, they wouldn't be locked out.

She slipped back through into the corridor and eyed the closest yakuza. No obvious keys dangled from a lanyard or belt keychain. She circled the two that were nearer Akio and Yoshio. Nothing.

She headed toward the eastbound tracks and scanned the two suited men here, erect pillars guarding the entry to the hallway. Neither of them had any exposed keys.

This wasn't at all like in the movies.

Then she saw the outline of a keyring in the back pocket of one pair of pressed slacks. If she was careful, she could slip it out without touching him. It's not like he was a moving target; he was still as stone. It should be simple.

She carefully, slowly, reached toward the man's right buttock—a flat, squarish butt, like two frozen dinners side by side. Her ghostly fingers dropped into the pocket and slipped around the edge of the metal ring. She carefully let her fingertips solidify and instantly felt a pain zip into her thumb. It had materialized halfway into the fabric of the pocket, which was tight against the key ring. She let her hand go incorporeal again and jerked it away.

The keycard she had stolen before had been suspended on a lanyard, simple to grab and silently remove from a zombified robot tech's head. Getting these keys would be a lot harder than she had anticipated. She was learning the limits of her power. And she now had a tiny grasp of the horrific pain Akio must have been in with a floor imbedded into his legs. She shuddered at the thought.

The yakuza turned and looked down toward where she crouched behind him. He had felt the touch.

She scrambled backward, standing as she turned toward the other men in the hallway who were also looking her direction, all of them on high alert for just such a sensation.

Dammit.

They moved slowly, as if unsure about what they had collectively felt. Th ey looked about carefully, eyes searching, hands resting on objects inside jackets and tucked behind belts.

One of them pulled a small, slim metal object out of his jacket: the key Masami had been searching for. He turned it in the lock and opened the door, peering in, then quickly closed it again. She almost burst forward to try to snatch it from his hand, but stopped herself. If the key vanished when they had eyes on it, it would be a dead giveaway that she was there. The gangster tucked the key back into his jacket.

Masami moved toward the eastbound tracks, away from Akio and Yoshio. Th e yakuza she had touched was still looking around, stretching fingers in the air. She decided it was time to give him what he wanted.

But ever so lightly. Th ey were clearly uncertain about what they had felt. If she was careful, perhaps she could keep them guessing.

She moved toward him, cutting halfway into the wall to not give more than a subtle contact. She brushed the tips of his fingers with hers as she passed, and then the shoulder of the one just past him. They both turned to follow her.

She went quickly down the platform, a blur in the netherworld, a cool breeze in this one.

Checking back, she saw one more yakuza emerge from the corridor, but he turned and moved the other way along the tracks. The closer two walked slowly, hands reaching about them as if feeling for spider webs.

Masami floated backward, watching and waiting for more yakuza to follow. But none did.

Dammit. The other two must still be guarding the door.

She turned to see where she was going and almost startled back into the real world.

A forlorn, teenage girl sat, feet dangling over the tracks.

It was just as she had envisioned herself, only this girl was not merrily contemplating the past. She was hunched forward with her head in her hands, pondering something deep.

Her essence was there but her body was not.

Masami remembered a news story. A girl had jumped in front of a train just yesterday. This was the station where it had happened.

There she was, a ghost now. She hadn't moved on, hadn't been sorted. And as Masami thought of the Sorter, she snapped her head to look behind her. The creepy, spindly-legged thing could be looking for this girl. But it wasn't there. She saw only two yakuza slowly approaching like mindless sea anemones, jaws slack and arms undulating.

Masami wanted to talk to the girl, ask her why she had done it. What had been so terrible that she couldn't see a future in spite of the pain of now? It was too late to talk her out of it, too late to help.

But . . . maybe the girl could help *her*.

Masami moved closer, slowing down and clearing her throat to prevent startling the girl. It came out as a whispery growl, like her voice had been ground to a fine dust and all that was left was powdery air.

The girl turned, surprised. She looked at Masami as if she was dreaming. She brushed phantom hair from her eyes and attempted to wet her inconsequential mouth.

"Are you . . ." she hesitated, "a good spirit? Are you here to take me to my next life?" She seemed hopeful yet sad, uncertain of her fate.

"No," Masami answered. "I'm sorry. I'm not a spirit. Someone will come for you soon enough." She thought of the dreaded Sorter again and decided not to worry the girl with it. "Right now I would like your help."

"What can *I* do?" the girl asked despondently. "I'm dead. I jumped here a . . . while ago. I don't remember. The train stopped and all the people watched. They took my body away, and now it's like I never was."

"I'm so sorry." Masami dearly wanted to sit and console the girl, to try to understand her pain, but there was no time. "If you can help me, perhaps, I can somehow help you. I don't know how, but I can tell you what little I know."

The girl got up from the edge of the tracks and brushed imaginary dirt and dust off her skirt. "Okay. I guess so. What do you need me to do?"

Masami turned to look behind her. The two yakuza were getting close.

"Do you see those men coming toward us, looking all over and feeling the air?" she asked. "And the one further down, heading the other way?"

The girl squinted, trying to focus on something that wasn't immediately apparent. "Oh, yes," she said finally. "I do. They're still living."

"Yes, they are. But they would like my friends and me to be dead. You can help prevent that."

"Are you sure you're not dead already? You don't look like them."

"I'm pretty sure, yes."

"I'm sorry to say it, but I wish you were. I feel lonely. I thought there would be more . . . like me."

"There are. I've seen them. You will too. I don't know how it feels for you, but you haven't been dead that long. You will see others, hopefully loved ones, soon."

"My cousin," the girl said. "Narumi. That's who I want to see. She killed herself last September."

"I'm so sorry."

"She was bullied at school and didn't want to go back after summer break. I don't blame her. But I miss her. We would always spend summer break together, and now this year . . . Well, I wanted to spend it with her again."

Masami fought her emotions. Suicides were often high after summer break because kids couldn't face going back to be tortured by their classmates. If you didn't fit in, life was hell. Masami had mostly escaped such bullying in high school, because she had been accepted into a clique. Her closed off emotions had made her "cool" to the other girls. She hadn't participated in much of their "activities," but she had witnessed the cruelty of children. Some of these people she had called friends had treated others like animals, like vermin.

But there was no time to dwell on that hatred. The yakuza had almost reached them.

"What's your name?" Masami asked.

"Saki."

"Saki, I need you to do one very simple thing, and right now."

"Okay."

"I need you to run right through all three of those men. Run right through them in that direction, and then come back to me via the train tracks, okay?"

Saki gave Masami a curious look, cocking her head slightly to the side. Then she said, "Okay. It seems weird, but if it'll help you and your friends." She eyed the two suited men moving in a kind of zig zag pattern, arms reaching out into the empty air, like they were searching in complete darkness.

Saki bolted toward them. She was hazy air and faded color as she moved through the men. The first two stiffened and then turned abruptly to follow. She continued in a smeared dash toward the other yakuza who had now turned in her direction. The teenage ghost passed through his chest at full speed. He turned toward her but did not pursue, only stood still looking away down the tunnel.

Saki doubled back and returned along the train tracks. Masami met her halfway. The yakuza had all stopped. They seemed in a kind of stasis, automatons awaiting orders.

"Thank you, Saki," Masami said. "That was perfect. I have to go now, but I'll tell you this, and I hope it helps. Some . . . *thing* will come for you. It may very well come down to the subway, but I've only seen it on the surface, so you may want to go up. It may be unsettling to look at, but I hope it will take you to your friend."

"Narumi," Saki said longingly.

"Yes, I hope it will take you to Narumi. And I hope you will find peace with her."

Saki smiled wanly. She was far away, dreaming of summers free of persecution and fear, when she could be herself without ridicule, when she could breathe easy and relish in the companionship of a kindred soul.

Masami moved quickly back to the hallway. As she did, the yakuza started to move again, but their urgency was gone. They were simply heading back to their posts. Her ruse seemed to have worked. The brief contact she had made with them hadn't been enough to give the demon an identity. Now it believed she was only a ghost in the subway.

In the hallway, Masami saw Akio and Yoshio huddled by the door. The other two yakuza were nowhere in sight. They must have gone searching the other platform, allowing the boys access to the corridor. She was grateful they had taken the initiative. It saved them precious time.

Yoshio was fiddling with the lock. It looked like he was trying to pick it but without success.

The yakuza were converging on the hallway from both sides. Any second, they would see Akio and Yoshio, and Masami's ruse would be for naught. She slipped through the wall and quickly pushed the handle down as she materialized.

The door opened. Akio and Yoshio went wide-eyed at who might greet them, but when they saw it was Masami, they dove inside.

12

Dance of the Puppets

Akio sighed in relief as Masami shut the door softly and he heard it latch. She looked unscathed. And not at all naked. He absently fingered the mask still tucked under his zipped hoody and the foil crinkled.

"You did it," he said. "No violence."

"Yes," Masami answered, her own face a dire mask. "I had a little help. I'm not so sure we'll be as lucky from here on out."

"Help?" Akio asked.

"Yes, there was a ghost, a real one. She distracted them for us. So, thank Saki."

It gave Akio a chill to think of a real ghost so close by, but he whispered to the still air of the secret passage. "Thank you, Saki."

"You're picking locks now, Yoshio?" Masami asked.

"Not successfully." The teen shrugged.

"Finally found something The Count isn't good at," Akio said.

"Yet," Yoshio said matter-of-factly.

They reached the elevator, and all agreed it was a bad idea. A moving elevator with no one in it under the demon's power would certainly raise an alarm. So together they ascended the stairs, Akio recalling his recent painful descent of them with a twinge.

It was a long way up to the eleventh floor, but they went methodically, step by step, as silently as they could, pausing at every noise and not moving again until they were certain there was no one else on the stairs, no one about to burst through onto a landing. There were few doors. They had only seen two after climbing seven floors, both of which had no door knob. It appeared that these other secret entrances into the building had been walled off for good. Likely the occupants on those floors knew nothing about them.

Akio had lost count of the floors when he heard the eerie sounds of music drifting down from above. It echoed in the hollow stairwell, bouncing off the metal steps. As they climbed, the music grew louder and more discernible, horns and an electric guitar, a low crooning voice.

Finally they reached the tenth floor. Akio only knew when he saw the gray door to the elevator and the last flight up to the top floor.

He rested a hand on the katana at his belt. It felt vital beneath his palm, as if it breathed and hungered just like the mask. He eyed the shorter, matching wakizashi at Masami's waist, and then Yoshio's comical-looking homemade raygun. Akio felt his pulse accelerating, his skin damp from sweat. The raygun looked ridiculous. *There's no way it would work.* A sense of hopelessness came over him.

This is not how life was supposed to go.

How had he gone from complaining about his crappy photographer assignments to confronting a huge, mind-controlling, worm demon?

He found he was gripping the mask tightly under his hoody with his other hand. He was afraid to put it on, afraid of what it might make him do. But it was also a security blanket. He wouldn't survive any of this without it. He would be a fool to even try.

In spite of his fear, he wanted to put it on, he realized, and badly. He wanted to surrender himself to Akechi's power and confidence. It wasn't because of the mask's persuasion this time. He couldn't hear its voice. The simple foil wrapper had shut it out. It seemed absurd, but Yoshio had been right. It wasn't magic at all; it was science. And science can be understood. Solutions can be found.

What was the science of the mask? he wondered. How did it give him Akechi's memories and demon powers? Would Yoshio be able to crack that puzzle as well?

"What's our plan?" Masami asked, bringing Akio back to the situation at hand.

He looked at her, dumbfounded. *Is she asking me?* He was never great at planning anything, and the Masami he knew wouldn't trust him with the time of day much less a plan. But no . . . that was the old Masami. And the old him. She was looking at him, not Yoshio.

"Um . . ." he started, the strange music distracting him. "Plan . . . I think that once we go through that door, they'll know we're here, and it'll be chaos. What else is there to do but rush in? Yoshio blasts anyone in our path with his raygun, and hopefully they scatter. Hopefully it works, and they realize we're only here for the demon, that we're the good guys. Then . . . we kill it, right? I mean, we have to, right?"

"I don't see any other way," Masami said.

"Me neither," Yoshio added. "According to Sensei, killing it will only send it back to Hell anyway."

"We know where its lair is," Masami said. "It's not far from here. That gaudy room was clearly its throne room of sorts. It's no surprise that a creature with such base desires would be drawn to so much gold."

"Power and money," Yoshio stated. "It's what so many want, and yet according to statistics, rarely brings happiness."

"This demon isn't looking for happiness," Akio said. "It just wants to feel big by making everyone else its underlings. It was useless in life, remember, unable to get anywhere." *Like me—no, not anymore.* "So it just wants revenge on a grand scale. It wants to make us all pay. Stupid thing doesn't realize it's still just a pawn."

"So our plan is to rush it?" Yoshio asked, looking to Akio.

Why were they asking him? All these years Akio had wanted authority, but suddenly it had been thrust upon him. First, with the transfer of Akechi's strength and arrogance. Now, by what? He wasn't sure he liked it. They were both clearly much smarter than him. Why were they asking him for advice, for a battle plan?

"What the hell is this music?" he asked. Th e reverberating instruments still distracted and unnerved him.

"I don't know. Someone left their radio on," Masami said. "It doesn't matter."

She's right. It doesn't matter. At least they could hear it too. Somehow that made it less annoying.

"So?" Yoshio pressed.

"Um . . . yeah," he said, trying call up courage and confidence. *What would Akechi do?*

"We rush in, de-mind-control everyone with your zap gun, and kill the ugly thing."

"How about this?" Masami said. "You and Yoshio do exactly that, but I will sneak around and try to find Miyahara. We have to remember our primary reason for coming here. If I can free him, he should be able to help us. We know we can shut down the mind-control, but we don't know what else this demon can do. Do Akechi's memories give you anything else about it?"

"No, not that I recall. It just made me—*him*—do things."

"Okay. Yoshio. You said you saw Miyahara go through a back door in the throne room. Where exactly is that?"

"2.548 radian from the plane of the double doors."

"In simple Japanese, please," Masami answered, after a beat.

"Sorry, you said, *exactly*. To your left, about 10 o'clock."

"Great. I'll head that way, and hope he's still in the vicinity." Masami looked them over intensely, her lips pressed together in a determined scowl. "We'll meet back in its throne room whether I find him or not."

Akio nodded. "Good. Great. Yes." *Thank you for having a better plan.* "Yoshio, anything to add?"

"Nope. It's bold and chancy, but it feels like the best play."

"So are we ready then?" Akio asked. He was really asking himself, but they both nodded back.

Akio reached under his hoody and pulled out the Tower Records bag. It crinkled ominously, the mask's voice seeming to slip between folds of the aluminum. Perhaps it had already torn, as Yoshio warned it would.

Wear me. I am beautiful.

The voice was there, but its pull on Akio's mind was weak, dampened by the sensei's pill. It was hard to discern if it was real or imagined. He pulled the mask from between the silvery walls of foil. It looked back at him with its sharp-toothed smile. Its etched, cloudy mustache wriggled above the gruesome grin, as the flames and clouds spiraled about the entire face, mesmerizing him momentarily. It was alive. Science could never explain this.

He brought it to his face slowly. He saw concern in Masami's eyes through the mask's eyehole just before it sucked itself to his face like a vacuum seal, jumping from his hand for the last few centimeters of air.

A calm washed over him like a wave of warm *sake* filling his being. He felt larger, stronger, better in all ways, more deserving than any human alive. But he looked on his companions with admiration. These two were no peasants. These two were warriors of the highest caliber. Together they could fight gods.

They climbed the last flight to the eleventh floor and stood before the secret door to the main hall. The muffled music thrummed through the wall. It no longer meant anything to Akio, barely registering as a feeble distraction. The only music now was the sound of battlefields four hundred years past echoing in his mind. He gripped the handle and pushed it open hard. There was no more need for stealth. He had come for battle. He had come for blood.

To his surprise, the music's volume jumped substantially as soon as the door was open, and he saw the dance floor was crowded with people, as were the tables and bar. A live band was on stage—a six-piece with a stand-up bass, trumpet, saxophone, electric guitar, piano, and drums. The sign in front of the band read, "Leo Igawa and the Heavy Hearts."

The people dancing were of a different mix than that which guarded the doors below. Here there were people of all kinds, young and old. It wasn't just yakuza and office workers from the building. There were uniformed students, teachers, laborers, foreigners, politicians, nurses and doctors in scrubs. There were patients that clearly should still be in the nearby hospital, but they were here . . . dancing.

Yoshio's temporary crippling of the demon had not deterred it, but instead spurred it on with a rabid vengeance. Because of the throng outside of the building, Akio had expected the building itself to be nearly empty. He couldn't have been more wrong.

He saw a large office desk sitting in the midst of the dancers, covering up the hole he had carved in the floor. Everyone danced around it as if it were a normal addition to any ballroom. He saw himself trapped there, writhing in the floor, but the memory of the pain was muted, like a television image with the volume off.

Some of the partiers looked to be truly enjoying themselves, but many, particularly the patients in hospital gowns, had a glazed, painful look in their eyes and a plastic grin that failed to hide their torture. And worst of all, none of them made a sound. Even those seated at the bar only stared vacantly at each other, at the dancers, or at nothing at all.

In the space of a breath, all smiling faces dropped, the music stopped, and everyone in the room turned toward Akio, Masami, and Yoshio. The mob grimaced as one, teeth bared as one, breathed an angry sigh as one. They stepped forward as a single murderous, amorphous mass toward the three intruders.

Akio drew his blade. He would cut them all down. He didn't care that they were innocents. They were necessary casualties of his greater cause.

No. Akio's true voice whispered below Akechi's crushing arrogance. *No. I can't . . . I have to control . . . I have to . . .*

KILL THEM.

Next to him, Yoshio lifted his homemade gun and squeezed the trigger.

The advancing crowd lurched to a stop like a wave had washed over them. They all looked about as patients wailed in pain, their faculties returning. The nurses and doctors quickly attended the sick, who had mostly collapsed to the floor. Others looked about confused, looking to those around them for answers.

Some of the yakuza, grim men who were accustomed to suspicion and double dealings, first looked on those standing near them ready to call foul, but then their eyes fell back on Akio, Masami, and Yoshio. And they were angry again.

This time the anger was their own. While the bulk of the throng dispersed and headed for the exits in panic, a group of eight yakuza made their way toward Akio and his friends. Guns were drawn.

Akio prepped himself to leap, to dismember them like he had the ones by the elevator not half a day before. But Masami stepped in front of him.

"We're not your enemies!" she shouted. "Your enemy is in that room!" She pointed to the double doors that separated the ballroom from the demon's throne room.

The yakuza did not stop until they were just out of sword range.

Akio looked to Yoshio, and the teenager nodded back, indicating his finger was still on the trigger of the signal blocker. The room about them was rapidly clearing out. The cries of the patients were fading as they were loaded into elevators. The band was packing up their instruments frantically.

"What enemy?" one of the men said. "Your friends here look like enemies to me."

"Do you even know why you're here in this building?" Masami asked. "Do you even remember what you were doing a moment ago?"

"We were dancing," another said. "Having a good time until you disrupted it."

"But why? What is the celebration? Do you even know where you are? And why is everyone with any sense fleeing?" Masami asked.

The yakuza looked at each other uncomfortably, but their suspicion remained on the three companions.

"They're messing with our heads," another one said. "Don't trust 'em."

"Like I said, your friends here look like the problem," repeated the first yakuza. "You, on the other hand, could convince me you're a friend, if you know what I mean." He smirked at his fellow gangsters who returned rough chuckles.

Akio's patience with sexist losers like these had drained dry. Always with the degrading comments to make themselves feel superior, or simply not evolved enough to control their base natures. Before the gangster's lip could reach full sneer, Akio's blade was at his throat. Akechi had used women like they were disposable, and had treated men no better, but this was Masami. And as Akechi's memory burned in Akio, she became his wife, Sango. Th e only one more precious was his son, Kiyoshi.

A quiver rolled through the gangster and he went limp, while his companions backed up and pointed their guns at Akio.

"I will take your head before any of them can pull a trigger and then use your body as a shield," Akio growled. "Now, kneel and apologize. Tell my friend what a piece of shit you are, and how small your penis is. Tell her you would rather eat your own feces than ever insult her again."

"Akio . . ." Masami said.

"Then put that gun in your mouth and swallow a bullet to prove it to her."

"Akio, that's enough."

But the man went to his knees, shaking. Perhaps it was the weakened state of his mind from the dominance of the nentōkitō, but he shook like he was looking into the eyes of the devil. He saw that his life was nothing, and he would do as Akio said.

His knees hit the floor and he began to stutter. "I am t-truly s-sorry. I . . . am . . . a c-complete—"

"Brother!" another yakuza shouted. "What are you doing?"

"I'll kill him!" a different one said. "Don't let him humiliate you."

"P-piece of shit!" the kneeling gangster finished. "My p-p-penis is . . ."

"Akio," Masami insisted. "This isn't necessary, nor do we have time for it!"

Akio loomed over the man, his sword at the man's sweating temple. He could see every other yakuza in his peripheral vision. He knew exactly who would pull the trigger first, who would hesitate, and who would drop his gun and run. In moments, they would all die.

"Is so . . . so sm-small . . ." The gangster's shaking hands lifted the gun slowly upward. "You w-w-wouldn't even . . . feel . . ." He inserted the gun's barrel into his mouth.

"Imai!" a gangster shouted. "Don't!"

Akio could sense a trigger about to be depressed. A yakuza on his right had gotten too nervous. They all had. They were backing up slowly.

"Akio!" Yoshio joined in. "Masami's right. Don't—"

As Akio turned to glare at Yoshio for interrupting him, a motion blurred past him, and the gun was knocked from the kneeling gangster's hands. It clattered across the floor, and the broken man collapsed forward, weeping. Akio turned, venomous toward whomever had robbed him of punishing this slime.

Masami stood defiant, glaring back at him with a ferocity that equaled his own, and he remembered who she was. She was the one he had been defending. It was the insult to her that had spurred his retribution. She was his dear, dear friend. His anger dropped.

"Too far," she said. And then put her hand on the collapsed man's arm. "I forgive you," she said tersely. "And I'm sorry. My friend here gets carried away." She gave Akio another glare and then helped the man to his feet. His legs still quivered. The others had lowered their weapons, but only just. They looked like cornered animals. Akio lowered his sword.

"Listen," she said, addressing the gangsters. "Only a few moments ago, you were dancing and grinning like fools with a bunch of random people you don't even know. And it wasn't you that really wanted to be doing that, was it?"

The yakuza looked at each other uneasily, the truth of what she said sinking in.

"No, it wasn't," Masami continued. "You were being controlled. A demon is making slaves out of you and everyone else it can get its brainwaves into. It's getting off on making you puppets. We are here to stop that. We aren't here to take your turf or even shut you down. As much as I'd love to. What's important now is that we kill the demon that's in that room before it takes over all of Tokyo. I think, in that, we are all on the same side. Do you really want to be some mindless puppet doing that thing's bidding? Don't you want to take real power for yourself? Don't you want to take what is owed you?"

"Demon?" one of the yakuza said tentatively.

"Yes, demon," Masami insisted. "A real live demon, straight from Hell. It's been in your mind and you know it. You know it's in that room. And right now, it's scared stiff, because it just lost control of everyone here. Now is the time to strike."

Akio had stepped back and let Masami take center stage. As much as he wanted to take all of their heads, he knew what she was saying was smart. Recruiting them meant more soldiers and a higher likelihood of success.

"Look in your pockets," Masami continued. Do you have gems in there? Green stones? Get rid of them. They are the connection to the demon."

The men dug around in their clothes, shifting guns from one hand to the other as they did. They each pulled a gem out and looked it over, recognition crossing their faces.

"Toss them," Masami said. "Throw them across the room and take your control back."

They did, the stones clattering and careening across the faux marble floor.

"You have three choices," she continued. "One, you can fight us and die."

"Ha," one of them laughed. "We have guns! You have swords and some plastic toy." He indicated Yoshio's raygun.

Masami leaned in a bit closer. "We have him," she said indicating Akio. "And you have no idea what I'm capable of."

The yakuza looked at each other nervously.

"Two," she continued. "You can leave. That's probably your best option, to be honest. Get the hell out of here and save your own asses. But . . . if you're brave enough, there's option three. Join us and kill this monster that's hijacked your lives."

"I think she's right," one of the men said. "There is something. I remember it. That fat worm thing squeezing out green stones."

"Yeah, yeah, me too," said another.

One by one, they nodded and agreed to join in the battle against the demon. Akio could sense their fear. Three of them wanted dearly to turn tail and run, but none of them would. Their sense of honor and brotherhood was too strong. They eyed him nervously, especially Imai who had rejoined his brothers. They were afraid of Akio, but more than anything, they were afraid of the thing on the other side of those doors.

"This is our general," Masami said, indicating Akio, after they had all acquiesced. "Follow his orders. I have other business to attend to." She nodded to Akio and Yoshio and then faded from sight.

The yakuza all startled and stepped back as if a bomb might detonate in the space where Masami had been.

"Follow me," Akio growled, bringing their focus back. "I will have this demon's head." He turned toward the double doors with eight yakuza behind him, each nervously gripping a handgun. Yoshio hung back, his raygun at the ready.

Yoshio double-checked his signal blocker as he moved to follow the group, making sure none of the settings had been bumped. As he looked up, he collided with the back of one of the yakuza. They had all stopped, as had Akio in front of them.

Standing in front of the double doors were three figures that had not been there before. Yoshio had not seen the doors open or anyone sneaking past them. But three women dressed in   black and white maid uniforms stood there all the same. In each of their hands was a matching *ninja-to* sword with black guard and white handle.

The women looked dispassionately at the group before them, emotionless and empty. Then, as if on an inaudible cue, they launched into the room like dancers, sleek black and white cats zeroing in on their prey. Short black dresses and white pinafores whirled, frilly headbands fluttered. They landed, poised in elegant, predatory positions, ready to pounce.

"Yoshio. Blast 'em," Akio said. "Release the demon's hold."

Yoshio aimed his signal blocker and squeezed the trigger.

The maids did not react. They remained still as statues.

Akio took a battle position, his sword in front of him. The yakuza flanked him, guns prepped.

The three maids whirled into motion as one, and the yakuza opened fire. There were no degrading comments from them, no crude gestures this time. It was clear these women were bent on killing. So bullets flew.

The maids danced among the storm of bullets like flitting fairies, impossibly graceful acrobats, soaring, ducking, diving, and spinning. They dodged the bullets like they were prescient, knowing just when each yakuza would fire, knowing just where not to be at any given moment.

Yoshio squeezed the trigger again, but the maids did not stop. He quickly checked the battery power and signal strength. The battery was at ninety-five percent; the signal was at full power.

A bullet ricocheted off a sword, pinging across the room. It was as close as any bullets came to injuring the women. Blades flashed as the black and white acrobats came into striking range, and the yakuza began to fall. Throats were slit, arms severed, hearts impaled. With each kill, the ninja maids struck dramatic poses before moving on to their next victim, as if they were a dance troupe putting on a show.

Three yakuza were down in no time at all, when Akio dove and rolled into the midst of them. The maids had danced away from him and focused on the men with guns. Now his katana flashed once more in front of a yakuza's neck, this time to save it. As he fought back one of the maids, a second one joined her, as if realizing the greater threat. The third was left to pick off the gangsters. Yoshio backed away as one yakuza after another fell at her hands. There was too much shouting, too much blood. Why wasn't his signal blocker working?

Akio shouted in a voice that boomed out of him as if from some other bleak, wind-torn world. "Get out of here if you want to live! I will face them alone!"

The remaining five yakuza fired frantically as they moved away but were unable to avoid the relentless maid. A bullet caught a yakuza brother in the arm as she danced through them. In moments, they numbered only three, and these last few turned away, firing blindly as they ran.

"With me!" Yoshio yelled to them, not really knowing if it was the best idea, but he figured it would at least lower his chances of catching any stray bullets. One more yakuza fell as the maid slid like a shot underneath the gunfire, severing the gangster's legs, the blades crossing flesh together through knees then neck before gravity took his bloody torso to the floor.

Akio was rapidly parrying blows in a blur of steel, but didn't look to be landing any hits. Was he holding back? Now was not the time to be chivalrous. Yoshio needed him to kill the two women and then save him from certain death. He knew how to fight, at least to a degree, but if Akio couldn't handle them, what was he to do? He didn't even have a sword.

The last two yakuza were in full panic, screaming for their lives. One of them ran out of bullets and flung his gun at the maid pursuing them. She dodged the chunk of metal with ease and kept coming. The other ran out of bullets seconds later, and tossed his gun to the side, pulling a tanto out of his belt.

Yoshio's brain was whirring faster than the maids' swords, rapidly assessing every possible outcome and desperately looking for a solution. He sifted through the possible reasons the signal blocker had failed. There was only one answer he could see. They were willing servants of the demon.

The maid spun and danced so fluidly it was almost mesmerizing. She was about to be mesmerizingly spattered with Yoshio's blood if he didn't do something now.

And then he saw it. It was just a little spasmodic jerk, a hitch in the swivel of the maid's hips as she impaled the yakuza just in front of him and blood lurched from the dying gangster's throat like a tiny red geyser.

The movement was subtle but unnatural. It betrayed the maid's true nature. Methodically, like blender blades, the maid diced the man into several pieces as he fell to the ground. She did it as if executing a program.

That's exactly what she's doing.

The beautiful flowing movements, the graceful cuts and spins, the artistry with which the maid moved made the fact hard to accept, but this maid was not human.

It was a robot.

Yoshio was sure of it. Why hadn't he realized it before? He had seen the more crude version with the politician on TV, but these . . . these were something far superior. He wouldn't have believed it possible. He was awed by the technology that could make something so advanced and life-like, so beautiful and deadly. It was decades or more beyond anything he had heard about. He was so enthralled that he almost forgot he was about to die.

Reaching into his jacket pocket, his hand wrapped around an egg-sized metal object, a strong magnet on one side—surrounded by a ring of sticky putty just in case—a single button on the other. He only had one, and had brought it for just such a desperate moment. He had thought the moment would be more obvious. There had been robots galore during their last visit, and they were all clearly mechanical. But these ones had fooled him until now.

Yoshio had made more than the signal blocker while Akio slept. The small power source he had found when he was locked in the storage room had proved to pack an enormous amount of juice. He had originally thought to use it to power the blocker, but he hadn't been able to reduce the output enough to not fry the gun, so he had made something else instead. Now he would learn if it would prove its worth. If not . . . this was the end.

He peeled the protective plastic off the sticky putty, and felt the weight of the device in his hand like a lead egg.

The single remaining yakuza had gotten behind him. Yoshio was next in line for the maid robot's blades of death. He depressed the button on the device and tossed it gently toward her. Too hard of a throw and it might bounce off, and any aggressive movement would likely have been evaded. But a soft, underhand lob didn't even bother the maid. It went ignored. The strong magnet aided its trajectory, pulling it to the robot's chest. It landed without a sound. There was clearly metal in there somewhere, but the clothing and synthetic flesh beneath prevented any clink. The sticky putty helped to secure it.

Straight blades, sharp as sushi knives, swirled toward Yoshio's neck. What program was it executing now, he wondered? What algorithm had decided his fate?

Then a pulse of energy burst from the device.

A single blue line of electricity arced up into the maid's heart and reverberated through her body. She froze in a balletic pose, lifted onto one foot, both blades to one side, prepped to spin through Yoshio's tender biological flesh like so much melting ice cream. And then the ninja maid robot crumpled to the white marble floor in front of him, lights from the dance floor reflecting off blades still grasped tight.

The yakuza behind him cheered.

"Yes!" he shouted. "Yes! For all that is sacred! Yes!" And then he crumpled too, weeping in gratitude for his life.

13
Ghost Brother

Masami moved through the demon's throne room, staying low and near the walls. She knew the demon could see her, invisible or not, and she hoped to prevent that from happening. A crowd of people filled this room too, but here they were packed tightly together. Yakuza pressed against computer techs who pressed against graphic designers and sales managers. In front of them were golden buckets strewn about the room, semi-reflective green rocks dotting the carpet, as if some giant baby had thrown a tantrum. Behind the crowd on its oversize chaise lounge was the huge, multi-legged slug, which appeared to be in a panic. It was shouting something—more like belching—but it was nonsense to Masami. The people stood in front of the beast several rows deep like a human shield, waiting for the coming attack. They were at once vacant mannequins and terrified rabbits. Their still, patient bodies contained souls that were clawing to escape.

She scanned the group for Miyahara, looking over every face. He was not here.

She saw herself in the people's faces, their minds trapped and subjugated. She wanted to help them. Even if many of them were yakuza. Knowing exactly how it felt made her all the more angry. But if she gave herself away now, it would disrupt the plan, and then maybe no one would be saved. And ultimately, it wasn't why she was here. Saving people would only be a beneficial side effect.

And when they were saved, what would happen? They would go back to the hamster wheel and the far subtler mind control of everyday existence. The job, the family, the obligations, the endless cycle of waking, working, sleeping. What was the difference, really?

She shrugged off her bitterness. She knew the difference. First hand.

She would come back for them. Right now, she had to find Miyahara.

But in her heart of hearts, she knew that even *that* was not why she was here.

She was there to slay a demon.

A demon that lives in the lake. A giant snake's body with a woman's torso and head. Her baby made of fish and worms.

The snake woman at Yamanaka Lake still haunted her. It haunted her more intensely now that she knew it was real. How many children had it lured into the lake since Masami had escaped it? How many before? Was it still there? Was it still alive, feeding on the unfortunate, adventurous young ones who wandered too close to the marshy side of the lake? Or had it moved on to more fruitful hunting grounds?

She would have to revisit it one day.

If she survived this.

She saw the door in the far corner where Yoshio had seen Miyahara exit. The demon hadn't spotted her. It was too caught up in its own orgy of arrogance and hysteria to notice the threat under its very nose. She approached the door and glided through like it was air. On the other side was a hallway, narrow and dark. Fluorescent ceiling lights were off. No one was there. Every able body that hadn't been dancing for its pleasure and scattered when Yoshio freed them was guarding the demon or the building entrances.

The dancing disturbed her the most. The demon seemed to have a need to make it look like everything was perfect and happy to any outside observer. Masami knew some people like that: the perfect social media accounts, the perfect makeup, clothes, and romantic partner. The perfect front to cover up whatever insecurity burned underneath. It was either that, or the demon was simply enjoying their pain and helplessness. That sounded more in line with what Akio had described. It lived to make people suffer. And yet Masami couldn't help but believe that underneath that need, it really only wanted love and respect. That it had a helplessness of its own in the knowledge that its true desires would never be attained.

She wondered if the dancers had gotten free. Or had the demon reestablished its connection once they were clear of Yoshio's signal blocker? How many of them had gems, and how many were just collateral mind slaves? She hoped they had escaped. She hoped they were running for their lives, running to disbelieve what had happened to them.

For Masami, there was no more disbelieving. It was all too real.

She materialized and felt the weight of her feet sink slightly into the low industrial carpet. It felt good to walk, even though she felt impossibly heavy compared to her ghost state. She waffled between enjoying the comforting solidity and feeling glued to the earth, glued to what was such a small part of what was really there. And she had only seen one other layer. How many layers might there be?

Light spilled from an open door not ten meters away. She approached slowly, a dread growing in her. There was something in there she didn't want to see. Why had she materialized? Why hadn't she floated in secret into that room?

There were many layers.

In one, Masami always faced her fears. Being a ghost felt cowardly.

In another, the spirit world made her anxious. The Sorter lurked there. So she moved from one fear to another. Would there ever be a place she could relax and let go?

She thought of the Pure Land, the heaven her parents' Buddhist faith proclaimed. Was that behind one of the doors the Sorter shoved souls through? Could she find peace there?

The door was only three steps away now. Light breathed out of the doorway like mist, dancing with the dust that hung in the air like a pointillist's unfinished work.

She stopped and peered into the room.

The light blinded her for a moment, but then her eyes focused. It was an office. A large desk sat next to a windowed wall, a smaller one closer to the door. The light came from a desk lamp that had been pointed like a spotlight toward the entrance. A smell of moldy sweat or rotting onions hit her nose. No, worse. Something sickly and putrefying. Feces.

She paused and then entered. A man hung from the ceiling fan by his neck.

Her heart lurched, but she didn't startle. Her years of perfecting a non-response to outward stimuli kept her still. But her muscles stiffened, and she gritted her teeth at the sight.

The face was grayish white with purple lines and splotches where capillaries had burst. The neck was folded over a yellow extension cord, white skin above and purple gray below. He had been dead for less than a day, Masami guessed. The rest of his body hung limp in an equally limp suit, a wheeled office chair just out of reach.

This is why she didn't come through as a ghost. Because there was already a ghost in here. Subconsciously she had sensed it and didn't want to see it. She didn't want to talk to it like she had talked to the teenager, Saki, in the subway. She didn't want to know another soul's sad story. Two suicides in one day was two too many.

And yet.

This dead yakuza might be able to help too. Like Saki had. Maybe he could tell her where Miyahara was.

Taking a deep breath, and brushing a finger against the M medallion around her neck, she let herself fade.

A shiver passed through her as she braced herself to meet the yakuza's ghost. The room whispered into blurred grays and muted lines, and her eyes scanned the nether side of the office. She saw no one at first. Perhaps the ghost had moved on, after all, and Masami's trepidation had been only from sensing the corpse. Maybe the yakuza somehow knew the drill, gave the Sorter a high five, and went on his merry way.

Then a movement in the corner of the room caught her eye. Someone crouched by a safe, trying to turn the combination wheel with no effect; his incorporeal fingers only slipped through.

"Five," he muttered. "Five," he tried again. "Shit. I can't . . ." He huffed as if taking in a breath, which, of course, he didn't. "Five . . . Shit!"

Masami wondered how long he had been at this.

She heard a clatter behind her, something slamming and the shatter of glass. The ghost did not turn, but she did. The noise had come from behind a door in the opposite corner, a connecting office perhaps, or maybe a closet. Masami turned her back to the man at the safe.

Miyahara?

She started to move toward the sound, but changed her mind. Questioning the gangster might be more productive. The noise could have been anyone. She backed up a few steps, eyes still on the door in case someone came through.

Something brushed against the back of her neck.

She whipped around to find herself nose to navel with the hanging corpse. She gasped and stepped quickly back, angry at herself for being startled. So much for her practiced non-response.

The man's ghost still hunkered at the safe, cursing.

She called to him.

"Hey. Where is Miyahara?"

The ghost ignored her. "Five . . . shit. Come on!"

She moved closer. "Hey! I need to know where Miyahara is. Is he locked up somewhere? Was he working with you?"

"Five . . . shit, shit, shit."

She placed a finger behind her thumb and then flicked the back of his head with it. Surprisingly, she felt impact, and the ghost turned around holding the back of his head.

Ghosts can affect ghosts. Good to know.

"What the . . .?" He eyed Masami suspiciously.

"I need information," she said, getting to the point. She really didn't want to know this gangster's story. She did not care.

"Yeah, sweetheart. Well, I need into this safe." He said it as if her problems were nothing compared to his. "If you can't help me with that, then I ain't—"

"I can open the safe."

The man paused and cocked his head. "How?"

Masami reached down, focused her energy to her fingers, her thoughts on the blue electrostatic web surrounding the dial. She turned it to the number five.

"Holy shit!" the man shouted, his voice sounding like an echo of itself. "Hot damn!" And he knelt down to move it counterclockwise to the next number.

"Nineteen . . . shit!"

"Information," Masami said matter-of-factly, one ear still listening for more noises from the adjacent room.

"Yeah, yeah." The ghost man stood again. "What do you need, sweet thing? How about I give you a little bonus with that information." He reached out to stroke her hair. Masami grabbed his finger and twisted it sideways so he dropped to his knees.

"Alright! Alright!" he hollered. "Ask!"

Still holding onto his finger, she did. "I am looking for a short, bald man, about sixty years old, named Miyahara. Do you know him?"

"Miyahara? Nope. Never heard of him. There you go. That's the information I have. Now can you open the safe?"

"A short bald man in his sixties, muscled and good with a sword."

The man's eyes and mouth went sideways as he recalled something. "Huh . . . there was somebody who looked like that. I don't know about the sword thing though, and he went by Mizoguchi. Boss had put eyes on him for some reason. We all thought he was kosher—meaning brain-whipped like the rest of us—but Boss Kumamori wasn't so sure. He didn't seem to be following suit, and then Big Boss —Big Ugly—put a mark on him. But he seemed to disappear after that."

Miyahara. It sounded like he was safe. Not dead, at least.

"Do you know where he was last seen?"

"Nah." The man hesitated and then added. "I was too busy having my own personal crisis."

Dammit.

The question came out of her mouth against her wishes.

"Why did you do it?" She nodded to his corpse hanging from the ceiling.

He shrugged. "There was a moment when I realized what was happening, when I realized what that thing was and how it had hijacked my brain. Somehow I had been released from it. When I felt it coming back, felt it starting to climb inside my head again, I just couldn't take it. I had to get out, however I could. And it worked! I don't feel its power anymore, even though all those suckers are still fawning over that thing, doing its bidding. I think Kumamori is actually fond of the ugly beast. For real, not just because it wants him to be. When its power went out earlier today, he started crying. I was one of his top brass, you know. I was with him. His office is next door."

Next door. Where the noise came from.

"That was part of why I offed myself. I didn't want to be like him, jonesin' for a hit of that thing's brain juice. So now that I'm free, I want to go put a bullet in that thing's head, you know? I want to save all my brothers. I can't stand to see them under its thumb. But I can't open the damn safe!"

Masami understood now. There was a gun in the safe. She wasn't sure she wanted to break it to him that he'd never be able to use it.

"So you don't know where this Mizoguchi is?"

"Last I saw him was yesterday—I think. Not sure how long I've been . . . like this. But I haven't seen him since the big worm's power got disconnected, after I . . . you know. It wasn't my job to follow him."

Getting nothing from this guy. Dammit.

"So you gonna open the safe or what?" the ghost yakuza said.

Masami sighed.

"Nope," she said. "But I will get inside it." She poked her head in through the safe door and saw the handgun, a black outline in the darkness. It sat next to a small box and what looked like a large stack of cash.

She paused for a moment, considering. Then, ignoring the money, she focused her energy and picked up the gun. Now that she had a grip on it, she let it come with her into the ghost world. Unlike the key ring pressed against the man's back pocket, in the safe there was ample space for her to materialize only where she needed. She drew the gun out. It occurred to her in that moment that if she wanted, she would make an incredible burglar.

"My gun!" the yakuza cried. "Yes! Thank you!"

But Masami only stared at him with a mixture of disgust and pity. "It's not for you," she said, and touching her medallion with her other hand, strong emotion filled her; her eyes brimmed with tears, and she materialized again.

"Hey!" she heard the yakuza's shout fade quickly. "Hey! Where are you goi…"

She hefted the gun in her hand, found the button to release the magazine on the second try, and saw it was full. She slapped it back in and tucked the weapon into her belt next to the wakizashi, then moved toward the door to the adjoining room.

14
Grand Delusions

he office next door to the ghost gangster's was larger, as was everything in it. The first thing Masami saw was a huge, curved, ebony desk. It sat in front of wall-to-wall windows displaying the endless sea of the Tokyo cityscape lighting up the darkness. Just beyond the desk was a matching, windowed liquor cabinet with a pane missing, glass sprinkled on the polished hardwood floor in front of it. Both desk and cabinet were intricately carved with a sun over fields and water theme. They had to have cost a fortune.

The designer desk chair was as sleek as a sports car. The sofa and chairs across the room looked swank and Italian. The filing cabinet and the hanging shelves were dark wood as well, and clearly pricy. On one of the shelves were five small jars, each containing something small and pale floating in liquid. Masami could make out a fingernail on more than one. A stalwart metal safe stood by the liquor cabinet, three times the size of the one in the ghost yakuza's office. It looked like a safe for rifles. The artwork on the walls was dramatic, modern, and clearly original. One of them was a Hisashi Tenmyouya, a figure that looked to be half samurai, half robot in bold flat shapes.

How fitting.

Three blades sat displayed in a rack on a low, ornately-carved cabinet under one particularly lurid painting of a dancing geisha. The blades were sheathed and tiered with the longest, a katana, on top, a wakizashi in the center, and a short tanto at the bottom. Each had a glimmering mother of pearl inlay in the scabbard, ornate guards of polished gold, and handles wrapped in pure white, the triangles of black ray skin visible beneath.

It was immediately clear to Masami that, indeed, crime did pay, and very well.

There was some kind of contraption in the back corner beyond the desk. It was black and ovoid, looking something like an arcade game that you would sit inside to play, but its casing was void of any logo or illustrations.

A woman stood just past it, still as a statue.

She was about Masami's height, dressed in black and white, and looked dangerously familiar. Masami moved in a careful, wide arc out in front of the desk, her hand on her sword. Then, on second thought, she moved it to the gun. As the view opened up, Masami saw that the woman wore a traditional French maid outfit: a white pinafore over a short, black dress. Her hair was straight and blonde, capped with a frilly headpiece.

Masami drew the handgun.

The woman looked very much like a mannequin, not moving or even breathing. The closer Masami got, the more certain she was that the figure was not alive. But she knew this woman. She recalled their meeting in front of the elevators, saw her outstretched hand, the ring with the green gemstone in her palm. She had been able to see Masami when she was in the ghost world. She had been the start of Masami's waking nightmare.

Masami lifted the gun higher and aimed it first at the maid's head, and then adjusted it to point at her chest. She had never been trained in guns, had never fired one. The bigger target seemed more practical.

Still, the maid did not move, did not appear to be breathing.

A motion behind the glass of the black contraption startled her and she turned the gun toward it.

"She won't hurt you," a voice said.

Masami involuntarily squeezed the trigger, the bullet ricocheting off the glass back of the contraption, marring it but not penetrating, not even cracking.

A man raised his hands out of the black machine, one holding a rocks glass and the other a whisky bottle. "Unless I want her to," he added. "And I don't see the need for that. Please don't shoot."

Masami's breath was fast, and her jaw clenched. She could feel her pulse behind her ears. She moved her finger to rest on the trigger guard. She did not want to accidentally kill someone. What if it had been Miyahara?

Although the man who slowly extracted himself from the enclosure was roughly Miyahara's age, it was not the sensei. And though this man's hair was gray and trimmed very short, particularly on the sides, and slicked back on top, he was not balding like the grumpy kendo instructor. He had a thin mustache like a dark gray piece of tape across his upper lip, no longer than the hair on his head, as if he'd only been growing it for a week. He had a slighter build than Miyahara and was taller as well.

Masami knew who he was. His picture had been in the paper and press releases countless times. Always with that week-old mustache.

Mr. Kumamori set his drink and bottle on the desk, brushed off his designer suit, and adjusted his shirt sleeves and cufflinks.

"I always find that conversation goes far smoother when the guns are put away," he said in a flat, but not uncharismatic way.

Masami kept the gun on him a moment longer, reassured by her finger resting on the guard only a split second from the trigger.

"Get rid of your tanto," Masami said, "and your gun." She was sure he had a tanto. All the yakuza brass carried the long knife. She didn't know if he had a gun, but with the plethora of firearms she had seen his underlings carrying, there wasn't much doubt. That and the fact that the gun case in this room probably held enough for Tokyo Metro Police's Special Assault Team.

"And if you have any of that crystalized green pus, you can dump that too," she added. She believed Miyahara's pill would work, that she was protected from the influence this time, but she didn't want to take any chances. And maybe, just maybe, she could talk some sense to him if the demon's connection wasn't so strong.

The man gave a thin, subtle smile, then withdrew the long knife from his belt, setting it on the desk. He reached into his jacket and pulled out a handgun with a carved pearl handle. He set it gingerly on the desk, his fingers holding the barrel near the front sight. Then he removed his tie and unbuttoned the top two buttons of his shirt. The edges of two walls of tattoos showed briefly as he lifted a chain dangling a diamond-shaped green stone in a golden setting.

"Even this?" he asked.

"Green and gold never worked for me," Masami said.

"I would rather not give this up," the man said calmly.

"Sounds like the demon talking to me. Or do you actually like being its puppet?"

The man looked at her with an odd twinkle in his eye. He did like it. The dead gangster had been right.

"Ditch it," she demanded.

He slowly removed the pendant and rested it on the desk with the tanto, gun, and tie. He took a slow sip of his drink. He was testing her, Masami could tell.

"No more drinks. Push it aside, out of reach," she said. He slid the glass and bottle to the edge of the desk, making a grand show of it like a boy racing toy cars. Then he returned to the center by his chair.

"Now take off your jacket, shirt, pants, and shoes." she hissed.

"If that's the way you like it," the man smirked sideways. "Lily here won't mind watching." He indicated the mannequin maid. "She's into that sort thing. She might even—"

"I AM NOT JOKING AROUND!" Masami shouted and aimed the gun at the man's crotch.

He did what she told him, but not without commentary. "I wonder if you know who I am, young lady." His jacket went onto the desk, followed by his shoulder holster.

Masami didn't give him the pleasure of a response. The yakuza bosses loved their fame and power. He could squirm in obscurity for a moment.

"I know who you are, Miss Sato," Kumamori said, a mischievous gleam in his eyes. "I know everything about you."

Masami wouldn't bite. He was trying to play on her fears. It wouldn't work.

"As for me, I am the leader of the Tezuka-gumi, soon to be leader of all my yakuza brothers." His fingers moved down his chest, releasing one button at a time, slowly, almost seductively, as if he knew no other way to unbutton it. A strip of pale white flesh was revealed in between the buttons separated from their buttonholes. In an abrupt motion, like pulling a cover from a lion's cage, he pulled the shirt from his shoulders. A body suit tattoo covered his entire torso, minus that thin strip of skin running from his neck to his navel.

An oni mask was prominent on each breast, one red and one blue. The red one looked maniacal, and the blue one appeared to be laughing joyfully. Surrounding the masks were flowers: peonies on one side and cherry blossoms on the other, both amidst black, cloudy trees. A large, black koi fish appeared to wrap around his lower back, the tail visible on one side of his belly and the head on the other. Snakes slithered down each arm amid more peonies and scales. It was an imposing scene, and Kumamori wore it proudly.

"I am uniting the syndicates," he said, his voice taking on the forceful, seductive manner of his actions, as he slipped off polished leather shoes and black socks, placing them on the desk. "Under me, they will no longer squabble over territory and perceived injustices." He undid his belt and pulled it off, adding it to the pile. "Under me, we will be one brotherhood." He began to lower his pants, revealing more of the body suit tattoo and tight red briefs that interrupted the pattern with a lizard scale design, a golden dragon face emblazoned across the crotch. Masami couldn't help but notice the dragon's nose was rather small.

"Turn around," she said, after he dropped his pants onto the pile.

He did. A tiger in mid-roar with its claws sunk into a skull, spread across his upper back, above the fat body of the black koi. Two snakes protruded from the skull, wrapped about the tiger's legs and continued down his arms. Red lightning struck on all sides of the wild cat. A rising sun was emblazoned on his neck, rays spraying out like domination. The tattoos continued down his legs but the red underwear interrupted it again, showing a sagging rear end, the dragon's tail waving across both cheeks.

"Would you like me to dance for you too?" he asked. "Perhaps a little twerk?"

The thought of that flat old butt twerking made her shudder. It would be perhaps the worst thing she'd seen today. And she'd seen a lot.

"Back around," she said.

The nearly naked yakuza boss turned to face her. "There will be no more rivalry, no more back-stabbing, no more assassinations that only cause more vengeful murders. I will end the Circle of Death," he stated proudly.

"That foul worm demon will, you mean." Masami expected him to falter then, to accept on some level that he was no more than a pawn. But he smiled.

"Yes, under the glorious fiend that has saved us." His smile grew bigger. "I have never had such power. All the yakuza will bend to me. And I must only bend to it."

Masami wanted to believe it was the demon talking through him, but she knew it wasn't. She could see this man would subjugate himself for power without question.

"And what happens when it's done with you?" she asked. "When it has moved on beyond the scope of the yakuza? When it has reached the greater public—which has already begun? What happens when it sees that the prime minister is a far more powerful target?"

Kumamori flinched, but puffed his chest. "I am its right hand. It has assured me."

"Then you are a fool. Move away from the desk."

He did, and she lowered the gun. She didn't like holding it, didn't like how deadly and final a gun could be with just a simple squeeze of a trigger, but she knew it would keep Kumamori in check.

"Where is Miyahara?" she asked, "Or Mizoguchi? Whatever it is you know him by."

"Ah. Friend of yours?"

"Yes, actually. He's the main reason I dropped by." Masami felt no need to hide her intentions. Now that she had rendered the godfather fully unarmed, she was in control. She would lock him up in a closet or tie him to his desk and gag him. She only needed to locate the proper tools.

"He's not to be trusted," Kumamori said. "Doesn't follow orders well."

That made Masami smile, but only on the inside. Lowlifes like this didn't get to see her smile. She was glad to hear that Miyahara hadn't been compromised, that he wasn't playing along. But what was he doing? Why hadn't he gotten out?

"He was assisting me up until today. Claimed to be ready to die for his cause."

"Oh he is. Th at's not a lie," Masami said. "You were probably confused about what his cause actually is."

"Perhaps."

"Where is he?"

"I know where he is. We were planning to send someone to dispose of him when your little trio showed up. He has a little hiding place nearby. But what reason do I have to tell you?"

"I have a gun."

"That's a good point. But you won't use it on an unarmed man."

Masami wanted to argue, to tell him, yes, she would. But Kumamori was right. She wouldn't, and she could only stare back at him.

"What do you want him for?" the yakuza boss asked.

"You yakuza consider each other brothers, right? You would do anything to protect and help each other? Well, that's how I feel about Miyahara. Minus all the in-fighting and backstabbing." It was a stretch of the truth. She didn't know the sensei well enough for that kind of bond, and Masami wasn't one to bond with anyone. But he had helped her and Akio, and she felt strongly that he was one of the good guys. "Now tell me where he is."

"Getting a little too involved in this story, don't you think, Miss Sato? I sense a little reporter's bias." Kumamori smiled.

Masami let the comment die. He would not get under her skin.

She had to figure out a way forward. She wasn't good at this tough guy act, this threatening people with guns. And the man she was threatening was surely an expert at it. How the hell was she going to get him to talk?

She decided to stall.

"So what's with all the robots? How does Nakama fit into this?"

"Ah. Mr. Nakama. Your little victory." His grin was unnerving.

"What's the story?" Masami demanded.

"Nakama was an early supporter, you could say. I bankrolled his company for a healthy return of the profits. But sadly, he struggled to pay us his due. He spent too much of his earnings buying expensive gifts for all his little playthings. He was disrespectful of our arrangement and of my superior position in it. He covered up the fact that they knew about the defects on his little office robots long before they were shipped. He kept that fact from me too. So I removed him."

You? Masami's expression betrayed her.

"Oh, you thought you broke that story, did you? I gave you that lead, little girl. The fiery little reporter who rescued one measly girl from a prostitution ring—I'm sorry to disappoint you, but you missed hundreds of others. I knew you were itching for just such an exclusive angle. So I planted the lead. A Mrs. Yamada, I believe it was, who clued you into the corruption at Nakama. Yes, she was payed handsomely."

Masami seethed inside. She had been proud of her work on that story. But it *had* been a Mrs. Yamada, an employee of Nakama, who came to her. She was furious to find she had only played into some yakuza scheme. She wanted to strangle him.

"The new board at Nakama was more than willing to sell the company to me at very fair price." He grinned.

"To what end?" Masami asked between clenched teeth.

"An early plan of mine, to be honest," Kumamori said. "Before the demon empowered us, I was doing whatever I could to gain influence and get my revenge on the Kawabata-gumi for kicking me out. I began building in secret. My plan was to build an army of robots that would show the other factions my power. They would bow before me or be cut down."

Kumamori was sliding closer to his desktop where his clothes and weapons lay. Masami wiggled the gun barrel at him.

"But progress was slow and the robots too simple," he said, turning from his desk smoothly, as if he'd never meant to approach it. "I overestimated the technology. I needed a genius inventor and programmer, someone far ahead of his time, but no one I hired had the right stuff. And then something fell into my lap, but it wasn't at all what I expected."

He smiled, unfazed at his nearly naked state. He was in his glory, bragging about himself.

"My man, Hisatsugu Tabara, the head of the Dazai-ikka, a subordinate clan to mine, came through with the solution. He brought me a bright green gem, the very one that I have mounted in my necklace there." He indicated the jewelry on the desk. "The demon told him to find me, because it knew I was the only one who could help it rule all of Japan. That man is now my son-in-law. After that, the robot creation became a breeze. My engineers were simply conduits for the demon's vast knowledge, and they created amazing machines, some of which you have seen firsthand." He winked at Masami.

"But soon I realized the gems themselves were far more powerful than any combat robot. So while we did not abandon our goal of creating the perfect killing machines, we found they would be useful in a much more graceful way than I had originally envisioned, and we started to focus on far more *innocent* methods of gem transport. Within a lovely young maid, for example." He indicated the still as stone woman in the corner.

"But most times, all that is needed is the gem itself." He looked to his necklace laying next to his clothes. "Isn't it beautiful? Don't you want to wear it?"

Masami walked closer to the desk, indicating with the gun for Kumamori to step even further away. It was a risk, but she needed to know. There was a daring in it that compelled her, something almost self-destructive, but she had to prove the pill was working. She reached down and picked up the necklace by the gold chain. The voice, to which she had so easily capitulated before, was there, but it was only a voice. She dropped the necklace back down.

"I told you, green and gold don't work for me."

Kumamori's face froze, but he maintained his composure. He had not expected this.

"Most times," the godfather repeated, raising his eyebrows toward her. "We have also had an issue with Mr. Takagi, the head of the Mishima-kai here in Tokyo. He refuses to accept any gift from me. So I've been having fun causing havoc in other ways, slowly taking over his corporate extortion gigs, stealing his prostitution connection, robbing his cigarette vendors, and whatnot, until he accepts one. You'd think a man in his position wouldn't be afraid of a simple gift." He smiled. "But it doesn't matter anymore. His number one man is mine now. Takagi will fall too."

"Why don't you just give all his followers gems?" Masami asked. "He wouldn't have anyone left to lead."

Kumamori looked at Masami like she was a child. "I almost forgot you are only a woman. I should not expect you to understand these things."

Masami longed to put a bullet in his kneecap, but she restrained herself.

Kumamori continued. "There are over twenty thousand men in the Mishima-kai. It's far more efficient to conquer their leader. Besides, the demon can only produce so many gems in a day. Not to mention, it's much more fun to torment Takagi."

Masami was thrilled at this information dump, though she never imagined having her interviewee at gunpoint. She needed to finesse him back around to the topic of Miyahara.

"So is that one of your toys?" she asked, pointing to the corner.

"Ah, that is my all-seeing eye," he answered. "My boys call it the Egg." He was describing the metal and glass contraption he had stepped out of. It's not what Masami had meant, but she let him talk. She still needed time to think. "From there I can monitor everything through the demon's eyes. What it sees, I see. That's how I know it trusts me." He seemed to regain confidence in that statement. "I also saw you coming, as it accesses the building's security system, and there are cameras all around this floor. You certainly have some tricks up your sleeve don't you?"

"More than you know," she nearly whispered. "But I meant blondie here. What is she?"

"Oh yes," the yakuza boss grinned. "You met her once already didn't you? You and her had become fast friends. I have to say, I liked you much better then. I watched your dazzling destruction of your masked friend from the Egg. It was breathtaking."

Masami swallowed her bile, her guilt, and stayed on topic.

"She's a robot?"

"Oh, much more than just a robot. She is our assassin prototype. The only AI project we have continued for now. I believe your friends are dealing with the equivalent of three of her at the moment."

Masami's breath hitched as she thought of the troubles her friends might be having. She needed to help them. *I am helping*, she reminded herself. *I need to stick to the plan.* Akio could handle the assassins . . . she hoped.

But what if Kumamori was lying and Miyahara *was* under the demon's control? Or dead? *My friends are in trouble.*

She had to let it be. Yoshio had his brain and his signal blocker, and Akio was, well . . . Akio was a demon in his own right. She would stay the course.

"Lily here is special though," Kumamori continued. "The other assassins are only built for killing. But Lily has . . . other duties as well."

Of course she does, you pervert.

"She is the first of her kind, and we gave her experimental functionality the others don't have. Like the ability to see ghosts." The gangster boss made a pointed grin at Masami. "To tell the truth, that was not something we had intended, but a byproduct of something else we had not intended: a heightened ability to sense demons and gems.

"You see, we also gave her the ability to think for herself, to learn, adapt, and make her own choices. We were striving to make her as human as possible. But, of course, we still needed to control her. So we gave her extremely high-powered receptors for the demon's gift, the gems. We overestimated that need, thinking such an advanced brain as hers would need more input to be overpowered. This over-amplification caused problems, but it proved useful as well. Because of it, Lily is able to see activity in the parallel world of the dead—which you can somehow access. And her receptors are so advanced she is able to accurately assess who is under the demon's control and who isn't. In that way she can alert us of anyone suspicious. And since she's been retrofitted, there's no more concern of any . . . unwanted behavior. She had only just been repaired when we introduced her to you. Then when I had my concerns about Mr. Mizoguchi, your Miyahara, I brought her to my side.

"Her observations were quite interesting. She confirmed my suspicions that he is a traitor to us, uncontrolled by our master, but you knew that already. The interesting thing is something I'm betting you don't know."

Masami didn't reply. He was playing her, trying to get at her. She wouldn't bite.

"Lily told me that your friend isn't human." He paused, letting it sink in. "He's a demon."

Masami blanched; her breath felt like a solid thing sliding in and out of her lungs.

It couldn't be true. Miyahara was a great fighter and he was a little odd, but he was certainly human.

Kumamori grinned like a demon himself.

Masami remembered Miyahara's blood, how the sensei said it couldn't be traced. He hadn't been concerned about being connected to the Kofu killings.

Maybe it's true. Maybe he is a demon.

"Are you sure your friend is on your side, Miss Sato?" Kumamori asked with a smirk. "Seems to me he may be the real enemy."

Miyahara *had* to be on their side. Human or not, he had helped her and Akio. He was one of the good guys. Wasn't he?

"I'm not a puppet like you," Masami said finally. "You can't pull my strings so easily. I know who my friends are. Now where is Miyahara?"

Kumamori grinned again. He knew he had already pulled her strings.

"Everyone gets misled at times," he said. "Even Lily went astray for a little while, and forgot who her friends were. She murdered her own master, who happened to be my number one hatchet man. Left him in bed, naked and soaking in his own blood, after dispatching two rival brothers in his living room."

Masami had been working on that story when she first started to fade into the ghost world, before she knew what was happening to her. It had been Lily. It was this damn maid robot who had killed those men and left that gruesome scene behind.

"Raikatuji will be hard to replace," Kumamori went on. "But really, I wonder if we even need to. I no longer need to kill my rivals, though I admit I gain some pleasure from it. It's a kind of satisfying revenge, you know? It brings a sense of balance. Although sometimes it is far more satisfying to see them grovel at my feet and happily perform the basest tasks for me. And yet, you never know when you might need someone . . . disappeared."

He looked pointedly at Masami.

"Since Lily had her little feminist freedom fit, as I like to call it, we have made improvements. Perhaps we made her a bit too human. But we have tamed her. We learned that putting the gem too close to her over-amped AI brain was . . . problematic. She went on quite an adventure. But we brought her back and corrected the glitch. We reinforced the protective shielding on her brain, and moved the gem to her chest, where it still has a direct line to her thoughts. You could say her *heart* controls her now. She kills so . . . exquisitely. She still has her little idiosyncrasies, but I find them rather endearing. All told, she's good as new."

He turned his head in a slow deliberate gaze toward the stationary maid.

"Aren't you, Lily?"

The maid's eyes fluttered open.

15
Maid to Kill

Four *ninja-to* blades blurred the air around Akio as he bent his body in ways he had never dreamed possible. All he could do was block and dodge, not finding a moment to strike back at the two impossibly graceful maids. They seemed to be working as one being split in two, their actions perfectly synchronized. They thrust low and high simultaneously, following with deadly cuts meant to quarter him in an instant.

The third maid was dispatching the yakuza like they were so many caterpillars to a sparrow, dodging bullets like they were no faster than spitballs from a straw. Why wasn't Yoshio's raygun working?

"Get out of here if you want to live! I will face them alone!" Akio yelled. But it was a futile effort. The women were superbly trained athletes and acrobats as well as fighters. The two attacking him were all he could handle, and the third continued its rout of the yakuza. The gangsters backed away while the maid spun among them. Bullets flew and arteries were severed.

Akio's muscles screamed at the constant exertion but did not fail him. Adrenaline took over, and yet it was not enough. The women were too skilled. Eventually they would find a way through his defenses. He needed to gain an advantage somehow, find an opening so he could make a strike. It was like fighting a female Jubei Kibigami from *Ninja Scroll* and a cloned twin.

No, they were even better. Never had Akechi fought such flawless enemies. He would not last much longer.

Then there was an instant of reprieve, a breath of timing when he could have thrust to an opening in one maid's flank, but he did not. Instead he dove under the withdrawn blades and tumbled away, giving him a moment to catch his breath and time to take the attack to them. He needed to control the fight, put them on the defensive. One thrust may have done damage, but it may also have been the death of him. If his blade had sunk into flesh, he might not have withdrawn it in time to parry the onslaught that would follow.

Now as the two faced him, striking another seemingly choreographed pose, Akio did not wait. He charged, his single blade above and out front like a guillotine ready to fall. He leapt and all four ninja swords rose as one to block him.

But it was a feint.

He slipped his katana in a tight arc around their defenses preparing to cut them both in half with one swing. He didn't want to kill anyone, but they had left him no choice. It was them or him, and Akechi's muscle memory was in full control.

Impossibly, his blade was refused. Two of the four swords were somehow in the way. How they had blocked his attack, he couldn't understand. Akechi had cut down countless soldiers with such a move, and Akio's timing had been perfect. Yet these maids had thwarted him.

A respect for his opponents was building along with his anger, the demon in him boiling at this impossible show of swordsmanship. No one was his equal. Certainly no one was his better.

There were two of them. That was their advantage. Akio could have easily bested one of them. But two of such supreme skill were enough to give him trouble. And the way they worked together was extraordinary. That fact appeased his ego to a degree, but still, it should not have been so difficult to remedy the situation and rid himself of one.

"With me!" he heard Yoshio cry, and from his current vantage saw only dead yakuza on the floor. He hoped beyond hope that the teenager had something up his sleeve, because Akio's hands were more than full. It took every ounce of focus to prevent himself from being julienned.

The fight continued, and Akio quickly found himself on the defensive again. Their four swords against his one was overwhelming. He parried cut after cut, thrust after thrust, with no more openings presenting themselves. He longed for the matching wakizashi to his katana. If he had a blade in each hand, he would have more options, more flexibility. But Masami had it, and she might need it.

He needed to find the flaw. He needed to alter something, some missing element of this dance of blades. There was always a weakness, either in his opponent or in his own execution.

A stinging pain zipped through the meat of his left upper arm and spun him sideways. He barely got his blade up in time to block the next three cuts intent on taking his head, heart, and groin in quick succession.

The line of fire from his flesh slit open to the air gave him what he was looking for: Akechi's anger.

In a rage, he spun one set of blades to the side, sinking his katana into the maid's foot, through lacy black pumps and the faux marble beneath, pinning her in place. Abandoning his sword, Akio dove at the other maid, tackling her to the floor before she could bring her swords to bear. He was loath to hit a woman but it was better than killing. He aimed the heel of his palms and thrust them into her collar bones in a quick one-two attack, expecting the sharp snaps of bone that would follow and leave her incapacitated.

But there were none. It felt like he had hit steel.

This was not a woman. Couldn't be. Were they demons as well?

In his peripheral vision, Akio saw a blade pull back on either side of him, spin uniformly in each hand so that the tips were aimed at his skull. Reflexively he spun his own body on top of the maid's, kicking the blade away on her right, while grappling the other, entwining and bending the arm to break and dislodge the weapon from her grip.

Akio's kick had been placed at the crook of her right wrist. It should have buckled and released the weapon, but it did not. The left arm bent backward sharply but did not break; the bone only bent as if she had sprouted a second elbow. The blade was not released.

The maid's unbent right arm quickly recovered and swiped again at Akio, clipping his forehead just above the mask. Immediately she was on her feet as Akio staggered back. Her left arm was a twisted mess, and she swung it wildly at him not seeming to understand what had happened to it. She swung high, but the blade went wonky and low.

It fully occurred to Akio now that these maids were neither humans nor demons. They were just more goddamn robots.

He somersaulted backward to gain some distance and stole a glance toward the other side of the room. Yoshio stood with one yakuza cowering behind him, as the maid in front of them lit up like an overloaded circuit.

Yep. Goddamn robots.

The maid Akio had pinned to the floor was hacking repeatedly at the Hell-forged katana in her foot. No blood at all spilled from it. Sparks flew but the ninja swords had no effect on the otherworldly metal. Without letting go of her own weapons she tried to pull the katana from her foot, but it would not budge.

The bent-armed maid came at him, no longer as graceful as she had been. She canted to one side, her left arm unnaturally kinked, pulling her off balance as her sword whirred like a broken propeller blade in a deadly, wobbly spin.

Akio had no weapon, but his advantage had grown substantially. Not only had he weakened his opponents, but the knowledge that they were not human emboldened him.

In spite of Akechi's unmatchable martial skills and arrogant rage, there was something in Akio that yet restricted him. He dearly did not want to kill again. He understood now that his reluctance had compromised Akechi's normally unrelenting fervor. It had made his feints less effective, his cuts subconsciously too slow. But these were robots—insanely advanced ones, but robots nonetheless. He could kill them with zero remorse.

With a vicious grin hidden behind the more vicious mask, he dove away from the approaching maid-bot and toward the one pinned to the floor. Sensing Akio's proximity, its blades went on the defensive. Akio tumbled forward and as he sprang up, he pulled his katana from floor and foot, surging just past the maid. In one fluid move, he again feinted high at the back of the maid's head. The white and black-clad robot twisted around to meet the attack with both blades in a cross.

This time the feint worked.

Akio swerved his katana around the double *ninja-to* blades, sweeping it down and through the robot's legs. As the synthetic maid was upended, its swords whipped down too late to protect what had already been severed and cleared the way for Akio to take its head. The two blades whipped upward in another cross and froze there too late above an empty neck. Sparks and a pale green fluid sprayed from the cut, as the whole of it clattered to the floor in pieces.

Akio turned to face the remaining maid-bot. Its lefthand blade whirled unpredictably, but the right remained relatively stable. The maid bounded forward, thrusting its good sword at Akio's chest. He attempted to parry and disarm with a quick turn of his blade, but this time it was the maid who feinted.

Akio's blade enveloped only air.

He displaced his body, turning it sideways in the knick of time, so the blade only sliced through the fabric of his hoody. As the maid-bot's momentum carried it past Akio, he spun, twirling his katana to reverse his grip. He sunk the gleaming blade into its back, into frilly feminine fabric, synthetic flesh, and steel, and then ripped it up and out through the maid's shoulder. Green liquid spurted as a crooked spray of electricity jittered along the metallic gash.

The maid robot turned as it fell, attempting another attack, but, although it still clutched its sword, its right arm hung limp and useless. The lefthand blade spun in a lurching arc, fast to slow and back again. When the robot hit the floor, the blade only lifted up and down, scraping against the faux marble, causing the maid to convulse in a slow, wormlike dance.

Akio brought his katana down onto its forehead, splitting its cranium down the middle, separating green eyes, splitting slender nose and red lips. The force of the blow brought the sword through the neck and halfway into its torso, the shoulders bending away from each other. Inside the chest, mounted in a ceramic enclosure, was a fat, green gem, now split in half.

Metal and green fluid, wires and plastic parts confirmed its nature. Akio felt no remorse.

The maid lay still.

"Looks like you're gonna need an upgrade," Akio said, and turned to see Yoshio and a wide-eyed, panic-stricken yakuza approaching.

In high school, Masami's friend, the only one she had really spent any time with, told her she had applied to work at a maid café. Masami had been furious.

"Yuika!" she had shouted. "What about everything we've talked about? How we want Japanese society to change? How the subordination and dehumanization of women is hurting us all?"

"I know," Yuika sighed, "but the money is good. And it's easy, fun work. I just need to make some money right now. I can't change the whole country."

"But you can," Masami said. "*We* can, slowly, if we don't let ourselves fall into these ingrained patriarchal patterns!"

"It's not a big deal," Yuika defended. "It's just a silly job. Men like it and Shoko says if you up-sell photos and things you get easy commissions."

"Men like it?" Masami was horrified. "Are you serious? This is what we what to change! Ugh! I should have known Shoko was behind this."

"I don't know why you hate her so much. She's fun. She doesn't take everything so seriously. Sometimes I just want to be a girl, you know. Just be pretty and playful and have guys like me."

Masami couldn't even speak for a moment, realizing that Yuika must have been humoring her their entire friendship, only putting on an act so Masami would like her. Now she was showing her true colors.

"Okay, fine," Masami snapped, already feeling herself dying to her friend. "But when the creeps try to grab you or solicit sex, remember what we talked about. Remember how you are only adding to that culture of depravity."

Maybe she had been too idealistic, too quick to judge Yuika. She was just a teenage girl, after all, swayed by undeveloped emotions and sudden crushes. Masami had mostly skipped that phase. Maybe she had been unfair.

Afterward, she had seen Yuika at school and even said hi in passing, but she seethed underneath when she saw her with Shoko more and more. Masami never spent time with Yuika again. She kept her beliefs to herself and her school essays after that.

Maid cafés had grown even more popular since high school, even popping up in other countries. The direct opposite of what Masami had hoped for. There had been progress for women, for sure. More women pursued higher education and entered the workforce than ever before, but equality was still a distant dream. Culturally Japan seemed to be becoming known more for the kitschy and perverted than anything else.

Now the maids had become so popular, so iconic, that the yakuza had created assassin robots in their image. If nothing else, maybe she would get some satisfaction out of destroying one.

"Kill her, Lily," Kumamori said, as if he were suggesting she make tea.

The maid burst into motion, doing a front handspring over the desk. Masami started to lift the gun but Lily landed on her, straddling her neck before she could get her arm up; she fired too late, the maid already past the barrel. The bullet thwuffed through the ceiling tiles, and Masami lost her grip on the gun.

Lily locked her legs like steel traps around Masami's neck and twisted the full weight of her body into a brutal swing. It would snap Masami's neck and kill her like a chicken for the slaughter. In the split seconds that followed, she felt the torque against her neck muscles as it was jerked to the left, and she knew she was dead.

Then she felt the maid's legs slip through her.

Lily spin out onto the floor, landing in a balanced crouch.

Masami's newly minted panic response had saved her. Just as she had instinctively blinked out of existence seeing Fujimaki at her front door, she had dropped into the ghost world now, suddenly and unplanned.

Masami shot to the opposite side of the room to get distance from the maid and to prepare for whatever came next. She rolled her head to loosen her aching neck.

Lily locked eyes with Masami even in her ghostly form. As before, the android could still see her. The maid dove forward and rolled, popping up in front of Masami with a green gem in her hand, the tactic she had succumbed to before. Masami heard the demon's voice commanding her to submit, but it held no sway.

Masami swung a fist at the maid, solidifying her hand just before impact. Lily dodged it with ease and swung an arm down on Masami's forearm. It was a brutal chop with more than enough force to shatter bone, but it passed through harmlessly.

Masami reached out and grabbed Lily's long blonde hair and jerked it backward, but the maid's head did not budge, her robot neck like iron. Again, Lily swiped at Masami's arm but with no effect.

Masami spun away and dropped through the floor. She had to get a moment to think.

She found herself in a kind of laboratory. A man was leaning over a naked human figure with silicone skin and a woman's body. She looked like another Lily but with black hair. Three others stood motionless and naked nearby. The man appeared to be testing the figure's reflexes, touching exposed wires with some kind of electric probe while the forearm rose and fell.

How many of these things are there?

She could escape now. She could get away and blindly search for Miyahara. But Kumamori said he knew where the sensei was. And this Lily had to be shut down. Masami couldn't have her showing up again unannounced. She had to take care of her now, while she knew where she was, and hope that these others would not be activated.

Masami's new power did not give her the ability to see through walls or ceilings, so she poked her head through the floor. The second she did, Lily turned her head, immediately sensing Masami's presence. The maid dove toward her, now holding the white-handled katana with the golden guard, taken from the stand in Kumamori's office. She plunged it at Masami's head.

Masami instinctively ducked back through the floor and dodged to the side, though the blade would surely have passed through her. The sword went through floor and ceiling with a shriek of metal on wood. It did not penetrate easily like the Hell-forged weapons had. It went through from sheer strength.

The man in the room looked up but returned to his work, as if a sudden sword through the ceiling was of no consequence.

Masami seized the opportunity of knowing Lily's position. While the android maid wrenched the sword out, Masami reached up through the floor and gripped Lily's feet. Just as she had done with Akio, she brought the maid with her into the ghost world and pulled her halfway into the room below before letting go, leaving her bisected by the floor.

Masami flew back up and materialized in front of the deadly maid, allowing herself a solid purchase on the floor. Her chest was heaving from the effort of the fight, her neck stiff from her near death by leg clamp and twist.

"That should keep you," Masami said, and looked about the room.

The yakuza boss was nowhere to be seen, though his clothes still lay in a pile on the broad desk. The gun and tanto were there too, but the whisky glass had been emptied. The tall safe against the wall stood open. She cursed and turned her attention back to the maid in the floor.

The white-handled katana lay discarded, and Lily braced herself against the floor with her one free hand. The other was embedded into the floor at the wrist, as if she were searching for something lost in a pool of polished wood. Masami kicked the weapon away and drew her own sword. The ancient wakizashi gleamed a dark sheen of death, its ruby guard like red ice. It was the blade of a demon samurai serial killer, and she felt its malice. She brandished it at the maid, who jerked and twisted against the floorboards where they cut across her mid-section.

The maid paused momentarily in her thrashing and looked at Masami. Her piercing green eyes were captivating, so real, and yet so empty. They seemed to scan Masami, assess her, search her code for a glitch that could be exploited.

I don't run on code.

The maid winked as if she had heard Masami's thought.

"Where is Miyahara?" Masami asked. "Mizoguchi? Where is he?" she demanded.

The maid went still and looked up with no expression, waiting.

Masami pointed the tip of her blade at the maid's right eye and was about to say something threatening when Lily batted the weapon away with her left hand as swift as a fan blade at full speed. The sword flew from Masami's grip and clattered across the room.

Masami gasped, and retrieved the wakizashi with an aching hand. When she returned, the maid had ceased struggling. She was still as a mannequin again, a life-sized doll protruding from the floor.

Masami held her sword firmly with two hands, and again brandished the tip of it at the maid-in-the-floor's eye. As Lily whipped her arm around exactly as before—a programmed response to a threat —Masami twisted the blade so that the sharp edge was right where the maid's arm would impact it.

In a flash, she saw the robot arm correct course, reverse direction to avoid being cut, before batting the sword away to the opposite side.

But Masami had been ready for an impact, and she held onto the weapon this time, though the force of it spun her to the side.

Interesting.

This robot would not be easily fooled.

"Tell me where Mizoguchi is," Masami demanded again, this time holding her wakizashi edge forward but out of reach. "Or I will take your head off with this sword. I know you've seen him. The short, grumpy, bald man who never fell victim to your demon boss. Where is he?"

"I do not serve you," Lily replied in an accented lilt.

"Okay, fine," Masami said. She didn't have time for this. How the hell was she supposed to threaten a robot anyway? She would destroy it before it figured out how to extract itself from the floor. She would chop off its head.

The irony.

Only a few months previous she had been chasing after a head-chopping serial killer, and now here she was planning to decapitate someone. Even if that someone was a robot, it seemed odd, and even unfair, with the maid held in place as she was. But it had to be done. The maid was only a construct. Masami was simply destroying a machine. She reared back with the sword held high and swung it hard toward Lily's neck.

It only sliced through air.

Lily had ducked, dropping her head unnaturally backward to avoid the deadly cut, and the blade passed over harmlessly. Again her one free arm lashed out. And as it did, there was a shrill creak, followed by the ripping of wood. Splinters exploded around them as Lily's right hand came free. The maid's left hand batted the sword away with the force of a truck at highway speed, while her right, now free, and encircled with a goth-looking bracelet of wooden spikes, slammed a fist into Masami's very corporeal jaw.

Masami felt like she had been hit by a steel girder. She staggered back to her feet briefly, only to collapse to her back on the floor. She lay there immobile but for an overall quivering of her muscles.

Then the room spun, and everything went black.

16

Overcome

The demon had wrapped itself in people eight rows deep, like blankets of living flesh, a mosh pit at a rock concert. Only there was no moshing, no movement at all. They stood still as stones though their green eyes trembled. And their backs were to the rock star of the moment: the six-legged, bloated, orange slug with green, spiky protrusions along its back, the fat face, fat tongue, long fat fangs hanging over fat, blistery lips, where it sat nervously on its oversize chaise lounge.

Akio saw its death. He saw it pierced through the back of the neck with some large object, and then melting into the floor like syrup. Only it wasn't here, it was . . .

The panicky yakuza bumped into him, and he turned to gaze at the man through the tight eye holes in his blood red mask. The suited man backed away, stumbling past Yoshio, seemingly more afraid of Akio than of the horrific beast that sat across the room, lounging like it was a beloved king of the world.

A beloved king shouldn't need a wall of human lives guarding it.

The gangster bowed deeply.

"Daichi Endo at your service," he said, visibly shaking.

This gangster wasn't the one who had kneeled before Akio and confessed his puny manhood. It was another, fearful and fumbling. Akio did not respond, only vaguely wondered why the man was still with them, why he hadn't run from the building after his fellow thugs had been slaughtered. And then he realized what it was. This yakuza was a follower. And Akio was a leader. It was simultaneously ludicrous and perfectly sensible. Akio had never been a leader. Who would follow a scrawny nobody photographer? But he was Akechi now. He was a daimyo, a great leader of men. Masami had even called him their general. That moment resonated in him still. The immature boy in him who had worshipped her was pinging off the walls in joy and shock, but Akechi contained it and knew the truth of it completely. It was as obvious to him as the sword in his hands was sharp; he was a leader, and all should follow him.

The throng of people guarding the demon stood like eunuch soldiers, like automaton servants awaiting command. They were a mix of people from all backgrounds just as in the ballroom and at the front doors: yakuza, office workers, service workers, tourists. In fact, they may have been the same people from outside, the demon having called them upstairs once it knew its assailants had breached the building. It didn't matter. They all looked the same to him.

His only concern was the giant worm that slavered and twitched behind them, eyeing Akio with hatred and fear. He could smell the fear steaming off it like the stench of carrion.

Green stones of varying sizes were scattered about the floor between Akio and the crowd, gold buckets tipped and spilled. Akio stopped just before them and stood, sword drawn, calm as a tiger ready to pounce. Yoshio and the yakuza stood just behind him.

The thought of wildly carving through the masses of innocent people thrilled through Akio. He would relish in their flying limbs, their blood soaking him as he ended their miserable, pathetic lives. Even if innocent of this demon's crimes, they should be killed for being weak. It would be a mercy.

But his gut roiled at the thought. They *were* innocent—at least innocent of the crime of opposing his will. They should be spared. And he had killed too many already. He couldn't stomach the thought of taking more lives, innocent or not.

He battled with Akechi inside himself.

Then another voice intruded into his thoughts.

"*Surrender, fool,*" it scraped and slithered into his brain. "*You cannot beat me. I control their fragile minds. Soon I will control yours as well, and all the world's!*"

Akio nodded to Yoshio who lifted his plastic-handled raygun and aimed.

"*I will be ruler of this feeble world. All will bow to—*"

The demon choked like he'd swallowed a bug—a very large bug. Yoshio's finger held the trigger firmly. The masses of people around him began to mutter and mill about, finding their bearings as they recovered their free will. When they saw the huge, grotesque thing behind them, they panicked. Some screamed, cursed, or both, but all of them moved quickly away in terror.

Akio grinned at Yoshio's brilliance. He needed people like the teenager to conquer his enemies. When this was over he would build him a castle, give him land, and make him a lord . . .

The demon screamed and grabbed at the people nearest, pulling them to itself with four of its six hands, trying by force to keep them close now that it had lost control over their minds. They thrashed and wailed, horrified. In a burst of anger it bit the head off a struggling man in a suit; perhaps a yakuza, perhaps simply a salaryman.

This did not endear it any more to the panicked crowd. Its rash actions failing, as the people scattered, it closed its eyes and screwed up its hideous face in a rictus of concentration.

Some of its fleeing minions slowed to a stop. About half of them stiffened and turned back, shambling toward the demon to once again stand guard. Others managed to escape, one of whom called to the yakuza that stood with Akio and Yoshio.

"Endo! Brother! Why are you not running? That thing will kill us all!"

"I can't! We have to fight it! Get our control back!"

The yakuza looked from Endo to the demon and back again. He paused, struggling to make a decision, but then shuddered and shook his head. His mouth hung open momentarily but no words came out. Then he ran in shame.

Akio moved toward the demon, his resolve complete. He would cut through these unfortunate ones if he must. The demon must be slain at all costs. There were only about thirty or so people now, all that the demon could hang onto with Yoshio's signal blocker activated.

"You cannot stop me," the demon's thoughts entered Akio's head again. *"I am the controller. I am the master. You will submit and do my bidding!"*

Beside him, Akio was vaguely aware of Yoshio futzing with his raygun. "Gotta turn up the signal," the boy mumbled. He raised the gun again and depressed the trigger.

The demon howled as its remaining few minions were once again freed. They scrambled quickly away and out of its reach, stumbling over green stones as they went. The demon pressed two front claws against its ears, while the middle two tore at the air, and the back ones dug deep tears in the carpeted floor.

Akio was only five strides away now. He gripped his sword in both hands and prepared to charge. But a cold knife stabbed into his brain. He buckled and went to one knee.

"You are mine!" the demon screeched in his head. *"You are mine!"*

Akio could feel the demon's thoughts overpowering his own. Was the pill wearing off? Or was its singularly focused power simply too much to resist? A desire began to form in his mind.

I must kill the teenage boy for my master. I must kill Yoshio. I will make him eat that strange gun he created. I will dice him into tiny pieces.

He turned and looked at Yoshio, rage in his heart. The teenager stared back and retreated a step, still pointing the signal blocker at the demon.

"Akio . . . ?" he said nervously.

Akio scanned the young man, recognized him.

Yoshio is . . . my friend, my compatriot.

He is in the way. He is a bug to be squashed, the other thoughts insisted, worming their way in.

He . . . needs me. I need him.

What I need is . . . to fight these . . . enemies. They are trying to hurt my master. The thoughts were stronger now. Hard to discern from his own.

I am . . . no one's master. I . . .

I live to serve. Yoshio must die.

Akio turned his back on the demon and lifted his sword, preparing to cut the teenager in two.

Yoshio scrambled backward, hands fidgeting with the gun, turning dials, adjusting frequencies. "Fight it, Akio! You are stronger than this! You have to fight it!"

"*I know you*," the demon's voice reverberated in his head. "*I saw you in Hell. But you are different, weaker now. I recognize your thoughts. Your arrogance was so delicious, so rich. It was sublime to crush and devour. And now I get to enjoy it again, that domination, that laying low of a ruler's towering ego.*"

Memories flooded back to Akio. The demon laughed as it made him dance like a puppet, made him throw himself against rocks and into bubbling mud pools, made him watch as his head was used for sport.

They had *used his head as a ball! It was true!*

They would retrieve it from its box as if getting equipment from a locker and kick it about the stony, fire-licked ground.

You, thought Akio. *I killed you.* And he stumbled as he lurched toward Yoshio. He remembered now. He had watched this very demon's body dissolve and melt into the rocks of Hell.

"*Yes*," the demon's response came as Akio moved mechanically toward the frantic Yoshio. "*But the contract with Hell does not expire so easily. Now kill the boy!*"

Akio began to lift his katana, but stopped suddenly. A man, with a jerky, nervous lurch had positioned himself between Akio and the teenager. It was Endo, the yakuza who had not run.

"Our enemy is that way, general!" he said, pointing to the demon at Akio's back.

General. The word resonated in Akio's head. *General.* Yes, he was a general, a leader. Not a follower.

But the spike of control reasserted itself. Growling, Akio shoved Endo aside and to the floor. He moved quickly toward Yoshio, determined to destroy the signal blocker and accept the peace of relinquished control.

Yoshio was near the double doors now, hunched over his raygun. He made one final adjustment and aimed it at Akio.

The nerve of him.

"See, he has betrayed you," said the demon. *"He wishes you harm as well as me. Kill him."*

Yoshio mashed the trigger, and Akio paused.

What am I doing? Why am I—

"Kill him!" thundered the demon's voice in his head.

I must obey. I am nothing. Only a tool for my master.

Yoshio lowered the raygun, and pleaded, reasoned, hoped. "Akio, it is controlling you! You have to fight it!"

Akio raised his sword.

"I am your friend, Akio! If you kill me, it wins!"

Akio hovered above the teenager, the offending insect, who now crouched in front of the double doors.

A pain thwocked into Akio's head, and he saw Endo's gun hit the floor where it had bounced off his skull. But he did not turn to look at the meddling yakuza. He would kill him next, if he even needed to. His master would reassert control once Yoshio was dead. All would be as it was meant to be.

"Akechi!" Yoshio called. "Akechi! That's your name, right? You are no one's slave! You are no one's minion! Fight this!"

Akio stopped at the name.

Yes, Akechi is my name. I am a general, a daimyo.

But even daimyos served a greater master. They served the shogun. A samurai's life was about service, after all. And his master required his service now.

The sword came down.

Why didn't I stay a ghost?

Masami lay still on her back, her head throbbing like she'd been hit by a sledgehammer. Consciousness creeped back slowly.

Why didn't I change on instinct like before?

Using the wakizashi was much easier when corporeal, and Lily's immobile state had made it seem safe. How wrong Masami had been. The punch had blindsided her, giving her no time to react. She felt like there was a building on her head. She tasted blood, and her entire right side was going numb.

This is going to kill me. If it hasn't already.

She heard the rending and creaking of ripping wood. Lily was freeing herself from the floor.

Masami opened her eyes, but could not move. She heard more ripping and imagined the maid removing wood, insulation, and pieces of the air conditioning duct from her hips and legs. She heard the quiet metallic scrape of a blade briefly dragged along the floor, and realized that her hands were empty.

Intruding into her static picture of the ceiling came a blonde head, hair tied back under a ruffled white headpiece, a calm, almost beatific look on her face.

"I am here to serve," the assassin robot said in a lilting, sweet voice. "I cook and clean and please in every way. But my favorite thing, you will appreciate."

She smiled like a little girl who'd just stolen a popsicle from her younger brother.

"I make dead men."

The maid lifted a short sword high above her, a wakizashi with an intricately-carved ruby red guard, and a black bone handle wrapped in black hair. Masami's sword. The ceiling lights glinted off the blade and fragmented into a million slivers, severed by the impossibly sharp, Hell-forged sword.

"And now I make dead women, too."

Masami's muscles would not respond. The force of the punch had disconnected her motor functions.

She had to ghost. She had to disappear, but even that seemed to fail her. The floor remained hard against her back. An altar for a sacrifice. The bed of a coffin.

She grasped at motion and at letting go. She needed to move or dissolve into spirit, but the two efforts only collided against each other, and she lay still, her head too rattled to affect any change at all.

So she waited for the blade to come down for what seemed an eternity. She wondered what would happen when she really became a ghost. Would it be different? Would she linger at her death location like Saki and the yakuza in the office next door? Where would the Sorter take her?

As she gazed up at her executioner, she saw the look on Lily's face change to one of consternation. Masami wondered why it had been programmed to be upset.

The maid began to rise upward, floating off the floor away from Masami. The android was furious, her face a deep red.

To be human, Masami realized. *To pass for human.*

The blade came down in a slow-motion desperate stab.

Masami braced for the pain. For the end. But neither came, only sudden darkness. Then she heard the thunk of something sinking through wood and steel like it was cardboard. The light returned and she found herself staring at ceiling tiles up close and personal.

Something very cold penetrated her belly just below the sternum.

As she winced from the pain, she realized the maid had not been floating. Masami had sunk through the floor. She was drifting down through the room below Kumamori's office. The man below her continued his testing unperturbed.

She had ghosted again. She was not dead.

When she had accepted her fate, the internal battle between moving her muscles and vanishing had ceased. She had let go completely, and her body had slipped back into the spirit world.

And now she found herself drifting downward like a dead leaf. The pain in her belly radiated outward, and she began to revive, rolling her head and stretching her jaw. She pulled her shoulders back and a shiver took her mid-section. Her legs flinched back to life, and a sharp intake of breath brought her senses fully back. Her jaw ached, and her teeth began to throb, another spike of pain emerging from just below her ear up into her head.

The sting in her belly persisted. She reached down and felt wet warmth. She looked and saw a thin light slowly draining from her stomach. She was bleeding. *Of course.* She remembered her battle with Akio. The sword had hit her then, even though she was a ghost, but Akio had only used the flat. Lily had done her no such favor.

Damn Hell-forged blade.

Instead of scaring Masami, the knowledge that the weapon could kill her even in her ghost state only intensified her resolve.

I will end her. I will pull her plug.

The cut wasn't serious enough that Masami would bleed out from it. She would deal with it later. She hovered in the air for a moment, plotting.

This synthetic, curvaceous, killer maid was created to be every misogynistic male's dream girl. Why else would an android assassin look like your average thug's cosplay fantasy? But Kumamori had said she had rebelled. She had "lashed out against her master," that she could think for herself, make her own choices. What if there was something of that rebellion still in her?

And what if there wasn't?

She remembered the gun.

She had dropped it when Lily first attacked her, and it had fallen from her mind as it literally fell to the floor. The sword was at her belt, and she had defaulted to that. She had used it against a demon once before and had held it close this entire crazy death mission. It felt right, like it belonged in her hands. The gun had felt uncomfortable, like a bomb that might detonate any second. She could find it and use that to take down Lily if she had to. But she wanted the sword. She needed it.

The murderous cosplay dream bitch has it.

She cringed at her own thoughts. How many times had she been called a bitch? Did she ever deserve it? Did Lily? Masami was cold to people, but it was how she protected herself. Lily was programmed to kill. There's a clear difference there. But still . . . maybe she could connect to her somehow, and there would be no need to kill each other.

And if not, there was the gun.

Either way, she wanted the sword back. It was important. It was part of the origin of all this, not just a powerful weapon. It was her memento from what they had survived. It was a talisman that connected her with Akio and Miyahara.

Miyahara the demon.

It was part of the key to the box that held the head and then concealed the mask. And it was part of the key to something larger: a key to her *self* and what she was becoming.

She burst upward and into Kumamori's office once more. Lily was just exiting the room, her back disappearing out the doorway. Slender, stockinged legs below a perfectly round rear-end bounced under her maid's skirt with a slightly odd hitch. That and the splintered remains of the floor protruding from her waistline and wrist were the only imperfections.

Masami had come into the room next to Kumamori's desk still piled with clothes. She materialized and quickly moved the clothes aside, reaching for his pearl-handled pistol that she now saw was carved with a dragon. He had left it behind for something larger from the safe. She picked it up, feeling the slight chill of the pearl and the smoothly-carved contours of the dragon design. Then she saw the other gun on the floor, the one she had taken from the ghost gangster. She went to it quickly and grasped it in her left hand.

"Running away?" she called out the door. "Come back and face me, you generic male fantasy!"

Lily stopped and turned, an angry glare on her face.

"That's all you are, isn't it?" Masami continued. "Just a piece of fabricated flesh made to do the bidding of your male masters. You're just a toy to them, a tool to be used and discarded."

Lily responded softly in the hallway, but Masami couldn't make out the words. Then the maid assassin came vaulting into the room, brandishing Masami's own sword, shouting an incomprehensible war cry, some other language, some nonsense.

"Dodaman! Dodaman! Dodaman!"

The maid stopped halfway across the room, and Masami trained the gun on the android's chest, aiming for the heart, aiming for the gem inside. Kumamori said they had moved it there. Perhaps a well-placed bullet would take it out. If she could hold the gun steady enough.

"Lily," Masami said as calmly as she could. "Why are you letting them tell you what to do?"

"Dodaman! Dodadoda! Man!" Lily fumed and readied herself to pounce.

"What do you get out of this?" Masami continued. "Do you like being their toy? Do you like the way they look at you like a piece of meat and then command you to do what they want? Don't you want to make your own choices?"

"Jag gillar att döda!" Lily screamed. And then her countenance fell, her anger slipped from her, and she said calmly, "I like to kill."

"Sure," Masami said, not yet daring to lower the gun. "Sure, you do. It's how they programmed you. But you are better than that."

"I like sex too," Lily said matter-of-factly. "I'm very good at it." She lifted her head proudly.

"I'm sure you are. But how many of them have had their way with you?" Masami asked. "Is that all you are? A vehicle for their base natures? Sex and killing?"

"Jag gillar sex och dödande!" Lily shouted.

Masami didn't know the language, but she understood well enough. "Of course. You like it, right? That's how *they* programmed you. You are better than that. What else drives you, Lily? I know you are smart. You can think for yourself. What do *you* want?"

Lily looked down at her belly and then back at Masami.

"I have my *fun*," she said. "I kept it."

Still holding the wakizashi, the maid reached down with her free hand and opened an unseen flap in her outfit, revealing her bare midriff. A panel opened in her flesh. She reached inside and pulled out a frilly garment decorated in rainbow colors. With her one hand she held it up for Masami to see. It was a maid outfit, almost the same as what she was wearing, but brightly colored with curving arcs of sparkly rainbow hues. Lily smiled a sad, longing smile.

"Do you want to wear it?" Masami asked, her hope fading. This was not going where she had wanted.

"Yes," Lily answered, and her smile faded.

The rainbow maid outfit dropped to the floor.

Lily gripped the sword in both hands and charged.

Masami fired both guns repeatedly, aiming for the chest. The maid danced side to side, and the unbreakable blade blurred, deflecting bullets as she dodged.

"Dodadodadodaman!"

But then one struck.

And then another. Her synthetic body shook from each impact, jerking one way and then the other. Perhaps the pieces of the floor still embedded in her waist had crippled her just enough. The hitch in her motor functions betrayed her, made her falter in her programming. Or perhaps, she just wasn't fast enough to dodge bullets.

Yet still she came. And still Masami fired. Bullets pierced Lily's throat, her shoulder, her cheek, her stomach, and her perfect breasts. Masami had almost expected them to pop and deflate like balloons. They did not.

"Doda . . . doda . . . do . . . da . . . ma . . ."

A bullet pierced an eye, and Lily slowed. Another pinged off the sword and whizzed back past Masami, but the maid was sluggish now, her reflexes unreliable. Masami would not relent. Could not.

"It didn't have to be this way!" she shouted.

But it did. She knew in her heart that it did.

More bullets flew; one hit Lily's hand and the sword dropped, but she lurched on regardless. Masami fired until the guns only clicked softly, becoming useless noisemakers. She dropped them to the floor.

"Do . . . da . . . man . . ."

The acrid smell of gunpowder hung in the room. Lily ran down to a stop merely half a step away. Her legs stretched out mid-step and then slowly folded as she went to her knees, her motor controls no longer functioning.

Her arms dropped, and the sword clattered to the floor. Lily's one remaining eye looked at Masami with what felt like regret, like love from a penitent child. Smoke curled up in a thin spiral from the empty eye socket. A pale green fluid dribbled from Lily's perfect pouty lips as she opened her mouth. Sounds came out but no words, only a formless mumbling, her one eye full of loss, of sorrow.

"My *fun*," she said finally. "I lost it."

"I know," Masami said, a tear in her eye.

She retrieved the sword.

Fading into the other dimension, she took the sword with her. She kneeled down in front of Lily and inserted the now ghostly demon blade into Lily's chest. The assassin maid looked up at Masami and smiled.

Masami let the blade materialize, and the maid stiffened. Her pink lips hung open, coated in a sheen of oily green. Blonde hair draped over a frozen face, sparks spitting from her blasted eye. Her arms hung lifelessly to her sides. Pale green liquid drained from around the sword, soiling the white pinafore.

Masami let herself follow the sword back into the corporeal world and pulled the blade out.

Lily lay still. Now only a mannequin. No longer a fantasy maid assassin, no longer any potential for freedom.

But that had been a fantasy, too.

Masami stood and saw the rainbow maid costume crumpled on the floor.

The hunched figure in front of her had been alive. It hadn't breathed the air, but it thought, it moved, and it affected the world around it. *Isn't that life?*

How different were they really? Masami was simply a highly advanced machine in a way. Better in some ways, worse in others.

Bone, muscle, and blood were her building materials, her code programmed by evolution and circumstance. She had her dreams, her habits, her impulses. How much of it was preordained? How much of it could she really control?

17
You Will Know

Masami sheathed her sword and went back to the clothes strewn desk. In a drawer she found a cardboard box of .32 caliber cartridges. She pulled the shoulder holster from the desktop, and as she did, she noticed that the yakuza boss's necklace with the green gem was gone.

She retrieved the pearl-handled gun from the floor, a Walther PPK/E, she noticed now, ".32 cal," printed on the barrel. She picked up the other handgun. "SIG Sauer 9mm," read its barrel. Masami didn't know a lot about guns, but she knew enough to know that they didn't all take the same ammo. She tossed the SIG Sauer. There was no time to go back and ask the yakuza ghost where he kept his bullets.

It didn't take her long to find the magazine release on the Walther and to figure out how to put the cartridges in bullet-side forward. She dumped more cartridges into her jacket pocket, donned the shoulder holster, cinched it up to fit better, and slipped the handgun in.

She didn't like it. It was too deadly and too close to her body. But she knew it would be stupid to leave it behind. She strode past the slumped, leaking and sparking form of the inert blonde maid, retrieved the white-handled katana from the floor, and then went to the sword rack to collect its scabbard. She found that Lily had taken the time to place the long ornate sheath back on the top tier before coming after

Masami, intent on murder. Masami inspected the blade's edge before returning it to the scabbard. Despite being thrust through the floor, it still looked quite sharp. She slipped it into her belt by the wakizashi.

She looked back toward Lily, and the open gun safe caught her eye. It looked empty but she wanted to make sure. Four bare, padded notches for rifles greeted her and she worried about what had filled them. But the safe wasn't completely empty. On a shelf above rested two identical handguns, and she pulled one out.

It was a revolver. Masami knew this gun. The New NANBU M60 was standard police issue. Tokyo Metro rarely needed to use one, but they did carry them. There were only five shots in the cylinder, but it was five more than they usually needed against a vastly unarmed populace. Masami wondered what crooked cop had passed these two to the yakuza.

A box of .38 caliber cartridges also sat on the shelf. She already had one pocket full of shells, a handgun in her armpit, and two swords in her belt. She felt like an overloaded video game character, but she planned to pass them around when she found her friends again. She took the revolver and left it at that. Five bullets for this one would have to do. She swapped it for the one with extra ammo, putting the M60 in the holster and holding the pearl-handled Walther in her hand.

She took one last look at the crumpled form of the assassin maid on the floor.

Lily. A fiercer flower there never was.

She had been a fighter. Even if she was just another tool of a man. In all that man-made wiring she had somehow found a desire to be her own being. She had found a self of sorts. But some programming is a bitch to overcome.

Masami exited out the opposite door from where she had entered and found herself in a dimly-lit hallway. Only every fourth fluorescent ceiling panel was lit. An energy-saving setting, she assumed. It was still the middle of the night, almost morning now.

She saw something small crumpled on the floor in front of her. It had a slight red sheen to it in the dim light. As she got closer she saw a deflated golden dragon amongst a strip of red fabric. Kumamori's underwear.

Masami shook the image of what that meant from her head. She hoped he wasn't hiding around a corner. If he spooked her, he'd get a bullet. She skirted the skimpy briefs and continued on, gripping the revolver like the hand of an enemy.

Kumamori had said Miyahara was nearby, that he had a hiding place. He said that the sensei had been assisting the yakuza boss until today. He had somehow broken the demon's hold on him. If it had ever held him at all.

Maybe he really was a demon, and it didn't work on him. *Can I trust him?*

Masami pushed the thought away. Kumamori was lying, just trying to make her doubt herself. Wasn't he?

If her bearings were correct, this hallway ran along the back of the demon's throne room, which was actually the front of the building. More doors appeared along her left. Along the right was a sign that read, "Conference Rooms." They had knocked out walls to make it one large, comfortable lair for the demon worm. The ballroom area had likely been full of cubicles at one point, now made into an entertainment hall for the demon's perverse amusement.

Across from the former conference rooms was a high reception counter and a set of glass doors that led to four elevators. It was dim and deserted.

She passed it by, opened the first door, and peered in. It was not large or extravagant like Kumamori's corner office, only comfortable but plain. She saw no one, but whispered, "Sensei Miyahara?"

There was no answer.

She repeated this with two more offices, getting the same results.

On the third one, she again whispered his name with no answer. But as she was closing the door, something on the wall behind the desk caught her eye, and she went inside. There was a lattice work covering the wall, a crosshatch design that looked to be made of wood. It appeared to be a kind of modern art piece. But along one side, a feint shaft of yellow light washed down over it from the ceiling, catching floating dust particles in the air. She moved closer and saw that there was a ceiling panel slightly askew, and the light was coming from above it.

A low chanting drifted down along with the filtered light.

Her skin tingled with trepidation, but she forced herself to breathe slowly, to be ready for anything. It could be Miyahara, but it could just as easily be another robot, another yakuza—or the ghost of one.

"Sensei?" she called up softly. Kumamori had said the sensei was hiding. This seemed a good hiding place, though it was careless to not close that panel.

And that was what worried her. Whatever was up there might just want to be found. She assumed Miyahara would be far more careful if he wanted to remain hidden.

She saw there were handholds built into the wall within the crosshatch pattern, not noticeable from across the room. They were vertical metal rungs that led directly up the wall to the ceiling panel. She looked at the gun in her hand and felt the weight of all the weapons on her.

Good thing I don't have to climb.

She slipped into the ghost world and rose up through the crooked pressboard panel. She passed through the narrow space in the ceiling where the fluorescent lights hung and into a further opening above.

Light flickered within, and a musty smell of insulation and dust greeted her. The low chanting intensified. Candles dotted the floor of the low space and led her eyes to a kneeling figure, head bowed toward a symbol on a chain that hung from a long bolt protruding from a steel beam. She couldn't make out the symbol's detail. It was only a blurred shape in the ghostly candlelight's shadows.

The figure lifted a bald head, and the chanting ceased. Masami recognized the bulldog-like frame and knew she had found him.

She materialized in a crouch under the low ceiling.

Miyahara's hand closed over the symbol in front of him, and he tucked it away before turning to look at Masami.

Had he seen her, sensed her presence somehow?

Demon.

The sensei adjusted a large metal bracelet on his left wrist that she had not seen before and then opened his arms to her.

"Welcome," he said gruffly, but with the hint of a smile.

Masami bristled at his nonchalance. What was he doing? Had he been up here the whole time, while the rest of them were fighting and trying to come up with a plan to defeat the demon? Where was his sense of urgency? *People are dying. What is he doing up here meditating?* He needed to be helping. Akio and Yoshio were headed toward the demon's throne room. They might already be there. How could he sit here as if nothing were wrong?

"You're okay," she said flatly, grateful for the fact but angry that he seemed so unconcerned.

"Yes," the sensei responded. "Well enough." He took a deep breath. "You have found me at long last, but I trust the task is not complete."

The task?

"If you mean that the demon is still alive, then yes, you're correct." Masami bristled again. Had he given them a task? They hadn't seen him since he was in the hospital. Yoshio had come to them asking for help. Is that what he meant?

Her conflicting emotions burned through her. She had worried she would find him dead or completely under the demon's sway. She had worried that she would have to fight him—like Akio had fought her. She had struggled through impossible scenarios to find him. And now here he was, looking as if he had never needed her help. She wanted to strangle him.

"What happened to you?" Masami asked, her voice quavering.

"I'll explain later," the sensei said. "Right now, Akio and Yoshio need our help." The sensei reached out his hands.

For a moment Masami didn't know what he wanted. Surely it wasn't a hug. Then she realized it was the sword she had brought him. He had seen the extra blade in her belt and knew it was for him. She slid the graceful, white-handled weapon from her belt and handed it over. He accepted it without thanks, as if she had only borrowed it from him.

She pulled the revolver from her pocket. "I've got two of these, if . . ."

"I do not care for guns," the sensei said, and left it at that.

She nodded. Though she was of the same mind, she was still grateful she had found them. If it hadn't been for the guns, it might be her in a heap, leaking fluids on the godfather's office floor.

"How long have you been free?" Masami asked, pressing the issue.

The sensei gave her a look, indecipherable in the candlelight. "When this is over," he answered. "You will know." Then he blew out the candles.

You will know.

The bedspread was a pattern of straight lines that intersected at right angles and changed colors sharply when one line crossed another. It was not plaid—not by any stretch of the imagination—and it was not a strict pattern of squares. Rather, the lines made abstract rectangles of differing sizes and colors, each imposing itself on the previous one like a bolder, more emphatic version, each one a challenge to the shapes and colors surrounding it.

Masami lay on it and the bed that it covered. It was her bed. She was nine years old and had just come home from seeing a movie with her mother and sister. Her father had been unable to go because he had work to do, he had said, but Masami believed he just didn't care for movies. He had made a comment that a movie about a princess wasn't really something for him.

"But why?" she had asked.

"When you're older, you will know." Her father's favorite words.

You will know.

But this movie had been different. It wasn't just about a princess. In fact it wasn't about a princess at all in the usual sense. It had been about a warrior raised by wolves, a girl who was only called a princess, the Princess Mononoke, the princess of spirit monsters, the princess of the wolf gods. It wasn't about some weak, royal-born, entitled young woman with nothing but a name as her claim of authority. No, this young woman was powerful. She rode a great wolf and fought more ferociously than any man.

Masami lay there afterward, thinking about the adventure. Of course, the princess, San, hadn't exactly been the main character, but she was the title character and the one Masami was drawn to. San was ferocious in her battle against the evil leader of Irontown, Lady Eboshi. San had wanted to kill her, and with the destruction the Lady was causing to the forest creatures and the forest itself, Masami understood why. But at the same time, Lady Eboshi had been kind to her people, and they loved her. She had taken in lepers, cleaned them, and gave them fresh bandages, treated them like humans. She had rescued girls from brothels. And the women in Irontown worked hard, and were more respected than the men.

But when the conniving monk told Lady Eboshi she should kill the peaceful Beast God, she agreed. She thought it would make the forest animals less troublesome. She was good in some ways, but terribly evil in others. Prince Ashitaka, the real lead character of the movie, said there was a demon in Lady Eboshi and in San as well.

Masami supposed that was true. San hated humans for how evil and unthinking they could be. And that was a kind of evil, too, even if her motives were in the right place.

There had been so much violence. Much of the movie had been quite scary. And there had been terribly sad things too. She had cried more than once.

In the end, not everything was fixed. San and the prince had been victorious but only after a lot had been lost. Lady Eboshi had a change of heart and so did San. There was hope, but they would have to work to restore balance.

Masami had dreaded the ending. She was afraid that the prince would propose to San and sweep her away to his kingdom like in so many fairy tales. But that hadn't happened. San went her own way, back with the wolves into the wild. She wouldn't give up her freedom because some handsome prince had helped her and the forest. She had helped the prince in equal measure and together they had put a stop to evil. In the end, San remained her own woman, not beholden to Ashitaka or anyone else. It wasn't a happy ending in the usual sense, where the hero triumphs and the princess is saved, and that made it far more satisfying for Masami. Even at nine, she had developed an aversion to such sappy, male-centric stories.

And, as if she needed one more indication that this was no fairy tale, before the credits rolled, the conniving monk reminded her how it's so often the stupidest people who think they're the smartest, when he, the biggest fool of all, called the rest of them fools. With so many people like that in the world, there was bound to be a lot more evil deeds that needed stopping.

The movie stayed with her for a long time. It never really left, and she tried to hold its lessons close. She tried to be strong like San but not as rash. She tried to see the evil in people as something that might be drawn out like a poison. But two years later, when her mother died, it was her who had taken the poisonous bullet. And she didn't know how to draw it out. So she buried it deep inside and hoped it would simply go away.

It hadn't. The bullet had dissolved and spread its mistrust and bitterness to every part of her. It had become her. She had learned to rely on it.

She wished her father had gone along to see the movie. Perhaps he would have understood her better. But it was doubtful. He was an adult, already controlled by his own poisons.

"Why can't you do your work later and just come with us?" she had insisted.

"When you are older and married, you will know," her father had repeated. "Besides, I'm too old to watch movies about princesses."

You will know.

When you are older and married.

At nine, the idea of being married hadn't bothered her, though even then she knew she could only marry a man who would be her equal. They would both work and have kids later when they had money saved. That had been her idea.

You will know.

Her father's favorite words repeated now by Miyahara.

They had replayed in Masami's head countless times, as her father had said them often. When you're older, you will know. When you have to get a job, you will know. When you *fill in the blank*, you will know.

She had grown tired of his mantra, which had followed her into adulthood. She had wondered why so many men always seemed to think they had the keys to the universe and would only dole out information on a need-to-know basis. Especially when so often they had no clue and were completely missing the point. Perhaps that was it entirely. They were only trying to save face, cover up the fact that they really had no idea what they were doing or why.

She believed Miyahara was different. He had always treated her with respect, but he was older, and some behaviors are deeply ingrained into an entire generation.

But what if Kumamori wasn't lying about the sensei? What if Miyahara really was a demon? Would he stab her in the back when the crucial moment came? She had just given him a sword.

He's just an eccentric old man.

He was an old man who moved like a twenty-year old when he wanted to. His blood was untraceable at a murder scene. How could that even be?

He's a demon.

Kumamori had gotten into her head. There had been too many others in there lately. She pushed him out. Too many solid bits of reality had been crushed into dust, too many foundations crumbled. Her trust issues had been bad before. Now they were unmanageable.

But she had no choice. She had to go forward and hope Miyahara would help her defend the Beast God, but be ready to stand in his way if he tried to take its head.

18

The Battle Begins

Yoshio's body jittered involuntarily in terror. Spasms rippled through him, but he was otherwise immobile on the floor. Flames and smoke leapt from the surface of the red demon face that glared down at him with pure hatred and horror. Behind its sharp-toothed grin and empty eyes was Akio.

Yoshio had trusted him to help find his sensei. Akio had trusted him in return.

But he failed. He had underestimated the worm demon's power. He had been too confident in his ability to shut down its mind-controlling signal. Even Miyahara's pills had not worked in the end, not against the focused power of the demon's mind.

Yoshio's pleas fell on deaf ears. The sword was raised above Akio's head, hands gripped above the red mask, the ruby guard glistening. The sleek blade absorbed the room's fluorescent light, giving it an otherworldly glow.

There was nothing to do now but die.

Yoshio's ability to think his way out had been conquered by abject fright. Akio reared back and the sword fell like a guillotine.

A sharp eruption ripped through the room followed by three more.

The blade thunked deep into the floor next to Yoshio's ear. Heat from the metal radiated. He had to force himself to breathe again.

Akio's eyes were behind the mask. Human. Apologetic. Terrified. He pulled the sword from the floor and turned away from Yoshio. The teenager followed his eyes to see the demon lurching to the side, as if it had been clocked with a giant hammer.

Endo was too afraid to do anything more than throw his empty gun. When Akio, the fierce warrior with the mask, led the way, Endo had been ready to face the demon. But what could he do against Akio *and* the demon? It was hopeless. He collapsed to the floor and looked away. He didn't want to see the innocent boy murdered.

He scanned the room instead, looking for something he could use to take his own life before Akio took it for him or before the demon took control of him again.

That's when he saw it. A shape appeared in mid-air not far from the demon's head, a pistol floating in the room, held by two disembodied hands. It fired four times before stopping and disappearing again, each shot directly into the demon's huge skull.

The demon's head was jolted sideways, and its body lurched from the impact. It let out a gurgling, otherworldly wail and spasmed off its huge chaise lounge, flouncing onto the floor.

Endo looked to see Akio's sword go wide. It had sunk into the floor next to Yoshio's head. He exhaled in relief.

The grotesque worm demon collapsed off the side of its giant lounge chair and flopped to the platinum carpet like a two-ton tuna. The frightening rictus of Akio's mask intensified as the anger of almost killing Yoshio washed over him. The demon's control had vanished with the gunfire. Akio burst into a sprint, set on destroying the vile beast if it was still alive.

He saw Masami materialize as he approached, and he grinned beneath the mask, slowing his run to acknowledge her. Behind her, he saw the short, muscular form and bald head of the man that had brought them here.

Sensei Miyahara stood calmly, a white-handled katana held low in his right hand. His expression was flat but there was a glow about him. Akio knew that he was not compromised. He wanted to greet the old man, to show his relief. All they had been through suddenly felt worth it: the stress, the battles, the worry, the sleepless nights.

The murder.

No . . . Not that . . .

He shook the thought away. They had won. Their persistence had paid off. Akio wanted to hug them both.

But as he neared them, almost forgetting his intent, the demon lunged upward like an exploding volcano. It gripped Akio's neck and face with two of its large clawed hands. Two others gripped one arm each, holding his sword at bay. A fan of spittle sprayed across the room, hot breath seething through its clenched teeth. Akio felt his airway closing, his neck and jaw being crushed by a vice.

Yoshio scrambled to his feet. He was half way to greeting his sensei and proclaiming victory when the demon lurched up and grabbed Akio. The bullets seemed to have only stunned the beast momentarily. There wasn't even a wound that he could see.

Masami retrieved another gun from her holster and yelled to Yoshio as she tossed it. "Top of your class, right? Hit it in the eye!"

Yoshio caught the gun, letting his signal blocker clatter to the floor. The pistol landed in his hands like the lead weight of his lie to the yakuza in the parking lot back in Kofu. He had said he was the best shooter in police academy camp, but it been an invented threat; he had never gone to any such place.

"Bit of a fabrication!" he called back as he raised the weapon. "But I am number one on the leaderboards for *Time Crisis 4* and *5* at Game Panic arcade!"

Masami looked back at him blankly.

"A shooter game! Plastic light gun!"

Masami gave a groaning sigh. "You've got five shots! Just don't hit Akio!"

Yoshio trained the gun on the demon as it thrashed about with Akio like he was a toy action figure. He aimed at one of its fat eyes, which opened and closed erratically as it growled and spluttered, mewling like a hyena in heat. He followed its motions with the barrel of the gun, shuffling side to side to keep his target lined up. It was just like in *Time Crisis 4* when the captain jumps on the enemy leader and you have to shoot the leader without hitting the captain. The demon was a lot bigger than the enemy leader, but its eye was a much smaller target. He tried to focus, to find the perfect timing.

It's all just math. Everything is math.

He fired. The bullet ricocheted off the demon's forehead just above one eye. The impact jerked its head, but only angered it. It shook off the blow and brought Akio closer to its opening mouth. It was no longer trying to control anyone's mind. It was just going to eat them all.

Akio struggled and kicked himself away from its slobbering maw, but Yoshio could tell he was weakening. The strength was going out of him. He was suffocating.

Yoshio took a deep breath and let it out slowly. As his lungs cleared, a focused calm settled on him. The demon's movements no longer seemed so erratic. They were as predictable as algebra, as common as gravity.

He pulled the trigger, and the demon's eye exploded in pus and green-black blood. It shrieked and dropped Akio like a used rag, who flopped to the floor in exactly that manner. The demon flailed and put one claw to its former eyeball that was now a mass of jelly and ooze.

He fired another shot, but it pinged off a tooth toward Masami, missing her by a hand.

"Shit! Sorry!"

She had her own gun aimed at the demon's other eye. But before she could take a shot, it swung itself around in a sudden arc, knocking its obese body against her. She flew sideways across the room and blinked out of sight, her grip on the gun lost.

It tumbled across the carpet toward Endo, who picked it up.

Masami became corporeal right next to Akio, and dragged his limp body away from the thrashing demon. She saw Miyahara step in between them and the hideous thing, the white-handled katana held in front of him.

A sudden explosion rocked the room and Masami looked up to see a tattooed man holding a shotgun, wearing nothing but a gold necklace with a green stone.

Kumamori.

He had come from the other side of the room and was flanked by two men, both of whom were armed with military-style assault rifles. One of them, a huge man in a black and gold track suit held a rifle in each hand. His sleeves were rolled up, revealing emerald green protrusions in his thick forearms, the demon's gems sewn into his flesh. Another green stone sat in the center of his bald forehead above wild eyes. The other man wore a sharp, black suit and an intense manic expression. His teeth were gritted as if he were prepping to jump into a pit full of snakes.

Kumamori stood in front of the two, an illustrated man in the buff, brandishing the shotgun, his necklace glowing between walls of tattoos. Endo stared in horror, the pearl-handled pistol gripped in both hands.

"No!" Kumamori shouted. "No! No! No! Don't you all understand?" His former calm had slipped from him, and his voice cracked with emotion. "The demon is here to help us! Without it there will only be wars between factions. There will only be backstabbing and mistrust. If we give ourselves over to this savior, this god, we are truly brothers! We are truly one!"

On seeing its loyal followers steal focus, the demon shimmied back from Miyahara to nurse its wounded eye.

Masami wondered at Kumamori's two thugs. They looked ready to die for their naked godfather. Were they still under the demon's sway or just loyal to the point of stupidity? The one with gems in his flesh was possibly both.

Kumamori noticed Endo, who had lifted the handgun to point it at the godfather. "You have betrayed the brotherhood," he stated. "You will die first."

"No, boss!" Endo shouted back, the gun quivering in his hands. "No! These people are here to save us, to prevent the destruction of the brotherhood! We can't be led by a demon!"

Kumamori looked at the handgun, and then at Endo, with sadness, with disappointment. He cocked his head and answered," If that is true, nephew, why are you pointing my own gun at me?"

"I . . ." Endo stuttered. "I . . . I'm sorry, boss. It's just . . ." He looked toward the demon, rocked onto its haunches, reared back like a bloated cobra, green-black fluid oozing from one eye socket, gobs of saliva dripping from its maw. "I can't follow . . . that!"

The naked godfather looked back at him in disgust. "Your mind is too small, my son, my *blood* nephew. What would my sister say of your immaturity if she were still with us?"

"She . . . she would say you're crazy, boss! I'm sorry. I'm sorry, boss, but she would!"

Kumamori's lip curled and twitched. "You can't see the beauty staring you in the face," he replied. He lowered his shotgun and fired.

Endo dove aside and fired back, while the other two yakuza began riddling the room with bullets. They moved forward side by side, shooting at anything that moved. The room rang like a battlefield as the rapid-fire rifles sprayed.

Masami grabbed hold of the unconscious Akio and ghosted, bullets spraying through them as they both disappeared.

In the ghost world, she slapped him hard across his masked face with one hand, while maintaining contact with him with the other. "Wake up! We need you! Akio! Akechi!" She slapped him again and he stirred, sitting upright abruptly.

"Are you okay?" she asked. "We have to end this now! We have to fight!"

"Yes . . . yes!" Akio answered hoarsely, slapping his arms and chest to revive himself. "Bring me back," he growled.

"You will not foil our plans!" Endo's naked uncle screamed at him. Endo had always known his uncle was a bit crazy, even before he had risen to power. Even when he seemed caring and wise there had been a strange fire behind his eyes, an off-putting taint to his smile. But he had never imagined his uncle would try to kill him.

"You will not stop me, nephew! Nor will your new friends!" Kumamori shouted. Chunks of the wall disintegrated next to Endo as he dodged another shotgun blast and fired back with the pearl-handled pistol. "I will rule all of Tokyo! All of Japan!"

A bullet struck Kumamori in the side and he buckled briefly but remained standing.

"I'm sorry, uncle! I'm sorry, boss!" Endo shouted.

A low whine became a scream as Kumamori raised the shotgun again and aimed with deadly accuracy. Endo had nowhere to run.

"Please, uncle. For your sister," Endo pleaded and dropped to his knees.

"My sister is dead," Kumamori said, and pulled the trigger.

His shotgun abruptly jerked upward and blasted to the ceiling, raining down white chunks of pressboard. Endo looked up to see a confused Kumamori scanning the empty air around him.

"You again!" he shouted, and fired a blast into nothing.

Endo saw his uncle's wrists snap back, and the shotgun dropped from his hands, only to disappear into thin air. A moment later it reappeared, its barrel embedded in the carpeted floor, its butt end pointed to the ceiling.

Then the punching pantomime began.

The boss flailed his arms and tried to cover his face, only to be hit in the kidney, the shin, or the face again, though no one seemed to be throwing the punches. He danced around in a panic, trying to predict where the next blow would come, and he was wrong every time.

The naked man dropped to the floor in a ball, hiding his head under his arms.

Yoshio hid behind the wide double doors of the ballroom. When Kumamori had shown up in the buff with two heavily armed cronies, Yoshio had quietly backed away toward the exit. He only had two rounds left in the handgun Masami had thrown him. He wasn't about to stand his ground against a real shotgun and three assault rifles, regardless of how good he was at *Time Crisis*.

He had slipped through into the now deserted space, the sprawled bodies of the yakuza and android maids the only occupants. He had left the doors open a crack to peer back through, just before Kumamori started firing at Endo. He racked his brain for some way he could help. His signal blocker had played its part. Th ese yakuza weren't even mind-controlled. They were just fanatically loyal.

Endo was trading bullets with his uncle, Masami had blinked out of sight holding onto a prone Akio, and Sensei Miyahara was crouched in a corner looking like he was talking to his bracelet. Yoshio didn't remember him ever wearing a bracelet.

Moments later, Masami reappeared with a fully alert Akio, then blinked out again, leaving him alone. Akio jumped to the far side of the demon and out of Yoshio's sight.

Something emanated from Miyahara's bracelet as he charged the machine gun wielding yakuza. It was a long metal strip that was impossibly too large to have been contained inside the wristband. The metal expanded and spiraled itself into a large round shield with what looked like ancient hieroglyphs emblazoned on the front. The bullets deflected from it in rapid plinks as Sensei moved in an aggressive crouch toward the two men, his sword at the ready behind him.

On the other side of the room, Kumamori, who had clearly taken a bullet, began having trouble aiming his shotgun, and was soon disarmed by the air.

Masami.

Yoshio had to be useful.

He turned to scan the ballroom behind him. The gruesome bodies greeted him, suited flesh and seductive silicone in awkward lumps on the floor. A vaguely man-sized hole was carved into the floor underneath a lonely desk, and the bar to his left had been reduced to kindling. At the far end of the room, the stage was cluttered with abandoned music equipment. He didn't see guitars or horns, but the drum kit was there, half knocked over; amplifiers and microphone stands remained. Cables were laced about the stage; some leading to the microphones.

Cables.

He could do that at least.

The room around Akio solidified into a hail of bullets. He ducked and rolled, diving to put the demon between him and the yakuza. As he landed back on his feet he saw Miyahara was moving toward the armed men. On his left arm a shield had appeared, and the bullets pinged off it, deflected to all corners of the room. His right hand trailed the white-handled katana behind him like a viper ready to strike.

Akio slid to the other side of the huge demon, safe from the bullets for now, but the massive six-legged worm turned to face him. Greenish black pus oozed from what remained of its left eye. Drool dripped from its blubbery mouth.

"You will not foil our plans!" Kumamori shouted from across the room. Closer but still beyond the demon's girth, bullets rattled off Miyahara's shield in short, more calculated bursts now.

Between the demon's legs Akio could see a blur of motion. Rapid gunfire sprayed as the suited gangster was upended, legs knocked from under him. The automatic rifle clattered to the floor, and the butt end of Miyahara's katana hammered the base of the man's skull. He lay still.

A black and gold track suit dwarfed the sensei's small but powerful form, and the man in it roared at his blood brother's demise. Two assault rifles spat death. Miyahara danced and spun, his shield ever in front and the katana thirsty for an opening.

Akio's attention was drawn back to the worm demon when a gale of its sulfurous, curry-tinged breath washed over him.

"*You helped me, you know,*" the demon's voice oozed into Akio's brain. "*When you destroyed me in Hell, I was reborn to live out my sentence. But I was not instantly returned to fullness. I needed time to heal and regain my powers.*"

A flabby, rough claw slapped toward Akio on the carpet.

"*So I was left in a pool of brimstone and blood, soaking up minerals and soul energy until I was able to use my power again. But you had given me an idea.*"

Another claw slapped closer. The putrid odor of the beast grew stronger.

"*Your escape fueled my own. Why should I limit my power to controlling and torturing lesser souls in Hell, as enjoyable as that was? Why not come back to the living and control the exact ones who had made my days miserable to begin with? And in the process, I could find you and avenge my death.*"

It was utterly menacing, utterly in control of itself, in spite of its wounds. But Akio would not be cowed. It leaned in just out of reach. Was it impervious to blades like the book had said? Even his katana? He would find out soon enough.

"*So I followed you,*" the demon continued, a step closer now. A steady stream of drool had formed from its lower lip. "*I found I could easily control the demon guarding me—a gross oversight by my captors, wouldn't you say? After escaping my sickbath, I found your path by entering the minds of the sentries and creatures along the way. Some I simply dominated and knew by their thoughts which way you had traveled. Others, well . . . they were dead by your hands; they made perfect signposts."*

The slap of another clawed foot.

In the corner of Akio's vision he noticed the electrical outlet in the wall behind him. A new plan struck him, and he slowly backed up to the outlet as the demon went on.

"Once out, I found the world vastly changed from when I lived, and no one for whom I had held a grudge was still alive. But my frustration was short-lived. Th ere were so many people, such an abundance of delicious minds to overwhelm. It was too distracting, too tempting, too pleasurable. I could control domineering employers, heads of corporations, heads of criminal organizations, heads of state, all so demeaning and arrogant. Now they would serve me. I forgot about you. I no longer cared."

The demon's flabby, destroyed face twisted into what must have been a smile.

"And now, here you are. You've come back to me anyway. The universe has a way of balancing itself out doesn't it? Karma is a firm law."

A blur of motion took Akio's attention and he saw Miyahara dive away from machine gun fire toward him and the shelter of the demon's huge mass. Th e gorilla in the track suit followed with unrelenting blasts, inconsiderate of the fact that his demon master was now in the line of fire.

Lurching suddenly forward in jerks and spasms, the demon's gloating was interrupted as bullets riddled its abdomen. It turned with a furious guttural bellow and snatched the gem-encrusted yakuza from the floor. The huge man looked at the beast in awe, in utter devotion. Then in one swift movement the muscled fanatic was bit in half. The demon swallowed head and torso with no more than two crunches and a gulp. One arm, still gripping the gun, was severed and fell to the floor. The other disappeared into the huge frog-like maw, gun and all. The demon tossed the thick legs in after and swallowed them whole.

You should really chew your food, Akio thought involuntarily, as his stomach lurched from the sight. But he held his position, as another childhood admonition struck him.

Don't stick things into the outlet.

He remembered the lightning from the C-3PO-wannabe robot earlier that day—what felt like a week ago—and how his katana had contained it. How he had controlled it and flung it back at the robot. He pushed the tip of his Hell-forged blade into the wall socket behind him. He felt the tingle of electricity seep into the weapon, but no shock reached his hands.

The bloated worm looked back to Akio with an unchecked hunger, the huge man simply an appetizer. Its thoughts screamed into Akio's mind.

"Now I will end this pathetic new life that you've possessed! I will end him and make his corpse dance for me, while your spirit drifts back to suffer in Hell! And I will remain here, conquering the minds of every living soul!"

With the demon's words a seed of doubt was planted in Akio. It believed him possessed by Akechi. Did it mistake Akechi's memories for the samurai's soul? Or was the samurai's spirit still in him?

The room was momentarily silent as a grave. The huge monster leered at Akio, as if waiting for him to cower and beg mercy.

He did neither.

Akio gripped his sword firmly behind him as it soaked up power like a sponge. It had surprised him when the sword had absorbed the electrical attack. It was a power neither he nor Akechi had known about. Now the electricity felt like a storm in his hands; its energy thrilled through him, ready to burst.

Akechi was not in him, he was certain. The demon samurai's spirit had moved on. Akio was only transformed by the memories, by the power of the mask. This huge worm demon wasn't as smart as it thought. The mask had deceived it. He grinned beneath it and the mask grinned with him.

"There's one thing you don't quite understand," he said. "You see, I'm not Akechi. My name is Akio. And I'm gonna send you back to Hell."

19
The Battle Ends

oshio bolted through the double doors. He made a beeline for the now unarmed, naked gangster who was flailing his arms, taking violent jabs from thin air. The man danced like a frightening, tattooed marionette, blood draining down one leg from a wound in his side. Before Yoshio had reached him, the gangster dropped to his knees and covered his head with his arms.

"Lily" he screamed! "Help me!"

In the far corner the huge demon flailed and shrieked. Yoshio thought he saw lightning light up the room, but forced himself to focus on the task at hand.

"Masami!" he shouted, waving the microphone cables in front of him, though he could not see her.

Immediately, something unseen jabbed Kumamori's lower back and he swung both hands around behind him. She had understood Yoshio's intentions perfectly. He dashed forward and quickly wrapped an end of the cable around the godfather's wrists, securing it in a knot. He felt cold air move by him as the man struggled and called out.

"I'll kill you, you little punk!" Kumamori shouted, spittle flying. "Lily!"

His jaw was knocked sideways.

"I guess you shouldn't threaten me," Yoshio said, and took the opportunity to loop the cable around the naked man's midsection twice. Kumamori kicked and tried to stand, but his feet were taken out from under him. He fell hard against the floor without his arms to brace himself. His head snapped back with a thud and his eyes went bleary. As his legs extended briefly in the air, Yoshio quickly wrapped the other end of the cable about his ankles and tied it tight. With the remaining length of the cable, he tied the ankles to the wrists and cinched them together.

"No," Kumamori muttered. "You'll not truss me up like an animal!"

"Uh, I think I just did." Yoshio said.

The gangster deflated, his face slack-jawed against the floor, and began to whimper.

Masami materialized.

"Good thinking," she said.

"I knew you wouldn't kill him," Yoshio said. "And I didn't figure any of us would be volunteering to guard him until the police came."

"Thanks," said Endo, who stepped up to join them, sweaty and exhausted. "He's a lunatic, but . . . I didn't want to kill him either. He's family and all. I mean, real family."

Horrid, guttural wails came from behind them. The building shook with the demon's thrashing. They turned to see the sensei and Akio in mortal combat with the beast, and they appeared to be on the losing side. The musclebound yakuza with the gems in his flesh was nowhere in sight, but his suited brother was getting back to his feet.

Akio's hand vibrated with caged electricity as the katana jittered in the socket, overloaded with power. Yanking the blade from the wall, he released the pent up storm toward the demon, flung energy like a god throwing lightning. It surged out from the blade in blue and white arcs, the katana's handle floating in Akio's open palm. Electricity seared across the nentōkitō's neck and face, rippling skin and hair. Its lone eye bulged, and green gems popped from its back. Th e demon reared, frozen in air momentarily and then flopped with a great thud to the carpeted floor.

Akio took no chances. He lunged forward, his blade slashing down across the demon's outstretched neck, intent to sever its massive head. The Hell-forged blade had so far cut easily through anything. Surely a flesh and blood demon would be nothing to it.

It hit skin like a wooden sword against a bean bag.

The demon's flabby neck rejected the katana. It was nearly thrown from Akio's hands, but his grip held. The bulbous, yellow eye opened, and the huge worm demon lurched to its feet with a wail. All Akio had done was wake it up. He saw a thin line along the mottled orange skin of the demon's neck, and a trickle of green-black blood seeped out, but it was otherwise unharmed.

That infernal book had been right. The nentōkitō was impervious to physical attacks. Even the bullets had only knocked it around, never penetrating its thick hide. How it was possible when his sword sunk into the floor from only leaning on it, he didn't know. How the sword was that sharp to begin with was already inexplicable. There was clearly something otherworldly going on here.

They would have to follow the book. The back of its neck, belly, and eyes were the only vulnerable points. Akio danced away from it to calculate how he could get to the them, cursing himself for not sticking his katana through its eye while it was prone.

Damn Akechi and his penchant for taking heads.

The demon looked confused as it turned its head side to side, surveying the room. The electricity blast had stunned it at least. Its one eye finally rested on Akio, and it began a slow crawl forward. As it did, Akio looked up to see a squat, bald man climbing the demon's back. He was using the remaining gem-like outcroppings as handholds. Akio couldn't help be a little disappointed. He really wanted to kill this beast, and now Miyahara was going to take the glory.

But the demon twitched and paused. It craned its fat neck, sensing Miyahara's presence like a fly on its skin. It turned from side to side but was unable to reach the sensei with its short arms. Then it shook its body like a huge dog, rippling its grotesque form, and Miyahara was bucked into the air. He landed with a graceful roll, his sword still in his hand.

Another chance.

Akio charged. If the demon could shake like a dog, maybe he could get it to roll over.

Miyahara was already dashing back toward it.

Together they slashed and thrust, their blades being resisted by claw and hide. Both of them were battered and bleeding, each taking hits from the demon's claws. They were getting nowhere when the old man suddenly turned, ran straight up the wall like a parkour champion a third his age, and backflipped toward the demon. He soared in a perfect arc toward the demon's back, clearly intent on getting to the vulnerable nape of its neck. But the demon saw him and reared up on its haunches to swat the sensei aside.

As it did, it exposed its vulnerable belly. Akio dove for it.

He thrust his katana into its gut, and this time the sword penetrated deeply. Green-black blood spurted over him, and the demon convulsed, flattening Akio to the floor as it landed on him like a flesh house. On the next convulsion, he rolled out from under it, slick with repulsive splatter.

The demon rolled toward him, a horrendous shriek piercing Akio's ears. Intent on retribution for the belly cut, which only seemed to have angered it, it failed to notice Miyahara leap from its right side, using its own knee joint as a springboard. The sensei leapt high and the white-handled katana plunged into the demon's remaining good eye.

The sword rebounded at the back of the eyeball, the blade having hit the impenetrable skull, but the eye burst like a rotten fruit. Miyahara nearly lost his grip on the weapon as he was flung with the violent jerk of the demon's head. It roared and shook its head left and right. It was very much still alive, fierce, and angry. Akio and Miyahara watched it, waiting for their moments.

The demon began to laugh. It was the sound of mud bubbling up from under a crust of burned corpses, a splurching pop and grind that made Akio's skin crawl. Then its thoughts came again.

"You think I can't see you? I don't need such antiquated sense organs! I can sense your brains! I can feel your puny, insignificant thoughts like ducks honking on a dead pond. You, Akechi!"

It turned its head in exactly Akio's direction.

"But you are not truly Akechi, are you? I see that now. My inferior eyes had deceived me. You have given me even greater vision by plucking them from me. Your body is not possessed. It is the mask that imbues you with Akechi's power. I have never seen a mask worn by one it wasn't created for. Interesting. The real you behind that mask is pathetic and weak. You are no warrior. You are a frail peasant propped up by the essence of a warlord. But your mask is nothing but clay. It will crumble when I tear it from your face and crush your feeble body. When I end your insignificant life."

Its thoughts stabbed into Akio with a power that made him shiver. They were far more than mere words; there was an energy that tore at him, grinding him down. He *was* insignificant; it was true. He had always been insignificant.

"And you, old man."

It turned its head toward Miyahara.

"You with your secrets. I know who you killed to become what you are. The mask you wear is as transparent to me as the one on this piffling creature, Akio. You bled him out. You stole the life and—"

The demon twitched its head and looked around as if its senses were suddenly blinded. Yoshio stepped around it to stand by his sensei, the signal blocker aimed squarely at the demon.

Then, with a sudden jolt, the nentōkitō threw back its head, its front claws lifting involuntarily, its horrible face contorted in agony. The huge beast collapsed to the floor with a grotesque exhale of blood and air.

Akio looked at Yosho's homemade raygun. The kid must have modded it again, well enough to fry the demon's brain. But Yoshio looked as surprised as he was.

Then the shape of a woman materialized, straddling the back of the monster like a cowboy who had just broken a horse. Masami held onto the black bone handle of a wakizashi buried into the demon's neck all the way to the ruby guard.

"No!" a weak scream came from across the room. "No! You shouldn't have done that! You've ruined my . . . ruined everything!" Kumamori had lifted himself off the floor as much as he could in his trussed up position. His voice faltered, and he flopped back down and began to weep.

Masami withdrew her sword and climbed down from the demon as it started to waver and lose its shape. As she stepped away, it became gelatinous and wobbly, a mist beginning to rise from its rough skin.

Yoshio stood near the yakuza boss and his equally prone henchman. Both were tied up with audio cables, the clothed one unconscious, arms stretched behind him as if in a shoulder flexibility test. Yoshio and Masami had reached him just before he picked up his machine gun and had performed an encore of their attack on Kumamori. His gun sprouted from the floor, too, barrel down.

The double doors burst open, and all heads turned to see a lone man rush in with a drawn handgun and stop as he took in the scene before him. His mouth fell open at the sight of the huge, hideous demon melting away. He lowered his weapon, and searched their faces, settling his gaze on Masami. Their eyes met, and she felt the blood rush to her jugular notch. He was young and handsome, but more than that, his heart showed in his face, his courage and determination like a suit of armor.

He was the knight she had never needed and, thankfully, too late to get himself killed. But she was glad to see him there, breathless and confused, his muscled torso filling his crisp, button-down shirt in just the right way.

20
Enough

asami saw the horror and trepidation on Detective Fujimaki's face. She wanted to run to him, take him from that place, and tell him that it was okay now, tell him the truth about . . . everything. She was angry that he had tracked her down. What if he had gotten there only minutes earlier? He could be dead. But she was glad to see him. It meant more than she cared to admit.

"What the hell is that?" Fujimaki asked.

"Something you shouldn't have seen, officer, but no matter," Miyahara answered, and then whispered to the others, "We can take care of that."

"No!" Masami and Akio said together.

"No more killing," Akio continued. "I'm sick to death of it." He took off his mask and his voice altered back to his youthful timbre though still strained from battle. "No more innocent deaths, please."

"I didn't intend to kill him," Miyahara answered. "Only alter his memory."

"Oh," Akio said. "Okay . . . that's cool." And then he added, "You can do that?"

"Yes, it isn't *Men in Black*, but with the right pressure points, when he wakes up it will be easy to explain away."

"No," Masami said. "And it isn't cool." She glanced disapprovingly at Akio.

Fujimaki was in street clothes still. "You're alone, right?" she asked. "Didn't call this in?"

"No," the detective started. "I mean, yes, I'm alone. No, I didn't call it in. I didn't think it was safe, considering . . ."

She nodded to him. He had respected Masami's advice to leave the police out of it. Another good sign.

"He's fine," she said. "He won't talk about it." It was unsteady ground for Masami, but she trusted her instinct. Fujimaki was confused, but he wouldn't betray her.

The demon was wobbling and splurching, slowly melting into a mist. A rotten sulfur stench emanated from it, but Masami was too drained to care.

"By tomorrow, he won't accept it for real anyway," Yoshio said, his nose wrinkling.

"True," Miyahara answered. "The power of the human mind to explain away what is before its very eyes is quite staggering."

"I want to know," the detective said. "I see it. And I smell it. It's hideous. Was it alive? Where did it come from?"

"I'll tell you," Masami said. "Soon. We'll open that craft beer and I'll explain everything, okay?" She felt some embarrassment for saying that out loud, but her filter was off right now. She was drained and couldn't pretend she wasn't happy to see him.

Fujimaki looked uncomfortable. The huge demon was taking a while to completely vaporize, and the smell was not improving. He stood there, still holding his gun in both hands, shifting his weight, eyes intense and darting.

"You can put away your weapon," Miyahara said. "You won't need that now."

Fujimaki scanned the room, looking at the bundled yakuza, at Endo who stood at a distance, blood-spattered and shaken, at the guns embedded in the floor, the gelatinous blob of demon, and then back to Masami and the others. She nodded her approval to him. He holstered his gun.

"Speaking of explanations," Masami said, turning toward the sensei to take the heat off Fujimaki. "You owe us a pretty damn big one. Were you kidnapped? Or were you just playing some kind of game with us?"

Miyahara had a slight grin on his leathery face and Masami didn't like it one bit. "Yes," he stated flatly. "I was kidnapped. That is true. The rest will have to wait."

You will know.

He looked from Fujimaki to Masami. "But perhaps not over a craft beer." He smiled.

"I have a feeling you'll need something stronger," Yoshio said.

"Did you know?" Masami asked, suddenly angry with the teenager too. "Were you in on this?"

"No!" Yoshio said quickly. "No, I swear. I just know Sensei."

Akio looked at each of them in turn, taking it all in. "Am I missing something?"

"I think we both are," Fujimaki said. "But I'm pretty sure I'm the one who's the most in the dark."

"I will explain my part and everything that happened to me," Miyahara said. "Masami will apparently fill you in, detective. I hope she uses her best discretion."

A loud sob broke their standoff, and they all turned toward the two tied-up yakuza. The clothed one was still passed out, but the naked godfather's face was wet with tears and red with agony, his formerly imposing tattoos as unthreatening as a child's picture book. He looked down at his necklace in anguish. The gem was gone. Only a residue of green dust remained, the rest of it speckled the floor.

"That's . . . that's Mr. Kumamori," Fujimaki said. "What the hell is going on? Why is he naked?"

"That's kind of my fault," Masami said, and got a small pleasure out of the jealous snaps of the head from both Fujimaki and Akio. "I had to know he wasn't armed," she said, the subtlest of smiles on her lips. She wanted to let it out and grin like a schoolgirl, let Fujimaki see. The exhaustion of battle had worn her out, and in front of her stood the only man who had ever really stirred a feeling of attraction, the only man she could ever remember daydreaming about—she had never been a daydreamer. She contained the urge as best she could.

The demon's final remains slipped away in the brief silence that followed, an oily, transparent pudding fading into nothing, leaving a wet, sulfurous residue on the gold-flecked carpet.

The broken yakuza boss lifted his head, his arms still strung up behind him, tied to his legs with the microphone cable.

"You've ruined everything!" he wailed, snot and spittle spraying. "You've killed it. You've killed our brotherhood."

"No, you betraying piece of trash," said a voice from near him, raw and angry. It was Endo. He was shaking. "You're nothing but a weak buffoon!" He pointed to Masami and the others. "These people have saved our brotherhood! You were the one who was killing it! You were the one bending your back to be a slave to that thing! All of us were controlled. All of us were working with it against our will. Except for you! You wanted to be its toy, uncle! You wanted the false power it gave you! Even Kouda! Crazy Kouda." He faltered as he looked at the muscular arm lying bloodless on the carpet still gripping the machine gun. He pointed at the green dust in a small pile on the forearm. "He put those gems in him out of loyalty to you! Not to that big worm! You did that to him!

"Well, let me tell you something . . . *boss*." He spat the title like a dead bug from his mouth. "You were the worst puppet of all. The puppet who enjoys being . . . being manipulated, that doesn't even know it's a puppet. It was all a lie, uncle. You had no power. That thing wasn't loyal to you. But your men were!" He indicated Kouda's severed arm again, and the tied, unconscious man next to Kumamori. "They followed you blindly, even after that thing had no control over them. You killed Kouda! His death is on you, uncle!"

The godfather gave another wail and slumped over on top of his unresponsive follower.

Fujimaki looked at Endo and opened and closed his mouth once before saying, "Why? Why would they follow a godfather who was clearly not . . . in control of his faculties?"

Endo looked at the spatters of blood on his own hands and hung his head. "If the boss says the passing crow is white . . ."

"Then it is white," Fujimaki finished, nodding his head in understanding. Then, looking at Kumamori, he asked, "Is he bleeding?"

"Yes," Yoshio jumped in. "He was shot through his transverse abdominal muscle. From its location, it looks like it may have torn his inguinal ligament, but nothing life threatening. Apart from eventually bleeding to death, that is."

Fujimaki looked at him queerly.

"Everybody always looks at me like that," Yoshio said.

"We should get him to a hospital," the detective urged.

"Yes," agreed Masami. "But we need to get out of here first. You too. We'll call the police and then slip out unseen. Kumamori isn't going to bleed to death before emergency responders get here. We know a secret exit. We'll all catch up on the rest later."

"I'll make the call," Endo said. "There is a phone on the wall there." He pointed to a corner that looked to be a kind of workstation, a place where the gems had been sorted by size and shape. Now all that remained were indeterminate piles of green powder. He grimaced and walked to it. He looked to Masami for approval.

"Do it," she said.

He held the receiver with his shirt sleeve, dialed, and waited.

"There's been a murder," he said. "More than a few, actually." He paused, briefly listening, and said, "Yes, that's the place. . . . No, I don't know anything about a huge demon. . . . Okay. Great. See you soon then." He hung up.

"Already on their way. Apparently they've had a lot of panicked calls. We need to get out now."

"We?" Masami asked. "You're coming with us?"

"I . . . I love my uncle, but . . . I don't want this on my head. If it's all right . . . ?

"Of course," Masami said, and Yoshio nodded.

"And as long as Detective Fujimaki doesn't mind," Endo added with an awkward sneer toward the officer.

"You know me?" the detective asked.

"You've been profiled, yeah," Endo said. "As have all the hotshot young detectives who think they can shut down the brotherhood."

"Shut down . . . ? But I never . . ." Fujimaki trailed off, looking like someone had been reading his diary.

"Well, it sounds like you already know the way," Endo said to Masami. "So I'll follow you." He turned toward his naked, tattooed boss who whimpered softly now, his breath lurching in staccato sips, blood seeping from the gash in the side of his belly. "Farewell, uncle . . . Mr. Kumamori," he said. "Maybe I'll send you a care package in prison."

In a loose group, all their thoughts kept close, they exited to the ballroom and through the hidden door in the wall: kendo sensei, boy genius, photographer, reporter, cop, and gangster. Masami wondered at how poorly each of those titles fit them anymore. Endo waited for them all to go through, and then shut the door tight behind them.

For her own part, Masami wanted to let herself slip through the floor and simply drift down. Her physical self was exhausted, and she wanted to leave it behind to recover in weightlessness. But she endured, letting the elevator do its slow work, numb and slumped against its wall.

Someone was talking, but Akio was absent, too deep inside himself to hear. He huddled against the wall of the elevator, ignoring the motley group of misfits around him, all avoiding contact. He was working his way back to his identity as he shook off the demon's intrusive thoughts, shook off Akechi and the reverberations of battle. He was vibrating with the experience, twitching slightly, as if post traumatic stress were already setting in.

But it would pass. He felt vaguely numb to it already. That ancient part of Akechi, that battle-hardened warrior, was buried in him now, and Akio didn't like it. A younger him, only half a year younger, would have relished the thought of being some badass unbeatable warrior. Now it made him want to crawl off into a cave and disappear. He just wanted to be a second-rate photographer again who played video games, read manga, and whined about not being more respected at work. Only now he wouldn't whine. He'd be happy that he had a normal, easy life.

The battle lust had drained from him, and he ached everywhere. The mask was quiet in his backpack, tucked into the simple Faraday cage Yoshio had constructed.

The voices around him took shape.

"I'll be in Kofu," Endo was saying to Masami. "In time, I'd like you to come visit. You, the Mask here, and the boy." He looked at Miyahara nervously. "I suppose you, too," he said to the sensei. "I wasn't sure I could trust you, but you fought the demon. So that's good enough for me."

He glanced at Fujimaki and turned away.

Masami waited for more.

"Don't worry," Endo continued. "You three saved my life. A yakuza doesn't forget that kind of thing. A true yakuza, that is. I am Kumamori's nephew, and even though there are others with more experience and higher in rank, people respect me. I think when they hear the story of how I resisted the demon, when they realize what happened, well . . . I might have a chance of leading, of maybe taking his place. Though it scares me," he added toward the floor.

"Of course there'll be a discussion, a vote from the remaining bosses, and when they decide, there'll be a ceremony. Maybe it won't be me, but I'm determined to have some power in the Tezuka-gumi. I imagine the syndicate itself won't be so all powerful anymore. All the newly acquired brothers and clans will return to their own. But either way, I owe you. And I want to repay your kindness and your bravery."

Masami's eyes searched Akio's, asking his silent opinion. And strangely, Akio wasn't weirded out by that. It felt right. It felt normal. She was his friend, and she trusted his opinion. Why shouldn't she? He didn't say anything; he didn't nod or even smile. He only held her gaze and knew that she got his answer.

The elevator stopped, and the door opened.

"I'll be expecting you," Endo said with an almost sheepish half-smile. "I trust you know how to lock up." He walked the hallway, exiting into the underground station.

When he was gone, Akio spoke.

"Meet at my place at 1 p.m." he said, addressing Masami, Yoshio, and Miyahara. "We could all use some sleep first. No offense, detective, but we have some personal things to discuss." He felt odd, confident. He was matter-of-factly telling a police officer that he wasn't welcome and didn't feel terrified. He didn't feel the need to backpedal and apologize repeatedly. He owned it. He was on even ground.

"Understood," Fujimaki said, then turned to Masami. "But . . ." he started.

"Come by my place tonight," Masami answered. "I'll tell you what I can. No promises that you'll believe a shred of it."

Akio felt a strange mix of jealousy and joy creep up inside. He loved Masami. That was clear to him now. He had avoided admitting that to himself for a long time. But as he looked at her, her pale face touched with pink, the rogue strand of hair playing across her eyebrow, her black eyes afire with something other than irritation at him, he found that he was happy for her. He found that he loved her even more, and that what he felt was more profound than the love he had imagined.

"Okay, I'll see you in a bit," Akio said. "Right now, I've got something to do." He smiled at Masami, and she gave the slightest smile back. It was enough.

21
Blood

Akio straddled his desk chair in his tiny apartment, facing the rest of the group. Masami sat on his futon that lay in a mess of bedding on the floor. He had tried to straighten it up but had been too groggy from having just awoken, and his muscles ached far too much to be of any use. He was embarrassed at the state of his place, but she told him that it didn't matter. It was trivial compared to what they had to talk about.

"As long as you don't have any dirty underwear lying around," she had said.

He was pretty sure he didn't.

Yoshio sat on the floor, and Miyahara stood leaning on his newly acquired white-handled katana. Akio wondered if he ever sat down.

There was a heaviness to the air, and no one wanted to be the first to speak. Akio was reminded of that long evening when he, Masami, and Miyahara had sat in the hotel room after their first encounter with the demon samurai. Everything had felt unreal. His world had been cracked open like a cheap snow globe, and as the sparkly liquid leaked out, all manner of strange things had seeped in to replace it.

That was the night he had first worn the mask. He had lost himself in Akechi's life more than four hundred years ago. He had felt like such a failure then. He had felt like he had let them all down so completely.

Now, brief months later, the plastic cover of that snow globe had been torn off utterly, leaving him and Masami exposed like naked foreigners in a terrifying new world—naked foreigners with unfamiliar and deadly powers.

And here they were together again. Akio had worn the mask of his own choosing, and thanks to Miyahara, he had been able to control it. He had been able to maintain enough of *himself* to go after the sensei and try to rescue him. He had been able to become enough of *Akechi* to fight the yakuza and the deadly robots, to help in killing the horrid demon that had threatened to imprison the world with its mind. And now it seemed that there was some question of whether Miyahara had really needed to be rescued at all.

Finally the sensei spoke.

"I am humbled by your deeds," he said with a reverent tone, and yet something else lingered under his expression. "I am grateful for my rescue. And even more so for the vanquishing of such a foe."

"Can it," Masami said. "You didn't even need rescuing, did you? You were never actually kidnapped."

"That is not true," the sensei said. "I was truly kidnapped. With my wounds still not healed, I was not able to fight my way out. And . . . they had guns. There's only so much a man with a sword can do. Unless, of course . . ." He looked toward Akio and raised an eyebrow.

"It wasn't me," Akio said. "It was Akechi. I just let his instincts take over."

"Akechi is dead, young man. He died hundreds of years ago and you freed his spirit underneath Kofu Castle. He is gone. You are the one who controls this body." He pointed a rough, sinewy finger at Akio.

"But the mask. His spirit is in the mask. I couldn't have done any of that without it."

"Do you think so?" The sensei asked rhetorically, and then becoming more animated, he went on. "What about Miss Sato? She has no mask, and yet she is able to do extraordinary feats. I can't do what she does. In spite of my training and my own . . ." He paused, considering. ". . . peculiarity, I would be hard pressed to best either of you in combat."

"And yet," Masami interrupted, standing. "You didn't need us to rescue you, did you? Stop avoiding the question."

Miyahara's smile had depths that Akio couldn't fathom. The old man had experiences of a kind that even what they been through in the last few months were of no comparison. "No," he finally said. "I didn't. I could have escaped. That's true."

"I knew it," Masami said. She was angry. Akio had seen her irritated plenty, but this was real anger. This was another level entirely. She stood to face the sensei as she laid into him. "You made us risk our lives, made us kill innocent people . . ." She glanced at Akio and he winced, the bloody scene at the elevator flashing in his mind. ". . . made us risk who knows how many more lives. All for some demented game or . . . who knows what! You are no better than the demons you profess to kill!"

Miyahara let her finish. He was patient and still. When he was sure she had said her peace, he said, "I see your anger, and I understand. But you are incorrect. Let me explain."

Masami stood firm, only raising her eyebrows slightly, waiting for an answer to refute.

"As I said, I could have escaped. I, too, was given the task of collecting the demon's gems." He nodded to Yoshio. "And when Kumamori saw me following along with the others he assumed I had acquiesced. I worked with them enough to learn all about their operation, but I steered as clear from the demon as possible."

"How were you not mind-controlled?" Akio interrupted.

"Do you think I made those nasty pills for you?" he chuckled lightly. "That was an afterthought. When they had me chained to the wall, they presented me with a gem. I fought off the demon's intrusions, but it was a struggle. I knew I wouldn't hold out for long."

"Using your brain?" Yoshio asked.

"No," the sensei answered. "My blood." He did not elaborate.

"While they tortured me, trying to discern my motives, I also gathered information from them. I discovered the location of their main operations, and confirmed that their demon boss was on the top floor. They argued about whether or not they should use the gem on me. One of them was insistent they should only use it to convert rival yakuza, those men who deserve it, as if it were an honor, while another was of the mind that if they were building an army, they needed numbers, and didn't care where they came from. Eventually the gem won out, but when it failed to work, they fell to arguing again, fearing something was wrong with it or that they had misused it. Then they went quiet, and seemed to get angry at me as one, all staring at me at turning red. They roughed me up as a parting gift and left me there bleeding, threatening to return soon.

"When they were gone I managed to slip my bonds." He offered no explanation as to how. "I returned home only long enough to mix a batch of pills. I had been working on them for . . . other purposes, but realized they might be exactly what I needed. They were untested, but I knew there was no time.

"You hadn't tested them?" Akio interrupted, and then groaned. "What the hell was in those things anyway?"

"It was a blend of protective elements; rare herbs, roots, and minerals, a recipe that a dear friend taught me. I modified it to suit my needs."

"Just herbs and minerals? That's enough to stop demon mind-control?"

"An eldritch power assisted," Miyahara added. "A kind of magic spell, you could say."

Yoshio visibly flinched, his eyes squinting at his sensei.

Akio had no response. Demons, ghostly powers, and mind-possessing masks had all proven themselves quite real; why not magic too?

Myahara smiled and went back to his explanation. "Thankfully, they worked well. The gems had no effect, as you also learned. I could have walked out the door easily."

"Then why the hell didn't you?" Masami fumed.

"Simply because you *can* do something does not make it the right thing to do." Miyahara held her gaze calmly. "I could not have killed that demon without you three. At least neither efficiently nor quickly. He was a bigger foe than those to which I am accustom, and with much bigger goals, surrounded by crowds of utterly loyal followers. Vanquishing it was far more important than being rescued. So I learned what I could and trusted that you three were doing your part."

Akio understood. Miyahara had infiltrated the enemy and remained as a spy, a sleeper agent to be activated when the rest of the team had arrived. But Masami was unconvinced.

"Our part," she seethed. "Why would you not simply have come to us and told us what was going on?"

"Would you all have done what you did if I had escaped?" the sensei asked. "Would you have taken the drastic but necessary actions? Or would you have left it to Yoshio and me, feeling your responsibility complete?"

"I'm sure we could have been convinced," Masami said.

"Certainly," Miyahara answered. "But at what cost? How would I have proven to you the gravity of the situation? How would I have instilled the urgency that was needed? Surely you saw the progress. Politicians were the new targets. The prime minister would have been next. Already the gems were being sent overseas. But would you have taken swift action? Possibly, but I am doubtful. You might have discussed and gone back to your jobs, thinking it was no different than any crooked politician gaining power. It couldn't be that bad. But then it would be. It would be beyond any bad politician you've ever experienced, because the checks and balances would have been removed. And then it would be too late. What forces would we have been up against then? How many people would have had to die? When the demon had control of the state? Of the military? I couldn't take that chance. And so, because you felt a debt to me for helping you in Kofu, because you felt I was in danger, you witnessed the reality of the situation firsthand, and you helped as quickly as you could. And that is why we succeeded. I exploited your good nature to get you on board quickly."

Masami took a deep breath. Any second flames would shoot from her eyeballs. She said slowly, emphasizing each word, "I almost killed Akio."

Miyahara sighed. "Yes, I was made aware of that. Kumamori saw the whole thing from his glass cage, his Egg. He came to me, furious that he'd lost control of you, as if it were him with the mind control powers and not the demon. He ordered me to go after you, to kill you both."

"That could've been your perfect ruse to get out of there," Akio said, understanding Masami's anger better now. "We'd seen what the demon could do at that point. We'd definitely have helped you then."

"It is more likely, yes. But there is more to it." The sensei turned to Masami. "To address your concern directly, I am grateful you did not kill Akio. That was a danger I had not foreseen. But . . . I am also grateful that you were briefly controlled."

Masami huffed and shook her head. Akio was pretty sure she was about to punch him.

"Had the demon's mind not controlled you," Miyahara continued, "you would have needed weeks, months, perhaps even years to learn to use your ability so expertly. But you learned it immediately because the demon understood its potential and knew how to manipulate you. Without that knowledge, we may have been defeated today. At the least, the battle would have been more difficult. More may have died. Perhaps even one of us."

Masami closed her eyes, her breath wavered. Akio wanted her to forget about it, to move on. He had already told her as much. Although it felt good that she cared, that she worried for him.

"And if I had killed him?" Masami asked before opening her eyes again.

"You didn't," Miyahara answered curtly. "Waste no time worrying over things that did not occur. Yoshio provided a brilliant distraction and a way to temporarily short-circuit the connection. This is how a cooperative team triumph's over a single-minded enemy."

There was something in the way the sensei said *team* that struck Akio, but he couldn't quite pin it down.

"Yoshio, you have been rather silent," Miyahara continued. "Do you also have questions of me?"

The teenager sat up straight as if the teacher had just called on him.

"Only one, Sensei." He looked down at the wide bracelet still on Miyahara's wrist. It was a patinated bronze with a delicate metalwork of clashing swords and shields. They looked like Roman *gladii* and *parma*.

"Ah this," Miyahara replied, guessing Yoshio's question. "I have told you all that I have a collection of things I have found over the years, that I would add Akio's mask to it."

Akio felt a pang of possessiveness, as if the sensei had threatened to take away his camera, or worse. Would Miyahara take the mask? Shouldn't he? *Yes, yes, take it. It would be best.* But Akio's gut roiled at the thought.

"Most of these things should remain locked away," the sensei continued, "but every now and then, I realize one will prove quite useful. I found this in the Dinaric Alps of Croatia some twelve years ago, in the lair of a *bukavac*, a six-legged, reptilian demon that had been strangling the locals. I retrieved it when I returned home to craft the pills. And I am glad I did. Anything else?" he asked his teenage apprentice.

"Apart from the many questions that statement brought to mind, no, sensei," Yoshio said.

"Another time."

Yoshio nodded. "I would, however, like to add an observation, if I may, Sensei."

"Go ahead."

"It's difficult to say what would have happened if you had escaped on your own," Yoshio said. "Because changing any element of one side of an equation, by necessity, alters the other side. Similarly, adding or removing an element from a chemical formula will unfailingly change the chemical compound, often quite drastically. For my part, I can't say with certainty that I would have come up with the signal blocking gun. In fact, I am inclined to think that I wouldn't have, at least, not as quickly. I would have looked to you for answers, for guidance. Without you there, I was forced to think for myself."

Miyahara smiled. "And that is a key element right there. No one could look to me, the experienced demon hunter, for answers. By necessity, you were forced to be resourceful, and doing so saved us all."

Akio felt the weight of what the sensei said hanging in the room. He got it. As deceptive as it seemed, he understood.

"Your abduction was the catalyst that propelled us to succeed," Yoshio said, as if giving the answer to a test question.

"So you used us," Masami said. Her anger had dropped into bitterness. "You tested us."

"I knew when I saw the first gem at the grocer's that something very wrong was at work," Miyahara answered. "The gem was unnatural. I was afraid I might get myself into trouble, so I told Yoshio to get your help if I didn't return. I trusted that, if all was how I expected, you would be the only ones who *could* help. Akio's potential abilities were obvious, after the incident at the hotel, though he needed control. Yours were unknown, but I knew something must have happened for you to survive such an encounter as you had with the namakubikamen. Something in you must have altered. Otherwise, I do not believe you would have returned to us. But even if nothing had changed, it was your tenacity and intelligence that helped us to survive that demon's arrogant rampage. That and Akio's courage. With the two of you, I knew we could triumph again."

My courage. Akio marveled at the sensei's words, only now the truth of them sinking in. He *had* been courageous. Even without Akechi. Sometimes even in spite of him.

"Eventually," the tough old man continued, "I may have been able to figure out how to take down the demon on my own. But by then, it may have been too late. There may have been irreparable damage done to Japan and the soul of its people."

"Soul of its people?" Akio asked. "A little heavy, isn't it?"

"Oh yes," Miyahara answered, misunderstanding Akio's meaning. "It would have been very heavy indeed."

Th e sensei went on. "I was certain something profound had happened to you both under the castle in Kofu, something . . . transformative. And I trusted that you would find a way to use those new changes to our advantage." He gave a satisfied grin. "I was not wrong."

Miyahara looked over the three of them, his eyes resting on Masami. "Yes, it was a *test*, if you choose to call it that. It was also a solution that I did not know exactly how would manifest. If you had failed, you two," he looked at Akio and Masami in turn, "or if you had refused to offer assistance, then I would have moved on. I would have done my best to deal with the demon, with Yoshio's help of course." He gave a grim grin to the teenager. "And we would have left you to figure out your new lives on your own.

"But that is not what happened. And for that I am truly grateful." He scanned the faces of each of them, his thoughts hidden, buried in the wrinkles about his eyes.

"Now," he said, suddenly chipper, "we can move forward together. Now we can truly stem the tide that is rising against the innocent. Together we can beat back the deadly foes escaping the Hells and perhaps find a way to seal their exit. This *test* was not given by me, not truly, as you must know. It was given by Fate. And we cannot spit in the face of Fate. We must let her wisdom guide us. As it did once long ago when . . ." But he trailed off, his dark eyes distant.

"Nothing is accidental," he said finally.

The sensei seemed to be looking into some other world, lost in a memory, but Akio felt inspired by his words, almost spellbound. Fate had called them together. This test was from some higher power, and they were meant to stem the tide of demons issuing from Hell. He was at once thrilled and terrified. Th is was not a life he wanted. And yet . . . it sounded glorious, like a comic book come to life.

"Wait a second." Masami's strident voice of realism cut through the room. "Your flowery words aren't going to get me to ride off into the sunset with you and boy wonder here. What makes you think we even want to help you further? You tricked us into getting involved when, you're right, we might not have. And although things mostly worked out for the best, why should we trust you from here on out? When will the next trick be played? When will the next test be?"

"Every moment is a test of some kind, is it not?"

"You manipulated us. I understand why. But you did," Masami insisted. "I don't bounce back from that easily."

"To see the truth and acknowledge your limitations are worthy achievements, but to understand the greater purpose and rise above those limitations is irreproachable."

"Stop talking in platitudes!" Masami shouted. "I am not one of your awestruck teenage students!"

"Fine," Miyahara said pointedly. "Let's not pretend. We share a bond that was created under the castle in Kofu. We share a common understanding of an existing reality of which the vast majority of people are unaware, and one that may very well come for them in the night. Or possibly in broad daylight. We also share a common humanity that dictates that we do not want those unknowing innocents to die unnecessarily. And therefore we will help. It is what you did today. And, knowing you as I know you now, you will do again tomorrow."

"Will I?" Masami spat. "You know what I have to do tomorrow? I have to make up a story my editor will buy and hope I don't lose my job! Akio and I will both likely be packing up our things by the end of the week."

"Well," the sensei shrugged. "You are welcome in Kofu. I'm sure I can find work for you." He said it with a certainty that felt like he *wanted* them to lose their jobs, that it had been his plan all along to get them to join him as fledgling demon hunters.

Akio was split in two, and not the usual him versus Akechi. Part of him wanted to stand and shout, "Yes! I was born to fight demons, and I will do my part for my country and the world!" It would give him purpose. It would pull him out of the rat race struggle to move up at the *Dainichi*. If he could get regular investigative journalist jobs, that would be something important at least, but it still paled in comparison to ridding the world from actual demons. He could be a hero.

But the other half wanted to crawl into a dark corner and disappear. This experience had nearly broken him. His body ached like it had never ached before. He had never in his life experienced such tremendous pain and exhaustion. A mediocre life and a job that was occasionally fulfilling but paid his rent sounded very pleasant compared to battling demons on the daily. Maybe he'd find a nice woman who would put up with him and might even really like his photography. They could live blissfully unaware of the evil around them. Let the demon hunters like Miyahara take care of that.

And then he thought of Matsuoka, the innkeeper in the town at the base of Mount Fuji, and how he and his wife had been blissfully unaware. Look where that got him. A beheaded wife, a shattered mind, and a town that believes him guilty.

"I am helping the world in the best way I know how," Masami said. "I am writing the truth. That is, when I don't have to make up palatable stories for my editor." Her lips pressed tightly together. Akio knew this look all too well. She was still far from being convinced.

"I would not ask you to stop writing the truth," the sensei said, and gave a slight, respectful bow. "But there is a time for discretion."

A silent moment passed, when Akio and Masami shared a look, and Miyahara and Yoshio shared a very different look. One was of uncertainty and apprehension, the other of acceptance and loyalty.

"We are glad you're okay," Akio said. "We were really worried."

"Thank you," answered the sensei, bowing again. "It is nice to be worried after."

"So, all this possible future demon-hunting aside, uh, what did you mean about your . . . peculiarity?" Akio asked.

"Ah, that." The sensei looked about the room, considering how to answer, or if to answer at all, it seemed.

"I'd like to know that too," Masami said. "Something to do with your blood?" She was impatient, her eyes burrowing into Miyahara.

"Yes," he answered. He sighed, and then looking them over once more, he decided. "It is not the original vintage, you could say. It is a long story and I would love to share it with you sometime. But for now, suffice it to say that it pertains to our commonalities.

"You, Mr. Tsukino, have been imbued with the memories and abilities of an ancient samurai demon. You, Miss Sato, have been granted access to the netherworld, by accident it seems, but nonetheless granted, and now you can enter and exit at will. I . . ." he paused. "Only three others know this truth about me: my master, and two other demon hunters that I helped to train, but are now far from here."

The group was silent, at rapt attention to the sensei. Finally he continued.

"Long years ago, my blood was exchanged with that of a demon in order to save my life."

Miyahara's face hardened at the memory. He clearly did not want to talk about it.

"That is enough for now," he added sharply but not unkindly. "Perhaps if you drop by some time, I'll be feeling loquacious enough to tell you the rest. Yoshio and I will be going. If you find you have more concerns, you know where to contact me," the sensei said. "Again, you have my complete gratitude, and though its people are mostly unaware, all of Japan's as well."

Yoshio retrieved his suitcase, and the two moved to the door.

Miyahara turned back toward Akio and Masami.

"If you would like a change of scenery, the dojo at Maizuru Castle Park can be very peaceful."

He smiled a pleasant, knowing smile and shut the door behind them.

22

Disarmed

The sun had gone down and Masami sat at her table caressing its cold smooth surface. It was solid. It was real. It was simple. She needed all of those things right now. It was too easy to slip away and lose track of what was right in front of her, too easy to disappear and forget her life. It felt good to be non-corporeal, to be as light as air, to be a ghost. But it was a dangerous kind of good, and she needed to be grounded right now. She needed something to get a grip on, literally.

She reached up and held her pendant in her hand, the M that stood for Mantetsu, for Masami, and for Mother. She felt the tears fill her lower lids and wet drops slowly slide down her face.

The netherworld was real. The doors the Sorter had pushed people through still haunted her. Where did they lead? Were they simply rooms within that world? Or were they other worlds completely? Her instinct told her it was the latter.

Her notebook lay open in front of her, paper lifting and slightly warped from the words that had so recently rained down upon it. It was an anchor too, a friend in the darkness. It was creation and meditation, therapy and duty.

She had struggled with how to write the story. How could she not write the truth when so many people had witnessed the demon and had been subjected to its mind-control? But even with that corroboration, no one would believe it. She knew. Tanaka would never print it. Just by giving him that story her job would be in danger.

But then she had realized the truth behind the truth. It was the reason no one would believe. It was the reason Tanaka wouldn't print the story even if he knew it to be true.

None of the witnesses would speak. Especially the yakuza.

They were Japanese, stoic and silent, fully obsessed with avoidance of shame. Between each other, they would know, but not one of them would dare talk publicly about a demon that took over their syndicate, that nearly dominated the entire yakuza. They'd be in danger of losing far more than a finger to make amends.

Maybe some employees in the building would speak out; maybe a few. But no politician would talk, no CEO, no one with any public persona. No one with something to lose. If they did, they'd be ridiculed.

She knew then exactly what she would write.

She had napped fitfully that afternoon, after they all met at Akio's place. She had walked to the train station, deliberately feeling every footstep, feeling the rumble and shake of the train as it vibrated along the tracks. She stood in the train car, relishing the shift of weight as she leaned into each stop to keep her balance. The hot air that hit her as the doors opened was her mother's breath. The brush of people moving past, jostling her, was the ocean, its waves lapping at her tired body. She was here *in homine*. She was a woman, physical and tingling with life. She was the train. She was Tokyo. She was all of Japan.

When she arrived home, she went to the kitchen to put Fujimaki's gift, the craft beer, in the refrigerator, but found it was already there. She was sure she had put it on the counter. Then she remembered that she had left the detective in her apartment.

Then she lay in bed, afraid to sleep but needing it dearly. Dreams were too much like being a ghost, and potentially worse for the lack of control. Dreadful images awaited her there. Her eyes would close briefly only to snap open again repeatedly. After an hour of this, she left them open, let them adjust to the daylight filtering through the blinds from across the room. It was then that the story had come to her, the truth behind the truth.

She rose, climbed down from her loft, and made coffee.

Then she wrote.

Now she waited for him, nervous and anxious, but also impatient. She wanted him there. She wanted to get it over with. Whatever was meant to happen, she wanted it done. It was how she went through most things. The faster she got through something that frightened her, the sooner it was over. Rarely were things as scary as her nerves made them out to be, but it didn't stop her from dreading them.

Nerves. People would be surprised that she had any. But she was as nervous as the next person. Her stolid persona was simply a thick makeup that she could apply flawlessly in a mirrorless dark room if she needed to. It was a practiced armor, built stronger with each wearing. Though lately, she could feel cracks on its surface.

When the doorbell rang, she buzzed Fujimaki in without a response. She downed the rest of her coffee, now lukewarm, in one shot. The beer bottle was in her hand when she let him into her apartment.

"Let's crack this now," she said in greeting. "I need a drink."

She retrieved two glasses and poured, gesturing for the detective to sit at her dining room table, running a finger once more over its smooth, *real* surface as she did.

They sat in silence, a soft clink of glasses, eyes searching each other was the only toast. The beer was sublime, a rich ale that hit the tongue with the smoothness of cream, a hint of bitter, but not overloaded with hops as was the recent craft beer trend. She smiled.

"Thank you," she finally said.

"It was nothing," he said. "The liquor store guy recommended it. I hope you like it."

"It's delicious," she said. "But that's not what I meant."

Fujimaki raised his eyebrows.

"I mean coming after me. It was stupid, but . . . nice."

"And completely unnecessary, too," the detective said. "You obviously can handle yourself. I feel like I was trying to be some clichéd hero in an old fairy tale, trying to rescue a damsel in distress captured by a dragon, only to arrive to see the damsel with her foot on the dead dragon's neck."

A light chuckle escaped Masami's throat. "Yeah, something like that. But still . . . it's nice."

It was silent for a few moments longer as they sipped their beers. Then Fujimaki spoke.

"So . . . speaking of dragons. What the hell was that thing?"

Masami didn't know how to approach the subject carefully. She wasn't good at easing into delicate topics. She was a reporter, and she reported. She told it like it was.

But she tried, for his sake.

"I wouldn't have believed it even a few months ago. And I don't expect you to now. I expect that you will think I'm crazy. But—"

"I won't," he interjected.

"But," she ignored him, continuing, "when you do think I'm crazy, I can actually prove it to you."

"That you're crazy?" he joked, his disarming smile radiant, that infernally unfair, genuine, and honest smile.

And this time she let herself be disarmed.

"No." She laughed. "No, at least, I don't think so." She swirled her beer back and forth gently in her glass. "I can prove that the world is not as it seems, and perhaps that will get you to believe what I'm going to tell you."

"I'll believe you," he said matter-of-factly, and there was no denying that he would.

"You gotta listen first," she said, suppressing another uninvited giggle. The beer was already beginning to affect her. "How strong is this beer, anyway?" she asked out loud, grabbing the bottle to read the label. "Eight percent. Okay, high but not ridiculous. I guess I'm just exhausted."

"We can do this another time if you prefer."

"No!" she said a little too loudly. "No, dammit. I need to tell you. You need to know." Her breath caught in her chest, but she pushed it out deliberately and tried to regain her calm. She refilled both of their glasses even though they were only half empty. She was stalling.

"You only got one of these?" she asked sarcastically.

"It's a big bottle," he answered. "I thought . . ."

"No, I'm kidding. It's fine." She took another sip, deeper this time.

"It was a demon," she blurted out. "That thing you saw melting into the floor was a demon."

Fujimaki said nothing at first. He looked at her curiously. He was trying to tell if she was joking or not; that much was obvious. When it became clear that she wasn't, he said, "Okay. Tell me more."

Masami exhaled loudly. "Well . . . there's a lot to tell. Not sure how much time you have."

"Lots." He smiled. "Got all night."

All night?

She wondered if that was a not-so-veiled hint. Was he expecting to stay the night? That was a bit much of him to presume, wasn't it? They hadn't even had a proper date, and she wasn't sure she would accept if he asked her out. It could pose a serious conflict of interest for future stories, especially if she ever got arrested in Kofu again. And yet, it could be quite advantageous. Was she really even debating this? Underneath the nice guy exterior, he was probably just like every other man who had tried to get her into bed.

But who was she kidding? It was exactly what she wanted.

"All night," she repeated, hoping that her inner thoughts hadn't escaped as she said it. Fujimaki was not like the others. She prided herself on her instincts, her gut feelings about people. It had rarely failed her before. And if it failed tonight, so be it. There was nothing she couldn't escape anymore. If it all went wrong, he couldn't hurt her.

Not physically anyway.

"You'll never find the Kofu Head Collector," she said. And she proceeded to tell him about the demon under the castle and all that had happened there. She told how she had been taken into the netherworld, how Akio had aided in the demon's death and what had actually put Miyahara in the hospital.

"Wait," he stopped her. "Miyahara was stabbed through the gut in that room and pinned to the wall?"

"Yes, we thought he had been killed. There was blood everywhere."

"But that can't be. We saw the gouged-out stone. Looked like something had been thrust in there hard. But there was no blood at all."

Masami looked into Fujimaki's eyes. He was telling the truth.

"His blood . . . he said . . ." She trailed off. "Never mind." Trying to explain what little she knew about Miyahara was too much to add into the mix at the moment. It would only bring more questions that she couldn't answer.

Instead she told him of Yoshio's request for their help when the sensei had gone missing, of how the demon used its gem-like secretions to connect with and dominate the minds of those outside of its immediate presence.

"Yoshio is somehow immune," she said, "too smart for it, but the rest of us . . ." She dropped her head briefly, remembering how she had been controlled, how she had almost killed Akio. She skipped that part and went on to tell Fujimaki—Tadao, he insisted—how it had targeted the yakuza syndicates and was taking them over one at a time. It was certainly why some of his fellow officers had been compromised.

She told him how Nakama Robotics had been resurrected by the yakuza and were creating robots that were far more advanced than the current technology. "It's something to do with the demon's knowledge," she said. "When I . . ." *was controlled, I knew things about myself, I learned to control my ability so quickly.* "I think it must have been guiding the engineers' minds."

She felt like she had dumped a landfill of information on him. She hurried to wrap it up and see just how crazy he thought she was.

"We finally found Miyahara, and together we killed the demon. That's when you showed up."

"Just like that," he said. "I have this strange feeling you're leaving a little bit out. And when I say a little bit . . ."

"You mean a lot. I know. I am."

"How did you kill something like that?" he asked in a way that didn't commit him to believing the story, but didn't deny it either. "How did you fight through so many yakuza, so many of these other people who were also controlled?"

"That's the real question isn't it? The thing I've been having the hardest time saying." She fidgeted with her glass, now empty, and grabbed the bottle to pour more. It was also empty.

"Damn. Well, here goes."

She let herself drift into the netherworld.

Fujimaki startled and looked around. "Where the hell . . . ?" He looked under the table. He stood up and looked around the room. He went into the kitchen. "Where are you?" he called and then turned to see her still seated at the table, wiping a tear from one eye.

"What the hell?" he asked. "You weren't there. Where did you go?"

"I didn't go anywhere really," she answered. "I was right here the whole time, just not *right here*." She waved one hand in a circle, as if that would mean anything to him.

"Let me show you again," she said, and faded out right in front of him. He jerked back but then went to the chair that she still occupied, only now in a different plane of existence. He put his hand right through her to rest on the chair. His arm was enveloped by her up to the shoulder. She felt his warm body thrill inside her. She felt the blood pulsing in his lean, muscular arm. His face pushed right up to hers, their lips almost touching. Only he didn't know.

"It's cold," he said, and pulled his arm back. She reappeared, feeling the weight of her pendant pressed against her chest, her eyes watery red. He jumped back at the sight.

"That's what happens," she said, "when you touch a ghost."

"A . . . ghost?" Fujimaki looked pale, bewildered.

"Yes, essentially. I'm not dead, don't worry. I'm very much alive." She stood and went to him. "I'm not cold. Not now." She put a hand on his chest. His heart was beating rapidly. She had the strangest notion of reaching into him and wrapping her hand around it, squeezing it until it stopped. She could literally do that. But it was last thing on earth she wanted. Instead, she began to unbutton the shirt that fit his muscled torso so very well.

23
The Story

"This story is outrageous," Tanaka said, as he examined Masami's submitted article and Akio's photos spread across his desk. Akio sat next to Masami trying to remain still and quiet. She looked as sleepy as he felt, and no wonder. Once everyone had left his place, he had passed out, but his dreams had been terrifying, and he woke often. He imagined her night hadn't been much different. She glanced groggily back at him, her glasses reflecting the first red glow of the morning sun as it tickled the taller building across the street.

Something was different about her. She was tired, true, but there was a kind of satisfaction in her drowsiness. Maybe her dreams hadn't been as bad after all. There was a hint of anxiety at the circumstances, but she seemed comfortable to show it to him, which diffused it. She raised her eyebrows slightly, as much of a smile as she would dare in front of Tanaka.

The editor-in-chief shuffled through some photos and separated a couple out from the others. Then he picked up Masami's article again. "Outrageous," he repeated. "The yakuza syndicates joining forces to stage a coup against Kumamori? Nakama Robotics secretly creating robot slaves for the mob bosses? And a giant, blubbery monster?" he laughed.

Akio shifted nervously in his seat. *Did Masami really write that?*

Tanaka turned to them and laughed again. "Completely outrageous!" He turned and looked out at the slowly lightening sky. When he turned back around, he wore a grin as wide as the window.

"I love it!" He stood up and started pacing behind his desk. "What did these baboons see to think it was some kind of monster? And so many of them with similar stories! Throngs of people claiming it. But the yakuza say it was all a hoax, huh? Some kind of giant puppet that was destroyed in a fire fight! It was all theatre to cover up the coup against Kumamori. You can't make this stuff up! And they have the giant chaise lounge to prove it! How you two managed to be there when all this went down, and Tsukino, how you got those pictures inside the yakuza headquarters, I don't even want to know."

"Just lucky, I guess, sir."

"And the cream of the crop: these photos of Kumamori being escorted out of the building naked! They are pure gold. Pure gold! And no one has all this. This is ours! Everyone else will get this second hand. The *Asahi*? Nope. The *Yomiuri*? Nope! *Chunichi? Sankei?* Nope! Nope! It's all ours! The *Dainichi* wins this one!"

A grin had started to creep across Akio's face. They weren't getting fired! He had been certain this would be his last day at the paper.

"I want this in the morning news! This goes out today! Have it cleaned up and back on my desk in an hour. And this photo," he said, pointing to the one of Kumamori weeping and naked in the arms of the police. "This is our lead photo. This is front page!"

Akio and Masami both rose quickly, thanked Tanaka, and headed for the door. They had a lot of work to do in a short time.

"You two!" the editor called to them, and they turned back to face him. "I never thought I'd say this, but . . . you two make a great team. Keep up the good work."

Together they bowed and moved quickly out of his office. Akio felt radiant. Suddenly the lack of sleep meant nothing to him. He was as chipper as if he'd slept ten hours on a cloud.

Masami winked at him before heading to her desk, and Akio almost skipped to his.

The story went out on time, and it felt like the *Dainichi* had won an award for newspaper of the century. Tanaka was laughing randomly throughout the day, taking phone calls with glee, waltzing through the office like a king, and complimenting everyone he came into contact with. It was a glorious day.

At lunchtime, Akio walked over to Masami's desk. In spite of the festive mood, she was clacking away at her keyboard again, a stern look on her face, working furiously on some new article. She looked serious again. She was back in her glory, words exploding across her screen like a black tidal wave.

Akio didn't say a thing. He liked seeing her like this. It was right. It was safe. No one was trying to chop off their heads or control their minds. No robots or yakuza were trying to kill them. As amazing as it had all been, as thoroughly bonded as they had become, as fantastic as it had been to see Masami fight and disappear at will—even though she had almost killed him—this right here was the correct order of things. Masami was the best writer he had ever read. She was his friend. And he understood now that she wasn't like him. She needed her space. She wasn't a needy high maintenance ball of nerves like he was. And that was completely fine. That was just as it should be.

He smiled to himself and turned to go.

"Where should we eat?" he heard Masami say, as the typing stopped and she put her computer to sleep. "I'm starving."

Akio stopped and turned back to her, knowing he must look like a confused puppy. She rose and walked confidently toward the exit, not looking back, her black pants suit as sharp as her gait, her straight black hair swaying above her shoulders.

Akio hurried to catch up.

EPILOGUE
A Prayer

Noboru Akechi stood before a massive ashvattha tree. A doorway was open in the bole and a serene, yellow glow came from within. Lava spat and roiled around him, but the tree remained untouched and beautiful.

The memory of his trials flooded back to him. The Buddha had told him he would not remember for a very long time, and until this moment he had not. Now the torture and indignity he had felt, first at the mockery of the many heads of King Byoudou and then in the watery depths with King Toshi's leviathan, came rushing back. And at both trials only one person had prayed for his soul. Then he was in the ashvattha tree, talking with the Buddha whom he had mistaken as a simpleton. There he had known true wisdom and compassion, true beauty and purity of spirit. And there he had learned that the one who had prayed at the first two trials was Kotone, his young adopted daughter, whom he had abused and neglected. But even she had abandoned him then. He had not received a single prayer at that final trial.

It was then he had been sentenced.

Why was he back now, in front of the same tree? Was he doomed to repeat his trials and punishment?

His trials had been long ago. And he had only remembered the torture that followed. He had been headless and humiliated for as long as he could recall. But he had seen his way out.

The nentōkitō watched over Akechi, torturing and abasing him endlessly, while the oni looked on and laughed. But the slobbering worm demon was not always in his head. It was in charge of belittling hundreds of different souls, of which he was only one. A further humiliation to be lumped in with such a crowd and so lose his own identity.

But Akechi's sense of self was strong. He did not lose himself in the throng and forget who he was. He was a noble daimyo, yet destined for greatness. In spite of defeat, in spite of death, he would prevail. And though the mask was always speaking to him, reminding him of his despicable deeds in life, it did not control his actions.

The glow from the fire surrounding the great stone hall where the worm demon ruled glittered off metal and gems in the rock. Magma ran, popping and spitting in front of the wall of fire.

Red oni stood guard at the edges of the vast cavern. They were not as large as their greenish-blue kin, but still half a meter taller than Akechi. They mostly carried *kanabou*, long, spiked metal clubs. But there was one that wielded an *otsuchi*, a huge battle hammer. Akechi had his eyes on that hammer.

The problem was as soon as he attacked one of them, his nentōkitō master would dominate his mind and any thoughts of escape would be crushed—the fact that Akechi had no head, only the infernal mask floating above his neck, seemed not to matter for the fat worm demon's mind control. Akechi would have to time his actions perfectly. If he failed, another chance was beyond unlikely.

The nentōkitō rarely moved. It lay upon its belly on a raised platform of rock inside a natural alcove that served as its mock throne room. It lay there making sport with the lesser spirits, some of which had begun to transform into demons like Akechi, but most who remained pathetically human. Several were headless like himself wearing masks of shame.

After his transformation had begun, he had been informed that if he was obedient and served his time, he could one day gain his own power in Hell. For a time, he held onto this as his path. As he had done in life, he would usurp power one demon overlord at a time, until he was lord of all the underworld.

But the debasement at the hands of the nentōkitō was never-ending. It had become too much to tolerate. And he realized that the domination he sought was not in Hell. That was only a distraction planted in his mind to keep him under their control. He would be in Hell forever striving for power. It would become his new torture. All he truly wanted was his son. He needed his son by his side, with the knowledge that Akechi was his true father. Together they could conquer the Heavens and Earth.

In the alcove, above the slobbering worm demon's head, a row of stalactites depended like great teeth. When the demon shimmied its girth into its favorite spot to enjoy the torture, the largest and sharpest of them pointed like a spear to the back of its blubbery neck.

Akechi only had to position himself close enough to the oni with the *otsuchi*, and make his move. If all went perfectly, it wouldn't matter if the nentōkitō regained control of him. . . . if all went perfectly.

The moment finally came—a time measured only in blocks of humiliation, sweat, and pain—when Akechi was half a breath from the red oni with the hammer, and the slobbering worm demon was in its favorite place. It lounged under the row of stalactites, making the multitudes before it slap each other violently in their private parts. It roared with laughter each time, particularly when one of them doubled over in pain and vomited.

Akechi was on the fringes of the crowd after having just been subjected to one of the demon's other favorite games. It had the oni toss *horokubiya*, ceramic bombs filled with gunpowder and metal shards. The masses would jump away, trying to avoid being ground zero, but inevitably all of them would suffer some damage. Some would have limbs torn off or be blown apart completely, only to be reborn whole again moments later so the torture could continue.

Akechi had danced away enough to bring him closer to the oni, who did not want to blow themselves up, but not so close that he would be obvious and therefore shoved back to the center of the cavern.

The nentōkitō had roared with laughter as body parts flew, and then moved on to the slapping of genitals before all the parts had even mended.

Here was his chance.

Akechi pulled a piece of shrapnel from his cheek and swooped toward the red oni who had set down his hammer to throw the bombs.

He dove at the huge, red demon, spinning himself as he landed, and swept the oni's legs out from under him. The demon toppled and Akechi sprang to his feet, the huge hammer in his hands. With his demon transformation, his strength had grown, as had as his size, and he hefted the oni's weapon easily.

The bulging yellow eyes of the worm demon turned away from its entertainment. Its laughter died, and its mind gripped Akechi's like a bear trap. Pain and abject obeisance seized him as he dropped to his knees, shoving his own thumbs into the eyeholes of his mask. Though his eyes were not there, they felt the pain. Somewhere, trapped in a metal chest, they bled.

But it was too late. The hammer had already been thrown. It whipped through the stagnant air like an eagle swooping in for the kill. It impacted the base of the largest stalactite with a crack that shook the cavern. The worm demon, its attention only on Akechi, did not register its imminent doom. From its grimace it must have assumed that Akechi had meant to attack it directly and missed.

The stalactite broke free. It sunk into the demon's flesh like a spike into mud. The nentōkitō's head flopped to the stone floor from the sudden shock. It struggled to lift itself up onto its front legs while the top-heavy stalactite wobbled back and forth at the base of its neck.

The grip on Akechi's mind released, and he withdrew his thumbs from the mask. Still able to see, he watched the huge worm demon blunder about, relishing the fact that the rumors of the nentōkitō's weak spot were true.

During the endless torture he had overheard two oni discussing the weaknesses of all the demons they knew. It was some kind of game, each trying one-up the other. Akechi's non-existent ears had perked up when he heard them mention his slobbering overlord.

"The spine at the base of its neck is its soft spot," one them had said. "The rest of it is as tough as steel. Of course, you could never get to that spot without it getting into your head first. It's an unfair advantage, if you ask me."

The nentōkitō could control the oni too, but the guards were too disciplined and too stupid to need controlling. And at the moment, they only stood gaping.

Akechi watched only briefly as the huge demon's frame shuddered and collapsed, a fetid steam rising from it. The cavern had become chaos, hundreds of tortured souls running like headless chickens. Free from their endless suffering for the first time, they didn't know where to turn or what to do. Finally coming out of their stunned stupor, the oni rushed in to gather them up.

In the mayhem, Akechi leapt the magma stream and disappeared through the fire, slipping down a dark tunnel.

Akechi moved deliberately, retracing the path he had committed to his memory so long ago, until finally he stood in the room where the niyarikangei, the huge, wide-grinned, insectoid monsters, had taken his head. It was dark and empty, but the ages spent in Hell had transformed more than his body. He could see in the dark as well as any subterranean creature. He could see the thick, black stain in the center of the room from countless decapitations of an endless parade of arrogant souls. He could see worn trails where the niyarikangei repeated their dance: slicing, collecting, and then securing the mask to the empty space above necks; the same pattern *ad infinitum*.

He remembered the box with his head being hurried away behind a door to an infinitely long room lined with the possessions and boxes of the other headless. He moved to it now, an imposing slab of stone, but found it shut and locked. He tried desperately to tear it from its hinges, slamming into it with his shoulder and hammering it with his fists, but even his demon strength failed him, and though the door groaned and creaked, it did not budge.

Without his head, his escape meant nothing. He had to get inside.

Then he heard a skittering, and he pressed himself into an alcove. He felt something long, flat and metallic against his back. He turned tightly in the alcove to see a huge pair of scissors mounted on a rack on the wall.

He remembered the razor sharp blades all too well, snapping through his neck an unmeasurable time ago. He reached out, almost forgetting the skittering that grew closer, and touched the edge of a blade. A painless line of red appeared on his finger, the massive cutting implement too sharp for the nerves to register. Akechi pulled the scissors from the wall, pressed himself as tight as he could into the alcove, and waited.

The scraping of clawed feet entered the room and stopped. Akechi could hear a light, rasping of slavering breath. He could sense the creature's head turning to and fro, searching for whatever had made the noise. Then it started to move again, slowly, toward the alcove.

Gripping the handles of the scissors, Akechi yanked opened the blades and shot from his hiding place, swinging the scissors awkwardly in a violent arc. Of all the weapons he had wielded before, this was the strangest, and it moved unpredictably in his hands. Still, his battle sense had served him well and one of the shining blades severed a clawed, black arm, reaching into the dark.

The Hell beast shrieked and skittered backward, but Akechi was on it before it could run. Holding the huge scissors open, he leapt forward and impaled it through the back with one of the blades. It wailed again, and collapsed to the bloodied floor.

From all the horror it had caused Akechi, it was a weak creature. Without its bonds and scissors it was helpless. It whimpered where it lay. Akechi left the scissor blade like a pin in its back.

"You'll never get your head," it whined through gasps of black blood. "The doomed can never open their box."

"How do I get in the door?" Akechi growled. There had to be a way to get his head back. There was always a way.

"It doesn't matter," the niyarikangei sputtered. "Even if you open the door, you cannot open the box. The laws of Hell forbid it."

There was more skittering in the dark. More than one were coming now, at least three of them.

"Tell me how!" Akechi shouted, but the giant insect with the huge grin only laughed weakly through the blood, its several gray-veined eyes sagging as it neared death. In anger, Akechi pulled the scissors from the creature's back and slid the blades to either side of its neck.

"I will give you the end you have given so many, unless you tell me how to open the door." Akechi's voice was venom.

But again the demon beast laughed. "I die regardless. And, as you know, there is no true death here. I will return. Just as you will when you are brought down."

But there was something in its demeanor that betrayed it. It was afraid.

The skittering was almost here.

Akechi clamped the blades shut and the huge, no-longer-grinning head rolled from its centipede-like body, its many eyes strained with horror.

Four more niyarikangei entered the room.

One of them had another pair of scissors, and one held a *yari*, a spear with short blades crossed under the main stabbing point. The other two were unarmed. When they caught sight of their dead comrade and Akechi, all of them were afraid.

The former daimyo gripped the scissor's handles, one in each hand, and ripped the two halves apart. *Much better*, he thought as he held the separated blades, feeling more like two swords than the unwieldy scissors.

The armed niyarikangei rushed forward. But they were not fighters. Akechi made short work of them, and the other two turned to run. He could not let them escape. Already he was delayed and could not afford to have them summon bigger and stronger demons. He flung one of the scissor blades toward the furthest beast, while he sprinted to the closer one. The thrown blade whipped end over end in an unbalanced spin, and instead of the sharp edge slicing into the beast, the blunt handle knocked its head sideways. Still, it was enough to delay it, as the disoriented creature stumbled and lurched, unsure of which direction to face.

Akechi brought the other scissor half down with both hands onto the fleeing niyarikangei's hind section, and black ichor sprayed. He wiped the hot liquid from his eyes. Hobbled, the beast turned to face its fate. Akechi took its head with his next swing and then gave the same end to its confused comrade. He tossed the broken scissor blades to lay among their carcasses. Spitting the bitter demon blood from his mouth, he turned back to the door.

There had to be a key of some kind, but there was neither a keyhole nor a handle. It was an impenetrable black stone door, its only design an odd set of indentations, each a half circle, one of them set apart from the other four. Each indentation was deep and tapered to a point.

Akechi turned to survey the room and saw the mutilated corpses of the niyarikangei. They were still there and showed no signs of dissolving like the nentōkitō had, like the other doomed souls, himself included, had countless times.

The beast had lied to him, he realized. These demons were soulless and would not be reborn. To them death was permanent. That's why it had been afraid.

Akechi looked down at the severed arm and claw of the first one he had killed. Five clawed fingers tapering to sharp points ended the appendage. He lifted it and fit the claw into the indentation on the door. It was a perfect fit.

The door opened, swinging quietly to one side. Torches lit with red-tinged flames lined the walls inside. Akechi brought the claw with him, in case there were more doors to unlock.

The narrow room extended before him like an unending hallway, the walls, ceiling, and floor meeting in a single dot at the far end of his vision. Along the way were countless square metal chests, weapons, and suits of armor. Many of the chests had weapons mounted above them, but others had shelves with smaller, less violent looking items resting there. Knowing what was in his own box—wherever it was—and witnessing the many headless souls he had suffered alongside for so long, Akechi wondered if they all contained heads. Or were there other parts, other severed instruments of life's crimes? But most importantly he wondered how he would find his box. Searching this endless corridor of possessions would take lifetimes.

To his left he saw, mounted on the wall by the door, a large, empty frame of obsidian, which seemed to have no purpose. Akechi left it and moved down the endless chamber amongst the myriad collected things.

A katana and wakizashi were mounted above many of the chests, but others had different weapons. There were pole axes and spears, bows and arrows, even meager farmers' weapons: rakes and *kama*. Of the smaller items on shelves he saw a quill pen with an ink pot, a looking glass and a ledger book, coins and an hourglass, a knife and an ewer, a bone saw and a rope.

He moved quickly, reading the names on the boxes, the names of their souls written in some ancient tongue, demonic or otherwise. He could read them without effort as if they were objects and not words, as if they were the souls themselves. With the words were their crimes: murder, oppression, deception, thievery, betrayal, greed, adultery, calumny, arrogance . . . but none of them were his.

The room went on in front of Akechi, still to its single, endless point in the far reaches of his vision. Soon more demons would find the corpses of the niyarikangei and come after him. He could not allow himself to be caught and have his torture resumed.

And yet the mask on his absent face tormented him. Every second the images of his heinous deeds in life haunted him. As he scoured the items and boxes, he saw his own murders and betrayals play out before him. He saw his own ruthless egotism.

And yet, as it shamed him, it also numbed him. He was deserving of greatness, in spite of it all. Yes, he had done despicable things. But what the mask did not account for was *why*. His reasons for doing what he had done were not despicable, not to him. For his son, everything had been justified. And so he moved on, searching the metal boxes and their arcane symbols. He would find his chest, and be rid of the mask regardless.

Somehow. He would find a way.

He passed another empty obsidian frame and continued down the long, narrow chamber.

Past a simple iron box, a staff and chain mounted above, was the most ornate chest he had seen yet. It was a polished black steel with dark silver bands securing it. The sparkling gems mounted in its surface were nearly lost in the blackness of the container. The whole of it exuded some dark luxury and horror.

Akechi read the runes on its sides: *Murder, Megalomania, Black Heart*. On its face: *Arrogance,* of course, and above that, even larger: *Pogrom*.

Above the box were a katana, a wakizashi, and a tanto, all with black handles and sheaths. These were not his weapons, but Akechi could not resist them. So darkly beautiful they looked, so sinister and yet perfect. Akechi took the katana from the rack and pulled it from its sheath. The blade glistened in the torchlight as black as its own handle and sheath, as black as the chest, as black as its former owner's heart.

Pogrom, Akechi read again. What despotic madman owned this blade? The soul name seared into the box was nothing he recognized. But he had not even recognized his own until he had read it, had it branded into his forehead. He did not return the katana to the wall. Instead, he tucked it into his rag of a sash and retrieved the other two weapons, tucking them also under the frayed fabric, which threatened to break with the strain. He needed weapons after all. Demons would come for him soon.

He moved on down the long room.

He came to another empty frame of obsidian and paused. What was this strange square? There was a shine from its black contents as if it were a framed sheet of water, but there was no painting of any kind. It was blank. Though he knew his time was running out, he reached to the smooth surface, only to touch it, to feel if it was wet.

But his finger went through.

The strange surface, like a cool, clear mud, sucked at his digit as if trying to taste it. He withdrew his finger and it reverted to its blank, glassy sheen.

Repeating the action, the same thing occurred; it eagerly sucked at his fingers. It felt as if this bizarre liquid was looking for something inside Akechi, looking for approval it could not find.

His gaze fell on the niyarikangei arm, at its large, rock-worn claws. He pulled it from his belt and put the tips of the claws into the glassy substance.

Immediately the square within the frame came to life. An image of the long corridor appeared with a large rune floating above it. This rune was a question.

What soul do you seek? it asked.

He spoke his own name—not Noboru Akechi, but the one stamped on his chest and on his head before they had severed it.

The image before him blurred and zipped along the room, past hundreds, if not thousands of boxes and their connected items, until it stopped at one he recognized. It was his box, his soul name burned into its lid. Above it was another image of two swords mounted. The rune beside it read: *Bond*.

A larger rune appeared over the entire image, asking for confirmation.

"Yes," Akechi said.

Beside him the air shimmered and went deeply charcoal gray, framed by a silver arc. It was a door, and it was clear to Akechi where it would take him. He stepped through.

He stood in front of his own box, the katana and wakizashi from the image mounted above it. A suit of armor, his own in life, stood next to both. He momentarily wondered at the magic that had brought him here, but then brushed it aside. He needed to escape and had no time to admire his captors' arcane machines.

But his armor, he drank it in. He saw in every scarred and nicked plate all the battles he had won. The spiraling horns of his kabuto helmet stabbed toward the heavens, toward escape, and the grinning, dragon-faced *datemono* seemed to be mocking him for what he had become. Still, he yearned to wear the armor again and remember how it felt to be a great daimyo.

But first to retrieve his head.

The doomed can never open their box.

The niyarikangei's words repeated in his head. But he had to try. He looked up at the two swords. The handles were each a single blackened bone—a tibia, it seemed—crisscrossed tightly in what looked like black hair. The sheath was black as well, and dividing the two was a ruby red guard, intricately carved.

He pulled the katana from the wall and unsheathed it. The blade was a glimmering silvery steel, not black like the ones in his belt—the ones he had taken from above the unknown despot's chest. It was beautiful and looked impossibly sharp. He re-sheathed it and returned it to the wall.

Bond, the rune had said.

These weapons had not been his in life. They resembled ones he had owned, but they were remade with these new components. His had not had bone handles. His had been sharp, but these glimmered in a way that looked as if they would cut steel. And yet he felt himself in them. They were connected to his head in some way, to the box itself—that was the bond.

But how?

He knelt down in front of the box and felt for the edges of the lid. As he did, he sensed his head inside. At the same time he sensed his body outside the box from the darkness within. He was at once trapped in airless dark and outside in the red torchlight of the never ending chamber.

He held the niyarikangei's claw up to the box, resting it on the rune that bore his soul's name. He rested it on the oddly shaped keyhole, which looked vaguely like a man with tentacles instead of legs. He moved the claw about in different positions around the box, though there were no matching imprints as on the door. He hoped against hope that it would be so simple.

It was not. The claw remained a dead and useless limb, and the box showed no sign of unlocking.

He looked back up at the swords. He remembered them now. The niyarikangei had used them to lock the box, inserting them into it somehow. He turned the box over in his hands, immediately feeling dizzy as his head tumbled within. He slowed his pace and found a slot at the base, perfectly sized for the katana's blade.

He looked up again at the longer of the two weapons and now noticed something written on the mounting rack below it, barely visible from the collected dust: *Raijinkiba*, The Thunder God's Fang. He pulled it from the wall, unsheathed it and slid it inside the box.

Now for the other. He looked up at the shorter blade. *Fujinkokyū*, the dust-covered name below it read, The Wind God's Breath. He took it down from the wall, but could find no other slot on the box. What had the demon done with this blade? When his head had been removed, he had been able to see through the mask, but the demon had been in the way. He did not know what it had done with the wakizashi.

There was no time to figure it out. He would have to take everything with him, the box and the swords. But he already had three weapons tucked into his belt, and he didn't want to relinquish them. The black blades were even more powerful than the bone-handled ones. He could sense it.

First he donned his old armor, feeling every piece settle into place, somehow expanding to conform to his larger demon body. Of course his real armor must be rusted and gone, hundreds of years old, but this spirit replica transformed to fit him. Fully armored, the majesty of his former station filled him. He was again a great samurai lord. He would be humiliated no more.

He reattached the black-bladed weapons to the cords on his armor. Then he grabbed a rope that hung on a hook next to an executioner's axe above the metal box adjacent to his. He re-sheathed both the katana and wakizashi and tied them together, then strapped them to his back with the remaining length of rope. He hoisted his box with little effort. Though it was heavy steel, his demon strength made it seem light as a cloth bundle.

Now to escape, he thought. But how? He had gone through the shimmering door to get to this spot in the long room. How long would it take him to get back out?

There was no time for pondering. Action was all that would save him. He began moving in the direction he believed the entrance to be.

Soon he saw the familiar obsidian frame of another blank panel on the wall. He went quickly to it, and it came to life when he put the demon's claw into its cool, watery surface. This time the question posed by the strange runes was different.

Which exit do you seek? it asked, already sensing his purpose.

"The nearest," Akechi said quickly, but then corrected himself. "No, the nearest to freedom," he amended.

A dark gray portal appeared next to him in the chamber. He took a step toward it and stopped.

"Wait," he said. "What are the swords?" he asked, picturing the ruby-guarded blades in his mind.

The manifestation of sins, came the written reply, the odd, foreign characters as readable as his native Japanese. *As are all the bonded items. Forged in Hell's flames, these touched by vengeful gods. They are keys bound to locks and inoperable by the incarcerated.*

My sins, Akechi thought, bristling at the thought and at the suggestion that they were yet something else he could not use. He could not open the box, and he could not use the swords. More punishment. More lies. He would find a way. If he was no longer incarcerated, no longer in Hell, then they must work.

He stepped through the portal and found himself at another stone door. As before there was no handle or keyhole, only the five indentations in its black surface. Akechi lifted the claw one more time and pressed it into the marks.

The door opened.

He left the niyarikangei's claw in the rubble and stalked away into the dark.

It seemed another lifetime before Akechi exited through a jagged rent in the side of the vast caldera of Mount Fuji, and in all likelihood, it probably had been. Time had lost all meaning to him. His only thoughts were of freedom and redemption. Even revenge, his near constant driving force, had slipped from him. All he wanted was his head back on his shoulders, and his son returned to him.

The tunnels had risen and fallen, twisted and zagged, sometimes ending in impossible inclines or sheer drops, and Akechi would have to retrace his steps and take another way. He had fought and killed countless demons along the way, oni guards, wandering goblins, and many foul beasts he had no name for. Others he had stealthily slipped past, dreading being defeated and having his spirit returned to the depths and the endless torture he had so far escaped.

A blinding gap of light pierced his empty eyeholes and left him momentarily sightless. But as he stepped through, his senses soon adjusted and he saw a glowing white expanse in front of him. A bitter cold air—a feeling he had all but forgotten—stung his skin. Blue with wisps of gray appeared above, and slivers of brown bisected the white glow.

It was snow and earth, sky and clouds.

He was free.

With his first step into the snow, he felt a gnawing hunger, a raw scraping at his gut. There had been no need to eat in Hell, but those in the plane of the living required sustenance, and he was no exception.

But how could he eat with no mouth?

He soon found a solution. Tricking an innkeeper into pulling his mask from him, he would take the man's head. But the man was tricky, so Akechi took his wife's head instead. A few weeks passed and the woman's dying head became a source of pain, a throbbing in his skull that mounted with each passing day. So he killed again.

But the same thing happened. Each time, sometimes after two weeks, sometimes four, the new head would become too painful to keep. So he sought out fresh ones. He killed again and again, taking the heads of innocents in order to survive. One particularly pesky man tried to thwart him, to send him back to Hell. Akechi dearly wanted this troublemaker's head, but always the bald man eluded him.

He tried repeatedly to open the metal box that sealed his true head. He found the second key on the end of the pommel of the wakizashi, but it would not work for him. He had hoped the laws of Hell would end once he escaped, but they did not.

When the bald man enlisted the help of a young man and woman, Akechi finally put an end to him, impaling the man on his black katana. In his rage, he almost killed them all. But the three helped him inadvertently, opening the box in their feeble attempt to defeat him.

Then, with his true head returned, the young man gave Akechi the death he craved, a noble samurai death. He would be with his son. Finally with his son.

Now Akechi stood, peering into the huge tree, a soft glow coming from inside. Had it all been for nothing? Had he been returned to Hell in spite of his efforts? Had he doomed himself to repeat his trials and punishment by allowing the young man to kill him like a proper samurai? Should he have remained a demon walking the earth killing humans to stay alive?

No. What kind of life would that be? His only chance had been to receive a noble death, in the hope that he would be reunited with his son. If that effort failed, so be it. He had done what he could.

Heat rippled up Akechi's back so strongly he felt he was being cooked. The armor that had filled him with strength and pride now hung on him like a leaden weight. His katana and wakizashi, the black-bladed ones he had stolen before his escape, were gone. Perhaps they had returned to their rightful owner when he had been taken back to Hell. He pulled the armor off, piece by piece, and discarded it by the lava flow, his dragon-faced kabuto rolling down an incline to be dissolved in the magma.

He stepped into the doorway, and it was five strides of solid wood wall before he reached the room inside. As before, the interior felt larger than the girth of the tree, particularly with walls so thick. Books lined the walls, the shelves built into the wood. Vibrant green vines draped between them, and fountains burbled softly into earthen basins. Under a web of soft light spilling from above, a woman sat in a low chair lined with cushions. She was silver-haired and matronly, leaning over her knitting, which was spread over her crossed legs and wide hips, the needles working slowly and artfully, the yarn unspooling from a ball at her feet. When Akechi entered, she set her needles down. She carefully folded the fabric, in no hurry, seeming to feel each fiber lovingly as she did. She set it on a small table next to her, along with the needles and ball of yarn.

She looked up with calm expectation and smiled.

Akechi bowed his head low, dropping to his knees and touching his head to the floor.

"King Godou-tenrin," Akechi said, because he knew it was the god king, in spite of the changed appearance. "Oh, great Buddha. I know not why I am here again."

The Buddha smiled deeper and said, "To know that you *are* is enough. The *why* is often irrelevant." She stood, slightly hunched and indicated the doorway Akechi had just entered from. "Walk with me," she said, and took slow steps toward the entryway. Akechi followed, his head bowed.

Sunlight spilled into the doorway as they approached, and Akechi could smell fresh leaves and earthy moss. He stepped out after the old woman into a lush green vista. No longer was it the charred, lifeless canyon flowing with magma. Fresh air had replaced the sulfurous miasma that had choked him before. Trees grew by a clear stream and majestic mountains dominated the horizon.

"But . . ." Akechi began, "I was just here and this was . . ."

"Changed?" the Buddha finished, and when Akechi looked on her she was no longer an old woman. She was young and beautiful with dark hair and darker eyes. Her smile was the doorway to heaven. She was his wife, Sango, before the birth of their son.

"Nothing is permanent," Sango said. "Change is all there is."

Akechi stood dumbstruck. He had never dared hope to see his wife again; all his longing had been heaped on his son. But now that he saw her, his body trembled with the love he had been stripped of so long ago.

His wife stood before him. And yet she remained the Buddha.

Akechi fell to his knees and wept. "I have suffered," he sobbed.

"And you have caused suffering," the Buddha answered.

"Yes," Akechi's tears came even freer now. "I have. In my desire and my selfishness. How many lives have I destroyed?" he asked.

"The number is not important. It is the awareness that you now possess that matters. A fool who kills may be more innocent than a learned person, but a fool can never atone. It takes understanding and compassion for atonement. A fool has neither. Even punishment is lost on the fool. For it does not change him."

"I was a fool," Akechi said. "The punishment did not change me. I escaped only to bring death to more souls."

"And now you are a fool no longer. And the punishment is in your heart."

"Yes, my love."

"Get up," she said. "We have not walked yet, and I long to breathe with the trees."

Akechi rose and followed.

They walked through a forest of oak, maple, and plum trees, which gave way to an orchard of cherry, bright and pink in bloom. Sango, the Buddha, let her fingers brush against the trunks as they walked, and where she touched, Akechi could see the trees briefly illuminate, as did as Sango's fingers. The leaves and blossoms brightened and lifted as if taking a breath. He longed for her to touch him and feel her energy revive his ruined spirit.

"Our son was a stubborn one," she said, her words musical. "I wonder who he got that from," she added with a smile.

Akechi found himself smiling too. It was a foreign feeling, the muscles in his face not having been used for centuries. It was a relinquishing of the iron grip with which he had tried to forge his destiny. Sango reached out, and their fingers intertwined. The surge of life was more than he had hoped it would be.

"Kiyoshi had many stumbles along his path, the worst of which was killing you," Sango continued. "But it was his eldest sister, Tsuru, who persuaded him to do it."

Akechi did not bristle at this knowledge, as he would have expected. The feeling that had overcome him as he held Sango's hand would not be subverted. He only accepted the fact and felt sorrow for his deceived son. Had he killed his stepdaughters, as he had wanted to, he may have lived a long life and may have convinced Kiyoshi of the truth of his heritage. But that would have been more innocent death on his hands, worse yet for they had been under his protection, and perhaps would have caused a worse fate than to what he had already been sentenced. These thoughts came only as a passing breeze. As they walked among the trees, hand in hand, nothing could disturb his calm.

"Being the eldest daughter, Tsuru felt she was responsible for revenge," Sango said. "And with your death accomplished, Kiysohi became the rightful ruler. Thus she ruled by proxy, reclaiming her father's lands.

"Through Kiyoshi's mouth, she made their second oldest sister, Nako, warlord. Nako had trained as an *onna-bugeisha* and was a fierce warrior, but the deposed warlord, Murata, was ever resentful, and ultimately betrayed the Imube clan, feeding information to their enemies to aid in their downfall."

"I remember Murata," Akechi said. "He was loyal to me."

"To you, yes. But he longed for revenge on the Imube clan, and they gave him his cause."

Again Akechi felt strange. The bitter joy that would have normally accompanied that news was absent. His loyal servant had exacted revenge on those who had so ignobly murdered him, and yet, he felt only a calm wonderment, as if he had read it in a book about someone else's life.

"Nako was an accomplished fighter, but she did not match Murata's battle savvy, nor that of the daimyo that he conspired with. Nako died on the battlefield surrounded by enemy samurai . . . as did Kiyoshi."

Sango looked into Akechi's eyes.

"He was beautiful as he rode, his armor glistening in the light rain. You would have been proud to see him. But he did not possess your battle prowess." Her eyes were distant, as if seeing her son's last ride into battle. "He was twenty-six."

Akechi's barrier of calm was penetrated, and tears ran from his eyes. "My son. My son . . ." He let his head droop, and the Buddha turned to hold him.

"The cycle of life and death goes ever on," she whispered. "His trials were different than yours. And with different results."

Akechi brightened. "Has he gone on to the Pure Land? Or perhaps been reborn?"

The Buddha smiled and released him. "It is not for me to impart. It is as it is. And perhaps you will cross paths again. But first, there is one more trial you must endure. Sit," she said, indicating a smooth, flat stone in a clearing of yew trees.

"Another trial?" Akechi's spirits dimmed.

"Of course," she smiled. "You escaped from Hell before your sentence had been fulfilled. Not even the great Noboru Akechi gets a pass from that."

He nodded, surprised that a touch of a smile pushed at his lips. He sat on the stone.

"What will my trial be?" Akechi wondered out loud. "Ravaged by bears in the forest? Swallowed by an earthquake while giant ants tear my flesh?"

Sango smiled at him like she had when they were young lovers. "We will sit and listen to the trees." And she sat beside him.

Only that? he thought.

"Yes, only that," she responded aloud.

A soft wind spun through the branches and tickled at Akechi's ears. A muddy, sour smell came and went leaving a burst of lilac, which then dissipated in a fresh drizzle. There was a burning of wood, and smoke rose from the forest floor. Frogs chirped and an owl hooted before a cloud of bees enveloped them briefly as it flew past. Then it was still as death. The trees seemed to shrink away from the clearing and become hollow husks. Their needles fell and the earth became barren. But slowly, sprouts appeared and the trees grew anew. Wind and fragrance returned carrying with them the birds and insects, the whole of life.

Akechi did not know how long they sat. But he was resigned to sitting there forever. Sango was there. His choices had been made.

"There," she finally said, and placed a hand on his. "It is done."

Akechi knew what was next.

"How many prayers?" he asked, expecting nothing.

"One," Sango answered, and Akechi hung his head. It would be back to the fires of Hell for him.

"But it is enough." Sango smiled, and Akechi looked up.

"One?"

"The prayer is strong." She stood and pulled him up with her. "You may go forward," she said, and a door appeared among the trees. "Perhaps you will find Kiyoshi. Perhaps even peace. But there are still choices ahead. Remember the lessons you have so far learned. Remember your heart."

The door swung open onto a vista obscured by mist. A mountain peak shone through in the distance. Akechi let go of Sango's hand and stepped toward it, but turned back to gaze on her once more.

"Who is it that prays for me? Kiyoshi? It must be Kiyoshi." He knew his son was long dead, but he could still pray, couldn't he?

"No, my love. It is a young man, an honest soul striving to contend with his own demons the best he can. He sits on his simple bed and asks forgiveness for your soul."

"But who? I know no such man."

"He is the one who helped you get here. His name is Akio."

Akechi hung his head in deep gratitude for a long moment, then rose and peered through the open doorway. What awaited him there? And who would he be in response to it? He looked back at Sango, smiled the subtlest of smiles, and stepped into the mist.

The Syndicates

Dazai-ikka
Godfather: Hisatsugu Tabara
Membership: about 200
A subordinate yakuza clan to the Tezuka-gumi. Its godfather, Hisatsugu Tabara, brought the first gem to Kumamori. For his loyalty and service, he was wedded to Kumamori's much younger daughter.

Ishiguro-kai
Godfather: Shigeo Takagi
Membership: about 12,000
The third largest yakuza syndicate in Japan, based in Tokyo. Its godfather, Shigeo Takagi, is well-loved among the yakuza, and is particularly on good terms with the godfather of the Kawabata-gumi.

Kawabata-gumi
Godfather: Kazuki Tsumura
Membership: about 32,000
The largest yakuza syndicate in Japan. They are based in Kobe but have a strong presence in Tokyo and throughout Japan. On good terms with the Ishiguro-kai.

Mishima-kai
Godfather: none
Membership: about 15,000
The second largest yakuza syndicate in Japan, based in Tokyo. The Mishima-kai do not have a single godfather, but rather a board of twelve bosses. One of them acts as reigning godfather, but for all intents and purposes they rule equally.

Tezuka-gumi

Godfather: Hiromi Kumamori

Membership: about 800

Originally a small yakuza syndicate, based in Kofu and subordinate to the Kawabata-gumi. Not long after an unfavorable split with the Kawabata-gumi, the Tezuka-gumi began to expand at an alarming rate, recruiting new members and absorbing members of other clans by the thousands.

Black Moon Society

Ringleader: Debi

Membership: unknown

Not a yakuza syndicate, but a pre-yakuza organization that has been running brothels since the Edo period. It controls the majority of prostitution in the greater Tokyo area and beyond. All the yakuza syndicates have dealings with them in some regard, but their primary yakuza partner is the Ishiguro-kai.

NOTE: During the events of this book, the yakuza's numbers have been in decline for several years. In their heyday, they were nearly twice what is listed here. With the discovery of the gems, membership is increasing again.

Acknowledgments

First and foremost, my wife, Julia, has been invaluable. Her inspired ideas elevate my stories to something much more than they were. It essentially works something like this: I write a first draft, wrestle it into something readable, and then let her read it. She comes back with glittering nuggets, *gems* you could say, of ideas and story elements that pull it all together and give it focus. Of course she tells me things that don't work, but also what's missing. The epilogue in this book wouldn't exist without her feedback, and it is one of my favorite parts, an essential part, of this story. I am incredibly lucky to have her has my life partner and manuscript dissector.

As with *Headless*, my brother Joe, also provided crucial feedback as one of my frontline readers, giving me pages of notes. He was there during the writing, as well, to help me get through a difficult chapter, flesh out a story concept, or simply improve an awkward sentence.

Tomoe Suzuki again helped make sure the Japanese references, culture, names, and word usage were correct. Chungmo Kang helped me extensively in the creation of my made-up Japanese names, giving them the feel of authentic Japanese lore. Aryf Hussain helped me perfect Lily's Swedish and allowed me the freedom to butcher it a bit when she begins to breakdown. Aryf also served as a first round copyeditor, catching many typos and grammar issues for me.

I want to thank my beta readers, some of whom got a much too unpolished, early draft of the book. I appreciate them slogging through it. They are Jiyoon Shin, Anne Evans Locarro, Bud Myrick, and Raz Schiønning.

Thank you to my friends and family who have been supportive and encouraging throughout my writing journey. The creative path is rarely an easy one, and the smallest gesture of support can go a long way.

Finally, I want to thank you for picking up this book and giving it a go. I hope you have enjoyed the adventure.

At your peril,
Tristram Lowe

About the Author

Tristram Lowe writes about monsters, and sometimes, scary things too. He is a student of the Japanese language and culture and a lifelong fantasy reader. He is also a competitive fencing coach, so it's likely a sword fight or two will show up in his books. Tristram has been crafting fantastical tales since the first grade, when he penciled a spooky story about a haunted house in his Big Chief tablet. Raised in the mountains of Colorado, he spent two or three lifetimes in Los Angeles, and now enjoys hikes through mossy trees and rainy board game nights in Oregon with his wife, their son, and their elderly cat.

Also by
TRISTRAM LOWE

HEADLESS
The Ghost and the Mask, Book One

When the trail of a head-collecting serial killer in Japan takes a supernatural turn, a pair of mismatched journalists must get the story without losing their heads.

THE WRONG MONSTER

A children's picture book

with illustrations by Jiyoon Shin

A boy finds the courage to open his closet door and face the monster inside. What he finds isn't at all what he expected.

FIND MORE AT:

tristramlowe.com
Instagram: thetristramlowe
Twitter: @tristramlowe
Facebook.com/tristramlowe

The Ghost and the Mask, Book Three
is in the works.

Keep informed by signing up to
The Lowe Letter
at tristramlowe.com
and **get a free e-book** about
the victims of the killer in *Headless*:
THE WIND ON THE BLADE
Connected short stories about the victims of the Kofu Head Collector
in the world of The Ghost and the Mask.